Q

Luther Blissett was until recently on the coaching staff at York City FC . He is perhaps best known for the brief period he spent playing for AC Milan in the early '80s. He had nothing to do with the writing of this book.

The four real authors of *Q* live in Bologna. More information about their work is available at www.wumingfoundation.com

'The quest for Utopia inspired the year's most entertaining historical blockbuster, *Q*, by the quartet of Italian pranksters who call themselves "Luther Blissett" after the ex-Watford and Milan footballer. It's almost a miracle that this learned, swashbuckling, multi-authored romp across Reformation Europe works as smoothly as it does.' *Independent*

'This remarkable novel throws the reader into the midst of one of the most turbulent eras of European history.' Peter Porter, *Guardian* 'Books of the Year'

'An audacious 16th century murder mystery epic . . . A truly unusual beast, a bubbling cauldron of politics, metaphysics and history.' *Arena*

'Throughout, the authors of *Q* avow their enthusiasm for radical social change and their disgust for traditional power structures. But it's *Q*'s action rather than its ideology that really inspires. This is a novel that drips with trickery and cant, that wholeheartedly rejects predestination while existing as a series of utterly gripping flashbacks, and overflows with blood, guts and passion. It may be rooted in the head of one man, but this is a novel of enormous scope and sharp detail. It will stain you.' *The List*

'An entertainment of much more serious intent . . . An energetic, daring read.' *Independent on Sunday*

'If you relish tales of schism, ecclesiastical politics and theological battles-to-the-death, then the 650 pages of this sprawling, compelling historical novel will keep you happy for hours . . . Compulsive in its portrayal of the realities and brutalities of reforming zeal and religious power.' *Church Times*

'Energetic . . . ridiculous . . . engaging . . . Between these examples of tyranny and chaos there is the novel itself, which is able to couple agreement and conflict, order and disorder; it is a living piece of anarchism, with all the fun and infuriation that implies.' *Telegraph*

'The air is full of blistering debate, revolutionary preaching and the smell of smoke, both from burning icons in the churches and the pyres on which the heretics are burned . . . The very chaos and crude violence of it mirror the madness and apocalyptic vision that must have propelled so many to their doom.' *Guardian*

Q

Luther Blissett

arrow books

Published in the United Kingdom in 2004 by
Arrow Books

9 10

First published in Great Britain in 2003 by
William Heinemann
Random House, 20 Vauxhall Bridge Road,
London SW1V 2SA

www.rbooks.co.uk

Addresses for companies within The Random House Group Limited
can be found at: www.randomhouse.co.uk/offices.htm

The Random House Group Limited Reg. No. 954009

A CIP catalogue record for this book
is available from the British Library

ISBN 978099439837

The Random House Group Limited makes every effort to ensure that the
papers used in its books are made from trees that have been legally
sourced from well-managed and credibly certified forests. Our paper
procurement policy can be found at: www.rbooks.co.uk/environment

Printed and bound in Great Britain by
Cox & Wyman Ltd, Reading, Berkshire

To Marco Morri

Prologue

On the first page it says: 'In the fresco I'm one of the figures in the background.'

The meticulous handwriting, no smudges, tiny. Names, places, dates, reflections. The notebook of the final fevered days.

The yellowed and decrepit letters, the dust of decades.

The coin of the kingdom of the mad dangles on my chest to remind me of the eternal oscillation of human fortunes.

The book, perhaps the only remaining copy, has never been opened.

The names are the names of the dead. My names, and those who have travelled those twisting paths.

The years we have been through have buried the world's innocence for ever.

I promised you not to forget.

I've kept you safe in my memory.

I want to recall everything, right from the beginning, the details, chance, the flow of events. Before distance obscures my backward glance, muffling the hubbub of voices, of weapons, armies, laughter, shouts. And at the same time only distance allows us to go back to a likely beginning.

1514, Albert Hohenzollern becomes Archbishop of Magdeburg. At the age of twenty-three. More gold in the Pope's coffers: he also buys the bishopric of Halberstadt.

1517, Mainz. The biggest ecclesiastical principality in Germany awaits the appointment of a new bishop. If he wins the appointment, Albert will get his hands on a third of the whole German territory.

He makes his offer: 14,000 ducats for the archbishopric, plus 10,000 for the papal dispensation that allows him to hold all these offices.

The deal is negotiated via the Fugger bank of Augsburg, which anticipates the sum required. Once the operation is concluded, Albert owes the Fuggers 30,000 ducats.

The bankers decree the mode of payment. Albert must promote the sale of the indulgences for Pope Leo X in his territory. The faithful will make a contribution to the construction of St Peter's basilica and will receive a certificate in exchange: the Pope absolves them of their sins.

Only half of the takings will go to the Roman builders. Albert will use the rest to pay the Fuggers.

The task is given to Johann Tetzel, the most expert preacher around.

Tetzel travels the villages for the whole of the summer of 1517. He stops on the borders with Thuringia, which belongs to Frederick the Wise, Duke of Saxony. He can't set foot there.

Frederick is collecting indulgences himself, through the sale of relics. He doesn't tolerate competitors on his territories. But Tetzel is a clever bastard: he knows that Frederick's subjects will happily travel a few miles beyond the border. A ticket to paradise is worth the trip.

The coming and going of souls in search of reassurance infuriates a young Augustinian friar, a doctor at Wittenberg University. He can't bear the obscene market that Tetzel has set in motion, with the Pope's coat of arms and the papal bull in full view.

31 October 1517, the friar nails ninety-five theses against the traffic in indulgences, written in his own hand, to the northern door of Wittenberg church.

His name is Martin Luther. With that gesture the Reformation begins.

A starting point. Memories reassembling the fragments of an era. Mine. And that of my enemy: Q.

Carafa's eye
(1518)

Letter sent to Rome from the Saxon city of Wittenberg, addressed to Gianpietro Carafa, member of the theological meeting held by His Holiness Leo X, dated 17 May 1518.

To the most illustrious and reverend lord and honourable master Giovanni Pietro Carafa, at the theological meeting held by His Holiness Leo X, in Rome.

My Most Respected, Illustrious and Reverend Lord and Master,

Here is Your Lordship's most faithful servant's report on what is happening in these remote marshlands, which for a year now appear to have become a focus for all manner of diatribes.

Since the Augustinian monk Martin Luther nailed his notorious theses to the portal of the cathedral eight months ago, the name of Wittenberg has travelled far and wide on everyone's lips. Young students from bordering states are flowing into this town to listen to the preacher's incredible theories from his own mouth.

In particular, his sermons against the buying and selling of indulgences seem to have enjoyed the greatest success among young minds open to novelty. What was until yesterday something perfectly ordinary and undisputed, the remission of sins in return for a pious donation to the Church, seems today to be criticised by everyone as though it were an unmentionable scandal.

Such sudden fame has made Luther pompous and overbearing; he feels as though he has been entrusted with a supernatural task, and that leads him to risk even more, to go even further.

Indeed yesterday, like every Sunday, preaching from the pulpit on the gospel of the day (the text was John 16, 2: 'They shall put you out of the synagogues'), he linked the 'scandal' of the market in indulgences with another thesis, one which is to my mind even more dangerous.

Luther asserted that one should not be overly frightened of the consequences of an unjust excommunication, because that concerns only external communion with the Church, and not internal communion. Indeed, only the latter concerns God's bond with the faithful, which no man can declare broken, not even the Pope.

Furthermore, an unjust excommunication cannot harm the soul, and if it is supported with filial resignation towards the Church, it can even become a precious merit. So if someone is unjustly excommunicated, it can even be seen as a precious merit. So if someone is unjustly excommunicated, he must not deny with words or actions the cause for which he was excommunicated, and must patiently endure the excommunication even if it means dying excommunicated and not being buried in consecrated ground, because these things are much less important than truth and justice.

Finally he concluded with these words: 'Blessed be he who dies in an unjust excommunication; because by being subjected to that harsh punishment because of his love of justice, which he will neither deny nor abandon, he shall receive the eternal crown of salvation.'

Uniting the desire to serve you with gratitude for the confidence that you have shown in me, I shall now make so bold as to convey my opinion of the things that I have mentioned above. It seemed clear to Your Most Reverend Lordship's humble servant that Luther had sniffed the air and smelt his own coming excommunication, just as the fox scents the smell of the hounds. He is already sharpening his doctrinal weapons and seeking allies for the immediate future. In particular, I believe he is seeking the support of his master the Elector Frederick of Saxony, who has not yet publicly disclosed his own state of mind as regards Friar Martin. Not for nothing is he called the Wise. The lord of Saxony continues to employ that skilled intermediary, Spalatin, the court librarian and counsellor, to assess the monk's intentions. Spalatin is a sly and treacherous character, of whom I gave you a brief description in my last missive.

Your Lordship will have a better understanding than his servant of the disastrous gravity of the thesis put forward by Luther: he wants to strip the Holy See of its greatest bulwark, the weapon of excommunication. And it is also apparent that Luther will never dare to put this thesis of his in writing, since he is aware of the enormity that it represents, and the danger it might present to his own person. So I have thought it opportune to do so myself, so that Your Lordship may have time to take all the precautions he considers necessary to stop this diabolical friar.

Kissing the hand of Your Most Illustrious and Reverend Lordship,

I beg that I may never fall from grace with Your Lordship.

Your Lordship's faithful servant

Q   Wittenberg, 17 May 1518

Letter sent to Rome from the Saxon city of Wittenberg, addressed to Gianpietro Carafa, member of the theological meeting held by His Holiness Leo X, dated 10 October 1518.

To my most illustrious and reverend lord and master the most honourable Giovanni Pietro Carafa, at the theological meeting held by His Holiness Leo X, in Rome.

My Most Respected, Illustrious and Reverend Lord and Master,

As Your Lordship's servant, I have been hugely flattered by the magnanimity that you have bestowed on me; since it is a great privilege for me to be able to serve you, being useful to you fills me with real joy. The official accusation of heresy levelled against the friar Martin Luther, to which the Sermon on Excommunication lent definitive support, should lead the Elector Frederick finally to adopt a position as regards the monk, as Your Lordship predicted. The facts that I am about to recount to you may perhaps be considered as an initial reaction on the part of the Elector to the unexpectedly hasty developments: indeed, he is preparing to bolster the ranks of theologians at his university.

On 25 August Philipp Melanchthon, from the prestigious university of Tübingen, was appointed Professor of Greek at Wittenberg. I do not believe that any university in the Empire has ever seen a younger professor than this man: he is only twenty-one, and with his gaunt and feeble appearance he looks even younger. Although a certain fame has preceded and accompanied him on his journey, the initial welcome from the doctors of Wittenberg has not been enthusiastic. But their attitude, and Luther's in particular, soon changed when this prodigy of classical knowledge delivered his inaugural lecture, in which he illustrated the need for a rigorous study of the Scriptures in the original texts. Since then he has had a strong and immediate understanding with Martin Luther. The two professors have certainly become a potent weapon in the hands of the Elector of Saxony, since the moment when they forged this agreement despite their considerable differences. Each supplies the other with what he lacked to become a real danger to Rome: Luther is ardent and energetic, however coarse and impulsive, while Melanchthon is highly cultivated and refined, but younger and more delicate, better suited to doctrinal battles than to armed combat. The first dangerous product of this union will certainly be the Bible in German, on which they are said to be working together, and for which Melanchthon's knowledge will be like manna from heaven.

Since I know that Your Lordship values detailed information on important matters, in the time to come I will continue to follow these two doctors with great attention, and refer everything to Your Lordship, only in the hope that I might still be of use to you.

I most humbly kiss Your Illustrious and Reverend Lordship's hands.

Your Lordship's faithful servant

Q   Wittenberg, 10 October 1518

PART ONE
The Coiner

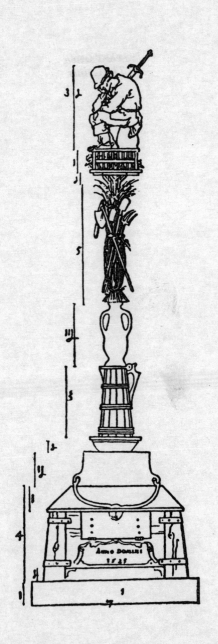

Frankenhausen
(1525)

Chapter 1

Almost blindly.

What I have to do.

Screams in my ears already bursting with cannon fire, bodies crashing into me. My throat choked with bloody, sweaty dust, my coughs tearing me apart.

Terror on the faces of the fleeing people. Bandaged heads, crushed limbs . . . I'm constantly turning round: Elias is behind me. Huge, pushing his way through the crowd. He has Magister Thomas over his shoulders, lifeless.

Where is the omnipresent Lord? His flock is being slaughtered.

What I have to do. Clutching the bags tight. Mustn't stop. My dagger bumping against my side.

Elias still behind me.

A blurred outline runs towards me. Face half covered with bandages, tormented flesh. A woman. She recognises us. What I have to do: the Magister mustn't be discovered. I put my finger to my lips: not a word. Shouting behind me: 'Soldiers! Soldiers!'

I move her aside, to get to safety. An alleyway on the right. Running, Elias behind us, running headlong. What I have to do: try all the doors. The first, the second, the third, it opens. We're in.

We close the door behind us. The noise drops. Light filters faintly through a window. The old woman is sitting in a corner at the end of the room, on a dilapidated wicker chair. A few pathetic objects: a shabby bench, a table, coals from a recent fire in a soot-black chimney.

I walk towards her. 'Sister, we have a wounded man. He needs a bed and some water, in the name of God . . .'

Elias is standing in the doorway, filling it. Still with the Magister on his shoulders.

'Just for a few hours, sister.'

Her eyes are watery, seeing nothing. Her head rocks back and forth. My ears are still ringing. Elias's voice: 'What's she saying?'

I walk closer to her. In the midst of the roaring world, a barely murmured dirge. I can't make out the words. The old woman doesn't even know we're there.

What I have to do. No time to lose. A staircase leads upstairs, a nod to Elias, up we go, finally there's a bed where we can lay Magister Thomas. Elias wipes the sweat from his eyes.

He looks at me. 'We've got to find Jacob and Mathias.'

I put my hand on my dagger and make as though to leave.

'No, I'll go, you stay with the Magister.'

I have no time to answer, he's already on his way downstairs. Magister Thomas, motionless, staring at the ceiling. Vacant eyes, eyelids barely beating, he looks as though he isn't breathing.

I look outside: a glimpse of houses through the window. It looks out on to the street, too high to jump. We're on the first floor, at least there's an attic. I peer at the ceiling and can only just see the cracks of a trapdoor. There's a ladder on the floor. Riddled with woodworm, but it'll hold me all the same. I slip in on all fours, the roof of the loft is very low, the floor covered with straw. The beams creak with each movement. There isn't a window, just a few rays of light slanting in between the chinks: the roof space.

More boards, straw. I'm practically lying down. There's an opening out on to the roofs: sloping. Magister Thomas will never make it.

I go back down to him. His lips are dry, his forehead is on fire. I try to find some water. On the floor below there are some walnuts and a jug on a table. The sing-song chant drones endlessly on. When I put the water to the Magister's lips I see the bags: better hide them.

I sit down on the stool. My legs hurt. I hold my head in my hands, just for a moment, then the hum becomes a deafening roar of screams, horses and iron. Those bastards in the pay of the princes are entering the city. Run to the window. To the right, in the main street: horsemen, pikes levelled, are raking the road. They are furiously attacking anything that moves.

On the other side: Elias pops out into the alleyway. He sees the horses, stops. Foot soldiers appear behind him. There's no escape. He looks around: where is the omnipresent Lord?

They point their spears at him.

He looks up. He sees me.

What he has to do. He unsheathes his sword, hurls himself at the foot soldiers. He's ripped one open, butted another to the ground. Three soldiers are on him. Their blows bounce off him, he clutches the hilt of his sword with both hands like a scythe, still slicing away.

They leap aside.

Behind him: a slow, heavy gallop, the horseman charging behind him. The blow knocks Elias flying. It's over.

No, he's getting up: a mask of blood and fury. Sword still in his hand. No one goes near him. I can hear him panting. A tug on the reins, the horse turns round. The axe is raised. Back at a gallop. Elias spreads his legs, two tree roots. His head and arms turned to the sky, he drops his sword.

The final blow: '*Omnia sunt communia*, sons of whores!'

His head flies into the dust.

The houses are being ransacked. Doors smashed in with kicks and axe blows. We'll be next. No time to lose. I lean over him. 'Magister, listen to me, we've got to go, they're coming . . . For the love of God, Magister . . .' I grasp his shoulders. He whispers a reply. He can't move. Trapped, we're trapped.

Like Elias.

My hand clutches my sword. Like Elias. I wish I had his courage.

'What do you think you're doing? We've had enough of martyrdom. Go on, get out while you can!'

The voice. As though from the bowels of the earth. I can't believe he's spoken. He's moving even less than before. A knocking and crashing from below. My head is spinning.

'Go!'

That voice again. I turn towards him. Motionless.

Crash. Down goes the door.

Right, the bags, they mustn't be found, come on, over my shoulders, up the ladder, the soldiers are insulting the old woman, I slip, nothing to hold on to, too heavy, come on, I drop a bag, damn! They're coming up the stairs, I'm in, pulling up the ladder, shutting the trapdoor, the door's opening.

There are two of them. Landsknechts.

I'm able to spy on them from a crack between the floorboards. I mustn't move, the slightest creak and I've had it.

'Let's just take a quick look and we'll be off, we're not going to find anything here . . . Hang on, though, who's this?'

They walk over to the bed, shake Magister Thomas. 'Who are you? Is this your house?' No reply.

'Right, then. Günther, look what we've got here!'

They've seen the bag. One of them opens it.

'Shit, there's just paper, no money. What's this stuff? Can you read?
'Me? No!'

'Neither can I. It might be important stuff. Go downstairs and get
the captain.'

'What's this, are you giving me orders? Why don't you go?'

'Because I was the one who found the bag!'

In the end they make their minds up, the one whose name isn't
Günther goes down to the ground floor. I hope the captain can't read
either, or we're fucked.

Heavy steps, the one who must be the captain climbs the stairs. I
can't move. My mouth is burning, my throat choking with the attic
dust. To stop myself from coughing I bite the inside of a cheek and
swallow the blood.

The captain starts reading. I can only hope he doesn't understand
it. In the end he lifts his eyes from the paper: 'It's Thomas Müntzer,
the Coiner . . . You might say the penny's dropped.'

My heart leaps into my throat. Delighted expressions: double pay.
They drag away the man who declared war on the princes.

I stay there in silence, unable to move a muscle.

The omnipresent Lord is neither here nor anywhere else.

Chapter 2

Finally, the light of dawn. I collapse, exhausted.

When I opened my eyes again, in the complete darkness of night and my existence, my first sensation is the absolute torpor in my limbs.

How long had they been gone?

Shouted abuse from drunks in the street, noises of merrymaking, the screams of women submitting to the laws of the mercenaries.

To remind me I was alive, a diabolical itch; on my skin, a carapace of sweat, straw and dust.

Alive, free to cough and groan.

Merely getting to my feet and hoisting myself up on to the roof with my bag and sword was a laborious task. I waited for my eyes to get used to the darkness, studying the face of the city of the dead.

Down below, the glow of scattered bonfires lit the grinning faces of the carousing soldiers, busy gulping down their reward for the easiest of victories.

Darkness ahead of me. The total darkness of the countryside. To the left, a few yards away, one roof jutted out more than the others, over the alley below, to the edge of absolute darkness. Creeping over the roofs, I have dragged my aching back to this boundary: walls ahead of me. As tall as three men, no one on duty. I managed to walk along them.

At first I wasn't aware of the smell: my mouth was a sewer, my nose filled with sweat and dirt . . . Then I noticed it: dung. Dung just below. I dropped, like that, into the darkness, hoping for the best.

A dungheap.

Running, away, thirsty, running, then I walked, tripping, away, and walked, away, away, hungry, faster, brushed by death and swathed in the stink of shit, until finally my legs gave in.

Dawn.

Lying in a ditch, I drink muddy water. I collapsed into darkness as the sun rose.

The sky is aflame to the west. Every corner of my body is on fire; encrusted with mud and shit: alive.

Fields, sheaves, the edge of a wood a few miles to the south. Have to get on with my escape. I'll have to wait for the darkness.

Alone. My companions, the master, Elias.

Alone. The faces of the brothers, corpses laid out on the plain.

My bag and sword seem to have doubled in weight. I am weak: I've got to eat something. A few yards away there are green ears of corn. I grab them by the handful and swallow them down with difficulty.

I wonder what I must look like and study the elongated shadow on the ground. It raises a hand to its face: the eyes, the beard, it's not me. It won't be me ever again.

Think.

Forget the horror and think. Then move and forget the horror. Then again, destroy the horror and live.

So think. Food, money, clothes.

A refuge, far from here, somewhere safe, where I can get some news and track down the brethren who got away.

Think.

Hans Hut, the bookseller. In the plain, running off at the sight of Duke Georg's suit of armour, before the slaughter began. If anyone got away, Hut will have been the one.

His printing works is in Bibra, near Nuremberg. Years ago it swarmed with brethren. A way station for many of them.

On foot, at night, keeping off the roads, through the woods and at the edge of the fields, it'll be a couple of weeks at least.

Chapter 3

A soldiers' bivouac.

Long shadows and coarse northern accents.

For two days and nights I've been walking in the forest, all my senses alert, jumping at the slightest sound: the wing-beats of birds, the distant howling of wolves that runs down the spine and loosens the bowels. Outside, the world could easily have come to an end, there might be nothing there.

Heading south until my legs wouldn't hold me and I fell to the ground. I've devoured whatever I could get hold of to ease the pangs: acorns, wild berries, even leaves and bark when hunger bit deeper . . . Exhausted, the damp in my bones, my limbs growing heavier and heavier.

It was after sunset when the embers of a fire appeared through the bushes. I went closer, creeping up behind this oak tree.

To my right, about fifty yards away, three tethered horses: the smell might give me away. I stay motionless, uncertain, wondering how long it would take to mount one of these animals. I peer round the trunk again: they're sitting around the fire, blankets over their shoulders, a flask is being passed from hand to hand, I can almost smell the spirits on their breath.

'Oh! And when we charged and they ran off like scared sheep? I skewered three of them on a single lance! A pig on a spit!'

Drunken laughter.

'I went one better than that. I fucked five of the women when we were sacking the city . . . and in between I never stopped killing the buggers . . . One of those whores bit half my ear off! Look . . .'

'And what did you do?'

'I cut her throat, the cow!'

'Waste of time, you prick. Another day and she'd have given you one just to get her husband's corpse back, same as all the rest of them . . .'

Another explosion of laughter. One of them throws another log on the fire.

'I swear it was the easiest victory of my whole career, it was just a matter of shooting them in the back and skewering them like pigeons. But what a sight: heads flying through the air, people praying on their knees . . . I felt like a cardinal!'

He jangles a full purse and with a snigger the other two supply an echo, one of them making the sign of the cross.

'How true. Amen.'

'I'm going for a piss. Leave me a drop of that stuff . . .'

'Hey, Kurt, make sure you do it a long way away, I don't want to sleep with the stench of your piss under my nose!'

'You're so plastered you wouldn't notice if I took a shit in your face . . .'

'Go fuck yourself, you cunt!'

A burp in reply. Kurt leaves the circle of light and comes towards me. He staggers past me, a few yards away, and continues into the depths of the bushes.

Decide, now.

Clothes. Clothes less filthy than the ones I've got on and a purse full of money on his belt.

I creep up behind him, hugging the trees, until I hear him splashing into the grass. I grip my dagger. As Elias taught me: one hand over his mouth, never a moment's hesitation. I cut his throat before he's worked out what's happening. Before I've worked it out myself. Barely a faint gurgle and he spits out his blood and his soul between my fingers. I support him as he falls.

I had never killed a man.

I undo his belt and take his purse, take off his jacket and trousers and roll it all into a bundle in his coat. Time to get away now, don't run, don't make a sound, holding one arm out to shield my face from the bushes and branches. The smell of blood on my hands, as there was on the plain, as there was in Frankenhausen.

I had never killed a man.

Heads flying through the air, people praying on their knees, Elias, Magister Thomas reduced to a shadow.

I had never killed a man.

I stop, in the total darkness, the voices are barely audible. My sword in my fist.

What I have to do.

Open wide the maw of hell for all those bastards.

I go back, one step at a time, the voices getting louder, closer, I drop the bundle and the bag, two of them, big steps now, two of them, no time to hesitate.

'Kurt, where the fuck . . .'

I step into the circle of light.

'Christ!'

A clean blow to the head.

'Holy shit!'

Blade straight into his chest with all my strength, until he spews blood.

A hand reaching for his weapon too late: a blow to the shoulder, then the spine.

He creeps towards the bushes on his elbows, the screams of a pig to the slaughter.

And here am I: ever slower, above him. I grip the dagger with both hands and plunge it between his shoulder-blades, splitting his bones and his heart.

Destroy the horror.

Silence. Just my hot panting breath, visible in the night, and the crackling of the fire. I look around: nothing stirs. Not now.

I've done them all in, by the power of God!

Chapter 4

I ride, bearing the device of wickedness.

It's the device that will protect me, now. Perhaps it's a shrewd move, I've got to get used to it, perhaps. The mask of a mercenary in the service of wickedness, when wickedness triumphs, that's all.

I've got to get used to it. I'd never killed before.

Another sunset streaking the fields and hills with purple reflections, blurring outlines, dissolving any remaining certainties.

I've travelled many miles, always heading south, towards Bibra, riding on a vague hope. The countryside I have passed through bore the signs of the passage of the murderous horde. Like the remnants of a natural disaster: land that will never again bear fruit; scrap metal and all kinds of leftovers from the vile armies; a few rotting corpses, the carcasses of poor unfortunates who had been standing in the horde's way; troops of mercenaries moving on from some massacre somewhere to fresh slaughter somewhere else.

Since the darkness swallowed up the horizon and the last shadows, I have been travelling on foot in the undergrowth. Between the trees I see glowing lights in the distance: perhaps they're more bivouacs. Another few steps and a faint sound comes towards me. Horses, the rattle of armour, reflections of torches on metal. My horse paws the ground, I have to hold its reins tight as I seek refuge behind a tree trunk. I stay there cautiously, stroking my horse's neck to ease its terror.

The noise is a river in full flood. It's advancing. Hoofs and gleaming weapons. A horde of ghosts rides past a few yards away from me.

Finally the commotion fades away, but the night doesn't fall silent again.

The light beyond the forest has become more intense. The air is still, but the treetops are swaying: it's smoke. I move closer until I hear the crackle of burning wood. All of a sudden the trees open up on a scene of total destruction.

The village is engulfed in flames. The heat blasts into my face, soot and embers rain down. A sweetish stink, the smell of burned flesh, turns my stomach. Then I see them: charred corpses, vague outlines abandoned to the pyre, while the vomit rises to my throat, taking my breath away.

My hands clutch the saddle, get out of here, headlong into the night, flee the horror and the terrible clutches of hell.

All around the way station, a coming and going of carts loaded with plunder from the villages; captains scream orders in various dialects; clusters of soldiers set off in all directions; barter and exchange of booty takes place in the middle of the street, between mercenaries even dirtier than myself, and tramps hoping for scraps. The other side of the devastation encountered along the way: behind the lines of a war without a front, the waste pipe to drain off the fat from the massacre.

The horse needs to rest and I need a decent meal. But more than anything I've got to get my bearings, find the shortest way to Nuremberg and from there to Bibra.

'It's not a good idea to leave a horse untended in times like these, soldier.' A voice to my right, on the other side of a column of infantrymen marching away. Stout and healthy, leather apron and high dung-covered boots. 'You'll just have time to get to your lodgings and they'll serve it to you for your dinner . . . It'll be safer in the stable.'

'How much?'

'Two crowns.'

'Too much.'

'Your horse's carcass will be worth less . . .'

The paid-off mercenary on his way home: 'Fine, but you've got to give him hay and water.'

'Take him inside.'

He smiles: crowded streets, plenty of business for him.

'Have you come from Fulda?'

The soldier returning from the war: 'No. Frankenhausen.'

'You're the first to come by . . . Tell me, how was it? A great battle . . .'

'The easiest earner of my career.'

The groom turns around and calls, 'Hey, Grosz, we've got someone here who's come from Frankenhausen!'

Four of them emerge from the shadow, coarse mercenary faces.

Grosz has a scar that furrows his left cheek and runs down to his neck, his jaw cleft where the blade cut the bone. The grey, inexpressive eyes of someone who's seen plenty of battles, who's used to the stench of corpses.

His voice echoes as though from a cave. 'Have you killed all the yokels?'

A deep breath to quell the panic. Attentive faces.

The soldier coming back from the war stammers, 'Every one.'

Grosz's eye falls on the bag of money hanging from my belt. 'Were you with Prince Philip?'

Another breath. Never hesitate. 'No, Captain Bamberg, in Duke Georg's troops.'

His eyes are motionless, possibly suspicious. The purse.

'We tried to get to Philip and join forces with him, but we were too late getting to Fulda. They'd already left: he made off like a lunatic, the great poof! We got to Schmalkalden, Eisenach and Salza in a forced march, didn't even have time to stop for a piss . . .'

Another one: 'There were just a few scraps left for us, we joined in with some sacking that was going on. Are you sure there are no peasants left to kill?'

The eyes of the soldier who exterminated the peasants in the plain: glass, like Grosz's eyes.

'No. They're all dead.'

The man with the twisted face goes on staring, thinking about the one thing on his mind right now: how risky it would be to take the purse. It's four against one. The other three don't move unless he gestures to them to do so.

He speaks slowly: 'Mühlhausen. The princes are planning to besiege the town. There's going to be a good amount of plundering to be had there. Merchants' houses, not peasant cottages . . . Banks, shops . . .'

'Women,' says the shortest one, sneering behind his back.

But Grosz, the ogre, doesn't laugh. Neither do I, my mouth dry and my breath trapped in my chest. He's weighing it up. My hand on the handle of my sword, hanging from my belt along with the bag full of money. He's understood. In a fight, my only blow would be for him. I'd cut his throat: I can. It's written in the expression on his face.

Barely a shiver, the batting of his eyelids is the verdict. It's not worth the risk.

'Good luck.'

They pass on, in silence, the sound of their boots sinking into the mud.

*

The fat man sits opposite me, taking great bites from a shank of kid, long draughts from an enormous beaker of beer run down his greasy beard which, with the bandage over his left eye, almost hides his face. His jacket, worn and filthy, barely covers the evidence of barrels consumed over decades in the pay of any master who would have him.

During a pause, the pig questions me: 'What's a fine little gentleman like you doing in a pig-sty like this?'

His full mouth dribbles. He wipes it with his hand and then burps.

Without looking at him, I say, 'The horse needs to rest and I need to eat.'

'No, my little chap. What you're doing in this shit-hole of a fucking war.'

'Defending the princes from the rebels . . .' I haven't time to go on.

'Ah . . . Right, got you, got you . . . from a few flea-ridden bums' – he chews – 'from a gang of beggars' – he swallows – 'what times we live in, young boys defending the lords from the peasants' – he burps again. 'I tell you, my little fellow, this is the shittiest of all the shitty wars that I've seen with my one eye. It's all money, my friend, nothing but money and business as far as those pigs in Rome are concerned. The bishops with all their whores and children to support! Hard cash, listen, the princes, the dukes, the lucky sods, they don't think about anything else. First they take everything the yokels own, and then they send us in to thrash the living daylights out of anyone who gets pissed off. Maybe I'm too old for all this bollocks. Fucking arseholes! But this time we should've turned the cannons on the princes and the Pope's lickspittles. They really showed what they were made of, the hayseeds did: they burned down the castles and everything in them, they fucked the countesses up the arse, disembowelled the priests, fuck's sake! Oh, they're always going on about God, but they smashed everything, I was that close to joining in as well, but I knew how things would turn out, the poor always get it in the neck. And we always end up with threepence. This is for that lot.' He farts, sniggers, swigs. 'Fuck it!'

I stop eating, somewhere between surprise and distaste. I like this fat guy, he's got a mouth like a sewer but he hates the lords. I'm encouraged: they're made of flesh and blood, not just hard, honed iron. 'And where were you?' I ask him.

'In Eisenach, then Salza, then I got fed up breaking my arms over the backs of the poor creatures. It was really disgusting. I've got too old for all that bollocks, I'm forty years of age, fuck's sake, twenty of them spent on this shit. And what about you, young sir?'

'Twenty-five.'

'No, no: where have you been?'

'Frankenhausen.'

'Bloody hell!!! You've been in the middle of the Last Judgement? From what I hear, there's never been anything like it.'

'That's right, mate.'

'So tell me . . . That preacher, that prophet, that, um, the tough bloke, what's his name . . .? Oh yes: Müntzer. The Coiner. What happened to him?'

Careful. 'They got him.'

'He's not dead?'

'No. I saw him being carried away. A member of the troop who caught him told me he fought like a lion, getting him was difficult, the soldiers were intimidated by the look on his face and the words he was coming out with. While they were carrying him away on the cart you could still hear him shouting, "*Omnia sunt communia*!"'

'And what the fuck does that mean?'

'Everything belongs to everyone.'

'Shit. What a man! And you know Latin?'

He sneers. I lower my eyes.

Chapter 6

A few hours' travel and the hills of the Thuringian forest were already a luminous patch in the deep grey of the sky behind me. I had just passed the fortress of Coburg and was making for the inn in the town of Ebern. Another two days of marching, three at the most, along the wooded valleys of High Franconia that were beginning to spread out before me. A wide road, normally crowded with merchants' carts between the Itz and the Main. That evening in Ebern, the next day in Forschheim, to avoid the prying eyes of Bamberg, then to Nuremberg and finally on to Bibra.

For the first time I felt I'd be able to do it. That exhaustion that's starting to flood back into me, I'd forgotten it, it was cancelled out by that strength that can drag us over the brink of defeat.

They came towards me from the distance, while the sky was filling with clouds: sorrowful, tattered, tragic. A thin mist advanced ahead of them, faint, greyish light mixed with the drizzle that blurs vision and breath, in the clearing in the narrow valley that I was hoping to have passed through by sunset.

They were moving slowly, they might have covered several hours since dawn, after a night pitched in some unimaginable camp somewhere, and ahead of them lay the unbearable darkness of a journey with no destination.

They had no carts, or oxen or horses. Bags over their shoulders. A torrent of refugees, a deluge of misery passing through the splendid towers of Coburg.

That column of massacred humanity crept onwards, crushed under heaven's massive heel. Exhaustedly dragging furniture with them, invalids groaning under sweat-drenched bandages, old people laid on improvised stretchers. Ceaseless litanies and the howls of babies wailing out their woes.

A few women tried to give the shambling bodies some kind of

direction: they would pass up and down the wretched line, comforting
the wounded or encouraging people to go on whenever they sank
beneath the weight of their misfortune. Always with children bound
to shoulders, arms and laps; tragic, proud faces. That unimaginable,
solemn strength had breathed life into the wretched flesh of who
knows what villages, perhaps the very one I passed through days ago,
or another one, or another still. Is there a single scrap of the world that
has escaped the cataclysm?

I followed the exhaustion of their footsteps, keeping my distance, a
few yards away on the right, motionless for a while, an eternity. Every
now and again a glance, an imploring lament would pierce me to the
quick. Hundreds of men under a single soldier: not a gesture of
contempt, not a sign of reaction. Exhausted, all of them, stupefied in
the face of their ruin. And it was to me, a runaway got up like a
murderer, that they addressed the prayer of the dispossessed.

Then, out of the lifeless mass, a woman's face turns towards me.
Vivid, in its terrible exhaustion, detaching itself from the weeping
column, entrusting to other arms the two starving children she was
bringing with her. 'We have nothing, soldier. Nothing but the
wounds of the cripples and the tears of our children. What else can
you steal from us?'

I had no words to soothe the remorse I feel for my powerlessness
and the guilt of being alive, as I stared into those proud eyes, nails
driven into my flesh. I should have got down from my horse, picked
up her children, given them money and help. I should have helped my
people, the army of the elect, lost in mud that they had no way out of.
I should have got down and stayed there.

I struck my horse's flanks, hard. Almost blindly.

This business of earning your daily bread is really sad and wearisome. People come up with the most pious lies about work. It's just another abominable form of idolatry, a dog licking the rod that beats it: work.

At the axe and chopping block from daybreak. I chop firewood in the courtyard separating the orchard and the stable from Vogel's garden.

Wolfgang Vogel: as far as everyone's concerned he's the pastor of Eltersdorf, Luther's successor; for Hut he's excellent help in the distribution of books, leaflets, manifestos; the insurgent peasants know him as 'Read-the-Bible', from that phrase he's always coming out with: 'Now that God is talking to you in your language, you have to learn to read the Bible on your own. You don't need teachers to help you.'

'Then we don't need you either,' was the most common riposte, but he never let it put him off.

And good for Read-the-Bible: a warm welcome, a slap on the back, keen to know who's alive and who's dead, and here I am with an axe in my hand, looking at a pile of firewood. I've only been here two days and I've got to earn my hospitality.

Hut wasn't in Bibra, the printing works were closed. They told me he'd passed that way the week before, but had soon set off for northern Franconia, to baptise as many more people as he could. Like a wayfarer arriving at an inn in flames and asking what's for dinner. When I learned that Vogel was back in Eltersdorf, after I'd changed horses and got hold of some provisions, off I went.

Eltersdorf. I've got a room, a plate of soup and a new name: Gustav Metzger. I'm still alive, I don't know how. I won't be setting off again for a while.

Long, unbearable days. Cleaning the stable, stacking wood, filling the pigs' troughs, waiting for the sow to spawn. Picking the fruit in the little orchard, mending the worn-out tools. Repetitive tasks, movements imposed on the limbs, for the equivalent of a bowl of dog food.

Meanwhile the news reaching us from outside tells of massacres all over the place: the princes' retaliation turned out to be more than a match for the gauntlet we threw them. The peasants' heads are still bowed over their ploughs: they're no longer the men who used their scythes as swords.

There's hardly anyone in the village that I can exchange more than a couple of words with. I go to the mill to have Vogel's grain ground and I bump into someone in the street, a few jokes about Pastor Wolfgang, the only person in the village with any wheat for the miller.

One of the few pleasant things about the day is chatting with Hermann, a slow-witted peasant who tends Vogel's orchard. He actually does almost all the talking, while axe blows fall on the logs of wood, because everyone, he says, is born with the hands he deserves and the ones he was born with had calluses already, and literate people like myself should only touch books. He smiles, his mouth half toothless, and he swears that this war was won by poor people like himself. He talks about the time they took the count's castle, and for ten days they had themselves served by the count and his men, while at night they fucked the lady and her daughters. That had been their great victory. No one imagines keeping the powerful low for long, apart from anything because if the peasants governed and the lords worked the land, everyone would quickly die of hunger, because everyone gets the hands they deserve . . . And yet, for a lord, licking the feet of a servant and having to stir some yokel's porridge is the most devastating defeat of all. For people like Hermann it's the most sacred of pleasures. He laughs like a madman, spitting and spluttering all over the place, and to please him even more I tell him that, perhaps, the next count will be his own son, and that's a good way of bringing down the powerful: get their wives up the duff and pollute their stock with plebs.

With Vogel, on the other hand, there isn't much talking to be done. He's a fine enough man, but I don't like him: he says that fate and the supreme will of God decreed that the terrible massacre of defenceless people was something that must take place, that the unfathomable supreme power exhorts us to understand through his signs, even signs that are tragic or gloomy, that the will of men, even the will of the just and meritorious men of the kingdom, is not enough to bring about his promise on earth. Vogel can go fuck himself, and his promises and everything else.

By now I automatically turn round when people call me Gustav, I've become accustomed to a name no less strange to me than any other.

At night, the candlelight is enough to read a few pages from the Bible: my room: wooden walls, small bed, stool and table. On the table, the Magister's bag, a shapeless, mud-encrusted lump. No one has moved it from there.

There's nothing left, nothing but the bag that's been brought here from Frankenhausen, to remind me of broken promises and the past. Nothing that would be worth the risk of keeping. I should have burned it straight away, but every time I've tried, when I went to pick it up it was like being at the top of a staircase and feeling the weight pulling me down, as I abandoned the Magister to his fate.

I open it for the first time. It almost crumbles between my hands. All the letters are still there, but the damp has eaten into them and rotted them. The sheets of paper are practically disintegrating.

To our magnificent master Thomas Müntzer of Quedlinburg, greetings from the peasants of the Black Forest and Hans Müller of Bulgenbach, who have rebelled in unison and with great force against the most vile Lord Sigmund von Lupfen, guilty of starving and oppressing his servants and their families winter after winter, reducing them to a state of despair.

Our Master,
I write to inform you that a week has passed since our twelve articles were presented to the Council in the town of Villingen, which replied promptly, accepting only some of the requests contained therein. Some of the peasants therefore agreed that no more would be obtained and chose to return to their houses. But a not inconsiderable proportion of them decided to continue the protest. I myself am attempting to reach the peasants in the adjacent territories to find reinforcements in this just struggle, and am writing to you with the haste of one who has one foot in the stirrup, sure that no other man living anywhere in Germany will be more willing than you are to justify my brevity, and hoping with all my heart that this missive reaches you.
May God be with you always.
Friend to the peasants
Hans Müller of Bulgenbach
From Villingen, 25 November of the year 1524

Müller, probably dead. I wish I'd known him then. And less than a year has passed. A year that now seems like somewhere on the other side of the world, like his words. The year when everything was possible, if it ever was.

I rummage around in the bag some more. A yellow, tattered sheet.

To the master of the peasants, Thomas Müntzer, defender of the faith against the wicked, at the church of Our Lady in Mühlhausen.

Master,
On the holy day of Easter, taking advantage of the absence of Count Ludwig, the peasants attacked the castle of Helfenstein, and after looting it and capturing the countess and her children, they headed for the walls of the town, where the count and his noblemen had taken refuge. With the help of the citizens, they managed to get in and took them. Then they led the count and another thirteen noblemen through the open countryside and forced them to pass under the yoke. Despite the fact that the count offered a great deal of money in exchange for his life, they killed him along with his knights, stripped him and left him in the middle of the wood with his shoulders bound to the yoke. Having returned to the castle, they set light to it.

It was not long before news of these events reached the neighbouring counties, sowing panic among the nobles who were now aware that they might face the same fate as Count Ludwig. I am sure that these occurrences will be a viaticum of primary importance for the acknowledgement of the twelve articles in all towns and cities.

On that Easter Day, Christ awoke from the dead to revive the spirit of the humble and revive the heart of the oppressed (Isaiah 57, 15). May the grace of God not abandon you.
The captain of the peasant armies of the Neckar and the Odenwald.
Jäcklein Rohrbach   Weinsberg, 18 April 1525

I clutch the musty page. I know this letter, Magister Thomas read it out loud to remind everyone that the moment of redemption was at hand. His voice: the flame that set Germany ablaze.

The doctrine and the marshland
(1519–1522)

Chapter 8

A shit-hole, Wittenberg. Wretched, poor, muddy. An unhealthy, harsh climate, free of vines or fruit trees, a cold, smoky pub. What have you got in Wittenberg, if you take away the castle, the church and the university? Filthy alleyways, muddy streets, a barbarian population of brewers and junk dealers.

I'm sitting in the university courtyard with these thoughts crowding into my head, eating a freshly baked pretzel. I turn it round in my hands to cool it down as I study the student throng that you usually see at this time of day. Equipped with hunks of bread and oil and soup, they take advantage of the mild sunlight to enjoy their lunch in the open as they wait for their next lecture. Different accents, many of us come from neighbouring principalities, but also from Holland, Denmark, Switzerland: the sons of half the world come here to listen to the lively voice of the Master. Martin Luther, his fame has travelled on the wind, helped along by the presses of the printers who have brought celebrity to this place forgotten by God and men until just a few years ago. Events . . . events are gathering speed. No one had ever heard of Wittenberg, and now more and more people are coming, younger and younger people, because anyone who wants to get involved in the enterprise has to be here, here in the most important bit of bogland in the whole of Christendom. And perhaps it's true: this is the place where they're baking the bread that will keep the Pope's teeth busy for years to come. A new generation of teachers and theologians who will free the world from the corrupt claws of Rome.

And here he comes, a few years older than I am, pointed beard, thin and pinched as only prophets can be: Melanchthon, the pillar of classical wisdom that Frederick was determined to install alongside Luther to give prestige to the university. His lectures are brilliant, alternating quotations from Aristotle with passages from the Scriptures that he can read in Hebrew, as though drawing on an inexhaustible well of knowledge. Beside him the rector, Karlstadt, the

Incorruptible, soberly dressed, some years older than his colleague. Behind him, Amsdorf and faithful Franz Günther, like puppies on an invisible lead. They nod, nothing more.

Karlstadt and Melanchthon talk as they walk along. They've been doing that a lot lately. You catch a few phrases, scraps of Latin every now and again, but you never quite know what the subject is. Along the walls of the university curiosity grows like ivy: young minds crave new topics to test their milk teeth on.

They sit on a bench directly opposite me, on the other side of the courtyard. With feigned indifference, little groups of students form all around them. Melanchthon's youthful voice reaches me. As captivating in the auditorium as it is strident out here. '. . . and you should be persuaded once and for all, my dear Karlstadt, that it has never been put more clearly than in the words of the apostle: "Let every soul be subject to the governing authorities. For there is no power but of God: the powers that be are ordained by God." Saint Paul wrote that in his Letter to the Romans. Consequently, he who rebels against authority is rebelling against what God has instituted.'

I decide to get up and join the other spectators, just as Karlstadt begins his reply. 'It's ludicrous to imagine that the Christian for whom, according to the very same Saint Paul, "the law is dead" – meaning the moral law imposed by God upon men – must blindly obey the laws, so often unjust, that have been created by men! Christ says: "Render to Caesar the things that are Caesar's, and unto God the things that are God's." The Jews used Caesar's money, acknowledging Roman authority. So it was also right for them to accept all those civil obligations that did not compromise the religious sphere. In that way Christ, in his words, distinguishes the political field from the religious and accepts the function of secular authority, but only on condition that it is not superimposed upon God, that it does not impinge upon him. Indeed, when it is substituted for God it ceases to promote the common good and instead makes slaves of men. Remember the Gospel of Luke: "Thou shalt adore the Lord thy God, and him only shalt thou serve."'

The air became thicker, ears tensed and eyes darting from side to side. An arena formed, a perfect semicircle of students, as though someone had sketched out a miniature battlefield. Günther stands in silence, wondering which side he is going to have to join. Amsdorf has already chosen his place: bang in the middle.

Melanchthon shakes his head and narrows his eyes, nodding with a magnanimous smile. He always has the attitude of a father telling his son the facts of life. As though his mind understood yours, as though it somehow encompassed it, having already understood everything that you will understand henceforward and until the end of your days.

He looks complacently at his audience; he has the New Christianity before him. He weighs his words before replying. 'You must dig deeper, Karlstadt, don't stop at the surface. The notion of things being "given to Caesar" actually means something very different from what you say . . . Christ distinguishes between the fields of civil authority and the authority of God, that is true. But he does that precisely because each is given its dues, since the two forms of authority mirror one another. That is the Lord's will. Saint Paul himself explained that concept to us. He says, "For the same reason you pay taxes, for the authorities are God's servants, busy with this one thing. Give each his due: tributes to whom tributes are due; taxes to whom taxes; fear to whom fear; respect to whom respect." Apart from that, my good friend, if the faithful behave honestly they have nothing to fear from the authorities; in fact, they will be praised. On the other hand anyone who performs acts of wickedness must be afraid, because if the ruler bears a sword there is a reason: he is in the service of God for the just punishment of those who do evil.'

Karlstadt says slowly, anxiously, 'But who will punish rulers who do not work honestly?'

Melanchthon, confidently: '"Do not make your own justice, my dearest ones, leave it to the wrath of God." The Lord says, "Vengeance is mine, I will repay." Unjust authority is punished by God, Karlstadt. God put it on the earth, God can destroy it. It isn't up to us to oppose it. And in any case, who could put it with greater clarity than the apostle: "Blessed be those who persecute you"?'

Karlstadt: 'Of course, Melanchthon, of course. I'm not saying that we mustn't love our enemies too, but you will agree with me that we must at least beware of those who, seated on Moses's throne, slam shut the doors of the kingdom of heaven in the face of men . . .'

Good Father Melanchthon: 'False prophets, my dear Karlstadt, they are the false prophets . . . And the world is full of them. Even here, in this place of study graced by the Lord . . . Because it is among the learned that pride takes root, the presumption of putting words into the mouth of the Lord in order to increase one's own personal fame. But He has told us: "I will destroy the wisdom of the wise, and the discernment of the discerning I will thwart." We serve God and fight for the true faith against secular corruption. Don't forget it, Karlstadt.'

That was below the belt, it was disloyal. A veil of weakness, the shadow of the conflict that is stalking him, falls upon the rector's face. He looks confused and unconvinced, and clearly wounded.

Melanchthon is on his feet: he has sown his doubt, now all that remains is to administer the *coup de grâce*.

At that moment a voice rises up from the audience. A firm, clear voice that could not possibly belong to a student.

' "Beware of men: for they will deliver you up to the councils, and they will scourge you in their synagogues. And ye shall be brought before governors and kings for my sake, for a testimony against them and the Gentiles." Perhaps our Master Luther is afraid to appear before the authorities to be judged by the courts? Doesn't his testimony alone make it clear to you? It is Luther's cry that rises from the fields and the mines, against those who have wrought havoc with the true faith: "He who comes from above is above all. He who comes from the earth belongs to the earth and speaks of the earth." Luther has shown us the way: when the authority of men is opposed to Christian testimony, it is the duty of the true Christian to confront it.'

We look at the face of the man who has just been speaking. His eyes are even harder and more resolute than his words. He never takes them off Melanchthon.

Melanchthon. He shuts his eyes, swallowing back his fury, taken aback. Someone has got ahead of him.

Two strokes of the bell. They are calling us to Luther's lecture. We've got to go.

The silence and tension melt away amid the hubbub of the chattering students, impressed by the argument and by Amsdorf's apt phrases.

They all stream towards the end of the courtyard. Melanchthon doesn't move, his eyes are fixed on the man who has stolen a certain victory from him. The two men confront one another at a distance, until someone takes the professor by the arm to accompany him to the auditorium. Before he goes, his tone of voice is a promise: 'We shall have occasion to talk again, I am sure of it.'

In the crowded corridor leading to the auditorium where everyone is waiting for Luther, I catch up with my friend Martin Borrhaus, whom everyone calls Cellarius, and who's also excited about what's just happened.

In a low voice: 'Did you see Melanchthon's face? Mister Sharp-as-a-Razor touched a nerve there. Do you know who he is?'

'His name's Müntzer. Thomas Müntzer. He's from Stolberg.'

Carafa's eye
(1521)

Letter sent to Rome from the city of Worms, seat of the Imperial Diet, addressed to Gianpietro Carafa, dated 14 May 1521.

To the most illustrious and reverend lord and most honourable patron Giovanni Pietro Carafa, in Rome.

Most Illustrious and Reverend Lord and My Most Honourable Patron,

I am writing to Your Lordship concerning a most grave and mysterious event: Martin Luther was abducted two days ago while returning to Wittenberg with the imperial pass.

When you commissioned me to follow the monk to the Imperial Diet of Worms, you made no mention of any plan of this nature; if there is something which escaped my attention and which I should know, I anxiously await Your Lordship to make your servant aware of it. If, as I believe, my information was not inadequate, I might stress that Germany faces a dark and a very serious threat. For that reason I consider it essential to keep Your Lordship informed of the movements of Luther and those around him throughout the days of the Diet, and the behaviour of his ruler, Frederick, Elector of Saxony.

On Tuesday, 16 April, at lunchtime, the city guard posted on the cathedral tower gave the habitual trumpet blast to signal the arrival of an important guest. The news of the monk's arrival had already spread throughout the morning and many people had gone to meet him. His modest carriage, preceded by the imperial herald, was followed by about a hundred people on horseback. A great crowd filled the street, preventing the cortège from advancing at any speed. Before entering the Johanniterhof Inn with the crowd on either side, Luther looked around him with demonic eyes, shouting, 'God will be on my side.' Not far away, in the Swan Inn, the Elector of Saxony had taken accommodation with his retinue. From the first few hours of his residence, he received a regular series of visits from the minor nobility, city dwellers and magistrates, but none of the most important figures of the Diet was willing to risk being seen with the monk. Apart from the very young landgrave

Philip of Hesse who put subtle questions to Luther concerning sexual customs in the Babilonica, receiving a severe rebuttal for his pains. The same Prince Frederick saw him only in the public sessions.

It was not, in any case, at the public sessions of 17 and 18 of April that the actual negotiations took place, as much as in private conversations and certain events that took place during Luther's stay in Worms. As Your Lordship will already be aware, despite the intense aversion that the young Emperor Charles has as regards the monk and his theses, the Diet did not succeed in making him retract, or in taking the correct measures before events got out of control. This was because of the manoeuvres that had been skilfully orchestrated by some mysterious supporters of Luther, among whom I believe I can number the Elector of Saxony, even if it is not possible to assert as much with absolute certainty, because of the obscure and underground character of those manoeuvres.

– On the morning of 19 April Emperor Charles V summoned the electors and princes to ask them to take a resolute position on Luther, showing the proper regret at not having taken energetic action against the rebel monk until recently. The Emperor confirmed the imperial pass of twenty-one days on condition that the brother did not preach on his return journey to Wittenberg. On the afternoon of that same day, the princes and the electors gathered to debate his imperial request. The condemnation of Luther was approved by four votes out of six. The Elector of Saxony certainly voted against, and that was his first and only open demonstration in favour of Luther.

– On the night of the 20th, however, two manifestos were nailed up by unknown people in Worms: the first contained threats against Luther; the second declared that four hundred noblemen were sworn not to abandon the 'just Luther', and to declare their enmity towards the princes and the supporters of Rome, and first and foremost the Archbishop of Mainz.

This event cast over the Diet the shadow of a religious war and of a Lutheran party preparing for insurgency. The Archbishop of Mainz, terrified, asked the Emperor to re-examine the whole question, and received an assurance from him that he would do this, lest he risk splitting Germany in two and exposing himself to rebellion. Whoever nailed up those manifestos thus achieved his aim of extending the cause by several days and spreading fear and circumspection about any condemnation of Luther.

– On the 23rd and 24th, therefore, Luther was examined by a

commission specially appointed by the Emperor and, as Your Lordship may already be aware, continued to reject the idea of a retraction. Despite this, his colleague from Wittenberg, Amsdorf, spread the word that an agreement was at hand between Luther, the Holy See and the Emperor. Why, My Most Illustrious Lord? I believe, on the Elector Frederick's suggestion, to gain more time.

Consequently, between the 23rd and the 24th many different mediators came to heal the rift between Luther and the Holy See, represented here in Worms by the Archbishop of Treviri.

On the 25th a private meeting was held, without witnesses, between Luther and the Archbishop of Treviri. Predictably, it brought all the diplomacy of the two previous days to nothing. Privately Luther, as he had already demonstrated during the sessions of the Diet in the presence of the Emperor, refused 'for reasons of conscience' to retract his theses. An unbridgeable and definitive rupture was thus imposed. Throughout that time, word of Luther's imminent arrest spread through the streets.

On the evening of the same day, two figures wrapped in cloaks were seen leaving Luther's room. The innkeeper recognised them as Feilitzsch and Thun, advisers to the Elector Frederick. What had been plotted at that late-night meeting? Your Lordship may perhaps be able to find an answer in the events of the days that followed.

On the morning of the following day, the 26th, Luther left the city of Worms quietly, with a small escort of sympathetic noblemen. The next day he was in Frankfurt; on the 28th in Friedberg. Here he persuaded the imperial herald to allow him to carry on alone. On 3 May, Luther left the main road and continued his journey on secondary roads, giving the reason for his change of itinerary as a desire to visit family, in the town of Möhra. He also persuaded his travelling companions to continue on in a different carriage. Witnesses say that when he continued his journey onwards from Möhra he was alone in his carriage, apart from Amsdorf and his colleague Petzensteiner. A few hours later the carriage was stopped by a number of men on horseback who asked the driver which one was Luther and, recognising him, took him away with them by force into the surrounding scrubland.

It will be clear to Your Lordship that one cannot avoid seeing Frederick, the Elector of Saxony, behind these machinations. But should you have scruples about leaping to too hasty a conclusion, I wonder if I might be granted permission to bring some questions to Your Lordship's attention? In whose interest would it be to delay

Luther's condemnation, leaving the conflict unresolved? And who, seeking to delay the sentence, would have an interest in conjuring the threat of a party of knights prepared to defend the monk by raising their swords against the Emperor and the Pope? Finally, in whose interest would it be to bring Luther to safety by staging a kidnapping, without revealing himself openly, and without compromising himself in the eyes of the Emperor?

I might be so bold as to believe that Your Lordship reaches the same conclusion as his servant. The air of battle is blowing, My Lord, and Luther's fame is growing by the day. The news of his abduction has unleashed unimaginable panic and agitation. Even those who do not agree with his theses still recognise him as an authoritative voice for reform in the Church. A great religious war is about to be unleashed. The seeds that Luther has sown, wrested from the impetus of conviction, are about to bear fruit. Disciples keen to move to action are preparing, with intrepid logic, to take his ideas to their conclusion. If sincerity is a virtue, Your Lordship will perhaps allow me to assert that Luther's protectors have already achieved their objective of transforming the monk into a battering ram against the Holy See, organising a large popular following around him. And now they are only waiting for the most opportune moment to take to battle in the open field.

I have nothing more to say but to kiss Your Lordship's hand, and take my leave in all sincerity.

The faithful servant of Your Most Illustrious Lordship

Q   Worms, 14 May 1521

Letter sent to Rome from the Saxon city of Wittenberg, addressed to Gianpietro Carafa, dated 27 October 1521.

To the most illustrious and most reverend lord and the most honourable patron Giovanni Pietro Carafa, in Rome.

My Most Illustrious and Most Reverend Lord and My Most Honourable Patron,

I am writing to Your Lordship to inform you that no doubt remains concerning Prince Frederick's abduction of Luther. Here in Wittenberg, some rumours refer to voluntary imprisonment of the monk in one of the Elector's castles in the north of Thuringia. If the rumours bearing out this truth, which are mounting daily, were not enough to dispel any remaining doubts, one would need only to read the message in the serene face of the effeminate and most learned Melanchthon, or in the daily tasks of education and training performed quite calmly by his disciples, or even more so in the frantic activity of Rector Karlstadt. So we may conclude that Luther has not been kidnapped, but brought to safety by his protector.

But I must reply to the question Your Lordship raised in your last letter. It may be true that the Emperor's forces have turned their attention towards the war on France, and it might be a propitious moment for Luther's followers to reveal themselves. But I do not believe that this will happen soon. If these eyes are fit for anything, they are confident that Prince Frederick and his allies will take their time. It is not in his interest to foment rebellion against the Pope, because he knows he might lose control of it and might be defeated. The Emperor, in fact, would fight in defence of Catholicism and he is still too strong to be challenged on the battlefield.

But there is another reason for the Elector's prudence. The minor landless nobility has gathered around two impoverished noblemen, sympathisers of Luther, by the name of Hutter and Sickingen, who might attempt an insurrection in the coming year. For this reason I believe that the princes, with Frederick at their head, will not wish to leave the way open for these tumultuous subordinates and will unite in destroying them, so that they alone remain in control of all reform.

But there is one more reason why the Elector is taking his time. The reason that I have not yet mentioned to Your Lordship is the popular mood, which has been gathering in the air for some months in these parts. In particular, events in Wittenberg, in Luther's absence, are exerting pressure upon the Elector. The rector of the university, Andreas Karlstadt, is actually at the head of a reform movement of his own that is finding a large following among the population. He has abolished monastic votes and celibacy for the men of the Church. Aural confession, the canon of the mass and the holy images have been subject to the same fate. He has unleashed popular fury against the pictures of the saints, and episodes of violence that have involved the despoliation of churches and chapels. He himself has promptly married a young lady barely fifteen years of age. He dresses in sackcloth and preaches in German in the street, talking of humility and the abolition of all ecclesiastical privileges. He has no scruples about maintaining that the Scriptures must be given to the people, who must be free to appropriate them and interpret them as they see fit. Not even Luther would have dared do as much. As regards civil administration, Karlstadt has installed an elected municipal council to rule the city on a par with the Prince, and this alarms Frederick to a quite considerable degree. Something he thought he would turn to his own advantage risks rebounding upon him: reform of the Church and independence from Rome could turn into reform of authority and independence from the princes.

For that reason I believe that it will not be long before the Elector has fetched Luther out of the lair where he has him hidden, in order to get rid of Karlstadt. I can also assure Your Lordship that if Luther were finally to return to Wittenberg, Karlstadt would be obliged to leave. He could not survive a clash with the prophet of the German reformation: he is still a little university rector and, after Worms, Luther is now the German Hercules as far as everyone in the country is concerned. So, My Lord, I am sure that this Hercules will bring down his club upon Karlstadt and on anyone who threatens to obscure his fame, as long as the Elector allows him to do so. Frederick, for his part, knows very well that Luther alone is capable of guiding reforms in the direction most useful to him; they need each other just as the navigator and the oarsman need one another to steer a boat. I am sure that Luther will soon be back in Wittenberg, and he will rid the field of all who have usurped his throne.

So, for all these reasons, Prince Frederick and his allies have not yet openly confronted the Church and the Empire.

Now, if ever a servant had been permitted to give advice to his own master, I am sure he would speak as follows: 'It seems to me, My Lord, that in order to strike the Elector and the princes who wish to rebel against the authority of the Roman church all at once, one would have to strike the German Hercules himself, the one they are using as a shield. The people, the peasants, are discontented and troublesome, they want more advanced reforms than those that Prince Frederick and perhaps this same Luther are disposed to grant them. The truth is that the portal that Luther has opened is one that he himself would now wish to be closed. Now, this Karlstadt isn't terribly important, he will not live long. But the fact that so many people here in Wittenberg have followed him is a clear sign of popular feeling. So, if from the waves of this stormy German ocean another Luther should emerge, more diabolical than the devil's friar, someone who would eclipse his fame and give voice to the desires of the mob . . . someone whose words would lay waste the whole of Germany, forcing Frederick and all the princes into war, forcing them to ask the Emperor and Rome for support to quell the rebellion . . . Someone, My Lord, who would take his hammer and strike Germany with such strength as to shake it from the Alps to the North Sea. If such a man existed somewhere, he would have to be held more precious than gold, because he would be the most powerful weapon against Frederick of Saxony and Martin Luther.'

If God, in His infinite providence, sent us such a prophet, it would only be to remind us that His ways are infinite, as His glory is infinite, which is why these humble eyes will continue in their work, and for ever serve Your Lordship, whose munificence I implore, and kiss your hands.

Your Lordship's faithful servant

Q   Wittenberg, 27 October 1521

The door is barely hanging from its hinges. I push it and slip inside. It's darker than it is outside and just as bitterly cold. Only splinters remain of the windows, the statues are mutilated in several places. The iconoclastic fury didn't spare the church. I can't understand why Cellarius arranged to meet me here, he just said he wanted to talk to me. He's been very agitated for some time. Everyone here in Wittenberg has. Preachers are going around the place, coming from Zwickau and being called prophets. We know one of them: Stübner, he studied here a few years ago. Their sermons stir people's indignation and win them widespread sympathy. Ideas both new and extreme: a mixture that Cellarius is unable to resist. The creak of the old bench as I sit down mingles with the creak of the door opening behind me. Cellarius, panting his way through the columns of the nave. He joins me, shaking the mud from his boots.

A glance around: we're alone.

'Great things are afoot. That argument with Melanchthon was spectacular. Heavyweight stuff: things like how baptising a child is like washing a dog, to take one example. The sight of Melanchthon! He was purple in the face! He managed to fight back, but he sure as hell wasn't expecting an attack like that. Now they're hoping that Luther will come back to confront him as well . . .'

'Well, they'll have a fair old wait. Luther won't be showing his face for a while, he's staying well hidden. The Elector's keeping Luther's arse nice and warm in one of his castles. As far as I'm concerned, all that business about Worms and the kidnapping sounds like a comedy written by Spalatin. Luther, the German Hercules . . . a mastiff on the Elector's leash.'

He growls and smiles. 'They won't have much trouble lengthening the leash, you'll see. It'll be just long enough for him to get here and bark at our friend Karlstadt, and put him back in his place.'

'That's for sure. Karlstadt's been exaggerating just a bit too much.'

He nods. 'But he's not on his own any more. There are those prophets. Then Stübner talked to me about that man Müntzer, you remember? He stayed with them in Zwickau and in Bohemia. It seems he inflamed the people and started riots with the mere force of his words. Everything that Karlstadt has done won't necessarily be lost . . .'

'As regards priestly marriage, preaching in German and that kind of thing there'll be no turning back, but the municipal order of the city won't survive Luther's return. Karlstadt isn't the kind who appreciates conflict. You'll see: rather than stand up to Luther, he'll pack his bags and go. You'd really need someone like Müntzer. When he was here he was more like Luther than Luther himself, and now that Luther's finished he might be our only hope. We should track him down.'

'We'll have to ask Stübner. He's bound to know more.'

Ankle-deep in snow and mud, the cold entering my bones. Cellarius says that Stübner usually stays with the brewer Klaus Schacht: ideal sanctuary for a German Isaiah. The incense a dense steam smelling of cooking and beer, the psalms the drawling songs and curses of the regulars.

Around a table about a dozen people, three or four students in a group of unkempt-looking workers. The centre of everyone's attention is a big man with a red beard and curly hair. He speaks without interruption, waving the air with his hand.

'Give up your fasting, and let the noise you make be heard aloft. Do you think that's the fast the Lord desires, the day when man mortifies himself? Letting your heads droop like rushes, sleeping on sackcloth and ashes, is that what you call fasting, is that what the Lord really wants? God wants fasting of another kind: He wants you to melt the iniquitous chains, break the bonds of the yoke and free the oppressed. That is true fasting: sharing your bread with the hungry, bringing the poor, the homeless into your house, clothing the naked, without taking your eyes off the people. Tell that servant Melanchthon . . .'

He's clearly the worse for wear. A tirade against everyone and no one, but applauded by the regulars who may be even drunker than the prophet. When the orator sits down again the chattering resumes more quietly.

I approach him. The table top is covered with carved graffiti. The clearest image: the Pope fucking a child. I introduce myself as a friend of Cellarius. Without looking me in the eyes he orders another beer.

'Cellarius told me you can give me information about what happened in Zwickau . . .'

He picks up his mug and takes two draughts from it, fills his moustache with foam. 'Why're you interested?'

'I had enough of Wittenberg.'

His eyes fix on me for the first time, suddenly clear: I'm not joking.

'Brother Storch and the weavers revolted against the city council. We attacked a congregation of Franciscans, threw stones at an insolent Catholic and dislodged a preacher . . .'

I interrupt him. 'Tell me about Müntzer.'

He nods. 'Ah, Müntzer, say the name quietly so that Melanchthon doesn't shit himself!' He laughs. 'His sermons are setting everyone's souls ablaze. The echo of his words has reached as far as Bohemia, he has been called by the city council of Prague to preach against false prophets there.'

'Who does he have in mind?'

He points his thumb over his shoulder, outside. 'Everyone who denies that the spirit of God can speak directly to men, to people like me and you or those workmen over there. Everyone who usurps the Word of God with their faithless talk. Everyone who wants a silent God, a God who says nothing. Everyone who claims to want to bring the food of the soul to the people, while leaving their bellies empty. Tongues in the pay of the princes.'

Light, a vanishing weight. The things that I have always thought become clear.

I would hug you, prophet.

'And what does Müntzer have to say about Wittenberg?'

'All they do is talk here. The truth is that Luther is now in the hands of the Elector. The people have risen up, but where is their pastor? Fattening himself in some luxurious castle! Believe me, everything we've fought for is in peril. We've come here with the specific purpose of confronting Luther in public and unmasking him, if he's brave enough to come out of his lair. Meanwhile we've challenged Melanchthon. But as far as Müntzer's concerned they're both dead already. His words are only for the peasants, the ones who thirst for life.'

Abandon the dead: get back to life. Get out of this marshland.

'Where's Müntzer now?'

'Travelling around Thuringia, preaching,' My expression tells him all he needs to know. 'It isn't hard to track him down. He leaves a trail behind him.'

I get up and pay for his beers. 'Thanks. Your words have meant a lot to me.'

Before I leave him he looks me straight in the eyes, almost issuing an order: 'Find him, son . . . Find the Coiner.'

Chapter 10

I rush along, almost slipping in the mud, my breath ahead of me cutting through the morning frost. In the university courtyard Cellarius is talking to some friends. I reach him and drag him into a corner, leaving the others speechless.

'Karlstadt's finished.'

He speaks in as low a voice as mine: 'I told you so. They've slackened Luther's leash. The old rector's for the chop.'

'Yeah. He was too good. His days are numbered.' I give him time to read the determination in my eyes, then continue, 'I've decided, Cellarius. I'm leaving Wittenberg. There's nothing left here to make it worth staying.'

A moment of panic in his face. 'Are you sure you're doing the right thing?'

'No, but I'm sure that the right thing isn't staying here . . . Have you heard what that wretch Luther has been saying since he got back?'

He nods, lowering his eyes, but I go on. 'He argues that it's the duty of the Christian to give blind obedience to authority, without ever lifting his head . . . That no one can dare to say no . . . He's disobeyed the Pope, Cellarius, the Pope, the Roman Church! But now he's the Pope and no one's allowed to breathe!'

He's getting more and more dark and disheartened under the blows of my words.

'I should have left two months ago with Stübner and the others. I've waited for too long . . . But I wanted to hear Luther speaking, I wanted to hear what I have heard from his own voice. Listen to me, our only hope is to get out of here.' A hand gestures towards the countryside that lies beyond the walls. 'He who comes from above is above everything; but he who comes from the earth belongs to the earth and speaks of the earth . . . Do you remember?'

'Yes, Müntzer's words . . .'

'I'll find him, Cellarius. They say he's somewhere near Halle now.'

He smiles at me in silence, his eyes are bright. We both know we want to leave together. And we also know that Martin Borrhaus, known as Cellarius, isn't the kind to throw himself into an enterprise of this kind.

He shakes my hand firmly, it's almost an embrace. 'Good luck then, pal. May God be with you.'

'See you. In a better time and place.'

Chapter 11

The man who brings me to the Coiner is like a mountain: a black cloud of thick hair and beard around the head of a bull, enormous miner's hands. His name is Elias, he's followed Müntzer from Zwickau, never leaving him, like a great protecting shadow. A glance to weigh up what he has before him: a few kilos of raw meat, for a stone cutter from the Erzgebirge. A little student with his head full of conjectures in Latin, asking to speak to Magister Thomas, as he calls him.

'Why are you looking for the Magister?' he asked me straight away.

I told him about the time when Müntzer's voice petrified Melanchthon, and about my meeting with the prophet Stübner.

'If Brother Stübner is a prophet then I'm the Archbishop of Mainz!' he exclaimed with a laugh. 'The Magister's voice, though, that's the one to grab you by the balls!'

It's a working men's house. Three knocks on the door and it opens up. A young woman with a baby at the breast. The massive form of Elias brings me into the only room. In the corner a man is shaving with his back to us, intoning a popular song that I've already heard in an inn.

'Magister, there's a man here who's come from Wittenberg to speak to you.'

He turns round, razor in hand. 'Good. Someone can tell me what's going on in that pigsty.'

A round head, a big nose, flaming eyes that trouble an otherwise affable face.

Without hesitation: 'Nothing can happen from now on. Karlstadt has been exiled.'

He nods to himself in confirmation. 'Who did he think he was dealing with? Behind Brother Martin you've got Frederick.' He waves his razor around in anger. 'And our friend Karlstadt . . . He thought he was going to carry out his reformation in the Elector's house! By the leave of Friar Untruth himself. In a menagerie of aldermen and little scholars who think fates of men depend on their little inkpots . . . Their pens won't write the reforms we're waiting for.'

For the first time he seems to turn towards me. 'Did Luther and Melanchthon banish you as well?'

'No. I left of my own accord.'

'And why did you come here?'

The giant Elias hands me a stool, I sit down and begin the parable of Old Karlstadt, the farce of the Luther kidnapping, the arrival of the prophets of Zwickau.

They listen attentively and understand my frustration, disappointment with Luther's reforms, the hatred for the bishops and princes that has matured over the years. The words are the right ones and come easily to the tongue. They nod seriously, Müntzer puts his razor back on the little table and starts to get dressed. The giant no longer looks at me with ill-concealed scorn.

Then the master of the humble folk puts on his coat and is already at the door. 'A day filled with things to do!' He smiles. 'Go on with your story in the street.'

As I speak I know that we will not part.

The bag and the memories

Chapter 12

Limbs stiff from working. The cold, more intense by the day, freezes my fingers, still on yellow, creased paper: an elegant hand, not hard to read, despite the flickering candlelight and the stains of time.

> *To Master Thomas Müntzer of Quedlinburg, most eminent teacher, pastor of the town of Allstedt.*
>
> *The blessing of God, first of all, to him who carries the word of the Lord to the humble and bears the sword of Gideon against the iniquity surrounding us. Greetings, then, from a brother who has been able to listen to the oratory of the Master in person, without being able to leave the prison of codes and parchments to which fate has confined him.*
>
> *The man who has travelled the labyrinth of these corridors in search of the ultimate meaning of the Scriptures knows how sombre and sad it can be when we lose sight of that meaning. And as the days move by, one after the other, along with the awareness, the preserve of the few, along with the brilliance of the Word, obscured by a thousand Spalatins who make a fortress of these mazes and, with these books, build walls around the privilege of the princes. If by some spell our lives were swapped around, and I found myself in Allstedt with the peasants and the miners, and you found yourself with your ear pressed to these doors, listening to the many intrigues hatched on behalf of charity and the love of God, I am sure it would not be long before you wrote inciting me to take a whip to those traitors to the faith. Therefore I have no doubt that you will understand the reason that leads me to take up my pen.*
>
> *The words of the apostle are confirmed: 'For the mystery of lawlessness is already at work, but only until the one who now restrains it is removed' (2 Th 2, 7). The sacrilegious alliance between the impious governors and the false prophets is mustering its troops, the pressure of great events is spurring the elect to keep the faith safe, and prepare to use any means to defend it.*

The man of iniquity, the apostate, sits in the temple of God, and it is from there that he spreads his false doctrine. Thus, one of the Medici of Florence, Giulio, is seated upon the throne of Rome, as Pope Clement. He is sure to continue the destruction of Christ in his name, like most of his predecessors.

Rome examines its own navel, and cannot see beyond. It is deaf to the trumpets which, all around, are heralding the siege. Immersed in the sin that dulls the senses, it will be unable to oppose who can bring fresh impetus and the light of the Holy Spirit to the way of the reformation of the Church.

And this is the great crux, Master Thomas: who will carry the sword that will run the wicked through?

Brother Martin has shown his true face as a soldier of the princes, a wretched role long concealed. So Luther will not be the one to bring the Gospel to the common man, not the man who has exiled Karlstadt and each day receives homage from the great of the earth. The purpose of the German rulers is clearly apparent. It is not faith that fills their hearts and guides their actions, but their greed for gain. They arrogate to themselves the glory and adoration of the Highest One, and turn their subjects into miserable idolaters.

Only the words that I had the privilege of hearing from your mouth have restored hope to this heart, along with the news that reaches us from Allstedt. The new liturgy that has now been inaugurated thanks to you and your most learned writings is the start of the reawakening. The Word of God can finally reach its chosen ones and regain its splendour. What better sign could there be that you are the interpreter of His will? What more conclusive than the spontaneous following that you are winning? Of humble folk, lifting up their heads and pursuing the redemption promised by the Lord?

So, where you are concerned, I tell you to stay staunch and never give up; as to myself, from this outpost, in times to come it will be my task to communicate to you any information that may be employed for the greater glory of God.

Certain that the protection of the Lord will always be with you,
    Qoèlet   *5 November of the year 1523*

I fold the page and blow out the candle. Lying in the darkness with my eyes open, I relight the fire in the chapel at Mallerbach.

When we'd been in Allstedt for a year, Magister Thomas had been called there by the town council. Each Sunday his sermons lifted everyone's hearts and during those days we could have done anything we wanted to: above all make the Franciscans of Neudorf pay, those filthy usurers suffocating the peasantry. We could have avenged all their years of feasting alongside the poor.

First we sack the building, then two faggots, a bit of pitch and up their little church goes in flames. While we stand there watching it going up, two hangers-on of Zeiss, the tax collector, show up, alerted by the friars. They immediately run to the well, with two buckets each: the boss had clicked his fingers and they'd hide in the flames of hell for him. Before a drop is spilled we come out of the shadow, black with soot, iron bars in our hands. 'If I were you I'd make sure the forest doesn't catch . . . There's nothing to be done here now.'

Ten against two. They look at us. They look at each other. They drop their buckets and off they go.

The flames subside, turn over in bed. Zeiss's piggy face emerges from the darkness. The Elector's census taker. Those flames had scorched his arse so badly that he called in people from outside to flush out the arsonists. Good for Zeiss! The town's been invaded by armed strangers? Nothing better to turn the people against you. All you have to do is utter the name of Müntzer once and his guardian angels come running: a hundred miners with shovels and picks emerging from the bowels of the earth to drag you under. The women of the town wanting to castrate you. Things are slipping out of your hands: like a frightened child, you clung to your mother's skirts and went crying to the Elector. I can imagine the scene: you creeping and trying to explain how you lost control of the town, and Frederick the Wise looking at you.

Zeiss: 'Your Grace, with your well-known foresight, will already have guessed the reason for your servant's visit . . .'

Frederick: 'I have guessed it, Zeiss, I have guessed it. But my foresight was not required in this instance. For some time all Count Mansfeld has brought me is complaints about your little village of Allstedt. It seems that the new preacher is giving you serious problems. In any case, you were the one who failed to tell me about the fact that he had settled in your parish, and I hope the problems that this has caused will make you think more quickly in future.'

Zeiss: 'Your Grace knows that the responsibility was not mine: it was the town council that decided not to tell you of the appointment of Thomas Müntzer. You know very well that as far as I'm concerned . . .'

Frederick: 'No excuses, Zeiss! You know that before this throne you cannot pass the blame on to anyone else. Fundamentally, this man Müntzer has caused me no problems. The fact is that too many people in Thuringia think too highly of themselves. First Luther unleashes his fury at Spalatin, so that he brings that preacher into line for not giving him enough respect, then Count Mansfeld writes to tell me that your council is defending a rabble-rouser who has openly insulted him. So, what else?'

Zeiss: 'Well, there's what I've come to talk to you about. But I expect you know something about that already, although I am sure that events in our town are not of the greatest concern to you.'

Frederick: 'Really? They tell me a little country chapel burned down.'

Zeiss: 'To be precise, it was the Chapel of the Holy Virgin in Mallerbach, on the road between Allstedt and Querfurt, owned by the Franciscans of the monastery in Neudorf. The bell was stolen during Sunday service, and they set fire to the church the next day. I sent two trusted men to put out the fire, but the men were there watching, and so they explained that they'd gone some way away to shield the forest from the flames, since the chapel was lost by now.'

Frederick: 'Nothing new so far. The Neudorf friars were unusually pedantic in their description of the situation when they asked me to intervene. If I remember correctly, I wrote telling you not to let the situation get worse and worse, to find some kind of culprit and keep him in jail for a day, and then for you to pay a symbolic sum in compensation.'

Zeiss: 'But everyone in the town knew that the arsonists were the preacher's acolytes. Just think, Your Grace, they've founded a league, the League of the Elect, they call it, and they've got weapons. It would be hard to avoid direct conflict without losing face . . .'

Frederick: 'So blame for all this should be laid at the door of this man Müntzer?'

Zeiss: 'Certainly . . . and his wife, Ottilie von Gersen. When I was in search of a culprit, that witch did more than anyone else to turn the whole population against me.'

Frederick: 'They're even setting their womenfolk on us now . . .'

Zeiss: 'From what I've seen, she's a raving madwoman, a crazy woman, worthy of her husband. And both other women and men fervently admire her.'

Frederick: 'Get on with it, Zeiss. How did things turn out in the end?'

Zeiss: 'I had to call in outside reinforcements, and the preacher's wife started screeching that foreigners were trying to invade Allstedt, that I'd sold myself . . . They wanted to lynch me!'

Frederick: 'And quite right too: you've fucked up mightily.'

Zeiss: 'But what was I to do? The Franciscans wouldn't leave me in peace. In the end a troop of miners from the county of Mansfeld turned up on my door, about fifty of them, asking me if Magister Thomas was all right, if everything was peaceful or if I needed their help, saying that if anyone touched a hair on his head they would have them to answer to . . . After that visit I gave up the use of any kind of force. I have no wish to be responsible for sparking a revolt in Your Grace's possessions.'

Frederick: 'Fine, Zeiss. And now I'll tell you what I think about all this. You wanted a fiery and innovative preacher to give a sheen to your country town. But this guy has turned out to be hard to manipulate; he's won over the town council, he's put a few stones and pitchforks in the hands of the common people, and you and Count von Mansfeld have been shitting yourselves. And now you're coming to ask for help.'

Zeiss: 'But Your Grace . . .'

Frederick: 'Silence! I think all this fits you like a glove. Still, for some time things of this nature have been happening more or less everywhere. It begins with the sacking of churches and ends with a request for a municipal order for any tiny village. The peasants are in turmoil throughout Germany and it would be unwise not to throw the hotheads in jail. In a few weeks you'll get a visit from my brother Duke John and my nephew John Frederick. Have a suitable welcome ready for them; inform them that the Elector will not tolerate this level of agitation and that if the people have any grievance against the Franciscans of Neudorf, they will have to turn directly to your envoys, via the burgomaster or their preacher. In any case, organise a meeting with this Thomas Müntzer. Just tell him that we've expressly requested it and tell him to prepare a sermon in which he sets out his ideas. Basically, he's still in his trial period; he will have to have our approval if he's going to be a pastor in your church.'

Zeiss: 'Your Grace always has the best solution for everything.'

Frederick: 'Fine, but too often the subalterns who are supposed to put it into effect turn out to be absolute dickheads.'

I laugh to myself. The darkness engulfs their silhouettes, bringing back to me the figure of Magister Thomas in the bright dawn of that great summer day.

'Open the Bible, my friend.'

The voice suddenly rouses me from the table where he must have been working all night. Barely awake, my mouth clogged, I growl, 'What?'

With the swollen eyes of someone who has been writing by too faint a light, he points at the book on the table. 'First Epistle to the Corinthians: 5, 11–13. Read, please.'

'No, Magister, you should sleep for a while at least, or you won't be strong enough to speak . . . Put down your pen and lie down on the couch.'

He smiles. 'I've got time . . . Read me that passage: 5, 11–13.'

I shake my head as I open the Bible and start looking. His ability to keep awake never ceases to amaze me.

'"But now I have written unto you not to keep company, if any man that is called a brother be a fornicator, or covetous, or an idolater, or a railer, or a drunkard, or an extortioner; with such a one you should not eat. Expel the wicked man from among you."'

While I read he nods in silence. He seems to be reflecting on the words, running them through his memory. All of a sudden he lifts his eyes, still, miraculously, awake. 'And what do you think the apostle means?'

'Me, Magister . . . ?'

'That's right. What do you think he means?'

I rapidly reread St Paul's words and my answer comes from the heart. 'That we did well to burn the temple of idolatry. That the Franciscans of Neudorf call themselves brethren but live on avarice and drive the people to worship images and statues.'

'You did it out of zeal. But do you not believe that there is someone to whom God has given the sword required for that purpose? Who is in the service of God for the just damnation of evildoers?'

'Paul asserts that that task is assigned to the authorities who are given that purpose. But were it not for us, no one would have punished that band of usurous idolaters!'

He brightens. 'Exactly. The zeal of the elect has had to wrest the sword from the powerful in order to do what the powerful refused to do: defend the people and the Christian faith. And does that not teach us, perhaps, that in allowing wickedness to thrive, the rulers are shirking their duty and becoming accomplices of iniquity? Therefore, like the wicked, according to the words of the apostle, they must be put away from us.'

The enormity of these words strikes me like a blow, as he starts reading from his manuscript: 'I affirm with Christ and Paul, and in conformity with the teaching of the whole of the divine law, that impious rulers must be killed, particularly the priests and monks who curse the Holy Gospel with heresy, while at the same time claiming to be the best of Christians.'

It can't be happening. I swallow hard. 'Magister, this . . . is this what you are going to preach today, in the presence of the Dukes of Saxony?'

A chuckle, a gleam in his eyes, more alert than ever. 'No, my friend, not just them. If I'm not mistaken, the chancellor of the Brück court will be there too, Councillor von Grefendorf, our own Zeiss, the burgomaster and the rest of the town council of Allstedt.'

I stay there, rooted to the spot, while he gets up, stretching his arms.

'Thanks for your help in dispelling any doubts. Now I think I'll take your advice and lie down for a while. Please call me when the bell tolls.'

Pastor Vogel wasn't speaking for me today, not to Brother Gustav. His voice was like a dull, distant rumble. I'm alone. Not a word can persuade me. Not after the slaughter of those unarmed people, not after that cry in the void. He can keep the comfort he takes from the Word – and I'm one of those who used to believe in its strength.

In the evening, in my room, blue with cold, I read the letters. And I feel something vague happening, getting closer with each passing day: something is struggling to get out, but I choke it back down again, to the pit of my stomach, with all my strength. It gets harder every night.

To the most illustrious Magister Thomas Müntzer, pastor and preacher of the town of Allstedt.

Most illustrious Master,
  May the Spirit of God, which instils wisdom and courage, be upon you in these hours of torment.
  I am writing to you with all the haste and agitation of one who sees danger creeping along in silence, suddenly leaping out behind the man in whom he has placed his hopes. I have already shown you how my ears might help you, given their proximity to certain doors behind which intrigues lurk. Well, I cannot say which is stronger in me, whether it is the joy of finally being of use to you, after the many months that have passed since my first missive, or my anxiety and contempt for that which is being plotted against you.
  The Elector, who had hitherto maintained a waiting position, really did not like your League of the Elect one bit. Likewise the sermon you delivered in the presence of his brother. Above all, he is alarmed by the fact that you have a printing press at your disposal, and that your words might reach the hearths of revolt that are gradually being lit throughout his territory and beyond. He has no

intention to attack you directly: I think he fears possible repercussions of a rash gesture. But he wants to remove you from Allstedt, from your press and from his Saxony. A certain Hans Zeiss paid him a visit here some days ago, and spent a long time talking to Spalatin, the court counsellor. They want to isolate you. Zeiss will pretend to be on your side, but in the meantime, in accordance with his promises, you will see a revolt against you, if not from the whole town council then at least from your burgomaster. He has said he is sure of success and it did not sound like a mere promise.

For his part, Spalatin will write you a letter on behalf of the Elector Frederick to invite you to Weimar, where you will be given the opportunity to expound your theses at length and before some important theologians. Do not grasp the hand they seem to be holding out to you! Do not imagine that you will end up playing the most important role. Do not count on the support of Zeiss and his colleagues: once they are far away from your people they will abandon you, swearing blind that your arrival has brought nothing but confusion to their town, that your theories are dangerous, that you are entirely lacking in the submission to authority that Martin Luther preaches.

You have one great strength: the strength of the Word of God that reaches His people through your lips. Between those walls, far from the peasants and miners, the strength will be sucked from you as though you were a new Samson. Zeiss will be your Delilah, and he already holds the scissors in his hands. I repeat: do not leave Allstedt. It is there that they fear you, for your sermons and your printing press, they fear the people's reaction to any violent action against you. They won't risk touching you. Do not leave for Weimar.

May the Lord God enlighten and sustain you.

Qoèlet   *the 27th day of July 1524*

This letter was certainly delivered to the Magister too late, after his return from Weimar, by which time the die had been cast. Perhaps, in those difficult days, he did not have the time to assess its importance, and yet he made no mention of it.

What is certain is that this letter revealed in advance what was about to happen. The man who wrote these lines was very close to the princes' rooms.

It was the clear-mindedness of Ottilie that saved us during those days. We could have been lost for good, but that woman pulled us up again and led us out of the black marshes of crazed desperation. Ottilie . . . you won't be there now to take me away from here. I don't know how you met your end: a plaything for mercenaries, food for crows. My arid heart almost leads me to hope that you did not survive to witness this void, the cold loneliness of Christmas in this year of death.

Ottilie is strong and resolute, with a magnificent bosom. The Magister, when those distillations of herbs and grape juice loosen his tongue, letting it slide cheerfully towards the lower parts both of the body and the spirit, says that those big, firm breasts contain the secret and the strength of creation, and that the impetus and revelations of these past frenetic months come straight from them. Then he adds, with a snigger, that the new faithful, poor things, have only second-hand knowledge of such matters. Never, though, does he issue such boasts or assertions in her presence, since she exerts an aura upon this great thundering pile of flesh, spirit and intuition that no one else, whether prince, bishop or constitutional authority, has been able to impose.

The gleam in her eyes is sometimes even brighter than the flame in the Magister's, when he sets whole public squares ablaze with his oratorical power. The strength of a human male, however big he is – and by God, Thomas Müntzer of Quedlinburg harbours a mountain of strength – often finds its origin and its discipline in the women who guide and accompany its flux.

The Magister's strength sometimes turns into profound despair: the outbreaks of rage, the sudden attacks of pride and the acute resentments of a man burdened with a ferocious task perhaps beyond human endurance. On such occasions Ottilie alone can calm his excesses, calling up the reason and genius that allow his vigour to re-emerge, to permeate the hearts of the common people of the whole of Germany.

One sultry night beneath the first August moon I tell you both, you and the woman sitting opposite me, my hope and my thoughts, such as they are, to get us out of a situation we have found ourselves in over the past few weeks, fraught with hidden dangers and as suffocating as a noose round the neck. As we stare into each other's anxious, tense and heat-flushed faces, sitting at the table where the pastor of Allstedt writes his own sermons, the Magister is wandering, at the mercy of a gloom-filled rage, through the streets and alleyways of this town, armed and in his warrior's garb, inciting the faithful to follow him, like the wolf which, on nights just like this one, gives up his lonely howl to the moon as he pleads for help. He walks under the protective eye of the indomitable Elias, who follows him from close by, some steps behind him in the darkness, ready to leap on anyone who might try to attack him.

Everything seethes with events, hard to interpret, apart from the one, the sole clear and distinguishable one: here, now, in Allstedt, a noose is tightening, a trap is about to snap shut on all our lives and those of the insurgent peasants. There's no time to lose, the Magister needs help.

'The snakes that rule this town will not harm us any more. Let's leave.'

The voice is firm, it has a solidity that contrasts with the woman's youthful face.

'What?' Ottilie's words suddenly lift the weight from my eyelids. 'But . . . what about the Magister?'

'He won't be long, you'll see. But we've got to get our minds working before they crush us like insects.'

Of course, Ottilie, the mind. That wasps' nest of unease that never stops buzzing. I turn towards the window. In silence, I try to listen to the Magister's far-off cries. I don't know whether I can really make them out or whether I'm just imagining I can. He is shouting that David is here among us, with his slingshot in his hand. The words of his last sermon to the League of the Elect, when the people almost turned round to look for little King David with the rock in his slingshot, so much did the Magister's words have the tone of a genuine evocation, rather than a mere rhetorical device. If we had to praise you as you deserve, Lord, our lips would burn with the ardour of your Word. Instead, fear extinguishes those flames.

'I imagine the Magister had the same idea in mind.' My words have a ring of hope.

She smiles. 'Ideas . . . Did you see his eyes when he left here? I know, he's got a thousand ideas and a thousand contacts, from the North Sea to the Black Forest. But now the decision's up to us . . .'

'Why don't we wait another little while? Is it that necessary to leave?'

Without a moment's hesitation, those softening lips: 'Yes, brother, after Weimar, yes.'

'Three days was really all it took . . . three days without the Magister for us to lose everything . . .'

'That was just the *coup de grâce*. Things had already started going wrong.'

'Not while the Magister was with us, they hadn't. A swamp of desperate people swelled that bog, you remember? They flowed here from all the towns all around, driven out by the lords . . . The flood could even have engulfed Duke John!'

As I walk back to my chair, for a moment she seems to be listening, too. Then she runs a hand over the table, full of the crumbs from dinner. 'You see?' she says, pushing them all into the middle and gripping them in her fist. 'That's what they did.' And she opens her palm and blows on it. 'Now they're about to sweep us away.'

The words emerge with difficulty from my parched throat. 'But one thing is certain, Ottilie. They are afraid of Magister Thomas as animals are afraid of fire. They had to remove him from the city so they could start their intimidations and their beatings. No one would have risked driving out our Wychart and closing down the printing press if the Magister had stayed.'

'And they won't try and get him tonight, either. Of course, of course . . . no one has said we've got to flee for the Indies. Just think about somewhere else where we could continue the work we've started here.'

I shake my head. 'How can I help? I know the peasants in Bavaria are fighting for their cause. But I don't have a sense that they need us there.'

'That's right. In the south things are coming along all on their own.' She studies the darkness beyond the window. 'Did Thomas ever talk to you about Mühlhausen?'

'The imperial city?'

'Exactly. A year ago the population even had fifty-three articles approved by the council. Today the power is in the hands of representatives chosen by the city inhabitants.'

A grimace. 'Do we still want to deal with a town council that is hostile to the papists out of pure self-interest? We'd be better off trying to find allies in the farms and the fields. They're the humble of the earth.'

She nods, staring into my eyes. Something she's ruminated about over time. 'Sure. But once we've got our hands on a town, it isn't difficult to get in touch with the peasants. On the contrary, that's what happened to the miners in the county of Mansfeld, isn't it? And if you start from outside you have to deal with walls and cannons.'

I gulp down the last foaming drop of beer. '. . . And once you're in the town the cannons are on your side already.'

'Yes, and if you're going to fight the princes, you need cannons!'

'Hm. These townspeople are all very easily manipulated. The Magister told me that even in Mühlhausen one of the leaders of the rebellion had some sort of strange contacts with Duke John.'

I refill my glass, after taking a first sip. 'You're talking about Heinrich Pfeiffer, I imagine. Yes, they've told us about his relations with the Duke. They say that John of Saxony has designs on the city and that he appreciates all the confusion down there; that's what he needs in order to present himself as a peacekeeper and assume control.'

I spread my arms to indicate the logical conclusion. 'So you think we should intervene and exploit the disorder for our cause, and get Pfeiffer working with us.'

'You were the one who said these people were easily manipulated.'

We laugh. Flashes of heat cut through the humidity of the night. Ottilie takes a lock of blonde hair off her forehead and puts it behind her ear. For a moment, she's barely more than a child.

'There's something important we haven't mentioned: how to get away from here.'

'It shouldn't be difficult. I really think the last thing Zeiss wants is to keep us here and muck the miners around by incarcerating their preacher. Believe me, they can't wait to get rid of us.'

'You never know . . . He might even take this evening's provocation badly, or use it as a pretext, or decide to humiliate Thomas Müntzer in order to make him harmless. It's better not to take risks.'

A bite of the lower lip to collect her thoughts. 'In that case, we'll leave at night.'

Chapter 16

Vogel's cow died of fever. I stayed to watch it die, its breath getting slower and slower, a muffled groan, glazed eyes filling with indifference towards the world, towards life.

They say that Magister Thomas, before being condemned, wrote a letter to the citizens of Mühlhausen. They say he invited them to put down their arms, because everything was lost now. I think of the man trying to explain why. Why the Lord abandoned his elect and allowed them to lose everything.

I can see you, Magister, lying in the darkness of your cell, with the marks from your tortures covering your body, waiting for the hangman to bring your journey to an end. But the scourge in your heart must have driven you to make your final message. Not their instruments . . . they could never have . . . perhaps it's because we've been thinking about ourselves too much? Perhaps because we've been so presumptuous that we've shocked the Lord? Because we've claimed to interpret His will? Perhaps because we've killed, because the rage of the humble was treated by the wicked agents of starvation so mercilessly? Is that what you wrote, Magister? Is that what you were thinking during those final moments, as the army of the princes marched to the siege of heroic Mühlhausen?

One single reason. Not one reason, not even the unfathomable will of the Lord our God, is enough to banish our despair. Because it is still a cry of despair, uttered from the depths of a dark cell. It's still the profound anguish of defeat that keeps me chained to this bed.

It came to me as clearly as one of those woodcuts made by that great artist of ours, to be more tasteful than you might expect, sometimes quite delicate and skilled. It seemed to burst out of the narrow space between those walls. The houses and the steeples of the churches rising one on top of the other like clusters of mushrooms on a tree trunk.

Of course, that's just how I could describe my memory of my first entry into Mühlhausen: four horses impelled onwards by our non-sensical shouts, along the road a few miles from the walls of the imperial town, Elias's thundering laughter and Ottilie's cries in the wind. Then at a walk, almost martial, approaching the gigantic portal, to give ourselves an air of authority that was undeserved but no less important for that, with a proud, direct gaze on that scorching mid-August day.

We could already glimpse the centre swarming with assorted humanity, like a menagerie designed to contain an example of every species, type, form or deformity within the human race. Animals and carts and noise, confused shouts, echoed curses and swearing. The stench of hops and the lively racket of the Steinweg, with shops and beer stalls opening on to it. The beer that has enriched the merchants of Mühlhausen more than any other town in Germany.

The Word of God uttered on every street corner, the black flag of the Teutonic Knights flying over the buildings; the corruption of the monks who attract curses in the streets, confirming the law of the world: where there is money you'll always find plenty of priests. In the maze of dry alleyways, dusty from weeks of drought, flanked on either side by the walls of dwellings and shops, inns and construction sites, thick with inscriptions and scratched names, symbols of all kinds, but a number of times glorifying the German Hercules – Luther – just like that, LUTHER was written on every wall of the first path we took towards the Church of St James; he went ahead of us and accom-panied us with his contempt, which we dutifully returned.

I remember it distinctly, the noise, the stench of sweat and cattle from the market in the big square, which would see very different events a few weeks hence, making us tremble, making our hearts race, while 'the just invoked the hammer of God', may it fall implacably upon the heads of those who have usurped His word. A tension that breathed in every alleyway, the strong smell of an injustice that called for retribution and seethed away uneasily beneath the pinnacles of the Cathedral of Our Lady and the big market. As though waiting for a spark.

Big Elias cut a swath through the crowd. 'I've been here before, to this shit-hole with its people in rags and its imperial envoys.' I came along behind him, losing my footing, distracted by shouted arguments of shopkeepers and the lewd suggestions of women who knew the soldiers in the pay of Duke John better than their own captains did. I found it hard to tear myself away, weeks of lustful dreams were consuming me with the anxious anticipation of pleasure, but there was Ottilie's caustic smile following me close by to discourage the offers and make my face flush bright red.

'Welcome to the powder keg!'

I can still distinctly remember the first smile and the phrase with which he welcomed us. Heinrich Pfeiffer, in the Church of St James, near the Felchta gate, a meeting point for the inhabitants of the suburb of St Nicholas. This shifty preacher, the son of a dairymaid, ex-cook, ex-confessor, ex-friend of the Duke of Saxony, sly supporter of the cause of the humble. And his connection with the Duke, which he had used to have a good fifty-six representatives of the people elected on to the council. His sermons had encouraged the plunder of the property of the Church and the destruction of sacred images. Without the support of the Duke he could never have survived for long in the town. We admired his cunning and intelligence; it wasn't hard to work out that, together, he and the Magister would be able to achieve great things.

And indeed, here they were, already busily engaged in serious discussions about things that needed to be done and incendiary sermons to be delivered for the townspeople and the ragged ones, the disinherited, the people of the region and also the nobles, who 'will soon be on the receiving end, their determination to shove their fat, swinish faces in a steaming plate of excrement'.

Now, from my hidden corner, Mühlhausen seems like a dream town, a spectre that visits you at night and tells you its story, but as though you had never seen it, a pen-and-ink drawing, that's how I remember it, like something by our brilliant painter, Herr Albrecht Dürer.

First article: [. . .] First, it is our humble petition and desire, as also our will and resolution, that henceforth we should have power and authority so that each community should choose and appoint a pastor [. . .]

Second article: [. . .] We will that, for the future, our church provost, whomsoever the community may appoint, shall gather and receive the tithe of our corn. From this he shall give to the pastor, elected by the whole community, a decent and sufficient maintenance for him and his people [. . .]. What remains over shall be given to the poor of the place, as the circumstances and the general opinion demand [. . .]

Third article: [. . .] It has been the custom hitherto for men to hold us as their own property, which is pitiable enough, considering that Christ has delivered and redeemed us all, without exception, by the shedding of His precious blood, the lowly as well as the great. [. . .] We, therefore, take it for granted that you will release us from serfdom as true Christians [. . .].

Shortly after vespers some news begins to mingle with the smell of the beer that is starting to fill the tankards. They have locked up someone or other, half drunk, for insulting the burgomaster.

To put it briefly, they aren't talking about anything else. Who was this person? What did he say, exactly? Where did it happen? They learn that he's been locked up in the dungeons under the Rathaus and everyone is furious. Many of them rise nervously to their feet, beat their fists on the table, and go out to tell as many people as possible. They'll pay for it this time, the bastards!

I stick my nose out of the inn. Half the suburb of St Nicholas has gone out into the street and the cries are getting louder as they pass from one set of lips to the next. The most excited of them, still clutching tankards or carding combs, as though they'd just been ambushed in the middle of the night, step out nervously on to the cobbles that lead to the Felchta gate and the Church of St James. They are looking for the Magister. He comes down, surrounded by a pulsing beat of voices impatient to express their own convictions about what should be done. Some way above us, the group slows down and starts to swell quite naturally, around the inn of the Bear, where the street widens towards the public wash-house.

In the month since we've been here I've come to appreciate how the spectre of agitation is an extra inhabitant of the town. Nonetheless, I still can't understand why people are reacting like this to an arrest that doesn't seem to be anything out of the ordinary. They don't even know who's ended up inside. It seems to revolve around one detail common to all the rumours: the unfortunate man has been locked up in the Rathaus dungeon, when they should have used the tower of the same building.

'What's this about the tower and the dungeon?' I ask an old man standing beside me observing the scene.

'Eighth article of our municipal ordinance: no more incarcerations in the dungeons, only in the tower. If you saw what sewers those dungeons were, you'd understand it's not just a matter of government codes!'

I look up above our heads: Magister Thomas is already standing on a bollard at the side of the road. He is railing against the abuse of power and scorn for the people. Below him there is a continuous coming and going of people running to get others and picking up tools and stones. Through the middle of the crowd, Elias is making his way towards me. When he sees me, he cries louder than all the rest, 'Go and get Pfeiffer! Tell him we'll soon be under the windows of the Rathaus and tell him to bring as many people as he can.'

I run to the walls. I am recognised by a sentry: not a problem, clearly they're not expecting any reaction. Still running, I find myself in the Kilansgasse. There's a clamour at the end of the street, towards the Church of St Blaise, and I find out that Pfeiffer hasn't wasted any time.

I turn the corner and find myself standing right in front of him. He too is standing on an improvised pulpit. He interrupts his harangue and, pointing at me, starts shouting, 'Here, here, we've got a messenger from the suburb of St Nicholas. Doubtless he is coming to tell us that Thomas Müntzer and his people are furious about the decision of that pig of a burgomaster . . . Isn't that so, brother?'

The heads of the audience turn towards me like a field of sunflowers.

'Of course, Brother Pfeiffer! The people of St Nicholas are already making their way from the Felchta gate to the Rathaus.'

As I approach the little crowd, Pfeiffer jumps down from his bollard and runs towards me. He throws an arm round my shoulders and whispers, 'Tell me, brother, how many of you are there?'

I exaggerate. 'You could count on two hundred.'

He grips my shoulder blade. 'Fine, this time we're going to fuck them over.' Then, louder: 'They'll regret this affront, believe me. To the Rathaus, brothers, to the Rathaus!'

His words are already battle-cries.

I don't know how the pitchforks, torches and iron bars have started springing up. But at a certain point they suddenly appear above the forest of heads, much more frightening than the halberds of the police closing the entrance to the building. One of them dashes up the stairs to ask for instructions. He comes back with about fifteen fellow officers behind him.

There is a heated discussion between the advanced lines of both groups. The news goes around that the precise insult directed by Willi Pimple at burgomaster Rodemann was 'kiss my arse', accompanied by a display of his posterior. For many, this was a very explicit invitation to repeat the gesture and dozens of arseholes peer up at the Rathaus.

All of a sudden, right at the front, there is a roar. I push my way through and clutch at people to see better, already anticipating the scene of Rodemann's definitive humiliation. Instead, I see Elias lifting high above his shoulders a tiny middle-aged man, almost bald, his purple nose covered with blotches. He is shouting with joy, and the outstretched hands receive him and roll him around above their heads: 'It's Willi! Long live Willi! Fucking shitheads! Long live Willi! Sewer rats! Willi the great!'

The crowd carries him in triumph across the square, a girl on someone's shoulders bares her tits and Willi hurls himself on them like a man brought back from the dead. The people throw him vegetables and sweets that daub him from head to foot. Laughing, I shout, 'Long live King Willi! Long live the hero of the people of Mühlhausen!'

And the drunk, as though he has heard me, turns in my direction and makes a sign of benediction in the air, a moment before a cauliflower catches him right in the face.

Chapter 18

Eltersdorf, Easter 1526

I remember that on the night of the coronation of King Willi few people in Mühlhausen slept a wink. Without a doubt, the people who didn't included Rodemann and Kreuzberg, the two burgomasters, beneath whose windows there raged an extraordinary tournament, dedicated to them, of insults, curses and violent slogans. The crowds of tramps couldn't have had much sleep, either. Eager for possible plunder, they filled the streets until the following morning.

Unfortunately, Morpheus embraced the two sentries posted at the rear of the Rathaus, so the burgomasters had little difficulty fleeing in the direction of Salza, with the town banner rolled up under their arms.

By the time we awoke, fresh news was spreading, there were fresh upsets and fresh assemblies beneath the windows of the Rathaus, demanding that the council intervene. The eight delegates of the people, already elected before our arrival, tried to convince the head of the guards of the seriousness of the gesture of the two burgomasters, and the need to erase that disgrace as soon as possible. But he replied that he didn't take orders from anyone but the legitimate representatives of the townspeople. And while we set about reordering our thoughts in our suburb of St Nicholas, he managed to gather a considerable proportion of the population around him, putting them all on their guard against anyone who might want to take advantage of this difficult situation in the town in order to organise forces as they pleased.

It wasn't long before comments along the lines of THE COPS NEVER CHANGE were flourishing on the city walls. Meanwhile, tired of waiting for events to explode, many practised plunderers were speedily going about their business, sowing terror within the walls of the town and among the lines of the palace defenders. For our part, we tried to assess as precisely as possible whether there was room for violent action. A messenger was sent to Salza to ask some of Magister

Thomas's followers if we couldn't intervene directly there, so as to make the two fugitives pay, and create a situation favourable to revolt in that town. The reply was a cordial invitation to mind our own business.

Mühlhausen was preparing for a second sleepless night. Groups of townspeople patrolled the town with torches in their hands while the guards crowded around the entrance to the Felchta gate and the palace. A pointless precaution: from our point of view it wouldn't have been difficult to break through that picket, but once we were inside, the town could be turned into a trap, boiling oil could fall from any window, death could come from any doorway. Furthermore, it had to be borne in mind that they had at least a hundred hackbuts in there, while we had five at the most.

So we waited. And the halo of twilight slowly enveloped the faces of this band of humble people, busy learning the art of throwing stones and sticks, knocking their enemies down, sleeping on cobblestones, eating rye bread and goose fat, listening with one ear to the Magister's sermon and the other to the erotic enterprises of their neighbour.

The following day, some hours after dawn, Ottilie and the Magister, seeing that long-distance confrontation was weakening most people and that many of them were insisting on returning to their business, sought help from the Bible. 'When God supported his people, the city walls crumbled at the sound of trumpets. Remember the end of Jericho. Since we are his elect, the Lord God will grant us just as easy a victory. But we must have faith and trust that God will not abandon his troops.'

Magister Thomas was a persuasive speaker, and this speech was received literally by about fifty of the comrades. Armed with seven imposing hunting horns, all with metal mouthpieces, they walked along the path flanked by the bastions, singing and playing as loudly as their lungs would let them. If nothing else, the scene filled everyone with enthusiasm and it certainly impressed many of the wealthy brewers who thronged the Rathaus square.

These fifty soldiers of Joshua never made their seventh circuit of the walls. They were just completing the fifth, and yelling at the tops of their voices 'Shit-eating lackeys!' at the guards lined up beneath the arch of the Felchta gate, when something that would finally dissolve the tension of those days appeared in the distance. A very large number of men, with a forest of long sticks growing above their heads, was advancing towards the town at great speed. Had they been reinforcements on their way from Salza, Mühlhausen would have fallen into our hands by evening. But Brother Leonard, whom we had sent to meet them, returned with the information that they were peasants from the surrounding district and they were coming to the aid of the town council. In a short while this news reached the people within the walls, and we soon found ourselves between the devil and the deep blue sea: on one side the peasants, already marching up the cobblestones, and on the other the townspeople, enjoying the scene as they peered out from behind the first row of sentries. Too many people, in short.

That's what happens when you ignore the peasants just to capture the town cannons. The council promises them a reduction in taxes on incoming foodstuffs and in a flash you find you're up against them. On a day like that one, with the peasants on our side . . . Instead of which the troop of the humble quickly disperses, with no blood shed, like butter in an oven. The peasants shook hands with the townspeople, smashing our hunting horns to smithereens, and got home in time for dinner.

So the council's resolution to elect two new burgomasters felt like a concession, an easy way to get rid of two idiots and reinforce control over the town.

The following morning, the town square was filled once again with a great crowd of people waiting to know the names of the new burgomasters. One of those elected, the producer of the best beer in the city, immediately celebrated by giving the population two enormous casks. Then it was the turn of the second man, who ran a textile shop. He said that thanks to the great foresight of the council, a situation of serious confusion had been resolved, that Rodemann and Kreuzberg had justly paid for their gesture and would not return to the town. Nonetheless, they were not alone in having acted against the interests of the citizenry; as might be expected from an outsider, Thomas Müntzer had done everything in his power to throw the town into chaos and Heinrich Pfeiffer had followed him blindly in his plan to incite rebellion. Mühlhausen had no need of such people to improve their own council ordinances. Thomas Müntzer and Heinrich Pfeiffer were therefore invited to abandon the city within two days. If they remained beyond that date they would deserve to be incarcerated in the Rathaus tower.

Even today I wonder what strange alchemies had been generated during the previous night and what paralysing fluid flowed at that moment over the pavement of the square. Certainly, the arrival of the peasants was a serious blow and so was that sense we had of being surrounded. Nonetheless, there must have been some explanation for

the silence that swept through that expanse of bodies, so strong as to
cancel out the stench for a moment. Something that Magister Thomas
must have sensed before I did, because that morning he stayed in St
James's, and when I went to see him he was getting his things together.

Outside the walls of Mühlhausen, we realised that we had committed
the gravest error. An unrepeatable error. With the town behind us, it
was to me that Ottilie murmured this lesson: 'You were right. We
can't do anything without the peasants.'

Chapter 19

Nuremberg, Franconia, 10 October 1524

*Fourth article: [. . .] Accordingly it is our desire if a man holds possession
of running waters that he should prove from satisfactory documents that
his right has been acquired by purchase in good faith. [. . .] But whosoever
cannot produce such evidence should surrender his claim with good grace.*

*Fifth article: [. . .] It should, moreover, be free to every member of the
community to help himself to such firewood as he needs in his home. [. . .]*

*Sixth article: Our sixth complaint is in regard to the excessive services
demanded of us, which are increased from day to day. [. . .]We ask that
this matter be properly looked into so that we shall not continue to be
oppressed in this way, [. . .] since our forefathers were required only to serve
according to the Word of God.*

We enter Nuremberg by the north gate. On the left, the imposing
towers of the imperial fortress remind us of what we know already: this
city is one of the biggest, finest and wealthiest in the whole of Europe.
Before us the towering steeples of St Sebald soar into the sky, and on
either side of the street painters and sculptors are at work in their
shops. Ottilie swears that the house of the great Albrecht Dürer is a
few yards away. The house of Johannes Denck, whom we are
supposed to be meeting this morning, is over towards Königstrasse, at
the southern corner of the rhombus that delimits the heart of the city.

We pass through the market square, intoxicated with the smell of
incense, perfumes and spices from India, the colours of Chinese silks
fluttering in the sun, the seven Electors bowing to the Emperor right
above our heads, on the clock of the Church of Our Lady.

Since we entered the city Hans Hut, the bookseller, has been
staying back with the Magister immediately behind us, keeping to a
deliberately slower pace. The reason: he maintains that in Nuremberg,
whichever gate you enter by, if you instinctively follow the flow of the
crowd you will sooner or later find yourself drawn by an invisible
current to St Lawrence's Square. So, lest he influence the result of the

experiment, he keeps himself at a distance, since these streets have no secrets for him. In spite of this precaution, the demonstration is also proved false, because the towers of St Lawrence appear in all their imposing presence the moment we cross the bridge over the river that divides the city.

There's a frenetic coming and going of people in the press. A day of important meetings: a ferment of contacts, dialogues, projects announcing new weeks of earthquake and revolution. The peasants are running wild: not a day passes without news of plunder, insurrections, everyday brawls turning into tumults, from one region to the next. The network of contacts that the Magister has been cultivating with obsessive precision for years is extensive and complex, forever broadening and supplying fresh information. And then, most important of all, there's the printing press; that stupefying piece of technology which, like a dry and windy forest fire, is spreading by the day, giving us plenty of ideas for ways of sending messages and incitements further and faster to reach the brethren, who have sprung up like mushrooms in every corner of the country.

The two apprentices are furiously at work in Herr Herrgott's printing room in Nuremberg. Their hands swiftly turn lead characters into ink marks on paper, a swarm of words on the page. Rapid glances and agile fingers composing the Magister's writings: projectiles fired in all directions by the most powerful of cannons. The press, in the corner, seems to sleep as it waits to print the final seal.

They didn't take much persuasion. Herrgott has been out of town for a week, and the presence of Hut, Pfeiffer, Denck and Magister Thomas all at the same time would have convinced anyone. The swirl of speeches, the passion and the faith of these men could get the dead back to work.

I smile dreamily, but I am listening attentively to the dialogue going on around the table, at the back of the print room. They are immersed in their discussion. Hans Hut is from around here, and he lives in Bibra, a few miles from here, an excellent distributor of printed material for some years now. He printed the first part of Luther's translation of the Gospel and that brought him a lot of credit, but he didn't put it in the princes' banks. Given the vast amount of work coming in, he is trying to open a printing press of his own, in Bibra: a major initiative, which may see the light of day one of these weeks. At any rate, he's familiar with all the current printing techniques and his advice is indispensable.

Johannes Denck looks about my age, sly as a weasel. He's from around here too, well known to the local authorities, but for some time he's been travelling around the countryside and the villages as far as the regions of the North Sea. A provocateur, an agitator by trade, he's someone you'd want to have on your side to ensure that his free spirit didn't turn against you. He also has a brilliantly intelligent way with the Scriptures: the city is in turmoil about a sermon of his in which he listed forty paradoxes encountered in the Gospels. He says that for the faithful 'there is no other guide' in our reading 'but the inner world of God, which comes from the Holy Spirit'. The Magister appreciates his acumen, his cunning and the huge amount of information that he's brought back from his travels. The text he wrote in Mühlhausen, and which we have brought back here, also mentions these things.

'That mass of flaccid meat that lives in Wittenberg, Friar Secrecy, wants to keep the Scripture far from the eyes of the peasants. He's afraid of being toppled from the throne on which he rests his arse. The peasants should keep their heads low over their ploughs while he becomes the new Pope. This scandal must come to an end, it's time he was unmasked! The Word of the Lord must be accessible to everyone, the humble in particular should be able to encounter it directly and meditate upon it consciously, without it having first to pass through the slobbering mouths of the scribes.' It's the Magister talking.

Denck nods and speaks. 'This is all true, no doubt. But we've got other problems to deal with too. The peasants aren't everything. And then there's the towns: you've seen Mühlhausen. As I told you, I've spent some incredible weeks in that port on the North Sea, Antwerp. The merchants there are wealthy and powerful, the shipping traffic is growing by the hour and the city is in ferment with unquiet souls. There's one brother there, a roof tiler whom many people consider coarse and ignorant, but who preaches and incites free spirits to rebel against the wicked. You'd be amazed to see whose ear he catches: furriers, shipowners, stone-merchants with their illustrious families, along with brewers, carpenters and tramps. It's cash, in the end, and cash supports all kinds of causes. The fucking townspeople of our city are bigots and inclined to barter small advantages for the submission of the peasants and the preservation of the princes. It's their arses we're going to kick!'

'If we manage to appropriate their shops to print our writings, there won't be such need for money!' Hut laughs to himself.

'Shut up, though; for months now you've been making projects for your new printing press and meanwhile you're forcing us to do somersaults!' mocks Pfeiffer.

'No, no, we're going to do it this time! We'll be ready in less than a month. They've assured me that the press is already on its way and if there wasn't so much trouble about the place it would have been ready weeks ago.'

Denck gives him a dig in the ribs. 'And you, mister lion-heart, aren't keen on trouble . . .'

We all burst out laughing.

Meanwhile Herrgott's apprentices haven't lifted their heads from the composition table: they won't for a while yet. For some time I've been staring at a basket full of strips of paper of various dimensions. I point it out to Hut: 'What's that for?'

'Nothing. That's the discards: this press prints four pages on each big sheet. When you cut them, there's always a bit left over.'

'Couldn't you cram the characters closer together and make the margin smaller?'

'Yes, but why bother? Isn't all this wasted paper enough for you?'

'Maybe it's a stupid thing to say, but I thought that apart from the Magister's writings, you could get some surplus sheets from each print run, then print our message on them in a few effective and memorable lines, and you could distribute them by hand, travelling around the countryside. We could circulate them via brethren scattered all over the place, we could reach everyone, I don't know, it's just a thought . . .'

Silence. Pfeiffer thumps the table. 'We could print hundreds of them! Thousands!'

The Magister's eyes gleam much as they do when he is fired up by one of his sermons, his smile makes me glow. 'You've grown up, son; you've just got to learn to stand up for your ideas more forcefully.'

Hut picks up a strip of paper from the basket, picks up pen and inkpot, and starts doing a few sums. He mutters to himself: 'It could work, it could work . . .' He almost leaps from his seat to turn round and shout at the printers, 'You two, stop! Stop everything!'

I'm repairing the chicken huts ahead of the coming winter, nailing the boards so that the creatures don't suffer too much from the cold. In the evening I sink back into my memories.

I remember when the föhn used to come, the same one that now blows upon a different world.

The föhn: a hot wind, dense with humidity and secretions that blows from the south, snakes through the Alpine chain and bursts into the fields and valleys, bringing with it the crazed moods and violent passions for which it is famous. It took us over, and throughout that winter of fever and delirium it clung to our bodies, making us shake uncontrollably, before hurling us into a dance of death that still etches all those names into my flesh. Names. Places, faces. Names of the dead. I first read them in the Scriptures and they flashed out of the pages of books, merging indissolubly with the joy in the eyes of the sisters, assuming the luminous expressions of their children, the sharp, rough profiles of peasants and miners liberated in the Spirit of God.

Jacob, Mathias, Johannes, Elias, Gudrun, Ottilie, Hansi.

Names of the dead, now. I will never have names again, never again. I will not bind the truth to the corpse of a name. That way I'll possess all names. I'm alive today in order to remember them, and I can listen to the rain beating on the roof while another autumn passes and Eltersdorf prepares itself for the snow, the icy cold that will come on the heels of this last hot breath.

October 1524 ended with another expulsion *extra muros*. This time it happened in Nuremberg. About a week previously the two adepts of Herrgott's press had delivered the fruits of their sleepless nights and days of furious toil; the two pieces of writing that the Magister had brought with him from Mühlhausen: five hundred copies of *The Manifest Interpretation*, more again of the *Confutation*. Apart from this, the changes made to the method of composition of the quartos had given us several thousand separate small sheets, on which was

reproduced a very short version of our programme, along with incitements, directed above all at women, and mentioning the blessings of
the Lord who would protect us with the sword if need be. We would
be able to distribute them freely as we travelled through the countryside, through villages and the outskirts of the towns. After one
discussion, which was not without its moments of hilarity, we decided
to call them *Flugblätter*, 'fly-sheets' or 'flyers', just because they were
small single sheets that could pass easily from hand to hand, adapted
to humble people, in a simple language that many of the peasants
would understand either by reading them themselves, or having them
read to them out loud.

That morning had passed with emissaries and couriers coming and
going, to guarantee the first round of distribution of the Magister's
texts to various regions: a hundred copies had already been sent to
Augsburg. But the climate in the city was not very reassuring. Great
commotion had been caused, for example, by Denck's umpteenth
enterprise when, on 24 or 25 of October, he had harangued the
students of St Sebald in no uncertain terms, issuing open invitations
to massacre anyone who claimed the exclusive right to interpret the
Word of God. A sermon at the end of which Johannes the fox, with
typical improvisation, had proclaimed himself rector of the school, to
the applause of the enthusiastic students. None of this had gone down
too well with the local authorities, who were under the additional
pressure of incessant information coming in about the spread of
revolts in the forest and all the surrounding regions, and from the
following day rumours began to spread about the imminent expulsion
of Denck beyond the city walls.

And that was what happened. On 27 October the load of books
from Brother Höltzel was stopped at the Spittler gate, as it was leaving
town for Mainz. Among the volumes found by the guard of the city
council, which had clearly been alerted in advance, were twenty copies
of *The Manifest Interpretation*. They impounded the whole print run
and kicked out Höltzel, to whom the Magister had assigned the task
of distributing and reprinting his works. In the course of the same day
rumours about the imminent expulsion of Denck became a certainty.
By daybreak on 28 October we were all under arrest. It would take the
police another whole day to track down our warehouse: Herrgott had
returned, he had had no qualms about denouncing us and letting the
guards interrogate the two apprentices for a long time. The whole
print run was impounded. Only Hut, on the first day, had managed
to have the flyers transferred to Bibra, along with some copies of the
Magister's writings.

The council didn't want any trouble. Two burgomasters visited us in our cell in the evening and informed us that the decision had been made: before dawn we would be led outside the city without giving notice of the arrest and the expulsion.

Magister Thomas, Ottilie, Pfeiffer, Denck, Hut, Elias and me. We found ourselves on the road once again, contemplating the incredible spectacle of dawn rising timidly behind the pinnacles of Nuremberg, tinging them with pink. This time the Magister didn't seem especially bothered by events. Hut led us to his house in Bibra, a few miles away, a safe place where we could decide what needed to be done.

There the Magister told us that we would have to split up and this worried us considerably: the fact that we had shared the misadventures of the past few months had brought us very close together and it seemed ridiculous to dissolve the company.

I remember the determination in his eyes. 'I know, but seven of us have to do the work of a hundred,' he said. 'And if we all stay together we'll never do it. There are tasks that have absolute priority and those we will have to share out among us. The time is ripe, we can get the godless into a corner, half of Germany is in revolt and there's not a moment to lose.'

He turned towards Hut. 'Before we do anything else, we've got to be sure that at least the books sent to Augsburg have reached their destination and try to distribute them as quickly as possible.'

Hut nodded but didn't say anything. It was his mission.

The Magister continued, 'As far as I'm concerned, it's vitally important that I get to Basle. I've got to meet Ecolampadius there, and find out whether the situation is really as heated as the brothers down there have written. If the most important city in the Helvetic Confederation passed to us, it would make life hard for the princes . . .' His eye fell on Denck. 'I think that you, Johannes, should come with me. You've worked in a big city before and your advice would be a great help.'

'And what about the rest of us?' Pfeiffer seemed worried. 'Where are we going to go?'

Magister Thomas picked up a heavy jute sack and opened it on the table, enough to let some of the contents fall out before our eyes. The flyers tumbled on to the boards as though moved by an invisible hand. 'These are the seeds. The countryside will be your field.'

My confused gaze met the eyes of Pfeiffer and Elias.

Ottilie picked up some sheets. 'Of course, the peasants . . . the peasants.' She looked at me. 'They must be told, we've got to let them know that their brothers throughout the whole of Germany are rising up. And for those who can't read, we'll read to them . . .' Then, turning to Pfeiffer: 'A troop, Heinrich, an army of peasants freeing this land from godlessness, inch by inch . . .' She sought approval from the Magister. 'We will march with the peasants on Mühlhausen; there are still plenty of people out there who want to shake off the yoke of tyrants and false prophets!'

I felt the heat of courage filling my heart and my muscles. That woman's eyes and words lit a fire that I thought nothing and no one could ever extinguish.

Pointing at us, Magister Thomas turned to her with a smile and said, 'Wife, I am entrusting these three men to you. Make sure that they are safe and sound upon my return. You will have to be prudent, the police of the princes have been set loose around the country. Never stop anywhere, never spend two consecutive nights in the same place, don't trust anyone whose heart you can't read like an open book. And trust in God at all times. His is the light that brightens our way. Be careful never to lose it. I am confident that we will meet at the church of Our Lady in Mühlhausen at the beginning of next year. Good luck, and may the Lord be with each one of you.'

Chapter 21

The wind beats against the panels of the door like a crazed dog. The candles seem to flicker even in here, as though the frozen breath of winter could get to them. So memories merge and tremble, still run through with the shudder of fury: those were turbulent days. Sleeping on straw, this makeshift bed a prince's four-poster in comparison: thin and dirty children, dignified faces beyond lamentation, filled with the desire for redemption; always on the road, passing through farm-steads, towns, villages. We were diligent sowers of the seed, lighting the spark of war against those who had usurped the Word of God, the tormentors of His people. I saw scythes hammered into swords, hoes becoming lances and simple men leaving the plough to become fearless warriors. I saw a little carpenter carving a great crucifix and guiding Christ's troops like the captain of the most invincible army. I saw all this and I saw those men and women take up their own faith and turn it into a banner of revenge. Love seized our hearts with that one fire that flamed within us all: we were free and equal in the name of God, and we would smash the mountains, stop the winds, kill all our tyrants in order to realise His kingdom of peace and brotherhood. We could do it, in the end we could do it: life belonged to us.

Themar, Unterhof, Regendorf, Swartzfeld, Ohrdruf, never two days in the same place. Halfway through November we decided to stop in a tiny village called Grünbach, a little over a day's walk from Mühlhausen. The village was inhabited entirely by peasants in the service of the knight of Enzensberg, to whom, some years before, the many-faceted Pfeiffer had acted as cook and confessor. He assured us that the knight was a sworn enemy of the imperial city and that he would certainly do nothing to obstruct our evangelical campaign on his lands.

In exchange for help with the most arduous labours, we were lodged in an old disused stable, next to the cottage of a widow by the name of Frida. Straw for a bed and blankets of untreated wool. From the morning of our arrival this woman proved very happy to have us, insisting that throughout the whole of the previous week she had had all kinds of premonitions about important people coming to her house. For the first time I felt the strange sensation of listening to a person talk my language without being able to make out a word of what she was saying. Apart from Pfeiffer, who was born hereabouts, the only one to grasp anything that the old peasant woman said was Ottilie who, in her travels with her husband, had begun to listen to the thousand different ways in which a single vernacular could be mangled.

Widow Frenner had a daughter, about sixteen years of age, who tended the master's cows and milked them every morning. The girl was the youngest of seven, and her six brothers had all ended up in the pay of a brave captain in the pay of Count Mansfeld.

From the day after our arrival in Grünbach, early in the morning, we started visiting fields, vegetable gardens and stables, and making contact with the people, distributing flyers and announcing the imminent fall of the powerful. Competition was very fierce: on the same day we met a Lutheran preacher, two tramps who were trying to get hospitality and food by explaining the Bible and predicting the future; and last of all a recruiter of mercenary soldiers who glorified life in his troop, the generous pay, the easy earnings, the glory.

Most of the peasants we met listened to us with a certain degree of attention, asked very punctilious questions about the end of the world, prided themselves at being called the elect, and showed a certain anxiety at the idea that to change their situation God would not descend in person to bring down the powerful, but rather that they would have to do it themselves with their scythes and pitchforks. Some of them, thanks to the flyers that we put in their hands, made acquaintance with the printed word for the first time, while others demonstrated that they were capable of reading something and told us that they had learned from a travelling salesman of almanacs and prophecies. One highly successful flyer was the print showing the image of Martin Luther beating bishops and papists with a big stick. We thus decided that in the next flyers we would print images more than anything else: sovereigns forced to hoe the land, peasants in revolt beneath the protective eye of the Omnipotent One and things of that kind.

That evening in Grünbach, we were invited into the shop of a certain Lambert, who worked as a blacksmith and mended tools. The furnace, which had recently gone out, spread its warmth through the room. We were offered bread spiced with cumin and coriander, and

Elias, without attracting attention, persuaded even Ottilie, who hated the taste, to eat at least a little. Later, when we wrapped ourselves in our coarse blankets, he explained to us that only witches and wizards refuse to eat cumin, because it is said to cancel all their power.

Lambert the smith threw down a challenge, in which we had to come up with songs involving contradictions, and proposed one of his own: 'I went out this morning just after dark, with my scythe to go hoeing, I went along the road and climbed up an oak tree, and I ate all the cherries, and the owner of the apple tree turned up and told me to pay for his grapes.'

Others replied with one about wolves bleating, shells carrying snails and chicks turning into eggs. But the final prize went to Elias, with his ogre's voice: 'I know a song of contradictions, I'll sing it to you straight away: I explained the Gospel to the parish priest, who kept on talking in Latin, I told him: you're going to have to pay for the wheat, and the part in excess belongs to the dispossessed. I went up to the palace on my own, my friend and I went to see the master, five of us told him the land was ours, ten of us explained it to him, twenty of us sent him running, fifty of us took the castle, a hundred of us burned it, a thousand of us crossed the river, ten thousand of us are marching to the last battle!'

Thanks to this song, which quickly became an actual hymn, we immediately won the sympathy of the peasants of Grünbach. Elias prepared them for the final battle: proper training, each day at sunrise, teaching them the use of swords and knives, disarming the enemy, bringing him to the ground and leaving him in a right state, all with their bare hands. I had never used any kind of weapon before that and I would have to admit that the peasants proved a good deal more skilful than I was.

And because country people aren't keen on abstractions, after a few days we put our little troop to the test. There still wasn't much fighting to be done, the parish priest fled as soon as they lifted their pitchforks over their heads and it wasn't hard to requisition the tithed grain to redistribute among the people of the surrounding villages.

Some days later we organised a big party at Sneedorf, in the course of which the new parish priest of the community was elected, and for the first time in many years the religious authority was allowed to perform what they called the dance of the cock, which had been forbidden until then because of certain very lascivious pirouettes that revealed the legs of the women. Before getting drunk as I had done several times, until my legs gave in, I danced with Dana, widow Frenner's young daughter.

Over the days that followed the news of a parish priest being elected by his congregation reached the neighbouring community, who sent messengers to Grünbach to intervene on their behalf, now against the parish priest, now against the lord. Without hesitation, our comrades left their work and ran to where they were needed, until three uninterrupted days of snow made travel impossible.

Apart from the icy winds, a storm of another kind reached our village. Shortly before dawn we were awoken by the cries of peasants who had gone into the fields to check the effects of the frost.

When we went out into the ploughed field, Frida was running madly around all over the place and Dana knelt weeping in the snow. Pfeiffer stopped the widow to find out what was happening, but in the state she was in, her speech became even more incomprehensible. Then I went over to Dana and, bending over her, asked her slowly, 'What's happening, sister? Say something.' Sobbing: 'The landsknechts are back. They've killed my father and taken my brothers away, and as to me and my mother, they . . . they . . .' She couldn't go on. Having emerged from nowhere, called away from who knows what war, hungry, cold and tired, a troop of mercenaries was advancing through the little village, hoping to carry off a bit of food, using threats of beatings, burnings and killings if they didn't find any.

Elias was the first to look for a solution. 'If I'm not mistaken, there are thirty men and twenty women here in the village. I'm sure there's much more of them than that. We can't beat them. I suggest we let them have the knight's cattle: four cows ought to be enough for them.'

Having said that he set off to warn the others. I walked behind him, while Pfeiffer stayed with the women.

The peasants were used to defending their masters' property on pain of death, because the alternative would have meant spending whole years giving the master almost their entire share of the harvest, to repay the damage he had suffered. For that reason it wasn't easy to convince them that this time, when the master came to claim his privileges, we would reply as he deserved us to. For the time being, isolated as we were, we could think only about saving our skins.

We met the mercenaries on the village street, up to our knees in snow and clutching all kinds of work tools. There were at least a hundred of them, but we spotted straight away that they were exhausted with marching and cold. Many of them couldn't stand upright because of their frozen feet, others were beginning to suffer from exposure. There were also a few women with them, probably prostitutes, in pitiful states.

'We need food, a fire and some herbs for fever,' said the captain, once we were within shouting distance.

'You'll get them,' came the reply from Lambert the smith.

'But', added Elias, who had grasped the meaning of the situation, 'free all the men and women who don't want to follow you.'

'No one wants to leave my company!' answered the captain, trying to sound convincing, but he hadn't finished speaking before at least thirty, both women and men, stamping their way through the snow, came to hide behind us.

The captain didn't move, his jaw set. Then he said again, 'Come on, then, show us the food and firewood.'

We dispatched four rather well-fed cows to the cooks, who immediately began slaughtering and butchering them. Blood mixed with the melted snow.

That night Dana, almost paralysed with cold and fear, came looking for me in my straw bed, asking me to stay there and protect her because she feared that the soldiers would do again what she and her mother had been subjected to two years before.

She slipped underneath me before I could breathe, before I could collect my thoughts. She was thin, with angular elbows, long, straight legs, little breasts pointing up at me. I struggled to control my breathing, more intense by the minute, and stared into her big, dark eyes. She made herself smaller, her face pressed against my chest, one leg gently wrapped round my hips.

'No one's going to hurt you.'

I dissolved days, months of tension and desire inside her, gasping at every touch, every smooth caress. Dana's quiet moans asked neither words nor promises. I bent over, my mouth sought her breast, first brushing, then pressing her nipple with my lips. I held her face and her hair, shorter than a shop-boy's, between my hands, and I stayed inside her for a long time, longer than I can remember, until she went to sleep, still holding me in a tight embrace.

They departed three days later, leaving the remains of the carcasses beside the blackened holes in the snow, and those thirty desperate people who hadn't been paid for months. The new arrivals proved useful: almost all of them were country people, but they knew how to wield weapons and draw up battle formations.

On the first Friday of every month there was a big craft fair in Mühlhausen, attracting people from the four corners of Thuringia, from Halle and Fulda, Allstedt and Sonderhausen. According to Pfeiffer, this was the day when we would have to try to get back into the city, hidden by the great mass of people passing through the gates.

December was approaching. We started to make contact within Mühlhausen, among the miners of Count Mansfeld, among the inhabitants of Salza and Sangerhausen. On the first Friday in December the brewers' city would be filled with a crowd looking for things other than new wicker baskets.

Chapter 22

Seventh article: We will not hereafter allow ourselves to be further oppressed by our lords. [. . .] The peasant should, however, help the lord when it is necessary, and at proper times when it will not be disadvantageous to the peasant and for a suitable payment.

Eighth article: [. . .] We ask that the lords may appoint persons of honour to inspect those holdings which cannot currently support the rent exacted of them, and fix a rent in accordance with justice, so that the peasants shall not work for nothing, since the labourer is worthy of his hire.

Ninth article: [. . .] In our opinion we should be judged according to the old written law so that the case shall be decided according to its merits, and not with partiality.

The pungent and revolting smell of the substances used in the tanning of hides makes the guards on the gate rush us through. The furrier is allowed through after a very perfunctory check, and so is his numerous entourage, so they don't have the chance to identify an old acquaintance from the imperial city, an ex-student from Wittenberg, a colossal miner and a young woman with jade-coloured eyes.

The streets of Mühlhausen are filled with carts, dragged into the marshy throng of people by the efforts of oxen, horses, donkeys and, in many cases, human beings. Loads like enormous sausages, crushed down by a tangle of ropes and cords, often high enough to block out the windows of the houses. Tools for all kinds of work, furniture for all kinds of dwelling, clothes for all kinds of individual. The carts emerge from every corner when you least expect them, the driver calling for a space to be cleared, always too quick to avoid people being shoved and hit and trampled.

In the broader streets to either side, the sellers are less well equipped, with the goods spread out on the ground; the traders in the square are the ones with at least two poles and a cloth to serve as a canopy, or luxurious carts which, with an intricate arrangement of joints and hinges, are turned into actual shops. Some loudly declaim the quality of their products, others prefer to attract your attention with a whisper, as though they had sensed that you, out of all those present, were the one who would be able to appreciate their incredible goods; others still send boys around to collar customers and give beer to the ones who stay to bargain. Many families walk about holding on to ropes for fear of being dragged away in the chaos.

Elias casts his eye over the crowd. In the area around the crockery sellers he has already recognised brethren from Allstedt. A glance towards the glassmakers confirms the arrival of the peasants of the Hainich. Further along, the ones greeting each other by raising the Bible must be from Salza.

Ottilie raises her eyes, waiting for a signal. She has already identified the sucker, a member of the city council, pointed out to her by Pfeiffer. They have to wait for the miners of Mansfeld, who have still not shown up. Without them, nothing will happen.

A little boy makes his way through the crowd. 'Mister, I'll get you a new suit of clothes! Come and visit my father's shop, I'll take you there, mister . . .' He clutches my jacket.

I turn round, annoyed, and he whispers, 'Our brethren the miners are here, behind a brick cart.'

Elias makes a jerking motion: 'It's starting, we're all here.'

I drop a coin into the outstretched palm of the little messenger, ruffle his hair and prepare to enjoy the scene.

Ottilie approaches her husband, at the densest point of the greatest crowd, opposite a lute player. She comes and stands behind him and lightly presses her breast against his spine, whispers something as she brings her lips to his ear, allowing her blonde hair to brush his shoulder. Then, with one hand, she starts working him between his legs. I see the nape of the poor bugger's neck turning crimson. He nervously smoothes his beard: he puts up no resistance. Still facing away from her, he bends forward slightly and starts to slip his arm under her skirt. As he makes his way towards the upper regions, Ottilie raises her tempting hand, takes a step backwards and, trapping his arm in that scandalous posture, she starts shouting her head off, slapping him with all her might with her other hand. 'You bastard, you worm, you revolting worm, may the curse of God be upon you!'

That's the signal. The brawl breaks out around Ottilie, while from the four corners of the square our brethren start advancing in a tight formation. They knock over the stalls, beat up the traders, trample the brewers.

'So that's what the gentlefolk of Mühlhausen get up to, eh? Sticking their hands up people's skirts?'

The first to reach us is a peasant who's rammed his way through the crowd, grabbing any townspeople who get in his way by the collar and butting them smack in the face. Immediately after him comes one of the miners, with a clutch of hackbuts, sticks and knives stolen from an armourer. 'These are for you,' he says. 'And there are a few more where they came from!'

'Blasted brewer,' Ottilie goes on shouting. 'I recognise him. He's on the council!'

I yell at the top of my voice, 'They've sold us to the brewers!'

The voices multiply and increase in volume. 'Bastard councillors, crooks, get out of Mühlhausen!'

Many of the people shouting weren't even present at the originally staged event and think it's a street demonstration to oust the council. And they're right.

Everything happens at the greatest speed. The tide, as though attracted by some mysterious magnet, starts to engulf the Kilansgasse, which leads from the market square to the Rathaus. Little streams of people scatter here and there: pious souls who suddenly need to go to church.

All of a sudden I look around and discover I've been left on my own; Elias, Heinrich and Ottilie have disappeared. A peasant beside me knocks down his enemy for being too well dressed, with an elbow to the throat and a fist under his ribs.

'Yes, brother, crush the godless as though they were dogs!' I yell, delighted.

The guards are careful not to show their faces. The city is ours.

The first bell of curfew rings out. I find the rest of our group by the Archangel Fountain, where we've arranged to meet in case we lost sight of each other. There are another two people there whom I don't think I recognise.

Pfeiffer does the honours: 'Oh, here he is, our student rebel! These are Briegel and Hülm, two of the eight representatives of the people of Mühlhausen.'

'And these', one of them says to me, waving around what looks like a big rattle, 'are the keys of our city!'

'. . . which is to say,' the other continues, 'the right to decide who stays out and who can come in.'

'We've done it. Thomas can come back,' Ottilie announces with a smile.

'As for you,' Briegel or Hülm goes on, 'the free imperial city of Mühlhausen welcomes you all.'

Tenth article: We are aggrieved by the appropriation by individuals of meadows and fields which at one time belonged to a community. These we will take again into our own hand unless they have been acquired legitimately.

Eleventh article: [. . .] We will entirely abolish the due called Todfall heriot and will no longer endure it, nor allow widows and orphans to be thus shamefully robbed against God's will [. . .]

Twelfth article: In the twelfth place it is our conclusion and final resolution, that if any one or more of the articles here set forth should not be in agreement with the Word of God, as we think they are, such article we will willingly withdraw the minute it is proved really to be against the Word of God by a clear explanation of the Scripture. [. . .] For this we shall pray God, since He can grant these and He alone. The peace of Christ abide with us all.

The news of his arrival flies from mouth to mouth, along the main street. The two wings of the crowd merge together to greet the man who has challenged the princes; people and peasants who have come running from the surrounding villages. I almost weep with emotion. Magister, I have to tell you everything, how we struggled and how we managed to get here, to welcome you, now, without a policeman anywhere around. They're very frightened, they're shitting themselves, if they try to show their faces, they'll be taking an enormous risk. We're here, Magister, and with your help we'll be able to turn this city upside down and flush out the council. Ottilie is beside me, her eyes gleaming, wearing a pretty dress so white that it makes her stand out against the mass of coarse townspeople. Here he is! He comes round the bend on a black horse and at his side is Pfeiffer, who has gone to meet him on the road. Two arms of steel grab me from behind and hoist me into mid-air.

'Elias!'

'My friend, now that he's here, the men from the council will be shitting themselves, you'll see!'

A vulgar laugh: even the rough miner from the Erzgebirge can't contain his enthusiasm.

Magister Thomas comes over as the crowd closes behind him and follows him. He sees the sign of greeting from his wife and gets down from his horse. A firm embrace and a whispered word that I don't catch. Then he turns to me: 'Greetings, my friend, I'm happy to find you safe and sound on such a day.'

'I wouldn't have missed it if I'd lost my legs, Magister. The Lord was with us.'

'And with them . . .' He gestures towards the crowd.

Pfeiffer smiles. 'Let's go, you're going to have to speak in church now, they want to hear your words.'

A gesture. 'Get a move on, you don't want to be left behind!'

He holds out his hand to Ottilie and helps her on to the horse.

I run to the portal of Our Lady's church.

The nave is full, the people are spilling out on to the little square in front of the church. From the pulpit, the Magister looks out over this sea of eyes and draws the power of his words from them. They quickly fall silent.

'May the blessing of God be upon you, brothers and sisters, and may it allow you to listen to these words with a steadfast and open heart.'

Not a breath.

'The sound of gnashing teeth that is rising up today from the palaces and the monasteries against you, the insults and curses that the nobles and the monks are hurling at this city will not shake your resolution. I, Thomas Müntzer, salute in you, in this crowd gathered here, the awakening, at long last, of the city of Mühlhausen!'

An ovation arises above the heads of the crowd, the people returning his greeting.

'Listen. Now you hear all around you the confused, impatient, angry hubbub of those who have always oppressed us: the princes, the fat abbots, the bishops, the notables of the city. Do you hear them yelling out there, outside the city walls? It's the barking of dogs with their teeth pulled out, brothers and sisters. Yes, the dogs which, with their soldiers, their tax collectors, have taught us the meaning of fear, have taught us always to obey, to lower our heads in their presence, to pay our respects like slaves before their owners. Those who have given us uncertainty, hunger, taxes, back-breaking labour . . . Now they, my brothers, are weeping with rage because the people of Mühlhausen have risen. When only one of you refused to pay their tributes, or revere as they thought fit, they could have him thrashed by their mercenaries, they could imprison and kill. But now there are thousands of you. And they won't be able to whip you any more, because you have the whip hand now; they won't be able to imprison you any more, because you have taken the prisons and removed the doors; they won't be able to kill you any more or steal from the Lord the devotion of His people, because His people have risen and turned their eyes towards the Kingdom. No one will be able to tell you, do this, do that, because from now on you will live in brotherhood and community, according to God's law. No longer will there be those who work the land and those who enjoy its fruits, because all will work the land and enjoy its fruits in community, as brothers. And the Lord will be honoured because the lords are no longer there!'

Another rumble of enthusiasm echoes in the great drum of the apse, like the roar of ten thousand people.

'Mühlhausen is a rock of offence, a source of horror for the godless of the earth, a premonition of the fury of God that is about to descend upon them, and that is why they are trembling like dogs. But this city is not alone. Along the road that I have travelled to reach here from Basle, everywhere, in every village, from the Black Forest to Thuringia, I have seen the peasants rising up armed with their faith. Behind you the troop of the humble is forming, desperate to spring the chains of servitude. They need a signal. You must be the first. Do what so many, elsewhere, are still finding it difficult to do. But be certain that your example will be followed by other cities, either nearby or so far off that we don't even know their names. You must open up the path of the Lord. No one will be able to take away from you the pride of this undertaking. In you I salute free Mühlhausen, the city on which God has placed His watch and His blessing, the city that wrought the revenge of the humble upon the godless of the earth! The hope of the world starts here, brothers, it starts with you!'

The final words are drowned by the noise and Magister Thomas has to yell at the top of his voice. I too leap into the middle of this joy: never again will we be driven out of any city.

The meeting is in the home of the cloth maker Briegel. Pfeiffer and the Magister are going to have to talk with the representatives of the people about which claims to present in the council chamber. They've invited me, too, while Ottilie will go to talk to the women of the city. Briegel is a small businessman and so is Hülm, a porcelain manufacturer and woodcarver. The spokesman of the peasants is small, hairy Peter, rough face and black eyes, disproportionately wide shoulders from working in the fields.

A humble house, but solid and clean, very different from the hovels we saw in Grünbach.

Briegel speaks first, and explains the situation. 'So this is how things are. We can put the representatives of the corporations in a minority. We propose the extension of the vote to citizens who don't belong to the guilds, but who live within the walls or in the hamlets outside the walls. Some of those fat bastards will be able to make a bit of noise, but they are well aware that all the people are on our side, and I believe that just to avoid rebellion they'll accept the new arrangement.'

He gives Hülm the floor. 'Yes. I think it's possible to impose our programme as well, they certainly won't want to risk their estates. Basically, all we're asking is that the citizenry can make its own decisions, without always being subjected to their rules.'

There's a moment of silence, a rapid exchange of glances between Pfeiffer and the Magister. Under the table a big grey dog slumps on my shoes; I stroke one of his ears while Pfeiffer speaks.

'Friends, allow me to ask you why we should lower ourselves to making pacts with an enemy that we have already beaten. As you have said, the population is on our side, the city can be defended without any need for municipal guards, we can do it without any difficulty. What interest do we have in maintaining some fat merchants in the council?'

He waits for his words to sink in, and then continues, 'Thomas

Müntzer has a suggestion that I support wholeheartedly. Let's throw out the corporations and the brewers, and set up a completely new council.'

The Magister intervenes impetuously, 'A Perpetual Council, elected by the whole of the citizenry without distinction. From which any representative and public magistrate can be dismissed at any time if the electors insist that they are not adequately represented and governed by him. The people could then organise into periodical assemblies to make judgements all together about the running of the council.'

Hülm, perplexed, nervously smoothes his beard. 'It's a bold idea, but you might be right. And what do you suggest we do about taxation?'

Pfeiffer answers, 'Everyone puts what he can afford into the council coffers. Everyone must be allowed to feed and clothe his own family. For that reason a proportion of the taxes will be sent to help the poor and the dispossessed, a kind of coffer of mutual aid for the purchase of bread, milk for the children, anything they might need.'

Silence. Then a murmur from the depths of Peter's chest. The peasant is shaking his head. 'That's all very well for the city.' The toothless words emerge with difficulty. 'But what's going to change for us?'

Briegel: 'You don't want the city of Mühlhausen to assume responsibility over every cottage in the region, I hope!'

The dog, tiring of me, rolls over and a kick from the head of the household sends him listlessly away. He crouches in a corner and starts gnawing on a dusty bone.

Peter starts again. 'The peasants are fighting. The peasants must know what they're doing it for. We want this city, and all the others, to decide to support our requests to the lords.' He isn't looking at Hülm or Briegel, but Pfeiffer, straight in the eyes. 'We want the twelve articles to be approved by everyone.'

I laugh to myself, reflecting that it was I who read the articles to him, yesterday, when the text reached the city fresh from the press.

Pfeiffer: 'It strikes me as a reasonable suggestion.' He looks at Hülm and Briegel, who are both silent. 'Friends, the city and the country are nothing without each other. The front has to stay united, we have common interests. Once we've got rid of the big crooks, the princes will be next to pay!'

His incitement hangs over the table for a moment, then Hülm erupts, 'And let the twelve articles be approved by the city and included in our programme. But before we do anything else, let's resolve these issues we have before us here, or everything's going to end up right in the shit.'

Last night I dreamed about Elias.

I was walking barefoot at night along a twisting path, and he was at my side. All of a sudden, a wall of white rock rose up in front of us, with a narrow crack above our heads. Elias lifted me up and I managed to stick my head into the hole. I asked him to pass me the torch so that I could see better: a kind of long, damp gallery. Once inside, I understood that he would never be able to reach me, there was no purchase on the wall. Then I turned back, but he had already disappeared. With some difficulty, torch in hand, I started creeping down that narrow passage.

I woke up and waited for Vogel's cockerel to herald the beginning of another day of toil. The image of Elias didn't leave me until evening. That vast strength, that voice, are still with me.

On 16 March the townspeople assembled in the Church of Our Lady to elect the new council. From that moment the city was ours.

The task assigned to me, along with Elias, was to organise the citizens' militia. In case of an attack, the princes wouldn't find us unprepared. Elias taught the people how to form themselves into a phalange, level their pikes, face a man in hand-to-hand combat. With the Magister's help he divided them into units of about twenty men and assigned each of them a part of the wall to defend in case of attack. Anyone with any military experience whatsoever was appointed captain by his own militia. I became responsible for communications between the units, and chose a few alert and trustworthy boys as messengers. I was handed a short dagger and in the evening I could practise using it with the unbeatable Elias.

Then, in April, the citizens of Salza revolted. The suggestion that we go to their aid was put to the vote and accepted unanimously. We assembled four hundred men, sure that this would be a good opportunity to put those months of training to the test. The Magister and Pfeiffer spent a long time talking to the heads of the insurgents, but they seemed more concerned about extracting minimal concessions from the lords than knowing what was going on around them. They gave us two huge barrels of beer for having gone all the way there and that was their only gesture of thanks.

That evening, while we were camped under the moon, I heard the Magister having a long discussion with Pfeiffer about the risks of each town acting independently. Only exhaustion brought their animated conversation to an end.

On the way back we were joined by a messenger coming from Mühlhausen, who had been sent by Ottilie. Hans Hut had reached the city with some very important news and letters. The Magister read some of them to the troop: by now the revolt was spreading throughout the whole of Thuringia, from Erfurt to the Harz mountains, from Naumburg to Hesse. Other cities were following Mühlhausen's example: Sangerhausen, Frankenhausen, Sonderhausen, Nebra, Stolberg . . . And, in the mining region of Mansfeld: Allstedt, Nordhausen, Halle. And indeed in Salza, Eisenach and Bibra, the peasants of the Black Forest.

This news lifted our hearts, there was no stopping us now, the hour had come. While we were returning towards Mühlhausen, we sacked a castle and a convent. No one was killed, the owners gave themselves up to us without resistance, trying to move us to pity so that we would spare their goods and concubines. As regards the women, not a finger was laid on any one of them. As to gold, silver and food, we didn't leave a scrap. Mühlhausen welcomed us in triumph and the two gigantic barrels of beer were quickly drained by the thirst of our fellow citizens.

The party lasted all night, with singing and dancing, in that place that was the centre of the world to us, a place of dreams, the last few days of spring, free and glorious Mühlhausen. It was as though all the forces of life had converged within those walls to pay homage to the faith of the elect. No one could have taken that moment away. Not a troop of soldiers or a shot from a cannon.

Before dawn I found Elias sitting on a chair, reviving the dying embers of a fire. The light from the coals drew strange outlines on that sombre face, which now seemed to have a shadow of fatigue or anxiety. As though something unimaginable were running through Samson's mind.

He turned round when I was close to him. 'Good party, eh?'

'Best I've ever seen. Brother, what's happening?'

Without looking at me, with the rare sincerity he sometimes

showed: 'I don't think . . . I don't think they'd be up to fighting a real battle.'

'You've trained them well. And anyway, I think we're about to find out.'

'Yes, that's just it. You've never seen the soldiers of the princes, the people the lords entrust with the defence of their safes . . .'

His expression was lost in the flickering of the flames.

'Why . . . have you?'

'Where do you think I learned to fight?' In barely a moment he read the question in my face. 'Yes, I was a mercenary. Just as I've done so many other crap jobs in my life. I was a miner, and don't imagine that it's all that much better just because you don't kill anyone. You kill, believe me: you kill yourself, under the ground, getting blinder and blinder like moles, and with the fear of being trapped down there, maybe staying down there for ever. I've done vile things, and I hope that the Lord God in his infinite mercy will have pity on me. But now I'm thinking about them, those wretches we're sending into battle against real troops.'

A hand on his shoulder. 'The Lord will help us, He's been with us so far. He won't abandon us, Elias, you'll see.'

'I pray for that every day, son, every day . . .'

To Herr Thomas Müntzer, brother in faith, pastor in Our Lady of Mühlhausen.

My good friend,
    Thank you for your letter, which I received just yesterday, and thank you to our Lord God for the news it announces. We hope that He has finally found in Thomas Müntzer of Quedlinburg the helmsman of the ship that will chase Leviathan into his abyss.

    Since our parting, it could not be said that my private situation is in accord with the magnificence of the events being prepared for the wretched of Germany; perhaps the Lord has decided to bring me back into that latter group, to make me a full participant in future glory. My family have stayed in Nuremberg, where they are the victim of continuous vexations and abuse. Right now I cannot be contacted, and they have driven me from the city, they are trying to get me by some means or another, to get me to shut up without causing an uprising. Fortunately our sisters in Nuremberg are close to my wife and helping her in this testing time. For my part, I visit inns only to sleep, and leave them before daybreak. But it won't be long before I'm living on the side of the road: my money is running out.

For these reasons I am telling you of my intention to join you in Mühlhausen: I am anxious to contribute to the enterprise of the elect, and I have to draw breath. Besides, in the city there must be plenty of opportunities to earn something with my lessons. See what you can do, among the many anxieties we are suffering at this time.

May the Light of the Lord illuminate your way.

With great gratitude,

    Johannes Denck   *Tübingen, 25 March 1525*

Hut brought us news from the south. Important, vital news. I search in the Magister's bag for that wonderful letter, the words of a man whose feats have found their way into the ballads of the storytellers and reached us here.

To the free city of Mühlhausen, to the Perpetual Council and to its preacher Thomas Müntzer, the echo of whose words instils hope in the whole valley of the Tauber.

The time is nigh. The forces of the enlightened ones have gone to war to assert the righteousness of God. The peasants have marched to the sound of drums along the streets of the imperial city of Rothenburg and, despite the rulings of the municipal council, no one raised a stick to them. In point of fact, the townspeople fear the violence of the countryside, and the possible consequences that being hostile to it might entail.

So I come, dear brothers, to set out the requests for reform with which the forces of the enlightened ones are advancing on the points of their lances.

Above all, they are explaining to the townspeople that law and agreement consist in the preaching of the Word of God, the Holy Gospel, in a free, clear and pure way, without any addition from human hands. But it is of great importance, because until now, and for a very long time, the common people have been oppressed and made by the authorities to bear an unsupportable weight, that the poor people should have such burdens lifted from them, and should be able to seek their own bread without being forced to beg. And that they should not be vexed by the authorities, and that they need not pay tributes, taxes, tariffs or tithes, until such time as a general reform has taken place, based on the Holy Gospel, establishing that which is unjust and must be abolished, and that which is just and must remain.

May I now be granted permission to speak openly to those who have lifted the hope and the hearts of the poor. The events taking place in these lands bathed by the river Tauber suggest to us the two precepts to be followed so that the cause of God may not be lost, and so that all that has been done is not in vain.

First, the forces must grow by the day, like the waves on a stormy sea they must continue to grow until they are so well-equipped and so numerous that they do not fear the sword of the princes.

It is also important to bear in mind that the various requests linking town and country find the same adversary at the end of their journey: the intolerable privileges of the great nobility and the corrupt clergy. We cannot allow such differences to be placed in opposition to one another, to the advantage of the common enemy. Further, since it is true that cities such as this one cannot be maintained without the payment of taxes, we must reach agreements on this matter among the councils, and with the peasant communities about what would be the best to do to sustain the cities. We do not want to abolish all tax burdens completely, but to reach a just agreement after hearing learned and respected people, lovers of God, expressing their opinions on the matter. To this end all ecclesiastical properties, without exception, will be impounded with a view to their being used, as agreed, to the benefit of the peasant community and the forces of the enlightened. People will be appointed to administer those properties, to preserve them and to ensure that a proportion of them are distributed to the poor. Moreover, that which is undertaken, ruled and decided for the benefit of the general good and for peace, whether for the townsman or for the country dweller, must be respected by both, so that all remain united against the phalanges of iniquity.

Wishing that these words may raise bright visions within you, in the hope that we will soon meet on the Lord's day of triumph, fraternal greetings from one fighting under the same banner as yourself, and the invocation of the grace of God.

The commander of the peasant forces of Franconia,
*   Florian Geyer*

Rothenburg on the Tauber, the 4th day of April 1525

Geyer, the legend of the Black Forest. The Schwarztruppe, which he trained single-handedly, had sown panic among the ranks of the Swabian League: impossible to capture, daring and fast, within a very short space of time they had become the model for the peasant armies.

Florian Geyer. A low-ranking rural aristocrat and member of the German knighthood, in 1521 he had disputed the excessive power of the princes and had abandoned his own castle, dedicating himself to brigandry and plunder inside and outside the forest, which he knew like the palm of his hand. Gifted with an astonishing degree of intuition and incomparable courage, even before he embraced the cause of the humble he chose men for his bandit band one by one: no drunks, no useless cut-throats, no rapists, just resolute people, alert and interested in booty out of necessity, or with a view to undertaking operations worthy of his approval.

I remember, in the days of the euphoria of Mühlhausen, how very much I wished to meet him, to be able to see, close to, the man whose name alone was enough to terrorise the great nobles of Franconia.

He laid assault to dozens of castles and convents, confiscated goods, arms and food, and distributed them to the poor. He appeared all of a sudden in villages, scattering to the wind from his red cloth bag the ashes of the last castle he had burned. Over a few months, his band of horsemen grew beyond measure until its recruits numbered many hundreds, well-armed, well-trained and loyal.

Very often, in the evening around the fireside, the peasants sang ballads about his deeds. Armed only with a hatchet and a knife, he hunted deer and boar. In Rothenburg, in the middle of the town square, he decapitated the statue of the Emperor with a single blow.

They caught him in Schwäbisch Halle, after following and trailing him for three days, setting fire to three hectares of forest where he had been spotted. They hastily hid his body, but many people are not actually convinced that he is dead, and swear that he escaped by plunging into the waters of an underground river. In every village of the Black Forest there is someone who says he has seen him riding at sunrise in the depths of the forest, brandishing his sword, ready to return to bring justice to the humble.

To Herr Thomas Müntzer, master of all the just in the true faith, most illustrious preacher in the Church of Our Lady in Mühlhausen.

Master,

The news that reaches me about you and your force of the elect now makes me certain that the hand of the Lord is upon you, after the thousand difficulties and the bitter humiliation of Weimar, which I was sorry not to have known about in time. God himself, who hates the powerful, 'hath exalted those of low degree' and is preparing to 'send the rich empty away, helping His servant Israel, in remembrance of His mercy'.

There is no time to lose: the princes are confused, because the area affected by the revolt is too vast, and the fire of faith is setting the hearts and the territory of Germany aflame each day. Although recruitment is proceeding apace, many are the obstacles one faces when putting a sudden manoeuvre into motion.

Among all of them, the young Philip, Landgrave of Hesse, is the most diligent, but his troops are not orderly, they move slowly and are forever running into difficulties, and have faced a succession of ambushes and attacks by peasants in all their regions. Thus it is apparent that not all the rulers are aware that the matter concerns each one of them, or that they will be destroyed one after the other. Consequently no one who believes he can put his own house in order by conceding benefits and making promises is going to give a sign of wanting to go into battle. Doctor Luther, privy councillor to Herr Spalatin, has visited the region of Mansfeld to placate the rage of the peasants, but has not been able to stop the revolt, instead having stones and insults thrown at him. The Hercules Germanicus is a spent force.

It is time, Master: give the princes a breathing space and they will lay waste our countryside, even at the cost of the year's harvest, until every last ear of grain is ash and the head of every last peasant has fallen. Therefore summon the elect together, lest they disperse. South of Mühlhausen, the Lord of the Armies has won many battles already, while in the north-east the situation is more uncertain. If you move solidly in that direction, the princes won't have time to think, they will have to try to stop you at all costs, and the Lord, through your swords, will show His righteousness once and for all.

Do not fear open encounter: that is where the God of the elect will show He is by your side. Do not hesitate: the All-powerful wants to triumph through you.

Be firm, then, and the Lord will enlighten you: the Kingdom of God on earth is nigh.

  Qoèlet   *the 1st of May 1525*

First of May. The troops of Philip of Hesse were already at the gates of Fulda, in force, ready to wipe them out. They moved quickly. What we met was not an army in difficulties.

Qoèlet. The third letter from an informer lavish with details reserved for the select few, as he had been with information about events in Weimar.

Important letters which had won the trust of the Magister. That crucial conversation comes back to me, Magister Thomas brandishing the letter . . . this letter.

'So, Heinrich, how many do you think we can count on?' The Magister's tone is urgent.

Pfeiffer shakes his head. 'We've lost Hülm and Briegel. They won't drag out so much as a barrel of gunpowder for the people of Frankenhausen. No one from here's going to come.'

The machine called Hans rang out three strokes on the steeple bell of the Rathaus clock.

'Who are they afraid of? Hasn't the Lord given enough signals? I've got at least fifty letters clearly stating: the army of the elect numbers twenty thousand men.'

Magister Thomas rummages in his leather bag and takes out a letter, which he brandishes like a banner. 'If they won't listen to the voice of the Lord, they can't hesitate in the face of the facts. A brother who lives in close contact with the Wittenberg clan wrote to me a few days ago to confirm that the princes are in the shit: the people hate them, their troops are slack and disorganised. Now is the moment to confront them, heading for the heart of Saxony, where they can't afford to let us come. Let me talk to the townspeople.'

'There's no point. Even if we forget about the burgomasters, the people of this town have already had more than they could ever have hoped for. They won't risk their own gains in a pitched battle with the princes.'

'You mean that Mühlhausen, the town that gave an example to all the cities in Thuringia, is going to stand and watch in the crucial battle for the liberation of the lands from the Bavarian Alps to Saxony?'

Pfeiffer, increasingly discouraged: 'Do you think the other towns are going to support this madness? It won't happen, I assure you. Even if Mühlhausen offered all its cannons, the situation would be no different. The insurgent cities have gained their independence and imposed the twelve articles; no one's going to see the point of risking everything in a single head-to-head conflict. And what if we were defeated? Listen. The path we've taken so far has yielded the best results. The rebellion in the countryside has opened up the way to reforms in the towns and cities. Things have got to continue in that direction, there's no sense in risking the lot.'

'Balls! It's the towns that have used the peasant revolt to wrest the councils from the hands of the lords! Now they'll have to run with the army of the enlightened, to sweep the evil tyranny of the princes away for ever!'

'It's not going to happen.'

'Then they'll be swept away by their own wretched selfishness, on the Lord's day of triumph.'

Peace returns for a moment. Denck, silent like myself until then, fills the glasses with wine robbed in great quantities from a Dominican monastery and brought out for the occasion. 'We'd need no less than a thousand men and ten cannon.'

The Magister doesn't even look at his goblet. 'What need have we of cannon? The sword of Gideon will smite their armies.'

He leaves the room, not looking at anyone. After a minute, Denck casts a glance at Pfeiffer, then at me, and follows him.

Heinrich Pfeiffer talks to me gravely. 'At least you've got to make him see sense. It's madness.'

'Madness or not, do you think it's wise to abandon the peasants to their fate? If the cities don't take to the field, it's going to look like betrayal in the eyes of the peasants. And who's to say they're wrong? It'll be the end of the alliance that we've taken so much trouble to build up. If we're defeated, Heinrich, you lot'll be next.'

A deep breath, sadness grips his heart. 'Have you ever seen an army charging?'

'No. But I have seen Thomas Müntzer rousing the humble just by the force of his words. I'm not going to leave him now.'

'Save yourself. Don't go.'

'We will save ourselves, my friend, by rising up and fighting by the side of the Lord, not standing there watching.'

Silence. We embrace tightly, for the last time. Our fates are sealed.

Chapter 27

The news of Thomas Müntzer's departure for Frankenhausen swept through the city before half the day was up. In the morning, barely awake after a sleepless night, when we look out of the window we see that the forecourt of the Church of Our Lady is already crowded. If we wished to delude ourselves we might conclude that the good conscience of the inhabitants of Mühlhausen has finally prevailed over their interests. But we know by now how these things work: the sermons of Magister Thomas, whether you approve of them or not, are a hard habit to quit, apart from anything because for many days now they have been one of the fundamental topics of conversation in the squares and shops. And it's clear to everyone, even to those who only know him by reputation, that Thomas Müntzer will not leave the imperial city without making one final, angry salute to his townspeople.

'Magister,' I shout so that he'll hear me in the next room. 'They're already down there!'

He joins me and appears briefly on the balcony, greeted by an exclamation from the crowd. 'Let's wait until the square is full, so that the Lord can choose his troops.' That's his only comment.

An excited noise rises from the churchyard. Four resolute knocks on the door. Then two more. 'Magister, Magister, open up!'

'Who are you?' I ask, rather surprised by the piercing tone of the voices.

'Jacob and Mathias Ziegler, Georg's sons. We've got to talk to you.'

I open with a smile to the sons of the tailor Ziegler, two devoted followers of ours in the face of the opposition of their father, who actually threatened the Magister a while ago and whom Elias dissuaded from his belligerent intentions.

'What are you doing here?' I ask, dumbfounded. 'Shouldn't you be with your parents in the shop?'

'No,' replies Jacob, the elder brother, fifteen. 'Not after today.'

'We're coming with you,' continues his brother, two years younger, with enthusiasm.

'Calm down, now,' I reply. 'Coming with us? Have you any idea what that means?'

'Yes, the elect are going to defeat the princes! The Lord will be on our side.'

The Magister smiles. 'You see? It's all happening as the Scriptures said: Christ is turning the son against his father and telling us to become as little children.'

'Magister, they can't fight with us.'

They won't let me get a word in. 'We've made our minds up and we're not shifting. Let's see, though. Stand firm, Magister, and let it be soon, we can't stay here.' Having said this, they close the doors behind them and dash down the stairs.

Magister Thomas senses the effect that the brief encounter has had on me. 'Don't worry,' he reassures me, pressing my shoulders. 'The Lord will defend His people, have faith! Chin up, now, it's time to go.'

I go to call Ottilie and Elias. Johannes Denck is no longer with us: he left yesterday evening, heading for Eisenach in search of cannon, arms and ammunition, and he's going to meet up with us on the road.

We leave via the passageway that leads straight into the church; Magister Thomas at the head, the rest of us behind him in silence. We slowly cross the nave, which is pierced with rays of sunlight. Elias opens the heavy door and we find ourselves, still in darkness, on the steps of the cathedral. The eyes of the crowd are all turned towards the windows of our room. Thomas Müntzer steps forward slightly, on to the cathedral steps. No one notices him. His first shout fills the square, already spilling over with at least four thousand people, and is immediately submerged by a wave of startled voices.

'People of Mühlhausen, listen, the last battle is at hand! Soon the Lord will deliver the godless into our hands, as he did Midianites and their king, vanquished by the sword of Gideon, the son of Jo'ash. Like the people of Succot, you too, doubting the power of the God of Israel, are refusing to lend your help to the forces of the elect, and are withholding your cannon and your weapons in order to defend your own privilege. Gideon defeated the tribe of Midian with three hundred men, of three thousand that he had gathered to him. It was the Lord who reduced their numbers, so that the people would not believe they had triumphed only thanks to their strength. Those who were afraid were sent back. In much the same way, today, the forces of the elect are being reduced by the defection of the citizens of Mühlhausen. I say that this is good: lest anyone forget what the Lord has done for his people, if need be I would be ready to move alone against the mercenaries of the princes. Nothing is impossible to those who have faith. But from those who do not have faith will be taken all that they have. So listen, people of Mühlhausen: the Lord has chosen his own, the elect; if anyone's heart is not filled with the courage of faith, let him not obstruct the way of the plans of God: let him go, now, towards his wretched fate. Off with him! Let him go back to his shop, back to his bed. Let him go, and let him never show his face again.'

The people start yelling and shouting, pushing each other and surging forward, and brawls are breaking out all over the place between those who consider themselves worthy and those who want to stay at home and who think Magister Thomas is a madman, shouting there at the top of his voice.

In the end, about three hundred are left, most of them people from outside the town, tramps who have come to the city to plunder the churches, poor people and some from St Nicholas, who wouldn't abandon Thomas Müntzer if the sun turned black. The Magister, who hasn't opened his mouth again, is about to turn to face his little army when it splits in two to let through a group of soldiers dragging three cannon.

'And where have these suddenly appeared out from?' asks Elias contemptuously.

'They're no use to us,' the guard says abruptly. 'You can take them. Heinrich Pfeiffer says the Lord might need them.'

Less than two hours later the column of the chosen leaves the city in silence, by the northern gate. Two carts loaded with victuals, the cannon pulled by mules bringing up the rear. An insect leaving the chrysalis that has protected it for so long, and slowly starting to creep towards new life, the new age, unknown and rapacious, which the butterfly's long wait has given it the strength to withstand.

Black, a long, silvery mane, its eyes two flaming coals and its nostrils dilated, foam at its mouth and its hoofs pawing the ground, the horse that will lead the sword of Gideon into battle. From the saddle hang bags full of messages from the insurgents, which the Magister has collected over many months of tireless travel: he will never give them up, they contain names, places and news that would give unalloyed delight to the guards of the princes.

I turn round; behind the cannons dragged by the mules, Mühlhausen obscured behind a blanket of dust. The walls are a vague outline, the towers pale like a print soaked in water, as my soul is heavy with all the anxiety I have ever felt. When I can see nothing more, I turn to look ahead. There's the Magister again, proud, reining in his horse, staring at the horizon, the day of reckoning, the scourging of the godless.

He fills me with strength; the time has come; we've got to go.

That's exactly how it was. That was how we left Mühlhausen. The memories of those final days are as clear to me as the outline of the hills on this clear day. Every word spoken by Magister Thomas, every phrase uttered by Ottilie, rises up from my memory like the notes of a Dutch musical clock, the weight of the past pulls on the ropes and sets the mechanism in motion. The sound of the wheels of the three cannon along the road, the greetings from the women in the fields, the excited happiness of Jacob and Mathias, who are like sparrows around a cart of grain, the meeting with the brothers from Frankenhausen, the first night spent on the plain, a little way outside the walls, waiting to move against the armies of the Landgrave of Hesse, which have come to punish the insurgent enemy cities.

That's exactly how it was. Elias furiously repeating that there are only eight thousand of us, and Elias is someone who can assess the size of a crowd in an instant. His ringing insults directed at the miners of Mansfeld who never came, held back by a promise of an increase in their daily wages. The news that Fulda was taken ten days ago, and so were Eisenach, Salza and Sonderhausen. Cut out, isolated. Landgrave Philip was quick to move and surround us. No word of Denck, but even if he had found men and weapons, he would already be behind the prince's lines by now.

'To the greater glory of God, to His greater glory!' The Magister's cry upon hearing this news. I feel like repeating it now, that incitement, here, in the yard of Vogler's presbytery, facing the geese and hens, I know it would be exactly the same. But I only have the strength to chew it between my teeth, in a whisper.

The mechanism starts turning. Ottilie organising the rearguard in Frankenhausen: lodging, defence, provisions.

It keeps on turning. So many faces, precise as portraits. The blue eyes and stumpy nose of a farrier from Rottweil, another with a fleshy chin and blond moustache, yet another with a flat nose and sticking-out ears. Faces and voices, one after the other. Hans Hut stacking the books on the cart, the horse ready to be harnessed: a little bookseller unfit for battle, who wants to get back to his press.

A sudden twang, the cord snaps and the notes ring out discordantly, shrieking, merging into a single buzzing hum. Colours blend together in the palette of memory. The image fades to make way for horror and confusion.

Chapter 29

The sign.

Striped, brilliant, purple, all of a sudden the rainbow flashes up in the sky beyond the hills and Philip's forces, before the rapt eyes of the humble.

For a moment it banishes fear, it wasn't heralded by rain, there's a clear sky, it's the sign of freedom that is already depicted on our ramshackle white cloth banners, the insignia of the people of the Lord rising to greet the blast of the heavenly trumpet in preparation for the day of reckoning.

A boom, the earth trembling somewhere, its bowels opening up to swallow them, the earth trembles, cracks, breaks open, thunders, erupts with the power of God.

A fist as big as a man hurls me to the ground, startled, my face in the mud. I turn on to one side, guided by a groan: a man like a blood clot, bone where his face should be. More shots, the dust hits our eyes, men taking cover under the horses, under the carts, in the holes blown open in the plain. I take refuge behind one of the few trees near a boy with a piece of wood stuck between his ribs, green with fear and pain.

The cannons keep on firing.

The head of the Magister impaled on a pole. That's what they're after. If they get that they might be merciful to the rest of us.

Evil troop of fucking lackeys. Filthy bastard cunting pig fuckers. You won't impose conditions on the troops of God. Worm-eaten carcasses drying in the sun. Godless phalanges of Darkness. We'll stove in your arseholes with our pickaxe handles. Lord, don't abandon us now. Your whoring mothers fucked goats in the forest. Back you go and kiss your masters' arses. Forgive us if we were wrong. Hell will open its vast maws, its bowels will swallow you up. If we have sinned, Thy will, Thy will alone be done. It will spit out the bones after sucking them dry one by one. Only love and the Redeemer's word, on the day of the Resurrection of the last men. There will be no pity for your corrupt souls. May our faith in the all-powerful Lord protect us.

'Magister! Magister!' Crazed shouts. Mine. Chasms of panic all around, the flight of the herd from the wolf pack.

I see him ahead of me, kneeling, flat on to the ground, frozen like a statue. Above him, I hear my voice shouting over the rumble that is approaching us on the horizon: 'Magister! Magister!'

His eyes empty, elsewhere, a prayer mumbled slowly on his lips.

'Magister, for God's sake, get up!'

I try to lift him, but it's like trying to uproot a tree or resuscitate a dead man. I kneel down and manage to turn his shoulders round; he falls into my lap. There's nothing more to be done. It's over. The horizon is hurtling towards us at ever greater speed. It's over. I support his head, my chest torn apart with weeping and my final cry, spewing blood and despair to the heavens.

It's barely daybreak when we start preparing to make our way towards the princes. Schnapps is poured down one throat after another as the flasks are passed round, trying to wash away anxiety and fear. It's barely daybreak and in the vague, pale light, beneath the cold mist that is gradually, slowly rising, as though facing a curtain, we can make out a black fringe on the edge of the hills to the north. No one has sounded the alarm, but they're already here. Magister Thomas spurs his horse, gallops from one part of the camp to the other, to revive the fire of faith and hope. Some men yell, raise their pitchforks, their hoes that have been turned into halberds, they fire into the air and yell words of disdain and defiance. Some kneel down and pray. Some stand motionless, as though caught by a basilisk stare.

A charcoal line stretches along the hill to the west, tracing the sinister outlines of the dawn, intensified by faint flashes of brightness. The army of George of Saxony is lined up, waiting on the western crest. Long black silhouettes point towards the plain: the cannons.

It explodes from the void of blood and bitter dust, the barded beast thundering down on a troop of unfortunates, paralysed with terror, crouched in prayer, or perhaps nothing but stiffened corpses awaiting their sentence of death. A pike held at waist level, hoofs and legs skirting a ditch, pierces a kneeling unarmed man right through, a shapeless pile of limbs, bone, skin and sackcloth. Drawing of a long sharp blade, armour rattling, the beast kicks its way through the bodies, the blade comes down on a poor soul who appears on its right, begging for mercy. Bends its heavy neck, pants, bends almost till it falls, the left arm sliced clean through, off it charges again towards fresh prey, up goes a cry of ferocious exultation.

The dust settles. A burst of daylight on the massacre. Nothing but bodies and wounded cries. Not a roar. Then I see them: the army appears, iron, pikes, standards in the wind, and the restrained fury of the horses pawing the ground. The galloping mass comes down the flank of the hill, the deafening clatter of hoofs and armour; black, heavy, inexorable as death. The horizon runs towards us, obliterating the plain.

It isn't the blow of steel running me through, it's the grip of Samson, hoisting the Magister into the air, towards the clouds and grabbing me by an arm. 'Get up, quick!'

Elias, an ancient warrior, his face black with earth and sweat, almost a dream. Elias, strength, showing me the way, shouting at me to run with him, away from death. 'Make way for me, boy, I need you!'

Magister Thomas on his shoulders, me finding my legs.

'Take these!'

The Magister's bags, I grip them tightly and run on ahead, pushing bodies out of the way, full tilt on the road out of hell.

Run. To the town. That's all. Not a thought. Not a word. That man's hope is shattered, I am opening the way of his salvation.

Almost blindly.

Carafa's eye
(1525–1529)

Letter sent to Rome from the Saxon city of Wittenberg, addressed to Gianpietro Carafa, dated 28 May 1525.

To the most illustrious and reverend lord Giovanni Pietro Carafa, in Rome.

My Most Honourable Lord,

It is with great satisfaction that I write to you to give you the happy news: Your Lordship's orders have been carried out as quickly as possible, and have had the desired result.

You may already have received news from Germany, and you will know that the army of the insurgent peasants there has been defeated. As I write these lines the mercenaries of the princes are preparing to douse the final flames of the greatest revolt that these marshlands have ever known.

The best-fortified rebel city, Mühlhausen, which was at the centre of the conflagration, surrendered some days ago to the princes' troops, and the head of their leader, Heinrich Pfeiffer, fell yesterday in the square at Görmar, along with that of Thomas Müntzer. It is said that during his last hours the preacher, although under torture, remained silent, without a word of complaint as he waited for the executioner, and that only once, in the last moment of his life, did he raise the voice for which he made himself so famous among the mob: '*Omnia sunt communia.*' They say that was his final cry, the same motto that has animated the popular fury of recent months.

Now that the blood of the two most dangerous men has commingled on the cobblestones, Your Lordship can doubtless take pleasure in his foresight and wisdom, in which your faithful observer has always had a blind trust.

But still: to come to the vow of frankness that you have requested from me, I shall confess that I had to act with considerable haste, risking the months of work and effort concentrated on the attempt to win the trust of the peasants' fiery preacher. Only thanks to such machinations, furthermore, was it possible to hasten Müntzer's ruin. Once I had offered him my services and information concerning the intrigues in Wittenberg, I gained his trust and was able to pass on to him the false news that spurred him on to his final battle. To tell the truth, I must say that our man has been a great help to us in hastening events onwards: the sole effect of my missive was to blot out the light of reason. A ragged army could never otherwise have hoped to defeat the well-armed forces of landsknechts and the princes' cavalry.

So, My Lord, given that you are so magnanimous as to request my opinion on the state of things so far, pray let your grateful servant unburden his heart of all that he has seen and his judgements upon it.

When Your Lordship's kind heart chose me to observe at first hand the dealings of the German princes with the monk Martin Luther, I could never have imagined what the Lord God had in store for that region. The human intellect could never have divined that apostasy and heresy would forge so strong a pact with secular power, and would root itself so firmly in the soul of the people.

Nonetheless, in these grave circumstances, your steadiness of resolve requested that I seek out an antagonist of the damned Luther, to foment the spirit of rebellion in the people against the apostate princes and weaken their unity.

When it was not within the power of human faculties to recognise the serious danger that that this would represent for the man who presented himself as the champion of Catholicism, Emperor Charles V, your wisdom lay in showing your humble servant the correct direction in which to guide our work and, hardly had we learned the news of the capture of the King of France on the field of Pavia, than you were immediately able to give the most appropriate order: hasten the end of the peasant revolt so that the princes friendly to Luther could become resolute rivals to Charles. In fact, the Emperor, after defeating and capturing the King of the French in Italy, is now rising like a predatory eagle which, while appearing to defend the nest of Rome, could cast it into the shadows with its wing and its pointed beak. The vastness of his possessions and his power are, in any case, such that they would endanger the spiritual authority of Rome, so much so that one might be forgiven for hoping that, in a region of the Empire such as the one I am writing about, the heretical princes might plant the sword between Charles's ribs, lest he be free to exert untrammelled power throughout the world. What the sinner learns is that merciful God never fails to remind us how mysterious and unfathomable His plan is: he who once defended us now threatens us, those who once attacked him are now our allies. And now, God's will be done. Amen.

So that is what the servant replies with the candour that Your Lordship requested: Your Lordship's judgement has been, in my most humble opinion, as far-sighted and as keen as ever. And it has been even more so in this last difficult situation, so much so that this arm of yours is extremely honoured to have been able to act as promptly as possible to put the directive into action.

No one could have sensed and predicted what was coming more fully than Your Honour has done. Dark and winding are the ways of the Lord and we must bend to His will. It is not given to us mortals to judge the workings of the Supreme One: our humble task, as Your Lordship never ceases to remind me, may only be that of defending a flicker of faith and Christianity in a world which seems to be losing it from one day to the next. It is for that reason we do all that we do, without regard for human laws or the sufferings of the heart.

So, I am sure that you will be able to guide me once again, through the hardships and the pitfalls that this age of ours seems to reserve for Christians, and which set our nerves atremble. It was the Lord's will to grant this sinner Your Lordship's valuable guidance, and He it was who granted that these eyes and this hand might serve His cause. It is this that allows me to stand firm as I confront the challenges to come and eagerly await fresh news from you.

Kissing Your Lordship's hand and, as ever, imploring your continued favour.

Your Lordship's faithful servant

Q   Wittenberg, the 28th day of May 1525

*Letter sent to Rome from the imperial city of Augsburg, addressed to
Gianpietro Carafa, dated 22 June 1526.*

To the most munificent and honourable lord Giovanni Pietro
Carafa, in Rome.

Your Most Illustrious Excellency wished to honour with an
undeserved compliment and an excess of grace one who aspires
simply and humbly to serve God through your mercy. But not
wishing to fail to carry out Your Lordship's orders, and abandoning
myself entirely to your wisdom, barely had I received your last
missive than I set off along the road towards this great imperial city
to carry out my master's command.

As regards this latter, I must inform you of the generosity with
which young Fugger received me on the basis of your recommendation. He is both shrewd and devout, with the wisdom and
calculating skill of his uncle, along with the courage and entre-
preneurial spirit granted him by his youth. The demise of old Jacob
Fugger two years ago has done no harm to the activities and the
boundless interests of the richest and most influential family in
Europe: the zeal with which the nephew takes care of the affairs that
were formerly his uncle's is second only to his most Christian
devotion and loyalty to the Holy See. One is immediately struck by
such simplicity and sincere abstinence in a young man such as
Anton Fugger, when one compares it with the vastness of his credit
in gold in all the courts of Europe.

Given the fresh outbreak of war and the new alliance that the
Holy See has forged with France, this man, who has bankrolled the
Emperor, has taken the trouble, perhaps hoping for an intercession
from me with Your Lordship, to reaffirm his neutrality; the same
neutrality, I might add, that only the purest gold can provide. My
impression is that this pious banker little cares who takes credit
from his coffers, be they imperial or French, Catholic or Lutheran,
Christian or Mohammedan; what matters to him is how much and
in what form. In his eyes it makes little difference whether one side
or the other wins this war, but it is clearly apparent that the ideal

situation for the young financier would be one of stalemate, a perennial war without winners or losers, and with the crowned heads of the whole world remaining tied to his purse strings.

But I have not been sent to Augsburg with a view to passing judgement on bankers. So, as regards the credit that Your Lordship has wished to open in my name, Fugger declared himself honoured to be able to number among his clients a man whom he holds in such esteem as Your Lordship, and said he was sorry not to be able to meet you in person. He deemed it necessary to provide me with a symbol which allows his legates to recognise me in every city in the Empire, and enables me to withdraw money from any of his branches, thus guaranteeing me the greatest possible freedom of movement. For reasons that I can easily surmise, he did not wish to inform me about the extent of open credit, barely allowing me to guess that it constitutes an 'unlimited' account. For my part, may the Lord grant that I do not lack respect for Your Lordship, I did not think it right to ask for anything else. Given that, I take care to inform Your Lordship straight away that I shall seek to administer the privilege that he has seen fit to grant me with parsimony and prudence, insofar as this lies within my competence, informing My Lord in advance of all use of the sums put at my disposal.

All that remains to me is to thank Your Lordship once again for his infinite generosity, and to implore Your Lordship's continuing favour while I await your news.

May merciful God send greetings to My Lord and may His magnanimous gaze stay upon this unworthy servant of His Holy Church.

Your Lordship's faithful servant

Q   Augsburg, the 22nd day of the month of June 1526

Letter sent to Rome from the imperial city of Augsburg addressed to Gianpietro Carafa, dated 10 June 1527.

To my most honourable lord, Giovanni Pietro Carafa, who has happily escaped the sinful forces of the barbarian heretics.

The news of knowing Your Lordship safe and sound fills my heart with joy and finally alleviates the pain that has deprived me of sleep throughout these terrible days. The very thought of St Peter's throne being devastated by new Vandals freezes the blood in my veins. I dare not imagine those terrible visions and those thoughts of death that must have struck Your Most Eminent Lordship during those moments. No one can be more familiar than this devoted servant with the brutality and wickedness of the Germans, sinful soldiers filled with beer and disrespectful of any authority, in any holy place. I know full well that they consider the plundering of churches, the decapitation of the holy images of the Saints and the Madonna, to be a reward for faith, as well as a pleasure.

But, as Your Lordship has been able to assert in your missive, the scandal cannot go unpunished: if the All-powerful Lord has been able to castigate the arrogance of those beasts by hurling pestilence upon them, he will not neglect to punish those who opened the cage to them, allowing them to flow through Italy. If not to the Holy Father, the Emperor will have to answer for this in the eyes of God.

The Habsburg, in fact, claims to be unaware that there are whole squads of heretics hidden in his army and in the armies of his princes: Lutherans without respect for anything or anyone. In fact, I have reason to believe that it was no coincidence that the conduct of the Italian campaign was entrusted to Georg Frundsberg and his landsknechts. Up here, they are well known for their viciousness and evil, as well as for the sympathy they nurture for Luther. I should not be surprised, to tell the truth, if something which seems today to be the undesirable result of an act of plunder by mercenary barbarians were revealed tomorrow to be the product of a military decision taken by the Emperor. The sacking of Rome weakens the

Holy Father and leaves him defenceless in the face of the Habsburg. The latter has thus found a way to be at once the saviour of the Christian faith and the prison warder of the Holy See.

So I can only share Your Lordship's harsh words of condemnation and contempt when I assert that Charles is placing the autonomy of the Church ever more closely and shamelessly under threat, and that he will have to pay for this final unimaginable affront.

I therefore pray to the Most High that He may help us to solve the great mystery of the iniquity that surrounds us, and that He may grant that Your Lordship stand up to the man who claims to be the defender of the Holy Church of Rome while having no qualms about allowing his evil battalions to lay it waste.

Faithfully and sincerely I beg your leave and kiss your hands.

Your Lordship's faithful servant

Q   Augsburg, the 10th day of June 1527

Letter sent from the imperial city of Augsburg, addressed to Gianpietro Carafa, dated 17 September 1527.

To the most eminent and reverend Giovanni Pietro Carafa, in Rome.

My Most Honoured Lord,

At this time heavy with uncertainty I have only been able to appeal to God's mercy, knowing that His light, through the goodness that Your Lordship continues to manifest towards me, can show this unworthy mortal the way to take in the darkness all around us. And that is why I am reporting on what happened up here in the rotten heart of the Empire, in the hope that even a single one of my words may advance Your Lordship's intentions.

Electoral Saxony is about to change its own ecclesiastical ordinance: the final act of the work begun ten years ago is about to be completed. Since the death of Frederick the Wise two years ago, his brother John's intention to continue where his predecessor had to leave off has become clearly apparent. So the new arrangement grants the Prince himself the role of choosing parish priests, who are now permitted to take wives; a consistory of doctors and super-intendents advises him in his selection; the possessions of the Church are placed under the control of the Prince – who will sooner or later proceed to annex them – along with the teaching of the doctrine and the management of the schools; the training of the new wave of Lutheran theologians is thus guaranteed. The first heretical university has been founded in Marburg.

Your Lordship's modest opinion is that the Lutheran plague is by now invincible by human forces alone, and that the only possibility is to attempt to contain it within the borders it has attained so far. But the events of the past few years have taught this poor soldier of God that often what appears to be an evil can, in the great design of the Supreme One, be transformed to good. The marriage between heretical faith and the German princes is such that the former can no longer be dislodged by the latter, or by the alliances that they will seek to forge. They may reveal themselves to be our best allies against the Emperor, and even now one frequently encounters French envoys and ambassadors along the roads of the German moorlands. Certainly it is premature to expect the princes to go into battle against Charles right away, but neither would it be deranged to imagine such an occurrence in the future. I believe, My Lord, that our calculations will reveal themselves over the course of time to be all the more acute and premonitory. If, therefore, the vicissitudes of the war in Italy turn to the advantage of the French, Your Lordship will be able to console himself with the thought that a few years hence Charles will risk seeing his own eastern territories crushed between the Turk and the Lutheran princes. Then his power would really start to look uncertain.

But there is a subtle evil creeping upon this unfortunate earth, about which I am about to bring you tidings.

The past few weeks have seen this city shaken by the suppression of the so-called Anabaptists. These blasphemers take to their extremes the perfidious doctrines of Luther. They refuse the baptism of children, maintaining that the Holy Spirit can be accepted only by the will of the believer who receives it; they reject the idea of ecclesiastical hierarchy and are united in communities, their pastors being elected by those same believers; they fail to recognise the doctrinal authority of the Church and consider the Scriptures the only source of truth; but – and in this they are worse than Luther – they also refuse to obey the secular authorities and claim that they are the only Christian community to accomplish civic administration. Furthermore, they abhor wealth and all secular forms of worship – images, churches, holy vestments – in the name of the equality of all the descendants of Adam. They wish to subvert the world from head to toe, and it is not insignificant that many of those who have endured the peasant war have sympathised with them, espousing their cause.

The authorities have a hard task ahead of them repressing these men seduced by Satan, who convened here in Augsburg last month for a general synod. Fortunately, within a few days almost all of their leaders were imprisoned. They did not number among them men of the stature of Thomas Müntzer, and nonetheless the danger that they represent is more serious than their actual numbers would lead one to imagine. Their heresies, in fact, seem to be spreading throughout the whole of south-western Germany with extreme ease and speed. They prefer the lower classes, mechanical workers, still infected by the hate that they nurture with regard to their superiors. The populations of the countryside, ignorant and discontented, often participate in their rituals in the woods, yielding to the spell of Satan. Precisely because they are not chained to any civil or religious ordinances, these Anabaptists, who refer to each other as brethren, are able to propagate their own plagues more easily and rapidly than even Luther has been able to do in recent times; it is easy to predict that their numbers will grow and that Anabaptism will soon enter the confines of this city. Wherever there is a discontented, hungry or ill-treated peasant or craftsman, there is a potential heretic.

That is why I shall not cease to collect information and to follow as closely as possible the fates of these unbelievers, to supply Your Lordship with new material to evaluate.

I have nothing further to say except that I kiss Your Lordship's hands, imploring one to whom I owe such unbounded respect, to let me continue to lend these poor eyes to the cause of God.

Your Lordship's faithful servant,

Q   Augsburg, the 17th day of September 1527

important appreciation of insisting. I can't think it is ridiculous to
be able to raise in person to the situation in Germany, and in
particular as soon. During this instant that Your Lordship will
remember the incoming a great times to the past
in the hope that I will not be risking the risk for our deposits
every day. And I beseech humble of solicit to our time.

*Letter sent to Venice from the imperial city of Augsburg, addressed to
Gianpietro Carafa, dated 1 October 1529.*

To my most eminent lord Giovanni Pietro Carafa, in Venice.

My Most Honoured Lord,
  This servant's soul is filled with gratitude and emotion at the
possibility of appearing in your presence. Do not fear that I might
miss this appointment: peace has made the streets of Lombardy
safer, and this fact, along with my urgent desire to see My Lord, will
make me speed my way as far as Bologna. My heart weeps to learn
that His Holiness Pope Clement has concluded such a wretched
deal with Charles, granting him this official coronation in Bologna;
the victory over the French in Italy and now this pontifical acknowledgement will elevate Charles V to the rank of the greatest
Caesars of antiquity, despite the fact that he does not possess a drop
of their virtue and rectitude. He will command Italy at his whim,
and in my opinion this union will see the Italian states, and this
Pope above all, as impotent onlookers of the Emperor's decisions.
But that is enough: *Vae victis*, no more for the time being, in the
hope that merciful God will grant such devoted souls as Your
Lordship's the grace to be able to thwart the arrogance of this new
Caesar.

  It is with regard to this very subject that I shall also permit myself
to be as frank as Your Lordship has so generously allowed me to
become accustomed to being, given that the free wandering of my
thoughts, unbiased enough to prompt My Lord's wise smile, leads
me to observe that today the enemies of Charles are three in
number: the King of France, Catholic; the German princes, of
Lutheran faith; and the Turk Suleyman, an Infidel; and that if they
were capable of making their common anti-imperial interests
prevail over the diversity of faiths, striking the Empire in unison
and concord, there would be no doubt that it would topple like a
tent in a whirlwind, and with it the throne of Charles. But these
eyes have been ordered to watch events in Germany and not
throughout the whole world, hence the need to be silent in

impatient expectation of meeting Your Lordship in Bologna and to be able to refer in person to the situation in Germany, and in particular to those Anabaptist heretics that Your Lordship will remember me mentioning several times in the past.

In the hope that I will not be a single day late for our appointment, I kiss Your Lordship's hands and submit to your grace.

Your Lordship's faithful servant

Q   Augsburg, the 1st day of October 1529

PART TWO
One God, one faith, one baptism

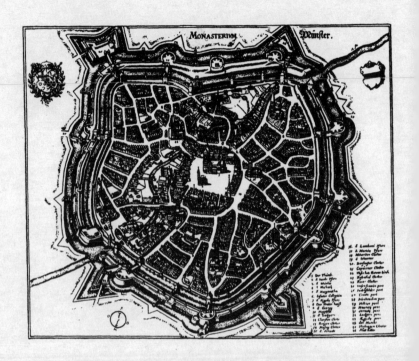

MONASTERIVM   Münster.

Eloi
(1538)

The 4th day of April 1538

Being imprisoned in Vilvoorde & condemned to death as Justice decrees, Jan van Batenburg, who, clinging most obstinately to heresy, could never bring himself to confess the holy faith, but determined to die in his perversity.

For the horrible Massacres & Homicides for which he has shown no repentance, but indeed satisfaction and diabolical boasting, he is condemned to death by the severing of his head, then to be burned & his ashes thrown to the wind.

Signed by the witnesses present:
Nicholas Buyseere, Dominican
Sebastian van Runne, Dominican
Lieven de Backere
Chrestien de Ridder

For Rijkard Niclaes, Commissioner

Chapter 1

Vilvoorde, Brabant, 5 April 1538

To you, Jan. To your merciless butchering. To the baying mob spewing forth humours of all kinds as the cart passed through it leading you slowly in chains towards the place of execution. To the vomit that rises in my throat and the fever that burns my bowels. To the Babylonian Whore as she drowns the mad David to whom she has given birth in his blood and the blood of his brothers. To the never-ending horror that has devoured our flesh. To oblivion, which has erected this tower of death beyond the sky. To the end, a pitiful end, a vicious end, an ordinary end and a definitive one. I have forgotten.

To you, Jan, brother, bloody, wicked man, your swollen face confronting hatred and the blows that come from all directions. To you, demon shat out by innumerable orifices, your ragged clothes drenched in blood, a shapeless blood clot where an ear should be. To you, pig to be flayed for the feast day, I hide and see you laying your head on the block, yelling once again the final insult: FREEDOM!

I have struck, plundered, killed.

The crowd would quarter you with their own hands, the executioner knows it and spins the axe round in a little dance, tests the blade, leaves time for the thirst of blood that rises to submerge everything in an unearthly noise.

I have destroyed, plundered, raped.

Everyone is an executioner here, and everywhere else. Everyone is insulting a son or a brother who has had his throat slit by the devil Batenburg and his Sword Bearers. That's not how it is and yet it is the truth. I have forgotten.

He raises the axe, sudden silence, he strikes. Two or three times.

A flood of vomit sullies the shoes and coat in which I drag myself bent double, the roar goes up once again, the dripping trophy is raised, sins cleansed, the vileness can continue.

They will kill me like a dog. What was the point, what, what was the point? Cold, in my mouth, cold, the cold of abandonment. I've got to get out of here, I'm dead already. Coughing, my left hand is burning madly above the wrist, down to the elbow, I'm dead already. What I had to do.

The crowd disperses, light rain, cowering among baskets piled up against a wall. Arse perched on unsteady heels. What.

They'll hang me from a pole, I'm finished, all the people I've ever been are calling for my death. Or I'll be kicked and knifed to death in a shitty dark street, away, for the love of God, my strength ebbing from me. To England, far from this blood puddle, maybe to England, crossing the sea, or going to sea and escaping the fate of the relic I've become. My names, the lives. Jan, bastard, come back here, you murderer. Bring those lives back, or else take what little remains.

'Start loading up!'

By daybreak I'm a drenched pile of rags, paralysed inside a basket of fat sticks with a little straw on the top.

'I'm going to settle the horses for the night, then I'll be back.'

I can't move, I can't think, the fire that got rid of the brand is burning, burning. Is this how it ends?

'Hey, what the fuck, ragman, shit, you're scaring me, get out of here.'

I don't reply. I don't move. I open my eyes.

'Bloody hell, this one looks like a corpse . . . Fuck, I'll turf him out, poor fucker . . . Christ.'

A tall youth with a beardless baby face, powerful arms, turning away slightly so as not to look at me. He stops.

'I'm dying. Don't let me die here.'

He gives a start. 'Jesus . . . What the fuck did you say? What? So you're not dead, but you scare me anyway, pal, you scare me.'

'Don't let me die here.'

'You're crazy, I can't load you on. My boss'll have my bollocks, I'm fifteen years old, what the fuck am I supposed to do now . . .'

He stares at me.

'Aaron! What the fuck're you doing, are you asleep? Move yourself please, or how the fuck I've got to tell you yes in the latinorum of the priests you great poof yes perhaps that's the language you like. Aaron!'

His terror is reflected in the terror in my eyes, he hesitates for a moment, babbles disconnectedly, yes, yes, boss . . . Of course just a minute, boss . . . he covers me with some more dry straw, here I am, just a moment and the load's complete, Aaron loads me on, it's in place, he puts the basket on firmly along with the others.

'Get moving, then! I've still got to eat, shit and rest, bollock-head, by dawn we'll have been up for ages, marching towards Antwerp, getting annoyed to hell with all those eggheads and the dockers in the port. Get a move on, Aaron!'

'You'll be fine here in Antwerp, they leave you in peace, the people in charge are the guilds and the money makers, apart from those comb-haired cunt chasers from the hidalgos and the imperial officials, the Flemish merchants who know the price of everything, they could tell you how many florins Cathay would cost, or even the whole world, they certainly know how to do their accounts, they have sound heads on their shoulders, not like those shit-eating Spaniards, who never do anything but come up with new taxes and get every slag in spitting distance up the duff.'

We met by chance, at the side of a road, outside an inn.

His name's Philipp.

He's in an even worse state than I am: he got his leg fucked, he says, when he was called up for the war by the Spanish, whom he hates more than the devil. Philipp is one long soliloquy interrupted by violent bursts of coughing and bloodstained catarrh. We cross the jetty, urged on by the traffic of the sailors and the dockers, an inter-section of different languages and accents. We run into a troop of Spaniards, gleaming oval helmets that get them the nickname of 'iron-eggs'. Philipp curses and spits. 'The other evening some whore stabbed one of them and they're not about to forget it. The sons of bitches will come on all heavy for a few days and then they'll come back to get the clap from our girls. And it's no more than they deserve. May the pox take the lot of them!'

Boats loaded with every kind of merchandise on the planet, rolls of fabric, sacks of spices, grain.

A little boy runs towards us, the limping man grabs him by the collar and murmurs something to him. The boy nods, frees himself from his grip and runs in the opposite direction.

'You're in luck, the Englishman's at the beer house.'

A big table in the open air, filled with sailors, ships' captains engaged in heated negotiations, some local shipowners, recognisable

by their black cloaks, elegantly cut and unadorned. The limping man
says to wait for him, he goes over to a big bloke who turns towards us
and points to me, and beckons me over.

'This is Mr Price, master of the *St George*.'

We bow to each other slightly.

'Philipp tells me you want to get to England.'

'I can work my passage.'

'It's two days' sailing to Plymouth.'

'Not London?'

'The *St George* is bound for Plymouth.'

There was no time or reason to think about it. 'Fine.'

'You'll have to make yourself useful in the galley. Make sure you're
at the ship by five tomorrow morning.'

A battered bed in an inn that Philipp brought me to, waiting for the
hours to pass.

Squares, roads, bridges, palaces, markets. People, dialects and different religions. The road through memories is hazardous and bumpy:
they're always ready to betray you. The dwellings of the bankers in
Augsburg, the gleaming streets of Strasbourg, the indestructible walls
of Münster . . . it all comes back to my mind confused, disconnected.
It wasn't even me, it was other people, with different names and a
different fire in their veins. The fire that burned right down to the
bottom.

A spent candle.

Too much devastation behind me, on this earth that I wish the sea
would swallow up once and for all.

England. Great man, that Henry VIII. Closes down the monastic
orders and impounds all the possessions of the monasteries. Eats and
fucks from morning till night and meanwhile proclaims himself head
of the Church of England . . .

A country without papists or Lutherans. Fine, and then maybe the
New World. In the end it doesn't matter where to, just away from
here, away from another defeat, the lost kingdom of Batenburg.

From the horror.

The image of the rolling head of Jan van Batenburg attacks me at
night and stops me from sleeping, and perhaps not even distance will
drive it away.

I've seen things that perhaps only I could tell. But I don't want to.
I want to get rid of them once and for all, and vanish into a hidden
hole, become invisible, die in peace, if I'm ever granted so much as a
moment of peace.

I've got a thousand years of war in the bag, a dagger, a shirt and the money that's going to hoist this anchor. And that'll have to be enough.

Just before dawn. It's time to go. There isn't a soul down in the street, a dog glances at me suspiciously as it gnaws on some scraps. I walk through the deserted streets, taking my bearings from the spars of the ships that stand out behind the roofs of the houses. In the area around the port I run into a few beer-soaked drunks. Their burps echo from a long way off. The *St George* must be the fifth ship along.

A sudden agitated noise from an alley to my right. Through the corner of my eye I see five men gathered closely around a sixth, busy kicking the shit out of him. It has nothing to do with me, I quicken my pace, the poor guy's screams are drowned by the noise of retching and blows to his belly. I recognise the egg-helmets. A patrol of Spaniards. I get past the alley and catch sight of the masts of the *St George*. From the gangway of one of the ships moored in the harbour half a dozen men come running towards me, clutching harpoons and grappling hooks. Calm, now. Passing me, they slip into the alley, screams in Spanish, the sound of thumps. Holy shit. I run towards my ship, there it is, nearly there, someone trips me from behind, I stumble and graze my face on the cobbles.

'You cunt, thought you'd get away from us, did you?'

Unmistakable accent. More iron-eggs, emerging from God knows where.

'What the fuck . . .'

A kick in the ribs catches the breath in my throat.

I roll myself up like a cat, more kicks, my head, got to protect my head with my hands.

They're fighting away in the alley.

I peep out between my fingers and see the Spaniards getting out their pistols. Maybe they've got a bullet for me, too. No, they're heading for the alley. Gunfire. The sound of footsteps running away.

The one who was kicking me puts the tip of his sword to my throat. 'Get up, wretch.'

I expect he's the only one who knows a few words of Flemish.

I stand up and get my breath back. 'I've got nothing to do with it.' I cough. '. . . I've got to get on to the English ship.'

He laughs. 'No, what you've got to do is thank God that I can't kill you like a dog: my captain ordered us just to give you a beating.'

The boot gets me right between the legs. I fall and almost faint. Everything spins, the spars, the houses, the bastard's ludicrous moustache. Then some sinewy arms lift me up and drag me away.

We pass through a confusion of kicks and shouted insults. By now my senses are dulled, my limbs have stopped responding.

I feel the street slipping beneath my feet, two of them carrying me. Shouts from the windows, objects falling, we get a move on.

The one to my right is tripped up and we fall. My face in a puddle. Leave me here. The shouts get louder, there are people at the end of the street, a cart shoved across it to bar the way: pitchforks. The Spaniards are yelling incomprehensibly. I raise my head: we're trapped against a building, the road is blocked by a barricade, insults are being hurled from behind it. Someone is throwing pots and pans out of the window on to the Spaniards. One of them lies unconscious on the ground. The other one who was dragging me is standing behind me, his pike levelled. I try to get up, but my legs won't straighten, everything's spinning. Darkness. Christ . . .

My head drops on to a soft surface, I must have been tied up, no, I move a hand, my legs don't respond, a foot, my limbs feel like they weigh a ton.

Set me free. The words stay in my head, saliva and something solid comes out of my mouth: a broken tooth.

I open one eye and there's the feeling of water on my cheeks. A cloth is cleaning my face.

'I didn't think you'd make it. But judging by your collection of scars you can take care of yourself in a fight.'

A calm voice with the local accent, a blurred shadow on a big window.

I spit clots of coagulated blood and saliva.

'Shit . . .'

The shadow comes closer. 'Yeah.'

'How did I get here?' My voice sounds cavernous and stupid.

'They carried you. You were brought here this morning. It seems that any enemy of the Spanish is a friend of Antwerp. That's why you're alive. And why you're here.'

'Where's here?'

I want to retch, but I hold it back.

'Somewhere the Spaniards and the cops never come.'

I manage to pull myself up into a sitting position.

'Why?'

My head falls on to my chest, I strain to lift it back up.

'Because this is where people with money live. Or rather let's just say that the kind of people who live here are the kind of people who make money. And they're the ones who make a difference, believe me.'

He hands me a jug of water and puts a basin by my feet. I empty the jug over my head, gulp down, spit, my tongue is swollen and cut in several places.

I can just about make him out. He's thin, about forty, grey at the temples, alert expression.

He hands me a rag and I dry my face. 'Is it your house?'

'It belongs to me and anyone who happens to be in trouble.' He points out through the window. 'I was on top of a roof and I saw everything. For once the imperial soldiers got it in the neck.'

He shakes my hand. 'I'm Lodewijck Pruystinck, roofer, but the brethren call me Eloi. What about you?'

'I ended up by chance in the middle of all this, and you can call me whatever you want.'

'Anyone without a name must have had at least a hundred of them.' A curious smile. '. . . and a story worth listening to.'

'Who says I want to tell anyone?'

He smiles and nods. 'If all you've got is the rags you're wearing, you could accept my money in exchange for a good story.'

'You'd be throwing your money away.'

'Oh no, on the contrary. It would be an investment.'

I've stopped following him. Who the hell am I talking to?

'You must be fucking loaded.'

'For the time being I'm the one who's tended your wounds, the one who's got you out of the shit you were in.'

We stay there in silence, while I do a roll-call of all the muscles in my body.

Evening is falling on the roofs, I've been unconscious all day.

'I was supposed to be leaving on the ship.'

'Yes, Philipp told me.'

I'd forgotten the limping man.

'. . . and disappearing for ever. It isn't safe around here. Above all, the rich have a cast-iron memory about the people who've fucked their daughters and made off with their jewels. And then, in the name of God . . .'

I lie there motionless, thunderstruck, too exhausted to collect my thoughts and work out what to say or do.

His eyes are fixed on me. 'Today Eloi Pruystinck saved the arse of a Sword Bearer. The ways of the Lord are truly infinite!'

I say nothing. I try to read a threat into the tone of his voice, but it's just irony. He points to my forearm, where until this morning a bandage concealed the brand.

The burned flesh is dirty, the brand almost indiscernible.

'The eye and the sword. I met someone who cut his arm off to escape the scaffold. They say Batenburg ate the hearts of his victims. Is it true?'

Still I say nothing, scrutinising him this time to see what he's getting at.

'There are no limits to people's imaginations.' He lifts a cloth covering a wicker basket. 'Here's something to eat. Try and get your strength back, or you'll never get out of this bed.' He makes as though to leave.

'I saw his head coming off. He shouted "freedom" before he was killed.' My voice shakes. I'm very weak.

He turns slowly on his chair, a determined glance. 'The Apocalypse didn't come. What was the point of massacring all those people?'

I slump like an empty sack, almost too tired to breathe. His footsteps move away behind the door.

Chapter 3

It's a big house. Two vast floors, with rooms opening up on to wide corridors. Half-naked children run up and down the stairs, some women prepare food in great cauldrons in a kitchen filled with all God's gifts. Someone greets me with a nod and a smile, without interrupting his work. They all seem relaxed and calm, as though they all shared in the same happiness. A long table stretches through the middle of what seems to be the biggest room, laid with silver cutlery: a beech log burns in the fireplace.

I feel the same sensation that you have in certain dreams a moment before you suddenly wake up: the knowledge that you're in a dream and the desire to know what's behind the next door, to reach the end.

Suddenly his voice reaches me from one of the rooms: 'Ah, you've finally decided to get up!'

Eloi is carving a large slice of meat on a marble table. 'Just in time to eat with us. Come on, come on, give me a hand.' He passes me a carving fork. 'Hold it tightly, like this.' He cuts thin slices and arranges them on a plate with a silver crest.

From the corner of his eye he studies my confused expression. 'I expect you're wondering where you've fetched up.'

My mouth is too sticky to get a word out, I reply with a mumble.

'The house has been put at our disposal by Meneer van Hove, a fish merchant and a good friend of mine. You might meet him when he comes back. Everything you see here used to be his.'

'Used to be?'

He smiles. 'Now it belongs to everyone and no one.'

'You mean everything belongs to everyone?'

'Exactly.'

Two children cross the room, chanting a nursery rhyme whose words I can't make out.

'Bette and Sarah: Margarite's daughters. I can never remember which is which.'

He picks up the plate and shouts, 'Dinner time!'

About thirty people flock around the big, laid table. I am seated next to Eloi.

A tall blonde girl serves me a tankard of beer.

'Meet Kathleen. She's been with us for a year.'

The girl smiles. She's extremely beautiful.

Before the meal begins, Eloi rises to his feet and calls for the group's attention. 'Brothers and sisters, listen. A nameless man has arrived among us. A man who's been fighting for a long time and who has seen much blood spilt. He was dazed and exhausted, and he has received care and attention in accordance with our custom. If he decides to stay with us, he will accept the name that we choose to give him.'

At the end of the table, a red-faced youth with an extravagant blond moustache shouts, 'Let's call him Lot, like the man who didn't turn back!'

An echo of agreement runs through the hall and Eloi looks at me with satisfaction. 'So be it. We'll call you Lot.'

I start eating with difficulty: my tongue and my teeth hurt, but the meat is tender, first-class.

'I know what you're wondering.'

More beer is poured.

'What?'

'You're wondering how we can afford all this.'

'I imagine it was all supplied by Meneer van Hove . . .'

'Not quite. He's not the only one to have opened up his coffers to give his property to the community.'

'You mean there are other rich men who give everything to the poor?'

He laughs. 'We're not poor, Lot. We're free.'

He makes a gesture that encompasses everyone seated round the table. 'Here we have artisans, carpenters, roofers, bricklayers. But also shopkeepers and merchants. What they have in common is nothing other than the Spirit of God. It is what all men and women have in common, in any case.'

I listen to him and can't tell whether or not he's completely insane.

'Possessions, Lot, money, jewels, merchandise, serve the body so that the spirit may enjoy them. Look at these people: they're happy. They don't have to kill themselves earning a livelihood, they don't have to steal from people who have more than they do, or work for them. And in turn, the man with more has nothing to fear, because he has chosen to live with them. Have you ever wondered how many families could be fed with what Fugger has in his coffers? I think half the world could eat for a whole year without lifting a finger. Have you ever wondered how much time an Antwerp merchant spends accumulating his fortune? Simple: his whole life. His whole life to accumulate it, to fill his safes, his strongboxes, to build a prison for himself and his own male offspring, and dowries for the females. Why?'

He drains his tankard: his dream was also mine. 'And you want to persuade the merchants down in the port that the best thing for their spirits would be to give everything to you?'

'Not at all. I want to persuade them that a life free of enslavement to money and commodities is a better life.'

'Forget it. I tell you, anyone who is rich has spent his whole life fighting for it.'

He closes his eyes and raises his glass. 'We don't want to fight them, they're too strong.' He gulps down the beer. 'We want to seduce them.'

The two leather armchairs in the study are very comfortable. I gently sink into one, trying to escape the pains in my ribs. A very long sharpened goose feather protrudes from a black inkpot on the table. Eloi gives me some liqueur in a little etched glass. 'Officially, Antwerp is faithful to the Church of Rome. The most devout Emperor insists that his officers maintain an allegiance to the true faith, which is to say, to his power. But many people here secretly support Luther's ideas. The merchant classes above all have had enough of the Spanish occupation and of priests who accuse anyone of heresy if they speak out against Catholicism or its lazy bishops. Merchants produce things, they make money, they construct buildings and build roads. The imperial forces impose taxes and inquisitions. It doesn't add up. Luther preaches the abolition of the ecclesiastical hierarchy and independence from Rome, his German princes have revolted and attacked Charles and the Pope in a formal act of protest. Conclusion: sooner or later, Flanders and the Low Countries are going to go up like a powder keg. With the difference that here instead of princes you've got fat merchants. The only reason they haven't clashed yet is that until a few months ago your crowd were still in the middle.'

'What d'you mean?'

'The Anabaptists wanted everything. They wanted the Kingdom: equality, simplicity, fraternity. Neither the Emperor nor the Lutheran merchants were willing to give them to them. Their world is based on competition between states and between commercial companies, on orders and obedience. In the words of Luther, whom I had the displeasure of meeting more than ten years ago: you can put all your goods in common if you really feel like it, but don't think of doing it with the goods of Pilate or Herod. Batenburg was as much of a bugbear to the Catholics as he was to the Lutherans. Now that the Anabaptists have been defeated, the two remaining parties in the struggle will soon be at each other's throats.'

I try to work out where he's headed. 'Why are you telling me these things?'

He thinks about it, as though he wasn't expecting the question. 'To give you an idea of the situation here.'

'Why me, though?'

'You've been through the wars. And you lost. You look like some-one who's been through hell and come out alive.'

He gets up and goes to the window after pouring himself another glass.

'I don't know if you're the right person. The one I've been trying to find for some time, I mean. I'd like to hear your story before making a judgement.'

Eloi fiddles with his empty glass.

I put mine down on the table. 'It's hard to take the smile off your face.'

'That's a good quality, don't you think?'

'How does a roofer come to be so well-informed, and to talk so shrewdly?'

He shrugs his shoulders. 'You just have to hang around with the right people.'

'You mean the merchants in the port.'

'News circulates around merchandise. As regards knowing how to talk, the friendships that gave me my way with words didn't leave me time to learn Latin, and I'm rather sorry about that.'

'*Omnia sunt communia*. You knew that one.'

A moment of hesitation that masks the usual half-smile of a man who is privy to some trick or an ancient secret.

'It was the motto of the rebels back in 1525. In that year I went to Wittenberg to meet Luther and present my ideas to him. Germany was in chaos. I was too young and full of ideals for a monk fattening himself in the princes' dining rooms.' A grimace. Then, unsure whether he should ask me, he says, 'Were you with the peasants?'

I get up, already too tired to go on, I need to lie down on the bed, my ribs are aching. I look at him and wonder why I was meant to meet this man, without being lucid enough to answer my own question.

'Why should I tell you my story? And forget the offer you made to me. I haven't got anywhere to go, I wouldn't know what to do with your money. I just want to die in peace.'

He insists. 'I'm curious. At least start off: when it all began, where.'

It's a deep well: a dull splash in the black water.

The words: 'I've forgotten. The beginning is always an end: the umpteenth Jerusalem, still populated with ghosts and crazed prophets.'

His face fills with horror for a moment, but it must be nothing compared with mine, faced with all those ghosts.

'Holy Christ, were you in Münster?'

I drag myself towards the door, my voice hoarse and thick. 'In this life I've learned only one thing: that hell and heaven do not exist. We carry them within us wherever we go.'

I leave his questions behind me, staggering down the corridor to get back to the bedroom.

Something still burns inside me. The girl is washing the sheets in the courtyard, the occasional glimpse of a young white body under her dress, belted tightly round the waist.

It isn't spring, not any more, April just makes me scratch my scars: the geographical map of lost battles.

It's Kathleen. She isn't anyone's wife, just as all the children don't seem to have a single mother or a single father, but have many parents. They don't show fear or reverence to the adults, who allow themselves to be teased and smile at childish jokes. Women with time to play, pregnant bellies, men who never raise their hands in anger, children sitting on their laps. Eloi has built the Garden of Eden and he knows it.

Thirteen years ago he confronted Philipp Melanchthon in the presence of Luther. Lean and Chubby both thought he was round the bend, and wrote to the papal authorities in Antwerp telling them to arrest him. A few months later Brother Fat Pig would incite the massacre of all of us, the devils incarnate who had dared to challenge their masters. Eloi and I have had the same enemies and we don't meet till now, now that it's all over.

Kathleen wrings out the washing: still that burning at the pit of my stomach. I've forgotten. The war's obliterated everything, the glory of God, madness, killing: I've forgotten. And yet there's still something there and it can't be obliterated, it's vague and present, lying in wait behind every twisting place in my mind.

She lifts her face and sees me: a smile.

It's a place where you could lock yourself in, far from your troubles, from the black wing of the cop who's been following me for ever.

You're beautiful. You're alive. You're a life that has slipped in the mud but doesn't want to give up, and still gives me a day of sunlight, and that burning sensation deep in my bowels.

'Gerrit Boekbinder.'

I give a start and turn round quickly, my arm drawn back to shield my body.

A short, stout man, a beard sprinkled with grey and a resolute expression.

He talks to me seriously. 'Old Gert-from-the-Well. Life really is full of surprises. I could have imagined anything, but not bumping into you again. And here, well . . .'

I scrutinise this anonymous face. 'You're mixing me up with someone else.'

Now he smiles. 'I don't think so. But it's not all that important, the past doesn't matter here. When I came here I was in a bad way and merely hearing my name mentioned made me start like a wildcat. You were with Van Geleen, weren't you? I was told you were seen when they took the Council House in Amsterdam . . .'

I'm trying to work out who I have in front of me, but his features tell me nothing. 'Who are you?'

'Balthasar Merck. I'm not surprised if you don't remember me, but I was in Münster as well.'

Eloi must have told him.

'I really believed in it too. I had a shop in Amsterdam. I abandoned everything to join the Baptist brethren. I admired you, Gert, and it was a severe blow when you left, and not just for me. Rothmann, Bockelson and Knipperdolling were crazy, they took us to the brink of pure madness.'

Names that hurt, but Merck seems sincere and willing to understand.

I look into his eyes. 'How did you get out of there?'

'With young Krechting. They hanged his brother from the shafts of a cart along with the others, but not him, he managed to lead us out just in time, when the bishops' supporters were already entering the city.' A dark shadow falls across his face. 'I left my wife in Münster, she was too weak to follow me, she didn't make it.'

'And you ended up here?'

'I spent months begging in the street, I even got arrested once, the soldiers, you know, when I'd already got back to Holland. They tortured me' – he shows his swollen fingers – 'to make me confess that I'd been a Baptist. But I gave them nothing. It was incredibly painful, I screamed like a madman while they pulled my nails out but I didn't give them a thing. I thought about my Anja, buried in that ditch. Not a word. They left me alone when they thought I'd completely lost it. Eloi took me with him, he saved my life . . .'

I turn round to look over the balustrade: Kathleen is putting the sheets in a basin and carrying them away.

'Isn't she beautiful?'

I want to reply that at this moment she's more important than our memories.

He puts his hand on my shoulder for an instant. 'There are no husbands or wives here.'

I pull a face. 'I'm old.'

He laughs, a great guffaw, as though I were hearing one for the first time, after abandoning my existence for years. 'You're just tired, brother. You're dead. Gerrit Boekbinder is dead and buried under the walls of Münster. Here you're Lot, the one who doesn't turn round. You just remember that.'

A hand on my shoulder. I watch the children down in the court-yard, as though they were children from a fairy tale. The baby executioners of Münster are far away, Bockelson's little monsters, the child inquisitors with blood on their hands.

'Who are these people, Balthasar?'

'Free spirits. They've conquered purity, they've decreed sin to be a lie and established the principle of freedom of their desires, their own happiness.'

He says this quite naturally, as though explaining the order of the cosmos. That burning in my stomach has turned to pain, for me, for this exhausted body and this simple joy.

The hand presses on my shoulder. 'The Holy Spirit is in them, as it is in everyone. They live in God's light, they don't need to take up a sword.'

The light fades from my eyes, it's as though they almost refuse to see. 'Do you think that's how it is? That we lost the Kingdom so that we would find it here?'

He nods. 'Eloi once told me that the Kingdom of God isn't something you wait for: there is no yesterday or today, and you won't get there, not even in a thousand years. It's an experience of the heart: it exists everywhere, and nowhere . . . It's in Kathleen's smile, in the warmth of her body, in the joy of a child.'

I feel as though I want to weep away the hate, the fear, the desperation, the defeat. But it's difficult, painful. I have to lean on the balustrade. 'It's too late for me.'

'It's never too late for anyone. If you stay here you'll learn that too, brother.'

'Eloi wants me to tell him my story. Why?'

'He believes in the simple people, the humblest ones. He believes

that Christ can resurrect in each one of us, particularly in those who
have been sunk in the mud of defeat.'

'All I see behind me is a great ocean of horror.'

He sighs, as though he really understood. 'Let the dead bury their
dead, so that the living can be born into new life.'

The lesson of the Saviour.

'Did he tell you that too?'

'No. It's something I worked out as I crossed the threshold into
where you are now.'

I don't know how it happened, it just happened naturally, without
anyone issuing instructions I suddenly found myself carving fence
posts for the vegetable garden. I started to return everyone's greetings
and a young carder even asked me advice about the best way to adjust
his loom.

I stack up the sharpened stakes in a corner of the garden at the back
of the house, the little hatchet is precise and light, it allows me to work
sitting down and without a great deal of effort. For a moment I see in
my mind's eye a young man splitting wood in Pastor Vogel's yard, a
thousand years ago, but it's a memory that I immediately dispel.

The little blonde girl comes over with a gappy smile. 'Are you Lot?'

It's still hard for me to frame words.

I stop, so as not to risk hurting her with the splinters. 'That's right.
And who are you?'

'Magda.'

She hands me a coloured stone. 'I painted it for you.'

I roll it around in my hands for a moment. 'Thanks, Magda, that's
very kind of you.'

'Have you got a little girl?'

'No.'

'Why not?'

I've never been asked questions by a child before. 'I don't know.'

Her mother suddenly appears, a little bag of seeds in her arms.
'Magda, come here, we've got to sow seeds in the garden.'

That old burning sensation again. The words come out on their
own. 'Is she your daughter?'

'Yes.'

Kathleen smiles, a smile to light up the day, takes the little girl by
the hand and looks at the fence posts. 'Thanks for what you're doing.
Without the fence the garden wouldn't last a day.'

'Thanks to you for taking me in.'

'Are you going to stay with us?'

'I don't know, I've got nowhere to go.'

The little girl takes the bag from her mother's hands and runs towards the vegetable garden, chattering away to herself.

Kathleen's blue eyes won't give my stomach peace. 'Stay.'

Chapter 5

Antwerp, 4 May 1538

Eloi is negotiating with two characters dressed in black, with the serious, urgent air of businessmen.

I wait, sitting some way off: he seems to be at ease with these people. I wonder if they know what he's really thinking.

They greet each other with great effusive gestures and phoney smiles, Eloi's smile winning hands down. The two crows leave without so much as glancing at me.

'They own a printing press. I've done a deal with them so that I can make use of it. I've promised them that they won't have problems with the censors, we'll have to be careful.'

He talks to me as though it were obvious that I was one of their own.

'I suppose your "acquaintances" put up the money . . .'

'Everywhere there are people who can understand what we say. You've got to contact them, get hold of extra money to print and distribute our message. Freedom of the spirit is beyond price, but this world wants to impose a price on everything. We've got to keep our feet on the ground: here we hold everything in common ownership, we live in serene simplicity, we work just hard enough to survive and we keep company with wealthy men to finance ourselves. But the world out there is governed by the war between the states, the merchants, the Church.'

I shrug my shoulders disconsolately. 'Is that what you're looking for? Someone who can move in that world of cut-throats? Someone who got out alive?'

The usual disarming smile, but now with the sincerity that the merchants didn't get. 'We need someone smart, someone who can dissemble and whisper the right words in the right ears.'

We look at each other.

'The story is long and difficult, sometimes there are gaps in my memory.'

Eloi is serious. 'I'm in no hurry, and you'll come back strengthened from your labours.'

It's as though we had always planned it, as though he were waiting for me, as though . . .

'I know you've met Balthasar. Did he get you to change your mind?'

'No. A little girl did that.'

The study is in semi-darkness, interrupted by a column of light filtering through the closed shutters. Eloi gives me a glass of liqueur and some silent attention.

'What do you know about the peasant war?'

He shakes his head. 'Not a lot. When I went to Germany in 1525, I met a brother who I'd been in communication with for some time: his name was Johannes Denck, a free spirit, ready to challenge the arrogance of the papists as well as that of Luther. But as I've told you, I was younger then and not so shrewd.'

The name chills the blood, sends memories flashing back, a face, a family.

'I knew Denck well. I fought with him alongside men who really thought they would put an end to injustice and wickedness on earth. There were thousands of us, we were an army. Our hope was shattered on the plain at Frankenhausen, on the fifteenth of May 1525. Then I abandoned a man to his fate, to the weapons of the landsknechts. I carried with me his bag full of letters, names and hopes. And the suspicion of having been betrayed, sold to the forces of the princes like a herd at a market.' It's still hard to utter the name. 'That man was Thomas Müntzer.'

I can't see him, but I sense his astonishment, perhaps the incredulity of someone who thinks he's talking to a ghost.

His voice is practically a whisper. 'You really fought with Thomas Müntzer?'

'I was young then, too, but alert enough to understand that Luther had betrayed the cause he had given us. We understood that we would have to go on where he had surrendered his weapons. The story could have ended like that, on that corpse-covered plain. And instead we survived.'

'Did Denck die there?'

'No. His task was to find reinforcements for the battle, but he didn't show up.'

Remembering is a terrible effort. 'I died for the first time in Frankenhausen. It wasn't the last.'

I sip the liqueur to jog my memory. 'For two years, two endless years, I hid in the home of a Lutheran pastor who secretly sympathised with our cause, while outside the soldiers were combing through the country, region after region, hunting out survivors. I was finished, I had a new name, my friends were dead, the world was populated by ghosts and people ready to betray you if you said one word too many. One day, when it seemed as though work and solitude had subjugated me, they unearthed us, I don't know how, but they managed to track us down. I had to flee once again.'

I take a breath. 'Thinking about it now, that sudden flight was a stroke of luck for me; it saved me from a slower, atrocious death.'

Perhaps he doesn't understand, he doesn't follow me all the way, but he doesn't dare to interrupt me, he's really fascinated by what I might say next.

'I took the name of a man who happened to have crossed my path. I wandered around for a long time in search of I don't know what, a place where I could disappear. At the end of the summer of 1527 I reached Augsburg and met Denck again.'

'The synod of the martyrs . . .' He speaks slowly and in a low voice: he knows how to listen to a story.

'That's right. The survivors' reunion. Stupid, useless survivors.'

Lucas Niemanson. Merchant of brocades in Bamberg. Full purse, fine clothes made of tough fabrics, a considerable load of goods and trinkets on a fairly new cart, pulled by two horses, both a bit rough but still young. I am resting my muscles, stiffened by miles of bumping, shouts and curses on the disconnected paths of these moorlands, on a reasonably decent bed in an inn just inside the western gate of the city. Before doing anything else, get a few hours' sleep to rest the bones; the next day, think of the load, the cart, the weariest of the quadrupeds. Glance around the streets of this crowded imperial city, with hotheads flowing in from all parts of the country to escape the new killing. Like Hans Hut, the prophet-bookseller, who must have founded a community at each staging post, and who delivered accounts of apocalyptic visions as soon as he'd skipped a meal. People say the city will soon be host to a synod of all the representatives of the communities that have come into being over the past few years, crushed in this new vice between Luther and the Pope.

Careful. Don't fall into the great maw, elude the ubiquitous eye of the enemy.

Observe, be careful, if necessary trust to chance. In the end how I found myself within these walls. Tragedy, fate, unfathomable destiny have supplied both the primary material and the spirit to this situation, in which I would never have imagined myself.

I've been in one place for too long. Torpor of the spirit generates torpor of the limbs. I went off wandering the minute I heard voices asking for Vogel. It was over again. Or rather I was off again, headed for who knows where. They're searching for survivors. Away, twenty-six years. The army of ragged insurgents. To destroy them. So, off again without a word. To a living soul.

A beggar among beggars, with a load of unbearable letters, memories and suspicions.

Chance has dragged my ragged clothes through paths and taverns, villages and inns, markets and barns. Chance joined the bitter and thoughtless fate of the merchant Niemanson with my own, on the twenty-seventh day of June, at the end of infinite and solitary roamings.

He nervously enquired about the safety of the roads towards the south, asking when would be the best time to leave. It was clear that he was transporting precious goods. Beneath his coat the enticing bulge of a pale leather purse: love at first sight. A servant forced to bed for a few days, infected by some whore or other, obliging him to travel on his own, at dawn the next day.

I follow him at a distance for about five miles, until the road takes a wide bend into a wooded zone, low hills, completely isolated. I run up alongside the cart and beckon agitatedly at him to stop. 'Excuse me, excuse me!'

'What do you want?' he asks, scratching his eyebrow and pulling his reins.

'Your servant, sir . . .'

'What's up, what do you want?'

'He doesn't seem as ill as all that. They picked him up this morning trying to sneak out of the inn. He had a big bag full of precious objects that I think may be part of your load,' and as I say this I show him the bag holding Magister Thomas's correspondence.

'The bastard! It can't be his stuff, he's skint. Wait there, I'll come and see.'

He gets down, comes over, I grip the strap of the bag with my left hand, he leans over to look. The stick quickly comes down on the back of his neck.

He goes down like a dry tree.

I block his arms with my knees, three times round him with the rope and a good tight knot.

I liberate the bag from the belt and roll him into a ditch. It's done.

I cut the tangle of cords holding the load and jump up to take a look; fabrics, rolls of various type and colour. Poor bastard, a bit of a setback to your business. And even your clothes won't be much use to you for the time being. Or the name that I read carved into the side of the cart: 'Lucas Niemanson, weaver in Bamberg.'

Chapter 7

Johannes Denck is in Augsburg. I've had some news of him along the way, and now I know exactly where to look for him. The most important figure behind the big meeting of the pastors of all the communities, which has been in preparation for the last couple of weeks, is the young veteran of the revolt.

The house pointed out to me is set back off a street of wool merchants. A tall, slim woman with a baby at her waist opens the door to me, followed by the uncertain running steps of a little girl who immediately hides between her mother's legs. I'm an old friend of her husband's, I haven't seen him for years. I stay in the doorway and the little girl stares at me curiously.

Johannes Denck: a firm embrace and clear eyes filled with disbelief.

He gives me a drink from a flask on his belt and a sincere, silent smile. He touches my arms, my shoulders, as though to be certain that I'm not a ghost re-emerging from the abyss of his worst nightmares. Yes, it's me. But forget my name unless you want to do the cops a favour. He laughs happily.

'What should I call you? Lazarus? The Resurrected?'

'For two years I've been Gustav Metzger. Now I'm Lucas Niemanson, textile merchant. Tomorrow, who knows . . .'

He keeps on staring at me in stupefaction. It's difficult for both of us to find words, to know how to begin. Then we stay there like that, in silence, for an infinity, thinking about everything. That afternoon Mühlhausen is an island far from the world and far from life, where we both turned up one day, perhaps, in search of the way of the Lord. Coming from distant places and heading for different fates.

'On your own?' His voice is heavy and thick with memories.

'Yes.'

He lowers his head to dredge up a face, an expression, a yell of euphoria and hope echoing into the far distance. 'How?'

'Luck, my friend, luck and perhaps a little bit of divine goodness that wanted to help me. What about you?'

His eyes widen with the effort of remembering, as though he's talking about his childhood. 'We got bogged down somewhere around Eisenach. I'd managed to recruit about a hundred men and get hold of a small cannon. But we ran into a column of soldiers who forced us to seek refuge in a village whose name I don't even remember.' His eyes stare at something over my head. 'I'm sorry, I didn't make it. I was no help to you.'

He seems more distressed than I am. I think about how many times during those two years he must have felt once more the powerlessness of that day.

'You'd only have been more cannon fodder. There were eight thousand of us and I don't know of anyone who got away.'

'Except you.'

I give a twisted smile and look for the irony in the disaster. 'Someone had to tell the story.'

'And that was you. That's what counts.'

'We've lost everything.'

His eyes smile, with a wisdom that I hadn't remembered. 'Can't you think of anything that it might be worth losing everything for?'

A grimace of amusement is all I manage to give him. But I know he's right and I'd like to be able to blow away the past as easily as he does.

He turns serious, he's had plenty of time to reflect. 'When I knew they'd sentenced Magister Thomas and Pfeiffer to death, I too thought it was over. They say another hundred thousand people were killed in the reprisals after Frankenhausen. I got away, I hid in the woods and tried to save my skin. For months I didn't sleep in the same bed two nights in a row. But I wasn't alone, no, I had the hope of making contact with the brethren in the other towns, all my friends and colleagues from university. That kept me alive, it gave me the strength not to sit down on the ground and wait for the final blow. If I'd stopped, I wouldn't be here to welcome you now.'

We move outside, into the courtyard behind the house, where some moth-eaten chickens are pecking about in the dust, and two boar-skins are drying in the sun like worn old sails.

It's my turn to talk: 'I sat where I was. And I died. I stayed underground for two whole years, chopping wood and listening to the lengthy disquisitions of the only man crazy enough to take me in: Wolfgang Vogel.'

'Vogel! Holy God, I heard he'd been executed a few months ago.'

'I only just escaped the same fate.'

He whistles anxiously through his teeth. 'How did they track you down?'

'They intercepted one of Hut's companions while he was heading south in search of some fugitive or other. I imagine they tortured him and forced him to name everyone. Vogel must have been one of them, and he had to make his getaway. And I went with him. Fucking sleuths. They followed us for two whole days, until we decided we'd better split up. I made it, he didn't. And here I am.'

He looks at me, astonished. 'You must have a guardian angel, my friend.'

'Hm. These days you'd be better off with a decent sword.'

The air is cool, the sounds of the city reach us faintly. We sit down on the chopping block. The intimacy of survivors melts our thoughts and our words sound calm, almost far away, like the noises of the street. We're alive and that miracle is enough for us now, that's what we want to say to each other, without adding anything else.

The alcohol roughens his voice. 'Hut should be coming in a few days too. He's got it into his head that the Apocalypse is just around the corner and he's going about the place like a saint baptising people. It's a wonder they haven't arrested him yet. He wanders around the countryside and stops to talk to the peasants, to ask them how they interpret the passages from the Bible that he reads to them.'

I laugh heartily.

'Apparently he's a great success.'

'Hut! A failed bookseller turned prophet!'

For a moment we roar with laughter, thinking about the timid Hans we knew so well.

'I heard that Störch and Metzler are trying to assemble an army by bringing together the survivors of the war. They're round the bend. They haven't a hope. But people have been coming here since last year. From Switzerland and nearby towns. There's a good climate here and at least we can meet freely. These people are clever, you've got to meet them, they've come from the universities. This synod we're organising will be a fresh start. Everything will begin all over again from here, more and more of them want to profess their own faith freely. But we'll have to be cautious.'

Maybe you're expecting enthusiasm, but this time I'm going to have to disappoint you, brother. I remain silent and let him continue.

'There's Jacob Gross, from Zurich, we elected him minister of religion, and Sigmund Salminger and Jacob Dachser as his assistants: they're from Augsburg, they know the people here very well. Then there are also the followers of Zwingli, Leupold and Langenmantel. We've set up a fund for the poor with them . . .'

He's talking about far-off events, telling the saga of a vanished people. Maybe he senses that, he stops, a sigh. 'Not everything is lost.'

I barely nod. 'At least we're alive.'

'You know what I mean. We've summoned all the brothers here.'

The same twisted smile. 'Do you really want to start all over again, Johann?'

'I don't want any new priests telling me what I must believe and what I must read, whether they're papists or Lutherans. There are enough of us to infiltrate the universities and undermine the friends of Luther and the princes, because it's in the universities, in the towns, that minds are trained and ideas are spread.'

I stare into his eyes. Does he really believe this?

'And you think they'll let you do this, that they'll stand around and watch while you get organised? I've seen them. I've seen them charging and massacring unarmed people, little boys . . .'

'I know, but things are different in Augsburg, we have greater freedom in the towns and cities, I'm convinced that if Müntzer were here now he'd agree with me.'

The name rebounds in my guts and makes me start. 'But he isn't. And whether you like it or not, that's quite important.'

'Brother, great as he was, he wasn't everything.'

'But the thousands who followed him were. Years ago I left Wittenberg because I was fed up with theological disputes and doctors explaining what I was reading to me, while outside Germany was in flames. After all that's happened, I still think that way. Your theologians won't be the ones to stop the repression.'

We walk in silence along the edge of the courtyard. Perhaps deep down even he himself doesn't believe in his own trust. He stops and passes me the bottle.

'At least let's try.'

Chapter 8

The house of the patrician Hans Langenmantel is big, the drawing room accommodates us all. About forty people, many of them already baptised by Hut, who arrived in the city just yesterday. When he embraced me, repeating the Magister's words: 'The time has come', I didn't know whether to laugh in his face or leave. In the end I simply kept my mouth shut – our bookseller hasn't noticed that time has gone marching on, as wicked as before. And how could he have done? He took to his heels at the first shot from a cannon.

Denck shows up and introduces me to the brethren, giving me the name of Thomas Puel. We stand aside from the vague chattering of the others, waiting for Hut.

'There's going to be a big fight.'

'What do you mean?'

'Hut was in Nicolsburg and he met up with Hubmaier, a brother from those parts who doesn't want to have anything to do with Hut's madness. It seems that our Hans has suggested not paying taxes any more, and refusing to serve in the militias. In the end the authorities locked him up in the castle and he managed to escape through a window with the help of a friend. I expect he's furious, and now he can act the martyr as well. He'll want to put forward the same suggestions here, too.'

Strange faces, serious expressions. I persuade Johann to sit down with me somewhat apart from the rest.

'Dachser and the others have got their feet on the ground. I'll have to try and limit the damage that Hut can do. If we immediately get into conflict with the authorities we won't have time to round up reinforcements. But go and explain that to him . . .'

Evoked by Denck's words, he appears in the middle of the room, in the pose of a prophet. Instead of being moved to laughter, I just feel sorry for him.

*

She gets dressed without a word. The light filters through the window and lets the evening in.

Lying on one side, I look at the bell towers against the sky, the flocks of swallows. A blackbird jumps on to the windowsill and studies me suspiciously. I feel the weight of my body, my muscles, inert as though suspended in the void.

'You still want me?'

I can't summon the will to move my head, to shift my gaze, to speak. The blackbird whistles and flies off.

My hand reaches the bag under the bed. I lay out the coins on the blanket.

'We could do it again with these.'

My voice murmurs something: 'I'm rich. And tired.'

The absolute silence tells me she's gone. I still don't move. I think about those lunatics arguing about what the Day of Judgement will be like. I think I left in too much of a hurry, offending everyone. I think that Denck must certainly have understood. And that I immediately liked the look of the street as I was walking aimlessly through the city. That she followed the right stranger and was young and miserable, like Dana, that she offered warmth and a smile that might almost have seemed sincere. I decided not to think.

My friends are dead and I've discovered that the words of the survivors mean nothing to me. God no longer has anything to do with it; He abandoned us one spring day, vanishing from the world with all His promises and leaving us with life as a pledge. The freedom to spend it between those white thighs.

The blackbird lands back on the windowsill, singing out to the towers. Sleep creeps beneath my eyelids.

I can't give you a face, you're like a shadow, a ghost slipping along the edge of events and waiting for darkness. You're the beggar who asks for alms in the alley and the fat merchant staying in the next room. You're that young whore and the cop who's been trailing me all around the town. Everyone and no one, your race came into the world with Adam: misfortune and an adverse God. The army in wait for us behind those hills.

Qoèlet, the *Ecclesiastes*. The prophet of doom. Three letters full of golden words for the Magister, important information and advice. In Frankenhausen we didn't find the army of muddled soldiers you had promised us, but a strong and warlike force. You wrote that we would defeat them.

You wanted us to go down into that plain. You wanted us all to be butchered.

Denck has a lovely family, they're tranquil enough, but they can't be doing all that well: their clothes are worn and darned in places, the house is bare. His wife, Clara, has cooked for me, and the older daughter looked after her brother while her mother served dinner.

'You shouldn't have left like that.'

There's no resentment, he pours the schnapps into the glasses and passes me one.

'Maybe. But I haven't the stomach for certain discussions any more.'

She shakes her head as she tries to bring the fire back to life by stirring the embers with the poker. 'Just because Hut isn't all that clear-headed it doesn't mean that . . .'

'Hut isn't the problem.'

He shrugs his shoulders. 'I can't necessarily force you to believe in this synod. I'm just asking you to put a bit more trust in people.'

'I've become suspicious over the past few years, Johann.'

I utter the name in a low voice, a habit by now. 'Magister Thomas didn't lead us to Frankenhausen to have us massacred: the information he had was incorrect.' I look Denck in the eyes, to make him feel the weight of my words. 'Someone, someone the Magister trusted, sent him a letter full of false information.'

'Thomas Müntzer betrayed? It can't be so . . .'

I put my hand under my shirt and pull out the yellowed pages. 'Read this, if you don't believe me.'

His blue eyes dart rapidly over the lines, while an expression between incredulity and disgust appears on his face. 'The All-powerful . . .'

'It's dated the first of May 1525. It was written two weeks before the massacre. Philip of Hesse was already isolating the South and route-marching his forces to Frankenhausen.' I let the words sink in. 'I've got two more letters here, written in the same hand, going back to two years before. Full of fine words, no one could suspect that they weren't sincere. It was someone who had been courting the Magister for some time to win his trust.'

I pass him the other letters. The grimace on his lips leaves no doubt about what is burning within. He quickly runs through the words that have, through some miracle, escaped destruction, until his face is made of stone, his eyes tiny. 'You've kept these letters all this time.'

We look each other in the eye, the reflections of the fire dance a witches' sabbath on our bodies. 'I was with him, Johann, I was at his side until the end. It was the Magister who ordered me to get to safety, to leave him to his fate. And I did it, without thinking twice.'

We stay there in silence, once again lost in memories, but it's as though I can perceive the flow of his thoughts.

Finally I hear him murmuring, 'Qoèlet. The *Ecclesiastes.*'

I nod. 'The man from the community, some man or other. Someone the Magister trusted, who sent him to the block. I don't trust anyone now, Johann, least of all doctors and pen-pushers. I have nothing against your friends, but don't ask me to sit and listen to every word they say.'

'If you stay out, I'll respect your decision. But I've got to ask you still to be my friend.'

I cast a glance towards the darkness in the next room.

'My family. If I was forced to leave the city in a hurry I couldn't take them with me.'

There's no need for any other words: we still have something that no cop or defeat can take from us. 'Don't worry. I'll keep an eye on them.'

Johannes Denck is the only friend I have left.

Chapter 9

Three knocks and a hoarse voice behind the door. 'It's me, Denck, open up!'

I jump down from the bed and undo the bolt.

He is red and sweating, and breathless from running. 'The cops. They've got Dachser, they broke into his house while everyone was asleep.'

'Shit!' I quickly start getting dressed.

'The district's full of guards, they're going into all the houses, they know where we live.'

'What about your family?'

'They're staying with friends, it's a safe place, you've got to go there as well, it's too dangerous here, they're looking for anyone from out of town . . .'

I pack my bags and fasten my dagger under my coat.

'That won't be much use to you.'

'You never know. Let's go, you lead the way.'

We go down the stairs and out into the street, he guides me through the first light of dawn down the narrow streets, where the shops are starting to open. I follow him, unable to get my bearings, we reach a wretched district, I bump into a flea-ridden dog, which I send flying with a kick, always behind Denck, heart in my mouth. We stop in front of a tiny door: two knocks and a murmured word. The door is opened. We go in, it's dark inside, I can't see a thing, he pushes me towards a trapdoor.

'Watch out for the ladder.'

We go down and find ourselves in a cellar, a light falls on anxious faces, I recognise some of the brethren I've seen at Langenmantel's house. Denck's wife and children are there too.

'You'll be safe here. I've got to tell the others, I'll be back as soon as possible.'

He embraces his wife, who holds a wailing bundle in her arms, strokes the little girl's head.

'I'll come with you.'

'No, you made me a promise, remember?'

He pulls me towards the ladder. 'If I don't come back, get them away from here, the cops won't bother them, but I don't want them to take any risks. Promise me you'll take care of them.'

It's hard to abandon him to his fate like this, it's something I never wanted to do again. 'Fine, but be careful.'

He presses my hand firmly, with a half-smile.

I draw the dagger from my belt. 'Take this.'

'No, better not to give them an excuse to kill me like a dog.'

He's already climbing the ladder.

I turn round, his wife is there, not a tear, her son at her breast. I think about Ottilie, the same strength in her expression. That's how I remembered them, the peasant women.

'Your husband is a great man. He'll come through.'

Three of them come back. One of them is Denck. I knew the old fox wouldn't get caught. He's managed to get hold of two more brethren.

The hours have been interminable, locked in down here, the weak light filtering through a slit.

She embraces him, choking back a sob of relief.

Denck's expression reveals the determination of someone who doesn't waste time. 'Wife, listen to me. They've got nothing against you, you and the children will be safe in this house and as soon as the waters have calmed you'll be able to get out. It would certainly be more dangerous to try to escape now that every gate in the city is watched by guards. Dachser's wife will put you up. I'll find a way of writing to you.'

'Where will you go?'

'To Basle. It's the last place left where you're not in constant danger. You'll join me with the children when the worst has passed, it'll only be a few months.' He turns to me again. 'My friend, don't leave me now, keep faith with the word I've given you: they don't know your name or your face.'

I nod without quite realising I'm doing it.

'Thanks. I'll be grateful to you for the rest of my life.'

I'm astonished by his haste. 'How do you plan to leave the city?'

He points to one of his two companions. 'Karl's vegetable garden abuts the city walls. With a ladder, and taking advantage of the darkness, we should be able to do it. We'll have to run all night through the fields. I'll find a way of letting you know when I've arrived safe and sound in Basle.'

He kisses his daughter and little Nathan. He kisses his wife, whispering something to her: an incredible strength that still keeps her from weeping.

I walk with him towards the ladder.

One last greeting: 'May God protect you.'

'May he light your way in this dark night.'

His shadow climbs swiftly, encouraged by the brethren.

'I never saw him again. A long time later I heard that he had died of the plague in Basle at the end of that year.'

My throat almost dries up, still, but time has diluted even sadness. 'What about his family?'

'They were welcomed into the home of the brother Jacob Dachser. Hut was arrested on the fifteenth of September, I remember that. He only confessed to his friendship with Müntzer after being tortured for a long time. He died in a stupid way, as stupidly as he had lived. He tried to escape by setting fire to the cell where they'd locked him up, so that the guards would run to open it. No one did: he died suffocated by the smoke that he himself had caused. Leupold, the most moderate of the brothers, proved to be the toughest nut: he never confessed or retracted anything. They had to release him, they banished him from the city along with his faction. I managed to join up with them. I left Augsburg in December of 1527 and never went back.'

Eloi is a dark outline in the chair behind the big pine desk. 'Where did you go then?'

'In Augsburg I'd learned that someone I'd studied with lived in Strasbourg. Martin Borrhaus was his name, known as Cellarius. I hadn't seen him for five years and he had heard nothing from me. When I wrote to ask his help, I knew he would prove to be a true friend.' The glass is refilled. It will help me to remember, or it will get me drunk, it doesn't matter much.

'So you went to Strasbourg?'

'Yes, to Baptist paradise.'

The usher's heels tap away ahead of me as we pass between the walls. One big room follows on from the next, the faces in portraits painted on canvas, tapestries, all kinds of ornaments crowding the pale wood and marble of precious pieces of furniture.

I'm invited to make myself comfortable on a sofa between two large windows. The curtains barely conceal the imposing shapes of the lime trees in the park. The usher walks on ahead with his little black boots, he knocks and appears on the other side of a door. A little boy's voice is chanting strange sounds that I, too, remember having learned by heart, back in the days when I studied ancient languages.

'My Lord, the visitor you were waiting for has arrived.'

The reply is a chair squeaking across the floor and a pleasant, hurried voice interrupting the student's words.

'Fine, fine. Now if you will forgive me for a moment: in the meantime, would you please conjugate *eurisko* and *gignosko* for me?'

He stops just by the door, the entrance of a consummate actor. 'A better time and place, don't you think so?'

'I hope so, my friend.'

Martin Borrhaus, known as Cellarius, is one of those people I never thought I would set eyes on ever again. I had received news of his employment as private teacher to the children of a nobleman and was convinced that our paths had taken us too far apart.

He, on the other hand, maintains that he has always hoped we would meet again and, since he has been in Strasbourg, that our meeting would take place here. He says that the students who filled the auditoria of Wittenberg, more sympathetic to Karlstadt than to Luther and Melanchthon, passed through this city in Alsace. So did Karlstadt.

He talks enthusiastically about Strasbourg, as we stroll past the building site of the cathedral, on the way to my lodgings. He describes it as a city where no one is persecuted for his convictions, where heresy can even be a source of interest and discussion, in shops and drawing rooms, if it is sustained by brilliant arguments and unimpeachable moral conduct.

A cart carrying blocks of sandstone struggles across the square. The bell tower of the Church of Our Lady is higher than anything I have ever seen before. It is on the left-hand side of the façade, and within a few years its twin on the right will double the magnificence of this extraordinary building.

'The printers,' Cellarius explains to me, 'have no problem publishing these most urgent writings. This privilege that they enjoy over their colleagues in the other regions they refer to as "Gutenberg's blessing", because it was here that the father of printing opened his first workshop.'

'I'd really like to pay it a visit, if that's possible.'

'Of course, but first we've got more important matters to deal with. This evening, as it happens, you're going to meet your wife.'

'My wife?' I ask, amused. 'You mean I'm married and no one's told me?'

'Ursula Jost, the girl who's turning the heads of half of Strasbourg. You, Lienhard Jost, are her husband.'

'All right, my friend, let's just slow down for a second. I'm glad she's a fine-looking woman, but more importantly, who's this Lienhard Jost?'

'You wrote to tell me you wanted to be quiet, change your name, become practically untraceable? Put your trust in Martin Borrhaus, I'm now an expert in this kind of thing. Strasbourg is full of people who want to kick over the traces. Furthermore, Lienhard Jost has never existed, and that makes things much simpler. Ursula isn't married either, although when she arrived here she said she was.'

'Why, if I might ask?'

'Lots of reasons,' Cellarius replies, with the same look that he assumed, in Wittenberg, when explaining St Augustine's theology to me. 'In the city, a woman travelling alone stands out as a witch might, while she prefers not to be too conspicuous. I don't even know if Ursula's her real name. And then all of a sudden the nobleman who's putting her up in his house started making rather pressing propositions . . .'

'. . . and telling him about her husband Lienhard, who would turn up sooner or later, cooled his ardour, I would guess . . .' I laugh. Meeting this old friend has really put me in a good mood. 'Fine. Anything else I should know?'

The sun filters through the middle of the dark clouds. A ray of light pierces the grey blanket and lights Cellarius's face. 'I've tried not to tell people too much about you. You were a colleague of mine at Wittenberg University. You've been held up on business and only now have you been able to join your wife, who came here to talk to Capito.'

Cellarius tells me about the two most important religious figures in the city, Bucer and Capito, decidedly tolerant characters, lovers of theological disputes and closer to Zwingli than to Luther. He says I'll meet them very soon, perhaps this very evening, on the occasion of a dinner presented by my future host.

She's in the garden of Herr Weiss's big house. From behind a column, without being seen, I follow her fine profile, the mass of hair that she wears loose, her slender fingers against the edge of the basin.

A cat goes and rubs against her cloak. Her caresses look like the repeated gestures of a ritual and her murmured words sound like a magic spell: there's something strange about her movements, casual in a strange and fascinating way.

I come out into the light that is raining down from above, but behind her, so that she can't see me. As I sidle up beside her, I become aware of the sharp smell of woman, an intoxicating blend of lavender and humours, that crossroads of earth and sky, heaven and hell, that makes you die and resuscitate in an instant. I fill my nostrils and study her from close up.

A cool voice: 'Are my monthlies driving you out of your mind, man?'

She turns round, with bright black eyes.

I'm astonished. 'Your smell . . .'

'It's the smell of low things: freshly turned loam, the body's humours, blood, melancholy.'

I plunge a hand into the icy water of the basin. Her eyes attract mine; her mouth a strange curve in her oval face.

'Melancholy?'

She looks at the cat. 'Yes. Have you ever seen the work of Master Dürer?'

'I've seen the *Imitatio Christi*, the cycle on the Apocalypse . . .'

'But not the melancholy angel. Or you'd know that it's a woman.'

'How so?'

'It has feminine features. Melancholy is a woman.'

I'm confused, I feel the itch of desire spreading through my body, beneath my clothes. I study her sharp profile. 'Would that be you?'

She laughs; shivers run down my spine. 'Perhaps. But the woman is in you, too. I've known Master Dürer, I posed for him once. He's a sombre man. Frightened.'

'Of what?'

'The end, like everyone else. And what about you, are you frightened?'

It's a serious, curious question. I think of Frankenhausen. 'Yes. But I'm still alive.'

Her eyes laugh, as though she'd been waiting for that answer for years.

'Have you seen blood flow?'

'Too much.'

She nods gravely. 'Men are scared of blood, that's why they make war, they're trying to erase its terror. Women aren't, they see their own blood flow every time the moon changes.'

We stay silent, looking at each other, as though her words had imposed a silence with their sacred wisdom.

Then, 'You're Ursula Jost.'

'Which would make you Lienhard Jost?'

'Your husband.'

The same silence, sealing an alliance of fugitives. Her eyes scan the details of my face. Her hand slips under her cloak, then on to my wrist, where an old scar is etched: her finger runs along it, marking it with the red of her blood.

I feel myself turning pale, a wave of cold sweat spreads beneath my shirt, along with the sudden desire to touch her.

'Yes. My husband.'

Chapter 13

'The city was calm, Michael Weiss, my host, was generous, and my "wife" was amazing. And just for a change I had a new name. I owed Martin more than I could have given him in return. The circle of doctors whose company Cellarius kept included people who were truly anomalous for that repressive age. They wanted to debate.

'Wolfgang Fabricius, known as Capito, was the one I was most curious about. Although he claimed to be a fervent devotee of Luther, he had a certain regard for the ones who were starting to be called Anabaptists, and seemed to want to include them within reformed Christianity. He asked me lots of questions, with a curiosity that seemed sincere to me. He had read and admired the writings of Denck. I didn't tell him I'd known the old rogue, but I enjoyed testing his tolerance with the occasional provocation.

'I also met Otto Brunfels, the botanist, an expert in the curative capacities of plants, who was compiling a universal herbarium and was interested in the natural world. I couldn't extract a great deal of information from him about his faith, but I sensed that he must have sympathised with the peasants at the time of the revolt. He was a mild character, opposed to violence, filled with guilt for the way the insurrection had ended. One day, when our mutual trust must have seemed solid enough to him, he even made me read some notes for a work he was writing, in which he argued that these were times in which true Christians, as in the time of Nero, would do better to hide their rites in the catacombs of the soul, concealing their faith and pretending to sway with the prevailing wind as they awaited the coming of the Lord. This private religion of his made me smile from time to time, but it was interesting to talk to him.

'The most difficult of them was Martin Bucer. I met him only once, at Capito's house. A gloomy, serious man, terrified of the ruin of the times. Resistant to life.

'It was an elegant city, Strasbourg, cultivated and at the same time peaceful and remote from the hatred that was ripening beyond its walls.'

Eloi pours me some water so that I can continue. He doesn't open his mouth, he silently savours each word, his eyes sparkle in the shadow like a cat's eyes.

'Ursula was a strange, witchlike woman. Raven-haired, sharp nose, a face both hard and sensual. We couldn't pretend for long: passion took us by the hand, it drove us wild straight away. She had no history either, I didn't know where she came from, her accent didn't give me a clue, and I didn't want to know, that's how it was, simple. She crept over to me, sinuous and silent as a wildcat, pressed her breast to my back and then I noticed her desire. What gripped us both was that uncertainty, not knowing. If we had been somewhere else it would have been different, everything would have been.'

'Did you love her?' His voice is hoarse.

'I think so. The way you love when you have no past, all you've got is an endless present, promising nothing. God no longer had anything to do with our lives: they had been erased completely, maybe she too carried the memory of a disaster, of some terrible misfortune. Maybe she, too, had died once before. Often, at night, after making love, I thought I could read it in her eyes, that suffering. Yes, we really did love each other. She was the only person to whom I could confide all my impressions about the circle of characters I moved among during the day. She didn't say a word, she listened attentively, then all of a sudden she would confirm my uncertain judgement with some lapidary phrase, a phrase which, a moment later, I found myself agreeing with entirely, as though she had read my thoughts, as though her reasoning were quicker than my own. And I am sure that that is how it was. She didn't have Ottilie's angry courage, although sometimes, in her rage, I saw the worry of that great woman, my master's wife. She was different, but nonetheless extraordinary, one of those creatures who make you thank God for granting you the chance to walk the earth by their side.'

I stare at the dusk that is entering our study and once again I see that sinuous body.

'We knew from the first moment. One day we would wake up somewhere else, far apart, for no necessary reason, following the twisted path of our lives. Ursula was a season, a fifth season of the soul, half autumn, half spring.'

Chapter 14

The new chisel does a terrific job. Balthasar wasted no time: I found it this very morning on the table in the study. The tip removed shavings of wood like a spoon in butter, while Eloi's incredulous gaze accompanied each blow of the little hammer, every scrap of sawdust that flew on to the floor, every detail of Strasbourg Cathedral emerging in relief from the little panel. 'Quite remarkable,' he observes, pursing his lips. 'Where did you learn to use your hands like that?'

'I've put more effort into swordplay than I have into this,' I reply, picking up the sharp tool. 'I was in Strasbourg. I was working as a compositor at a printing press in the city. There was a bloke who did the illustrations for the books. During his breaks he put down the plate and burin, and picked up his gouge: he made portraits of all of us and gave us all dozens of copies. He was forever saying that a beautiful thing need never be unique. He was the one who taught me to carve wood.'

He studies the drawing for a moment, then points to the date in a corner. 'You haven't practised your hobby for a long time.'

I shrug my shoulders. 'You know, I'm always on the road. I used to keep my hand in by carving little statues that I would give as presents to children. I took it up again in Münster, as well. But, you know . . .' A smile covers my excuse. 'I lost my tools somewhere.'

Eloi leaves the room and reappears with the usual bottle of liqueur. By now I know what that means. He fills my glass to the brim. 'I didn't know you'd found yourself a job in Strasbourg.'

'Thanks to Cellarius. I'd always been attracted by the printers' workshops. Books have a special fascination for me.'

The chisel removes some shavings. It's time to move on to the knife for the smaller details. Eloi breaks off to follow the phases of the work, then he starts talking again. 'Fill me in. In Strasbourg you had found a certain tranquillity, an affectionate friend, a woman who was full of life, a trade. Why didn't you stay there?'

I look into his eyes, speaking slowly. 'Have you ever heard of Melchior Hofmann?'

This time he's incredulous. 'You're not going to tell me you knew him too?'

I nod, in silence, smiling at his reaction. 'You might say that he was the final reason for my leaving. A lot of things had happened by then.'

I realise that I'm starting to enjoy telling the story. I enjoy creating suspense and interest. Eloi, too, must have noticed the change. Every now and again he helps me along; at other times, like this, he stays silent, waiting for me to go on.

'With the passing months Ursula started getting more and more impatient about the prevailing atmosphere in the city. She kept telling me there were plenty of people in Strasbourg with innovative and brilliant ideas, but the only thing that distinguished it from other German cities was the possibility of expressing those ideas in a cultivated and refined form. Her battle-cry became "In Strasbourg, living is the real heresy".'

I raise my eyes from the delicate lattice-work of the rose window of the cathedral. Eloi listens with his chin resting on the back of his hand. The pleasure of my rediscovered pastime frees my tongue even more than the drink does.

'She used to go around the squares performing spectacles, especially doing dances that were thought to be lascivious or lewd, playing the lute and singing the songs of the street people. She even got me involved.'

Eloi laughs enthusiastically. He puts his glass down on the table. 'I heard you singing something while you were pulling up the fence around the vegetable garden. If your intention was to put people's nerves on edge, then Ursula was right to rope you in.'

'No, no singing, please! I started working as a bricklayer. The first action we came up with was going into a church at night and building a brick wall in front of the stairs to the pulpit. Above it we wrote a sentence from Cellarius: "No one can speak to me of God better than my heart."'

Meanwhile the drink is starting to take effect. The chisel misses its mark a few times, so that I mess up a bit of bell tower. Time to stop.

'Best of all, though, must have been the joke we played on Madam Goodheart Carlotta Hasel. You must know that Carlotta Hasel was one of the many ladies of the city who organised feasts at her table for the poor and tramps. She made them pray and eat, drink and sing psalms.'

'I know the type, unfortunately.'

'Ursula couldn't even bear to hear her name mentioned. She hated her, and in that special way that only one woman can hate another. On the other hand, Madam Goodheart had the annoying characteristic of seeing the poor as saintly. Her motto was, "Give them bread, and they will praise God." Ursula wasn't of the same opinion. She said that those who have nothing, once their stomachs are filled, have other things in mind than praying: drinking, fucking, enjoying themselves, living. Let's just say that events tended to bear out her theory.'

'What happened?'

'The colossal orgy we provoked in the Hasel drawing room.'

'I don't know what I'd have given to take part in the demonstration of the theory!' Eloi exclaims, amused. 'Nonetheless, I don't see what that story has to do with Melchior Hofmann.'

Just a moment of concentration for the *coup de grâce*. I blow away the sawdust and raise the little panel to eye level. Perfect.

'It's hard to believe, my friend: even Melchior the Visionary, in the end, was one of the spectacles produced by the theatrical company of Lienhard and Ursula Jost.'

Chapter 15

Antwerp, 6 May 1538

'The day of the apocalyptic preachers has passed. The last one was beheaded before my eyes in Vilvoorde a month ago. But during these past ten years I've known so many of them, on every street corner, in every brothel, in the remotest churches. My peregrinations have been so studded with those encounters that I could write a treatise about them. Some of them were merely charlatans and actors, others believed in their own sincere terror, but only a very few had the stuff of prophets, the brilliance, the ardour, the courage to repaint John's great fresco in the souls of men. They were capable of choosing the right words, seizing situations, taking the gravity of the moment and filling it with the imminent event, bringing it into the present moment. Mad, of course, but skilful too. I don't know whether it was God or Satan who suggested their words and visions to them, that's irrelevant. I didn't care then, and I still don't. Frankenhausen had taught me not to wait for a host of angels: no God would descend to help the wretched. They would have to help themselves. And the prophets of the kingdom were still the ones who could lift them up and give them a hope to fight for, the idea that things would not always be like this.'

'You mean you joined the battle again?' Eloi looks astonished.

I take a sip of water to clear my throat. 'I didn't know what to do. Ursula and I started to hate those theologians who went on talking and talking, presenting themselves as great thinkers of the Christian faith, talking about the mass and the Eucharist in the drawing rooms of the wealthy people of Strasbourg. Their tolerance was a luxury for the affluent, which would never go beyond granting a plate of soup to the poor. These well-fed shopkeepers could afford to maintain that band of doctors, and even to bestow their magnanimity upon the heretics, because they were rich. It was wealth that guaranteed the fame of Strasbourg. It was that fame that brought writers and students flooding to the city.'

I sigh. 'They were scared, oh yes, really scared, when we pointed out to them that the poor, the humble, the ones they wanted to help with alms, in order to ease their mercantile consciences, aspired to steal their purses and even to cut their lovely white throats. We didn't have long to wait because Capito and Bucer responded to our provocations, introducing subtle distinctions between "peaceful" and "seditious" Baptists. We clearly fell into the second category.'

Eloi smiles crookedly, perhaps he's thinking about his Antwerp, but he doesn't interrupt me.

'It wasn't a matter of restarting a war that we had lost. That would have been stupid. But Ursula had brought me back to life, it was as though her belly had given birth to me for a second time. We wanted to cause some trouble, exasperate the hypocritical philanthropy of those people so that they would reveal themselves for what they were: an army of the wealthy attached to gold, disguised as pious Christians. It was one of the most carefree times of my life.'

I stop to draw breath, perhaps I'm waiting for a question to pick up the thread of the story.

Eloi asks one. 'How long did it take?'

An effort of memory. 'About a year. Then, in the spring of 1529 the man who would be responsible for the start of my journey arrived in Strasbourg. Now he's rotting in that city's dungeons. He committed the fatal error of setting foot there again after everything that we'd done.'

'Melchior Hofmann.'

'Who else? One of the oddest prophets I've ever met, pretty much one of a kind, and in terms of madness and oratory maybe second only to the great Matthys.'

'I'm all ears.'

I take another drink and reconstruct that far-off face. 'Hofmann had been a furrier. One day he had a Damascene experience and started preaching. He had courted Luther until he managed to get him to write a letter of introduction to the communities in the North. That signature had opened the doors of the Baltic countries and Scandinavia to him, allowing him to acquire notoriety and even a certain following. He had travelled a great deal in the North. Then one fine day he had convinced himself that the kingdom of Christ and the Saints was at hand, and had started preaching repentance and the abandonment of all worldly goods. It wasn't long before Luther renounced him. He told me he'd been expelled from Denmark with the promise that if he ever set foot there again his head would end up on a pole. He was really a mad genius. He'd known good old Karlstadt and he shared his complete rejection of violence. He arrived in Strasbourg convinced that he was the prophet Elijah, in search of the martyrdom that would confirm that the coming of the Lord was nigh. He immediately fell in love with the local Anabaptists, and managed to fall foul of all the Lutheran reformers, first Bucer and then Capito and the rest.

'Ursula and I knew immediately that this was the man we were looking for to turn the city upside down. It came to us spontaneously, we didn't even have to talk about it: over dinner we improvised some complicated revelations, Ursula worked herself up to a state of ecstasy before his very eyes, while I told him how the rich and powerful would be swept away by the fury of the Lord. In the weeks that followed, we gradually dictated our visions to him and he didn't miss a single word. When everything was ready, I found the way to send everything he had written to the printers: two treatises containing Ursula's prophecies and my own. He started preaching to the crowd in the main square. Some people spat in his face, others tried to hit him, others still tried to attack a pawnshop to distribute the goods to the poor. When the writings were distributed by the booksellers, Bucer tried to have him put in prison. Those were days of ferment. It was a year of fire, I felt the blood boiling in my veins, the rope on the point of snapping.

'And so it was, at the beginning of 1530, if I remember correctly: Hofmann had himself rebaptised and preached for the last time, proclaiming the imminence of the Kingdom of Christ, denouncing attachment to worldly goods and demanding that the Anabaptists be allowed to use one of the city churches. It was the final straw. Bucer put the most severe pressure on the council to have him expelled from the city. At Easter, he received the injunction to leave Strasbourg. If he failed to comply, that would be him done for.

'Things were looking difficult for me, too. Cellarius could no longer protect us from the fury of Bucer and Capito: he was quite open with me, well aware that he would lose me again, this time for ever. That was the fate I had chosen for myself and old Martin couldn't do a thing about it. I hugged him again and said goodbye, just as I had done years before in Wittenberg when I went in search of a master and a new fate. My old friend, who knows where he'll have ended up: I expect he's either still in Strasbourg or in some new university talking about theology.'

I shrug to wipe out the sadness. Eloi, all ears, wants to hear the ending.

'I'd decided to go with Hofmann. To Emden, in eastern Frisia.

Southern Germany was lost, it was a desolate moor that I was glad to leave to Luther and the wolves. Huge numbers of people had been expelled from the Low Countries for their profession of faith: new people, much less attached to Luther's habit than those in Strasbourg. There was ferment, this was the place where things could happen. I had backed the right horse: my Swabian Elijah prophesying the imminent coming of Christ and preaching against the rich. As passports go, he was difficult to manage, but enthusiastic enough to be successful.'

'And what about Ursula?'

A moment of silence allows him to regret his question, but it's too late. I still smile at the memory of that woman.

'The season passed, to make way for a new year.'

Chapter 16

I explode inside her, unable to contain the yell that mingles with hers. Pleasure shakes my body, twisting me round like a dry branch in a fire. She lowers herself on to me, damp, the black cloud of her hair envelops me, the smell of the humours on her mouth, on her hands, her breast against my chest. She stretches out beside me, white and amazing: I listen to her breath slowing. She takes my hand, in a gesture that I've learned to indulge, and puts it between her thighs, to touch, in a single delicate gesture, her still contracting sex. Ursula is something I will never feel again: she is Melancholy, cut into the soul and the flesh.

'You've decided to leave with him.'

'For Emden, up north. Hofmann says the refugees from Holland are gathering up there. Great things are about to happen.'

She turns on to her side, facing me, allowing me to see her shining eyes. 'Things worth dying for?'

'Things worth living for.'

Her index finger runs along my twisted profile, my red beard, down my chest, stopping at a scar, then down to my belly. 'You'll live.'

I look at her.

'You're not like Hofmann: you expect nothing. Your eyes are filled with defeat, desperate defeat, but what afflicts you isn't resignation. It's death. You've chosen life once before.'

I nod silently, hoping she will surprise me again.

She smiles. 'Every creature follows its own destiny in the cycle of the universe. Yours is to live.'

'And I owe that to you.'

'You know I won't come with you, though.'

Whether it's sadness or emotion, words fail me.

She sighs serenely. 'Melancholy. That's what my husband called me. He was a doctor, a highly cultivated man, he loved life too, but not like you. He loved its secrets, he wanted to extract the mystery from nature, from the stones, from the stars. That's why they burned him. Perhaps a loyal wife would have followed his fate. But I ran away: I chose to survive.' She strokes my face. 'You will too. You'll follow your star.'

The vegetable garden's ready. Everyone compliments me. No one asks any questions; who I really am, what I did before fetching up here . . . I'm one of their own: one brother among the rest.

Magda, Kathleen's daughter, still gives me presents; Balthasar asks me after my health at least twice a day, as you would a recovering patient.

'I'm still alive,' I tell him, to make him laugh. He's a good fellow, the old Anabaptist. It seems that his job is to find buyers for the goods manufactured here and he does it well.

I don't ask him any questions either, I'm learning by the day, studying these people's secrets.

I asked Kathleen about her daughter's father. She said he boarded a ship two years ago and then not a word. Shipwrecked, abandoned on some enemy island, or alive and indolent in a palace filled with gold and diamonds, in the kingdoms of the Indies. The same fate that I was after before I ran into these men and women.

Eloi keeps prodding me gently, he wants the next part of the story: clearly he wants to hear about Münster. The City of Madness has the fascination of fantastic things, it's the shiver that the name still provokes, a shiver that was once an earthquake. He's already asked Balthasar all about it, but I followed that path to the end: Gert-of-the-Well was a hero, lieutenant to the great Matthys, the best at carrying out reprisals, at pillaging inside the bishop's camp, at putting out flyers and the message of the Baptists: Balthasar must have told him that as well.

Yes, Gerrit Boekbinder tempered the iron with his own hands.

Then one day, without a word, he left, tired, sickened, all of a sudden aware of the abyss of horror that had opened up beneath the New Jerusalem.

Gert thinks again about the child judges, their index fingers raised. He remembers those people who died of hunger, dragging themselves through the snow like white maggots. Once again he feels the pangs of starvation and the relief of that final dash beyond the walls, towards the iniquity of the world, but far from the omnipotent and bloody delirium.

And yet once he was out he didn't find Eloi Pruystinck waiting for him with open arms, just more blood and fresh visions of glory and death. Gert fell again, recruited for the Last Battle, with the mark of the elect branded on his arm. Once again Gert saw the same banner billowing behind Batenburg the Terrible, and he couldn't stop. Gert fell in love with that blood and he went on, he went on.

He went on.

Eloi has that expectant look that I know by now; he pours a glass for both of us, which makes the story easier to tell.

I pick up the thread of my memories: 'We headed northwards, Hofmann and I, following the course of the Rhine, on a merchant's barge. We passed through Worms, Mainz, Cologne, up to Arnhem. I had managed to impose silence upon my travelling companion until we found ourselves in Frisia: I didn't want to risk seeing myself being stopped along the way. It was hard for him, but he kept his word. Once we had left the course of the Rhine, we set off on foot and on mules, always heading northwards. We moved from one village to another, along the borders of the Low Countries, towards the countryside of East Frisia. Hofmann had already been in these parts during his long itinerant preachings, and this time, too, he didn't neglect to instruct the peasants of these moorlands about the obligatory choices that the events of the time required all Christians to make: following Christ in his example of life. He rebaptised them all, like a new St John.

'Meanwhile he told me about the situation in Emden, our next stop. There were many refugees in that town, most of them Dutch Sacramentists, as he called them, those who no longer accepted the sacraments of the Church of Rome and didn't believe in transubstantiation. This, he explained to me, pushed them beyond the positions held by Luther, opening them up to the clear promise of the millennium. He described them as stray dogs, waiting for a prophet to bring them the message of hope and the light of renewed faith. He defined that journey as "our desert", which would temper us, putting our faith to the test and improving the justification of the Lord through absolute obedience to Christ. I indulged him, without trying to extract myself from the fascination that his words managed to exercise over the humble: I was really dumbfounded by that strength.

I hadn't told him that I had fought beside Thomas Müntzer: his condemnation of violence held me back. He used to reserve a lapidary phrase for me, every time I provoked him, by referring to the possibility that Christ would call His army of the elect to Himself, to exterminate the wicked: "He who lives by the sword will die by the sword."

'We reached Emden in June. It was a cold little town, a stopover for merchant ships between Hamburg and the Dutch cities. The community of foreigners was a large one, as Hofmann had predicted. The reigning prince, Count Enno II, allowed the ideas of the Church reformers to take their course on his lands, without trying to obstruct them in any way. My Elijah began to preach in the streets from the day we got there, drawing everyone's attention. It seemed clear that the other preachers wouldn't have been able to compete with him, he'd have made mincemeat of them. After a few weeks he had rebaptised at least three hundred people, and was in a position to found a community that would bring in discontented people of the most diverse origins and conditions. Above all they had left the papist Church and were dissatisfied with the Lutheran Church, which, even without priests and bishops, already boasted a hierarchy of theologians and doctors not much different from the one it had wanted to abolish.

'The notoriety of the Anabaptists reached us almost immediately, and frightened the city authorities half to death.

'Events were going on around me. I felt the earth moving under my feet and a strange sensation in the air. No, I hadn't been infected by my travelling companion: it was the sense of imminent events, the call of the life that Ursula had talked to me about. That was why I decided to leave Hofmann to his preacher's fate and follow my own path. A path that would take me elsewhere, into the eye of the storm. It's hard to say whether I was the one who guided my own life towards the boundaries that needed to be crossed, or whether it was the torment itself that pulled me along with it.

'The authorities in Emden expelled Hofmann as an undesirable troublemaker. He told me he would come back and start writing again, that his task up here was done. He assigned the leadership of the new community to a certain Jan Volkertsz, a maker of clogs, known as Trijpmaker. This Dutchman, from Hoorn, was not a great orator, but he knew his Bible and had the expression of the man who had inspired him, and the same spirit of initiative. I bade farewell to old Melchior Hofmann at the gate of the town, as they escorted him out of the territory of Emden. He was smiling, naive and trusting as ever, confessing to me in a low voice that he was certain that the Day of

Judgement would come within three years. I too gave him my last smile. And that's how I remember him, a distant farewell, as he sways out of my view on a bony old mule.'

I'm still not clear about what Eloi is after. He sits in silence behind the table, rapt by the story, perhaps even with his mouth open, in the semi-darkness that prevents me from clearly making out his face.

I continue, having decided by now to get to the end and astound him with each page of this unwritten chronicle.

'I wouldn't see Melchior Hofmann again until two years later, when he came to Holland to reap what he had sown. But I was telling you about Emden. Trijpmaker and I had stayed there to look after the well-being of the Anabaptist community, and it was almost Christmas when we received the injunction to leave the city. I wasn't displeased: I felt I had to move on, that I couldn't stay here in this northern port. We decided at night, with the determination and the spirit of someone who knows he is confronting a major task: the Low Countries, with the exiles who were slowly managing to cross the border and return to their towns of origin, opened up at our feet like an unexplored territory, ready to receive the message and the challenge that we represented for the governing authorities. Nothing would stop us. For Trijpmaker it was a mission, as it had been for Hofmann. For me it was another push towards the horizon, a way of driving things along, new land, new people.

'We would make for Amsterdam. Along the way Trijpmaker would teach me a few phrases in Dutch so that I could make myself understood, but he would be the one who did the preaching and the baptising. He started straight away: before leaving Emden he baptised a tailor, a certain Sicke Freerks, who then returned to the town of his birth, Leeuwarden, in western Frisia, where he had the task of founding a community of brothers, and where instead he was put to death the following year at the hand of the executioner.

'While we were travelling towards the south-west, passing through Groningen, Assen, and Meppel to Holland, Trijpmaker enlightened me about the situation in his country. The Low Countries were the commercial and manufacturing heart of the Empire, it was from there that the Emperor derived the majority of his income. The port cities enjoyed a certain autonomy, but they had to defend it tooth and claw against the centralising desires of the Emperor. Charles V was still annexing new territories, allowing his troops to roam through the country, doing severe damage to communications and crops. Additionally, the Habsburg seemed to prefer exposed Spain to his native land, and he had placed his officials in many important positions and inaugurated an imperial government in Brussels, before going to live in the South.

'The state of the Church in that part of Europe was as tragic as could be imagined: what prevailed there was a religion of blow-outs and banquets that went on behind the peasants' backs, the profitable decadence of the monastic orders and the bishoprics. The Low Countries were without spiritual guidance, and many of the faithful had begun to abandon the Church, to join lay confraternities that led them to a communal life and cultivated the study of the Scriptures. They would be able to receive our message before anyone else.

'Luther's ideas had spread through the lower classes, and even to the merchants who grew rich on their backs. Events in Germany were still a long way off, the obedience to which the German peasants had been brought back did not affect the workers in the Dutch factories, the weavers, the carpenters in the ports, the artisans in those ever-expanding cities. Luther's reformed religion brought with it new dogmas, new religious authorities, which alienated the faith of the believers almost as much as that of the papists. Equality in faith, communal life, called for a different kind of lifeblood, and we were there to supply it.

'I was impressed by the landscape of that highly fertile land. Coming from Germany, with its dark forests, it was astonishing to see the way the inhabitants of the Low Countries had subjected nature to their will, extracting from the sea every inch of cultivable land, to plant grain, sunflowers, cabbages. Windmills along the road in impressive numbers, tirelessly hard-working people, capable of standing up to natural adversities and overcoming them. The city of Amsterdam was no less striking: the markets, the banks, the shops, the network of canals, the port, every corner seethed with feverish activity.

'It was the beginning of the new year, 1531, and despite the intense frost the streets and the canals were crammed with incessant comings and goings. A captivating city where I could have lost myself. But Trijpmaker knew some brethren who had been living there for some time and we would start with them.

'We contacted a printer with a view to bringing out some selections of Hofmann's writings that Trijpmaker had translated into Dutch, and some flyers to distribute by hand. I took care of that while Trijpmaker devoted himself to bringing together everyone he knew in the city. We won a good following among the craftsmen and mechanical workers: people discontented with the way things were going. You could feel in the air the imminence of something that might manifest itself from one moment to the next.

'In less than a year we managed to organise a consistent community, the authorities didn't seem too worried about these fervent Anabaptists who disdained wealth and announced the end of the world.

'In my heart I felt that things couldn't go on like this for very long. Trijpmaker continued to preach meekness, witness, passive martyrdom, as Hofmann had directed him to. I knew it couldn't last. What if the authorities took it into their heads that we were a danger to the order of the city? What would happen if men and women who had converted to the imitation of Christ found themselves faced with weapons? Did he really believe they would allow themselves to be crucified without putting up any resistance? He was sure of it. And then the time was nigh: Hofmann had predicted the Day of Judgement for 1533. There was not much to be done to counter such arguments, so I shrugged my shoulders and left him to his boundless faith.

'Our numbers kept on growing, morale was high, the devotion of the rebaptised was immense. From the villages around Amsterdam came ungrammatical messages from new adepts, peasants, carpenters, weavers. I had a sense of being in a great cauldron topped by a lid that would sooner or later blow away. It was intoxicating.

'Finally, preaching against riches in one of the wealthiest cities in Europe had an effect. In the autumn of that year the Court in the Hague ordered the Amsterdam authorities to put down the Anabaptists and execute Trijpmaker.'

Eloi poured me some water. 'You're tired; do you want to go to sleep?'

The question contains a plea to continue, he's a child conquered by storytelling, despite the fact that I'm probably telling him things he knows already.

'First I should really tell you what they did to Trijpmaker and how I decided to take up arms. At first it was only to resist the people who wanted my head on a plate.' I stretch my arm and laugh derisively. 'Then I met my own true John the Baptist, the one who would persuade me once again to fight the deadly yoke of the priests, the nobles, the merchants. And Christ, I did it: I took that sword and I started. I'm not sorry about that. Not about the choice I made at that time, faced with those severed heads fixed on the top of a pole. The first was the head of the man who had brought me to Holland, a madman possessed, perhaps, a stupid man who had sought martyrdom and who had found it. But he was the one they had done it to.'

I can almost hear Eloi shivering.

'Yes, Trijpmaker chose his death, the death of Christ. He could have fled if he had wanted to: Hubrechts, one of the city burgomasters, was on our side and had tried until that moment to prevent him from being captured. It was he who sent a servant to our house to warn us that the police were about to come and arrest the leader of the community. I took a moment to get my things together and so did many others. But not he, not Jan Volkertsz, the clog maker from Hoorn who had turned missionary. He sat down and looked at his guards: he had nothing to fear, the truth of Christ was on his side. Along with him they took another seven and brought them to the Hague. They tortured them for days. They say they burned Trijpmaker's balls and drove nails under his fingernails. The only thing they didn't touch was his tongue: so that he could give them the names of all the others. And he did. Mine included. I never held it against him, torture can break the strongest souls, and I believe his faith had already been so crushed by the glowing iron that he didn't need anyone else's rancour. None of us blamed him, we managed to get away, there were many safe houses around to put us up.'

'Did they execute all eight?'

I nod. 'On the point of death they all denied everything that had been extorted from them with torture: small consolation, and I don't know how many were able to die in peace because of it. Their heads were returned to Amsterdam and displayed in the square. A clear message: anyone who tries again will face the same fate.

'It was November or December 1531, around the time Lienhard Jost kicked the bucket. That name attracted the police as shit attracts flies. The family that was hiding me gave me their name, explaining that I was a cousin who had emigrated to Germany and returned after many years. Boekbinder, they were called, and their cousin really existed, except that he had died in Saxony, drowned in a river when the boat he was travelling on went down. His name was Gerrit. So I was the ghost of Gerrit Boekbinder, Gert to his friends.

'It was early in 1532 that I received a letter from Hofmann. He was in Strasbourg, he'd had the gall to go back there. Clearly when he'd received the news of the treatment meted out to Trijpmaker and the others, old Melchior had shat himself. The letter announced the beginning of the *Stillstand*, the suspension of all baptisms, in Germany and the Low Countries, for at least two years. From that moment onwards we would have to move in the shadows as we waited for the waters to calm: no more disturbances in broad daylight, no more proclamations, let alone declarations of war on the world. As far as Hofmann was concerned, we should have been a herd of meek preachers, skilled and not too noisy, lining up to be butchered one after the other in the name of the Supreme One. That's more or less what he was writing during those months in Strasbourg.

'As to myself, I still wasn't clear what I was going to do, but I wasn't going to sit there twiddling my thumbs, hidden away like a kicked dog, even if the people who were looking after me were kind and generous. One day in the woodshed I found a rusty old sword, a souvenir of the war in Gelderland, in which some member of the Boekbinder clan must have taken part. I felt a strange shiver as I clutched a weapon once again and I understood that the moment had come to try something magnificent, that I had to abandon peaceful proselytising because all we would ever encounter on the other side was iron, the iron of the gendarmes' halberds and the executioner's axe. But I knew I wouldn't go much further on my own. It was a new, blind beginning, I felt myself trembling, more lucid and determined than I had ever felt before: I wasn't frightened by my knowledge that the adventure was about to turn into war, because it would be the only one worth fighting: the war to free ourselves from oppression. Hofmann could go on making martyrs, I would look for fighters. And I would cause trouble.

'And now, my friend, I really think I'm going to leave you for my bed, it must be very late. We'll continue with the story tomorrow, if you don't mind.'

'Just one moment. Balthasar calls you Gert "from the Well". Why's that?'

Nothing escapes Eloi, every word contains a possible side road from the story.

I smile. 'Tomorrow I'll tell you about that as well, about how casually nicknames can come into being, and how once they have you can never quite shake them off again.'

Chapter 18

Fortunately the chain holds my weight, clutching the bucket, dangling like a hanged man, instinct, instinct more than anything else, he caught me on the ear, if he'd got me full in the face I'd have been in the water down there, what a thump that was, I can't hear anything now, everything sounds far away, the shouts, the flying chairs, hold on tight, if I faint I'll drown, at least here they won't get me, shit there are too many of them, and I'm bang in the middle of them like a cunt, all for someone I don't even know, my arms, I've got to hold on, my arms or I'll drop, if I jump back up they're going to thump me again, if I stay here sooner or later my muscles will give in, what a fucking situation, everything's spinning, my shoulders hurt, an enormous great fucker, I couldn't have done it on my own, no way, he's going to kill me if I go back up there, but shit, the other poor bastard, they must be butchering him, how many are there, three, four, who's had the time to count them, we found them on top of us, it began all of a sudden, he started yelling, what did their mothers do? Got fucked by whose pigs? A table flew over my head, wonder it didn't kill me, and if they pick up their knives, they didn't look armed, fuck, you don't bring weapons into a pub, to drink a beer, no, to talk some nonsense or other, to talk deals, but that bloke says that stuff about their mothers, my arms, Christ, my arms, I'm holding on tight, yes, I'm holding on tight but not for long, I can't drown like this, what a way to die, after all I've been through, all the places I've escaped from alive, or maybe yes, it's something that's coming to an end, you escape the armies, the police, and then you die like a drowned rat all because of someone who couldn't keep his trap shut, I found myself in the middle of it, I had nothing to do with it, and I found myself in the middle of it, that's the cunt of it all, four against one, because they were jingling those purses full of money, well-fed shipowners, frigid wife once a year if they're lucky and syphilitic slags every holiday, exploiters, all prayers and big business, so let's wind up the

Anabaptists in the pay of the Pope, the Anabaptists are just plague spreaders who need their throats cut and feed their guts to the dogs, sleek great greyhounds with their country houses, fucking moneybags, the Anabaptists in cahoots with the Emperor, sneak their way into your house to convert your wife with their dicks, we should make a clean sweep, my arms, Christ, they're giving way, but why did I get mixed up in it, that other nutter was the one who started it, there was no need to get up and spit beer in his face, and then say that thing about their mothers, right enough they probably were a bunch of whores but obviously they were going to take it badly, they'll have slit his throat by now, if he'd stuck to spitting he could've been just another drunk, but no, he had to come out with it, and that's why I'm stuck here, because of his big words, which I'd have liked to say myself, my arms, shit, my arms, I've got to pull myself up, come on, up we go, I can't end up at the bottom of this filthy well, I can't die like this, like a cunt, he could still be alive, he might say something else before they kick his brains in, fine big words, my brother, because yes, you're a brother, otherwise you'd never have risen to your feet, never have said what you said, I wouldn't have done it for the world, that's what I want to tell you, I wouldn't have got mixed up in it for some drunken Anabaptist, I've known too many of them, my friend, but you had the guts, up we go, Jesus, up we go, got to get out, that's the way, gently now, up, nearly there, got to get out, oh shit, here I am, on the rim, one more shove and we're there.

There are five of them now. It looked like four to me, I could swear I'd counted four. Now there are five, all around him, he's fucked, the landlord's on the cobbles in the courtyard, he's clutching his head, the pot I threw shattered but at least it did some damage. And this unknown friend who's standing there stock-still challenging them with his eyes as though he's the stronger one, and go on, say something, what was it like? What did you say before the world crashed down on my back, before that giant threw me down there?

I get to my feet and start picking up the chain, I don't even notice myself shouting. 'Hey, that thing you said . . . About Jesus Christ and the shit-eating merchants . . .'

He turns round, astonished, almost as astonished as the others. The scene freezes, as though printed on a page, I nearly lose my balance. I must look like a bloody idiot.

'Yeah, I agree with you completely! And now take the advice of a fellow brother: get your head down.'

The giant who thought he'd drowned me turns purple, he moves ahead, come on, come on, now I've wrapped the chain round my waist and I've got the bucket in my hand, come on, fellow, come here and lose that big fucking head you've got on your shoulders.

It's a dull sound, a dry thud, just one, that dents the metal and sends a rain of teeth flying through the air. He goes down like an empty sack, without a groan, spitting out bits of tongue.

I start swinging the chain round, faster and faster, showing these fine gentlemen just how annoying an Anabaptist can be. The bucket hits heads, backs, it's spinning further and further from me, the chain's cutting into my hands, but I see them go down, crouch on the ground, run towards the door without quite making it, the Bucket Justice is implacable, round, round, faster and faster, I'm not holding it any more, it's dragging me round now, it's the hand of God, I could swear, sirs, the God that you've been pissing the hell out of. He's down, another one, where did you think you were going to hide, you stupid rich piss artist?

A jolt, the bucket's come to a halt, stuck in the branches of a little tree that nearly goes down too.

A glance at the battlefield: uh, they're all on the ground. Someone's moaning, he's licking his wounds, semi-conscious, staring at his bollocks.

The brother was sensible. He threw himself on the ground first time it came round and now he's getting up dazed, a gleam in his eyes: I haven't done too badly as an exterminating angel.

I jump up and stagger towards him. Tall and slim, dark pointed beard. He shakes my hand too firmly, the chain's cut it to bits.

'God was with us, brother.'

'God and the bucket. I'd never done that before.'

He smiles. 'My name's Matthys, Jan Matthys, a baker from Haarlem.'

I reply, 'Gerrit Boekbinder.'

Almost emotional: 'Where are you from?'

I turn round and shrug my shoulders. 'From the well.'

'I became Gert "from the Well". Matthys liked to use that silly name, but he also liked to think that our public encounter had not come about by chance. In any case, nothing was coincidence as far as he was concerned, everything had a meaning in the eyes of God, a meaning that went beyond simple appearance and spoke to men, to us, the elect. Because he thought the Baptists were the elect of the Lord, the chosen ones. It was an enterprise to be taken to its conclusion, something magnificent, something final. My John from Haarlem knew Hofmann, he had been personally baptised by him and he had read his prophecies. The day was nigh, the day of liberation and revenge. But I immediately understood that this baker had made a different choice from old Melchior: he wanted to fight this battle, he wanted to fight it with a passion, he was just waiting for a sign from God to declare war on the wicked and the servants of iniquity. He had a plan: assemble all the Baptists and lead them out of the world, this world of servitude and prostitution to which the powerful wanted to condemn them for all eternity. Fine, but how would you recognise the elect? Matthys never tired of repeating that Christ had chosen poor fishermen as his followers and apostles, spitting on the merchants in the Temple. Because that was what it was all about: lucre, the accursed lucre of the Dutch traders. That kind of people would select the faith they professed on the basis of their own interests, and that made them a terrible enemy. The more involved the faith was with indisputable rites and dogmas, the more attached they would be to it: basically the only reason they didn't sympathise with the Church of Rome was that its greatest supporter, Emperor Charles, oppressed them with excessive taxes and wanted to swagger about the Low Countries like a tyrant, obstructing their business deals. It was of little importance that so many wealthy merchants were sincere in their good faith: that good faith – my Haarlem baker often said – wasn't enough, what was needed was truth. If good faith were enough, there would be no point in redemption: "Good faith doesn't abolish errors: many Jews, in good faith, shouted 'crucify him'. Good faith is an idea of the Antichrist."

'But even more surprising than that was the way in which Matthys had unmasked the hypocrisy of the priests and the doctors who had served up the Bible from the pulpits and thrones: that wretched theology of "moral rectitude" and the inevitable "honesty", often and gladly bestowed only by superior ranks, by the authorities. "The Gospels, on the other hand, praise the dishonest, they are addressed to the prostitutes, the panders, not repentant prostitutes, but prostitutes as they are, the criminals, the dregs of the earth." Praise of honesty and morality was, as far as he was concerned, the religion communicated to us by the Antichrist.

'For that reason, it was among the common people, the artisans, the beggars and the dregs of the streets, that we would find the elect, among those who endured more than anyone else, and who had nothing to lose but their condition as the world's rejects. It was there that the spark of the faith in Christ and His imminent return might survive, because the conditions of those people were closer to His choice of life. Christ had chosen the disinherited, the whores and the panders? Then it was among them that we would recruit our captains for the battle.'

'What was he like? I mean what kind of man was Jan Matthys?'

Eloi's question comes down slowly like the evening, at the end of that day devoted to the garden and to Kathleen's smile.

'He was the most determined madman I had ever met. But that was before we went to Münster. He was determined, determined enough, perhaps, to devour Hofmann and his rejection of violence. If old Melchior was Elijah, then he would be Enoch, the second witness of the Apocalypse. I had a sample of his strength when a certain Poldermann, a Zeelander from Middelburg, said that he was Enoch: Matthys leapt on to a table and subjected all the brethren assembled there to a furious torrent of abuse. Anyone who didn't recognise him as the true Enoch would burn in hell for eternity. After which he said nothing for days. His words had been so convincing that some of our number locked themselves in a room without food or water, begging God's mercy. It was a test of strength, oratory and determination: he won. Perhaps it wasn't yet clear to him, but I knew that Jan Matthys was already Hofmann's greatest rival, and something else besides: he knew how to address the rage of the humble. I felt that if he learned to channel that rage, he really would become God's captain, with the potential to turn the world upside down and make the last the first, to give a great shake, perhaps a final one, to the fat province of the North.

'He had come to Amsterdam with a woman, by the name of Divara, a magnificent creature whom he jealously kept from the eyes of everyone. They said that in his country he was married to an old woman and that he had left her to escape with this very young girl, the daughter of a Haarlem brewer. So Enoch, too, had a weak point, the same one as most men, halfway between his dick and his heart. That woman always frightened me, even before she was the queen, the prophetess, the great whore of the king of the Anabaptists. She had something terrifying in her eyes: innocence.'

'Innocence?'

'Yes. That quality that can make you be and do anything at all, it can make you commit the most terrible and gratuitous crime as though it were the most innocuous action in the world. She was a woman who would never have wept, whom nothing could have upset, an ignorant little girl, unaware even of her own white flesh and for that very reason even more terrible when she finally understood.

'But it was only later on that I would learn really to fear that woman. In those first months of 1532 we had other things to think about. Above all, the fact that the clandestine preaching of Matthys, our curious recruitment, had been on a collision course with the *Stillstand* proclaimed by Hofmann. During those days word had reached us that the German Elijah would soon be coming to Holland to visit our community, and Matthys knew he would have to assert himself against the master, if we wanted the brothers to awaken and join up with us. It was a fight to the death: Hofmann, for his part, had the authority of his past as a preacher. But Jan of Haarlem had the fire.'

Chapter 20

Amsterdam, 7 July 1532

'No! No! No! And four times no!' The voice rises high above the hubbub in the room. 'It isn't time to resume the baptisms! To do so right now would be to challenge the Court of Holland and send ourselves to the scaffold! Is that what you want? Who will announce the Coming of the Lord when you've ended up like poor Trijpmaker and all his companions?'

Our good old Swabian Elijah hadn't expected to be challenged like that, he had hoped to be welcomed like a father. And instead . . . Here he is, red in the face and ready to contradict himself with exasperation.

Enoch doesn't lose his composure, his acute-angled beard points towards his adversary, one prophet against the other: nothing about that in the book of Revelation. He looks into his eyes with the beginnings of a smile.

'I know it can't be martyrdom that's frightening brother Melchior, I know it because no one more than he has endured the pains of exile and the difficulties of testifying.' A studied, masterful pause. 'What he fears is that in a few hours, without giving us time to escape or send a letter, the authorities in the Hague will track us down and descend upon us, capturing the lot of us.' By now he has everyone's attention. 'But how many of us are there? Have we ever asked that question? And what are we willing to risk for the Final Day? I tell you, brothers, that with the help of the Lord we can be swifter than the swords of the wicked, maybe that's our message, the sign of judgement.'

Hofmann, furious, fights down the bitterness that is welling up in him.

Matthys insists, 'It's true: they can follow us, infiltrate us with their spies, discover our names, our safe houses. But why should we stop just because of that? It is written in the Bible that Christ will know his saints. Peter, in his letter, incites the faithful to hasten the coming of the day of the Lord.' He quotes from memory the passages we have discussed a number of times: '"We look for new heavens and a new earth, wherein dwelleth righteousness." And John asserts that "he that knoweth God heareth us: he that is not of God heareth not us". But how are the just to hear us if we won't talk to them? How will we be able to distinguish the spirit of truth from that of error, if we do not go into the open field to fight? How can we do that if we do not have the courage to baptise them, to preach, to reach them with the message of hope, challenging the edicts and the laws of men? We must be more cunning than they are! Or perhaps we believe that it is only by writing theological treatises and fine words that we will be able to accomplish our task!' Voices are raised, the words inflexible: hammer blows on the anvil. 'How much, bothers, how much have the holy apostles put us on our guard against the Antichrists, false prophets and the seducers who will swarm upon earth at the final hour, to distract the elect from their task? Our task. The Bible says, "And of some have compassion, making a difference. And others save with fear, pulling them out of the fire." The fire in the hearths that are being got ready for us all around the Low Countries, brothers, to seal our mouths and impede the preparation of the battlefield for the Coming of Christ and the New Jerusalem! And are we to bend our heads and await the axe?'

His voice dances, an explosive music, a rumble that starts a long way off, bounces into the stomach and suddenly erupts. The brothers are divided, the charisma of Elijah against the fire of Enoch, souls are coming aflame.

Hofmann rises to his feet, shaking his head. 'The day of the Lord is nigh. All signs bear witness to that, prime among them the power of the iniquity that is persecuting us so cruelly in Germany and here in Holland. That's why our task is to wait and to bear witness. Wait for Christ, yes, brothers, wait for that power which alone will bend the nations and abolish evil for all eternity. Brother Jan' – he turns to Matthys alone – 'the wait will be a brief one. The darkness is already withdrawing and the true light is already resplendent. John tells us, "Love not the world, neither the things that are in the world!" And so does Paul. We must guard against the sin of pride in this critical moment, we must be humble and wait, brother, wait and suffer, keeping firm the peace within us.' A glance at our faces. 'It will be soon. That much is certain.'

Matthys: eyes narrowed to slits, his breathing seems to have stopped. 'But the hour has come! It is now! Now Christ is calling us to move! Not tomorrow, not next year, now! We have talked so much about the return of the Lord that we don't notice it's already here, it's happening, brothers, and if we don't get marching the Kingdom will vanish once more without our noticing, being too much immersed in our theological treatises!' He runs to the window; when he swings it open over the suburbs of Amsterdam, a shiver runs down my spine. 'What are we waiting for? Why have we not abandoned Babylon, this merchants' brothel, to march out there! Let us call an assembly of the people of the elect and fight the armed battle of the Word of the Lord!'

Hofmann hobbles forward, troubled. 'These ideas will lead to civil war! And that is not what we were called to do!'

Matthys's glazed eyes are fixed, murderous, his reply is ready, the hiss of a serpent: 'That's entirely your decision.'

The two factions explode, by now they're quite clear and divided, insults fly, and some well-aimed spits. I try to calm our side down, unaware that Hofmann's compassionate eye is upon me, upon the one he really didn't expect to find on the opposite side. Maybe he's looking for help, he asks me to bring Matthys to his senses, in the name of our Strasbourg sodality.

'Brother, will you at least talk to these madmen? They don't know what they're saying.'

I have only a few words to dismiss him with. 'Let madness and despair speak: that's what we have to offer.'

That puts his fire out completely. He stands there, thrust into a deep, dark chasm. He knows the fire of Enoch will engulf the plain.

Chapter 21

'Here we are, the street you're looking for is the first on the right. You can't go wrong from here.'

The little boy who has accompanied us stops, waiting for a coin or two, and points to a little street at the end of the block. He seems almost paralysed. A whisper, eyes downcast. 'My mum works there, she doesn't want to see me around here.'

He opens his hand to accept the small change. Jan Matthys doesn't lose his composure. 'You will have your reward in heaven,' he solemnly intones.

'But meanwhile,' I add, getting a florin out of my purse, 'a little earthly advance can't do you any harm.'

The blond-haired boy darts away, giving us the beam of a toothless smile, while Jan Matthys tries to look at me with disappointment, although he's unable to hold back a laugh. 'We've got to get them used to the urgency of the Kingdom at a young age, don't you think?'

It could be the mother of our little guide who welcomes us in the alley. Blonde-haired, like him, clear eyes lined with black, she rests her tits on the cracked sill of a window on the second floor. Almost before we turn to see her, we hear the sharp smack of ten kisses carried on the wind. As in the gallery of portraits of some noble family, the generous busts of the prostitutes of Leyden line up to right and left, leaning at various different heights on the wattle walls of the houses.

Although distracted by a welcome of this kind, it doesn't take long for us to find the green door we're looking for. It's the last building on the street, on the corner with a little bridge without a balustrade that arches over one of the many canals leading to the Rhine.

Matthys, tall and thin, is radiant. On the stairs leading to the first floor, he claps his hand on my shoulder and nods his head. 'Among whores and pimps, Gert!'

'And among the drunks in a pub,' I add with a smile, alluding to the recruitment of Gert from the Well.

This time we are welcomed by a girl, fully clothed, but not exactly like a lady going to market. 'You're looking for Jan Bockelson, Jan of Leyden, aren't you? Just right now I can't . . .'

'Show them in!' A shout from the end of the corridor breaks in. 'Can't you see that they're prophets? Come on, come in!'

The voice is low and corporeal, one of those voices that start from the abdomen and boom into the throat. It certainly doesn't sit very well with the scene that confronts us once the door from which it issued is flung open.

Our man is lying stretched out on a short little sofa, clutching a blanket with one hand and his balls in the other. He is naked from the waist up, with his chest smeared with oil. A woman, also half naked, is holding a razor and shaving him.

'You must excuse me, my dear friends,' he says, in that voice of his that always sounds like mockery. 'I didn't want to keep you waiting too long. You always meet some shady types in our ante-room.'

We introduce ourselves. Matthys looks at him for a moment, then looks around the room. 'Is this your work?'

'My work is anything that doesn't make you sweat,' is the immediate answer, like the joke of an actor on the stage. 'I deny Adam's sin as firmly as anyone can, and in consequence I do not accept the curses derived from it. I used to be a tailor, but I soon gave it up. Now I impersonate the great protagonists of the Bible in the street.'

'Ah, so you're an actor!'

'Actor isn't quite the right word, my friend: I don't recite, I impersonate.'

He takes a sponge from a bowl and covers himself with soap. He leaps to his feet, tugging away resolutely between his legs. His face is a mask of painful resignation, his eyes directed straight at mine.

' "I go the way of all the earth. Be thou strong therefore, and show thyself a man. And keep the charge of the Lord thy God, to walk in His ways, to keep His statutes, and His commandments, and His judgements." '

The girl applauds enthusiastically, pushing her breasts between her arms. 'Bravo, Jan!' Looking at me: 'Isn't he fantastic?'

King David gives a deep bow. Strange noises come from the corridor: thuds, screams, muffled shouts. At first our Jan seems not to notice, intent as he is on his personal hygiene. Then something that makes him jump into action, perhaps a cry of 'help' that is either higher than the others or simply more convincing. He grabs a razor and dashes out.

His voice echoes through the house. Matthys and I look at each other, uncertain whether or not to intervene. A moment passes and Jan of Leyden reappears in the doorway. He is breathing deeply, he straightens the crotch of his trousers and plunges the razor into an enamel bowl. The water turns red.

'What do you think?' he says without turning around. 'Have you ever heard of a pleasant pander, well-mannered and respectful of his fellow man? Pimps are cruel, brutal people. I, on the other hand, want to be the first holy pimp in history. Yes, friends, I'm a pimp who dreams of sitting at God's right hand. And yet every now and again the dream is interrupted and the pimp wakes up . . .'

'It isn't a matter of sleeping and waking.' The other Jan has the voice of Enoch, not the voice of an actor. 'Pimps, prostitutes, thieves and murderers: those are the saints of the last days!'

Jan of Leyden puts a hand to his lips and then to his balls. 'Agh! Don't talk to me about the end of the world. My friend, I've known plenty of prophets in here and they're all jinxes, every one.'

'No wonder they are,' I reply immediately. 'Sitting and waiting for the Apocalypse brings you bad luck. Revelation only comes from below. From us.'

He turns round with a laugh. It's hard to tell if it's ironic or enlightened. 'I understand.' The corners of his mouth go on rising, revealing his hard gums. 'It's a matter of doing neither more nor less than *making* the Apocalypse!'

The emphasis with which he pronounces the word *making* really strikes me. With my old passion for Greek and etymology I try to find a new name for the final undertaking. Apocalypse, like apotheosis, contains the prefix referring to something that comes from above. Hypocalypse would be much more suitable: you only need to change a couple of letters.

I look at Jan Bockelson with his hand resting between his thighs, a half-naked woman stretched out on the sofa, a bloody razor lying in the water: and my arguments don't quite cross the threshold into my brain. The words of the Haarlem baker would be much more convincing.

Jan Matthys smoothes his pointed black beard. He seems to like the holy pimp, even if the pimp hasn't yet quite grasped the situation. In any case, the Amsterdam Baptists who suggested that we meet him didn't mention his lucidity or his faith, but only his visceral hatred of papists and Lutherans, his fascination with the theatre and his rather rough manners.

Matthys presses his lips between his fingers and decides to get to the point. 'Listen to me, Brother Jan, here's our idea: twelve apostles will travel the length and breadth of this country. They will baptise adults, invite people to prepare the way for the Lord and preach in His name. Above all, they will sniff the air of each town and city to assess how best to bring the elect together.' He turns to me with a nod. 'We're looking for people who are capable of doing all that.'

The other Jan gestures to his attractive companion to leave the room. His eyes become attentive as he lowers himself on to the sofa, arranging himself in his trousers. 'Why all in one city, friend Jan? Wouldn't it be more useful to involve the biggest territory possible? The strength of an idea can also be measured by its capacity to involve the most distant people.'

Matthys has already replied to this objection several times. He narrows his eyes and speaks slowly. 'Listen, only when we govern a city and abolish the use of money, private ownership of goods and differences in wealth, only then will the light of our faith be powerful enough to enlighten one and all. That will be the example! If, on the other hand, from this moment onwards, our sole concern is to spread our ideas as widely as possible, we will end up weakening the disruptive effect we expect from them, and they will die between our fingers like rootless flowers.'

Jan of Leyden claps his hands together, shaking his head. 'My blessings be upon you, my friends! For a long time now, this street actor has been waiting for some lunacy like this so that he can finally bring his favourite characters to life: David, Solomon, Samson. And by God, this Apocalypse of yours is what I've always dreamed of. I accept the part, if that's what you're looking for: as of today, you've got one more apostle!'

'A whoremaster? The King of Münster a pimp?' For a moment Eloi loses the acquiescence that I've become accustomed to. For the first time he seems unable to believe me.

I reassure him. 'If the legend has painted him as a terrible, bloody king, that does indeed correspond to the truth, but neither before nor after our entrance to Münster was he any different from what he had always been: an actor, a charlatan, a pimp. And, of course, a prophet. That makes the epilogue to our vicissitude even more grotesque, because the actor forgot that he was reciting and confused his performance with real life. The farce turned tragic.'

Eloi is uneasy, and he lets out a loud laugh to subdue his astonishment.

'The Anabaptist epic and the legends of our enemies turned us into monsters of cunning and perversion. In actual fact they were the Horsemen of the Apocalypse: a baker-prophet, a pimp-poet and a nameless reject, forever fleeing. The fourth was a man possessed, Pieter de Houtzager, who had tried to become a monk but had been turned down for the violence of his language: he went crashing into people in the street, the visions he evoked were full of blood and destruction, the Lord's only justice.

'Then the Boekbinder family supplied another member to the Matthys gang, young Bartholomeus, who was officially my cousin and who joined us in the autumn of 1533 along with the two Kuyper brothers: Wilhelm and Dietrich.

'We also convinced such a calm and pious man as Obbe Philips, and in Amsterdam Houtzager baptised another follower, Jacob van Campen. And in that way the disciples of the great Matthys reached the considerable number of eight. Reynier van der Hulst and the three Brundt brothers, boys who still stank of milk, but with hands as big as shovels, joined us from Delft in the last days of November 1533. Almost without noticing, our numbers had grown to twelve.

'The sign was more than clear enough to our prophet. You could clearly see in his face that he was planning something. At the end of the day, the world around us really seemed to be on the point of exploding, our words always had the desired effect. We were only a band of misfits, actors, madmen, people who had abandoned work, home, family to devote themselves to preaching in the name of Christ. Choices that had been made for a great variety of reasons, from a sense of righteousness to impatience with the life to which they had been condemned, but all of them leading to the same conclusion: an act of will involving as many people as possible, demonstrating to mankind that the world could not go on like this for ever, and very soon it would be turned upside down by God in person. Or by someone on his behalf, which is to say, us. That was why we were the ones who could really blow things sky-high.'

'Did you obey Matthys's orders?'

'We followed his intuitions. We were in perfect harmony with one another, and furthermore our prophet was anything but stupid: he was a good judge of character. He took my opinions very seriously and often consulted me, while he preferred to use Jan of Leyden as a kind of battering ram: Jan's theatrical attitude was very useful to him. And his physical attractiveness didn't do him much harm, either. He was very young, but he already looked very mature, athletic, blond, with a dazzling smile that broke girls' hearts. Matthys had taken to sending him all over the place, all around the imperial territories, checking the lie of the land, while Houtzager remained active in the Amsterdam suburbs.

'Towards the end of 1533 Matthys divided us up into pairs, just like the apostles, and gave us the task of announcing to the world, in his name, that the Day of Judgement was at hand, that the Lord would soon be slaughtering the wicked, and that only a few would be saved. We would be his standard-bearers, the messengers of the one true prophet. He had harsh words, although not ungrateful ones, for old Hofmann, imprisoned in Strasbourg. He had predicted Judgement Day for 1533: the year was drawing to a close and nothing had happened. Hofmann's authority was officially dismissed.

'He didn't talk about weapons. I couldn't say if he ever talked about them. He said nothing about involving the apostles in the Lord's battle and I don't know if he was pondering that solution even then. As far as I could see we were all unarmed. All except me. I had shortened the old sword I had found in the Boekbinders' stable, turning it into a short dagger, a more agile and familiar weapon that I could keep hidden under my coat and which allowed me to travel with my mind at ease.

'I paired up with Jan of Leyden at Matthys's wish – my determination and his appeal to the public: a perfect combination. I didn't mind. In fact, Bockelson was someone I'd never have got bored with, unpredictable and just crazy enough. I was sure we'd achieve great things.

'It was then that, for the first time, I heard of Münster, the city in which the Baptists were making their voices heard most loudly. Jan of Leyden had passed through a few weeks previously, and had brought back an excellent impression. The local preacher, Bernhard Rothmann, was a close friend of some Baptist missionaries who were followers of Hofmann's, and he enjoyed great success among the townspeople, standing up to both the papists and the Lutherans. Münster was included on the itinerary that we were planning to follow.'

'Were you and Bockelson the first to arrive?'

'No, as a matter of fact we weren't. Bartholomeus Boekbinder and Wilhelm Kuyper had got there a week before. They'd left again, but not before they'd rebaptised more than a thousand people. The enthusiasm in the city was at fever pitch, and we got an impressive taste of it when we turned up.'

Carafa's eye
(1532–1534)

Letter sent to Rome from the city of Strasbourg, addressed to Gianpietro Carafa, dated 20 June 1532.

To my most honourable lord Giovanni Pietro Carafa, in Rome.

My Most Munificent Lord,
   The news of the signature of the alliance between Francis I and the Schmalkaldic League – for which we have hoped so devoutly – fills me with hope. The Protestant princes and the Catholic King of France are uniting their forces to limit the power of the Emperor. There is no doubt that war will soon resume, especially if the rumours that have reached me, via rather select channels, about a secret negotiation between Francis and the Turk Suleyman, are confirmed over the months to come. But Your Lordship is without a doubt better informed than this his humble servant, looking across from this corner of the world in which your generosity has allowed him to carry out his little task.
   And yet, as My Lord rightly observes, the times require of us a constant and diligent vigilance, never allowing ourselves to be overwhelmed, I might add, by a fire that is smouldering beneath the ashes, preparing to explode with an unprecedented violence. I refer once again to the Anabaptist plague, which continues to claim so many victims in the Low Countries and the border towns. Merchants are coming from Holland, reporting that there are already large communities of Anabaptists in Emden, Groningen, Leeuwarden and even Amsterdam. The movement's ranks are growing by the day, and spreading like an inkblot across the map of Europe. And this at a time when the most Christian King of France is about to succeed in his intentions to assemble in a redemptive – albeit bizarre – alliance all the forces hostile to Charles and his untrammelled power.
   As Your Lordship knows very well, the imperial province of the Low Countries is not a principality, but a federation of towns, connected to one another by intense commercial traffic. They consider themselves free and independent, so much so as to be able to confront Emperor Charles with obstinacy and courage. Up

there, Charles V is the representative of Catholicism, and it is not difficult to read in the aversion of the population for the Church of Rome the ancient hatred that they feel for the aims of the Emperor.

At this moment, the Emperor is busy organising resistance against the Turks and resisting the diplomatic manoeuvres of the King of France. So he is unable to pay a great deal of attention to the Low Countries.

To this we must add the miserable state of the Church in those lands: simony and profit are in undisputed control of monasteries and bishoprics, provoking the discontent and rage of the population, and leading it to abandon the Church, or to seek another one in the promises of these wandering preachers.

And consequently heresy, taking advantage of the general discontent, is managing to find new channels along which to spread.

In the judgement of Your Lordship's servant, the danger represented by the Anabaptists is more consistent than it might at first appear: if they managed to gain the sympathy of the countryside and the commercial cities of Holland, their heretical ideas could no longer be contained and they would travel on Dutch ships to who knows how many ports, until they would finally threaten the stability established by Luther and his men in northern Europe.

And since Your Lordship flatters your servant with the request for an opinion, might I be permitted to say in all frankness that, in the face of the spread of Anabaptism, the advent of the Lutheran faith is a great deal more desirable. The Lutherans are people with whom it is possible to forge alliances favourable to the Holy See, as can be demonstrated by the alliance between the King of France and the German princes. The Anabaptists, on the other hand, are indomitable heretics, resistant to compromise of any kind, contemptuous of all rules, sacraments and authority.

But I do not dare add anything else, leaving all evaluation of the matter to the wisdom of My Lord, impatient to serve Your Lordship once again, with these humble eyes and the scrap of sense that God has been good enough to grant me.

I sincerely implore Your Lordship's goodness.

Your Lordship's faithful servant

Q   Strasbourg, 20 June 1532

Letter sent from the city of Strasbourg, addressed to Gianpietro Carafa in Rome, dated 15 November 1533.

To my most honourable lord Giovanni Pietro Carafa.

My Most Illustrious Lord,

I am writing to Your Lordship, after a long silence, in the hope that you will still have cause to bestow upon your faithful servant the attention and care that you have shown him hitherto.

The facts that I wish to report to Your Lordship are, in my view, useful, and perhaps even necessary, if we are to read between the lines of events in the northern lands, which, as I have mentioned on a number of occasions, are becoming more complicated by the day.

The theatre of the facts that I am reporting with such urgency is the episcopal principality around the city of Münster [. . .], on the borders between the territory of the Empire and that of Holland, now entrusted to the wise guidance of His Eminence Bishop Franz von Waldeck.

He appears to be a resolute man, most devoted to the Holy See, but also prudent and careful not to lose the power that both the Pope and the Emperor have placed within his hands. He rose to become Prince Bishop in a climate of furious arguments and conflicts with that part of the population that professes the Lutheran faith, most of the merchants, members of the guilds which control the city council, and which he has confronted with the greatest determination.

None of this would merit so much as a moment of Your Lordship's attention, were it not for the fact that everyone is now talking about recent events in this city, so much so that even Landgrave Philip of Hesse has seen himself obliged to send peacemakers to quell the rebellion that is occurring there.

I must confess that for some time now a name familiar to me reached my ears, returning along the course of the Rhine, bringing me the echo of fiery sermons. Until yesterday, when I received the witness of a poultry dealer who had come from Münster and who was resident there.

This merchant spoke to me of a new Isaiah, hailed by the common people, with many followers in the inns and alleys, aware of his ascendancy over his fellow citizens, and in a position to raise them up against Bishop von Waldeck. Only then, when I had a physical description from an eyewitness, did I associate the name with the face of the man whose fame had reached me.

Bernhard Rothmann is his name, and I remembered having caught sight of him here in Strasbourg about two years ago, when his Lutheran sympathies led him to visit the most important Protestant theologians. At that time I hadn't thought of him as a dangerous person, at least, no more so than his other peers who had left the Holy Roman Church, but now I hear his name being mentioned once again, and loudly.

He is a Münsterite preacher, about forty years old, the son of an artisan, but they say that since childhood he has shown signs of great intelligence and ability, and for that reason he was sent into the ecclesiastical life, and subsequently to study in Cologne, by the churchmen who were looking after him. During that journey he passed through these parts, but also through Wittenberg, where he met Martin Luther and Philipp Melanchthon.

It would appear that when he returned to his birthplace he became an official preacher, launching a most harsh attack against the Church. The merchant guilds immediately supported him, seeing him as the best possible battering ram to break down the portals of the bishopric. Within a short space of time he won the favour of the common people and became fired with ambition.

To arrogance he seems also to bring the blasphemous eccentricity of someone who claims to administer his religion as he sees fit: my merchant described to me the very strange way in which he administers holy communion, dipping little pieces of bread in wine and serving them to the faithful. Furthermore, for some time now he has begun to deny baptism to children.

This detail aroused my keenest suspicion and prompted me to find out more. And indeed, interrogating the merchant and persuading him to give me any useful information that he might have, I discovered that this false Isaiah had Anabaptist sympathies.

I found out that at the beginning of the year some Anabaptist preachers came to Münster from Holland. I have carefully jotted down their names, at least those retained by the merchant's excellent memory. They so excited the preacher as to convert him to their false doctrine and reinvigorate his acrimony towards the bishop.

It also appears that for some months Luther has kept an eye on this character, clearly impressed by the noise that he is managing to provoke, and it is said that in various letters sent to the city council of Münster Luther tried to put the Protestants on their guard against a man of this kind. But it is known that the monk Martin is terribly frightened of anyone who might compete with him in popularity and oratory, threatening his primacy. However, what revived my attention more recently in this city was news which reached me to the effect that Landgrave Philip felt duty bound to dispatch to Münster two preachers to guide this Rothmann back within the banks of Lutheran doctrine. When I asked my providential merchant why Landgrave Philip had put himself to such trouble for such a little preacher, who, furthermore, does not even live within the confines of his principality, he replied by supplying me with an even more detailed account of the most recent events in Münster.

So, as Your Lordship will be able to read, such events confirm the worst suspicions that this humble observer has expressed in his previous messages, meagre consolation for such a disaster.

The moment this Rothmann embraced the doctrine denying child baptism, many among Luther's friends turned their backs on him, setting themselves against the man they had previously hailed. But while many turned their backs on him, just as many must have chosen to follow him, if what I have been told corresponds, as I believe it does, to the truth.

The city was thus divided into three faiths, three parties equally remote from one another: the Roman Catholics faithful to the bishop, the Lutherans, most of them merchants, who control the city council, and the Anabaptists, artisans and mechanical workers following Rothmann and his preachers, who had come from Holland. Not even the fact that the latter were foreigners managed to separate the mob from its preacher, and in fact, when the council tried to expel them from the city, they were brought back in at night and the people expelled the local preachers in their place!

Who is this man, My Lord? What incredible power does he exert over the common people? One's memory runs straight to that man Thomas Müntzer whose acquaintance Your Lordship also made through these humble eyes.

But it is better to bring this chronicle to an end; it would seem to be a product of the imagination were I not certain of the wisdom of the man who reported it to me.

So, faced with a situation of this kind, it was considered

appropriate to hold a public debate between the three different confessions on the question of baptism, lest matters degenerate into open warfare.

It was in August of this year that the best minds went into battle in the arena of doctrine. Well, My Lord, Bernhard Rothmann and his Dutchmen won a resounding victory, bringing the townspeople on to their side.

On a number of occasions, Your Lordship reminded this servant of yours how the Lutherans, heretics who are strangers to the grace of God, have revealed themselves to be useful, albeit undesirable, allies, against yet worse threats to the Holy See. Münster has once again given proof of that, producing an alliance between Lutherans and Catholics against the seductive Rothmann.

The burgomasters of the city ordered him to remain silent and shortly afterwards they exiled him. But, strong in the support of the common people, he treated the orders with contempt, continuing to stir people up and spread his pernicious doctrines.

The city appeared on the point of exploding, so much was blood seething in the veins on both sides.

And this explains why it was that Landgrave Philip hurried to send his peacemakers. The two Lutherans, a certain Theodor Fabricius and Johannes Lening, were both learned and diplomatic, and they set about trying to distract everyone's attention from the question of baptism.

But from the account of the man who reported the facts to me, they only managed to obtain an armed truce, in which a single spark would have been enough to set the whole city alight. My merchant had no doubt. If it came to a test of strength, Rothmann and the Anabaptists would gain the advantage in a flash.

To this we might add two events that are no less significant. The head of the guilds, one Knipperdolling, openly supports the preacher with his head held high, bringing the city's artisans with him. Not least, it appears that the spread of Rothmann's fame is bringing into Münster many Dutch exiles, Sacramentists and Anabaptists, shortening the fuse to the powder keg with each passing hour.

And now I wish to tell Your Lordship of my fears concerning the gravity of the situation. Everywhere the Anabaptists have proved their tenacity and their perfidious seductive power, just as Satan does to mortals. They are spreading their plagues all around the Low Countries and within the border of the Empire. If there are few of them now, quite scattered among the regions of the North, they have still demonstrated the fascination that their doctrines exert, specially among the ignorant mob, seditious by its very nature.

So, what would happen if they joined forces? What would happen if they started to enjoy ever greater success as they crept through the alleys, through the workshops, far from the control of doctrinal authority? What if no one, not a bishop, not a prince like Philip nor Luther, appeared capable of halting their subterranean advance; when, in fact, they fear them like the plague, trying to keep them far from their own borders, unaware that they are advancing invisibly and could easily cross them?

We have all the answers we need before our eyes. The first actual case is already in existence and it is that of Münster, where a single man has a whole city in check.

Landgrave Philip and Martin Luther, having scented the grave danger represented by these Anabaptists, do not, in fact, know how to stop them, and they really think that they can contain their perverse violence and keep them in isolation. I fear, My Lord, that it is an illusion and that they will become aware of their error only when they find the Anabaptists at the doors of their own houses.

Well, what I think is, as Your Lordship has wished so magnanimously to teach me, that the threats should be thwarted in time and destroyed before they can come into effect. For that reason I have never neglected to inform Your Lordship of everything that could be useful, however minimally, in assessing the risks that lurk in this part of the world.

In the case in question the facts are already becoming apparent, but it may not be too late: this sickness must be stopped, stopped at birth, before it can spread throughout the whole of Europe and contaminate the Empire, something that is already happening, not even stopping at the Alps, and descending into Italy and who knows where. Before that can happen, action must be taken.

So I look forward to hearing your instructions, if you still wish to gratify a servant of God by allowing him to pursue your cause at this difficult time.

I kiss Your Lordship's hands as I wait for your reply.

    Your Lordship's faithful servant

    Q   Strasbourg, the 15th day of November 1533

Letter sent to Rome from the city of Strasbourg, addressed to Gianpietro Carafa, dated 10 January 1534.

To my most honourable and reverend lord Giovanni Pietro Carafa.

My Most Illustrious Lord,

Today I received Your Lordship's missive, which I awaited more expectantly than ever. Indeed, it would be senseless to conceal the fact that time is of the essence where this grave matter is concerned, and Your Lordship's authorisation is a matter of great concern and urgency to me, since what needs to be attempted will require all the providential protection of the Supreme One if it is to turn out to the good.

So allow me now to reveal to Your Lordship what I think must be undertaken against the Anabaptist pestilence.

First of all, My Lord, the situation as it stands: Anabaptism spreads underground, it does not have a single head that can be severed from the neck and there's an end to it; it has no enemy to defeat in battle; it does not have true and genuine borders; it springs up now here, now there, as the black plague does when, jumping from one region to the other, it harvests its victims without regard for state or language, exploiting the vehicle of the bodily humours, breath, a scrap of a piece of clothing; where the Anabaptists are concerned we know that they prefer the mechanical classes, but we can say that they may be found anywhere, and so no borders can be safe; no militia, no army, in fact, can obstruct the advance of this invisible army.

So how will we manage to halt the danger that threatens the whole of Christendom?

How many times, My Most Munificent Lord, have I asked myself that question over the past few weeks . . . How much have I racked my brains, almost reaching the conviction that in this matter Your Lordship's servant could never help his Lord.

May God will that I am mistaken, and that you will receive what I am about to suggest in a favourable manner.

So, I hope the solution will be suggested to us by the same plague spreaders; the Anabaptists themselves are showing us the way to strike them efficiently.

If, indeed, My Lord casts his mind back to the events that he was obliged to resolve ten years ago, at the time of the peasant war, availing himself at that time of this modest servant, he will recall that in order to fool the fanatic Thomas Müntzer it was useful to become familiar with him, to pretend to be on his side, so that he might, first, more easily obstruct Luther, in accordance with his nature, and then plunge into hell, once he risked turning the world upside down, let alone inadvertently helping the Emperor against the German princes.

While one is sure that the memory of those moments is still vivid in Your Lordship's mind, allow this servant to remind you that Thomas Müntzer was indeed a perfidious man, guided by Satan, but also intelligent and cunning, with a power over the mob and great oratorical skill.

And what are our Anabaptists if not so many Müntzers, except on a smaller scale?

Among them, too, there seem to be stronger personalities, spiritual guides, such as this Bernhard Rothmann, but also others, whose names might mean nothing to Your Lordship, but who are roaming the length and breadth of these lands: the names of Melchior Hofmann and Jan Matthys prime among them.

So my advice is that it is a matter of urgency for us to thwart their apparent ubiquity. We must succeed, that is, in bringing together all their leaders, all the Müntzers, the coiners, the plague spreaders, in a single place, all the rotten apples in a single basket.

But in this respect, let us remark too that we have also been placed at an advantage, since, as Your Lordship has learned from my previous missive, it is not only the attention of the Anabaptists that is flowing towards the city of Münster, but also a great crowd of people, whole families, who, bearing weapons and household objects, are heading in that direction from Holland and the Empire. Münster has become the Promised Land of the most impenitent heretics.

So I believe that it would be easy for someone to join in that flow and enter the city. He would then have to win the trust of the leaders of the sect and pretend to be friends with them in order to influence their actions without attracting too much attention, encouraging the influx of as many Anabaptists as possible.

Once the bad apples are gathered together, the prospect of being able to sweep away the most dangerous elements at a single stroke will be enough in itself to forge an alliance between Landgrave Philip and Bishop von Waldeck, Protestants and Catholics, against the most dangerous rabble-rousers.

So, since the implementation of such a plan will require involvement of a single person, the one who will be there on the spot, I consider it natural that the one who proposes the action should also, in this case, be the one who carries it out. That is why I am leaving for Münster, with the intention of borrowing a considerable figure from the Cologne branch of the Fuggers, and bringing it as a dowry to the ignorant Anabaptist husbands.

Since I will be acting undercover, it is important that I should be able to count on Your Lordship's recommendation to Bishop von Waldeck, and that he be informed of my presence in Münster and of the fact that I will contact him beforehand in order to plan what is to be done.

Once I have reached my destination, I shall hasten to give the most detailed information about what is happening there. For the moment all that remains to me is to consign myself to the will of God and His protection, in the certainty that Your Lordship will mention this humble servant in your prayers.

I kiss Your Lordship's hands.

Your Lordship's faithful servant

Q   Strasbourg, the 10th day of January 1534

The Word made flesh
(1534)

Chapter 23

On the outskirts of Münster, Westphalia, 13 January 1534

I jump to my feet at the sound of the distant rumble, the cannon in my ears, my eyes narrowed to slits, more men fleeing on the plain.

No. It's just the thunder that's been following us along the road for days. Different time, different vision. The straw, stinking and warm: the animal warmth of cows and men that brings me back here. And a sudden cold gust that drags me from sleep, not far from the breath of the ox. A huge round eye is studying me: the daily rumination has already begun.

At the window, a very strange, ferrous light beneath a low sky, filled with clouds and frost that awaits the courageous people on the road towards the city.

There goes the second, another shiver in my memory: the uneasy animals know more than we do about what awaits us out there. I try to banish the images of the past.

The third thunderclap is a flicker that splits the horizon. It is coming quietly closer, as the sparrows cry out with hunger and the frustration of not being able to fly. It will crush us, an even blackness spread across the whole of the sky.

And who can say whether the end won't come like this: the undertow or the flood, rather than the earthquake of the cannons. I don't think I'd do it a second time.

And yet it isn't something to ask yourself at dawn, on a stomach that's been empty for two days and with all those miles behind you.

That's the fourth, much closer. It's almost on top of us. A crash that shakes the earth, and the sudden roar of rain bouncing off the leaves and hammering down from the roof.

I look at the road, already a channel of mud sliding down the low hill: only two madmen would travel in weather like this.

Two men like us.

I hear him groaning in the shadow of the stable, cursing quietly to himself.

The horizon is completely closed: the city, too, might easily have ceased to exist.

'Oh, Jan . . . Have you never thought that the Day of Judgement might be like this? Come and see, the countryside's in a terrible state. It seems unbelievable that the earth and the sky could ever return to the way they were . . .'

Rustle of crushed straw, balance still uncertain: he staggers out, blinking his eyes. 'What the fuck are you on about? It's just winter.'

'There it is! Down there!'

A grey outline, blurred by the flood, is barely visible.

'Are you sure?'

'That's it.'

'How do you know? We've lost our way.'

'That's it, I tell you. I've been there before.'

We almost start running.

We appear on the rim of the hill and there it is, just a few miles away, but the clouds have spared it. It isn't raining on the city: the sky is split above the church towers and a column of light descends to envelop the walls.

That is exactly how I've always imagined the celestial city . . .

'I tell you they'll remember this day, brother, they'll remember it as the beginning.'

His eyes are bright, the water runs from his beard and from the brim of his hood. 'Definitely. They'll remember the day when the apostles of the great Matthys came to bring them hope. This is the beginning.'

I can hear that he's about to explode, chaotic zealous apostle pimp, overwhelmed by the ecstasy of being here.

He makes an ostentatious chivalric gesture to allow me to pass, but he is genuinely excited. 'Welcome to the New Jerusalem, Brother Gert.'

Our eyes are laughing. 'Welcome to you, Jan of Leyden, and take care you don't get left behind.'

We charge down the hill, slipping on the rain-soaked grass, getting back to our feet and laughing like drunks.

Chapter 24

Münster, 13 January 1534

The Latin name, Monasterium, would make you think of a place of peace and remoteness from the world.

Münster, on the contrary, asks to be shod with fire.

Nine gates to pass through. Above each gate three cannon: thick walls, narrow passageways.

Four low, massive towers protrude towards the cardinal points, turning the city into an outpost.

The whole thing surrounded by walls that can be walked by three men side by side.

The water in the moat is the deviated course of the River Aa, which bisects the city. It's a double moat, black water before the first piece of wall and black water behind it, crossed by little bridges leading to the second, lower piece, with its stocky towers.

Impregnable.

'Brothers and sisters, the wayfarers that we were waiting for have come. Enoch and Elijah have crossed the world and arrived in Münster to tell us that the time is nigh, that the days of the rich are numbered and the power of the bishop will be abolished for ever. Today we know for certain that what awaits us is freedom and justice. Justice for us, brothers and sisters, justice for anyone who is held in servitude, forced to work for a starvation wage, anyone who has faith and sees the house of the Lord sullied with images, and children being washed with holy water like dogs under a fountain.

'Yesterday I asked a five-year-old boy who Jesus was. Do you know what he replied? A statue. That's what he said: a statue. In his little mind, Christ is nothing but the idol before which his parents force him to say his prayers before going to bed! For the papists, that is faith! First learn to venerate and to obey, then understand and believe! What kind of faith can that be, and what pointless torment for children! But they want to baptise them, yes, brethren, because they fear that without baptism the Holy Spirit won't descend upon them. In that way the act of faith becomes secondary: consciences are washed with holy water before sins can be committed. And so their baptism covers the most unutterable acts of vileness: taking money from the work of their neighbours, the accumulation of possessions, ownership of the lands that *you* cultivate, the looms that *you* put into operation. The old believers don't want to allow anyone to choose what life to lead, they want you to work for them and be contented with the faith that the doctors hand down to you. Theirs is a faith of condemnation, it is the faith passed off on us by the Antichrist! But we, brothers, we want Redemption! We want freedom and justice for all! We want freely to read the Word of the Lord, and freely to choose who will speak to us from the pulpit and who will represent us on the council! Who decided the destinies of the city before we kicked him out? The bishop. And who decides now? The rich, the important burghers, illustrious admirers of Luther only because his doctrine allows them to resist the bishop! And you, brothers and sisters, you who make this city live, you can't object to their decisions. You can only obey, as that same Luther bawls from his princely lair. The old believers come and tell us that good Christians can't be preoccupied with the things of the world, that they must cultivate their faith in private, suffer abuses in silence, because we are all sinners condemned to atone for our wrong-doings.

'But here are the messengers of hope, here are people who will announce the end of the old heaven and the old earth, so that we can lay claim to others. These two men have heard our cries of indignation and have come to bear witness, like Enoch and Elijah, to tell us we are not alone, that the time has come. The powerful of the earth will be toppled, their thrones will fall, by the hand of the Lord. Christ comes not to bring peace, but a sword. The gates will be open to those who dare. If they think they can crush us with a blow of the sword, then we shall parry that blow with the sword to return it one hundredfold.'

Bernhard Rothmann. Before me I have courage, rage, balls, the vast force of a faith that I haven't encountered for a long time. Magister, if you were here now, if things had turned out differently, perhaps you would have a sense that all wasn't lost, that something, creeping beneath the ashes and emerging from them, survived to fertilise a new earth. One hundred, two hundred? I've forgotten how to count crowds; you had taught me, I've forgotten. I've forgotten the strength, Magister, and you can no longer teach me anything. I'm someone else, maybe a son of a bitch, disillusioned and furious, and yet for the first time, after so many years, in the right place. It was here, here and nowhere else, that we had to reach this truth: no faith without conflict. That's how it's always been and even if none of my faith means anything any more, something's coming back today, something fiery that I had lost on that plain in May. It's the knowledge you gave me: we will never free our spirits without freeing our bodies. And if we can't do that, we won't know what to do with them: there are times when misery and the gallows are not all that different from one another. And then it's still worth breaking the yoke and accepting what destiny will hand us in the end. We'll go on fighting. Again. Or we will die trying.

Now it's Jan of Leyden's turn, ready, resolute, and he's got an audience. His gaze glides about in the void above their heads, don't miss it, Jan, this is your moment: an actor's pose, excessive and ridiculous as ever, he vomits forth absurd words that gradually acquire meaning in the mind and find a particular sequence, hit home. It might be his movements, his gestures, his eyes, gaping wide one moment, bewitching the next, it might be his beauty, his youth. What do I know? I know that it works.

'Jan walks these streets, without a destination, like a drifting shipwrecked man, and searches for a sign, a clue to tell him whether this is the place where he will find what he's looking for –' His voice suddenly rises. 'Stupid fucker, son of a Leyden whore. The sign isn't anywhere around you, it isn't in the walls, in the bricks, in the limestone, in the cobbles, no, that isn't where you'll find what you're looking for. The sign is the search itself, the sign is you hobbling out of the mud of the roads. It's you. We who are questing: we who are the now, the past and that which is yet to come. The old are stationary, they've already been. Old believers, dead already. The bricks of the cathedral say nothing. But your eyes say that God is here, God is here now, His Spirit is among us, in this youthfulness, in these arms, these muscles, legs, breasts, eyes. Something immense is in view on the threshold of life, dirty, cursed, inane fucking life that you thought was a silent fart in the divine plan. And it isn't! God will make a soldier of you. Listen to Him: He is calling you to work. Listen to Him, listen inside yourselves. There it is, you can hear Him calling the roll for the last battle. Jan, listen, you cursed worm!' His eyes suddenly narrow, two blue slits, they fly close over the people's heads, they float, then they rise again, in a hiss: 'Yes, you, idiotcharlatanwhoremonger, because that's what we're talking about, what do you think? Do you think you're fighting for a scrap of paper daubed with your civic freedoms? To hell with it! God is talking to you about something else: not about Münster – no, not about these houses, these stones, these

streets, not about everything as it is now. But of what it will become.
Of you and me in the city, brethren! God doesn't ask you to fight for
a treaty, not for an equitable peace: but to fight for the New Jerusalem.
A new heaven and earth! A world, our new world beyond the ocean!'
Panic and, once again, astonishment on people's faces. 'This is the
promise that bans the charlatans, the indecisive, the inept, the voice-
less dregs from the call. Let them make their way right now to the
cemetery of the old faith. We will erect the pyramid of fire, we will
found the New Jerusalem. Alone, you ask? No, Jan, son of a whore!
Now you're thinking that these dirty, calloused hands that have never
been able to build anything other than castles of shit will never
manage to mix the celestial mortar. You're wrong, moron. The
promise is clear: I'll send you a prophet who will lead you into battle
and gather all your strength to spew it in the face of my enemies. Hark!
Make way for the prophet who has sent two of his emissaries today,
Jan of Leyden and Gert from the Well, to light the spark. When the
prophet arrives, we will no longer be alone and Münster will be a great
fire, a gigantic huge great pyramid of fire standing out against the sky,
splitting the clouds and building the ladder to the Kingdom. I know
it, the name already chills the blood of the powerful, the rich and the
godless, they run and hide beneath their brocade covers as soon as they
hear it echoing among the ranks of the wretched. They utter edicts,
issue rewards, stupid clay-footed giants, unaware that he is everywhere, that his apostles have reached the cities, the villages,
announcing the end of time. Jan Matthys is that name, brothers! He
is the true Enoch, the one who will come at the end of time to
inaugurate the celestial city! After us, Matthys the Great!'

Dumbfounded, embarrassed, silent. Anxiety has spread among the
rows of people while Jan was speaking, a dazed unease that makes
people look each other closely in the face, just to be sure that they are
still the same. Burghers, workers, artisans, mothers, rough faces,
strong hands. Young, all of them, since poverty doesn't give you time
to grow old. Have I really come to say that somewhere the hope of
redemption and the Kingdom still exists? The handsome maturity of
Rothmann, their preacher, and Bockelson's twenty-five years whisper
in their ears that it is possible.

A stout man, beer belly and powerful shoulders, embraces Jan of
Leyden, kissing him on his beard. Rothmann's gauntness and his
flattering voice, along with the bear-like mound of the representative
of the artisans' guilds of Münster: Berndt Knipperdolling, tanner and
tailor. He jumps on to the table we're standing on and it creaks
alarmingly. 'Welcome to the apostles of the Great Matthys, on behalf

of the entire community of the brethren of Münster. You who are present today will tell the story of this day to your grandchildren, because this is the beginning of everything. God has looked upon our city of Münster and decided: this is the place where it will all begin. We have begun the struggle, and we will take it to its conclusion. And you may be certain that it will not be easy: we will have to stand up to the bishop, we will have to wrest the power from the hands of the notables, that task may involve the shedding of sweat and perhaps even blood. But the moment has come, it cannot wait much longer. That is why I say: if anyone does not feel it, may they leave us now and go to hell. Amen.'

A single clamour of raised fists, clapping hands and clattering tools.

'Your name flies on the wings of the wind: Bernhard Rothmann, preacher of the oppressed.'

He laughs, persuasive, sincere, with a way of moving his hands and his body that wins the sympathy of the people. I couldn't say whether it's deliberate or natural, but I have already been told of the rumours circulating about the irresistible power that Rothmann exerts over the ladies of Münster. They say that more than one husband would like to see him dangling from the shafts of a cart, and not for reasons of faith. It seems that women find his sermons truly irresistible and they linger for a long time, after the functions, to discuss them in private with the preacher. Furthermore, he's not short of presence, he really doesn't show his forty years.

'Matthys's name has been talked about just as much, if not more. We anxiously await him.'

'He'll be here soon. It's important for all of us that you meet one another.'

He nods as he offers me a drink. 'There's a huge amount to be done. You've seen, we're solid, but we're few in number. We've got to gain advantage one day at a time.'

'Hm. Do you know how many of you there are?'

He shows me to a battered armchair, the only piece of furniture in the room where he's staying, apart from his wicker bed. 'It's difficult to assess the effective forces we can rely on. The situation is uncertain. Bishop von Waldeck sneaked off the minute things in the city started swinging in the direction of the Protestants, and now he's a few miles from here, conferring with his feudal lords. The Catholics have gone into hiding and are keeping their heads down as they wait for the pig to come back, possibly armed, to sweep away us Baptists and all the Lutherans.'

'And why doesn't he do it?'

'Because he knows that if he did he would reawaken the municipal spirit of Münster and everyone would form a coalition against him. The city doesn't want to go back to being his personal possession.' A smile. 'We've done something good and we've got to acknowledge that. Von Waldeck is sly, my friend, very sly. We mustn't make the mistake of underestimating him or thinking that he's out of the game. He remains our greatest enemy.'

I'm starting to understand. 'And inside the walls?'

He brightens. 'The Lutherans and the Catholics will join together to oppose our success among the people, the workers and Knipperdolling's artisans. Almost all the big merchants who vote for the council are Lutherans, and they've elected two of their own as burgomasters: Jüdefeldt and Tilbeck. Jüdefeldt is unreliable, he's a spineless wretch who's as frightened of the bishop as he would be of the devil. Tilbeck seems to have a certain regard for us, he'd do anything just to avoid having the bishop's men back in the city, but even him we can't trust too much. The common people are all on our side and that frightens them, they're afraid of being toppled. And they're right to be. In turn, however, they don't trust the Catholics, because they're afraid that the Catholics will give the city to the bishop.' He shrugs his shoulders. 'As you see, the situation is anything but certain. We've got to play on two fronts: the bishop out there, with his spies in the city, and the Lutherans inside, his adversaries but certainly not our friends. So far we've managed to beat them every time they've tried to throw us out. The population defended us, that's our strength.'

'The people, yes. Your words today reminded me of a man I knew years ago when I was more or less Jan's age. I fought for those words. And I admit that I didn't think I'd do it again.'

'Is that supposed to be a compliment?'

'I think so. But you should be aware that I lost everything back then.'

His face shows that he understands. 'Are you frightened? Is the apostle of the Great Matthys afraid of being defeated for a second time?'

'No, it isn't that. I just wanted to say that you've got to be alert, you've got to be cautious.'

He runs a hand through his hair and adjusts the pleats of his clothes, a poor fabric worn with incredible elegance. 'I know. But now I've got the very best allies by my side.' He always manages to flatter you. 'Jan of Leyden spoke with fire in his veins.'

I laugh loudly. 'Jan's a madman, a colossal rogue, a great actor and a successful whoremonger. But he knows how to do it, without a doubt. It's important to have him with us, I've seen him at work. He's a real war machine when he wants to be.'

This time we laugh together.

Chapter 25

'Good God, friends, if the faith of the inhabitants of Münster is as abundant as the tits of the women there, then I've never been anywhere so close to paradise!'

Jan of Leyden buries his excited face in the opulent bosom of his first Münsterite admirer. His words are the reason for Knipperdolling's laughter.

'And you've never seen the abundant span of the head of the city guilds,' he replies immodestly, after a few attempts to articulate a comprehensible phrase.

'A span, friend Berndt?' asks Jan with an edge of sarcasm. 'Then the indigenous people of the Americas are going to reach the Heavenly Kingdom before us!'

'What do you mean?' asks Knipperdolling, his curiosity roused, as he unlaces the bust of his lady companion.

'Oh, drop it, my friend. I wouldn't want to injure your pride.'

A cushion catches Jan full in the face. The two women giggle, amused, and repay their cavaliers with increased attentions.

The girl looking after me isn't interested in chattering, she doesn't waste time. Two or three kisses on the lips, then down she goes with her head to take care of the rest. I'd barely caught her name before I'd forgotten it again.

Meanwhile Knipperdolling is wallowing heavily among the covers. He tries to turn round and sit without detaching himself from his friend, but his paunch is giving him some problems. 'So, Jan, you're in the trade, do you have some comfortable position for those of us whose torsos have slipped?'

'Well, friend Berndt, I couldn't say. But I can tell you about when I was working with the fattest whore in Europe. You can't imagine how many customers that slut had!'

'Really! But how fat was she?'

'Listen, she was a disgusting fat pig. But people like yourself loved her to pieces.'

'In what sense?'

Jan purses his lips and squeezes the blonde's tits between his hands. His voice comes out higher than usual. ' "Yes, Matilda, your billowing plumpness makes me come. Not the thin ones, not me, because I'm a fat-fucker." '

'Oh fuck off!'

'I swear. They were all at it, even if it was just to say they'd had a woman it took five men to lift.'

A kiss aggressively administered makes Knipperdolling shut up. For my part, I don't need that kind of gag on my mouth. Half lying on the floor, with the back of my neck against the wall and a girl slowly swallowing me, I lost the power of speech some time ago.

Jan is now half suffocated by his exciting companion. You could say she'd succeeded in her attempt to shut him up.

So, it is in a general silence that Knipperdolling begins to emit a dull, puffing, definitive roar.

'Are you always in such a hurry to get to the finishing post, friend Berndt?' Jan interrogates him with his usual snigger. 'I've got a cure for cases like yours. Boil some onions in water and when it's cold you squeeze it inside.' He waves his arms in the air. 'Infallible, I guarantee it. Otherwise, if you're passing through Leyden, ask for Helen. She used to work for me. She's the only whore I know who could give you pleasure without once making you come.'

'And how does she do it?'

'No idea, but she really does. Imagine: I paid her by the hour and I really had the bookings coming in. I tell you, one time we had someone come in who wanted a quick fuck, you get me? But she managed to keep him there for at least an hour. It seems this fellow was banging away like a man possessed, but nothing happened. After a while he started getting really furious. He took out his knife and he slashed her on me, you get me? Of course it was the last thing he did in his life. Fuck's sake, spoiling my capital like that!'

Knipperdolling brushes away the hair from his girl's sweating face and looks towards Jan. 'Fuck!' is his only comment.

A small laugh escapes me, but I haven't the strength to illustrate our actor's strange habit to him: when he tells a story he can't keep from saying 'you get me?'. It's an infallible way of gauging the truth of his anecdotes.

Now Knipperdolling doesn't want to miss any of his friend the pimp's stories. 'What were you saying before about the indigenous people of the Indies?'

'When?'

'Before, remember? The story about them being ahead of us in the Kingdom of Heaven!'

'Oh nothing. I was told it by a sailor who used to be a customer of mine, who's been over there. They're much shorter than us, but they've got dicks like this. And if you're interested, another customer who's been in Africa told me that they have themselves circumcised there because the women like it much better.'

'Fucking Jews! So that's why they do it, not just because they're the chosen people.'

By now Jan, too, has reached the end. The nod to Israel gets him even more excited. He raises his arms to the sky and can't hold himself back: 'And ye shall be unto me a kingdom of priests and a holy nation.'

He holds the last word like a long lament, as he slowly subsides on to the bed.

If I know him well, that's the last we'll hear of him.

A few minutes later he's back in the saddle. So I don't know him that well.

'Ladies, gentlemen, friends, *por favor*.' Naked, arms spread, kneeling on the bed. 'Some instructions first of all, or requests if you prefer: you, friend Berndt, do you want me to die of thirst, you stingy fucking shopkeeper, is that it? Because then the heavens will punish you . . .'

'Yes, yes, yes, fuck, I'm going, I'm going right now, but, but you're worrying me, you drink like a fish, I hadn't noticed.' Knipperdolling's paunch staggers towards the next room.

'Well, look at this, bravo, bravooo!' he applauds noisily. 'And you, my friend, my devoted holy whore, go on playing with the font between my legs, while the holy pimp tells you the story of his noble origins. Yes, my dear, yes.'

Knipperdolling comes back in with three bottles of schnapps and an idiotic smile on his face, which fades when he notices that his lady has her face buried halfway up Jan's arse.

'Fine, I'm ready, or rather I'm not. Gert! Gert, is there someone there? Are you sure that the young lady hasn't dissolved you completely? She's been sucking away on you for an hour now, you're going to suffocate the poor girl!'

'Shit yourself!' is my reply.

'Ah no, my friend, that wouldn't be right, even for the good of

Madam Kiss-my-arse down there. But that's enough, now. A little attention, *por favor*!'

Knipperdolling isn't very convinced; he tries clumsily to interpose himself in the midst of the writhing flesh and regain his position.

'My mother was a German immigrant, unmarried she was. Got shagged in a ditch by old Schulze Bockel, a great womaniser in the Hague, and she brought me into the world with the name of Johann, or, in Dutch, Jan. At the age of sixteen I set off on a merchant ship: England . . . Flanders, Portugal . . . Lübeck . . . then the captain started coming on to me. One night during a storm I split his head open with an oar and threw him overboard. Two days later I disembarked in Leyden and slipped into his wife's bed. I consoled the widow for a couple of years, living in her house, going through a fair amount of her savings. The lady found me work as a tailor: she said I was cut out for the trade, I don't know what made her think that, I didn't want to do a stroke. She was a great big whore, that one: she'd swapped a fat drunkard of a husband for a wonderful twenty-year-old. But my true vocation was different, I didn't want to break my back working my whole life, I was called to do something better, something higher and more spiritual, to be an actor, write verses, I had to dump the old bag . . . live my life . . . yes. Where was I, oh yes, when I duped the widow and opened my inn . . . a real luxury whorehouse, good money and not many troubles . . . I cheered up the customers by declaiming my verses, before the girls took care of them. Once I even recited in a church, passages from the Old Testament from memory, not at all bad. The Chamber of Rhetoricians made me an honorary member. You know, they were assiduous visitors to my brothel and I gave them exceptional discounts, special rates. I was closer to God among my whores than all those literati with a bad smell under their noses, the ones who came for a good servicing.

'One day two pilgrims came, sent to me by God. One was Jan Matthys, and the other one was that guy that Inge's busy massacring on the carpet. Gert, are you still alive? And they say to me, "Jan of Leyden, the Lord hath need of thee, drop everything and follow us."'

'And you did . . .'

'Of course, because I felt it was the right thing to do, my destiny, fuck's sake, God spoke to me and said, "Jan, bastardwomantupper, I've shat you on to the earth for a reason, not so that you can roll about in the mud and the humours for the whole of your life! Arise and follow these men, there's a job to be done." And here we are receiving your welcoming committee. And our gratitude, friend Berndt, will follow you to heaven, where you will receive what you deserve!'

Knipperdolling sniggers with his hands on his balls. 'You are a cunt, Bockelson, but listen, that stuff you were saying about the indigenous people over there, listen, it's bollocks.'

'As long as your arm, Berndt, as long as your arm.'

Knipperdolling grows gloomy. Jan takes a drag from the bottle and sprawls out on the bed. He starts blethering: 'Who am I? Guess, who am I?'

Silence.

'Go on, go on, it's easy.' He picks up a corner of the blanket with two fingers and slowly begins to cover himself. 'Who am I?'

'Dead drunk.'

He pulls himself up, very serious, wrapped in the blanket. '"Cursed be Canaan; a slave of slaves shall he be to his brothers!"' A shout towards Knipperdolling: 'Who am I?'

The head of the guilds looks at me, perturbed and visibly frightened.

I'm about to reassure him when Inge raises her head, turns towards Jan and says, 'Noah.'

Chapter 26

Münster, 28 January 1534

Münster has a fascination all of its own, narrow alleyways, dark houses, the market square with the Church of St Lamberti rising at its edge: the architecture and the arrangement of the buildings, everything seems casual, chaotic, and yet as the days pass you realise that there's a hidden order in the labyrinth of streets. I have spent my free time getting to know the city by wandering aimlessly for hours, losing myself in the maze and then getting my bearings back, always at different spots in the city. I discover half-secret passages, I chatter with the tradesmen, the people here are open with strangers, perhaps because Anabaptism came here on the feet of wandering Dutch prophets. I have met one of them, Heinrich Rol, who has been assigned a parish inside the walls. We spent a long time talking about Holland, he told me the names of brethren from there, I didn't recognise any of them. They say that Münster has fifteen thousand inhabitants, but on market days it must be more than that. The burghers here are the kind that travel, textile factories, loads of workers. Getting rid of the bishop allowed them to abolish taxes on textiles and compete with the products of the monasteries: the friars have a tough time, the merchants get fat. I've learned how to harness the strength that comes out of places, those walls exude excitement, discontent, life: it's a major crossroads, between northern Germany and the Lower Rhine, but there's a vital energy that comes from the city itself, from the conflict that is being born among the dirt and the cartwheels.

Münster is one of those places that give you the sense that something is bound to happen sooner or later.

I'm dashing through the mud of the street, already enveloped in darkness, paying no heed to the dirt splashing my trousers, I'm flying fast, on the tips of my boots, all the way home. It was Knipperdolling who sent us to get everyone, they found me in the inn, lingering over a theological dispute between two blacksmiths. Quick, quick, big trouble, the boy who tracked me down told me to run to the house of the leader of the guilds, and to wear the pin on my coat, a little piece of copper showing the acrostic of our motto: DWWF, The Word Made Flesh, without which I wouldn't get in.

Three knocks on the door, and after a moment a voice asks, 'Who are you?'

'Gert from the Well.'

'What's the password?'

I show the brooch: 'The Word made flesh.'

Bolts running back: Rothmann nods to me to come in, a rapid glance at my shoulders before closing the door again.

'It's a stroke of luck that we found you. There's a nasty wind blowing.'

'What's happening?'

'Haven't you heard?'

I shrug my shoulders in apology.

Worry is clearly apparent in his face. 'The bishop, that son of a bitch, has issued an edict: he's taken away all our civil rights, from us and anyone who supports us. He threatens repercussions on the townspeople if they continue to cover for us.'

'Shit.'

'Von Waldeck is preparing something, I know him, he wants to divide us, he hopes he can win the Lutherans over to his side and leave us isolated. Come on, we've called this meeting to decide how to react. We need everyone's opinion.'

The dining room is already crowded, about twenty people are jostling around the circular table, the noise is like the sound of the market from a distance. Knipperdolling and Kibbenbrock are whispering among themselves, the purple faces of the two representatives of the weavers' guilds speak for themselves.

When they see me, they gesture to me to sit down next to them. I push my way through, Bockelson is already there, a grave nod of greeting. 'You've heard about the edict?'

'Rothmann told me, I didn't know anything about it, I've been farting around all day.'

Rothmann calls for silence with broad gestures; the other brethren hush one another.

'Brethren, this is a serious time, there's no point hiding it, von Waldeck's offensive is aimed at isolating us in the city, putting us outside the law so that we can be persecuted, possibly with the connivance of the Lutherans. Tonight we've got to decide how to defend ourselves, now that the bishop has shown his cards and is giving battle, and we face great danger.'

A knock at the door, startled faces, someone runs to see, the password echoes through to us, more than one, there are a few of them.

About a dozen workmen, hammers and hatchets in their hands, at their head a tiny, thin, dark man, a huge pistol in his belt, the face of a right bastard, rapid movements. It's Redeker, highwayman by trade, who joined the Baptists to relieve the rich of their purses and then converted to the common cause. Rothmann himself baptised him a few days ago, after he had given proof of his affability by donating to the Baptist fund the proceeds of his most lucrative plunder: five hundred gold florins taken from the bishop's knight, von Büren, a memorable enterprise.

Rothmann rages at everyone with his expression. 'What does it mean?'

'That people don't want to sit twiddling their thumbs while the noose is being tightened around their necks.'

'It isn't a good reason for coming armed into Knipperdolling's house, Brother Redeker. We mustn't give our enemies a pretext for attacking us.'

'It's going to happen anyway, what do you think?' The little man is black with rage. 'Strike at the right time, that's what we've got to do, and soon. The Lutherans are ready to kiss von Waldeck's arse and sell the lot of us! They've seen weapons being transported on the other bank of the canal, to Überwasser monastery: they're preparing to attack us.'

'Redeker's right, fuck it. We can't wait until they come through that door to slit our throats!' The echo comes from everyone who's been listening, a chorus of incitements. 'That's right! Let's give it to them right now, finish them off once and for all!'

Rothmann narrows his eyes, a wolf. 'What do you want to do?'

Redeker stands up to him, rooted solidly in the middle of the room: 'I say, get rid of them. Let's cut the papists' throats, let's cut the Lutherans' throats. I'd rather trust a snake than Jüdefeldt and his mates in the council.'

'And what about Tilbeck? The other burgomaster isn't hostile to us, do you want to slit his throat too?'

'They're all in it together, Rothmann, can't you see that? One plays nice cop, the other plays nasty cop, they're corrupt, they'd a thousand times rather have von Waldeck than us, they're just waiting for the chance to stab us in our sleep and the bishop's offering them that chance on a silver platter. Let's put an end to all this, and anyone who's got to go to hell, let them go there right now.'

Rothmann folds his arms and takes a few dramatic and meditative paces. 'No, brothers, no. That can't be the way.' He waits until his words have attracted everyone's attention. 'We've been struggling for two years, together, sometimes alone, winning the support of the population of Münster, of the workers, step by step, scattering the seed of our message, collecting members first in the city and now from outside, too.' His eye falls on me and on Bockelson. 'Matthys's apostles are here. And other people are coming in too, led by hope all the way to our city. They are the ones, those men and those women full of faith in God and in us, yes, brothers, in us, in our capacity to win this battle, they can't see everything destroyed in a single night on a wave of panic. It isn't just their faith that gives us strength, but their material contributions, even their legacies, brothers, the money that is donated to us.' A murmur runs through the room, questioning eyes looking for the donors.

Redeker's restrained fury interrupts him: 'I've donated a bag of money to the cause as well. And now I'm saying, with that money, let's buy cannon!'

'Yes, a cannon and swords!'

'And pistols?'

'No, we're not going to sort everything out that way, not our efforts, Redeker, not our work. If we start a massacre now, what will the neighbouring cities say, what will the brethren say, the ones who are looking to Münster as a beacon of revitalised Christianity? They'll think we're bloodthirsty madmen and they'll hold back. What you've given to the cause, what others are giving today, isn't the booty of war. And I say that it can be employed very differently and put to good use.'

'What the fuck does that mean?'

'It means that today the bishop is trying to turn the population against us, threatening the population if they support us. So we've got to act in such a way that they stay on our side. We have to be the captains of the humble, not only of ourselves. Don't you understand what von Waldeck wants? I'm not going to play his game, we will react, Redeker, but more effectively.' A pause to create a sense of expectation. 'I propose that the assembly deliberate on the use of the money collected in favour of a fund for the poor. To which all the needy can have access, in a manner which we will decide, a mutual aid kitty, and the ones who have more should contribute to it as they can.'

Seated, Knipperdolling and Kibbenbrock nod, convinced.

Redeker sways on his legs, undecided: it isn't enough.

Rothmann insists, 'Then the poor will understand that their cause is our cause. The mutual assistance fund will be worth more than any sermon, something tangible in their lives. The Lutherans can plot as long as they want, but we'll be stronger, the bishop can issue a thousand edicts, but we'll have the people on our side!'

He has finished, they stand and look at each other for a long time. Behind Rothmann there is a nodding of heads, behind Redeker a rumble of uncertainty.

The brigand twists his mouth: 'And what if they decide to fuck us over?'

I stand up, sending my chair flying. From under my coat I throw my dagger on the table, Rothmann and Knipperdolling give a start. 'If it's force they want to try, we'll give it back in plenty, brother, on the word of Gert from the Well. But if the people are with us, the swords will be raised by the thousand.' The silence of the grave throughout the hall. 'Now let's go out there and tear up the bishop's edict, and the Lutherans will see that we aren't afraid of von Waldeck or of them. Let them think twice before attacking us.'

Everyone's astonishment quickly fades, as does Rothmann's tension.

Redeker stares at me cockily, over my sword, and barely nods. 'Fine. We'll do as you say. But none of us plans to make a martyr of himself. If I've got to be fucked over, I want to do it with my sword in my hand, taking a good few of those bastards with me.'

The agreement is reached, thanks to the words of Rothmann and the effective action of Matthys's apostle. The foundation of a fund for the poor is put to the vote: passed unanimously. Kibbenbrock, paper and pen, writes up everything in his accounting books, while Redeker organises five-man teams to tear down the edict from the walls of the city.

Rothmann and Knipperdolling take me aside as the brothers are leaving in groups of three or four so as not to be conspicuous. The night swallows their silhouettes one by one.

A slap on the shoulder and a compliment: 'The right words. That was what they wanted to hear you say.'

'And that's what I think. Redeker is crazy, but he knows his stuff. We've managed to bring him to reason and he's understood.'

Knipperdolling shrugs his shoulders. 'He's a highwayman, hard to deal with . . .'

'A bandit who steals from the rich knights to give to the poor. We need people like that. Matthys says it's among the scum of the street that we'll find the soldiers of God, among the last men, the outlaws, the acrobats, the pimps . . .' I gesture towards Bockelson, who is crouching on a chair near the fire, half asleep with his hands on his balls.

The big weaver scratches his beard: 'Do you think it'll come to an armed fight?'

'I don't know; von Waldeck doesn't strike me as the kind of man to give in easily.'

'And what about the Lutherans?'

'I think that'll depend on them.'

Knipperdolling goes on rubbing his chin. 'Hm. Listen, it's less than a month to the elections to renew the council and the burgomasters. Kibbenbrock and I could stand as candidates.'

Rothmann shakes his head. 'Our supporters are too poor to be able to vote; either you change the ordinance or you're lost before you start.'

The opinion of Matthys's apostles seems to be essential. I insist, 'I wish with all my heart for you to succeed and take the city peacefully, but in this atmosphere things might turn out differently.'

Rothmann nods gravely. 'Sure. We'll see. Meanwhile let's get the fund for the poor working straight away. Elections or no, we'll manage to put the Lutherans and the Catholics in a minority. As a precautionary measure, we'll shift the services from the parishes to private houses to protect against spies.'

'May the Lord help us.'

'I don't doubt it for a moment, my friends. Now if you will permit me, I'm going with the brothers to make confetti out of the bishop's edict.'

'And what about Jan, are you leaving him here?' Knipperdolling reminds me of my friend's body sprawled by the fire.

'Let him sleep, he wouldn't be much use to us anyway . . .'

Outside the night is icy, there's no light. I shiver in my cloak as I look for the way to the market square. I'm helped by my memory of drifting at length through those alleyways. Barely a shadow, the hint of a presence and I've already got my dagger ready, pointing into the darkness ahead of me.

'Stay your hand, brother.'

'Why should I?'

'Because the Word is made flesh.'

A face emerges from the darkness. It was at the meeting.

'A bit closer and I'd have run you through without a second thought . . . Who are you?'

'Someone who's been admiring your way of doing things. Heinrich Gresbeck is my name.' A diagonal scar runs across his eyebrow, blue eyes, well-built, more or less my age.

'Are you from around here?'

'No, from not far away, although the last time I found myself in these parts was ten years ago.'

'Preacher?'

'Mercenary.'

'I didn't think there were any Baptists who had been trained to fight.'

'Just you and me.'

'Says who?'

'I can tell a good swordsman. Matthys knows how to choose his men.'

'Is that all you wanted to tell me?'

His face is hollow, the scar makes his features look darker and more menacing than they really are. 'I admire Rothmann, he was the one who baptised me. We've got a great preacher, sooner or later we'll have a captain, too.'

'You mean me. Why not you?'

He laughs, white teeth. 'Enough of your jokes. I'm little Gresbeck, you're the great Gert from the Well, the apostle. They'll follow you, the way they listened to you this evening.'

'They're not mercenaries, brother.'

'I know. They won't be fighting for booty, they'll be fighting for the Kingdom, so they'll be able to smash everyone's head in. But someone's going to have to lead them.'

'I'm taking Matthys's place until he . . .'

'Matthys was a baker, let's not beat around the bush, that guy from Leyden was a pimp, Knipperdolling and Kibbenbrock are weavers, Rothmann's a man of the Bible.'

I nod, saying nothing more. A reassurance: 'When the time comes you'll know where to find me.'

'We'll all be there. And now let's go and wipe our arses with that edict.'

He is already heading off into the night of the alleys, in search of the ghost of von Waldeck.

Chapter 27

Tile Bussenschute, known as the Cyclops, a box maker by trade, is a gigantic, mythological creature.

Bussenschute is one of those people you hear mothers using as warnings when they've reached the end of their tether: 'If you don't go to sleep I'm calling the box maker . . .'

Everything about him is enormous, apart from his brain. I don't know what Kibbenbrock told him when he fetched him from his shop, but even if he had explained matters line by line, backing them up with sign language, I'm quite sure the box maker wouldn't have had the faintest idea about what he was on about. He's cross and uncomfortable in the only elegant piece of clothing we could manage to get him into: it came from Knipperdolling's wardrobe and has considerable difficulty containing the belly, arse and countless double chins of the leader of our delegation. As a rule he doesn't speak, he grunts; they say he was ruined by three years' imprisonment for murder: he was working as a porter and on the steps of some building or other he threw an assistant a weight so heavy it knocked him off balance and rolled him down the length of a ramp before finally crushing him.

Right behind Bussenschute, completely obscured by his vast bulk, comes Redeker, who shared a cell with our box maker in the bishop's prison for a time. He certainly hasn't given up his vice of pinching other people's wallets, but he's got the even worse habit of bragging publicly about his activities, and sooner or later it's going to get him into trouble.

Last in this trio is Hans von der Wieck, pettifogging lawyer, who recently stood for election to the delegation. He really thinks he'll be able to negotiate peace with the bishop and the Lutherans, and he didn't know how to get out of it when we decided to turn the encounter into a bit of a carnival.

The bishop called that Diet to find a compromise between the two sides that would allow him back into the city, and if it were up to

Burgomaster Jüdefeldt, who is able by right to participate in the delegation of townspeople, a compromise would be reached, to our disadvantage: von Waldeck would concede a few municipal freedoms to keep Jüdefeldt's rich Lutheran friends happy, he'd regain control of his principality and liquidate the Baptists and the people would get shat on. *Divide et impera*, the old story.

There wasn't much option but to send the whole caboodle sky-high. We forced Jüdefeldt and the council to accept the presence of the representatives of the people of Münster we had chosen for the occasion: a monstrous giant, a highwayman, a pettifogger and us lot all standing right behind them.

We climb the stairs one after the other, in an orderly line, trying to strike a pose. Knipperdolling has tears in his eyes, spluttering away as he tries to control his laughter. He was the first one to put the big man's name forward, when we were looking for the right person to head our delegation: 'Tile the Cyclops! Yes, yes, he's the man to put our case!'

The hall where the Diet is being held, in the home of the knight Dietrich of Merfeld, one of the silverest tongues ever to lick a bishop's arse: inlaid beams, coarse tapestries on the walls in a vulgar style, tuppenny swank. The thrones on which the bishop's vassals are seated open up like the wings of a bird. The host sits to the right of the throne, swollen with pride: all the banners are spread to impress the poor ignorant burghers.

Throne in the middle, lion's-head wooden hand rests, the episcopal coat of arms next to his family escutcheon perched atop the seat back.

Very impressive, dressed in black from head to toe. Shiny boots; fine woollen breeches and an elegant blouse; the buckle on his belt, keeping his sword in place, a thoroughbred Toledo to judge by the inlay; the episcopal ring gleams on his finger, gold and ruby, and on his chest gleams the princely medallion of the Empire. Inside, a thin, upright body.

The face of the enemy.

Silver hair and grey beard, a hollow face, no cheeks to speak of, the woodworm of power devouring him for years.

Von Waldeck: five decades worn lightly, the expression of an eagle that has spied its prey from above.

Here he is.

Tile Bussenschute, overawed by the gold and the decorations, manages a bow, placing the stitches and buttons of Knipperdolling's clothes in the gravest danger.

One of the bishop's knights twists round in his chair, stretches his

neck and hoists himself up, hands on his armrests, to see who is hiding
behind this mountain of flesh making sluggishly for the centre of the
room. Until the cyclopean box maker bows deeply to reveal, behind
him, the nonchalant grin of Redeker.

It's a moment to cherish. Melchior von Büren, attacked on the road
near Telgte not more than a month ago and robbed in broad daylight,
finds himself face to face with the man who ran off with his land taxes.
Perhaps he doesn't recognise him immediately: he squints to see
better. Heinrich Redeker can't help himself, he darts forward as
though he's about to leap the great back in front of him in one bound,
face red, chest out. 'Your arse still giving you gyp, my friend?' he
mutters between his teeth.

In reply, the robber's victim draws his sword in a flash and waves it
in the face of the startled Bussenschute. 'Fight, you dog, you'll pay
back every florin with a drop of blood.'

'In the meantime, have a few drops of this!' our delegate yells at
him, spitting him full in the face, over the shoulder of the head of the
delegation.

The episcopal knight tries to reply with a blow of his sword. The
gesture makes Tile Bussenschute more than a little nervous, as he feels
the blade passing an inch from his ear. He reacts immediately: he
opens his hand wide and, using all the strength in his arm, pushes it
full in the face of the swordsman, who falls to the ground along with
his chair, knocking over two other knights.

Jüdefeldt yells at them to stop it and tries to hold Redeker back.

Von Waldeck the eagle doesn't lose his composure, he doesn't say
a word: he observes us with the best look of contempt in his repertoire.
Redeker delves into his own: insults directed at his parents, the dead,
the holy protectors. He uproots and topples his adversary's family tree
with the force of his obscenities.

Our own von der Wieck starts screeching into the midst of the
confusion, trying to adopt the tone of the serious advocate that he has
never been. 'Within the venue chosen for a Diet, immunity for all and
a complete ban on weapons!'

Von Büren's comrades hold him back as he tries to get at Redeker.
Jüdefeldt makes vain attempts to calm everyone down, embarrassed
and as purple as a helpless baby.

Everything comes to a standstill when von Waldeck rises to his feet.
We stand rooted to the spot. His gaze turns the hall to ash: he now
knows that the burgomaster is nothing, we're his adversaries. He stares
at us in silent fury, then turns round contemptuously and leaves us, he
limps towards the door, escorted by von Merfeld and his personal guard.

> Full many a nun crept o'er the walls that night
> And from the cloister made her reckless flight;
> With concupiscent lusts they were afire
> And brazenly indulged their keen desire.

Redeker concentrates on the coin he's turning over in his hands. He looks at the wall for a moment and then half closes his eyes, and knocks back his fifth beer and schnapps chaser. 'It's the last one,' he assures us immediately as we are heading back to our table.

There's a great crowd gathered around the two arenas set up between the tables in the Mercury Tavern. It's the Carnival tournaments this evening: on one side they're dancing to the sound of the lute and the last one to stop dancing wins a barrel of beer; on the other there's a pint of beer and schnapps for whoever throws a coin as close as possible to the wall without touching the wall itself. Redeker is the undisputed champion.

Knipperdolling has a tab with the landlord and he's plunging into it for all he's worth. Four empty beakers are already lined up in front of his spongy nose. He gets up on his rather unsteady feet and stands on his chair, trying to call the attention of the room and starts improvising, to the lute music, a song about what everyone's talking about:

> What drove them from the cloister must have been
> A serpent bold, a spirit most unclean.
> And then, when in their folly they had fled
> They sought out impure company instead.

Two tables away, someone picks up the guild leader's rhymes and continues the description of the fugitives from Überwasser. He doesn't get to the end before someone else has taken up the invitation and celebrates Rothmann's actions beneath the walls of the convent. It goes like this: whoever started the song, in this case our Knipperdolling, buys a drink for the one who brings it to an end. It's a competition to see who will leave the whole tavern without a verse to add.

'The best bit was when he reminded the nuns of their procreative functions. I don't know how he kept a straight face,' Kibbenbrock recalls, shaking his head in disbelief.

'Right, though, wasn't he?' someone else throws in. 'What's so funny? Even the Bible says we've got to multiply.'

'Of course, and what made me laugh was the abbess facing the window, trying to call her sisters back to the love of their only true husband!'

'That old whore von Merfeld! She's an old bitch and the bishop's spy! So long to all those lovely novices.'

A round of beer arrives, paid for by Redeker with the booty collected in Wolbeck. The little bandit dances on a table to the rhythm of the chants in his honour. He's drunk. He lets his trousers down as he swings his hips, loudly repeating the invitation made to the nuns by Rothmann's supporters a few hours ago: 'Come on sisters, consolation for these poor men!'

An old man with a pair of big whiskers hugs me and Knipperdolling from behind. 'The next round's on me, boys,' he exclaims contentedly. 'Ever since I discovered my dick, I've been standing under the convent windows with my mates at Carnival time propositioning the nuns but, my God, I'd never managed to get them to escape like that. Fair play to you, well done!'

We raise our beakers to drink to the compliment. The only one who leaves his on the table is Jan of Leyden. Strangely, he still hasn't said a word. He's sitting stock still in his seat, looking apathetic. If I know him well, he's pissed off because he didn't come with us to raise hell under the Überwasser tower. He tried to get a similar result with the prostitutes in one of the city brothels, inviting them to give a free fuck to anyone who would have himself rebaptised by Rothmann, but he got only insults for his pains.

He raises his eyes and sees that I'm staring at him. He starts irritably scratching his shoulder as though to act nonchalant, but it doesn't work. He exploits a moment's silence and butts in, 'Hey, people, this is an easy one, look: Who am I, eh? Who am I?' He scratches himself harder and harder, using a soup-covered spoon. Knipperdolling stiffens in his chair. Some people look elsewhere to avoid the direct question. I feel duty bound to save them: 'You're Job scratching his boils, Jan, it's obvious.' Then, turning back to the others, 'How come you didn't work that one out? He was brilliant, wasn't he?'

A chorus: 'Yes, yes, bravo Jan!'

The actor mocks himself: 'Yes, fine, all right, that was an easy one. But pay attention now.' He slips from his chair and under the table with a catlike movement, blowing hard between his teeth. 'Who am I? Who am I?'

Knipperdolling stands up as quietly as possible, murmuring that he has to go for a piss.

From below the voice insists, 'Don't leave just because you don't know! I'll give you a hand: "Yet hast Thou brought up my life from corruption, O Lord my God. When my soul fainted within me I remembered the Lord my God." '

'Who's reciting the Book of Jonah from memory in the pub?' The incredulous, rather amused voice belongs to Rothmann, who has just arrived at our table. The prophet barely has time to re-emerge from the belly of the whale before a roar of admiration explodes for the conqueror of Überwasser. A week ago he made all the women of Münster give up their jewels and hand them over to the fund for the poor, now he's persuaded a throng of nuns to embrace the renewed faith.

'You used to need money to attract women,' observes a weaver, 'now you've got to have an interest in the Scriptures. What on earth are you doing to our ladies, Bernhard?'

'I'm not going to say a word about your ladies, but all you had to say to the novices of Überwasser was that if they didn't leave, God would bring their bell tower crashing down around their ears.' An explosion of laughter. 'And yet, people, there aren't that many vocations in there: it's those fat shopkeepers, their fathers, who are persuading the novices to renounce the world just so that they don't have to stump up for a dowry.'

A glass of spirits from the landlord in person, 'for the most fascinating of all the Münsterites', lands on the table. Rothmann sips slowly. A glance at Bockelson: 'Jan has a disheartened look about him! What's happened to you this evening, where did you get to?'

The holy pimp leaps to his feet. 'I was looking for inspiration, you know? For the big show this evening. I utterly reject the idea of original sin! So now I'm going to take all my clothes off and, as naked as our father Adam, I'm going to walk through the streets inviting the inhabitants of the city to rediscover the uncorrupt man within.' He starts taking off his jacket, getting more and more excited, and taps

Knipperdolling's fat belly. 'Come on, Berndt, you and I will take the main parts in our play, all about the Garden of Eden!'

'Christ, Jan, it's practically snowing out there!'

Knipperdolling looks anxiously about, but allows himself to be persuaded. Jan is already undoing his belt. 'Mend your ways, citizens of Münster, strip yourselves of your sins!'

The shout makes the locals jump. Some of them start repeating it as a joke and, almost as a challenge, given how cold it is outside, about a dozen people start undressing. In an attempt to understand what's happening, Redeker gets distracted and throws his coin against the wall, losing the first of at least fifteen games.

Jan is yelling at the top of his voice. Jan is completely naked. Jan leaves the pub. Knipperdolling follows his every movement. Behind them, at least a dozen Adams. A crowd assembles in the doorway of the Mercury Tavern. They have to push their way forward to see what's going on.

Knipperdolling, despite his layers of fat, can't stand the cold, and runs like a river in full flow to try and get warm. Jan joins him. He puts himself at the head of the strange procession. The people walk down the street making the sign of the cross, although whether it's out of devotion or to avert calamity it's hard to say. We make our way through the various clusters of people, throwing ourselves to the ground in fake agitation, but we manage not to laugh. Rothmann declaims the visions of the Book of Ezekiel, Redeker foams at the mouth, I slash at imaginary demons with my sword.

Many people imitate us, amused, thinking it's a bit like a carnival. Others take it far too seriously. Some start weeping and fall on their knees pleading to be baptised. Some demand to be whipped and some throw their possessions into the street. An old man, among the first to strip naked, falls to the ground, unable to move. Kibbenbrock covers him with his fur and carries him off.

The tailor Schneider, whose daughter has already been carried away by angels once before, cries, staring into the sky, 'You see: God is enthroned among the clouds. Behold the victorious army that will crush the godless!'

He starts to run along the walls, clapping his hands; he makes the gesture of flying with his arms; he jumps, but being wingless he falls into the mud, looking very much like a crucifix.

Chapter 29

I'm woken by a burst of knocks on the door.

Instinctively my hand goes under the mattress for the handle of my dagger.

'Gert! Gert! Get up, Gert, get a move on!'

My sleep recoils, hitting me right between the eyes: who the fuck?

'Gert we're in deep shit, wake up!'

I swing out of bed, trying to keep my balance. 'Who is it?'

'It's Adrianson! Get a move on, everyone's running to the square!'

As I put on my breeches and slip into my old jacket, I'm already thinking the worst. 'What's happening?'

'Open up, we've got to get to the council!'

As he's saying the last word, I swing the door open into his face.

I must look like a ghost, but the cold sharpens my senses in a moment or two.

Adrianson, the farrier, doesn't have the jovial air that he usually brings to our evening discussions. He's completely out of breath. 'Redeker. He's just brought a stranger into the square, a man who's arrived . . . He says he saw the bishop getting an army together at Anmarsch, three thousand men. They're about to rain down on us, Gert.'

A twinge in my stomach. 'Landsknechts?'

'Move it, let's go. Redeker wants to consult the burgomasters.'

'Are you sure, though? Who is this stranger?'

'I don't know, but if what he says is true they're about to put us under siege.'

In the corridor I knock at the front door: 'Jan! Wake up, Jan!'

I open the door of my mate from Leyden, which, despite advice, is never locked. His bed hasn't been slept in.

'He's usually having a shag in some barn or other . . .'

The farrier drags me down the stairs. I almost fall to the bottom. Adrianson goes down the street ahead of me, it's been snowing all night, the slush splashes up from our boots, someone tells me to fuck off.

We run to the main square: a white meadow. At its centre, the dark mass of the cathedral looks even bigger than usual. Agitation spreads through the clusters of people collected under the Rathaus window.

'The bishop wants to enter the city with his army.'

'He can fuck off. Over my dead body!'

'It was that bitch of an abbess who called him.'

'With our taxes. That bastard's paying an army to fuck us over.'

'No, no, that big slag of an abbess of Überwasser . . . it's all because of that business with the novices.'

In spite of the frost, at least five hundred people have surged into the square on the wave of the news.

'We've got to defend ourselves, we need weapons.'

'Yes, yes, let's listen to the burgomaster.'

I spot Redeker in the middle of a group of about thirty people. He has the cocky air of someone determined to go against the grain.

'Three thousand armed men.'

'Yes, they're at the gates of the city.'

'You only have to get up on the tower over the Jüdefeldertor to see them.'

I feel a blow on my shoulder and turn round. Redeker versus the rest, snowballs in hand. Someone must have tried to shut him up. Suddenly there's turmoil. People glancing upwards: Burgomaster Tilbeck is at the window of the Rathaus.

A roar of protest.

'The bishop's army is marching on the city!'

'Someone's ratted on us!'

'We've been sold to von Waldeck!'

'We've got to defend the walls!'

'The abbess, the abbess, lock up the abbess!'

'Never mind the abbess, it's cannon we need!'

The little clusters merge into a general mob. They look even more numerous than before.

Tilbeck stiffly raises his arms to embrace the whole square. 'People of Münster, let's not lose our calm. This story of three thousand men has not yet been confirmed.'

'Bollocks, they've been seen from the walls.'

'That's right, that's right, someone's arrived from Anmarsch. They're on their way.'

The burgomaster doesn't lose his cool. He shakes his head and, with a seraphic gesture, tries to calm them down. 'Don't get worked up: we'll send someone to check.'

The crowd glance at each other impatiently.

'Army or not, Bishop von Waldeck has personally given me every guarantee that he won't violate municipal privileges. Münster will remain a free city. He's personally committed to it. We'll show them we haven't lost our heads: this is the moment to act responsibly! Münster must live up to its ancient tradition of civic tolerance and cohabitation. At a time when all adjacent territories are involved in internecine wars and revolts, Münster has to be exemplary in . . .'

The snowball catches him full in the face. The burgomaster collapses on to the windowsill, submerged in a sea of insults. One of the councillors helps him to his feet. Blood flows from his split cheekbone: something must have been hidden in the snow.

There's only one person in the whole of Münster with an aim like that.

Tilbeck beats a retreat, followed by the most furious shouting.

'Corruption! Corruption!'

'Tilbeck, you're a whore: you and all your Lutheran friends!'

'What the fuck do you expect? If it wasn't for you bloody Anabaptists, von Waldeck wouldn't raise a finger against the city.'

'Bastards, we know you're in league with the bishop!'

Some people start shoving. The first blows fly. Redeker is still on his own. There are three of them, all pretty well-built. They don't know who they're up against. The biggest of them aims a fist at face height, Redeker bends over and takes it on the ear, stumbles back and aims a kick between the other man's legs: the Lutheran bends double, his balls in his throat. Then a knee to his nose and his two comrades have a tight grip on Redeker, who is kicking away like a crazed mule. The big one hits him in the stomach. I don't give him time to do it again: a two-handed blow to the back of the neck. When he turns round, I rain blows down on his nose. He falls on his arse. I turn round. Redeker has freed himself from the clutches of the other two. Back to back, we defend ourselves against attack.

'Who thought up the story of the three thousand knights?'

He spits at his adversary and nudges me in the ribs. 'Who said anything about knights?'

I almost burst out laughing as we strike out, each man for himself. But by now it's a general riot, we're swept along by it. A troop of fifty men emerges from behind the cathedral: the weavers of St Egidius, roused by Rothmann's sermons. In a moment the Lutherans are on the opposite corner of the square.

Redeker, more of a son of a bitch than ever, looks at me with a mocking laugh. 'Better than the cavalry!'

'Great, and now what are we going to do?'

From the market square, the sound of the bells of St Lamberti. As though we're being summoned.

'To St Lamberti, to St Lamberti!'

We run to the market square and invade the stalls under the astonished gaze of the traders.

'The bishop's about to enter the city!'

'Three thousand soldiers!'

'The burgomasters and the Lutherans are in cahoots with von Waldeck!'

Among the carts, the tools of daily work are turned into weapons. Hammers, hatchets, slingshots, hoes, knives. In the blink of an eye the carts themselves become barricades, blocking all access to the square. Someone has taken the prie-dieux out of St Lamberti to reinforce these improvised walls.

Redeker grabs me in the confusion: 'The people from St Egidius have brought ten crossbows, five hackbuts and two barrels of gunpowder. I'm off to speak to Wesel the armourer to see what else I can get hold of.'

'I'll go and get Rothmann, we need him here.'

We set off without wasting any more time, quick, dashing through the furious crowds.

Knipperdolling and Kibbenbrock are also in the presbytery of St Lamberti. They're sitting disconsolately at the table and all three leap to their feet when they see me come in.

'Gert! Good to see you. What the hell's happening?'

I look hard at the preacher of the Baptists. 'An hour ago news came in that von Waldeck has prepared a force to march on the city.' The two guild representatives blanch. 'I don't know how much is true, the news must have got exaggerated along the way, but it's certainly not a carnival prank.'

Knipperdolling: 'But they're already pulling everything down, they've rung the bells, I've seen the church being emptied . . .'

'Tilbeck made an arse of himself in front of everyone. It may be that the Lutherans have drawn up an agreement with von Waldeck. The people are going wild, the weavers are already in the square, they've erected barricades, Rothmann, they're armed.'

Kibbenbrock kicks the cobblestones. 'Bloody hell! Have they all gone mad?'

Rothmann nervously drums his fingers on the table, he has to decide what's to be done.

'Redeker's gone in search of more weapons, the Lutherans might try to get us out, to hand the city over to the bishop.'

Irritated, Knipperdolling swings his great belly from side to side. 'That fucking cut-throat. He's the only one who could have come up with a story like that. But didn't you tell him he risked fucking up everything we've done? If we go all the way to armed confrontation . . .'

'We're there already, my friend. And if you don't place yourselves behind those barricades now we'll be cut off, and the people will have to advance on their own. You've got to be there.'

A long silence.

The preacher looks me straight in the eyes. 'Do you think the bishop decided to take action?'

'That's a problem we'll deal with later on. For now, we need someone to take care of the situation.'

Rothmann turns towards the other two. 'It's started, long before we could have expected. But to hesitate now would be fatal. Let's go.'

We go down into the square, there are at least three hundred men and women shouting behind the barricades, their work tools transformed into lances, clubs, halberds. Redeker pushes a cart covered with a tarpaulin towards the middle of the square. When he takes it off the blades flash in the winter sun: swords, axes, a pair of hackbuts and a pistol. The weapons are distributed, everyone wants to be holding something so that he can defend himself.

At a rapid pace, sword and pistol in his belt, the former mercenary Heinrich Gresbeck comes towards us. 'The Lutherans have stored their weapons up at Überwasser. They're bringing them to the central square.' He studies us as though he's waiting for an order from me or Rothmann.

The preacher grabs a stall from the market and drags it out, jumping on to it. 'Brothers, we mustn't start fighting each other. But if anyone doesn't understand that the true enemy is Bishop von Waldeck, then it will be up to us to defend the freedom of Münster from those who are threatening the city! And anyone who joins in this battle for freedom will not only enjoy the protection that the Supreme One reserves for his elect, but will have access to the mutual assistance fund which is, from this moment, made available to our common defence force.' A roar of acclaim. 'The Pharaoh of Egypt is outside these walls and he wants to return to enslave us once again. But we will not let him. And God will be with us in this undertaking. In fact, the Lord says, "They also that uphold Egypt shall fall; and the pride of her power shall come down: from the tower of Syene shall they fall in it by the sword. And they shall know that I am the Lord when I have set a fire in Egypt, and when all her helpers shall be destroyed!'"

Hearts rise in unanimous excitement: the people of Münster have found their preacher once again.

The imposing Knipperdolling and red-faced Kibbenbrock wander about among the clusters of the weavers; most of the members of the most organised and sizeable corporation are already there.

Gresbeck takes me aside. 'This looks like the moment of truth.' A glance behind him. 'You know what's needed.'

I nod. 'Assemble the thirty fittest men in front of the church, people who are familiar with the city and not overburdened with scruples.'

We join Redeker, who has finished emptying the cart.

'Form three squadrons of four men each, and send them off to walk around Überwasser: I want a report every hour on the positions of the Lutherans.'

The little man darts away.

To Gresbeck: 'I've got to be mobile. You're in command of the square. Don't let anyone take any spontaneous initiatives; don't let anyone take us by surprise; man the barricades; put a sentry on the church bell tower. How many hackbuts have we got?'

'Seven.'

'Three in front of the church and four by the entrance to the central square. They won't be much use if they're scattered around the place.'

Gresbeck: 'And what will you do?'

'I've got to work out how the battlefield's to be organised and who's in which positions.'

Redeker, in seventh heaven, is getting the men together. He sees me, raises a huge pistol and shouts, 'Let's get the fuckers!'

The reconnaissance from the walls has been reassuring: as far as the eye can see there isn't a trace of the three thousand mercenaries we'd been warned about.

The second patrol turns up to say that the Lutherans have placed men armed with hackbuts on the cathedral bell tower, and from there they are dominating the Rathaus square, the entrance to which is barred by two carts placed sideways across it, exactly opposite ours. There are no more than ten Lutherans behind the carts, but they're well armed, with supplies from Überwasser: in case of attack they wouldn't need to spare their bullets. We, on the other hand, have to make do with what we've got and we're short of ammunition.

The market square where we've barricaded ourselves is easily defensible, but it could also prove to be a trap. We've got to go round the barricades, close the bridges over the Aa and cut the Rathaus square off from the monastery.

'Redeker! Ten men and two hackbuts. We want to close off Our Lady's bridge, behind the square. Right now.'

We leave the garrison to the south of our fortification. We manage the first stretch quickly, no one in sight. Then the road forks: we've got to go to the right and follow the bend leading to the first bridge over the canal. We're there, the bridge is right ahead of us. A shot from a hackbut smashes into the wall a yard away from Redeker, who is at our head. He turns round. 'Lutherans!'

More hackbut fire booms from a narrow little alleyway leading to the central square.

'Come on, come on!'

As we're going back up the street we are followed by shouting and a general hubbub: 'The Anabaptists! There they are! They're getting away!'

We stop when we reach St Egidius.

I call to Redeker, 'How many did you see?'

'Five, six at the most.'

'Let's wait for them here and when they come round the corner we'll fire.'

We load up: two hackbuts, my pistol and Redeker's.

They leap out about ten yards away: I count five of them, they weren't expecting this, they slow down, while our guns fire in unison.

One of them is hit in the head and goes straight down, another falls backwards, injured in the shoulder.

We go on the attack and they retreat confused, dragging the wounded man behind them. Others appear round the corner, some of them slip into St Egidius. More shots, then impact: I parry a blow with my dagger and the barrel of my gun splits open the Lutheran's head. This is one hell of a mess. More gunshots.

'Come on, Gert! They're firing from the bell tower! Come on!'

Someone grabs me from behind, we're running like crazy with the bullets whistling around us. We're not going to get through here.

We reach our barricades and slip in behind them. We count ourselves straight away: we're all there, more or less intact apart from a sword slash to a forehead, which is going to need stitches, a shoulder dislocated by the recoil of a hackbut and a good dose of fear for everyone.

Redeker spits on the ground. 'The bastards. Let's get a cannon and bring St Egidius down round their ears!'

'Forget it, it was a fiasco.'

Knipperdolling and some of his men come running towards us. 'Hey, anyone injured? Anyone killed?'

'No, no one, luckily, but we've got a head here that's going to need stitches.'

'Don't worry, needle and thread's our speciality.'

The weavers take in the wounded man.

In our absence, in the middle of the square, where the traders' stalls had been, a fire has been lit to cook lunch: some women are turning a calf on a spit.

'Where the hell did that come from?'

A fat, red-faced woman carrying crockery comes up beside me with a nudge: 'Generously donated by Councillor Wördemann. His grooms wouldn't accept our money, so we took it . . . ever so politely!' She giggles contentedly.

I shake my head: 'Cooking, that's all we need.'

The fat woman puts down her load, puts her hands on her hips and stands there defiantly. 'And how were you planning on feeding your soldiers, Captain Gert? With lead? Without the women of Münster you'd be finished, believe me!'

I turn to Redeker. 'Captain?'

The bandit shrugs.

'Yes, Captain.' Rothmann's voice comes from behind us, he's with Gresbeck, they're holding some parchments. The preacher looks as though he doesn't want to waste time on explanations. 'And Gresbeck is your lieutenant . . . He notices Redeker's immediate agitation, as the man stretches his neck in between us to get himself noticed, and immediately adds with resignation, 'and Redeker your deputy.'

'It hasn't gone well. I wanted to go round the square, but they took us by surprise before we could cross the canal.'

'Our patrols tell us they're barricaded in at Überwasser. Burgomaster Jüdefeldt is with them, along with most of the councillors apart from Tilbeck. There's about forty of them, I don't think they'll try to attack us, they're on the defensive. They've got a cannon in the convent cemetery, the building's impregnable.'

I breathe out. What now?

Rothmann shakes his head. 'If the bishop really has got a force together, things could go very badly.'

Gresbeck unrolls the parchments in front of me. 'Have a look at this, in the meantime. We've got hold of some old maps of the city. They might be useful to us.'

The drawing isn't precise, but they show even the narrowest passages and every bend and corner of the Aa.

'Excellent. Let's see if they suggest anything to us. Now, though, we've got things to do. Redeker gave me the idea. Let's drag a cannon down from the walls, quite a small one, not too heavy, one which could be easily transported here.'

Gresbeck scratches his scar. 'We'll need a winch.'

'Get one. Seven hackbuts would barely be enough if we had to resist an attack. Take the men you need, but make sure you get the cannon down here as quickly as you can, time's moving on, and when it starts to get dark we're going to have to be well protected.'

I stay alone with Rothmann. The preacher's face shows admiration mixed with a hint of reproach. 'Are you sure you know what you're doing?'

'No. Whatever Gresbeck thinks, I'm not a soldier. Cutting off the people in the square seemed to me to be the right idea, but they've clearly organised troops to search the streets all around. The bastards are covering their arses.'

'You've fought before, haven't you?'

'A former mercenary taught me to fight with a sword, many years ago. I've fought with the peasants, but I was a boy then.'

He nods resolutely. 'Do whatever you think is necessary. We'll be with you. And may God sustain you.'

At that moment, behind Rothmann's back, Jan of Leyden appears at the end of the square. He spots us too and comes over, an almost amused expression on his face.

'Finally! Where have you been?'

He moves his hand up and down in an allusive gesture. 'You know how it is . . . But what's been happening, have we taken the city?'

'No, you fucking whoremonger, we're barricaded in here; the Lutherans are outside.'

He follows my gesture and gets excited. 'Where?'

I point to the barricade fronted by the carts at the entrance to the central square.

'Are they in behind there?'

'Exactly, and they're armed to the teeth.'

I recognise the expression on my holy pimp's face, it's the one he uses for special occasions. 'Careful now, Jan . . .'

It's too late, he's making for our defences. I haven't got time to think about him, I've got to go and instruct our patrols. But while

I'm talking to Redeker and Gresbeck, out of the corner of my eye I
see Jan approaching the defenders of the barricade – what the hell is
he thinking about? I calm down when I see him sitting down and
taking the Bible out of his pocket. Good man, you just read
something.

The map of Münster shows us how many different paths we could
take to get round the Lutheran fortifications. Redeker gives us a lot of
advice, telling us which are the most exposed areas, which buildings
could be used as cover if we were to try to approach them. But all
conjecture comes to a halt in the face of the impregnability of
Überwasser: getting the novices out was one thing, taking the place
when it's held by forty armed men quite another.

All of a sudden the hubbub reaches us from the other side of the
square. Shit! I've just got time to cast a glance towards our defences,
when I see Jan of Leyden standing open-armed on the top of the
barricade.

'What the fuck are you doing?'

'Run, Gert, they'll kill him!'

'Jaaaaan!'

I dash across the square, almost crashing into the calf on the spit, I
stumble and get up again. 'Jan, get down here, you mad bastard!'

Shirt open, he shows his hairless chest, calling to be shot. His eyes
flame over at the Lutheran carts. 'Shortly mine anger shall be accomplished and I will cause my fury to rest upon you. By your works will
I know you, and I will do unto you that which I have not done,
because of all your abominations, sinful Lutheran.'

'Get down, Jan!' I might as well be invisible.

'And neither shall mine eye spare, neither will I have any pity, but
I will hold you responsible for your conduct and your abominations
will be apparent within you; then you will know that I, the Lord, am
the one striking you. You have understood, you great Lutheran son of
a whore, your bullets can do nothing to me. They will bounce off this
chest and return to you, while the Father is in me, He can gobble them
up and fire them back out of His arse whenever He wants, right in
your faces!'

'Jan, for God's sake!'

He's standing bolt upright with his mouth wide open, making a
terrifying noise. Then the mad blond from Leyden raises his voice to
the heavens: 'Father, listen to your son, hear your bastard: clear these
pieces of shit off the cobbles! You heard me, Lutheran, go on, shit
yourself, you'll drown in the spit of God and the Kingdom will be
ours. I will dine with the Saints on your corpse!'

The hackbut goes off and Jan freezes. For a moment I think they've hit him.

He turns towards us, a stream of blood coming from his right ear, his eyes filled with enthusiasm. He drops and I catch him before he hits the ground, he faints; no, he's coming to. 'Gert, Geeert! Kill him, Gert, kill him! He almost took my ear off! Give me my gun till I kill him . . . please, give it to me! Shoot him, Gert, if you don't shoot him I'll do it . . . He's down there, you can see him, there he is, Gert, the gun, the gun . . . He's ruined me!'

I lean him against the wall and say a few words to our defenders: if he tries to do that again, tie him up.

The sun is sinking behind the cathedral bell tower. The dogs are gnawing on the calf bones piled up in the middle of the square. I've established a roster of guards at the barricades: two hours each, so that everyone can get a bit of sleep. The women have prepared makeshift beds made out of whatever they had to hand and lit us fires for the night. The cold is intense: some of the men have opted to have a roof over their heads. But the most determined have stayed, people you can count on.

We are warming ourselves round a fire, wrapped in our blankets. A sudden hubbub at the barricade closing off the square to the south makes us leap to our feet. The sentries are escorting a boy of about twenty to us, breathless and frightened-looking.

'He says he's Councillor Palken's servant.'

'The senator and his son . . . they dragged us away, they're armed, there was nothing I could do, Wördemann . . . Burgomaster Jüdefeldt was there as well, they've been taken . . .'

'Calm down, get your breath back. Who were they? How many?'

The boy is drenched in sweat, I have somebody bring him a blanket. His eyes dart from one face to the next. I hand him a mug of steaming soup.

'I'm a servant in Councillor Palken's house. Half an hour ago . . . about a dozen armed men . . . came in. Jüdefeldt was leading them. They forced the councillor and his son to follow them.'

'What do they want with Palken?'

Knipperdolling, furious: 'He's one of the few people who support us in the council. Wördemann, Jüdefeldt and all the other Lutherans hate him.'

Rothmann doesn't seem convinced. What's the point of a hostage? They're invulnerable to attack in Überwasser. Panic in Rothmann's eyes: 'The keys!'

'What?'

'The keys, Palken's got the keys to the gates on the north-western side of the walls.'

'That's exactly right.' The servant lifts his nose out of his mug. 'It was the keys they were after!'

'Gresbeck, the map!'

I unroll it in the light of the fire, with the help of Knipperdolling. The Frauentor and the Jüdefeldertor: the gates behind Überwasser, the road to Anmarsch: 'They want to bring the bishop's men into the city.'

Things are looking bad.

You can see it in everyone's faces. Crammed into the narrow market square, cut off from the opposite shore of the Aa, where the Lutherans are committing the atrocious crime that will finish us off. Should we try a sortie? Escape from this impasse and launch a surprise attack on Überwasser? An unreal silence has fallen over the whole city: apart from the combatants, everyone is locked up in their houses. Mute, sitting round flickering fires, waiting for our imminent and unknown fate. Who's coming to the city? The three thousand paid men following von Waldeck? A vanguard waiting for daybreak? This night will give us our answers.

Knipperdolling is in a rage. 'Those great arseholes. Rich fuckers. I remember all those fine speeches against the bishop, the papists and everyone talking about municipal freedoms, new faith . . . But they've got to tell me to my face if they're going to sell themselves to the bishop for a handful of silver! We expelled the bishop together! I want to talk about it, Gert, until yesterday I couldn't have imagined them handing over the city to the mercenaries. Let that pig Jüdefeldt tell me himself what kind of promises von Waldeck has made to him! Give me an escort, Gert, I want to talk to those charlatans.'

Redeker shakes his head. 'You're mad. Their words aren't worth a fuck, they only think about their wallets, you'll be a halfwit if you waste your time talking to them.'

Rothmann intervenes. 'It might be worth a try. But without taking any pointless risks. They may not be as firm as they appear. They may just be bloody frightened . . .'

Two squadrons set off. One straight to the Frauentor on the south, then walking along the walls, about ten ghostlike figures in all. Redeker heads in the opposite direction, for the Jüdefeldertor.

No initiatives or desperate attacks, not yet. Keeping an eye on the entrances that have fallen into their hands, checking any movements in and out of the city. Trying to read the future from their activities.

The two squadrons have the task of keeping watch and posting look-outs along the way and on the road to Überwasser: eyes to scrutinise every twitch and couriers ready to bring messages at any moment.

With me to escort the head of the weavers' guilds, about twenty, almost all of them boys, sixteen or seventeen, but they have courage in spades and keen eyesight.

'Are you scared?' I ask the boy with the fluffy attempt at a moustache.

In the rough voice of sleep he drawls slowly, 'No, Captain.'

'What's your trade?'

'Shop assistant, Captain.'

'Drop the "Captain", what's your name?'

'Karl.'

'Karl, are you a fast runner?'

'As fast as these legs will carry me.'

'Fine. If they attack us and I get injured, if you see that things are going badly, don't waste time picking me up, just run like the wind and give the alarm. Do you understand?'

'Yes.'

Knipperdolling takes three of his men with him and marches at their head carrying a white flag as a sign of truce. We follow him twenty or thirty feet behind.

The head of the weavers is already close to the monastery, and starting to ask someone to come out and parley with him.

We stop a little ahead of St Nicholas's Church, our guns loaded and catapults at the ready. Silence from Überwasser. Knipperdolling continues to advance.

'Right, Jüdefeldt, out you come! Some bloody burgomaster! Is this how you defend the city? Kidnap a councillor and open the gates to von Waldeck? The city wants to know why you've decided to have us all killed. Come out and talk to us like men!'

Someone calls to him from a window, 'What the fuck have you come to do, Anabaptist wanker? Did you bring any of your whores with you?'

Knipperdolling staggers, loses his cool. 'You son of a bitch! Your mother's the whore!' He steps forward again, too far this time. 'You're joining forces with the papists, Jüdefeldt, with the bishop! What the fuck are you thinking about?'

Come back, you fool, don't get so close.

The gate swings open and about ten of them, armed, are on top of him.

'Attack!'

We hurl ourselves forward, Knipperdolling is yelling at the top of his voice, four of them have hold of him. They retreat as we fire at them with catapults and crossbows. The first hackbut fire is heard, some of us are hit, they're shooting from the tower. The gate closes again and we are exposed, we scatter, spreading out around the square, returning fire, the place echoes with the cries of Knipperdolling and the shots from the hackbuts. They've fucked us over. There's nothing to be done, we've got to withdraw, picking up the wounded.

I give the order: 'Back! Back!'

Curses and laments accompany us towards the market square.

They've fucked us over and we're in the shit. We cross our barricades and stop on the steps of St Lamberti, hubbub, shouting, curses, everyone crowding around us. We lay down the wounded, entrusting them to the women, the news of the capture of Knipperdolling immediately spreads, along with a roar of rage.

Rothmann is dismayed, but Gresbeck stays calm, orders us to hold our positions, we've got to contain the panic.

I'm furious, I feel my blood boiling, my temples pulsing. We're in the shit and I don't know what to do.

Gresbeck shakes me. 'Redeker's back.'

He's exhausted too, face like thunder. 'They're in. No more than twenty, galloping like mad, von Waldeck's knights.'

'Are you sure?'

'I've seen their banners, their blazons. I expect that pig von Büren's there too.'

Rothmann, his face in his hands: 'It's over.'

Silence all around.

Kibbenbrock tries to revive our spirits: 'Let's stay calm. Until the bulk of the bishop's troops enter the city they can't touch us. There are more of us and they know we have nothing to lose. But we have to do something.'

The weaver's right, we've got to think. To think.

Time passes. We reinforce the sentries on the barricades. Our only cannon is placed in the middle of the square, to repel an attack if one of our defence lines is breached.

The men mustn't have time to lose heart. More patrols and weapons collections, we manage to get hold of some more hackbuts. They say the Catholics are hanging garlands on the doors of their houses, so that von Waldeck's troops will spare them. Other squadrons are taking them back down again.

The city is motionless. The square, lit by fires, could be an island in

the middle of a dark ocean. Out there, like terrified animals, everyone
is waiting, hiding in their houses.

In their houses.

In their houses.

I step aside with Gresbeck and Redeker. We put our heads together.
It can be done. We can try, at least. It couldn't be worse than
this . . .

A final order to Gresbeck: 'So we agree. Tell Rothmann. Tell him
to move; give him the smartest men; we've barely got time.'

'Gert . . .' The former mercenary hands me his pistols, holding
them by the barrel. 'Take these. They're accurate, a present from the
Swiss campaign.'

I slip them inside my belt. 'See you in an hour.'

Redeker makes way for me in the almost total darkness, I walk
resolutely past him. We pass through two or three narrow streets, a
few yards more and he shows me the door. Whispering: 'Jürgen
Blatt.'

I load the pistols. Three loud knocks on the door. 'Captain Jürgen
Blatt of the municipal guard. The bishop's troops are entering the city.
The burgomaster wants us to escort the lady and her daughters to the
monastery. Right now. Open up!'

Footsteps behind the door. 'Who are you?'

'Captain Blatt, I said, open up.'

I hold my breath, the sound of keys, I lean the barrel of the gun
against the chink of the door. It opens a crack. I blow half his head
away.

Inside. The man at the top of the stairs hasn't time to aim his
hackbut. I grab him by the leg, he falls, shouts, draws a knife, in two
bounds Redeker is at the top of the stairs and finishes him off with it.
Then spits on the floor.

Dagger in hand, at the end of the corridor the sound of women
screaming. An old woman appears before me. 'Take me to the lady.'

A big bedroom, a four-poster bed and various ornaments. Frau
Jüdefeldt, in a corner, presses her two children to her, and a terrified
servant kneels to pray.

Between us and them stands a moron with a sword in his hand,
twenty years old at the most. He trembles, not saying a word. He
doesn't know what to do.

Redeker: 'Put it down, you might hurt yourself.'

I stare at her. 'Milady, the convulsive events of this night have made
my visit a necessity. I mean you no harm, but I am obliged to ask you
to follow us. Your daughters will stay here with all the others.'

Redeker sniggers: 'I'm going to take a look around the house, to check there aren't any other overzealous servants.'

Burgomaster Jüdefeldt's wife is a beautiful woman of about thirty. Dignified, she holds back her tears and raises her eyes over my head. 'You villain.'

'A villain who's fighting for the freedom of Münster, Milady. The city's about to be invaded by a troop of murderers in the pay of the bishop. We have no time to lose.'

I whistle to Redeker, who comes back up the stairs to us with a little wooden box under his arm. He isn't discouraged by the expression on my face. 'We kill his servants, we take his women. And why not take his florins?'

In the doorway, the old woman throws a pelisse round her lady's shoulders, murmuring an 'Our Father'.

We escort Frau Jüdefeldt to the market square. When the prisoner is recognised, we receive a stirring ovation, weapons are raised to the sky: the Baptists are still alive!

Rothmann comes towards us from the other direction, with his arm round the shoulders of a distinguished-looking lady, wrapped in a sable, a long black plait hanging down to her shoulders. 'May I introduce Frau Wördemann, the wife of Councillor Wördemann. Our lady is a sister: I baptised her myself.'

Redeker leans over to my ear. 'When his spies informed him about this baptism, the husband confirmed her new faith by giving her a sound thrashing. The poor thing thought she was going to die; for days afterwards she couldn't crawl along the ground, let alone walk.'

Frau Wördemann, an austere beauty, wraps herself in her pelisse. 'I hope, gentlemen, that you will allow us to warm up by a fire, after dragging us from our houses by force in the middle of the night.'

'Of course, but first I am obliged to deprive you of a personal object.' I slip the rings from her slender fingers, two inlaid pieces of gold. 'Karl!'

The boy comes running, his face filthy with sleep and smoke.

'Take the white flag and run over to Überwasser. The message is for Burgomaster Jüdefeldt. Tell him that we're going to present ourselves at the monastery, we've got to talk.' I push the rings into Karl's fist. 'Give him these. Is that clear?'

'Yes, Captain.'

'Go on, quick as you can!'

Karl takes off his shoes, which are too big anyway, and stands barefoot in the snow. Then he dashes off like a hare across the square, while I nod to the sentries to let him go.

'Which of us is going?' Rothmann asks.

Red-haired Kibbenbrock goes at the head, loosening the belt that holds his sword and giving it to Gresbeck. 'I'll go.' He looks at the preacher and me. 'If they see one of you two they might have an irresistible desire to shoot you. I represent the weavers' guild; they won't open fire on me.'

Gresbeck butts in, 'He's right, Gert, you're more use here.'

I draw the pistols from my belt. 'These are yours. It's dark, they won't recognise me, I'll use a different name.'

'You'll get yourself killed.' His tone is already resigned.

I smile at him. 'We've got nothing left to lose, that's our strength. The map, quick.' To Redeker: 'Do you recognise this passageway behind the cemetery?'

'Of course, you get there via the little footbridges of the Reine Kloster.'

'They'll probably have placed sentries here and here. Form groups of three or four and get them over to the other bank.'

'How many in all?'

'At least thirty.'

'And the sentries?'

'Knock them out, but do it quietly.'

'What are you planning to do? We'll be here unarmed.' Gresbeck follows my finger on the parchment.

'The monastery is impregnable. But the graveyard isn't.'

Gresbeck scratches away at his eyebrow. 'They're armed to the teeth, Gert, they've even got a cannon.'

'But it's easy to get to and it's out of range of the monastery.' To Redeker again: 'Get as close to it as you can; they're barricaded inside, they won't be checking the outer wall. But hurry, it'll be daybreak in an hour at the most.'

A glance of agreement with Kibbenbrock. 'Let's go.'

While we're making for the edge of the square, Rothmann's voice comes from behind: 'Brothers!'

Silhouetted against the torchlight, tall, very pale, his breath disappearing into the frosty night: he could be Aaron. Or even Moses. 'May the Lord be with you along the way . . . and may He watch over you all.'

Just past our barricade we come across Karl, still running, his feet frozen, so breathless he can hardly speak: 'Captain! They're telling us to go . . . that they won't open fire.'

'Did you hand over the rings?'

'To the burgomaster in person, Captain.'

A clap on the shoulder. 'Fine. Now run and warm up by the fire, you've done your bit for tonight.'

We go on. Überwasser is silhouetted like a great black fortress over the Aa. The Church of Our Lady flanks the monastery: our patrols heard Knipperdolling's anguished screams coming from the bell tower for an hour, until his voice gave out.

Now there's only silence and the faint flowing of the river.

Kibbenbrock and I advance side by side, with a white sheet stretched in our hands.

The door creaks half open. An alarmed voice says, 'Halt! Who goes there?'

'Kibbenbrock, representative of the weavers' corporation.'

'Have you come to keep your mate company? Who's that other one with you?'

'Swedartho the locksmith, spokesman of the Münster Baptists. We want to talk to Burgomaster Jüdefeldt and Councillor Wördemann, their wives send their greetings.'

We wait, time stands still.

Then another voice: 'I'm Jüdefeldt, speak.'

'We know you've brought the bishop's vanguard into the city. We have to talk. You and Wördemann come outside, to the cemetery.' No useless leniency. 'And remember that if we don't get back to the square in half an hour the workers of St Egidius will take your wife, fore and aft, and maybe she'll give you that son you've been wanting for so long!'

Silence and cold.

Then, 'Fine. To the cemetery. The men won't fire on you.'

We walk round the convent: the cemetery – where at least three generations of nuns lie rotting beneath the wooden crosses – is surrounded by water and closed off at the end by a low stone wall. It's been turned into a camp. About twenty horses tied to the wall facing the monastery indicate that our patrols have counted accurately. There's a small cannon pointing out from behind a pile of sacks, guarded by three Lutherans, another two with hackbuts stand at the entrance, watching us carefully. Von Waldeck's knights flash their swords, bivouacked round the fires, menace and superiority written all over their faces: the affairs of these burghers don't concern us.

The burgomaster and the richest man in Münster come towards us, torches in hand, with a dozen armed men behind them.

I put them on guard. 'Keep your cops at a distance, Wördemann, or your wife might find out whether Rothmann's dick really is better than yours . . .'

The merchant, austere and menacing, gives a start and looks at me with disgust. 'Anabaptist, your preacher is nothing but a rebel buffoon.'

Jüdefeldt nods to him to be quiet. 'What do you want?'

He is bare-headed, his hair dishevelled by a sleepless night, his sweating, nervous hand on the stiletto in his belt.

I let Kibbenbrock speak first. 'You're about to make the biggest fuck-up of your life, Jüdefeldt. A fuck-up that you will regret for the rest of your days. Stop while you still have time. At daybreak, von Waldeck's troops will take possession of the city, he'll regain dominion over it . . .'

The burgomaster interrupts, irritated, 'The bishop has assured me that he won't touch the municipal privileges, I've got a document written by his own hand . . .'

'Bollocks!' spits Kibbenbrock. 'Once he's back in power he'll be able to wipe his arse with your municipal privileges! Who's going to be able to tell him to do anything when he's the boss of Münster again? Think, Jüdefeldt. And you too, Wördemann, just do your sums for a minute. How exactly is your business going to benefit from paying duties to the bishop? The production of the monasteries will put the squeeze on yours again and the Franciscans will get rich while you pay your taxes to von Waldeck. Think about it. The bishop is a clever son of a bitch, promises cost him nothing. The papists are used to this kind of subterfuge, you know that better than I do.'

Kibbenbrock has raised his voice too loudly. The rattle of armour and spears announces the approach of the horsemen, torches illuminate the well-trimmed beard and leather gloves of Dietrich von Merfeld von Wolbeck, brother of the abbess of Überwasser, the bishop's right-hand man. At his side, Melchior von Büren: he's probably here because he hopes to settle his scores with Redeker in person.

Jüdefeldt anticipates their question. 'My lords, these men are Baptists, they are here to negotiate. We have promised them their safety.'

Dietrich Pointy-Whiskers gives a snort of astonishment. 'What's happening, Jüdefeldt, are you still dealing with these wretches? In an hour's time there'll be nothing left of them but a pile of bones. They're the walking dead, forget about them.'

'Herr von Merfeld is not mistaken,' I intervene. 'Of all the parties involved in this struggle tonight, we are the only ones with nothing to lose. As far as we're concerned, the bishop's entrance into the city would only mean certain death. So you'd better believe that we're not going to give up without a fight. You'll have to take the city one inch at a time.'

Von Büren sighs. 'You're a bunch of cowards. You won't last as long as a yawn from His Lordship. Pinchpurses and street thieves, that's what you are.'

Kibbenbrock smiles and shakes his head in a way that attracts the nervous attention of the two merchants. 'You're so frightened of losing your power that you've allowed von Waldeck's vassals into your house out of fear of our four hackbuts. Do you know what I think, Jüdefeldt? Von Waldeck has known this from the first. He was able to use the division between you and us to cut the city in two.'

The burgomaster's high forehead is covered with wrinkles, his eyes dart from Wördemann's face, gloomier than ever, to Kibbenbrock's and mine.

Kibbenbrock won't leave him in peace: 'It's a bloody mess, haven't you noticed? The bishop's been playing a double game from the start. He's reassured you so that he could be sure of support within the walls, someone to open the gates to him at the right moment, and once he's in he'll suddenly remember that you're Lutherans, rebels like ourselves against the Pope's authority.' A pause, time for that to sink in, and then: 'You can forget your municipal freedoms: after us, it'll be your turn on the scaffold. Think about it, Jüdefeldt. Think long and hard.'

The two burghers are motionless, looking at Kibbenbrock and then over their shoulders, in search of an invisible adviser.

Von Merfeld says in disbelief, 'Jüdefeldt, you're not going to listen to these two wretches? Don't you see they're trying to save their skins? They're in a state of desperation. When His Lordship gets here we'll sort things out. We've made an agreement, so don't forget it.'

Still silence.

I listen to my heart beating out a rhythm to the passing of time.

Wördemann mentally tells the rosary of his accounts.

Jüdefeldt thinks about his wife.

Jüdefeldt thinks about the bishop's army.

Jüdefeldt thinks about his forty men barricaded inside the monastery.

He thinks about von Merfeld's ludicrous whiskers.

He thinks about that bitch Merfeld's sister the abbess, and yes, everyone had always known that she was the bishop's spy in the city.

He thinks about the garlands on the houses of the Catholics . . .

I spread my arms. 'We've come here unarmed. Let's stop fighting and defend our city together. What the fuck have the nobles got to do with it? Münster is us, not the papists, not the bishop's men.'

Von Merfeld explodes, 'For God's sake, you can't allow yourself to be won over like that by two silver-tongued roughnecks!'

Jüdefeldt sighs and grasps an imaginary snake. 'They weren't the ones who convinced me, Herr von Wolbeck. You brought us promises.'

'The word of His Lordship Franz von Waldeck!'

'But these . . . roughnecks, as you call them, are offering peace, with no need for any armed mercenaries in the city, it's a proposal that's worth taking into consideration.'

Von Merfeld explodes again, 'You're not really going to believe these shitheads?'

'I'm still the burgomaster of this city. I've got to think of the interests of its inhabitants. We know that the Catholics have received the order to hang garlands outside the doors of their houses. Why, sir? Can you explain that to me? Might it be so that the bishop's mercenaries can tell which houses are to be spared sacking? That wasn't part of our agreement . . .'

Von Merfeld stiffens, a fucking Lutheran is openly accusing him, but von Büren is the first to jump in: 'If that's how it is, I've got a way of dealing with turncoats!' He draws his sword and puts it to the burgomaster's throat.

The Lutherans react, but a nod from von Merfeld is all it takes to get the knights up on their feet: twenty horsemen, armed to the teeth and ready to fight a dozen frightened burghers. In direct combat that would be that.

Von Merfeld gives me a triumphant grin.

It is extinguished by a horrible scream, like the screech of a bird of prey, from the wall at the end of the cemetery, a scream that freezes the blood and makes the hairs on our arms stand up, creeps up our spines like a spider: 'Stop, you bastard!'

Long shadows of spectres advance between the tombs, the army of the dead resurrected. Some of the men drop to their knees to pray.

'I'm telling you, you fucker!'

Weird figures, they cross the field, emerging from the darkness, in the torchlight, the army of the shadows, thirty ghosts with raised crossbows and hackbuts, their captain at their head. And on his back, two pistol-lengths taller than the man himself, the wings of the Angel of Death. 'Von Büren, you son of a whore.' He stops, spits on the ground and hisses, 'I've come to pull your heart out and eat it.'

The knight blanches, his sword trembles.

The Angel of Darkness, Redeker, pushes his way forward until he's a couple of yards away from us. 'Everything all right, Gert?'

'Just in time. The situation's been turned upside down, you might say, now it's up to you to decide, gentlemen. Either we settle our scores right now, on the spot, or you get back on your horses and set off the way you came.'

His whiskers still standing to attention, von Büren has already given his vote by lowering his sword and Jüdefeldt finally breathes again.

There are twice as many of us and we're the more determined. We have nothing to lose and von Merfeld knows it.

A click of the tongue and a whispered curse, one final contemptuous glance at the burgomaster, he turns on his heels and rejoins his men with a great jangle of spurs.

Redeker puts the barrel of his gun against von Büren's chest. Von Büren closes his eyes and waits, frozen, for the shot. An expert hand unlaces the purse from his belt. 'Clear off, you bastard. Off you go and kiss your bishop's arse.'

The sun is dimly appearing from behind the Church of St Lamberti as we return to the market square. The horsemen are leaving the city, escorted by both Redeker's men and the Lutherans. Some people swear they saw von Büren weeping with rage as he passed through the gate of the city.

Frau Jüdefeldt and Frau Wördemann have been reunited with their husbands, and Knipperdolling is walking beside us with Councillor Palken and his son, a hint of hoarseness in his voice, one black eye, but in good humour, as though he were walking along absently in search of an inn.

In the camp, we are welcomed by a cry of exultation, the hackbuts fire into the air, a forest of hands lifts us up above everyone's heads, the women kiss us, I see people taking their clothes off and Jan of Leyden being carried in triumph by a group of girls as though the mere force of his words had seen off misfortune. The people demolish the barricades and pour back into the streets, those streets which, for a whole night, have been under the most terrible threat. Windows open up, women, old people and children go down into the street, despite the intense cold, despite the fact that dawn is beginning to scatter the darkness.

Knipperdolling pours beer for everyone.

Rothmann comes over to me with satisfaction, his face tired but smiling. 'We've done it. I told you the Lord would protect us.'

'Yes, the Lord and hackbuts,' I smile. 'And now?'

'What?'

'And what are we going to do now?'

The reply comes from Gresbeck, blackened by torch smoke, crumpled and dirty, the white scar on his eyebrow looking even bigger on that sombre face. 'Now we're going to hold our breath, Captain Gert from the Well.' He smiles, and I press his hand as I thank him.

Knipperdolling is listening to the message from one of the patrols. Looking worried, he staggers towards us. 'Gert, I didn't want this to . . .'

'What the fuck's happened now?'

'Von Waldeck has set his peasants against us. They're coming here. It's said there are three thousand of them, they want to sort things out in the city once and for all.'

The pub is the latrine of war.

If it's the blood of men that drenches its rotting body, the piss that soaks the battlefield is beer.

Beer that swells the stomachs of fighting men, that reduces their fear before the battle and intensifies their intoxication after victory. Piss that enriches the latrine attendants beyond measure. No less important than the profusion of blood and courage that decide the outcome of a battle.

Piss on your enemy before you strike him, he might wake up, placate his rage, disperse the fog that surrounds the thirst for blood. He might suddenly see the absurdity of the fate that he's about to inflict or suffer, and withdraw.

They arrived in a black rage, they went home pissed as farts.

Twenty barrels of beer, the reserve of the municipal beer hall. The homage paid by the townspeople of Münster to their brothers from the surrounding area, received with such pomp and splendour at the Jüdefeldertor.

The obtuse animus of the three thousand peasants melted away along with the foam on their beer.

Once another danger has been averted, the festivities become a bacchanal, rich in grotesquery.

A group of dishevelled women run into the market square, half undressed or actually naked. They throw themselves to the ground in the pose of the crucifix, they roll around in the mud, weep, laugh and beat their breasts, invoking the Heavenly Father.

They see blood raining from the heavens.

They see black fires.

They see a man crowned with gold on a white horse, clutching the sword that will smite the wicked.

They call out to the King of Zion, but the only man who might satisfy them with his theatrical presence is getting plastered in some tavern.

People are laughing and enjoying themselves, getting involved as they might in a play staged by Jan of Leyden. But not the farrier Adrianson, annoyed by the hysterical shouting, who grabs a hackbut and brings down the weathercock from the roof of a house with a single shot. It comes down with a terrific crash. The scene immediately freezes. The women come to their senses as though they had woken from a nightmare. Adrianson is given a great round of applause.

Over the next few days it becomes increasingly clear that von Waldeck won't be coming back to the city.

Many Catholics are packing their bags.

The balance of strength is all in our favour, not even the Lutherans can oppose us now: Burgomaster Tilbeck, as a good old opportunist, has even had himself baptised by Rothmann, perhaps in the hope of being re-elected. Jüdefeldt welcomed us into the council chamber and had to accept our decision to give all family heads the vote in the next elections, regardless of class. This was hard for him to swallow, but a refusal on his part would have been even more so, as the townspeople are all behind us. Knipperdolling and Kibbenbrock have stood for election.

It's clear by now that the wealthy merchants will no longer have the city in the palms of their hands.

Many Lutherans are packing their bags.

They're gathering together their gold, their money, their jewels, their silverware, even their finest hams. But they'll have to get through the inspection of Sündermann, tireless sentry of the market square during the days of our victory. Wördemann the wealthy, blocked at the Frauentor, with a pistol to his head, has been forced to shit out the four rings he'd slipped up his arsehole, while his lovely wife submits to an indecorous body search and her servants can't keep from laughing.

Female protests lead to Sündermann's removal from his post: anyone who wants to leave can do so freely. And that's exactly what nobleman Johann von der Recke plans to do, except that his wife and daughter are of the opinion that anyone who wants to stay can do so freely. They fly into the arms of the amiable Rothmann, who welcomes them into his house. When he goes to get them back, the old fool gets only insults for his pains: he discovers he is no longer either a father or a husband, that he can no longer thrash the ladies of his house, or dictate the rules as he sees fit. He even learns that it's better for him to forget he ever had a wife and a daughter, and fuck off away as far as possible. By the time he leaves the city, word of his pathetic figure has already spread through the female population of Münster: von der Recke leaves under a hail of all kinds of objects.

Adrianson uses the tools of his trade to pick the lock. A great hall, luxurious furniture and tapestries. The legitimate owners haven't even extinguished the embers of the fire before leaving. One of the Brundt brothers gets it going again. The staircase leads to the floor above. A bedroom, a smaller room. In the middle, a wooden tub, a jug and ewer. Bath salts and all the equipment required for a noblewoman's personal hygiene.

Adrianson appears in the doorway with a quizzical expression.

I nod. 'I like it. Put on some water to heat up.'

I get undressed, kick away my shirt and jacket, a single black, foul-smelling pile. Off with my socks, too. Burn them. In a big wardrobe I find clean clothes, elegant material. They'll do fine.

Adrianson pours the first two steaming jugs into the tub, glancing at me uncertainly. He goes out shaking his head.

The chorus comes in from the street.

> They came all pompous, haughty and affected,
> They went away all gloomy and dejected.
> That night amid the tombstones dark and drear
> A shady phantom filled them all with fear.
>
> He commandeered the burgomaster's wife,
> And stripped the bishop of the joys of life.
> Take care, then, not to cross Gert from the Well.
> He'll slit your throat send you straight to hell.

'Do you hear them?' Knipperdolling sniggers. 'They love you! You've won them over! Come, come and see.'

He drags me to the window. About thirty fanatics, who cheer in unison the minute they see me.

'You've made it into their songs. The whole of Münster is singing your praises.' He leans over and puts a hand on my shoulder. He shouts to the people below, 'Long live Captain Gert from the Well!'

'Long live Gert!'

'Long live the liberator of Münster!'

I laugh and step back. Knipperdolling holds me there, shouting, 'It was with you that we liberated Münster and with you we'll make this city the pride of Christendom! Long live Captain Gert from the Well! All the beer in the city would never be enough to drink your health!'

Shouts, cries, things being thrown in the air, Knipperdolling you great poof, we'll hoist your belly to the top of the Rathaus, laughter, beakers flying . . .

Knipperdolling shuts the window, waving at them with broad gestures. 'We're going to win. We're going to win the elections, all we'll need is a word from you and there'll be no competition.'

I point to the city beyond the glass. 'It's easier to get rid of a tyrant than it is to come up to their expectations. The hard part may well be just around the corner.'

He looks at me, puzzled, then erupts, 'Don't be such a misery! When we've won the elections we'll decide how to govern the city. For the time being, bask in the glory.'

'Glory awaits me in a tub of steaming water.'

Chapter 31

The tide has gone on rising until this crucial day. Yesterday Redeker delivered a solemn speech to the ordinary people in the Rathaus square: as a result, twenty-four of them were elected to the council. Blacksmiths, weavers, carpenters, manual workers, even a baker and a cobbler. The new representatives of the city will cover the whole range of the minor trades, the dregs that one would never have imagined deciding the fate of this world.

The night was spent in festivities and dancing, and this morning the last formalities were undertaken: Knipperdolling and Kibbenbrock are the new burgomasters. Let the Carnival commence.

It begins with the beggars of Münster, who enter the cathedral and, Last Men that they are, catch a glimpse of what might await them in the kingdom of heaven: the gold, the candelabra, the brocades of the statues all disappear, and the alms for the poor pass straight into the hands of the people concerned, without the priests being able to pinch it all. When the thread maker and carder Bernhard Mumme, axe in hand, finds himself face to face with the clock that has called him to his labours for so many years, he doesn't think twice about smashing those infernal cogwheels to pieces. Meanwhile his colleagues crap in the chapterhouse library, leaving foul-smelling calling cards in the bishop's big liturgical tomes. The altar pieces are pulled down and, so that they can serve as a stimulus to the constipated, they are used to build a public latrine over the Aa. The baptistery is demolished to the sound of hammers, along with the pipe organ. They yield to unbridled gluttony beneath the vaults, a banquet is held on the altar, finally they all eat in enormous quantities, finally they fuck, against the columns of the nave, on the ground, their spirits freed of all burdens, everyone pisses on the tombstones of the lords of Münster, on those most noble skeletons that lie there beneath the stones. And after fertilising those aristocratic corpses, they all wash their arses in the font.

Weep, saints, pull out your beards, your cult is at an end. Weep, lords of Münster, surrounding Christ's manger with your gilded devotion: your time has come and gone. Nothing that has represented the abominable power of the priests and the lords for centuries must be left standing.

The other churches are subjected to visits of a similar kind, crowds of loot-laden poor wandering through the streets, giving sacerdotal robes to whores, setting fire to the property documents seized from the parish churches.

The whole city is celebrating, Carnival processions pass through the streets on carts. Tile Bussenschute, dressed as a friar tied to a plough. The most famous whore in Münster carried around Überwasser cemetery to the accompaniment of psalms, the waving of sacred standards and the sound of bells.

'Are you Gert Boekbinder?' Distracted assent. 'I've been sent by Jan Matthys. He wishes to inform you that he will be in the city before sunset.'

I take my eyes off the stage. A young face. 'What?'

'Jan Matthys. Aren't you one of his apostles?'

I look in his eyes to see the gleam of a joke, in vain. 'When did he say he was coming?'

'Before evening. We slept thirty miles from here. I set off early in the morning.'

I clutch him by the shoulder. 'Let's go.'

We push our way through the crowd. The spectacle has brought in large numbers of people: on stage is the best imitator of von Waldeck in the whole of Münster. Every square has its attractions today: music and dance, beer and roasted pig, games of skill, world turned upside down, biblical representations.

My young friend is distracted by a pair of tits casually revealed on the corner of the street.

'Come on, let's go. I'll introduce you to another of the apostles.'

We need him now. Bockelson is the only one who could improvise something at a moment like this. If I remember correctly, he's giving a recitation in front of St Peter's Church.

A Carnival cortège comes towards us, crushing us against the walls of the houses. It begins with three men being ridden by a little donkey. Behind them lurches a cart, pulled by about ten kings. In the centre is a little tree with its roots in the air, in a tub a naked man covering himself with mud. In the corner the Pope is praying, in a dignified pose, 'Let Samson die, along with all the Philistines!'

Jan's voice reaches us from the distance, giving it his best: it's as though it's vibrating in superhuman effort to demolish the columns of the temple of Tyre. The enthusiasm of the spectators is undiminished.

I jump on to the stage beside the holy pimp and the roar of applause falls silent almost at once. A sense of expectation, a babble of voices growing subdued.

In an ear: 'Matthys will be here before sunset. What'll we do?'

'Matthys?' Jan of Leyden isn't capable of whispering. The name of the Prophet of Haarlem is a pebble thrown into the pool of yelling voices below us. The ripples spread quickly.

'This evening we were supposed to be having the festival banquet at the expense of the councillors, the fur sellers and all the rest . . .' He strokes his beard. 'Stay calm, Gert, I'm thinking about it. Go and tell the others if you haven't done so already, Knipperdolling will be keen to meet the great Jan Matthys.'

I nod, still undecided. I leave the stage to him, almost pleading, 'Jan, please, no nonsense . . .'

Towards evening a terribly cold wind blows up, blasting with it a harsh, icy snow. The streets turn white.

Everyone in the city has had word of the arrival of Matthys. Around the Aegiditor, along the street leading to the cathedral, people have already taken up their positions. The torches are being lit one by one as the light fades.

'Here he is, it's him! Here's Enoch!'

Kibbenbrock and half the council on one side, Knipperdolling and the other half on the other, push the heavy wings of the door from outside. The creaking of the hinges is a signal. Necks strain towards the gate. The little light of day that remains first filters in like a blade, then slowly spreads to fill the whole arcade.

Jan Matthys is a dark shadow, straight-backed, stick in hand. He walks slowly, without so much as a glance for the crowd. The two new burgomasters, along with the whole of the council, walk a short distance behind him, torches held high above their heads. A subdued chant accompanies his passage.

I take a better look: in the snow that is still settling on the cobbles in increasingly large flakes, the feet of the Baker Prophet are shoeless, bare. He isn't holding an ordinary stick, but a thresher: the tool used by the peasants to separate the chaff from the grain.

As Matthys advances, the impassioned crowds of onlookers on either side of the street merge together behind him and the procession grows. Jan of Haarlem stops, grips the thresher with both hands and points it towards the sky. The chants stop all at once. 'The Lord is going to sweep His threshing floor!' he shouts, at first on his own, then with the thunderous accompaniment of hundreds of voices. The long blade swings furiously through the snow. 'The Lord is going to sweep His threshing floor!'

His voice is already being echoed by the crowd, who are telling the new arrivals, 'The Prophet, the Prophet is here.'

'He is come!'

'Jan Matthys, the great Jan Matthys is in Münster!'

They push their way forward, they crowd towards the central square. Everyone wants to see God's messenger, tall, gaunt, black, shaggy, barefoot.

Here he is.

Here is Enoch.

He stops, perhaps there's the hint of a smile, just perhaps.

Bockelson appears before him, open-armed. 'Master. Brother. Father. Mother. Friend. An angel told me you would come today. The angel I saw entering the city beside you and now flying about your head. Today, not yesterday, not tomorrow. Today, now that victory is ours and the enemy is routed. Angel of God. How I love you.'

Matthys comes towards him and delivers a punch to his cheek that knocks him over. Everyone freezes. Bockelson gets back up. He smiles. The two Jans embrace as though they are going to crush each other, they stay like that in their double grip, swaying back and forth for a long time. Bockelson weeps with joy.

I walk over, try to catch his eye. 'Welcome to Münster, Brother Jan.'

He embraces me too, very firmly, crushes the breath out of me. I hear him murmuring with emotion, 'My apostles, my sons . . .'

His eyes are black torches, the same ones which, a thousand months ago, entrusted me with a mission. There's something wrong, a strange unease: only now do I realise that I haven't once thought of Matthys all the time we've been here. Events have overtaken me. He knows nothing of the struggle and the danger that these people have lived through. We've done everything all on our own, but now that he's here I remember in whose name we came here, with his words on our lips. Münster has absorbed our energies, it has made us fight, take up arms, risk our lives. How can I explain that to you, Jan, how? You weren't there.

I say nothing. I watch him climb up on to the stage, erected alongside the cathedral. The torches frame his elongated shadow along the façade of the church, a dancing demon gesturing to everyone to join him, grimacing at the crowd. The snow cuts through the light, swirls around above everyone's heads: an icy shiver.

Taller and thinner than I remembered, he studies the faces one by one, as though trying to remember their features, their names.

An unreal silence has fallen. Everyone is looking up at him, up through the torches, the breath of hundreds of men and women is suspended above the square, along with their lives.

His voice is a profound gurgle, which seems to come from some cleft in the bowels of the earth.

'Not me. Not me. I am not the one that you adore, O happiest mob of God's elect. Not me. The fire tonight burns on the altars, it licks at the statues, it burns to hell with everything that has been. And will never be again. The old world is consumed like parchment in the flames. The world, the sky, the earth, the night. Time. None of it will ever be again. It is not me that you are raising up to the glory of eternity. Not me. The Word knows not the past, the future, the Word is the present alone. It is living flesh. Everything you knew, knowledge, the rotten common sense of the world that was. Everything. All ashes. It is not me that you are leading to victory. It is not me that you are granting this day of glory. Not me that you are defending, fists clenched, against your enemy. I am not the captain of this war. Not this mouth, these passion-ravaged bones. No. It is the Lord your God. The one they have always forced you to worship in churches, on altars, prone before statues. He is here. God is that blood, those faces, this night. His glory is not the glory of a day, it does not last festivities of a season, but seeks eternity. It seizes it with an iron grip, it grinds, pounds, crushes. Out there, beyond these walls, the world is already finished. I have crossed the void to arrive here. And the fields plunged away behind my footsteps, the rivers dried up, the trees toppled and the snow fell like a rain of fire. And blood, a surging sea of blood. A rising ocean, a wave of fury. Four horsemen galloped by my side, faces of death, pestilence, famine, war. Cities, castles, villages, mountains. Nothing is left. God only stopped by these walls, to call to your souls, your arms and your life. And now He tells you that the Scriptures are dead and it is on your flesh that He will etch the new Word, He will write the last testament of the world and engulf it in fire. You, Babylon of mud and lies. You, the last of the earth. You are the first. Everything starts here. With these towers. With this square. Forget your name, your people, your godless merchants, your idolatrous priests. Forget it all. Because the past belongs to the dead. Today you have a new name and that name is Jerusalem. Today you are led into battle by the one who calls you.

Guided by your hands, His axe will build the Kingdom, step by step, brick by brick, head by head. All the way to heaven. The humblest dregs, the oppressed people of a distant age, you will fight with no fear of evil, the army of God of the Kingdom to come. Because your captain is the Lord.'

I tremble. A frozen moment. Suspended in time, night wipes out the world beyond the square, there's nothing left, just us, here, brought together in a single breath. United in the terror of the words, the army of Light. His eyes scan the ranks, enlisting us one after another. Fear and pride, and certainty, because nothing else can banish the fear of these words. To be up to the task.

I tremble. We wanted the city. He has placed the Kingdom before us. We wanted the Carnival of freedom. He gave us the Apocalypse.

My God, Jan. My God.

Chapter 32

Are the flames of hell freezing? Will we wait in line half-naked, famished, mute, for Cerberus to hurl us through the gate into the eternal ice of godlessness?

The threshing floor must be swept.

What ineradicable wickedness marks these weeping children, clutching their disgraced mothers, these terrified old men, pissing in their own rags? Who will tell them why they were banished from Eden?

Head upon head, Enoch ruled. Heads stacked on towers, on the city walls, adorning the battlements, piled up in an orderly fashion, clearly visible to the bishop and the wayfarer, the nun and the soldier, the pious man and the thief, and more than anything else to the army of darkness that will soon besiege the New Jerusalem: that's what the Prophet has ordained.

So it seems an act of clemency for Matthys merely to shout through the blizzard, 'Depart from here, ye wicked! And never return, enemies of the Father!'

The exodus of old believers creeps quietly away across the mantle of snow. Naked. Eyes to the ground, counting the steps remaining before the freeze. Some of them might hope to reach Telgte, or Anmarsch. No one will make it, perhaps the strongest of the adults might, if anyone, but they won't abandon their wives, their children, their parents.

'There must be no delay. The Father wants justice.'

'What do you mean by that?'

'They must die.' Almost serene as he says it, seraphic, staring straight ahead.

They slip. They weep. They bear their pregnant bellies. Papists, Lutherans: the old world buried in the storm evoked by Matthys. You can read the sign: the will of God.

'It's written, that's all you need to know, is that what you mean?

They are damned, they must die. You want to cut everyone's head off?'

'This is the chosen place. This is the New Jerusalem: there is no place for the unregenerate. They can still choose, they can convert. But the time has come for the last tolls of the bell. They must be quick.'

'And if they don't?'

'They'll be swept away along with everything that is obsolete.'

'Then send them away. Let them go at least, let them get back to their fucking bishop, their wretched Lutheran friends.'

The scores are being settled before our eyes. We've won, then. But where is the unutterable joy, the life-filled laughter, the desire for bodies to be united, all the bodies of the ordinary women and the men, embracing with abandon in radiant warmth?

Our task is accomplished: time is over, God the Omnipotent will think of all the rest. The Apocalypse is coming from above, it is capturing us in a tragic and terrible pantomime that we cannot escape, unless we are to renounce everything we have fought for, unless we are to lose the very meaning of our presence here, to challenge the world.

We've won? Then why does that acrid taste fill my mouth? Why do I avoid the eyes of the brethren like the plague?

'Let it be a warning, a warning to everyone.'

The curses of the most agitated seem obscene to me, and cruel the spittle that rains down on the defeated, the kicks dished out to them. They are no longer the enemies of the people of Münster, no longer the people who have oppressed us for centuries, they're no longer men, women, children, but creatures deformed, monstrous, repulsive. Only their extinction can give us life, can confirm God's word about the fate that awaits us.

Might I be the defeated of all battles ever?

The holy jester of Leyden runs along the row of people, touching their heads gently with a little stick. The counting stops on the head of a little boy. Jan stares at the sky.

'Why? Why must it be an innocent?' He falls on his knees, weeping. 'He's not to blame! The angel of light is flying around him!' He beats his breast, shrieks even louder, sighs. 'Why?'

The little one buries his face in his mother's skirt. She draws away from the pit of despair, kneels down, embraces the boy and lifts him to her breast, her eyes filled with tears. Then, in a definitive gesture, the woman removes the boy from her and her own death, and implores, 'Save him. Keep him with you.'

Matthys's apostle gets up again, touches his beard and, turning back towards the angel, announces, 'The Father separates the grain from the chaff,' then lowers his eye to the boy. 'From today you will be Shear-Jashub, "the returning remnant", the one who will convert and thus escape punishment. Come.'

He takes him with him, while the gate is already absorbing the exodus of the damned.

The torment obscures my vision like the darkest of omens.

The Carnival is over.

Chapter 33

Things are looking bad. Ruecher, the blacksmith, bolted to a great cartwheel and tied up with heavy chains, probably forged by himself, is surrounded by four guards, improvised like everything else at this time, waiting.

The population of the city, along with the new arrivals whose numbers are mounting each day, has been summoned to meet at two o'clock in the afternoon, by the supreme Prophet: angry, disappointed, melancholy, bestialised by the behaviour of his sainted subjects.

Ruecher, the blacksmith, that great piece of shit, dared to offer up heavy comments of disapproval about the outcome of three days of meditation, total abandon, the full descent of the light of the Supreme One into the earthly body of the Great Matthys, all of which had yielded important decisions.

What the fuck, said the blacksmith, expressing something that many people were thinking, it's all fine with me, abolition of property, common ownership of everything available, wealth of no one and for everyone, of course, we'd thought of it ourselves, and some time ago, the fund for the poor, all sacrosanct, new rules, but fuck, you go and appoint seven deacons for the administration and distribution of all resources, for the solution of all conflicts or emergencies and not one, not a single one of them, was born in Münster or had been resident there, they're all Dutch, all disciples of Matthys, and we're absolutely fucking not having it, he said, we've risked our lives for municipal freedoms, we weren't far off having our heads adorning the battlements of the city walls, fuck's sake, and then along comes someone, a great prophet, illuminated by the holy word, certainly, but fuck not a single one, all of them Dutch, and he wasn't even there when we took the city, what the fuck's that all about? Someone shows up, finds everything in place and starts issuing orders, issuing orders and installing his own men to issue orders, issuing orders and suddenly we're all being fucked over again.

Arrested, on the spot.

Hubert Ruecher. Ironmonger and blacksmith. Münsterite. Baptist. Hero of the barricades of 9 February. Hubert Ruecher. Son of the cause. Forger of projectiles. Fighter for the liberation of Münster from the tyranny of the bishop.

Hubert Ruecher is being dragged in chains to the market square: a traitor, a scoundrel who has raised a doubt, spoken out, said that Matthys prayed for three days before appointing his own most loyal followers as deacons. Community of goods, fine: collect them together in big warehouses, one per district, and distribute them to those who have need of them, fine, but why put the Dutchmen in charge of them? Why? Why exclude the Münsterites? It's a fuck-up, Jan, an unforgivable fuck-up. Are you scared? Of what? Of whom? We're all saints, that's what you said, we've been chosen, we're brethren. Do you think that by concentrating all the power in your hands you'll prevent everyone from having any doubts? Someone who's fought to free his city might now, after the appointment of those seven Dutchmen, find himself thinking it had all been for nothing, if he can't make his own appointments in his own house.

Someone like Hubert Ruecher.

They've told you everything – perhaps you've unleashed your spies on the city? – you sent your cops to arrest him by force. In chains, now, foaming at the mouth with rage: a warning to everyone. You've lost your mind, Jan, this isn't what we fought for.

I see you as you come impressively on to the stage, ice in your eyes, your beard more pointed than ever.

I see you talking about the lack of faith, waving your thresher about.

I see you.

'The Lord is enraged because someone has raised doubts about His Prophet's task.'

He fought along with me, that man, he obeyed my orders and now I know he regrets it. He may well hate what he has done. I try to catch his eye so that I can understand: but maybe it's better not to. There he is, bolt upright and paralysed by his chains, waiting for God to tell Jan Matthys the Prophet how to behave.

'The time is over. The choice has been made. Anyone who abandons the Lord's banner shows that he was always undecided, that he followed the others without ever really receiving the inner call to holy arms: he is an enemy. And now he is spreading uncertainty among the ranks of the saints in order to throw our victory in jeopardy. But that victory is inevitable, because the Lord leads us.'

You're a madman, a mad scoundrel of a baker, and I'm a madman too, because after all, I was the one who handed you all this on a plate.

'If we don't immediately remove the sinner from the midst of the holy people, the wrath of the Lord will fall upon everyone.'

Sword in hand, he walks around Ruecher, whose face is purple and startled.

The pettifogger, von der Wieck, along with three other notables, objects that in Münster no one has ever been executed without due process, that there should be witnesses, an advocate . . .

Matthys walks round and round in silence; he weighs these words, goes on walking round, the tension rises from the people and reaches him. He stops.

'Due process. Witnesses, an advocate. Come forward, then.'

Hesitant looks, they come uncertainly forward to the stage.

What the hell are you doing, Jan? I realise I'm clutching my pistol. A few heads away, Gresbeck looks at me, his face harsh, impassive, the scar quivering on his eyebrow, his only sign of nerves.

Careful, Jan, these men have learned to fight.

'Today you will bear witness to the greatest of events. You will bear witness to the birth of Jerusalem: Münster is no more, in the city of God His word alone is law. And He speaks and acts through the hand of His Prophet. You are the witnesses.'

The blade swings up and comes down on Ruecher's throat, killing him with a single blow.

Despair.

Von der Wieck, drenched by the deluge of blood, stands devastated in the middle of the square, Knipperdolling and Kibbenbrock stare at the ground, Rothmann moves his lips in prayer, Gresbeck is motionless.

A silence more chilling than the coldest ice of hell, broken only by humble invocations of the will of God: some people fall to their knees.

Bockelson takes the stage. 'How privileged we are to have the blood that washes the people of the saints of the shame of doubt!' He puts a hackbut to his shoulder, walks forward and runs a finger down von der Wieck's face for some of Ruecher's blood. He smears it on his own face. 'That bastard. That wretched worm has been granted the highest of honours. Why? Why him?'

He fires point blank into the corpse's chest, plunges his hands into the wounds and blesses the crowd with generous splashes of his blood: 'I bless you in blood and spirit, my most holy brethren!'

No one moves.

Matthys spreads his arms to welcome us all. 'Flock of the Lord, God the Father has given us a great lesson. He has revealed impurity, He has dug to the bottom of the yearning for privilege and ownership that still spreads among us and He has cleansed us of it. There were some who still believed that the spirit could be encompassed within the mean municipal privileges of a city. They were mistaken. The New Jerusalem is now a beacon for all the people of the saints, who are coming here from the whole of Christendom to share the glory of the Supreme One. We are not fighting for the privilege of the few, but for the Kingdom of God. And indeed, that is the wonderful message: I tell you that by Easter this year there will be a new heaven and a new earth, the beginning of the Kingdom of the saints. God the Father will come and sweep away every scrap of earth beyond these walls. In the short time left to us, not me, it will not be me who keeps the flock from the temptations of the old world. God the Father says it is good, that anyone appointed by men to this task will be carrying it out in His name' – he hands his sword to Knipperdolling. 'Don't hesitate, brother, it's the will of the Father.'

The burgomaster takes it, incredulously, then looks to Matthys's face for help, finding none. 'We are merely His instrument.'

The Prophet intones the psalm and gradually everyone turns to follow him:

> The Lord is known by the judgement which he executed:
> the wicked is snared in the work of his own hands.
> The wicked shall be turned into hell, and all the nations that forget
>   God.
> For the needy shall not always be forgotten:
> the expectation of the poor shall not perish for ever.
> Arise, O Lord; let not man prevail: let the heathen be judged in thy
>   sight.

Knocking at the door. I don't move. I'm tired, in the darkness. Sharp taps, repeated.

'Gert, open up. Open the fucking door.'

More knocking. I get up, slowly. He isn't going to go away.

I open up.

Wrapped up in a heavy dark cape, ready for a long journey, Redeker is standing before me.

He's going.

I sink into my sofa with my head on one side. As I was just before he came in. As I have been for the last three hours. What can I tell you now? My brain won't respond. A whisper, lacking conviction. 'I didn't think things would turn out like this.'

'What did you think? What the fuck are you on about? It was you who brought him here.'

I stammer something.

Redeker's fury slashes my words. 'I believed in your God, Gert, because He came out on to the barricades and got drunk in the taverns; He sacked churches and He frightened the horsemen. I still believe in Him, if you want to know. Do you happen to know where He went after He left here?'

The echo of the phrases that have been rattling around in my head since Jan of Haarlem arrived.

'Matthys is a fool, Gert. The judges, the cops, the executioner are the worst enemies of the poor who have been fighting on our side. That son of a bitch talks of the God of the last men. But who is his God? Another judge, another cop, another executioner.'

Three hours ago, in the square, clutching my pistol. I gulped air and saliva. I waited.

The others were waiting. For me.

'That fucking madman has ruined everything. It chilled my blood.'

'So why are you standing there? Why don't you get rid of the son of a bitch? Come on now, Gert, get off your arse, Gert from the Well! You're the saints, remember, I'm the thief. I've taken what's mine. When I leave here I'm off.'

I clench my fist, my fingernails sticking into the palm of my hand. I have no answer.

Faint light on a man who doesn't look as though he's from hereabouts, a nervous little hawk, on his feet – his only protruberance – his big solid boots, filthy and fast. I can just make out the swell of his pistols and his little bulging rucksack, short, curly hair and a strange, sparse beard trimmed and combed to a point, the honed black blade pointing to the ground, his supple whiskers curling to his chin, a weird crossbred geometry, the kind of sharp corner you don't want to stumble against on the uncertain nights in these parts.

Chapter 34

He's aged. Sitting on the edge of the bed, the aura of the amiable preacher fled. His face hollow, pitted with cold. Bent over, he abandons his reflections for a moment, looks at me blankly, then lowers his head again.

'What are we going to do?' Bernhard Rothmann runs his hands over his face and shuts his eyes. 'We don't want to throw everything away. It isn't happening the way we thought it would, but it's happening.'

'What? What's happening?'

A sigh. 'Something that's never happened before: the abolition of class, the community of goods, the redemption of the last men on this earth . . .'

'The blood of Ruecher.'

Sombre, his hands on his face again.

'It has abolished hope, Bernhard. New laws won't give it back to us. Before, God was fighting at our side. Now He's come back to terrorise us.'

Rothmann stares into the void, murmuring, 'I'm praying, Brother Gert, I'm praying a lot . . .'

I leave him alone with the anguish that is bending his spine, whispering invocations that no one will hear.

What I have to do.

I turn up in front of Wördemann's mansion, embellished with bronze plaques and bulbs, artfully carved wood right up to the top. It is here, in the residence of the richest man of the city, that the Prophet has made his home.

Immediately inside, four armed men: faces I don't recognise, people from elsewhere, probably Dutchmen.

'I have to search you, brother.' He looks me up and down, perhaps he recognises me, but he's had his orders.

I glare at him. 'I'm Captain Gert from the Well, who the hell are you?'

He tenses. 'I can't let anyone go up without frisking him first.'

The other guard nods, hackbut at his shoulder, moronic expression on his face.

I reply in Dutch, 'You know who I am.'

He shrugs, embarrassed. 'Jan Matthys told me not to let in anyone armed. What can I do?'

Fine, I leave my pistol and my dagger. A second glare is enough to put him off, he doesn't dare touch me.

He walks me up the stairs, lighting the way with his lantern.

What I have to do.

At the top of the second staircase there is a corridor, another light catches the eye, it comes from a room off to the side, the door is open: she is sitting down, brushing her radiant hair, which reaches almost to the floor. She repeats the movement, from top to bottom. She turns round: terrible beauty, innocence in her eyes.

'Move.' The guard's voice.

'Divara. I didn't know he'd brought her here.'

'And as a matter of fact she doesn't exist. You didn't see her, it's better for everyone.'

He guides me to the drawing room. A gigantic fireplace holds the fire that lights the room.

He is sitting brazenly on an imposing throne, his eye fixed on the flames that are consuming the log. The Dutchman nods to me to go in, turns on his heels and disappears.

Alone. What I have to do.

My footsteps echo like the tolling of a bell, lugubrious, heavy.

I stop and try to look into his eyes, but his mind is elsewhere, the shadows draw strange features on that pallid face.

'I've been waiting for you, my brother.'

The pokers are lined up on the wall of the hearth, like a row of pikes.

A massive candelabrum on the long walnut table.

The knife that he's been using to cut the meat of his dinner.

My hands. Strong.

What I have to do.

He barely turns round: a face without determination, without menace.

'Fearless hearts love the depth of night. It's a time when it's hard to lie, we're all weaker, we're all vulnerable. And blood-red fades with all the other colours.' He swings his leg over the arm of the chair and lets it dangle there inertly. 'Some burdens aren't easy to bear. Difficult choices, that the coarse minds of men can't grasp. We make an effort, each day we struggle to understand. And we ask God to give us a sign, a nod of assent to our miserable deeds. That's what we ask. We want to be taken by the hand and guided through this dark night, till daylight comes. We want to know we are not alone, not to be in error as we raise our knife over Isaac. So we wait to see the angel come and stay our blade, and reassure us of God's goodness. We really want to see the futility of our gestures confirmed, we want it to be nothing but a ridiculous pantomime, its sole purpose to test our absolute devotion to the will of the Lord. But that's not what happens. God doesn't put us to the test in order to amuse Himself with these wretched mud-forged creatures, just to test our devotion. No. God makes us His witnesses, He wants us to sacrifice ourselves, to sacrifice our mortal pride, which makes us love being loved, exalted, elevated as prophets and saints. Captains. The Lord doesn't know what to do with our good faith, with our goodness. And He turns us into murderers, unscrupulous sons of bitches, just as He converts murderers and panders to his cause.'

Matthys's voice is a murmur that reaches the ceiling, touching the heads of our elongated shadows. It is the voice of mortal illness, of a profound gangrene: there is something chilling in his words, in his body that now looks exhausted, something that makes me shiver despite the fact that I'm only a few feet away from the fire. It's as though he knew why I came. Like a mirror reflecting the image of what I felt within.

'Sometimes the weight of that choice becomes unbearable. And you feel like dying, like blocking your ears and deserting the Lord. Because the Kingdom, Gert, what we've been dreaming of since we were in Holland, you remember? The Kingdom of God is a jewel that you can win only if you get your hands dirty with mud, shit and blood. And you're the one who has to do it, no one else, that would be easy. No, you're the one. Reciting your part in the plan.' He smiles crookedly at his ghosts. 'Once a man saved my life. He jumped out of a well and, all alone, he faced the men who wanted my blood. When I entrusted that man with a mission, to come here, to Münster, and prepare the coming of the Kingdom, I knew he would not fail. Because that was his role in the plan. As mine is to keep the throne of the Father until the established day.'

What I have to do.

The poker.

The candelabrum.

The knife.

'When is the day, Jan?'

I was the one who was speaking, but it was a different voice, the thought formed within me and came out without passing through my lips. It was the voice of my mind.

No, he turns round without hesitating. 'Easter. That's the day.' He nods to himself. 'And until then, Gert, my brother, I entrust you with the defence of our city against the forces of darkness that are gathering out there. Do that for me. Protect the people of God against the last tremor of the old world.'

Yes, you know what I've come to do. You knew the moment I came in.

We stare at each other for a long time, promise in our eyes: you're a fixed-term prophet, Jan of Haarlem.

Chapter 35

We're on a reconnaissance mission, tracing trajectories that gradually fan out further and further from the city walls. A group of seven, we are testing the solidity of the bishop's encirclement. We move in silence, some distance apart, within reach of signals in light or sound, often aided by darkness, on the bare stone paved by Master Winter and turned polished by Blacksmith Wind. As soon as we see the lines of mercenaries, we begin to skirt them, hidden, until we can find gaps between them.

Waiting patiently, frozen, slight movements, furtive incursions, signals disseminated and annotated on improvised maps to record our journeys, gaps in their defences, escape routes.

We've already escaped von Waldeck's blockade twice and we'll do it again, we've worked out that it's disjointed, ineffective, sluggish.

We're short of a stretcher where we could lay the bones of the brave brothers Mayer, heroes of the February barricades; we're short of a cup to pour herbal infusion, copiously topped up with schnapps by the farrier Adrianson; beer for the bigger of the Brundt brothers, Peter, simple and enthusiastic as the noonday sun.

Although he doesn't say anything, Heinrich Gresbeck misses the lamp that usually illuminates the incessant nocturnal reading of that exact and impassive soldier, whose thirst for knowledge must have been born in a very different time from this one.

On the other hand we have Arrow, the falcon that Bart Boekbinder, a young cousin picked up along the way, is raising with paternal care and surprising results.

As to myself, I don't know what I can say with any clarity about my own condition during these days: my mind and body are going in different directions, not in open opposition, but remote nonetheless. My thoughts, in turn, are divided within themselves, accumulating page by page, action and memory, reflection and decision, leaving me like a great onion, layer after layer. At its deep heart, searing and profound, lie the words of the Great Matthys, the Baker God.

We spur our horses the minute we're out of the Jüdefeldertor, heading north-west, to circle the bishop's positions.

Gresbeck is riding at my side, along with five of his best men. I've chosen people who fought under my orders on the ninth and tenth of February: the new arrivals from Holland don't inspire great trust in me; they bear arms, certainly, but they've also brought women and children, more mouths that need to be fed in a terrible winter: they barely know who von Waldeck is and they don't even know how this all started. All they can see is the beacon of Jerusalem in the night. It's the ardour of the Prophet.

The bishop has recruited a ludicrous army, a thousand men, well-armed but underpaid, with little reason to risk their lives; once toppled from his throne, the pig in purple is nothing. They say that Philip, Landgrave of Hesse, has sent two enormous cannon, bearing the impressive names of 'The Devil' and 'His Mother', but refused to send troops. I'm convinced that von Waldeck is trying to persuade all the minor lords in the vicinity to help him fight the Anabaptist plague. For the time being all he has done is to dig embankments to close off the exit roads towards Anmarsch and Telgte. And given that he isn't stupid, he'll be putting all the noblemen of the lands between here and Holland on the alert, to block the flow of heretics heading for Münster.

We gallop into the Wasserberg forest, travelling along the path that connects with the road to Telgte. We dismount in silence and bring the horses to the edge of the pond, an obligatory stopping point for anyone coming from the north: the horses can drink, and an old abandoned cottage shelters us from the snow and rain.

In the intense cold, our breath forms clouds in front of our beards. We squat on the damp moss.

We count a dozen men, hackbuts, a row of banners, a small cannon. 'The bishop's mercenaries.' His scar stands out even whiter than usual.

'Do you recognise their standards?'

Gresbeck shrugs. 'I don't think so. It could be Captain Kempel . . . I told you, it's a lifetime since I've been in these parts.'

'These people are fighting for tuppence ha'penny. Jackals, they are. With everything that's been requisitioned from the Lutherans and the papists, we could offer them more than von Waldeck could afford.'

'Hm. It's an idea. But we should be careful, our strength lies in our brotherhood.'

'We could print flyers and distribute them in the countryside.'

'Münster can't go on taking in people indefinitely.'

'You're right. We'd have to make contact with the Dutch and German brethren. Münster could be the example. We've shown that it can be done. But why not Amsterdam, or Emden . . .?'

We return to the horses and set off to complete our mission.

I decide to tell him. I've got to know whom I can depend on. 'Matthys is dangerous, Heinrich. He could destroy everything we've done in a single day.'

The former mercenary looks at me strangely, something's bothering him.

Again: 'I don't want things to end up this way. I knew Melchior Hofmann, he'd established a date for the end of the world as well. The day came, nothing happened and his reputation evaporated.'

We ride on ahead of the others, they can't hear what we're saying.

'That man has balls, Gert: he's abolished money and since the day I was born I'd never thought such a thing could be done. And he did it with a click of his fingers . . .'

'And he's shutting up anyone who opens his mouth.'

'Tell me. What do you plan to do?'

I've got to tell him. 'I want to stop him, Heinrich. I want to stop him becoming the new bishop of Münster, or dragging us all into a fearsome bloodbath. I'm the one who's got to do it. Rothmann is ill, he's weak. Knipperdolling and Kibbenbrock would never attack the authority of the Prophet, they're shitting themselves.'

We fall silent for a moment, listening to the hoofs ringing on the ground, the horses panting.

It's his turn to speak. 'Nothing's going to happen on Easter Day.'

Maybe it's a statement of intent on his part.

'That's exactly the problem. What plans does Matthys have for that day? He's a madman, Heinrich, a dangerous madman.'

It seems incredible: just over a month ago we were in charge of Münster; now we're talking in whispers, far from the ears of everyone, as if doubt were a mortal crime.

'He gave a date and on the basis of that date he has assumed absolute power. We can get him.'

'Run him down in front of everyone?'

I swallow hard. 'Or kill him.' My bones are chilled the minute the words are uttered, as though winter wanted to freeze them with an icy bite.

A few yards more in silence. It's as though I can hear the hubbub of his thoughts.

His eyes remain fixed towards the end of the road. 'There would be a war in the city. Those people who have come from elsewhere, they all love him. The Münsterites might follow you, but with every passing day they're becoming more of a minority.'

'You're right. But we can't just stand and watch as something we've fought for goes up in smoke.'

Once more, the sound of his thoughts. 'Anyone who's tried to challenge him has left his blood on the cobbles of the square.'

I nod. 'Exactly. And that wasn't what you were fighting for when you used your pistols against the Lutherans and the bishop's men.'

The city seems deserted. Silence, no one in the streets. We look at each other anxiously, like people who scent that a disaster has taken place; but we don't speak, we leave the horses and set off together, as though drawn by a magnet towards the central theatre, the great cathedral square. With each step we take we sense the mounting anxiety of some menacing disaster, unknown but clear and present, that has fallen upon the city and engulfed the inhabitants. Where is everyone? There's nobody there, not even a flea-ridden dog. We all quicken our pace.

The whitish cloud puffs above the row of buildings along the narrow street leading to the square.

It is full.

The noise of a crowd arranged, rapt and respectful, around its centre, where there stands a pyre shooting tongues of flame. An obscene altar raised to oblivion, the Word of God erasing that of men, spewing forth its triumph over our bent backs, burying our eyes beneath an impenetrable blanket of smoke; its breath pouring out above our heads; its implacable eye fixed upon us, hunting us down to where we cannot hide, within our own thoughts, within the desire to be, one day, wiser. Stifling all curiosity, all brilliance.

The smoke rises gently from the pile of books. They're picking up armfuls of the volumes loaded on the backs of the carts, and throwing them into the bonfire; a column of fire rises until it licks at the sky, to attract the angels with the smoke of Peter Lombard, Augustine, Tacitus, Caesar, Aristotle . . .

The Prophet, standing bolt upright on the stage, clutches a Bible. I am sure he sees me. Mumbled syllables which do not rise above the exalted cheering of the people or the crackling of the fire, but are uttered for my benefit by those thin lips. 'Vain words of men, you won't see the day of thunder. The Word, and it alone, will sing the Lord's judgement.'

The pile grows and is consumed, it rises and turns to ash, I spot a copy of Erasmus, showing that this God no longer needs our language and will not give us peace. The old world is consumed like parchment in the flames . . .

By my side, the pale face of Gresbeck, furious and strong. 'I'm on your side.'

I wake with a start from agitated sleep, drenched in cold sweat despite the rain hammering furiously against the shutters, throbbing with ancestral fear, I catch my breath with a dull, hoarse wheeze. I narrow my eyes, defenceless.

Yellow lights pierce the gloom of early morning.

Day of Resurrection.

Scenario number one: at sunset the square is full, everyone's there, waiting for a speech from the Prophet. Matthys comes out on to the stage, addresses the crowd, gives some kind of explanation of the non-existent Apocalypse, probably attributing blame to those members of the elect who are not yet pure. The stage is erected to the south of the cathedral. Twenty men, including myself, enter by the western façade and leave by the transept window right behind the Prophet. The other ten are in the first few rows. The guards haven't time to react. Gresbeck grabs Matthys by the shoulder and puts his blade to his throat. Captain Gert explains why Enoch must die.

Scenario number two: Enoch guides the people of the saints to the final battle. Let him. Von Waldeck's ragbag of troops can be defeated. Twenty of my men in the key battle positions. The rest are arranged around the Prophet, keeping an eye on his personal guard. In the confusion of battle, find the right moment. Captain Gert's pistol leaves Enoch dead in the field.

The cathedral spreads wide its jaws.

Four broad and shallow steps, each one a span across, lead up to the two supporting pillars of the arch that precedes and dominates the portal; pointed at the top, the underside jagged with thirteen stone protrusions like sharpened fangs. Two steps, then four more, narrower and steeper, up to the two doors. In the middle, a kind of uvula formed by a statue supported on a slender column. On either side of the second staircase three niches gradually restrict the opening. All the way from the arch that forms the lips and teeth to the dark throat in the depths of the building, a host of statues clusters on the palate like the souls of the damned swallowed by the monster.

Above the entrance are the huge eyes of a window with fine lattice-work, flanked on either side by two smaller, coarser windows. The face is finished off with a triangular forehead, topped by three pinnacles: its horns.

The façade is enclosed by the massive square towers, outlined by two orders of hanging arches, the first order simple, the second double, opened up by two orders of mullioned windows, growing progressively larger. On either side the two wings of the transept are claws planted heavily on the ground.

Rain-drenched, I am swallowed up.

Almost half the present population of Münster has been gathered between these three imposing naves since vespers on Saturday. On their knees, hands clasped together, they wait, chanting quietly, for the event that the Prophet has predicted for today.

'Today everything will vanish from the earth, says the Lord. I will destroy men and beasts. I will exterminate the birds from the sky and the fishes from the sea, I will smite the wicked. I will exterminate man from the earth. The final day will be like a flood. This city of ours is the ark, built with the wood of penitence and righteousness. It will float upon the waters of the final retribution.

'God did not ask Noah to tell the world what was about to happen. And when the waters withdrew, He promised that He would never again smite all living creatures as He had done that day. From that point onwards, every time the Lord intends destruction, He chooses a prophet to instruct his fellow men in the ways of conversion. Jeremiah spoke to the King of Judaea, Jonah crossed Niniveh, Ezekiel was sent to the Israelites, Amos travelled through the desert.

'If I send my sword to destroy a country and the people of that country choose a sentry, and the sentry, seeing the sword fall upon the country, sounds the trumpet and gives the people an alarm; and if he who hears the sound of the trumpet pays no attention and the sword reaches him and takes him by surprise, he is responsible for his own destruction. If, on the other hand, the sentry sees the sword coming and does not sound the trumpet and the sword reaches a man and takes him by surprise, that man will be surprised because of his own iniquity: but for his death I will demand an answer from the sentry.

'I do not enjoy the death of the wicked, says the Lord God, I want the wicked to cease their evil ways and go on living. If God wanted to judge the world as it is, He would not send prophets. If God wanted to convert all the godless, He would instil his Spirit in them, but He would not use prophets.

'Jan Matthys of Haarlem was called to spread the Word of God as far as his voice could reach. Beyond these borders the Lord must have appointed other prophets to himself: in Turkey, the New World, Cathay.

'Outside these walls, where death is sharpening its scythe, there are men who were deaf to the trumpet, and not because they were careless. The mercenaries in the pay of the princes, the desperate men forced by hunger to fight wars that have nothing to do with them, those who have heard only lies about us. How many of them would enter the ark if they were told that money had been abolished, that all goods have been placed in common ownership, that the only erudition is that of the Bible and the only law the law of God?

'If the Prophet of the New Jerusalem does not speak to them, does not dissuade them from conduct dictated by their poverty of spirit, then he is the one the Lord will hold to account for their destruction.

'There is a time and a place for all things with a beginning and an end. Our time is at an end. The Lord is coming and His Prophet will be as nothing. The doors of the Kingdom are open wide. He will fulfil his mandate, as it is written in the Plan.'

Knipperdolling doesn't understand. With an incredulous expression he follows Matthys's steps to the door. He tries to ask Rothmann something, but gets no reply. The preacher's ravaged face betrays no emotions, his lips are moved by the trembling of a prayer. Perhaps knowledge of the Bible and its prophets makes him more far-sighted than Gresbeck and myself about Matthys's behaviour. Heinrich, leaning against a pillar, looks like a statue. He cranes his neck, straining to catch my eye. What do we do now? Jan of Leyden flicks frantically through the Bible in search of passages that might be translated on to the stage. Someone intones the *Dies Irae*. A kind of spontaneous procession runs along the central nave.

I push forward to get to the door, ready for whichever scenario has been chosen.

A sickly ray of sunlight accompanies his resolute bearing.

The Prophet of Münster passes through the Ludgeritor and leaves the city behind him, escorted by a dozen men. No one else has been able to follow him: everyone has his role in the Plan.

We crowd on to the city walls.

The bishop prince's camp is clearly visible a short distance away, slightly blurred by the mist rising from the damp earth.

We see them advancing towards the embankment dug by the bishop's mercenaries. There is commotion in their ranks, they take aim with their hackbuts.

Matthys gestures to his men to stop.

Matthys walks on alone.

Matthys is unarmed.

Everyone's astonished. What's he trying to do?

No one breathes.

Matthys raises his arms to the sky, very high, his black hair rain-sodden.

He's out of range, but a marksman would only have to take a quick run, a few dozen yards at the most.

Everyone silent, as though the wind could carry his words to the earthworks.

Thousands of eyes concentrated on a single point. The final moment.

The Plan.

He keeps on walking. He climbs up on to the first low wall of the fortifications.

My God, he's really going to do it.

Until Easter.

A fixed-term prophet.

People seem to hear something, perhaps the echo of a word that has been uttered more loudly than the others.

A sudden movement behind the Prophet. Someone climbing, the gleam of a sword. They drop forward.

A troop of horsemen emerge from the camp and hurl themselves into the road to block Matthys's retinue. Men and horses in a single confused mass.

Everyone's eyes are frozen with horror, like dry leaves in the ice.

Not a shout, not a breath.

Shouts of exultation from the bishop's men.

A hand on my shoulder. 'Come away, Gert.' It's Gresbeck, his face sombre.

'What the fuck's going on now?'

'He really did it . . .'

The Münsterites are all still on the walls, waiting for something to happen, for Matthys's body to rise up and open the heavens with a fiery word.

'What the fuck are we going to do, Gert?'

He shakes me. I almost discharge the tension with an idiotic smile. 'That bastard has managed to scotch our plans . . .'

'The important thing is that we've got rid of him. But what now?'

We watch the people flowing through the streets as we go in search of the burgomasters. Drained, lifeless ghosts and sleepwalkers without even the strength to be frightened. They've been deprived of their Apocalypse, the Prophet is gone. Not the merest hint of God. But this is really the Last Easter, with the tombs uncovered and the souls of the dead wandering as they wait for judgement. Someone saw him being carried into heaven by the angels, someone else saw him being dragged to hell by a demon. They are crowding the streets, the market square, no longer with any desire to pray, because they don't know who or what is worth praying for. Clusters of people talking in low voices form all over the place. The situation needs to be taken in hand, we have to find Knipperdolling and Kibbenbrock before discouragement turns to panic.

We find the second burgomaster sitting on the steps of St Lamberti's, head lowered.

'Where's Knipperdolling?'

Confused: 'He was with me at the walls and I haven't seen him since then.'

'Are you sure he's not in the church?'

He shakes his head. 'He hasn't come this way.'

We hurry towards the cathedral square. I don't need to look at Gresbeck: we are harbouring the same dire presentiments.

Shortly before dark, macabre confirmation arrives.

The body of Jan of Haarlem in a basket catapulted beyond the walls. Butchered, in pieces.

Knipperdolling seems to have gone mad. Running through the torpor of the city, he is yelling at the top of his voice the name of Jan Bockelson, the new David.

Standing on the stage next to the cathedral is the unmistakable outline of the Madman of Leyden.

Scene one: the dream of King David (KNIPPERDOLLING *in the role of* MATTHYS, BOCKELSON *as himself*).

MATTHYS: Yes, yes. You're a bastard, Jan of Leyden. A son of a bitch. The bastard and the son of a bitch who will succeed me as leader of the forces of the Lord.

BOCKELSON: No, no! I am a slimy and disgusting worm, unworthy, unworthy!

MATTHYS: Jan, my namesake and my apostle, you know how much I love you. And my love is nothing but a reflection of the greater love that the Father has for you. Worm, yes, that's exactly what you were. And I dragged you out of the mud of your filthy whorehouses to make you fight at my side in Münster. Worm. Regal worm who will assume the task of taking up my sword and ushering in the Kingdom. In a week the Prophet will have to make way for the Lord. And the Lord will choose you, to be the leader of the New Zion.

BOCKELSON (*holds back his tears; either he can't see anyone, or perhaps he sees everything very clearly. Much more clearly than me and* GRESBECK): Step forward, Berndt.

Intermezzo: (KNIPPERDOLLING, *dressed as himself, comes forward clumsily, clutching the great sword of Justice*).

KNIPPERDOLLING: It's true. A week ago Jan of Leyden told me he had had a visit from Matthys in his sleep, and that in that dream he entrusted him with the task of taking the Plan to its conclusion.

Scene two: the Plan is carried out (BOCKELSON *in the roles of* GOD *and* DAVID, KNIPPERDOLLING *as himself*).

GOD: Men and women of Münster, look at this little man. Look at David. Men and women of the New Jerusalem, the Kingdom is yours! By God, I have won. All that was promised has come to pass. You are in charge of the Kingdom. Run on to the walls to laugh in the face of your enemies, fart out your joy upon their bestial grunts! There is nothing they can do, Matthys has shown as much. He wanted you to know that the godless shit eaters may be able to reduce him to tiny bits the size of pickings from your nose, but they will not even tarnish the Plan! And my plan is to win! To win! A slingshot for David!

KNIPPERDOLLING *hurries to pass a slingshot to* BOCKELSON, *of the kind that the peasants use to keep the crows away from their harvest.*

DAVID: Citizens of the New Jerusalem, I am the man who is coming in the name of the Father: the new David, the bastard stepbrother of Christ, the chosen one! Admire the Father, who chose a whore master, a brothelkeeper, to appoint as His apostle, His captain. And through the mouth of the archangel Matthys He announced His pregnancy. Yes, the pregnancy of the Plan accomplished. Jan Matthys is not dead! Matthys the Great fertilised me with the Word of the Lord and lives in me, he lives in all of you, because we are destined to go on to the end, we are the strength of the Lord, we are the best, the chosen, the saints, the ones who inherited the earth and can use it as we will. There are no limits now on what we can do: the world is over, it is at our feet! (*He draws breath; with his blue eyes he scans the crowd, by now so great that it fills the square.*) Brothers and sisters: Eden is ours!

KNIPPERDOLLING (*at his side*): Long live Zion!

The response is a leg-breaking kick, a frenzy, a pistol shot, a blow to the chin, a bucketful of icy water that leaves me utterly dazed. It's a shout of celebration by thousands of people at the tops of their voices, to banish our despair, our discouragement, our knowledge of having followed a madman now lying in bits in a basket. Better to maintain our beliefs right to the end, better to go on dreaming than become aware of the collective madness. I read it in their eyes, in their distraught faces: better a charlatan pimp, yes, yes, the son of Matthys, he's what we want, give us back our Apocalypse, laugh at our faith. Laugh at our God.

I stumble in silence, I see Bockelson hoisted aloft by a forest of hands and borne in triumph around the square. He is laughing and blowing kisses to everyone, sensual, provocative, maybe he's got one for the comrade who has hauled him out of troubles more than once and accompanied him all the way here. Or perhaps the holy pimp no longer thinks about that. Never again will he leave this role, the best performance of his life. Jan, you've finally managed to put on the world like a glove with your theatrical repertoire. Or else, on the other hand, it could be that your characters have found their proper stage in the hearts of these men and the events of the world. Now you are Moses, John, Elijah and whoever you want to be. You are those people for ever, you have no intention of going back. It is written in your smile and in the fact that you would have no reason for doing so.

Grand finale: The crowd flows through the city, carrying the new Prophet of Münster to the Aegiditor so that the bishop's men may see that the morale of the people of Zion is high, and that they have a new leader. But a cry of horror freezes the triumphal procession in its tracks. The women who have opened the gate point to one of the two great pillars.

An arrow has fixed something to the wood, like a small bloody bag. A macabre joke by the bishop's men: they must have taken advantage of the absence of the sentries to approach the walls and then make off again.

The crowd opens up and JAN OF LEYDEN *walks resolutely forward, pulls out the arrow and, without batting an eyelid, picks up the scrotum of* JAN MATTHYS, *clenches it in his fists and nods to his own angels. He raises his voice and the balls of the* PROPHET, *in full view, so that everyone can see.*

BOCKELSON: Yes. Although I left a legitimate wife in Leyden to follow the Great Matthys, he told me I should have been husband to his wife. I must marry the Prophet's widow and use my bollocks in his place. (*He stuffs the bloody lump into his pocket and announces*): Bring Divara! My wife to be!

Applause.

End.

'Don't call me crazy!'

The fist catches me on the cheekbone and I go down.

Jan is a red and blond mask of fury.

I collapse on to a chair. 'Now you really have shown that you're a wretched charlatan.'

He holds his breath, takes a few steps massaging his bruised knuckles, lowers his head, sways back and forth. The outburst of rage is suddenly veiled by despair. 'Help me, Gert, I don't know what to do.' He looks exhausted: a wretched, whining little tailor. 'Help me. I'm a worm, help me, tell me what I have to do. Because I don't know, Gert . . .' He sits down on the throne that belonged to Matthys and looks at the floor.

'You've done enough already.'

He nods. 'I'm a buffoon, yes, a real buffoon. But they wanted hope, you saw them, they wanted me to tell them what I told them. They wanted me this way and I did it, I made them happy, I restored their strength.'

I sit there in silence, lifeless, my head, the blow, the confusion of the past few hours.

He seems to recover a little. 'Yesterday they were lost, today they could resist von Waldeck with their bare hands!' He looks over at me. 'I'm not Matthys. We can start over, we can fuck, you know, we can stuff our faces, we can do everything we want to do. We're free, Gert, we're free and in charge of the world.'

I don't feel like talking, there's no point, but the words come out all by themselves, for me and this crazed character with whom I've shared the stench of the stables: the new Prophet of Münster. 'What world, Jan? Von Waldeck is no fool, the powerful never are. Powerful man helps powerful man, prince supports prince: papists, Lutherans . . . it doesn't matter, the ones at the bottom rebel and you find them all united, with their horsemen and their gleaming armour, lining up to fire. That's the world out there. And you can be sure that that hasn't changed just because you've given these people the lovely dream of Zion.'

He is whining like a puppy, his fingers clutching at his blond curls. 'Tell me. You know how things happen. I'll do whatever you tell me, but don't leave me, Gert . . .'

I rise to my feet in astonishment. 'You're wrong. I don't know either. I don't know any more than you do.'

I reach the door amidst his childish whinging.

She's behind the door. She's been listening to everything.

Her hair is so bright and luminous it could be made of platinum.

Divara: a low-cut dress that shows off her perfect body to marvellous effect. In her face the innocence of a child, white child-queen, daughter of a Haarlem brewer.

A light touch raises my hand and slips a tiny blade into it. 'Kill him,' she barely murmurs, indifferently, as though talking about a spider on the wall, or an old dying dog that needs to be put down.

Her dress opens over her full breast, to reveal the prize. Her eyes of an intense blue that sends terror through my very bones, sending my hair straight up, making my heart thump like a tambourine. A pile of corpses: the vision of what could happen, the abyss opened up by a girl of fifteen. I have to clutch the banisters as I hurl myself down the stairs, far from Venus, Dispenser of Death.

Münster, 22 April 1534

Torpor. Of the limbs, of the mind. I don't recognise anyone, these aren't the same people who defeated the bishops and the Lutherans in a single night. My men, yes, they are that, they would follow me to hell, but I won't be able to take them with me: someone has to stay, to control the jester, the White Queen and their Kingdom of Wonders.

All alone. Get away from here, get away right now, to find the outlet of the sewer before it's too late.

The events of the past few days have been frightening. Yet morale is as high as it could be. In one sortie I captured a troop of horsemen trying to attack the Jüdefeldertor and now we're trying for an exchange of prisoners. We've also stopped the bishop's men lining up below the city walls, just out of the range of the hackbuts, and showing off their pale arses crying, 'Oh, Father, give it to me, I crave your dick!' a habit that they had developed over long evenings of drunkenness and debauchery. With a bit of decent ballistics, all we had to do was get one of them with a cannonball, right between the cheeks, turning him into dog meat.

For a week, all the men in the bastions pissed and shat into a barrel, which was then rolled into the bishop's camp. When they opened it up, the stench almost reached all the way here.

Along with Gresbeck I organised shooting practice for everyone, women and boys included. We are teaching the girls to boil pitch and to pour quicklime on the heads of our besiegers. The walls are guarded on a shift basis, shared out among all the citizens, of both sexes, between the ages of sixteen and fifty.

I've had them put a bell on each bastion, to be rung in case of fire, so that we know where to run with water.

We've discovered that Matthys wrote an inventory of the goods impounded from the Lutherans and the papists, as well as the supplies of food in the city. He jotted down everything, down to the last chicken and the last egg. We can survive for at least a year. And then? Or rather, and in the meantime?

It isn't enough; it can't be enough. The tall tales of Prophet Charlatan won't get us very far.

The Low Countries, the brothers. Tell them what's happening in Münster, organise them, select them, maybe even train them to fight. Request money, ammunition.

I don't know. I don't know the right thing to do, I've never known, I've chosen a different path each time. You just feel that things can't go on like this, that the walls, inside and out, are getting too close for you and that your mind needs some fresh air, your body needs to feel the miles passing beneath you.

Yes. There's one more thing you can do for this city, Gert from the Well: ensure that it is not abandoned to the madness of its prophets.

Münster, 30 April 1534

My luggage is light. Inside there's the old leather bag: biscuits, cheese and dried herrings, enough for a few days; a map of the territories between here and the Low Countries; a full powder horn, make sure it doesn't get wet; the two pistols that Gresbeck insisted I carry with me; and three old faded and greasy letters that betrayed Thomas Müntzer. Relics that I won't be parted from, those last, the only tangible souvenir of what died and was buried beneath the debris of the failed Apocalypse.

'Are you really sure you want to go? The rough voice of the ex-mercenary comes through the door. It isn't the tone of someone who has an objection to raise, but someone who's wondering why I don't take him with me.

'We've miscalculated, Heinrich.'

'You mean with Matthys?'

'I mean with these people.' A fleeting glance as I do up the last straps. 'They want to believe that they're saints. They want someone to tell them that everything has gone smoothly, that Münster is the New Zion and there's no longer anything to fear.' I test the weight of the sack: perfect. 'Whereas in fact they should be shitting themselves. Have you taken a look outside the walls? Von Waldeck is raising fortifications and I'm sure I saw trees being felled to the north-east. Do you know what that means? War machines, Heinrich, they're preparing for a siege. They have every intention of keeping us here for as long as possible, at least until the last tales told by the last prophet kissed on the lips by the mouth of God have left us well and truly fucked. The ships carrying the Baptist brethren here from Holland have been intercepted on the Ems. They were bringing weapons and supplies. Von Waldeck's men are closing the borders, the roads. All the signs are there, but no one can see them. They've got it very well planned.'

Gresbeck gives me his surly look. 'What do you mean?'

'A long siege. They want to shut us up in here, tighten the noose, and wait: hunger, the next winter, internecine rebellions, what the fuck do I know. Time is on their side. If I were von Waldeck here's what I would do: I'd point the cannon and fold my arms.'

The bag is already over my shoulder, Adrianson should have my horse saddled down below. I'm almost serene. 'We need new contact with the Dutch brethren. We need money to buy von Waldeck's mercenaries and turn them against him. We need to discover safe routes to force the blockade. And above all we need to understand whether anyone out there is willing to take up arms and follow us or whether, as Matthys said, it really is a desert out there. We've got to do it quickly: each passing day is a gift to those vultures.'

'And what are you going to do about Bockelson?'

I burst out laughing. We go down the stairs; the mares are ready. The farrier tightens the belts of my saddle. 'If they've chosen him, what can I do?' I jump into the saddle and pull on the reins to restrain the animal's ardour. 'Jan's pathetic, he's a scoundrel. That's why I'm not taking you with me. I want you to keep an eye on him, you're the only one who can do it: Knipperdolling and Kibbenbrock have gone soft, Rothmann's ill. Be careful to choose men you can count on and keep the city defences solid. This above all: Von Waldeck will try to exploit any blunder, any distraction. Give him as good as you get, deluge his mercenaries with flyers, they can be worth more than cannonballs, remember that. I'll be back soon.'

A strong handshake: life-defining choices are still being made. Gresbeck shows no emotion, it isn't his way. It isn't mine either, I now discover.

'Good luck, Captain. And always make sure you've got a good pistol in your belt.'

'See you soon, my friend.'

Adrianson walks ahead of me. My heels strike the flanks of the horse: I don't look at the houses, the people, I'm already at the Unserfrauentor, I'm already out of the city, I'm ten miles along the road to Arnhem.

I'm alive again.

Chapter 38

The wind stirs the tufts of grass on the low dunes, like beards on the chins of giants. A miracle seems to hold up the little shed where the fishermen's boats are kept, battered as if by storms and seawater.

The sun is about to rise, night is over and day has not yet begun: a pinkish light falls upon the gulls as they wheel placidly about, occasionally fighting with the crabs for the dead fish that have fallen from the night's nets. Slow backwash, low tide, a fine mist hides the edge of the beach from north to south. Not a soul.

Little insects run along the trunk of wood brought here from who knows where. I run my hands along its damp bark. The guide assigned to me by the brethren in Rotterdam told me that this was the spot. He didn't hang about: van Braght isn't the kind of person you're pleased to see.

Three long shadows on the sand, to the south. Here they are.

My hands slide to my pistols, crossed under the hooded cape that protects me from the North Sea breeze.

They approach slowly, side by side.

Dark, inexpressive faces, bushy beards, crumpled shirts and swords tucked under a shoulder-belt.

I don't move.

They come within earshot. 'Are you the German?'

I wait for them to get closer. 'Which of you is van Braght?'

Tall, stout, face worn by sun and sea, a small-scale pirate who claims to have attacked twenty Spanish vessels. 'That's me. Have you brought the money?'

I jangle the little bag on my belt.

'Where's the gunpowder?'

He nods. 'It showed up last night. Ten barrels, is that right?'

'Where?'

Three pairs of eyes upon me. Van Braght barely moves his head.

'The imperial forces are covering the coast, it wasn't safe to leave it here. It's at the old dyke, half a mile on.'

'Let's go.'

We set off, four parallel tracks in the sand.

'You're Gerrit Boekbinder, aren't you? The one they call Gert from the Well?' There's no curiosity, no special emphasis in his question.

'I'm the buyer.'

The dyke is a palisade of rotten wood. The sea has penetrated it, forming a narrow channel that disappears into the hinterland. At the top, the low cottage of the coastguard stands out against the sky.

The barrels are covered with worn sailcloth on which terns are walking. When they lift it up, a swarm of flies abandons the stinking fish crammed into boxes. Underneath: the barrels, lined up. One of the three lets me choose. I point to the barrel in the middle, he takes off the lid and steps aside.

The pirate wants to reassure me: 'It's from England. The stench of the fish will keep the cops away.'

I plunge a hand into the black powder.

'It's very dry, don't worry about that.'

'How am I going to transport it?'

He points behind the dunes, where I can see the head of a horse and the high wheels of a cart. 'You're on your own from here.'

I untie the purse and hold it out to him. 'While you're counting it, your men can load up.'

At a nod of his head the two reluctantly lift the first barrels, starting to stagger clumsily towards the path.

A gull lets out a cry above our heads.

The crabs slip beneath the carcass of an old boat.

The sunlight begins to weaken the morning breeze.

Absolute peace.

Van Braght finishes counting. 'There's enough there, mate.'

I reach for my pistols. 'No there isn't. It's less than half what we agreed.' A moment's indecision, he can't see the guns under my coat. 'The bounty on Gert from the Well must be twice as much as that.'

I don't give him time to move, my shot explodes right in his face.

The other two come bounding back, swords drawn. Two against one, I pour the powder into the unloaded pistol, load the bullets, more powder, faster, prime the guns, pull the trigger, they're a few yards away, arms outstretched, a deep breath, no shaking. I aim at the moving limbs: two shots, almost in unison, the first one collapses at my feet and the other falls, his pistol explodes, perhaps I'm dead already, but my ghost draws a short dagger and plunges it into his throat.

A groan.

Silence.

I stay where I am. I watch the gulls coming back to settle on the beach.

I'll have to load the barrels on my own.

Rotterdam, 21 July 1534

'And that makes fifty.' Adrianson finishes checking the weapons, then gives me the list of what we've got. 'Fifty hackbuts, ten barrels of powder, eight bars of lead. And ten thousand florins.'

'We're going to need two carts. Did Reynard give you the passes?'

'Here they are. He says they're practically authentic: the seal is the same as the one they use in the Hague.'

'They'll get us as far as the border. Then we'll have to think about something else. We'll leave as early as we can. We're going to have to stop at Nijmegen and Emmerich, and I don't know how much time it'll take us to get there. It'll be a long journey; we'll have to avoid the busier roads.'

The farrier offers me one of the rolls of dried tobacco from the Indies – he says he was taught to smoke them by the Dutch merchants. The Spanish call them *cigarros*, they smell of another world, of shacks, leather and green pepper. The smell is aromatic and leaves a pleasant taste in the mouth.

We throw ourselves into the hammocks offered to us by Brother Magnus, preacher of the Baptist community in Rotterdam. He keeps a frugal table, but his generosity to the cause makes up for the banquet one might have wanted.

We let the smoke swirl along with our thoughts, and it hangs there in the middle of the room, in the attic of the house.

The brethren over there are meek people. They admire Münster, and they've been a great help to us. But they wouldn't challenge the authorities with an insurrection: they content themselves with practising their own faith in secret, in nocturnal meetings and communal readings. I haven't come across the combative spirit I was expecting. On the other hand I have encountered generosity and esteem in abundance.

It's hard to blame them; things don't work the same way in the big mercantile cities as they do in our German city-state. And the Spaniards are here too, which means the locals have the Emperor right in their own backyard.

But I've discovered that there is a party of discontents, there are a few turbulent brethren who want to follow our example. Few in number, inexperienced, lacking a real leader. One of them is Obbe Philips, who has denied his past as an apostle of Matthys and pretends he's always followed the same moderate line as he does today. Then there's young David Joris of Delft, a brilliant orator whom our host identified as a promising guide. It seems that the future of the movement depends to a large extent on Joris. His mother was one of the first Baptist martyrs, beheaded in the Hague when David was a child. He is wanted as a highly dangerous criminal throughout the whole of Holland, so it's difficult to meet him. He has no fixed abode, he's always travelling about the place, he turns up and off he goes again, he often uses false names with the brethren for fear of infiltrators. It seems that he doesn't shirk the sacking of churches, but even he, like Philips, vociferously denies murder.

The situation is far from stable, but likely to end up with nothing but a lot of fine words being bandied about.

Meanwhile, we'll be on the road again tomorrow, heading back with our precious cargo to hide from the roadblocks and prying eyes. Another two communities to visit. Back in Münster in a month.

'Goodnight, Peter.'

'Goodnight, Captain.'

It appears grimly from behind the hill. The cold wind hurls the rain into our faces, forcing us to narrow our eyes. I can make out the black silhouette in the plain, the banks of the Aa, the line of the walls, the sentries' lanterns, the only stars in a black-dark night.

I spur the horses on to one final sweat-drenched and exhausted effort. Adrianson, who's bringing the other cart, is close behind me. We've done it. The wheels throw up mud from the path, we travel slowly, ever closer to our goal. Further to the north, I can make out a black row of fortifications: von Waldeck's earthworks have become an insurmountable barrier closing off all means of access and all escape routes.

'There's something wrong.' The farrier's voice is lost in the rain. He's right, I have a strange feeling of anxiety in my stomach, a deadly sense of catastrophe.

'The bell towers, Gert . . . the towers. What's happened to them?'

That's what's missing. The city is flat. And the bishop's cannon can't reach so far and so high. Where have the bell towers gone?

It isn't the cold of the night that sends shivers into my limbs; an invisible hand is strengthening its grip on my innards.

We identify ourselves to the sentries of the Ludgeritor. I don't know any of the guards, or perhaps I do, one, Hansel, the shoemaker, white-haired, decrepit. 'Hansel, is that you?'

The shifty eyes of a guilty man. 'Good to have you back, Captain.'

A slap on the shoulder. 'What on earth's happened to the towers of Münster?'

A gloomy expression, his eyes still fixed on the ground, no reply. I grab his arm as I try to suppress the panic rising in my throat. 'Hansel, tell me what happened.'

He frees himself from my grip, a thief before the court. 'You shouldn't have gone away, Captain.'

The night air speaks of a crime committed, something horrible, unspeakable. Filled with anxiety, we walk down the deserted streets towards Adrianson's house. No one says anything, there's no need, we hurry, soaked to the bone.

I see him knocking at the door, tightly hugging his wife and his little son. There's no joy in their faces, these are the gestures of someone sharing a misfortune.

His wife offers us a hot infusion, by the embers crackling in the fireplace. 'That's all I can give you. Since rationing was introduced it's been hard to get hold of milk.'

Thin, the nerves standing out in her neck, the strength of her grief sustaining her. Her eyes turn to her son with each sentence she utters, as though to protect him from some obscure danger.

'Are things as bad as that?'

'The bishop has intensified the siege, with each passing day it's got harder to go out and get food. And we have to queue every day to get food for our children. The deans in charge of rationing are giving us less and less.'

Adrianson has managed to get the fire going, as though the performance of these simple domestic gestures could alleviate the imminence of despair.

'What's happened to the bell towers, Greta?'

She looks at me without trembling, strong, she doesn't share the men's cowardice. 'You shouldn't have left, Captain.'

It's almost an accusation. Now I'm the one avoiding her glance.

Her husband is ready to reproach her. 'Don't get angry with him, he's risked his life for everyone. In Holland we got hold of money, lead for the cannon, gunpowder . . .'

The woman shakes her head. 'You don't know. You haven't heard anything.'

'What is it, Greta? What's happened?'

Adrianson can't control his fear and anger. 'Tell us, woman. What's become of the bell towers?'

She nods, those hard eyes are meant for me. 'They knocked them down. Nothing must rise to challenge the Supreme One. No one must be proud; we have to keep our eyes down when we walk in the streets; we can't wear necklaces, they get requisitioned. He's appointed two little girls and a boy to be judges of the people. They strip you of any superfluous objects, any coloured clothes. All the gold and silver fetches up in the court strongboxes.'

Adrianson takes her hand. 'What about your ring?'

'Everything . . . to the greater glory of God.'

I breathe deeply, I've got to stay calm, try to understand. 'What court, Greta? What are you talking about?'

She speaks with hatred, with profound fury. 'He's made himself king. King of Münster, of the elect.'

I'm so angry the words stick in my throat, but she goes on, 'It was Duesentschnuer, the goldsmith, that old crock, along with Knipperdolling. A horrible recitation: they flattered him, they implored him to accept the crown. They said that God had spoken to them in a dream, that he had to accept the crown from the Father and lead us into the promised land. And that vile charlatan was there prostrating himself, mocking us, saying he wasn't worthy . . .'

Protective and raging, the blacksmith hugs his wife's shoulders. 'Revolting pig. Threepenny whoremonger.'

I murmur, 'No one stopped him . . . Where were my men . . . Heinrich Gresbeck?'

'You mustn't blame them, Captain, they're not here. They're acting as escorts to the missionaries who were dispatched to find reinforcements. The king has surrounded himself with armed men, anyone who dares to speak out against him is carried off, disappears, no one knows where, to some underground prison, perhaps . . . then to the bottom of the canal.'

I've got to ask, I've got to know: 'Bernhard Rothmann?'

The silence heralds a horror even worse, if possible, than I was expecting.

'He's been appointed court theologian. Knipperdolling, Kibbenbrock and Krechting received the title of count. The king says he will soon lead the chosen people across the Red Sea of the enemy armies and conquer the whole of Germany. He's already assigned the principalities to his most loyal followers.'

Anger and fear are becoming a dead weight that drags me down. I'm exhausted, but there's more, I can read it in that steadfast expression, in that proud, tired beauty.

'Rothmann said we had to follow the customs of the patriarchs of the Scriptures. Go forth and multiply, he said, and let every man take as many wives as he can satisfy, to increase the number of the elect. The king has fifteen wives, none of them much more than children. Rothmann has ten and so have the others. If my husband hadn't come back within a month I'd have been assigned to one of them.'

Adrianson's hands, white with tension, want to smash the fireplace to pieces.

'Oh, we shouted, yes we did, we said it wasn't right. Margaret von Osnabrück said that if the Lord wanted procreation, then women should be allowed to choose more than one husband as well.' She swallows back her compassion with a sigh. 'She spat in the face of the preachers and pissed on the heads of the ones who came to get her. She knew what awaited her, but she wouldn't keep quiet. She shouted to the whole city as they dragged her away, that the women of Münster hadn't fought side by side with their men only to become common concubines.'

Another pause, holding back her tears of hate. There's an infinite dignity in those words, the dignity of someone who has shared in the extreme gesture of a brother or a sister. 'She died killing them with her words. Many women followed her example, preferring to die insulting the tyrants rather than accept their laws. Elisabeth Hölscher, who dared to leave her husband. Katharina Koekenbecker, who lived with two men under the same roof. Barbara Butendieck, denounced by her husband because she dared to contradict him. They didn't execute her, no. She was pregnant, that was why she got away.'

Nothing but the crackling of the fire. The deep breathing of little Hans in his cot. The drumming of the rain on the roof.

'Didn't anyone rebel?'

She nods. 'The blacksmith Mollenhecke. Along with another two hundred of them. They managed to lock the king and his followers in the Rathaus, but then ... What could they do? Open the gates to the bishop? That would have meant condemning the city to death. They couldn't imagine doing that. Someone freed the king and two hours later their heads rolled into the square.'

Peter Adrianson picks up the old sword he fought with on the barricades in February. Exhaustion on the furrows of his face. 'Let me kill him, Captain.'

I get to my feet. What remains to be done. 'No. A martyr wouldn't be much use to your wife and son.'

'He'll have to pay for it.'

I turn back to Greta. 'Get your things. You're going tonight.'

Adrianson clutches blindly at the hilt of his sword. 'He's got us fucked, he can't get away with it.'

'Take your family far away from here. That's my final order, Peter.'

He's about to cry, he looks around: the house, the objects. Me. 'Captain . . .'

Greta is ready, her son in her arms, wrapped in a blanket. I wish Adrianson had her strength right now.

'Let's go.' I pull him by one arm, we walk out into the deluge, I let her pass. We keep close to the walls, along a route that seems interminable.

All of a sudden Adrianson's wife gives a start.

Instinctively I put my hand on my sword. Two short, hooded silhouettes.

One holds a lantern. They approach, small footsteps in the mud.

The light is raised towards our faces. I glimpse young eyes, smooth cheeks. Not more than ten years old.

A shiver.

The little girl points her finger at the bundle that Greta is holding pressed to her chest. A small white finger.

Terror in the woman's eyes. She lifts the corner of the blanket and reveals Hans, stiff with cold.

The girl doesn't take her eyes off my face.

Blue eyes. Blonde curls dripping with rain.

The lofty indifference of a fairy.

Pure horror.

The instinct to crush her. To kill.

My heart beating like a drum.

They pass on.

At the Ludgeritor.

They've unloaded our carts, the animals have been lodged under a canopy.

'Halt! Who goes there?'

'Captain Gert from the Well.'

I come forward so that he can recognise me. Hansel, his face spectral with hunger.

'Harness the horses up to one of the carts.'

Uncertainly: 'Captain, I'm sorry, no one can leave.'

I point to the bundle that Greta is pressing to her chest. 'The little one has cholera. Do you want an epidemic to break out?'

Terrified, he runs to call his companions. The horses are hitched up again. 'Open the gate, quickly!'

I push Adrianson on to the cart, putting the reins into his hand. 'Get as far as you can.'

His tears mix with the rain dripping from his hood. 'Captain, I can't leave you here . . .'

I grip the collar of his coat. 'Never deny yourself what you have fought for, Peter. Defeat doesn't make a cause unjust. Always remember that. Go now.'

I strike the horse hard on its rear.

I can no longer feel the rain. My breath precedes me along the street leading to the cathedral square. No one. As though they were all dead: a single silent cemetery.

The stage is still set up against the church, but now it's topped by a heavy canopy that covers the throne. Beneath it, carved in clear letters, is the name of the place to which the minds of these people have decided to migrate: THE MOUNT OF ZION.

I go on, until the sound and the light of the party reach me from above, from the windows of the house that used to belong to the gentleman Melchior von Büren.

I've found the court of the Jester King.

He is wearing a crown on his head.

He is wearing a velvet cloak.

He is holding a sceptre in his hand; an orb, topped by a crown and two swords, dangles from his neck. He has a ring on each finger, his beard combed and curly, his cheeks rouged and unnatural, like those of a beautified corpse.

He is sitting at the centre of the table, arranged in a horseshoe shape, covered with piles of bones that have been sucked dry, bowls of goose fat, glasses and beakers holding dregs of wine and beer. The motionless grin of a suckling pig on a spit stands in the middle of the hall. To the right of the king, Queen Divara, dressed in white, more beautiful that I remembered, a garland of wheat wrapped round her hair. To the left a tiny pug-faced man: must be the famous Duesentschnuer. The wives are seated beside the courtiers, serving wine to their lords and masters.

At the end of the hall, on the throne of David, a little boy sits awkwardly, his legs on either side of the arms. Bored, he is playing with a coin. His outfit, too big for him, is covered with gold necklaces, his sleeves are rolled up to his elbows. I barely recognise Shear-Jashub, Bockelson's favourite, dragged from the fate of the old believers one winter's day.

The king puts his hands on the table and gets up from the chair. He cranes his head in search of an eye to catch. Unease among the diners. Eyes lowered. 'Krechting!'

The minister gives a start. Everyone else heaves a sigh. The king begins: 'For the Dukedom of Saxony, Krechting!'

Imitating a broad peasant accent: '"Now why dost thou cry out aloud? Is there no king in thee? Is thy counsellor perished? For pangs have taken thee as a woman in travail. Be in pain and labour to bring forth, O daughter of Zion, like a woman in travail: for now shalt thou go forth out of the city, and thou shalt dwell in the field, and thou shalt go even to Babylon; there shalt thou be delivered; there the Lord shall redeem thee from the hand of thine enemies." Who am I? Who am I?'

Krechting blushes and stares at the gnawed drumstick beneath his nose, he nudges his neighbour, in hope of a suggestion.

The king, bitterly: 'So, you don't know . . .'

His eye studies the people around the table. 'Knipperdolling! For the Electorate of Mainz!'

He taps the jug with the tip of his sceptre. Then he shatters it to pieces with a clean blow. Water flows on to the table. '"Is the Lord among us, yes or no?"'

The burgomaster quickly answers, 'Yes, yes!'

'No! You've got to tell me who am I, who am I?'

Wrapped in a brocade housecoat, probably made from the von Büren household's tapestry collection, Knipperdolling fiddles nervously with his beard. His belly, imposing a little while ago, has drooped flaccidly along with his double chin. His black hat falls limply on either side of his head, like the ears of a hound. He wears the defeated expression of a beaten dog. An old animal, grown soft and tired. He tries to brighten up with an answer: 'Isaiah?'

'Nooooo!'

He's nervous. He climbs on to the table. 'Palck! For Gelderland and Utrecht!' He approaches the head of the piglet and struggles desperately, amidst much shouting and roaring, until he has torn it in two. He drops the pieces and suddenly turns round. 'Who am I, who am I?'

The deacon is clearly drunk, he has started rocking in his seat and has to lean on the table. A satisfied smile. 'Yes, yes, that's easy: Simeon!'

'Wrong answer, fool.'

He takes a rib of pork and throws it at him. He sighs deeply and turns towards Rothmann, almost hidden at the end of the table. 'Bernhard . . .'

A little thin body, wrapped in filthy clothes, death painted on its face, tiny eyes. Years seem to have passed since an affable preacher welcomed the disciples of Matthys in Münster, and as many since the convent of Überwasser was emptied by his words. 'Micah, Moses and Samson.'

The king applauds, immediately followed by everyone else.

'Fine, fine. And now Divara, my queen, do Salome. Go on, go on, Salome! Music, music!'

Divara jumps on to the table and begins to spin and sway sinuously to the sound of the lute and the flute. Her dress slips to her shoulders, her legs are revealed. She whips the air with her hair and brings her hands together above her head, her back arched.

Salome's dance for the head of John.

The head of Jan Bockelson, tailor and pimp of Leyden, actor, apostle of Matthys, prophet and king of Münster.

Of Jan and all the rest.

A pile of corpses. She knows.

I watch death dancing, choosing them one by one, until I decide to leave the shadows and allow her to notice me.

She's the first to stop, all of a sudden, as though she's seen a ghost. Everyone else at the table, petrified, mouths open as they watch me come back to life, seeing themselves for a moment with my eyes: limp, mad, goddamned wretches.

And then there's Divara: she gives me a cheerful smile as though we two were the only people here.

Take them away, the lot of them.

Carafa's eye
(1535)

Letter sent to Rome from the city of Münster, addressed to Gianpietro Carafa, dated 30 June 1535.

To the most illustrious and reverend Giovanni Pietro Carafa, in Rome.

My Most Honourable Lord,

By the time you take these pages between your hands, the news will already have reached Your Lordship's ears of the end of the kingdom of Zion in the city of Münster. The attention of every state is focused upon the outcome of the siege and Your Lordship will be particularly attentive to events that concern him. I therefore appeal to your concern, and to the natural curiosity of a highly cultured and educated man, so that my letter may have a purpose, illustrating some particulars that have struck me as significant over the past few months of silence, never forgetting that Your Lordship has always shown great appreciation of first-hand information, in the full awareness that the most alarming occurrences are the most likely to be enriched by non-existent details, false interpretations and wild inventions.

But perhaps I might begin the story with an almost intimate reflection, which may help Your Lordship to read my exposition, and that is that never, in the thirty-six years granted me by God, have I endured months so tiring to the body, so exhausting to the mind, so unsettling to the spirit, as those endured by a sane man who must become a madman among madmen. Such a man, however rigorously he may survey the provinces of his mind, will often nurture the atrocious suspicion that he has irremediably lost his own nature, in spontaneously assuming the attitudes of the mob and forging friendships with lunatics until he ends up understanding them better than he does those of sound mind. So his return to normal life will be neither easy nor immediate.

During the crucial months of the fall of Münster I have seen the food supplies becoming ever more meagre, as the faces of the city's inhabitants grew increasingly gaunt. In a single week I have seen all the rats disappear from the streets of the city, and I have begun to suspect that it is not out of madness, but out of clear-sighted calculation that Jan Bockelson has begun to execute an ever greater number of so-called 'disobedients': fewer mouths to feed and more meat to eat.

I may say that, had the Anabaptist front been truly solid, my task would have been much less burdensome. I would easily have identified the people barricaded behind the walls with the forces of Satan and the mercenaries camped outside with the troops of the Lord. As things transpired, however, it became increasingly difficult not to consider the King of Zion and his court as the sole true enemies and the rest of those under siege a blameless flock. Bockelson's great madness made the Anabaptist madness of all the others all the less horrible.

So, on more than one occasion, when I heard him promise his people that the cobblestones would be transformed for them into bread and pheasant legs, I felt an inextinguishable desire to kill him, to erase him from the face of the earth, to release those poor people from that yoke, which was borne only because of the presence of a greater danger outside the walls.

Nonetheless, Your Lordship's correspondent has been responsible, in person, for the division created within the city. Since the arrival of Jan Matthys I have begun to win the friendship of the chief preacher of the community, Bernhard Rothmann, a highly cultured man with a fine mind, whom I mentioned in my last letter more than a year ago now. When I saw the way in which he was brushed aside by the new prophet Matthys, I immediately realised that his wisdom could be useful to my plans. I could use the dissatisfaction of the failed leader, the man of the Bible excluded by rogues and panders. But Rothmann fell gravely ill, and with his health his will to fight gradually faded as well. In the end he settled for the role of theologian at the court of Jan of Leyden. And yet no reasonable person, however feeble and exhausted, could bear the spectacle of the Kingdom of Zion for long.

I don't know how I hit upon the idea of polygamy, it was probably inspired by the legend that the Anabaptists practised community of wives as well as goods. I spent a long time talking to Bernhard Rothmann about the practices of the patriarchs of the Holy Scriptures where marriage was concerned, with the result that the preacher advised Bockelson to take up this custom, one so odious as to make the people hostile to him. From that point onwards everything was submerged in a tide of blood and Rothmann finally took fourteen wives. But the spirit of the besieged city, which had until that moment solidly resisted the attacks of Bishop von Waldeck, would never again know unity.

So no traitor would have been required had the besieging forces been better organised and less afraid of failure. And yet the siege seemed destined never to come to an end. It is true that the New Zion was by now on the point of collapse through hunger, and it is also true that the tight grip that the bishop's troops managed to put upon the city began, after a year, to be properly effective, but in the long term a mercenary army usually breaks down and loses its vigour the longer its pay is delayed.

I reached the episcopal camp at dawn on 24 May, with the hackbuts of the mercenaries aimed at my head and the shouts of the city sentries telling me to turn back. I overcame the diffidence of Captain Wirich von Dhaun by constructing clay models of the fortifications of Münster and describing in detail the gaps in sentry duty. I had to confirm the precision of what I was saying by climbing at dead of night into the bastions of the city and slipping unharmed out of one of the gates.

A month later the episcopal troops entered Münster. Of the battle that took place within the walls I have no details to give, because I did not have the opportunity to be present. What happened next, on the other hand, is something that no human eye would ever wish to see and no mouth will ever be able to describe. The searches, the first few killings, the massacres are still taking place. Everyone is being run through on the spot. Only Jan Bockelson and his two most trusted men, Krechting and Knipper-dolling, were captured to be interrogated. In that fateful hour the king of the Anabaptists was not seen fighting in the square along with the strenuous defenders of the city, but was discovered in the throne room, hiding under a table, begging them to spare a little tailor and a miserable pander. As for Bernhard Rothmann, his fate is a matter for conjectures of the most various kinds: he was not taken prisoner and his corpse is nowhere to be found, but some people say they saw a Hungarian planting a sword between his shoulder blades and then, having recognised him as one of the men the bishop had ordered to be taken alive, concealing the corpse.

Bodies lie in all the alleyways and the city is plagued by an unbearable stench. In the central square a pile of white bodies mounts, stripped naked and heaped up one on top of the other.

The arrival of Bishop von Waldeck did not contribute a great deal more to the health of Münster. The streets of the city are still empty, even at midday, and the grocery stalls have not yet reappeared beneath the pinnacles of the Rathaus. A long time will pass before life returns to the city of Münster, although work on the reconstruction of the cathedral has already begun. I am still trying to regain the strength and resolution that I lost in that carnival of death, but this city's *danse macabre* catches all of us in its whirl, like a pestiferous contagion, as though the smell of the corpses were turning even the living into corpses.

And that's how it will be for the Anabaptists between here and the Low Countries, now that the beacon of their hope has been extinguished. Many supporters of Münster sent by Bockelson to stir up the people of Holland are still travelling about those regions, but their days are numbered and ever fewer will be the fools willing to listen to them. That is why I think that the fate of this execrable heresy is sealed and the danger has been averted.

For the same reason I think I have accomplished the task assigned to me by Your Lordship, a task to which I have sacrificed all the strength of my body and my mind, having been put most profoundly to the test by the horrendous tragedy in which I have been both spectator and minor participant. So it will not be difficult for My Lord to understand why I ask to be removed from the nauseating and deadly stench of these lands, and to continue to serve him, if my services can ever be of use to him again, in other places and circumstances.

I take my leave of Your Lordship's benevolence, and humbly kiss your hands.

Your Lordship's faithful servant

Q   Münster, the 30th day of June 1535

Chapter 40

Antwerp, 28 May 1538

'I didn't wait for the end. I left Münster at the start of September. I never set foot there again.'

Eloi lights me a cigar with the embers in the hearth. The swirls of smoke rise around me, as I savour the great peace that slowly descends into my limbs. I wouldn't have expected to find this peaceful product of the Indies here.

The swallows are flying low above the roofs streaked by the sunset, a sign that it's going to rain. The regular creaking of a cart passing in the street, voices, dogs barking in the distance.

I have run through names, faces, sensations, all nestling in the furrows of my scars. Something has disappeared, forgotten for ever at the bottom of the dark well.

Memory. A bag full of trinkets rolling out by chance and finally amazing you, as though you weren't the one who picked them up and turned them into precious objects.

I smile at time, at the tragic enterprises, the casual heroes of other days. I smile.

Eloi is a man who can take the time that needs to be taken. You don't often come across a man who knows how to listen to a story told by the fireside.

He breaks the smoky silence surrounding us: 'And then?'

'I plunged in. Without managing to think, without asking myself anything. And many others did as I did, getting out just in time from that city of madmen, exiled and exhausted. We bore within us the rancour of a huge missed opportunity, a slow gangrene that gnawed away at the mind. We no longer had a place in the world.

'The Low Countries were in turmoil, it seemed as though everything might explode from one moment to the next. So we all found ourselves there, with no particular aim, putting ourselves back together again. In Holland, discussions among the brethren were more fervent than ever. On the one hand there were supporters of the way of peace, with Philips and Joris. On the other there were the most determined, the stalwarts who were willing to take up arms. We met them in the street, young, ready for anything.'

Eloi interrupts me with a fit of coughing: 'You're forgetting our lot. Joris hated me, still does. Wait, wait a moment, how did he describe me? "A libertine dedicated to copulation and debauchery." Couldn't have put it better myself!'

He smiles, by now we're on to subjects he's very familiar with.

'Then, in December, Van Geelen turned up, that big Limburger I had known in Münster, where he had gone in search of hope for the oppressed, finding only an old, mad God devouring his people. The task Bockelson set him was to seek new pupils among the communities of the Dutch brethren, but the New Zion wasn't going to see him die like a rat in a trap to realise the follies of an actor. He had no intention of going back there.

'So I went back to fighting. By now it was the only thing I knew how to do.

'In March of 1535 we were in Bolsford, taking the monastery of Oldeklooster. We barricaded ourselves inside for a week. Van Geelen thought that from such a strategic position we would be able to dominate the Gulf and at the same time relieve Frisia, where the peasants were already rebelling. But contacts turned out to be harder to maintain than we had expected.

'In May we took the Council House in Amsterdam. Van Geelen's plan was that the common people should rise up and join us. That duty fell to me, while he barricaded himself inside the municipal building, keeping the Civil Guard at bay.

'It was a complete disaster, the final act. No one followed us. Van Geelen was wrong. The humble folk had no intention of risking their lives for us, we'd gone too far, we'd pushed too far ahead, failing to notice the extent to which fear and poverty had ravaged our people's souls. The occupants resisted through to the last bullet and in the end they attempted an exit bearing only their swords. They were massacred to a man.

'There was nothing we could do. Van Geelen was dead, I had about thirty badly armed men with me and an old fishing boat. In these circumstances I took the decision to dissolve the brigade: with a bit of luck some of them would get away. If we stayed together we would soon be identified and captured. They understood, no one asked any questions. That was the final order of Captain Gert from the Well.'

Eloi tries to smile at me. 'Another name?'

'No name. No friends. The soldiers were scouring the whole region, nowhere was safe, all the peasants could have betrayed you, any wayfarer along the road could be a bounty hunter on your trail.

'I walked for days, I slept in barns, begged for food. I had no news of the brothers, I didn't know what was happening away from the precise place where I happened to be. I also started to lose my bearings, my mind grew cloudy. I only knew I was heading northwards. I had lost everything: Münster, my men, Van Geelen, the brethren who had believed in me in Amsterdam. Finished. After four days of fasting my legs were beginning to collapse under me, I saw things that heralded impending madness. I was dead, a ghost, I might as well just lie down on the ground and wait. I no longer had a reason to drive myself on and survive.

'They found me there in the mud, ragged and as good as dead. I found myself hoping that I would be stabbed by a brigand's blade; I almost wept because I had nothing on me worth stealing. They wouldn't grant me that *coup de grâce*; they picked me up and took me with them.'

I let the cigar go out over the fire, my memory is confused, they seem like events that I have lived through in a dream. 'And I looked, and behold a pale horse: and his name was Death, and Hell followed with him.'

Eloi is grave, crouching, a nocturnal predator sunk in his armchair. I hear him murmuring that name: 'Jan van Batenburg.'

'The Sword Bearers. A ragged army of survivors, almost all men who had escaped from Münster, who formed a column behind the last Horseman of the Apocalypse left standing. Our time was over, as Jan Matthys had said. We couldn't help believing that the mystery of iniquity had spread across the earth, head by head, brother by brother, to lead us into that blind fury. All that remained was to devote ourselves to the death of the world and swear fidelity to its final conflagration. We would end up like that, swords in our hands and patches on our arses, high on fear and ostentation, while we still had breath to fight. We no longer expected anything, we were already beyond Apocalypse, far from everything, we were nothing but murderers. There was no longer any room for innocence, in our eyes it became cowardice, damnation. So we spat the scraps of our lives in the face of anyone left.'

Eloi has disappeared into the shadows, into the depths of his armchair, I'm not quite sure he isn't actually shrinking.

'I don't have a clear memory of that period, that wouldn't be possible. I have killed, tortured, destroyed. I have seen whole villages burning, the terror of the peasants escaping the moment they saw us appearing on the horizon. I have seen friars impaled like pigs on the spit, I've seen the scarecrow figure of the Pale Horseman galloping along the edge of the hills, with us behind him, on the rim of that abyss, tracing the borders of holiness. After Matthys and Bockelson, the third Jan of my life: the third curse. When they finally caught him he laughed in the face of torture and death. He delivered a great yell of victory from the scaffold: I heard him . . .'

I relax into the armchair, stretching my legs. 'And that's really it, glory and wretchedness.'

I listen to the silence. I'm tired.

His faceless voice cradles my exhaustion: 'It's the most magnificent story I've ever heard. And without a doubt you're the person I've been looking for.'

I strain my eyes, but he's just a patch of deeper darkness beyond the desk. 'I'm tired, Eloi. Too tired.'

'You're alive. That's what counts.'

I'm tired.

The corridor that separates me from my bed is very long, the light flickering from the candle barely illuminates it, while I grope my way along it.

I'm tired.

And yet I have the feeling I'm not going to get any sleep. Eloi's thirst for knowledge has awakened my own. Münster fell on 24 June 1535. Gert from the Well had been gone nine months. And what of the others?

A sleepy voice replies to the knocks on the door.

'Who is it?'

'It's Gert.'

The light of a candle is added to mine, I study the face of Balthasar Merck. Without asking any questions, the old Baptist points to a chair beside his bed. 'Take a seat by all means, but I'm not sure I can be of any use to you.'

'Just this: who got out?'

He puts the candle down on the little table and sits on the edge of the bed, massaging his face. 'All I can tell you is that there were five of us: Krechting the young one, the miller Skraup, Schmidt the armourer, the carver Kerbe and me. All Krechting's men. Kerbe they got in Nijmegen, shortly after we split up. I heard that Schmidt and Skraup were executed in Deventer two years ago. Krechting I know is still around the place and some people say Rothmann is too: his body wasn't among the corpses in Münster.'

'None of my men?'

He shakes his head. 'I have no idea. Some of them weren't even in the city. Bockelson had got rid of them because he was terribly scared of you.'

'Gresbeck, the Brundt brothers . . .'

He nods his head. 'They came back just in time to witness the final delirium. They hoped to see you, but you'd gone, never to return.'

'Why did they stay?'

'Gresbeck and the Brundts tried to get away, but the bishop's men caught them just outside the walls. Horrible end.'

I sigh, exhausted, no longer having the strength to imagine, my questions are coming out automatically. 'Which front caved in first?'

'The Kreuztor and the Jüdefeldertor, the most undefended parts of the walls: someone must have told the bishop's men. A squad got in during the night and at dawn it opened the gates to the rest of the army. The massacre lasted for days. I entrusted my sick wife to the care of a beguine, making her promise that she wouldn't denounce her, and made off with the others. I haven't heard anything of her for three years.'

We stay there in silence, listening to the roar of memories, savouring the bitter solidarity of survivors.

I get up, almost regretfully. 'I'm sorry.'

'Captain . . .'

I turn round: his eyes are swollen with tears and fatigue.

'Tell me that what we were fighting for wasn't a mistake.'

I clench my jaw, my fists clenched. 'I've never thought so, not for a moment.'

The sea
(1538)

Chapter 41

Dawn. Pewter sky. Thoughts creep beneath sleep and pull away the covers.

Kathleen is asleep, an unbelievable spectacle of hair and mouth and warm breath.

Get up quietly lest I wake her. Early morning chill that hobbles you, gets to the guts, wrap yourself in a big goatskin, while you drag your feet in search of a bucket to piss in, a bit of water to rub your eyes and a drop of hot milk to wake you up. The years have passed, getting out of bed isn't as easy as it was: sometimes the cold gets to your limbs, the rheumatism suddenly seizes hold of you to tell you you've been overdoing it for too long. Your muscles start aching to tell you that you're going to have to be a bit careful with the fifth decade of your life if you don't want to be bedridden while you still have your wits about you. Wretched end that would be, terrible.

So stay. Stay here, too old to learn a trade and too tired to start fighting again. The cobbler's needle or the potter's wheel, perhaps, I'll leave to rust in the canal where I threw it.

Magda watches in silence, her eyes wide with curiosity, as I slip the last pivot between the arm and the shoulder of the puppet. 'Who's it for?' she asks, shaking her curls with instinctive flirtation.

'It's for you children,' I reply. 'But you're its mum, all right?'

'Yeees!' A high note that would burst your eardrums and the smack of a kiss on my hairy cheek.

I've never been kissed by a child before.

Eloi watches and smiles as he walks among the columns of the portico. He hasn't time to say hello before Magda jumps out in front of him waving the little wooden doll. 'Look, look! Lot made it!'

Eloi kneels to move the puppet's arms. 'Is it yours?'

'It belongs to all the children,' Magda replies as she's been taught.

'But I'm going to take care of it. Lot made some spoons and soup dishes for mamma, did you know that?'

Eloi nods, while the little girl runs to show everyone her new toy.

A thought spoken aloud and a wave of the arms: 'This is my adventure. Over the past ten years it's all I've done.'

With irony: 'A small thing . . .'

'I don't know if it's a small thing or a big one. Certainly my story isn't a match for yours.'

I hold out my hand with a grin. 'If you want to swap, let's shake on it right now.'

He looks at me seriously. 'No, it's not your past that I want. I just want to understand what weird alchemies have decreed that I have never been involved in the things that you have seen, and vice versa.'

'Fine. And if you can, try to explain to me how come my past has nothing like this in it: Magda, Kathleen, this place . . .'

'We were born and bred in two different worlds, Lot. On the one hand you've got the lords, the bishops, the princes, the dukes and the peasants. On the other the merchants, the bankers, the shipowners and clerks. Antwerp and Amsterdam aren't Mühlhausen and they aren't even Münster. This city is the most important port in Europe. Not a day passes without whole ships being loaded with wool, silk, salt, tapestries, spices, furs and coal. Over the past thirty years the merchants have transformed their shops into commercial agencies, their houses into palaces, their boats into tall-masted ships. Here there is no ancient and unjust order to turn upside down, no yokels to sit on thrones. There's no need for an apocalypse, because it's already been under way for a while.'

I interrupt him with a tap on the knee: 'That's where I first heard your name! It was Johannes Denck, in Mühlhausen, talking to us about the way you seduce merchants from your country. You had convinced him that without money, in the city, you can't amount to anything.'

Eloi pulls out a coin and turns it round between his hands, throws it in the air and catches it a few times. 'You see? You can't topple money: whichever way you turn it, one side always shows.'

He half shuts his eyes to enjoy the ray of sunlight filtering between the branches as he tries to find an order, a starting point for his story.

He smiles. 'At first I was thinking of something along the lines of the Hutterite community.'

'Those lunatics over by Nikolsburg?'

'They're the ones. They live completely isolated from the rest of the world and claim to be self-sufficient.'

With studied emphasis I turn my whole torso towards him, visibly surprised. 'They certainly wouldn't say what you were saying about money a moment ago. What made you change your mind?'

He searches for words, it's difficult, he realises that he has to take his time, he might even get lost in the twists and turns of too long a speech. 'The Apocalypse isn't an objective to be sought, it's all around us. Over the last twenty years I've heard so much talk of the Apocalypse that if it came right now we'd have terrible trouble telling it from the fate that mankind endures every day. The true Kingdom of God begins here' – he points to his chest – 'and here' – he touches his forehead. 'Being pure doesn't mean cutting yourself off from the world, condemning it, in order blindly to obey the law of God: if you want to change the world of men you've got to live in it.'

I get up to draw water from the old well in the middle of the courtyard. My back hurts as I pull the rope to lift the bucket. I look at Eloi: if he hadn't told me he was the same age as me, I'd have thought he was much younger. 'If you're trying to convince me that Batenburg was a madman, spare yourself the trouble, I knew that already. But perhaps his ideas weren't very different from your own: he thought the elect were already pure, incapable of sinning, he thought he was already in the midst of the Apocalypse. That's why he killed and slaughtered without a second thought.'

He sips the cold water. 'Within anyone who exorcises in others the contempt he feels for himself, for his own defeats, within anyone who blames and judges lest he himself be judged and blamed, there lurks a priest who, even if he wants to conceal the fact, is still cawing away among the crows of the old faith. Anyone with enough intelligence to understand the world and too little to learn to live, cannot hope for anything but martyrdom.' He turns to smile at me. 'I've never talked in terms of the elect. I've only said that anyone can discover within himself the spirit of God, which is free, removed from any code, incapable of doing harm. I have said that sin is in the mind of the sinner.'

I'm starting to understand.

He goes on calmly, 'At the age of twenty I thought that Luther had given us a gift of hope. It didn't take me long to understand that he had immediately sold it back to the powerful. The old friar freed us from the Pope and the bishops, but he condemned us to expiate sin in solitude, in the solitude of internal anguish, putting a priest in our souls, a court in our consciences, judging every gesture, condemning the freedom of the spirit in favour of the ineradicable corruption of human nature. Luther stripped the priests of their black garb, only to put it on the hearts of all men.'

He takes a breath, playing with wood shavings on the ground. He really feels like telling me everything, almost in exchange for my story. And I feel like listening. 'I want you to understand that you and I started off with the same disappointment. The same people who wanted to reform the faith and the Church also reformed the old power, they supplied a new mask for it. You Anabaptists had legitimate hopes: to deny Luther and continue where he had left off. But your vision of the struggle made you divide the world into black and white, Christians and anti-Christians.' He shakes his head. 'That kind of vision will help you win a just battle, but it isn't enough to realise the freedom of the spirit. On the contrary, it can construct new prisons in the soul, new morals, new courts. The meaning of everything is contained in the story you have told me: Matthys, Rothmann, Bockelson, Batenburg . . . The only disagreement between a pope and a prophet lies in the fact that they are fighting over the monopoly of truth, of the Word of God. I think everyone ought to be able to find that Word by himself. I've stayed outside the battle and worked for that.' He makes a sweeping gesture, taking in the courtyard around us. 'Don't imagine that it's been easy. Several times I've risked being incarcerated and for many years I've had to lead a clandestine life.'

'Kathleen told me.'

He nods. 'I've been put on trial too, a number of times. Contempt for municipal laws and swindling a textile merchant. I got away with it: I used the fact that many people travelling around Europe have used my name, including old Denck, may his soul rest in peace. I've always been turning up in places other than the ones where the authorities had spotted me. In that respect you and I are very similar . . .'

I think about how many people I have been until that point, but I can't remember the exact number.

'I've been many people and so have you. Yes, the difference is minimal.'

We are sitting side by side on the steps. Almost instinctively I pick up a bit of wood and start carving it with my penknife. The intense odour of moss growing everywhere in the garden is intoxicating I like it, it reminds me of the forests of Germany.

I realise that he wants to go on, tell me something else, something I've been waiting to hear for a long time.

'It all looks clearer from Antwerp. Even a little roofer like myself can work out a lot of things that wouldn't be noticed elsewhere. I've learned to read and write, I've learned to speak by frequenting the merchants of this city, luring them to the free and happy life. But above all I've learned how the world works, and men, and religions.

You see, merchants from all countries come here, all kinds of merchandise comes and goes: Polish copper bound for England and Portugal; Swedish furs for the imperial court; gold from the New World wrought by local artisans; English wool, minerals from the mines of Bohemia. This traffic employs an incalculable number of people: traders, shipowners, sailors, craftsmen, porters . . . and, of course, soldiers, guaranteeing the safety of life, conquering new lands, putting down revolts. The lives of whole countries and populations revolve around commerce. Charles V's Empire couldn't keep going without the commerce of the Low Countries. The Low Countries are the lung of the Empire: Charles raises most of his taxes in these lands, and most of them come from these traders and craftsmen.'

'Is that why they're in fiscal revolt against the Emperor?'

'Exactly: they're tired of financing his wars and the unproductive affluence of his court.'

He takes out the coin again and throws it in the air, catching it as it falls. 'Paying workmen, transporting products, equipping a ship, putting together an army to defend their cargoes from pirates . . . To do all that you need one thing: money.'

I don't know why, but when he says that word I have a kind of shiver, the one you get from a truth that may be predictable but is chilling nonetheless.

'Everything depends on money: merchants and the Emperor, princes and the Pope, luxury, war and commerce.'

He stops, as though he has had a sudden idea. 'If you've finished carving puppets, I'd like to show you something.'

I look at him, puzzled. He gets up and nods to me to follow him. 'Come on, a quick walk will do us good.'

'This is the port that circulates the greatest quantity of goods in the whole of Europe.'

We have come to a halt in front of a big three-masted merchant ship; the coming and going of the loaders on the walkway is impressive, carrying sacks over their shoulders with an almost superhuman effort. The jetty is crowded with men engaged in negotiations, sailors and recruiters. In the distance I can make out a patrol of Spaniards and give a start.

'No, really, don't worry. No one's going to recognise you in all this chaos. They aren't looking for trouble. Live and let live is more their style. You were unlucky, you got caught up in some reprisals. Come on.'

Eloi brings me in front of a little walled office with a discoloured sign: I can't read it, I haven't learned much of the written language of these parts.

'This is a foreign exchange office. The merchants can change their English or Swedish coins, or coins from the German principalities, into florins or any other currency, according to which country they've done their business in. The currency changes, but the money is always the same: it doesn't matter whose face is stamped on it.'

We stop again in front of a big, three-storey building. This time I manage to decipher the sign: HOUSE OF MERCHANTS AND SHIPOWNERS.

'Here the merchants decide what business they're going to do: what the best deals are going to be.'

We push our way through to get out of the crowd. The languages and dialects of half of Europe surround us like a single incomprehensible chant, an inverted Babel, in which everyone seems to understand everyone else.

'You see those carts? They come from Liège. They're transporting woollen fabrics made by the weavers of the Condroz: they'll be loaded on to those boats, which will in turn reimport, back to England, the wool that the merchants of Antwerp have acquired from the English sheep farmers.'

'But that's ridiculous!'

Eloi laughs heartily. 'No. It's profit. Perhaps one day the English will realise that it's more convenient for them to develop textile factories in their own country, but for the time being that's how it works.'

We continue on our way, leaving the canal and heading towards the centre of the city, along narrow alleys that the rays of the sun don't reach.

'The whole mechanism is driven by money. If it wasn't for money, no one would lift a finger in Antwerp, or perhaps anywhere in Europe. Money is the real symbol of the Beast.'

'And what do you mean by that?'

We stop close to a kiosk selling cabbages and smoked sausage, its penetrating smell envelops us.

'How do you think Charles V managed to get himself elected Emperor in 1519? By paying money. He bought the electors, someone put at his disposal a greater sum than the one offered by Francis of France. And the war against the peasants? Someone lent the German princes the money to equip the troops that defeated you. And how do you think Charles V is financing his war in Italy against the French? And his expeditions against the Saracen pirates? And his campaign against the Turks in Hungary? Maybe you think the merchants here have that kind of money to equip their commercial expeditions? Not in their dreams. Money, rivers of money lent in exchange for a percentage of the profits. That's how it works, my friend.'

The question has been in the air for a while. 'Who's got money like that?'

He looks straight ahead of us, then he points at the building in front of us and murmurs, 'The banks.'

'Now you know where to find the Antichrist you've spent your whole life fighting.'

'In there?' I point at the imposing building in front of us.

'No. In the purses that pass from hand to hand all around the world. You've fought against princes and property owners. I'm telling you that without money those people would be nothing, you'd have defeated them long ago. Instead, there's always a banker hanging around to finance their initiatives.'

'I can see how that applies to commercial enterprises, but what does a banker get out of financing a war against the peasants?'

'Do you need to ask? So that they'll go back and till the fields of their masters, dig in their mines. From that moment, the bankers will get a considerable share of everything produced. You see, Charles V and the princes are a class of parasites who produce nothing, but have a huge need to squander money: wars, courts, concubines, children, tournaments, embassies . . . The only way they have to pay off the debts they contract with the bankers is to grant them concessions, to allow them the usufruct of mines, factories, lands, whole regions. In this way the bankers are always getting richer and the powerful are becoming more and more dependent on their money. It's a vicious circle.'

Eloi's crafty air leaves no doubts about the fact that he's enjoying himself depicting the world to me from his point of view. He buys a steaming sausage and blows on it before biting into it.

He points to the bank. 'I'm sure you've heard the name of the Fuggers of Augsburg: the bankers of the Empire. There isn't a port in Europe where they don't have a branch. There isn't a business in which they don't have an involvement, however small. Our merchants would be lost without the money that the Fuggers put at their disposal to finance their journeys. Charles V wouldn't be able to move a single soldier if he didn't have limitless credit in their strongboxes. Further-more, the Emperor owes the Fuggers his crown, the war against France, the crusade against the Turks and the maintenance of all his whores. He's paid them back by giving them the usufruct of the mines in Hungary and Bohemia, tax collection in Catalonia, the monopoly of mineral extraction in the New World and who knows what else.' The sausage points towards the building that looms up in front of us. 'Believe me, without the Fuggers and their money that man would have been ruined a long time ago.' He looks all around him. 'And perhaps none of this would exist.'

He sucks his greasy fingers with the most natural air in the world.

I take a few steps towards the middle of the street and study the massive, anonymous construction, and then look around in confusion. Conflicting emotions pile up within me, anger, astonishment, even irony. I stop and let it all out: 'Why has no one ever talked to me about banks before?'

'Your story, the incredible story of Gert Up-and-Down the Well, took my breath away. I couldn't even sleep after we parted in the small hours. That's why I like people who know how to tell a story, whether with words, brush or pen. You have painted Münster with the mastery of the Brueghels, father and son. Now I've lived through the story myself, and you've done it twice.

'Twice, Lot: once for the experience and the second time as a way of shaking it from your shoulders. As the name we've given you demands, look straight in front of you, look straight ahead, beyond the great ships that wait to set off each day, along the estuary that slowly widens, mile after mile, before finally opening up into the sea. The sea, Lot. Not a day passes without fresh information about new lands and people coming from across the sea. And new crimes as well. Across the sea the Apocalypse rises each morning along with the sun.

'Don't turn back, don't be imprisoned by your history. Take to the sea, sever the hawsers that have kept you moored to the land, keep your mind on the prow and take to the waves. Let's take to the waves. One world is ending, another beginning; this is the Apocalypse and we're in the midst of it. Help me to equip the boat that will weather the storm.'

Eloi gets up and moves a few steps away from the sausage kiosk and the big grey building, then goes and sits down on the steps.

'What did you have in mind?'

He looks at the bare façade, the massive wooden portal. 'Kill the Beast. And make a stack of money.'

I walk along the quay, boards nailed to poles protruding from the stagnant water, down one of the branches of that endless labyrinth of putrid water and wood, trying to keep up with Eloi as he quickens his step.

It's a little merchant ship, round-bellied and inelegant: a capacious hold, two very high masts, a little cabin on the quarterdeck. The figurehead is a great bird with its wings spread, which gives the ship its name: *Phoenix*.

'Lodewijck Pruystinck!' The man who greets us is leaning from the parapet of the bridge: grey beard and hair, pock-marked complexion, tiny darting eyes.

'Polnitz, the mathematical wizard!'

Eloi grips the railing of the gangway and with one leap he's on board. I'm behind him.

He fires his smile at him: 'Gotz, this is Lot who came out of a well. A master of the art of getting out of wells.'

'Come in, come inside.'

I have to lower my head to get into the cabin. A table hooked to the front wall, two chairs at the sides, a bench nailed to the floor. Apart from a lit candle on the table, the only light comes from the door through which we entered.

Eloi lets me have the chair and sits down on the bench at the side, Polnitz opposite me. He doesn't look like a sailor.

'Well, gentlemen.' Turning back to Eloi: 'I suppose our friend will be wanting some kind of explanation.'

'Sure. But I've brought him here because he's the man we were looking for.'

I pull a little face and wait.

Polnitz adjusts himself on his chair. 'Let's get down to it, then. You know about the Fuggers of Augsburg?' His eyes stay on me.

'The bankers.'

'The bankers.' His eyes study me carefully, he already knows what he wants to say to me. 'Let me tell you a story.'

Eloi lights a cigar and disappears, silent and sly, behind the swirling smoke.

'Ten years ago the most powerful banker in Antwerp was a certain Ambrosius Höchstetter: a hard-hearted, mean old man who dominated the market for decades. Every florin spent by King Ferdinand of Hungary came out of his purse, in exchange for all the mercury in Bohemia and much else besides. In order to reach that position old Ambrosius, many years previously, had shown great foresight. Apart from the important fact of his being friends with the Habsburgs, he had worked out that if the princes gave him rights of usufruct over mines and territories, the money would go on passing through other hands, dirtier and more nimble than his own. The hands of the merchants of Antwerp. So he started to take in their savings; the fruits of commercial deals, factories and all the exchanges, both big and small, that take place against the backdrop of this port. He granted a substantial interest rate to anyone who deposited even small sums with him. He lent money to the rising merchants, he financed their activities, he had such power over the fortunes of anyone transporting anything to Antwerp that no one could ever have imagined him being toppled from his throne.'

Gotz von Polnitz keeps his eyes on my face, to be sure that I don't miss a word of the story.

'In 1528 Höchstetter was still the king of Antwerp, but he had problems. He was old, he was almost blind and many people outside the city wanted to take his place. In the same year Lazarus Tucher, a merchant originally from Nuremberg, was responsible for a considerable volume of traffic between Lyon and Antwerp. Tucher was well off and clever, but he didn't enjoy Höchstetter's favours: so he knew that his business wasn't going to grow. From the spring of that year, rumours started pouring in from Lyon about the amounts of money that Höchstetter actually had at his disposal; the old man found himself being exposed on all fronts, people were calling in considerable sums, while he was lending money to merchants and bankrolling the Habsburgs, and the war for the mercury monopoly was becoming extremely expensive. The savings of the small merchants and the crafts corporations in Antwerp were hopelessly far off on boats making their way to the New World, in the court of Ferdinand and in the mines of Bohemia. It seems incredible, but very soon a crowd was demanding the return of its own deposits.'

Gotz draws breath, allowing me to imagine the scene, then he goes on, 'Bankruptcy was inevitable. Höchstetter hadn't enough money in his coffers to satisfy their demands. He desperately tried to get away by asking for help even from his most ferocious competitors, but his fate was now sealed. In 1529 the young, aggressive Anton Fugger, nephew of the patriarch Jakob the Rich, made his triumphal entrance into the city, serving as a guarantor for the masses of creditors and at a stroke taking on all of Höchstetter's obligations, storehouses and general activities. Accused of having deceived his savers, the old man ended his days in jail.

'In fact, young Fugger was putting the finishing touches to an operation that he had begun more than a year before, when he had brought Höchstetter into discredit through the skills of his most ambitious agent: Lazarus Tucher. Antwerp crowned a new king.'

The question emerges out of me of its own accord: 'What happened to Tucher in the end?'

He weighs his words. 'That doesn't matter, he's no longer in town.

What this story teaches you is the fundamental law of credit: anyone wishing to take on the savings of a large number of people must enjoy the trust of a large number of people.'

Another pause. Eloi is listening attentively at my side, he doesn't move a muscle.

Gotz takes a small piece of paper from his jacket pocket and puts it on the table. 'You won't believe it, but most of the deals here are done via letters of credit. Pieces of paper like this.'

I turn the sheet round in my hands: a kind of letter, written in elegant calligraphy with two seals and a signature at the bottom.

'Anton Fugger or whoever guarantees with his own seal the entity of his deposit in his strongboxes. When you're holding in your hand a piece of paper like this one, it's exactly as though you were holding your money, although it's actually safe in Fugger's safe. Then you set off, you travel, avoiding the risk and discomfort of bringing it with you. The minute you want your silver and gold coins back, you just turn up at any branch of the Fugger bank scattered around Europe and withdraw it by showing your letter of credit. But the point is that, on the basis of the law of credit, you might never need to do that.'

Gotz stops at the sight of my furrowed brow, puts his hands together, searches for the right words and continues, 'Right, I'm a spice merchant, you want to buy my goods and you're carrying the letter of exchange that guarantees your credit with the Fuggers at two thousand florins. You can pay me directly with that.' He points to the letter in his hand. 'All you have to do is turn it over and write on the back that you're transferring your credit to me. From that moment onwards I can withdraw two thousand florins from Fugger's coffers, because it's his seal, not yours, that guarantees it. You see? I'm not obliged to trust you, you're not the one who promises to pay me, it's enough that I believe in the word of Anton Fugger.'

I turn over the paper and see a series of five or six annotations, all followed by various signatures. On six occasions the letter I am holding has stood in for the metal of the coins, without that money ever leaving the bank's safe.

'All clear so far?'

'There's something I don't understand: what does the banker get out of all this?'

Gotz nods. 'While the letter of credit passes from hand to hand, the actual money is at his disposal. Remember old Höchstetter: he took people's savings and reinvested them in profitable affairs. That's what the banker does. Your two thousand florins, along with the money of many other creditors, go to finance the equipment of mercantile fleets, the recruitment of armies, mineral extraction, the maintenance of the princes' courts and much else besides, to return doubled to the Fugger safes. Fugger has his money in the bank, Fugger lends it to princes and merchants, Fugger invests it again with interest.' He grants me a moment to realise what he means. 'The money generates money.'

His silence alerts me to the fact that we have reached a salient point in the exposition. Eloi has stopped smoking, his arms folded. He wears a thoughtful expression.

Gotz continues to address himself to me. 'Now you can understand why Fugger is willing to increase your hoard if you deposit it with him for a long time.'

'Which is to say?'

'That he pays you interest too, since effectively by depositing a certain amount in his coffers you have put money at his disposal, thus allowing him to increase the volume of his investments.'

I try to make head or tail of it all. 'You're saying that if I deposit my two thousand florins in the bank and leave it there, a year later it will have turned into two thousand one hundred?'

Gotz smiles for the first time. 'Exactly so. That way the creditors won't be tempted to withdraw their deposits too frequently and they won't leave Fugger exposed to the possibility of money haemorrhaging out of his coffers.' He points at the letter of credit once again. 'From that point of view, this piece of paper makes it possible for the sums deposited to keep on growing, because until someone goes and withdraws them, they just stay there growing away in Fugger's hands.'

I'm starting to feel a little light-headed, the mechanics of it all seem simple enough as Gotz explains it, but I have a sense that I'm inevitably missing something.

'Hm, let's see if I've got it. The letter of credit is worth two thousand florins. You can decide to exchange it immediately as though it were money, or keep it and wait for the deposit to grow with interest.' Gotz follows my reasoning with emphatic nods of the head. 'Well, I think your choice depends on whether or not you need to use the money immediately.'

'Very good.'

'It's a devilish mechanism.'

Eloi laughs loudly, and finally he speaks: 'Let's leave the devil out of this. Things are complicated enough already.'

Gotz grabs my attention again. 'The whole mechanism is based entirely on the trust that everyone puts in the signature of Anton Fugger. It's his word that governs the exchanges.'

'Yes. That's clear enough.'

'Fine.' For the first time he looks to Eloi for confirmation. A little nod from his friend, and Gotz's pock-marked face turns back to me. 'Let's get to the point, then. What would you say if I told you that the letter of credit you're holding was fake?'

I turn the yellowing sheet over again, take a good look at the signatures, the seals. 'I'd say it was impossible.'

Gotz reveals his satisfaction. From the little purse at his side he takes an anonymous little black box, a sheet of the same dimensions as the one I'm holding, an ink bottle and a long goose quill.

He writes slowly, careful not to stain the paper, the scratching of his pen the only sound that fills the silence of his two onlookers.

With the candle flame he melts two drops from a little stick of red wax, letting them fall on to the paper. Then he opens the little box and takes from it two little lead stamps, which he presses into the hot wax. He turns the sheet over and spreads it out on the table in front of me.

The writing is identical, the same words, the same hand. The stamps are the same, even the signature of Anton Fugger is in the same position, the same faint smears of ink on the consonants, where the hand has pressed down more heavily.

I look into Gotz's face, trying to imagine what on earth kind of person I have before me.

It doesn't bother him in the slightest. 'Yes, they're both fake.'

'How did you get hold of the stamps?'

He stops. 'All in good time, my friend. Now take a good look at those two letters.'

My eye moves from one to the other a few times. 'They're identical.'

'Not exactly.'

I look more carefully. 'On this one there are marks in the right margin, at the bottom, but they're almost invisible.'

'That's right. It's a secret code. The code that the exchange agents who work for Fugger in his branches scattered around Europe use to communicate among themselves. The first mark indicates the branch that issued the letter of credit, that is, where the money was paid in. The scribble you see there, for example, tells you that the money was deposited in Augsburg. The second is the personal signature, also in code, of the agent who wrote the letter, in this case Anton Fugger in person. The third sign shows the year in which it was issued.'

'How come you know the code?'

Gotz pretends not to have heard the question. 'If you turned up with an uncoded letter at one of the Fugger agencies, you'd be arrested immediately. However good you are at reproducing the signature of a

Fugger agent, unless you know the code you can't fake a letter of credit.'

'So how come you know it?'

Silence. We stare at each other.

Eloi encourages him: 'Tell him, Gotz.'

He sighs. 'I spent seven years as a Fugger agent in Cologne.'

My mind is racing, I'm confused. I turn back to Eloi. 'Is that the deal? Faking letters of credit and making off with Fugger's coffers?'

Eloi laughs. 'More or less. But it isn't as simple as that.'

Gotz speaks again. 'Fugger and his agents know their biggest creditors personally, they're the ones they do their most lucrative deals with. They also have a fairly precise idea of the circulation of exchanges passing through the ports between the Baltic and Portugal: that's their realm and never forget it. Antwerp is right in the middle of the commercial traffic: it's their base. So tomorrow, if some stranger in need of a few bob turned up with a letter giving him fifty thousand florins' credit, it wouldn't be easy for him to get out with that sum. You have to take care. Gently does it.'

Gotz is skilled at it, if he were cheating me he wouldn't make it so complicated. But now I've got to know what we're really talking about. 'How much?'

Without hesitation: 'Three hundred thousand florins in five years.'

I gulp at the thought of such an unimaginable amount of money: a strike against the wealthiest bankers in the whole of Christendom.

'How?'

He nods. I'm still here and that in itself is a good sign.

'I'll explain it to you now.'

'Before you do anything else, you've got to set up a cover operation. What do you know about goods trafficking?'

'I robbed a merchant on the road to Augsburg and killed three pirates near Rotterdam. I'm sure it's profitable, but it seems to be a risky business.'

Gotz looks pleased. 'Great. Another thing these bankers do is insure cargoes, because with the times being as they are the merchants have difficulty shouldering all the risks themselves.'

'Go on.'

'Imagine you're a merchant who has the chance to do an important deal on an exchange of goods with someone in England. You've bought refined cane sugar from factories in Antwerp and Ostende, and you're selling it on in the markets of London and Ipswich. It's a very lucrative deal and you plan to develop it as best you can. You've hired two boats, but the owner has asked you to take on all the risks of the transport, ships included. What do you do to protect yourself?'

I think about it for a moment and work out what the answer is: 'I go to the Fugger office in Antwerp and tell them my story, so that I can insure the cargo and the ships.'

Gotz's little black eyes don't move. 'Are you up for it?'

'What about the cargo and the ships?'

Eloi butts in, 'The first cargo of sugar lands safely in London. The second time, the cargo destined for Ipswich and the two ships transporting it will be ambushed by pirates from Zeeland.'

Gotz goes on. 'So you can legitimately claim back the fifteen thousand florins of insurance.'

I think about it calmly, until everything is clear. 'And then?'

'Rather than withdrawing the cash, you get him to write to you in letters of credit confirming your intention to pursue the activity and continue as an agency customer. And, in fact, you'll ask the Fugger agent to place your letters on a fixed sum of deposit for three years, so that whoever calls them in at the end of that term will receive a considerable amount of interest, but not before.'

'Three years?'

'To take your time. The later our letters are called in, the better it'll be for us. Because during those three years you'll go about your business with letters of credit attesting to your savings in the Fugger safes, but in the meantime you'll also start to circulate the false ones that I'll supply you with. We'll use all the letters, the real ones and the fake ones, to buy goods in a wide range of markets and then we'll exchange them for hard cash. Part of that will be deposited back in the bank. That'll be enough to keep relations with the agency alive and attest to the fact that our commercial enterprise is moderately prosperous. The rest will be a very well-deserved prize for our cunning.'

'How can you be sure they won't spot you straight away?'

'That's my job. It's just a question of balancing the payments made with the letters that actually correspond to the money really deposited in the bank and the payments made with the fake letters. We'll circulate most of the fake ones in peripheral markets, and in that way we'll gain more time and at the same time it'll be harder for the Fuggers to make their checks.'

'How long will the whole business take, if we don't get killed first?'

'According to my calculations, if we're careful to distribute the fake letters in different markets, it'll take them no less than five years to uncover us. And anyway, that's as long as we need to insure our old age. A hundred thousand florins a head. Does that sound all right, gentlemen?'

Absolute silence falls, even the lapping of the waves against the belly of the ship seems to stop.

I look at Eloi. 'And your role in all this?'

My friend's eyes are shining, but it's Gotz who replies: 'He'll be your colleague in the enterprise.' A fit of coughing. 'One last thing, we mustn't neglect the details: you'll have to get yourself accustomed to using a false name.'

While Eloi bursts out laughing, I reply: 'No problem.'

I listen to the echo of our feet as we set off along the jetty. Gotz von Polnitz, the mathematical wizard, has said goodbye to us, giving us an appointment for the day after tomorrow.

We walk along, deep in the same thoughts. Perhaps Eloi is waiting for me to object. I say, 'There's something that doesn't seem right to me.'

He nods. 'I know what you're thinking. Why does he need us? Why doesn't he do it all on its own, or turn to people who are already in commercial activity?'

'Got it in one.'

He knows there's no point in playing at secrets now, from this point onwards we're business associates. 'For the same reason that he can't show his face in Antwerp. Polnitz is a name of convenience. The man you've just met has been dead for three years.'

'So who on earth is he?'

He smiles. 'The man to whom the Fuggers owe their dominion over Antwerp. Their best agent: Lazarus Tucher.'

My eyes stand out on stalks. Eloi guffaws and puts his finger to his lips: 'Sh. After he finished off old Höchstetter and prepared the way for the ascent of Anton Fugger in Antwerp, his merits brought him the post of first agent at the Cologne branch. But in 1535, when Fugger decided to equip an expedition that would finally go off and bring back gold from the New World, the management of such an important operation was entrusted to the diligent Lazarus. Except that a storm off the Portuguese coast sank the whole fleet as soon as it set off. That's what any sailor down at the port can tell you: the biggest fiasco since Anton has been in charge of his family's activity. What isn't known is that one ship was saved, the flagship, and with it all the money that was to have financed mineral excavations in Peru.'

'And Tucher was on that ship.'

I can see where the story's going, but Eloi isn't about to interrupt himself halfway through. 'He set sail for Ireland and from there he moved on to England, where he hid out for three years, dealing with the friends of Henry VIII.'

'And now he's decided to perform a sting on the coffers of his former bosses.'

'Precisely.'

We walk down the narrow little street that runs along this stretch of the estuary. The bell towers of Antwerp appear through the mist on the horizon, the gulls inspect the water from above, a stork watches us motionlessly from its nest, on the flagpole of an abandoned wreck.

Eloi's eyes are on the ground as he thinks about what to say to me.

He stops. 'It isn't just a swindle on a magisterial scale.'

A few steps on I wait for him to come out with it.

'It isn't just about money.'

'What then?'

'Credit. How do you think traders would react if they thought fake Fugger credit letters were circulating around all the markets of Europe?'

'I don't think they'd accept a single piece of paper with Anton Fugger's signature on it.'

'Exactly so. What's a banker without credit? He's like a sailor without a ship. If people stop accepting his signature as a guarantee because they think it might be fake, he's finished, he's a dead man. You remember the story of old Höchstetter? That's how they finished him off: by discrediting him. People start withdrawing their deposits from the bank. Mistrust is a contagion that quickly spreads: who's going to want to do deals with someone who's losing customers rather than acquiring them?'

'So you're saying that Tucher wants to do the Fuggers of Augsburg over, cheat the cheaters?'

He shakes his head. 'He's interested in money. And so am I. But if we really do manage to put Fugger's credit in jeopardy, he could be ruined within a few years.'

My heart beats hard at the pit of my stomach, my guts turn to jelly: Ferdinand, Charles V, the Pope, the German princes. All tied to the purse strings of Anton the Sly.

I murmur it quietly, as though a vision were revealing itself to me: 'And along with them the courts of half of Europe.'

Eloi too lowers his voice, although there's no one else there as far as the eye can see. '"And I saw a new heaven and a new earth: for the first heaven and the first earth were passed away."'

Chapter 43

'Has he seen the cargo?'

'Yes.'

'The ships?'

'Yes.'

'Did he raise any objections?'

'A few questions about the route we're planning to follow.'

Lazarus Tucher, the man who came back to life, Gotz von Polnitz, the mathematical wizard, shakes his head disconsolately. 'They must think they're omnipotent. They're so certain of their strength that they can't even imagine that someone might try to cheat them. The bastards.'

'And that certainty is all to our benefit, isn't it?'

Gotz ignores the question, following his own train of thought. 'Did he go for the fifty thousand florins?'

'He didn't bat an eyelid. He asked us for three thousand as a deposit, which he'll return to us after the first expedition. I did as you said: I handed them over without a murmur, so he'd think we've got a considerable amount at our disposal.'

'Fine. But if I'd been in his shoes it wouldn't have gone so smoothly.'

'Then we're lucky we've got you on our side.'

The former Fugger agent pours me a little glass. 'Time to drink a toast. You've done well. We've taken the first step.'

The barge on which Lazarus Tucher hides the secret of his existence is hidden in a bight of the river. Inside it looks like a normal house, apart from the strange objects hanging from the walls in every corner: swords, pistols, musical instruments, maps, the clear shell of a tortoise.

I know it would be better to say nothing, but you don't often meet someone like this. 'Eloi told me your story.'

He doesn't seem surprised. 'He shouldn't have done. If they get us, the less we know about each other the better it is for everyone.'

I make myself comfortable on the leather sofa. 'Do you mean to say Eloi's told you nothing about me?'

Gotz shrugs. 'All I know is that you were in Münster with the madmen and I tell you in all sincerity that if those had been your only credentials, I wouldn't have involved you. But Eloi said you were the man for the job and I trust his intuition: someone who's managed to keep his head above water for twenty years amidst Antwerp's sharks, without getting himself done over, must be a pretty good judge of character.'

I chuckle and pour the spirits. 'You're right, they were madmen. But they took over a city. Have you ever done that?'

Gotz's eyes are two black dots set deeply among his scars. He has no need to reply, it seems that the Anabaptist and the merchant understand each other very well. 'You have to be fanatical to attempt an enterprise of that kind.'

'You have to believe in it.'

'And did you believe in it, really?'

A good question. 'Let's say that it wasn't the money that attracted me in those days.'

He smiles and fills a second glass. 'Do you want to hear a really interesting story about Münster?'

'Something I don't already know?'

'Something known only to me, Anton Fugger and perhaps the Pope.'

'It sounds like a state secret.'

He nods slyly, smoothing his moustache. The gulls shriek outside the little window, the only sound. 'At the beginning of 1534 I was in charge of the affairs of the Fuggers in Cologne. It was there that I learned the tricks of the trade and everything that's going to come in useful for our operation. What happens is that one day I receive a letter on which is written only a sum of money. No signature, just a seal: a big letter Q.'

'Q?'

'Stamped on the wax. I ask for an explanation from the agency's accountant, who's been in the service of the Fuggers for more than ten years, and he tells me that, when you get a letter like that one, you have to prepare the money and wait for someone to come and get it, showing the seal.'

I interrupt him: 'I don't see where Münster comes into it.'

Gotz flinches slightly. 'Let me finish. At this point I ask to be told more: how do we go about getting money into the hands of an unknown man? The old accountant tells me that a few years previously, word came from Rome to open unlimited credit on the Fugger coffers for a secret agent working in the imperial territories. "Herr Q", the accountants of the German branches called him.'

'A spy.'

He won't interrupt his story. 'So I prepare a letter of credit for the sum requested, and get ready to receive it. And you know who turns up? A cleric. Wrapped in a dark habit, with a hood covering his eyes and half his face. He shows me the ring with the Q, identical to the one stamped on the letter. However, when he sees the letter of credit he tears it into a thousand pieces in front of my eyes and tells me he wants hard cash. I point out that it's dangerous to travel with that kind of money in your pocket, but he insists: he wants the gold. Fine, I open the strongboxes and give him what he asked for. After that he asks me if I can tell him of a horse-hiring company that would cover the distance between here and Münster. I direct him towards the biggest stables in Cologne.'

He falls silent. The story is finished. A dark presentiment forces its way into my head, but I can't articulate it. I put my glass on the table, my hands trembling slightly.

Gotz waits for a reaction. 'Isn't that a great story? Maybe if you want to take over a city you need fanatics who believe in it, but if you want to infiltrate a city with a spy, you need money. Cash always comes into it.'

He notices my unease.

The dark line of the spirits in the bottle swishes gently back and forth in time with the boat.

The tortoiseshell gleams darkly.

A white heron slices through the fragment of sky framed by the little window.

The map of the English coast has, in the bottom left-hand corner, a wind-rose that looks from here like a black-and-white flower.

Gotz, sunk deep into his armchair, doesn't move a muscle.

Gotz. Lazarus. Different names, different men. Same story.

Gustav Metzger, Lucas Niemanson, Lienhard Jost, Gerrit Boekbinder.

Lot.

'No one is what he seems to be.'

I don't know if the words were spoken by Gotz or myself, or whether it was just a thought bouncing around in my head.

The questions come flooding out of their own accord. 'Who opened that credit?'

'I've never known. Probably some high-up in Rome.'

'Describe that man to me, the one who came to collect the money.

'His face was covered, as I told you. His voice suggested that h
wasn't all that old, but four years have passed since then . . .'

He's following me, he's understood, he's making an effort. '
remember wondering what he was going to get up to in Münster with
that kind of money, although it wasn't a huge sum, two or thre
thousand florins as far as I remember, but why set off on a journey o
that kind with a full purse?'

'To avoid leaving a trail or raising suspicions.'

I look at him. Now it's my turn to think out loud and provide
story in exchange. 'Early in 1534 the Baptists of Münster received thei
first conspicuous cash donations, contributions to the cause from
various communities, and also from single brethren.'

'You're saying that the money could have been used to make friend
with the Baptists . . .'

'What better passport for a spy?'

Once again we listen to the slow lapping of the waves and th
creaking of the wood.

He's the first to speak, somewhere between false modesty and
disbelief. 'I don't know too much about religious issues. Tell me wh
Rome would have wanted to infiltrate an agent into the Baptis
community of a little town in the North.'

The answer takes shape as I utter it. 'Maybe because that little tow
in the North was becoming the beacon of Anabaptism. Mayb
because that community was going to kick the lords up the arse and
raise up the people where no one else had ever succeeded in doing so
Maybe because someone far-sighted, down at the Pope's court, wa
shitting bricks.'

Gotz shakes his head. 'No, that doesn't work: the cardinals hav
other things to think about.'

'They have to think about defending their power.'

'Then why not break the balls of the Lutherans?'

'Because the Lutherans are sometimes the best allies against th
rebellion of the humblest classes. Who massacred the peasants i
Frankenhausen? The Catholic princes and Lutherans together. Wh
lent cannon to the bishop of Münster so that he could retake the city
Philip of Hesse, an admirer of Luther.'

'No, no, that one won't wash. Luther brought the Pope low, h
chucked him out of Germany with a series of kicks up the ars
and all the goods of the Church were impounded by the Germa
princes . . .'

'Gotz, it takes two pillars to hold up an architrave.'

The ex-merchant thinks about it and looks across at me. 'Adversaries, yet allies. Is that what you mean?'

I nod. 'A secret agent active in the imperial territories. For how long?'

'More than ten years, was what they told me.'

Once again that dark presentiment, an excruciating pressure behind my eyes.

Metzger, Niemanson, Jost, Boekbinder, Lot.

The many and the one. The ones I've been.

The many and the one. Someone.

The man in the crowd. Hidden within the community. One of ours.

'"For God shall bring every work into judgement, with every secret thing, whether it be good, or whether it be evil."'

Gotz is perplexed. 'What does that mean?'

The pressure eases, the presentiment melts away. 'It's the conclusion of Qoèlet's book, *Ecclesiastes*.'

The estuary broadens as far as the eye can see, as the ship glides quickly towards the sea, already visible on the horizon. The dawn casts its rays on the mirror of water before us and lights our way.

The sea. Eloi was right: it gives you a sense of freedom to detach yourself from a coast, to cast your eye over that infinite mass of waves. I've never sailed the sea: a strange anxiety, an intoxication, eased only by thoughts of the night just past.

The crew consists of a bo'sun and eight sailors under the orders of Captain Silas, all Englishmen who have worked before with Gotz, whom we can trust implicitly. They speak their strange language, of which I can already make out a few of the more frequently used expressions: what I take to be expletives and curses.

I had come to Antwerp with the idea of sailing for England and never coming back. Now I'm going to do business there. You never know how things are going to turn out: yesterday I was a ragged man being hunted down by the police, today I'm a respectable sugar merchant, with an insurance of fifteen thousand florins on my cargo and ships.

I glance back, the second boat is following us a quarter of a mile away. It's under the command of Silas's deputy, a young Welsh buccaneer who has sailed in the Indies.

The merchant Hans Grüeb is going to sell sugar in London. The flat, gull-crowded islets of Zeeland, land clawed back from the sea, stretch out ahead of him. Gradually they thin out and the North Sea receives him placidly with its intense blue, as dark as the thoughts that have been crowding his mind since the previous night.

The incredible story of Lazarus back from the dead forces me to return to my memories of Münster, perhaps more vivid today for having been told to Eloi.

The question is always who. Who was the spy? Who was working for the papists from the start? Who put up cash for the cause, having himself welcomed by the regenerate?

Who?

Who was the wretch?

I run faces, places, occasions through my mind. My arrival in the city, my reception, the barricades and then the delirium, the madness. Who worked to ensure that it would all end up like that? I've already told Eloi. They all died. No one survived. Only Balthasar Merck and his friends. The boy Krechting? Not a hope.

But that too is just another way of stifling the worst presentiment.

One of us, an ally, in a position to gain trust. And to send you off to be massacred when the right moment came.

The letters.

The letters to Magister Thomas.

A spy already active before 1524.

In Germany.

Someone and no one.

Frankenhausen. Münster.

The same strategy. The same results.

The same person.

Qoèlet.

TRATTATO

VTILISSIMO

DEL BENEFICIO DI GIESV CHRISTO CROCIFISSO, VERSO I CHRISTIANI.

Venetiis Apud Bernardinum de Bindonis. Anno Do. M.D.XXXXIII.

Letter sent to Naples from the pontifical city of Viterbo, addressed to Gianpietro Carafa, dated 1 May 1541.

To my most honoured lord Giovanni Pietro Carafa in Naples.

My Most Reverend Lord,

The news that Your Lordship gives me about the Emperor's defeat in Algiers, and the routing of his troops in Hungary at the hands of the Turks, fills this heart with the hope that we will soon see the Habsburg collapsing beneath the blows of his adversaries and his vast power toppling. If we add to this the news from France, of Francis I's intention to resume war, I feel that the moment is especially propitious to Your Lordship's hopes and to those of his devoted servant. Never before has the Emperor had such problems controlling his immense territories; never before have his debts with the German bankers been so great and so far from being paid.

So it should come as no surprise that he is attempting to unite Christendom beneath his banner, making concessions to the Protestant princes in Germany so that they may come to his aid in the plains of Hungary and in the Balkans in order to resist the advance of Suleyman. The Lutherans have now consolidated their position in Saxony and Brandenburg, and the Emperor is willing to take account of this and to allow Rome to remain outside those principalities.

Yet anyone planning to see Charles V's power diminished must hope that the princes will not yield to his flattery, and will continue to consider him a powerful enemy with whom one might forge a pact, but whom one would not choose as an ally. The sympathies of Philip of Hesse are not, in fact, a good sign: the Emperor has turned two blind eyes to the landgrave's bigamy just in order to win him back as an ally, and the latter has struck a cowardly deal.

But be that as it may: forcing the Roman Church and the Lutheran theologians to sit down at the same table is the plan that Charles V is pursuing with all the means at his disposal, and there is not the slightest doubt that he will go into battle: since his failure to defeat the Lutheran princes, he now wants to be the champion of Christendom, united under the banner of the new crusade against the Turks, and he is sure that this would make him invincible. To this end he is willing to spend all the resources he has at his disposal.

Fortunately, I have the pleasure of learning that the Diet of Worms has not yielded the results that Charles so hotly desired: the Lutheran doctors remain a menace to the Holy See and the Catholic princes.

Having met Luther and Melanchthon personally during their rise to prominence, I may add that they are too proud and suspicious to agree to a reconciliation with Rome. This plays in favour of Your Lordship's plans, and for the time being it prevents the rapprochement between Catholics and Lutherans, which would be fatal to us.

Nonetheless the danger, rather than coming from beyond the Alps, could arise within the very bosom of the Holy Roman Church.

The new garb that Your Lordship's generosity has allowed me to don so that I may continue to serve the cause of God, and the privileged vantage point to which I have managed to gain access, have allowed me to gather information at first hand, and to assemble many elements which my service to My Honourable Lord requires me not to conceal. Once again Your Lordship's foresight has proved more than valuable.

So I can state with certainty that what is forming here in Viterbo, within the Patrimony of St Peter, is a genuine party that is favourable to dialogue with the Lutherans and could lend its support to the Emperor's aspirations. Your Lordship is in the habit of referring to them as *spirituali*, in allusion to those cardinals receptive to the dangerous doctrines of Luther and the new heresiarch in Geneva, John Calvin; at any rate, while it is certain that the Viterban circle gravitates around the most learned Cardinal Pole, I must inform My Lord that the circle of people that has formed around him since his appointment as Papal Governor of the Patrimonium includes all kinds of men of letters, laymen and clerics from everywhere one could think of, united in their common aim to lay the Church open to the demands of the perfidious Luther. This naive acceptance of any intellect willing to serve his cause meant that Your Lordship's diligent servant was able to become part of the circle and win the favours of its most illustrious members: they have been more than happy to have within their ranks a literate German with a good knowledge of the writings that are currently being produced in the German universities.

I should therefore like to be allowed to deliver my impressions of the man who should, beyond a doubt, be considered the inspiration behind this congregation: the English cardinal Reginald Pole. He enjoys the distinct fame of being a Catholic martyr, having been obliged to flee his country as a result of the schism of Henry VIII, and this in itself makes it difficult to raise any kind of suspicions about his orthodoxy. He is a man of great culture and refinement, incapable of suspicion or bad faith, a genuine supporter of the possibility of engaging in a dialogue with the Protestants, with a view to bringing them back within the bosom of the Holy Roman Church.

So, as I remarked above, it should come as no surprise that the Emperor sees this pious man of the Church as a champion of his own interests.

Pole also enjoys the friendship of Cardinal Contarini of Bologna, the man chosen by His Holiness Pope Paul III to conduct fresh negotiations with the Lutherans in Regensburg after the collapse of the Diet of Worms. To this we may add Cardinal Morone, Bishop of Modena, Gonzaga of Mantua, Giberti of Verona, and Cortese and Badia of the Pontifical Curia. All these men are fairly flexible in their response to Protestant doctrines, preaching the use of persuasion upon those brethren who have deviated from the path of Rome, and consequently abhorring the persecution of such ideas with coercive force.

Reginald Pole, as Your Lordship is well aware, is a man of letters who studied in Oxford with the same Thomas More whose experiences have so shaken the Christian world. A martyr and a friend of martyrs: his credentials really do appear unimpeachable. After Oxford he completed his studies in Padua and is consequently most familiar with the realities of Italian life.

So it is not difficult to guess how well he relates to the men of letters with whom he surrounds himself, and in particular with Marco Antonio Flaminio, the poet and translator who enjoys the friendship of His Holiness Paul III, whose name Your Lordship will surely have heard mentioned for that very reason. The association between Pole and Flaminio, who are very close here in Viterbo, is not, in my view, any less dangerous than the one consolidated more than twenty years ago in Wittenberg, between Martin Luther and Philipp Melanchthon. When a faith stubbornly maintained comes into contact with learning, the product of that encounter is always something magnificent, whether it be for good or ill.

The sooner I am able to bring Your Lordship further news about events in Viterbo, the sooner my desire to serve you will be satisfied.

Kissing Your Lordship's hands and imploring your continued favour.

Your Lordship's faithful servant

Q   Viterbo, 1 May 1541

Letter sent to Rome from the pontifical city of Viterbo, addressed to Gianpietro Carafa, dated 18 November 1541.

To my most reverend and honourable lord Giovanni Pietro Carafa in Rome.

My Most Respected Lord,
   It is with satisfaction that I learn of the collapse of the initiative conducted by Cardinal Contarini in Regensburg. As I had predicted, the Lutherans remained immovable on the doctrine of justification by faith alone and, despite Contarini's willingness to accommodate them, Your Lordship's skilled diplomacy was able to impede and repel the agreement that appeared on the point of being ratified.
   It is a bitter disappointment for the members of Reginald Pole's circle and I can still see the horror on their thunderstruck faces.
   But it is not time to sheathe our swords; the danger that these minds represent is far from weakened. And I shall now give you a detailed account of a new menace, so that Your Lordship may advise his servant about the measures he will consider it opportune to undertake.
   The Diet of Regensburg posed the threat that the doctrine of the Holy Roman Church on the subject of salvation might be contaminated by the teachings of the Lutheran heretics.
   As Your Lordship knows, the Protestant theologians, reinforced by certain ill-interpreted New Testament passages (Mt 25, 34; Rm 8, 28–30; Eph. 1, 4–6), assert that those whom God has chosen as his saints since the beginning of the world, and only they, will be saved on the Day of Judgement. The accomplishment of good works as a pledge to gain eternal salvation is, according to this, pure illusion. Salvation is guaranteed to the elect not by meritorious actions, but by the divine gift of faith and nothing else. Consequently no good work carried out by a Christian could intervene in order to alter this original gift, which is received by some men, the elect, those who are predestined to salvation according to the plan of God. I do not need to remind you of the danger that this

doctrine presents for good Christian order, which must instead be affirmed on the basis of the free choice of faith or its rejection on the part of men. Furthermore, I have no hesitation in asserting the doctrine known as justification by faith alone as the pillar supporting all the abominations committed by the Lutherans over the past twenty-five years. This is the architrave of their upside-down theology, and it is what gives them the strength to inveigh against the Holy See without the slightest humility, and to call into question the hierarchies of the Holy Roman Church, on the basis that it is senseless to appoint a judge of human deeds, or establish an ecclesiastical body to administer the law and assess just who is worthy to enter the Kingdom of God and who is not. Your Lordship will of course recall that one of Luther's first bold moves was to refuse to recognise the Holy Father's authority to perform excommunications.

So what Cardinal Contarini was unable to do – crippling and mutilating the Catholic doctrine of salvation through good works – the increasingly broad circle of Cardinal Pole's acolytes could well achieve today.

I have already had cause to inform Your Lordship of the dangerous fascination exerted upon naive minds by the writings of that young Genevan who seems to have picked up Luther's baton where the dissemination of heresy is concerned. I am referring to that John Calvin, author of a putrid work, *The Institutes of the Christian Religion*, which confirms and reinforces many of the ideas that have emerged from the heretical mind of the monk Luther, prime among them the one known as justification by faith alone.

This work has inspired what I consider to be the most dangerous publication in these Italian lands since the days of the perfidious sermons of Savonarola, which we owe to the twisted genius of the minds of Viterbo, in whose company I find myself.

I am referring to a brief treatise whose danger far exceeds its volume, since *in it is fully expounded,* in a language easily under-standable to anyone, *the Protestant doctrine of the justification by faith alone as though this did not run entirely contrary to the doctrine of the Church.*

There can be no doubt that this is an attempt on the part of this circle of learned men and clerics to introduce at a doctrinal level elements favouring rapprochement between Catholics and Lutherans, in complete acceptance of the doctrine of salvation maintained by the latter.

The author of the work in question is a Benedictine friar, one

Benedetto Fontanini from Mantua, currently resident in the monastery of San Nicolò Arena, on the slopes of Mount Etna. But the hands which have worked on the writing of the text, introducing almost literal translations from Calvin's *Institutes*, are those of Reginald Pole and Marco Antonio Flaminio.

Enquiries conducted with extreme care led me to discover that Cardinal Pole had an opportunity to meet Friar Benedetto as early as 1534 when, on his flight from England, he found himself passing through the monastery on the island of San Giorgio Maggiore in Venice. At that time, in fact, Fontanini was staying there. Your Lordship must be aware that the abbot of the monastery of San Giorgio Maggiore at the time was none other than the same Gregorio Cortese who is today a fervent supporter of the *spirituali* in the Curia.

To this precedent we may add the fact that two years later, in 1536, Marco Antonio Flaminio went to that monastery, called there by Cortese himself on the pretext of undertaking the printing of the Latin paraphrase of Volume XII of the *Metaphysics* of Aristotle.

So: Cardinals Pole, Cortese and Flaminio. All friends and all very close to the conciliatory policies of Cardinal Contarini of Bologna. These are the minds that have brought this terrible work to life. If Friar Benedetto of Mantua supplied the clay, it was the circle of the *spirituali* who moulded it into a vessel filled with heresy.

The title of the treatise speaks for itself, literally picking up as it does on an expression used several times by Melanchthon in his *Loci communes*.

The Benefit of Christ Crucified, or *A Most Useful Treatise on the Benefit of Jesus Christ Crucified for Christians*. That is the title of the work the editing of which was completed in the past few days by Flaminio, in which it is clearly affirmed that:

> the righteousness of Christ shall be sufficient to make us righteous, and the children of grace, without any of our good works. Neither can those works be good except that before we do them we our own selves be made good and righteous by faith.

Your Lordship can easily judge the threat that the distribution of ideas of this kind would represent for Christendom and in particular for the Holy See, should they meet with approval. If, then, this little book were to be endorsed by the important men of the Church, an epidemic of agreement with the Protestants could break out within the heart of the Church of Rome. I do not dare to think

what odious consequences that might have for the policies of the
Holy See in its dealings with Charles V.

I am therefore preparing to receive new directives from your
ingenious mind, certain that you will once again be able to advise
in the best possible way this your zealous servant.

I implore your protection in faith, kissing Your Lordship's
hands.

Your Lordship's faithful servant

Q   Viterbo, 18 November 1541

Letter sent to Rome from the pontifical city of Viterbo, addressed to Gianpietro Carafa, dated 27 June 1543.

To my most honourable and reverend lord Giovanni Pietro Carafa in Rome.

My Most Honoured Lord,

I am writing to tell Your Lordship that I now know for certain that *The Benefit of Christ Crucified* has been sent to Venice for printing. A few days ago Marco Antonio Flaminio returned from his journey as part of the Holy Father's entourage to Busseto, to meet the Emperor. By questioning one of Flaminio's page-boys I was able to discover his movements. My suspicions proved to be justified. Indeed Flaminio, after taking part in the meeting in Busseto and spending May in that town, made an unusual detour via Venice on his journey home. The page-boy mentioned that he visited the printing press of one Bernardo de' Bindoni, but he was unable to tell me more. At any rate I am sure that his purpose was none other than the delivery, or perhaps even the final revision, of the text in question.

Since Pope Paul III placed the revived Congregation of the Holy Office in Your Lordship's hands a year ago, establishing that heresy may be persecuted wherever it may lurk, and with every means necessary, the *spirituali* have become more cunning. His Holiness's bull *Licet ab initio*, the consequent rebirth of the Inquisition and not least the death of Cardinal Contarini, have led Pole and Flaminio to work with extreme caution. I suspected that they had printed the little book away from Rome; furthermore they know very well that Venice enjoys an unusual level of freedom as regards the printing and selling of books, and if I still had any lingering doubts concerning Flaminio's visit to the Venetian press, they would be dispelled by these reflections.

My Lord is fully aware how dangerous a weapon the printing press can be: without it, Luther would still be teaching in an unknown university in a muddy little Saxon town.

In the expectation that I shall soon be able to supply My Lord with fresh and useful information, I kiss Your Lordship's hands.
Your Lordship's faithful servant
Q   Viterbo, 27 June 1543

Letter sent to Rome from the headquarters of the Fugger company in Augsburg, dated 6 May 1544.

To the most illustrious and eminent Cardinal Giovanni Pietro Carafa in Rome.

To Your Most Reverend Lordship I send greetings and very best wishes, nurturing the hope that these lines, penned by a pious Christian servant entirely devoted to the Holy Roman Church, shall reach no eyes but those of Your Lordship.

The long years of friendship linking my family with Your Lordship free me from the obligation to use false words to embellish the favour that I am about to ask of you. On more than one occasion Your Eminence has been so good as to grant us the honour of lending our services to the affairs that you have conducted on German soil: on more than one occasion this soul has been honoured to lend his assistance, with the means granted him on earth by the good Lord's munificence, to the deals and negotiations that Your Lordship has undertaken here. Among those services one might certainly number the fact of my having made available a considerable sum of money for the agents that Your Lordship maintains on German soil and at the Emperor's court.

Well, such a debt could be wiped out at a stroke, as though it had never existed, from our company accounts, were you to grant us our request.

You should be aware that our company has been the object of a huge and terrible fraud, which must be remedied as soon as possible; and since I consider it injurious to our family interests to allow the matter to come to the public attention, I am impelled to request Your Lordship's intervention.

Without going too much into the details of the infernal ruse, it should suffice for you to know that for some time I had noticed a certain incongruity in the company's annual accounts; something was not quite right: a matter of a few commas, a few unimportant figures in the accounts books. And yet a nagging doubt remained. Since the vastness of the interests of the Fuggers throughout Europe is almost by definition incalculable, it is far from easy to spot every little leak. But a leak there was, and with each passing year it assumed the features of a suspicion and gradually of a certainty. It was as though the peripheral branches of the company were making minimal errors in their accounts, as though they were being excessive in their approximations of the sums issued in the form of letters of credit. So at first I thought one of our agents might be responsible for the fraud. And yet that seemed strange, since before choosing the men to whom to entrust the care of our interests, we vet them from head to toe and often bind their personal fortunes to ourselves, in such a way that they are entirely at one with the interests of the company.

And in fact I was mistaken. The parasite came from without.

Your Lordship cannot imagine how much time and expense it has taken to discover the guilty parties: we have been obliged to send a special commissioner to each branch and agency of the Fugger bank, to supervise their loan activities for a whole year. Taking agencies and branches together, there are more than sixty of them across the continent of Europe.

It took a whole year to trace back, from merchant to merchant, the trajectories of the letters of credit that we had issued and to understand what was going wrong in our accounts. In that way we were able to discover that some of the letters of credit drawn on our agencies were fake.

Well, the factor common to all the deals under examination was the presence of an apparently innocuous merchant of linen, sugar and furs. Peculiar as this appeared to us, we followed up his commercial movements and found them quite unusual. Although he was not trading in very precious goods, he was covering twice the distances that he would have needed to sell his own merchandise: goods from Sweden that could have been sold on the market in Antwerp were transported to Portugal: goods from Brest that would have found an excellent market in England ended up being sold in Hamburg, and so on. In short, our merchant preferred peripheral markets. At first we thought he was doing this in the hope of making bigger profits, but we discovered that that was not in fact the case, since his prices were not significantly higher than the average. But an even more curious detail is that he turns out to be a creditor of our company, who opened an account with our Antwerp branch six years ago.

His name is Hans Grüeb, which would indicate that he is German by birth. Yet my commissioners have found no trace of that name on any of the German markets. He seemed to have made his first appearance in Antwerp in 1538. So we made enquiries there, discovering that his business associate is an even more shady and suspect character, a certain Loy, or Lodewijck de Schaliedecker, or Eloi Pruystinck, who was until ten years ago a simple roofer and who is already known to the authorities in Antwerp, where he is suspected of heresy.

By now we were sure that we had identified the parties responsible for the terrible fraud done to us. We still do not know how they managed to reproduce perfect copies of Fugger letters of credit; nevertheless, we have no intention of waiting any longer and subjecting ourselves to further damage.

So, the reason why I decided to request Your Lordship's intervention is that I do not consider it useful, in a situation of this kind, to denounce the two suspects to the local authorities. Irreparable damage would be done to the company if news got out that fake letters of credit of ours were circulating on the markets. It would cause a terrible crisis of trust where we were concerned and in a short time we would risk seeing the creditors withdrawing their money from our coffers. I might add that this would have dreadful consequences for many people, and not only for the Fuggers: the company's interests are closely linked with those of many courts, not least that of the Holy See.

So, there is a path that we can take to our common benefit, which would allow us both to resolve this problem without either of us suffering any great harm. As I said, this Eloi Pruystinck has already been suspected of heresy for some time, since he practises and preaches common ownership of wives and abandonment of private property and denies, my most trustworthy informants tell me, the existence of sin. Hitherto, this little heresiarch's cunning has been such as to allow him and his peers to escape accusations of blasphemy and apostasy. But since His Holiness Paul III reestablished the Inquisition, putting it under Your Lordship's command, I would entertain the hope that these Loists might finally be indicted and put on trial. I should like to beg Your Lordship to be so magnanimous as to direct the attention of the Tribunal of the Holy Office towards these damned heretics and low tricksters, that they may desist from the dissemination of their blasphemous ideas and at the same time stop doing harm to our company, while also ensuring that no one knows about the damage that they have done to us already.

Humbly trusting in Your Lordship's intervention, and confirming the friendship that binds us, I kiss Your Lordship's hands.

Anton Fugger, servant of God

Augsburg, the 6th day of May 1544

Basle
(1545)

Chapter 1

'Don't come to me and say I didn't warn you, Oporinus, old pal. For two years now I've been telling you to keep an eye on that Sebastian Münster. A pupil of Melanchthon, with an attitude like that, *capito*? Writes a *Cosmography* the like of which you've never seen, all geography and romance, cartography and anecdotes, words and illustrations, a real firework display if you know what I mean. And you leave it to be printed by those dusty old typographers Hericpetrina, five thousand copies in five months, we're not talking chicken-feed here!'

Pietro Perna is in full flow, talking his laboured German mixed with the odd phrase of Italian and Latin, having burst without warning into the printing press of Oporinus, one of the most important in the whole of Switzerland.

'Do we want to do an Italian translation of this genius straight away, or do we want to wait for someone else to get there first? What's this?' He grabs a book from a shelf and flicks through it, almost tearing it in half between his fat hands, then throwing it on the table with an expression of disgust. He walks over to Oporinus and throws his arms round his shoulders, clumsily, because he's at least a head shorter. With a wave of his hand he presents him to our attention.

'*Signori*, the great Oporinus, who recently published the book that will guarantee his imperishable fame, the extraordinary *De Fabrica* by the unparalleled anatomist and draftsman Vesalius, is also interested in a collection of nonsense about the circulation of the blood, a volume entirely without illustrations, which would look old-fashioned to even the most loyal follower of Aristotle! Can we get it into our heads, pal, that scientific treatises which do not show what they are talking about deserve simply to be thrown in the waste-paper basket?'

He walks nervously round the tables, rubbing his hands, while Oporinus casts us sorrowful glances. An Italian, one of the shortest men I have ever come across apart from actual dwarfs, inveterately foul-mouthed, almost completely bald and incapable of standing still, Pietro Perna is a very well-known character in Basle. It seems that he passes through the city every month, advising on publications, coming up with new ideas, ripping other people's works to shreds and above all, stocking up on prohibited underground books, suspected of heresy, which in turn he sells on to bookshops in every duchy, every republic, state and *seignoria* in northern Italy.

'Stancaro? Drop him, Oporinus my old friend. He's boring anyway!'

'Boring, you say?' Oporinus's voice is full of resentful astonishment. 'Francesco Stancaro is a highly cultivated man, a refined student of Hebrew. In his next book he's going to establish parallels between the Anabaptists and the Hebrews in terms of the advent of . . .'

'Most wonderful, most interesting and most honourable!' He lowers his tiny arm and sweeps the air in front of him. 'How many sleepwalkers do you think are going to buy that stuff?'

'Selling, that's all you think about. But some books are useful in other ways: they give you prestige, they humble your detractors.'

'My only prestige is the following, my old pal: the books that I recommend and distribute keep the printworkers up all night. In short, no one likes frontal attacks, hair-splitting arguments, accusations any more. The keyword now is "heterogeneity", *capito*? "Het-er-o-gen-e-i-ty"! Mixing genres! Things that keep you guessing, *capito*? and right up to the end you haven't a clue whether you're reading a heretic or an orthodox believer. Books like *The Benefit of Christ Crucified*, written by a Catholic friar, but full of themes dear to the German faith. Stancaro! Who recommended him? Our Anabaptist over there?'

He's pointing to me. He comes over to me. A series of quick little slaps on the shoulder. 'Of course! And it's not a bad idea. It's not original, but it's clever. This Stancaro hurls anathemas on the Anabaptists. Not your usual commonplaces. Serious stuff. Fine: how better to expose the features of your faith to the whole of Italy?'

I look at him askance. 'Me? Faith?' I laugh heartily and return the slap. 'You can't know me that well!'

Pietro Perna gets back up from the floor, dusting down his clothes. '*Puttana miseria,* you're free with your hands, mate! I remember this guy in Florence . . .'

Oporinus intervenes with a paternal air, knowing very well that when he talks about Italy Perna becomes unstoppable. 'Come on, Messer Pietro, let's get down to business. These gentlemen are waiting for me and you've jumped the queue. What sort of thing can I interest you in?'

The Italian is still walking around between the tables and the shelves, grabbing a book with each step he takes. 'Not this one, not this one, not . . . this one either. This one!' He taps the cover with the back of his hand. 'Give me twenty copies of this and a hundred of the Vesalius.'

Meanwhile the chimes of the bell remind me that it's really getting late. I nod to Oporinus to indicate that I'll drop in again and make for the door.

'No, wait!' Perna's shrill voice and his rapid footsteps behind me. As though he hadn't spoken. 'I'm talking to you, wait for me. Oporinus, one to keep your eye on: the third volume of Rabelais, translate it and see what happens, don't you think? Then there's Michael Servetus, you must have read his treatise against the Trinity, well, you don't feel offended because of what I said about faith, do you?'

He catches up with me after following me for half a mile, drying the generous expanse of his forehead with a handkerchief. 'You're a touchy one, aren't you, mate? You Nordics haven't got the hang of irony!'

'Could be,' I reply, breaking away abruptly from his sweaty hand, 'and you must forgive me for striking you back then; as you know, Nordic people don't touch each other unless they're going to fight.'

The Italian attempts to catch his breath after his long run, while at the same time trying to keep up with my rapid pace. 'I've been told you're quite rich, that you've seen more than anyone could imagine, that you're an Anabaptist and you're interested in the book trade. I seem to have worked out where you stand on Anabaptism. What about the rest?'

'Put it this way: if the rest was true, what would you ask me?'

'I'd suggest going into business.'

I shake my head. 'The last person who did that was executed a few months ago. Drop it, that would be my advice!'

He insists on gripping my arm with that hand of his. 'You wouldn't be superstitious about Italians, would you, pal?'

'It isn't a question of superstition. It's what's happened so far: everyone who's been involved with me has met a terrible end.'

'But you're still alive!' he shrieks in that irritatingly high-pitched voice of his. 'And I'm very lucky.'

He's in front of me, walking backwards with his arms spread. 'At least listen to what I have to say! It's about that book I mentioned before, *The Benefit of Christ Crucified*. An ex-plo-sive piece of writing. Let's agree on this: what he says, in itself, is fine for bores, you know? Some stodgy stuff about justification by faith alone, but the important thing is that it was the cardinals who wrote it. That's a scandal, don't you see? And scandals mean thousands of copies.'

I put up the fur collar of my jacket to shield my ears from the freezing wind. 'Talk to Oporinus about it, why don't you? I'm sure he'll be interested.'

'Oporinus is out of the picture, mate. Only Italians are going to be interested in *The Benefit of Christ Crucified*. You can't publish a book like that in Basle.'

'And where's it being published?'

'In Venice. That's actually where they published it. But they're about to ban the printing of it. It's a matter of a few months; the current publisher may have to stop making copies, *capito*? And it could be that the people who are distributing it at the moment will drop it like a hot stone. You know very well that in Venice . . .'

'I don't know a lot about Venice. Someone told me they've got canals there like they have in Amsterdam.'

My unwanted companion abruptly comes to a standstill as though he's suddenly been taken ill. He clutches a ring protruding from the wall, the kind you tie horses to, and slowly turns his head towards me. 'Are you telling me you've never been to Venice?'

'I'll tell you more than that: this city is the southernmost place I've ever set foot in.'

Sounding offended and still clutching the ring, he says, 'But in that case everything I've heard about you is mistaken. Not only are you not an Anabaptist, *capito*? But you can't have seen such incredible things as all that if Venice isn't one of them, and certainly you can't be all that interested in the book trade if you've never visited the capital of printing, and finally you can't be as rich as all that, because nowadays no one with the money to spare would deny themselves a trip to Italy.'

I look at him for a moment, still unable to understand why it is, in the end, that I can't help liking this awkward, petulant little man. At any rate, it's time to say goodbye to him, he's already dragged me quite a long way from the place where I was supposed to be. 'If you want to spend the whole morning hanging on to that ring, that's fine by me. But as to myself, I've got to get an important letter to the post by midday.'

He looks half dead. 'Off you go, pal. I already know you're going to accept my proposal. You don't need any other reason. It's your chance to see Venice.'

Chapter 2

I've jotted down a few inadequate lines that will cross the hills, beyond Franche-Comté, turning into the Seine, following its ever-broader, ever-flatter course, where the boats will make for Paris and the sea. And then the Channel and the English coast. A month, maybe more. That way they'll be able to escape the war, the mercenary troops of the German princes, the armies massed at the Dutch border by the Emperor's vassals.

I hand over the letter.

Addressed to a ghost by the name of Gotz von Polnitz, in the city of London. No one had said so openly, but we knew we were close to the end. We'd already got two hundred and fifty thousand florins stashed away. And a sense that Fugger was beginning to suspect something.

Gotz von Polnitz, the only one who always stayed in the shadows, beyond suspicion. Apart from anything else he died a few years ago under the name of Lazarus Tucher.

It was to him that I entrusted the fate of the people dearest to me: Kathleen, Magda. If things go wrong, he's the one to turn to. Lot's going to have to run faster than the police, without looking back.

I had just disembarked when a little boy came over and advised me to go home. 'They've taken everyone away.'

My agreement with Gotz. If you take them with you, put a red cloth in the window of the house where we've hidden the money.

The cloth was there, perhaps it still is. The house belonged to an old merchant who had moved to Goa, in the Indies. And the money was still there: a hundred thousand florins.

I should have joined Kathleen and Magda, in safety, and lived the rest of my days in peace.

But I didn't have the guts: history tells me if I touch anyone they die. Friends, brethren, fellow travellers. There's a lake of blood behind me that begins far away, one day in May, and reaches all the way here.

Thomas Müntzer: tortured and executed, twenty years ago.

Elias the miner: beheaded with the sword of a mercenary in a muddy street.

Hans Hut: suffocated in jail when he burned his own bedding.

Johannes Denck: carried off by the plague in this very city.

Melchior Hofmann: probably rotted away in the prisons of Strasbourg.

Jan Volkertsz: first martyr on Dutch soil.

Jan Matthys of Haarlem: in pieces in a wicker basket.

Jan Bockelson of Leyden, Bernhard Knipperdolling, Hans Krechting: tortured with red-hot pincers, executed and publicly displayed in three cages hung from the steeple of St Lamberti.

Jan van Batenburg: beheaded in Vilvoorde.

The names are the names of corpses.

The last survivor of an unfortunate race, a race of people that history has decided to exterminate. Sole survivor, along with the women who gave sustenance to the minds of the warriors. Ottilie, Ursula, Kathleen. Magda is safe, under another sky. Her twelve years of age are the leak through which life can slip away, escaping from half a century of defeats.

I am the last remnant of an era, and I drag myself along with all that era's dead, a heavy burden that I wouldn't wish anyone else to be condemned to bear. Let alone the family that I might have had. They're safe, that's what matters. Gotz will take care of them. He promised.

Maybe you'd have done the same for me, mathematical wizard, but I was a risk, I was plague-ridden, a face that they would always recognise. So you said nothing and you hoisted anchor even though you didn't want to. You said so from the start: if it goes badly, we will never have known each other, we won't help each other, it'll be every man for himself. You took your share and Eloi's on behalf of Magda and Kathleen. You proved to be a kind-hearted son of a bitch.

Kathleen. These lines won't explain things, a thousand letters wouldn't. It was me they were after, not you, they would have taken the women and children too, of course they would, but not Gotz the ghost, so keep them safe, England, safe in the arms of your English friends and their drunkard king.

Kathleen. Maybe you read in my face that day that everything was coming to an end. That we would never see each other again, even if I'd managed it, even if I'd got away. Because an ancient destiny had caught up with me and a thousand lost friends died again with Eloi.

They took Balthasar, who will never see his wife again, they took

Davion and Dorhout. They took Dominique, whose writing dies with him. And then van Hove, the money wasn't much use to him this time; and Steenaerts, Stevens, van Heer. The big house was left empty. I got away and I'm on my own, yet again.

We feared the wrath of Fugger the Sly; we hadn't reckoned with the Pope's sleuths.

He didn't give up so much as a name. His spirit flew free from his torn flesh. They say he laughed, that he laughed loudly, that rather than screaming he laughed. I prefer to think of him that way: while the smoke envelops him, he's laughing his head off in defiance of the black crows. But he should still be here, offering me schnapps and those perfumed cigars from the Indies.

It is my destiny to survive, always, to go on living in defeat, taking it a little at a time.

I'm old now. Every time thunder shakes the heavens, I start at the memory of the cannon. Every time I close my eyes to sleep, I know that by the time I open them again I'll have been visited by many ghosts.

Kathleen, now, in a place far away from war. I am spending the time that still remains to me hidden, among refugees from half of Europe, hunted, like myself, by the Pope's Inquisition, or the Inquisition of Luther and Calvin. Peaceful people arriving with their own piles of books, their own stories and adventures: men of learning, persecuted clerics, Baptists. I'm only one face among many, wealthy enough to buy myself a bit of peace. Money to end my days. A hundred thousand florins. And no decent way of spending them.

I'm old. Perhaps that's all it is. I've lived ten different lives without ever stopping and now I'm tired. Despair stopped visiting me some time ago, as though my mind had closed itself off from suffering and could now see things from a distance as though reading them in a book.

And yet, from those pages there rises still the Black Shade that has always walked with me, telling me that no amount can pay your bill, that you never stop paying and that there is no safe hiding place. This is a game that demands to be played to the end; if that is the case, then so be it. All my loved ones are safe. I'm the only one left. There's just me and the ghosts that go with me. All of them.

Including Lodewijck de Schaliedecker, alias Eloi Pruystinck: burned *extra muros* on 22 October 1544.

'You can get lost in Venice, mate, even when you think you know it well, *capito*? You can find yourself completely at the mercy of this city. A maze of canals, alleyways, churches and buildings that appear in front of you as though in a dream, without any apparent connection to anything you've seen before.'

Pietro Perna, as usual, is losing himself in his talk about Italy, as he uncorks a bottle of 'the best wine in the world'. From the window of Oporinus's back room, the sky of Basle is of a grey tending to white as though someone had drained it of colour, but whether it's the smell of the wine or the Latin accent of my interlocutor, I feel as though the room is flooded with sunlight.

'Weren't you just talking about the alleged authors of *The Benefit of Christ Crucified*, Pietro?'

'That's right,' he answers, wiping his moustache with the back of his hand, 'let's not lose sight of the main issue. The book is officially anonymous, while unofficially it's said to have been written by Brother Benedetto Fontanini of Mantua, and in the underground it's claimed that it is the work of minds not a million miles away from the English cardinal Reginald Pole.'

I immediately interrupt him. 'I don't imagine you'll mind if I ask you for a bit more information about what's happening in Italy, because what you've just said about cardinals quoting Calvin doesn't make sense to me. And maybe wine isn't the best thing to be drinking if we're to have this discussion.'

He opens his eyes wide and pours himself another glass. 'This is wine from Chianti, my good man, you drink as much of it as you like and it will seem as though your head keeps getting lighter. My parents bottle it, in a farm near the village of Gaiole. It's a wine that has honoured the table of Cosimo de' Medici, *capito*? An in-im-it-ab-le beverage!'

He notices my gesture and continues, 'Let's get to the point, my friend. The Spanish doctor Michael Servetus described the Italians as being different from each other in every respect: government, languages, customs and physical characteristics. The only thing that links us, he says, is our dislike of each other, our cowardice in war and our haughtiness towards people from across the Alps. Where faith is concerned, you might almost say the same thing: on the one hand there are those adopting a conciliatory position towards the Lutherans, on the other there are those who give absolute precedence to the war against heresy and want to dust down the Holy Office of the Inquisition. Hatred of priests is very widespread among the people, hence the sympathy for what everyone calls the "German faith". But you could say the opposite too, *capito*? Just as you could say that many peasants don't know what the Trinity is, but they still take communion and confess at Easter to keep the parish priest happy, and the rest of the year they live on their superstitions.'

I try to imagine the country described by Pietro Perna, as I sip the second glass of his exquisite wine. Italy: maybe it's true that I can't die without having been there. However, I do have a sense that much of what I've been through started there, not least the killing of Eloi and the Free Spirits, identified by the Inquisition, who reported them to Charles V as heretics, dangerous citizens and infidels.

Meanwhile Perna hasn't drawn breath, accompanying each sentence with eloquent gestures. 'The Schmalkaldic League set up by the Protestant princes has an ambassador in Rome, *capito*? And loads of people would be delighted if Lutheran ideas triumphed in the Serenissima Repubblica of Venice. But you can't afford to lose a city like this one, comrade. Thanks to commerce, they've got everything a rich man could wish to buy, everything that a curious spirit could wish to see, everything that the flesh could ask of the capital of prostitution, where one woman in five is or has been, however irregularly, engaged in the profession. Finally, thanks to books, there is a way to fill your purse, as long as you've got a bit of that courage which, it would seem, only we Italians lack.'

Third glass: 'While you're on the subject of money, Pietro, I've got an idea for you. Write a book about Venice, to fill the notables of Europe with the desire to visit the city, and tell them where to eat, where to drink, where they can find female companions, where to sleep. I'm sure the book would be very successful and that the owners of the places you listed would pay you for the mention.'

He stretches his hands out on the table and takes mine before I have time to draw them back. 'Listen, my friend, you're wasted up here. Basle, as you know better than I do, is the city where the most innovative thinkers, the most dangerous heresiarchs, the most rebellious minds of Europe come to shake off their traces, to rest, to breathe quietly for a bit. None of this, be honest, is for you. You're a man of action.'

'Maybe. But my last injury was too recent, the skin hasn't grown back yet.'

'Then drink, comrade, there's no better balm for it.'

Fourth glass: my head really is light.

Chapter 4

Basle, 28 March 1545

Johann Oporinus's house is big enough to hold us all. The community of fugitives here in Switzerland numbers about twenty people, more or less illustrious Protestants, wild cards who have known the best minds of the Reformation: friends of Bucer, Capito and Calvin who, here in Basle, published the first edition of his *Institutio Christianae Religionis*.

Many of these learned men don't agree with the fathers of the Reformation about the constitution of a new ecclesiastical organisation. The decision of Bucer in Strasbourg and Calvin in Geneva to transform the capitals of the Reformation into city churches isn't welcomed by everyone. Many of those who have fled down here have been ostracised by those same masters who are now busy rebuilding a new church to replace the old one: new doctors to take charge of catechistic education, new deacons, new pastors, and old men keeping an eye on the religious and moral life of the faithful.

Discipline is the watchword that now echoes from one end of the reformed countries to the other. A word that leaves these free thinkers dissatisfied: awkward people for those who aspire to order and hierarchy.

Oporinus summoned us here to talk to us all, he wouldn't say what about, but I think it has something to do with rumours that are going about the place, to the effect that the ecumenical council announced several times by the Pope is actually going to happen this time, at the end of the year.

The only famous face is David Joris, until a few months ago the leader of Dutch Anabaptism. He's down here with a few followers, fleeing the crushing vice of the Inquisition. Bocholt, August 1536: the council of Anabaptists; Batenburg against everyone else, against Philips and Joris, I remember it well, sword against word. I don't think he'll recognise me, almost ten years have passed.

I see Pietro Perna slipping towards a chair clutching a few books, which he is now flicking through, bored, shaking his head to himself as though finding his worst suspicions confirmed.

I sit down too, slightly apart from the rest. I have no suspicions, no expectations, particularly about Oporinus and his circle of friends. I appreciate the work of our friend the printer: Paracelsus, Servetus, Socinus are all authors who could do damage, cause trouble, people whom Calvin is willing to sacrifice just in order to become a new Luther. But courage of that kind isn't enough on its own and even if it's all that the times can give us, I've been fighting too hard to get worked up over a theological dispute.

Our host nods to us to stop chattering, he wants to speak.

'My friends.' His voice is mild, his tone peaceful. 'I've summoned you here today because I think an exchange of ideas about the forthcoming event could be useful to us all.' He raises his voice. 'You will probably have heard that a council is to be summoned in which the whole divided Christian world will participate, with a view to finding a point of agreement and reconciling all the different parties.' He reads agreement in the faces of everyone present. Perna yawns in a corner, perched on a chair that's too high for him, his legs dangling.

Oporinus continues, 'Well, we can't stay aloof from so major an event, we can't just be silent onlookers. In all likelihood, in order to facilitate the intervention of the best doctors of Lutheran Protestantism, the place chosen for this council will be the neutral city of Trent, between Rome and the German lands, not too far from our own city of Basle.'

'Are you going to get us all invited to the council?' The tone is halfway between irony and disbelief, the joke comes from one of the chairs opposite Oporinus.

The printer shakes his head. 'That's not what I'm saying. But it might be useful to write to Geneva to inform Calvin and his men that we don't want to be left out, that we too want to have our say, maybe even publishing something, even if it's only a document that can be read before the Catholic cardinals. We could drop a line to Servetus in Paris, who might write us something for the occasion . . .'

From the second row a pale, thin man gets to his feet; he has a French accent. Oporinus must have introduced him to me, but I can't remember his name. 'You don't really believe that Luther, Melanchthon and Calvin are going to participate in this council?'

'Why not? If the cardinals have decided to call a council, it means they're worried that the Reformation will spread and they're up for a compromise, they might even be open to certain requests . . .'

Leroux, that's his name, speaks excitedly: 'If Luther attends the council, he won't come back. And the same is true of all the rest of them. If the papists can get them all within firing range, they won't be able to resist the temptation. They'll get hold of them and burn the lot . . .'

Heads nodding, some grimaces, Perna dangles his legs and indolently turns the pages of the books in his lap.

Joris is standing behind the Frenchman, tall and blond, waving a white hand: 'Listen, if Calvin and Luther managed to get their hands on some of the people there they'd do the same to them. What does the council matter to us? Even if we accept that it's really going to happen, it's going to be a trap for everyone, and if one of those old crows from Geneva or Wittenberg walks into it, I'm not going to feel sorry for him!'

Oporinus intervenes to put people's minds at ease. 'No, Joris, you mustn't say that. The disagreements separating some of us from Luther and Calvin shouldn't make us lump everything all together. And I don't even agree with your opinion about the council.'

The Dutchman shrugs and sits down again. 'If you allow this council to happen, they'll end up imposing one single opinion.'

'As I see it,' the printer goes on, over the noise that the Anabaptist's intervention has provoked, 'Calvin and Luther will do everything they can think of to exclude us from any negotiations, and if they ever do reach an agreement with Rome, it will be damaging to anyone who is not fully in accord with their proposals. What will become of people like Michael Servetus, Laelius Socinus, Sebastian Castellius?' Oporinus's eye runs across the sequence of faces. 'What will become of us, brothers?'

From the furthermost chair, at the end of the row, the preacher Serres from Basle speaks: 'There will be no agreement, Oporinus, because the papists will never give in on the doctrine of justification by good works, and Luther and Calvin aren't willing to budge an inch from justification by faith. As far as they're concerned that would leave room for the Pope, the Antichrist, for indulgences, for the buying and selling of faith . . .'

'We can't be absolutely sure of that, Serres. Some Italian cardinals, remember, value the idea of reaching a peaceful accord with the Protestants and appreciate Lutheran theology. There's already a literature on the subject, small things, perhaps, but important signals nonetheless. You've all read *The Benefit of Christ Crucified*. Its author is said to be a friar backed by important Italian men of letters, and even by a cardinal! These are facts, my brothers, we cannot ignore them. If there is a chance that this council might represent a chance for the reunification and radical reform of the Roman Church, I say that we must not leave the initiative to Calvin and Luther alone. Our liberty depends on it.' His eye runs across the row of heads until he comes to Perna's bald pate. 'I'd like to hear your opinion, Messer Perna, you are better informed than anyone about Italian affairs.'

The little man stretches out his tiny short arms; he hadn't expected to be called to account; he scratches his forehead and gets to his feet, still not rising above the heads of the assembly.

A long sigh. '*Signori*, I have heard many fine words, but no one has managed to get to the heart of the problem.' Everyone looks at him in puzzlement, craning forward to catch the Italian's curious pronunciation. 'You can write or commission the finest theological works of the century if that makes you feel better, but you won't change the reality of the facts. And the reality, gentlemen, is that it won't be doctrinal questions that decide the fate of the council, but politics.'

A sepulchral silence has fallen. Little Perna is a stranger to half-measures, I can see that his logorrhoea is about to seize hold of him. 'If this council does take place, it will be because of the pressure that the Emperor is exerting on the Pope. It is the Habsburg who wants to reunite Catholics and Protestants, because the Empire is slipping out of his grasp and the Turk Suleyman, a man who, it is said, can satisfy twenty women in a single night and who is not called "the Great" for nothing, is giving him serious problems. Charles V doesn't care what agreements the theologians reach or how they do it, he's interested in reunifying Christians under his banner to resist the Turks and retake control of his borders.' He shakes his head. 'Now, and listen to me carefully, down in Rome there are a considerable number of cardinals who take great delight in burning people at the stake. But you mustn't imagine that these holy men are dying to see Luther, Calvin, Bucer and everyone else roasted on a spit. Because, you see, as long as these heretics, as they are called, are in circulation, they will be able to unleash the Inquisition on anyone whose way of thinking fails to fit in with theirs, prime among them their political adversaries within the Roman Church. Since the beginning of time, external enemies have been handy when it comes to going after enemies within. Oporinus is right when he says some cardinals are in favour of dialogue with the Protestants and that's exactly what the Emperor is counting on to carry his project through. But let's see who's lined up on the other side.' Perna counts on his fat fingers. 'Right: we've got the German princes, which is more or less the same as saying Luther and Melanchthon. If they're to maintain their autonomy from Rome and the Empire, it's not in their interest to send their theologians to the council. Indeed, if the council decides that they're all apostates, the Emperor won't cry *lèse-majesté*, and will resign himself to losing the German principalities. Then there's the King of France, which means all the French cardinals: twenty years of war bear witness to the enmity Francis I feels towards the Habsburg Emperor. Doesn't that in itself tell you that the French cardinals are going to vote against possible reconciliation? Finally there are the hard-line Roman cardinals of the Inquisition, who are standing in the way of dialogue with the Protestants.'

Perna draws breath; everyone looks utterly astonished, as though a dancing bear had come into the room. A moment later the Italian is on the attack again. 'The council, gentlemen, will be a settling of scores among the powerful men of Europe. Write, write as much as you like, write all the theological treatises in the world, but it won't be you, or Calvin, or Luther playing this game. If you want to survive you're going to have to come up with something else.'

'Pietro, wait!'

The little man stops struggling on through the mud, turns round just enough to see me and comes to a halt in the middle of the road. 'Ah, it's you. I thought . . .'

I'm too far away to catch the rest of the sentence. I catch up with him. 'What did you mean by that? What do you mean they've got to come up with something else?'

The Italian smiles and shakes his head. 'Follow me.' He drags me by an arm to the edge of the street and we slip into an alleyway. His ridiculous skipping gait puts an irreverent smile on my face. Strange how the man always manages to lift my spirits.

'Listen, mate. There's nothing more to be done here. All your friends . . .' He stops at my raised hand. 'Forgive me: all the friends of Oporinus, very nice people, you know? But they're not going anywhere.' His little dark eyes examine the wrinkles of my face in search of something, 'They aren't interested in anything beyond divergence or agreement between their way of thinking and Calvin's. And people like me, and like you, my friend, are very well aware that that isn't how the world works, you know?'

'What are you getting at?'

He pulls my arm again. 'Come on! Let's not beat around the bush: if it takes an Italian bookseller to tell them what's what, it means that those fine minds can't see beyond the ends of their own noses! They write theological treatises for other doctors, you know? And when all of a sudden they find themselves tied to a stake with a pile of kindling underneath it, maybe that'll open their eyes! Except, of course, by then it'll be too late. What I mean, my friend, is that the die is cast. Up in Germany you made a bit of noise and pretty damned impressive it was too, and then there were the Dutch, jolly characters they were, mad as hatters, and now you've got the French and the Swiss, and Calvin who's becoming the star of the revolt against the papacy. All complete nonsense, my good sir, power, power, that's what they're after. Don't get me wrong, I'm not saying that old Luther doesn't believe in it all, I'm not saying that our stout friend Calvin isn't convinced of it, but they're just pawns. If they didn't happen to suit the powers that be, those prelates would be nobody, I'm telling you, no-bo-dy!'

I free myself from his grip, drunk on words.

Perna shrugs and spreads his unbelievably short arms. 'I get on with my job, you know? I'm a bookseller, I travel around, I see a load of people, I sell books, I discover talents hidden under mountains of paper . . . I propagate ideas. Mine is the riskiest job in the world, you know? I'm responsible for the distribution of ideas, maybe the most awkward ideas in existence.' He points towards Oporinus's house. 'They write and print, I distribute. They believe that a book has its own value per se, they believe in the beauty of ideas as such.'

'You don't?'

A glance is enough. 'An idea has value if it's spread at the right place and time, my friend. If Calvin had printed his *Institutio* three years earlier, the King of France would have burned him in the wink of an eye.'

'I still don't understand what you're getting at.'

He skips nervously round on the spot. 'For fuck's sake, will you just pay attention?' He takes a yellowing book out of the bag he always carries. 'Take *The Benefit of Christ Crucified*. Small, handy, clearly written, fits in a pocket. Oporinus and his friends see it as a sign of hope. But do you know what I see in it?' A short pause for effect. 'War. This is a low blow, this is a powerful weapon. Do you think it's a masterpiece? It's a mediocre book, it's a watered-down and synthesised version of Calvin's *Institutes*. But where does its strength lie? In the fact that it tries to make justification by faith compatible with Catholic doctrine! And what does that mean? That if this book is distributed, and if it enjoys success, perhaps among the cardinals and the doctors of the Church, then perhaps you and Oporinus, and his friends, and everyone else, won't have the Inquisition breathing down your necks for the rest of your days! If this book wins approval from the right people, the intransigent cardinals risk finding themselves in the minority, you know? Books only change the world if the world is capable of digesting them.'

He draws breath and looks at me for a moment, then, with his eyes narrowed: 'And what if the next Pope was disposed to dialogue? What if he was one of those opposed to the methods of the Holy Office?'

'A pope is always a pope.'

A gesture of disapproval. 'But being alive and saying what you think is very different from dying at the stake.'

He's about to pick up his bag and go but this time I'm the one who holds him back. 'Wait.'

He stops.

I look at him, shrewdness and strength emanating from all his pores. There's something of Eloi in his flashing eyes, something of Gotz von Polnitz in the determination of his words. 'What would you say if I told you I no longer cared about changing anything?'

He smiles. 'I'd say you should set off for Italy straight away, before the Swiss mud clogs your brain.'

'Whores, business, banned books and papal intrigues? Is that what you're promising me?'

He makes a little skip as he sets off, already trying to gain some distance on me. 'And what else gives life its flavour?'

Chapter 5

'I heard you were leaving. Should we talk business?'

He laughs radiantly and brings me into the sitting room, where the fire is flickering and two armchairs are waiting for us. The inevitable wine bottle stands on the table. It's almost as though I were expected.

He rubs his hands, leaning forward, all ears.

I can't help smiling when this man's around. 'If I'm going to invest my money, you're going to have to explain to me what you have in mind.'

He nods violently. 'Of course, it's sacrosanct. But in return you'll have to tell me what it was that made your mind up.'

'That seems fair enough.'

He skips to his travelling bag, from which he extracts the little yellow book. 'Here it is: *The Benefit of Christ Crucified*, by Brother Benedetto of Mantua. This is the big one at the moment. Bindoni printed it in Venice in 1543 and managed to shift a few thousand copies. I myself helped to distribute it, my contract with Bindoni guarantees me half the profits.'

'Get to the point.'

On tiptoes, he moves his armchair closer to mine, with the sly expression of someone who thinks he can sell furs to the Swedes. 'Bindoni is a brave man, you know? But he hasn't got the money or the necessary breadth of vision. Let me put it more clearly: in the Republic of Venice it isn't hard to sell books like this one, which aren't, you might say, orthodox: the Venetians want to remain independent of the Pope even on religious matters, and Bindoni managed to print the *Benefit*. But if someone with his eyes open, and with that modicum of cunning that helps you travel the world, took on the task of transporting copies around Italy, to Ferrara, Bologna, Modena, Florence . . . he'd reach a potentially limitless market.'

'Hm. You'd have to increase the print run. Are you sure this man Bindoni will be willing to help us?'

'Why wouldn't he be? The Venetians can smell a deal a mile off and even if he wasn't interested we'd find another printer in no time at all, you know? Venice is the capital of printing!'

He stands there in silence, searching my face for agreement.

Out in the street, a group of students sing a vulgar song that fades away down the street.

Other miles, other lands and cities.

'I expect I'd be the one travelling around Italy with copies of the book.'

'We'd divide the job equally, *capito*? I'd concentrate on the area around Milan, and Rome. But someone's got to go to Venice and contact the printers and set them to work on the *Benefit*. Listen, this book could sell tens of thousands of copies.'

I pull a face. 'I've been fighting Luther and the priests all my life, and now you want me to work for cardinals who are in love with Luther?

'A well-paid job. And a useful one to anyone, like you and me, who thinks it's better for books and ideas to go on circulating freely, without the courts of the Inquisition getting in the way. I'm not asking you to marry the authors of this book, just to help them to make our lives easier, maybe even to save our lives, *capito*?' Silence again, just the fire and a cart creaking its way down the street. The Italian knows his subject, his arguments are sound. He pours the wine and hands me the glass. He sighs and then goes on in an almost fraternal voice, 'My friend, do you really want to spend the rest of your days in Basle? Are you really not getting bored with those people and their endless discussions? You're a man of action, I can tell that from your hands and your face.'

I barely smile. 'What else does my face tell you?'

In a low voice: 'That you no longer cared much about where things were going, but you were still fascinated by an unfamiliar landscape. And that you could embark on this enterprise for that very reason. Otherwise you wouldn't have come to see me. Or am I wrong?'

Perna is a peculiar character, hard-nosed and practical, but at the same time a keen and refined judge of character. He combines doctrinal wisdom with a concrete sense of things: a mixture that I have rarely encountered in my life.

I sip my wine, the strong taste fills my mouth. I let him go on, I've learned that it isn't easy to get him to hold his tongue.

'You've known the world of letters and the world of arms. You've fought for something you believed in and you've lost your cause but not your life. You understand, I'm talking about the sense of life that people like you and I share, the inability to stop, to grow comfortable in some hole somewhere, waiting for the end; the idea that the world is nothing but one great piazza in which peoples and individuals come face to face, from the most drab to the most bizarre, from cut-throats to princes, each with his own unique story, which contains everyone's story. You must have known death, loss. Perhaps you had a family somewhere in those northern lands. There must have been many friends, lost along the way and never forgotten. And who knows how many scores to be settled, destined to be left open.'

The fire lights half his face, making him look like a fairy tale creature, a gnome, wise and scheming, or perhaps a satyr, whispering secrets in your ear. His little eyes flash with the flames.

'That's what I'm talking about, you see? The impossibility of stopping. It isn't right. It never is. We should have made other choices, a long time ago, it's too late now. Curiosity, that insolent, stubborn curiosity to know how the story is going to end, how life will end. It's about that and nothing else. It's never a question of profit alone that leads us around the world, it's never only hope, war . . . or women. It's something else. Something that neither you nor I will ever be able to describe, but which we know very well. Even now, even at a point when you seem too far removed from things, the desire to know the ending is still within you. The desire to see some more. There's nothing left to lose when you've lost everything already.'

A detached smile must have remained etched on my face while he was talking. And yet it is born of the sensation of listening to the advice of an old friend.

He touches my arm. 'Tomorrow I'm leaving for Milan, I'm going to sell Oporinus's books down there. I'm going to have to stay down there for a while to sort out some unfinished business. After which I'm going to make for Venice. If you like my proposal, the meeting is at the bookshop of Andrea Arrivabene, at the sign of the Well, remember that name . . . Why are you laughing?'

'Nothing, I was just thinking of life's coincidences. The Well, you said?'

'That's right.' He looks at me, puzzled.

I drain the glass. He's right: forty-five years old and nothing left to lose.

'Don't worry, I'll be there.'

Letter sent to Rome from Viterbo, addressed to Gianpietro Carafa, dated 13 May 1545.

To my most illustrious and reverend lord Giovanni Pietro Carafa in Rome.

My Most Honourable Lord,

I am writing to Your Lordship to inform you that the die is cast. Reginald Pole has actually decided to make the first move.

As I am sure Your Lordship will be aware, His Holiness Paul III has entrusted Pole with the task of drawing up a document illustrating the intentions of the council, in anticipation of its opening in December.

So today I was able to listen to a conversation between the Englishman and Flaminio, in which they discussed the contents of the document in question, which bears the entirely neutral title of *De Concilio*.

It seems that the first argument introduced by the Englishman is the definition of the doctrine of justification. In his exposition of this problem he used mild and apparently innocuous words that were nonetheless tendentious, guaranteeing some degree of compatibility between the Protestant and Catholic doctrines. So it is now certain that from the outset the cardinal wants to keep the council fathers busy searching for a compromise with the Lutherans.

The printing and distribution of *The Benefit of Christ Crucified* are now being revealed in their true light: as part of a well-planned strategy.

For two years now Pole and his friends have managed to scatter the seeds of their crypto-Lutheran ideas through this accursed little book, and to provoke debates concerning its contents, and now they hope to reap its fruits in Trent.

May the All-powerful Lord guard us against such a misfortune, enlightening My Lord's mind and advising him of the indispensable measures required to prevent such an occurrence.

Kissing Your Lordship's hand, I humbly implore your continued favour.

Your Lordship's faithful servant

Q   Viterbo, 13 May 1545

Q's diary

Viterbo, 13 May 1545

In the fresco I'm one of the figures in the background.

At the centre stand the Pope, the Emperor, the cardinals and the princes of Europe.

On the margins the agents, discreet and invisible, peeping out from behind the crowns and tiaras, but in fact supporting the whole geometry of the painting, filling up its space and, without making themselves conspicuous, keeping those powerful heads at the centre of the composition.

With this image in mind, I resolve to keep these notes.

Throughout my life I have never written one word for myself: there isn't a page from the past that could compromise the present; there is no trace of my passage. Not a name, not a word. Only memories that no one would believe, since they are the memories of a ghost.

But things are different now: they could be more difficult and risky today than they were in Münster. The Italian years teach us that palaces can be just as deadly as battlefields, except that in here the noises of war are muffled, absorbed by the animated chatter of negotiations and the keen and murderous minds of these men.

In the Roman *palazzi* nothing is as it seems.

No one can grasp the whole picture all at once, see both the figure and the background, the final objective. No one but those who hold the threads of these conspiracies, men like my master, like the Pope, like the deans of the Holy College.

Note: understand, make notes, never ignore apparently irrelevant details that might turn out to be the keystones to an entire strategy.

The elements of the painting: a dangerous book; an imminent council; a very powerful man; the most secret servant.

On The Benefit of Christ Crucified

The book was printed about two years ago. It has provoked diatribes (Cardinal Cervini has already banned it in his diocese), but nevertheless continues to circulate undisturbed, even enjoying wide distribution.

The 'Viterbans' are acting as though nothing's going on, and in the meantime they're preparing to bring the book's theses to the Council of Trent (Reginald Pole: 'Ideas have a time and a place, which, if carefully chosen, may prevent new courts from putting a stop to them'). Pole hopes he will be quicker than Carafa over a period of time: the spread of reformation ideas versus the construction of the Inquisition.

Could *The Benefit of Christ Crucified* become a double-edged weapon, which might strike the one who forged it? And how?

Ensure that the Council excommunicates it immediately and unmasks its authors? Attribute it to Pole and his circle of friends?

No, the Englishman would deny everything, his credibility is too high for him to be charged with heresy and there is no proof that he wrote the book. If he managed to exonerate himself, he would emerge stronger than ever. My Lord knows this; he is too prudent to concede such an opportunity to his greatest adversary.

It would be better to make a net into which all the cardinals who look favourably upon the reformers will fall, one after another. A book passing from hand to hand, from library to library and contaminating everyone who touches it. And when you haul in the net, you get all the big fish all in one go. It's important to let it go on circulating, even if the council excommunicates it, to allow Pole's friends to read it and to be fascinated by it, just as they are fascinated by that fine English intellect. Meanwhile Carafa works away, slowly building the machine that will enable him to get them all at a stroke. Yes, that's how My Lord's mind is working. But such a game could get out of hand; it could grow too big even for his ubiquitous mind.

On the council

29 June 1542: publication of the papal bull convoking the ecumenical council.

21 July 1542: papal bull *Licet ab initio* establishing the Congregation of the Holy Office of the Inquisition.

Between these two dates, resumption of the war between Charles V and Francis I.

It would appear that if there is no council there will be war; it doesn't make much difference whether it's fought out between armies or intellects.

De Concilio: a veiled defence of the theses contained in *The Benefit of Christ Crucified*. The *spirituali* wish to turn the Council of Trent into the chief arena for tackling the question of justification. They want the council to become the opposing force to the Inquisition, which is becoming ever more robust under Carafa's astute leadership. There is no doubt that My Lord will do all he can to ensure that the theses of the *Benefit* are condemned even before they have been discussed.

On Carafa

One might wonder what Vesalius, that necrophiliac, would find were he to dissect this man whose eyes seem forever fixed upon a remote, unearthly horizon. Perhaps all the fear that he has at his command. Or the divine grace of the unfathomable mind of the Creator concealed beneath the lineaments of cruelty.

Who on earth is this man?

My patron is a monk, a master of simulation and dissimulation, born to command. A bishop, before he took the vows of a poor Theatine. Enemy of the Emperor, whom he dandled on his knee when he was a child, hating him already; possessed of an intuition that would seem diabolical if he did not have faith; supreme architect of the Holy Office, reborn for him and in his charge, the custodian of its secrets and aims, nurturing it like a beloved child, with boundless energy, at an age when most men have already been long underground and keeping company with the worms; apostle of that which he exalts above all things: spiritual war, the inner and the outer struggle, giving no quarter, battling against the seductions of heresy, in whichever form they may appear.

Who on earth is he?

On myself

Carafa's eye.

Chapter 6

St Gotthard Pass, 17 May 1545

I should never have done it. Am I going to go back over my movements, my thoughts?

Funny, sublime, terrifying vision.

Or abandon myself altogether?

The undulating woods of the Mittelland down to the Aare, then slowly on the flat wide boat via Olten, Suhrsee and finally to Lucerne, at the very end of the dark lake of the cantons where it meets the Reus. From there, on mule, two mules, one for the luggage and Perna's books, among the hundreds of burdened creatures puffing their way up the grim slopes of Mount Pilatus, along paths often almost impassable, but filled with traffic and human beings and carts and animals. Up and down this unavoidable tract of sunlit slopes and Alpine pastures, wonderful wild woods, surrounded by sharp crags, swept by bitterly cold air cut at the summits by the wings of the peregrine falcon. A clear spring morning, I inhale the bracing intoxication of the heights. I observe the improbable threshold of a new season, the pass leading from Andermatt to Airolo, St Gotthard looking out over Italian soil.

I must be out of my mind. An old madman rolling down from the mountains towards the great brothel of the world, staring the Turk in the face.

A vision both funny and sublime.

Panic spreading torpor through my limbs. A chamois darts between the trees.

I could die right now. In the grip of a terrible euphoria, in the paralysis of hot sun on aged, aching muscles. Now. Without knowing who I am. Without a plan and with two heavy bags of books. Before the absurd inertia returns, before the crazed intellect returns on the back of that mule. Two bags. I contemplate the steep Italian valleys leading down to the plain, all the way to the sea. To meet the ghosts, at the sign of the Well. Come with me, roofer, because I don't know who I am. And my legs aren't as solid as they were. Now.

Bergamo, Republic of Venice, 25 May 1545

So, just a few drags on those long rolled leaves, the aromatic cigars from beyond the sea that I had brought with me from the Netherlands: can they induce such intense and unbalanced emotions among these dizzying peaks?

I'm still agitated. But mostly with that fear that is like the vertigo of disorientation, the fascination of the unknown, extreme possibilities, regions unexplored, depth of vision. Not like the drunkenness you get from wine, beer or spirits. Without the blurred head you get, the curious mishmash of thoughts, the crazed logorrhoea.

Another creature within you. Which fades away quietly, leaving no traces on the body, your questions unaltered.

Along the Ticino river to the little village of Biasca. From there, accompanied by a guide, across the mountain paths, eastwards towards Chiavenna, crossing the valleys of Calanca and Mesolcina, on Perna's commission, to bring books to the exiled reformers who are flowing from northern Italy into the Swiss Republic.

On the banks of the River Mera, a place marshy and treacherous, obstructed here and there by the remnants of old landslides, where dry land meets the waters of Lake Como and high, sterile mountains impede access. Chiavenna, key to the valleys: apart from its strategic position and the autonomy that make it an ideal refuge, not a place to recommend to travellers.

Two days' break to rest my bones after my march through the Alps, north to south, to the point where the Adda emerges into Lake Lario. Half a day to reach Lecco, within the borders of the territory of Venice, La Serenissima.

From there, after so much climbing, the road runs straight across the plain to Venice. With good connecting services, four days' journey.

Venice

Chapter 7

When you see it in the distance for the first time, still veiled by the mist that makes the sun a white disc, you can't tell if the mirage is floating on the sea that you are crossing, when in fact it's on dry land; you can't be sure that the palaces and churches resting on the water might not really be fantastic architectural rock formations.

Then the boat enters a wide canal. Windows, balconies and gardens dance in bright patches of colour that spread between the banks.

Alleys open up on either side, navigable by one small boat at a time, some of them so narrow that the roofs of the houses seem to touch, preventing the rays of the sun from filtering through. Perna has talked to me of churches, palaces, squares and brothels; but I wasn't expecting the miracle of the waterways, the impressive number of boats of every kind and dimension that replace carriages, sedan chairs and horses. The city seems to be a stranger to the wheel, and to main streets crowded with traffic. It's an absurd construction that challenges all the laws of architecture and seems almost to be floating on the sea, making Amsterdam and the Netherlands, dragged from the ocean by the tenacity of the northern people, fade into insignificance.

The gulls cut through the pale sky and come to rest on stout, thick poles, many of them colourful and decorated with shields, which protrude from the canal bed like tree trunks in a forest, serving as moorings of various shapes and sizes.

The narrow horizon gradually widens to embrace another island on the right, and a majestic set of constructions in muted colours, surmounted at a great height by a stout, square bell tower as pointed as an arrow.

Another waterway opens up to the left, a real undulating street, with the doors and staircases of the buildings leading directly to the water, something I have never seen before in any country with a river or anything like it. The city and the sea seem to have grown up together.

The boat moors just below the magnificent balcony of a palazzo entirely clad in pink marble, next to a column bearing the statue of the winged Lion and what I take to be the stage for public executions. The symbols and instruments of the power of the Venetian republic are designed to be the first images that strike the stranger.

Immediately upon disembarking, however, I'm struck by the hub-bub, the throngs of people coming and going, the shouts, the crowds, the greetings, the quarrels; perhaps the only element that separates the sea, a place of muted sounds, from the rest of the city.

Barely have I set foot on dry land when I'm immediately recognised – by what particular characteristics I don't know – as a German-speaking stranger and surrounded by about twenty boys determined to explain to me that it's impossible to get around Venice without an intimate knowledge of the place, that there's a terrible risk of getting lost, of ending up in the wrong hands, getting swindled; and while they are politely enumerating these dangers, they are trying every way they can think of to slip their hands into my wallet.

'Your magnificence, your lordship, over here, over here, follow me, my great lord, you want somewhere to sleep? You do? Come with me, O most illustrious one, I'll show you the loveliest city in the world. Where's your luggage, O finest of lordships? At the station? Bad place, sir, not worthy of a great man such as yourself.'

The voice issues from a completely toothless mouth and sounds decidedly like that of an old man, but the boy who has offered to show me the city for a handful of coins can't be more than fifteen.

'Come on, come on, you want to drink some wine? You don't? You want a woman? Here you'll find the most beautiful women between Constantinople and Lisbon, not expensive, sir, not expensive, no, come on, you want a woman? I'll take you where you'll find the most beautiful ones of all, very clean, no diseases, no, no, very young. Are you here on business, most noble lordship? Silk? Spices? No? I'll take you to the right place, it's not far from here, come on, lovely place, great lords like yourself, merchants, come on . . .'

As we cross the square his tongue doesn't let up for a second, he lapses into Venetian dialect if anyone tries to approach me, keeping the other man at a proper distance, putting a hand to his chest to indicate that the stranger belongs to him and that no one else is to touch him.

'Follow me, *signore*, in just a moment we'll be at the Rialto and the Fondaco dei Tedeschi, the German Warehouse. There you can change all your money, conduct your business, all that. But if you want a good deal, I'm your man: I'll give you fifty ducats for thirty-two regular-weight florins.'

St Mark's Square doesn't seem like part of a city; it's more like a great salon in some palace or other, the covered deck of a huge vessel, the mainmast being that robust campanile, wide at the base and narrow at the top, and the clock tower the fo'c'sle, beneath which we are now passing, with two admirals perched at the top ready to ring the big bell.

'This is the headquarters of the Procurators of Saint Mark, great magistrates of the Republic, the Procuratoria it's called. Now we're about to pass the Mercerie, the haberdasheries if you like, you want to buy fabrics? Spices? I can tell you where to buy them and where to sell them at a good price. You want to do some business on the Rialto? Then stick with me, and don't get involved with the dealers, dreadful people, my most noble lord, dishonest people.'

I'm not sure if I've understood everything the boy has said. When he talks he looks straight ahead, without turning his neck too much, in a language that I can barely make out, and in the midst of an indescribable confusion of faces and voices. I stammer an encouragement to set off and in a moment find myself fifty yards behind him, nose in the air, like a cork in a stream. I study the faces of the people crowding these narrow streets of shops and stalls; I listen to the dialects and the stranger cadences, one language that sounds Slavic to me, another that I would guess was Arabic.

All at once this cobbled street takes me a long way from the world that I have known so far. I have inhaled the fragrance of spices on other occasions, at other times I have inhaled tobacco smoke, but never before had I had such a sense of finding myself at a crossroads of possible places. A souk in Constantinople, a port in Cathay, a way station in Samarkand, a fiesta in the streets of Granada.

'So, my great lord, do you want to buy something? Ask me, I'll advise you.'

The guide has joined me again and is tugging me violently by an arm. He studies me with a strange expression, and I almost have the impression that he's beginning to doubt my mental capacities.

'You see, *eccellentissimo*? In all the cities in Italy, this here is called a piazza, here in Venice you call it a *campo*, and the roads, and the streets, are narrow *calli*, that's a *fondamenta* along the canal, and that's a *salizada*, that's a *ruga* . . .'

The street reappears on the water, where it meets an imposing wooden bridge. From the number of ships moored on the banks of the canal, to the right of the bridge, and the incessant traffic of goods being loaded and unloaded, we really seem to have reached the commercial heart of La Serenissima.

'The Rialto, *signore*!'

A splendid wooden bridge, the upper part of which can be opened to allow the bigger ships to pass underneath.

On the right an enormous loggia, its outer walls painted with frescos that stretch the whole length of the house.

'Painted by Giorgione, your eminence, and by his pupil Titian, you know him? No? A great wonder, signore . . . Famous painters, Titian is painting the Emperor.'

In the inner courtyard, the vague murmur rising from the commercial negotiations consists of at least four different German dialects. People from the North, blond heads, bushy moustaches, and beers being poured.

'The Fondaco dei Tedeschi, most noble one, for your business. Banks, agents, wealthy people. You see that agency down there? Fugger, the biggest bankers in the world. I know the agent, I can introduce you if you like, *signore*, he's my friend, I find whores for him and he's teaching me your language . . .'

'If I'd wanted to meet Germans I'd have stayed in Germany, don't you think?'

'Quite right, *signore*, business isn't so interesting, pleasure is better, isn't that right? Lovely ladies . . .'

'I've got to sort out a place to stay. Decent bed, decent food.'

'Somewhere you don't want to stand out too much? Of course, *magnifico*, no sooner said than done, come on, I'll take you there, a discreet place, good cooking, good beds and good women . . . Very good women, no questions asked, Corte Rampani, in San Cassiano, come on, it's not far, past the bridge, Donna Demetra will be delighted to meet you, an important *signore* like yourself.'

'Calle de' Bottai, my magnificent lord, we're almost there.'

'There are whores all over the place. Do the women in this city practise any other trade?'

'Nothing quite so lucrative, sir. The council wanted to confine the brothels to Corte Rampani, but there wasn't room for them all so, as you might say, they closed an eye, you know? So, here is the Caratello Inn. I will announce my lord to Donna Demetra.'

The two girls standing on the threshold say something in Venetian, big smiles and breasts peeping out through their scanty clothes. It's a house made of wood and plaster, three storeys high. On the door there is a sign showing a small barrel – a *caratello*. The guide slips inside, leaving me in the company of the young whores.

'German?'

I give them a small bow, which they both return. The younger-looking one tries to find words in my language.

'Merchant?'

'Traveller.'

She translates for her friend and they laugh together.

She reveals an ample breast. 'You want some?'

In the nicest tone of voice that I can find: 'Not now, my dear, I need to rest these old bones.'

She may not have understood, but she shrugs her shoulders and covers herself up again.

The little clearing in the forest of houses is interrupted by a bridge, apparently too slender to carry the weight even of two men. The muddy canal runs placidly beneath. I realise I have lost all my bearings; we've crossed an endless maze of streets, bridges, squares, and I'm almost certain that we haven't gone in a straight line. That's something you can't do in this city.

The guide points to the door, beckoning to me to enter.

A big space, a tavern, with enormous barrels lined up against the wall, a big fireplace and tables in the middle.

A woman in her forties comes towards me and I bow to her; raven hair and a sharp profile, exotic features redolent of the Mediterranean.

'I'm Donna Demetra Boerio. Young Marco tells me you're looking for somewhere to stay. You are welcome here.'

She turns to me, speaking a strange but comprehensible language, it's cultivated Latin, which suggests that she's done a considerable amount of studying, although her greeting was in German.

I opt for Latin: 'I'm Ludwig Schaliedecker, German. I'd like to stay here for a few days.'

'Stay as long as you like. We have capacious beds and the rooms aren't expensive. Marco told me you'd left your luggage at the way station. Don't worry, I'll send the boy to get it, you can trust him, he's been working for me since he was a child.'

Things are starting to look up and I manage a smile. 'When the luggage gets here, I'll pay for the room in advance.'

Toothless Marco drops the bag on the cobbles and wipes the sweat from his eyes with his sleeve.

A gold ducat immediately banishes the exhaustion from his face.

'Thank you, most munificent lord, thank you a thousand times over. If I can be of any other use to you, just ask for me and you will always be satisfied.'

'For the time being all I need is some directions. There's a place I have to get to.'

His face lights up. 'Tell me, tell me, sir, I know the whole of Venice, there's somewhere you want to go? I'll take you there whenever you want.'

'Not right now. You know Andrea Arrivabene's bookshop?'

'Arrivabene the bookseller? Of course, sir, it's in the Merceria.'

'At the sign of the Well?'

'Of course, most noble lord, not a long way on foot, just beyond the Rialto. You want to go there?'

'Tomorrow. Now I want to rest.'

He leaves, bowing several times.

From the little window I can see the big domes of the cathedral and the campanile. So that's where I disembarked, away over there. And somehow or other I've crossed the labyrinth of this strange city that now separates me from St Mark's. I wouldn't know where to start if I wanted to go back the way I had come. Doubtless I'd find myself a few yards away from that enormous church without being aware of it and end up who knows where. And that's exactly the prevailing sensation: that you could go on walking endlessly without ever getting anywhere, or else finding yourself in places you'd never imagined, hidden places. Wonders await you behind every corner, at the end of every alleyway.

Venice. Merchants, whores and canals, alongside frescos, churches, palaces, building sites. Perna was right: you inhale contrast and possibility in the humid air of these streets.

The bed is spacious, my legs need to rest. It's not that far from the cathedral to here, but there's all that going up and down bridges, all those twisted streets. The first thing to do is to get hold of a boat.

Chapter 8

Pietro Perna has arrived in town. He's left a message for me at Arrivabene's bookshop, arranging an appointment in the workshop of Jacopo Gastaldi, a painter from whom he wants to commission a painting.

The master is instructing one of the apprentices about the colour that needs to be used for the completion of a drawing.

'Hasn't Messer Perna shown up yet?' I ask from the door.

With a nod of the head he invites me to come in. The canvas on the easel is very big, and it shows Venice, a bird's eye view, an incredible maze of water and land, stone and wood, home to at least a hundred and fifty thousand people of all kinds of different races, more than a hundred churches, sixty-five monasteries and perhaps eight thousand houses of ill repute.

For a few moments I'm flying over it.

I'm immediately struck by the absence of walls and doors, defensive towers and bastions. The water of the lagoon seems enough to discourage the most dangerous enemies. A considerable number of buildings, all around, are as high as, and higher than, the walls of many cities, and I would bet that it would take all the colours of the painter's palette to render all the colours, all the different kinds of marble, that crowd on to those façades.

With Gastaldi's permission, I spend my time waiting by walking around looking at the paintings, some of them finished and some still works in progress.

One painting, much smaller than the earlier one, shows a canal full of boats: from the most imposing galley, with negro oarsmen, to the simplest little dinghy, with a single rower. On the *fondamenta* alongside it you can make out a Turk, in an Arabian-looking kaftan, and at least three women, unmistakable, because they soar above the crowd on those enormous heels that I've seen them wearing, blonde, as almost all the girls around here are, not because they're born fair, as they are in Germany, but because of their habit of exposing their hair to the sun, drenched in potions and stretched out over those strange, capless, wide-brimmed hats.

Immediately behind that there are two other canvases of similar dimensions. Two unfinished portraits: one of a woman and one of a magistrate. The woman is bejewelled from head to toe, big golden rings dangling from her ears, in accordance with the habit that the women of Venice have of exposing quantities of jewels, pearls and precious stones all over their bodies. The magistrate wears a vividly coloured toga, which is supposed to indicate his membership of one of the many associations within the government of La Serenissima.

From blasphemy to fighting, from foreigners to nightlife, there is no aspect of the life of the Venetians that is not governed by a particular magistracy. Pietro Perna maintains that the system really is very complicated, so much so that the people have probably given up understanding any of it, and abstain from protesting and contesting it, discharging all their tensions into more brutal games such as bull-running, and the traditional battles between the two factions called the Castellani and the Nicolotti, for the conquest of a bridge, by means of blows and kicks.

A precious cornice, covered with stucco and openwork, is followed by a rather mysterious painting: in it, the lagoon appears crammed with all kinds of vessels, among which one stands out, decorated with flags and colours. From the top of it a man who might be the Doge is making a curious gesture towards the open sea.

'You're interested in paintings, my friend?' Perna's shrill voice startles me from behind. 'Or are you stupefied by their subjects?'

I point at the figure in the centre of the picture. 'That's the Doge, isn't it?'

'The very same, his most serene self, seen here in the ceremonial act of marrying the sea, throwing a gold ring into the waves, in accordance with the "Festa della Sensa", the Ascension of the Virgin. The Venetians go crazy about that kind of ritual.' He shakes my hand and his smile broadens. 'Welcome to Venice!'

'Glad to see you again, Pietro. Now that you're here, I hope you'll guide me through this maze. I still haven't managed to get my bearings. And perhaps in exchange I can be of use to you in some way . . .'

Looking rather circumspect, he comes very close to me. 'As a matter of fact you can, you can . . . and it involves a woman, you know? I've got a letter for her here, but I can't take it to her servant, because if he sees me he's likely to get rather nasty. I wondered if you wouldn't be so kind . . . Without being too conspicuous, obviously.'

'Will you finally give me that dinner you promised me in Basle?'

'Ask and ye shall receive, my friend, a heart that's mad with love doesn't fret about the cost!'

Chapter 9

The racket from below makes me leap to my feet. Shouts, chairs being knocked over. Someone comes running up the stairs. I reach for my dagger.

The door flies open and I find myself staring into the terrified eyes of Marco.

'What's going on?'

'Terrible business, sir, terrible . . . They're going to kill her, I'm sure they're going to kill her!' He goes on rambling in Venetian.

'I don't know what you're talking about. What's going on?'

'The Mule, my lord, the Mule is down below, with two of his men, he wants to punish Donna Demetra, Holy God, he's going to kill her!'

I push him out of the room. 'Who's the Mule?'

'He keeps whores on the Calle de' Bottai, he says Donna Demetra's been stealing his girls . . .' The rest is unintelligible.

I go downstairs. It looks as though the landsknechts have passed through the tavern: tables knocked over, smashed chairs. The girls are huddled, terrified, in a corner and there are three men standing there, one of them with a knife to Donna Demetra's throat.

Five paces between me and the nearest one: early thirties at the most, grasping a pointed stick. The tallest one is clutching Donna Demetra by her hair, with his blade to her skin, the third is at the door.

They see me. The tall one says something in Venetian. Stupid, murderous face. He's the boss.

The one with the stick creeps towards me. An inexpert jab. I grab his arm and head-butt his nose in. He tumbles back in surprise. I pick up the stick, look into the Mule's eyes and spit on the ground.

A twisted sneer. He hurls Donna Demetra to the floor and shouts something, pointing his finger at her.

He's about to come in my direction. I break the stick over his shoulders and whack him in the belly with the stump. He bends double, I've hurt him.

I draw my dagger and slip it into one of his nostrils, holding him by the hair.

A glance at the other two: his hands to his bleeding nose, that's him out of play, the other one's already planning to sneak off, to judge by his face.

'Marco!'

The boy is behind me. 'Holy Christ, sir, do you want to kill him?'

'Tell him if I see him in these parts again I'll rip his head off.'

The boy growls something in Venetian.

'Tell him if he touches Donna Demetra or any of her girls, I'm going to hunt him down and rip his head off.'

Emboldened, Marco puts more rage into it than I could have mustered.

I push the Mule towards the door and finally give him a resounding kick up the arse. His two partners slip out behind him.

Donna Demetra gets up, arranging her clothes and hair. 'Thank you, sir. I'll never be able to make it up to you for what you've done.'

'If you could tell me whom I've just thrashed, Donna Demetra, we'll be quits.'

She sits down in a chair, while the girls throng around her attentively and Marco hands her some water.

'The Mule runs the brothels along the Calle de' Bottai.'

'And he hates you that much?'

She smoothes down her hair. 'Some of the girls who worked for him decided to come to me. They weren't satisfied with the treatment that the Mule meted out to them. Low pay, and he hits them. I don't know if you quite understand . . .'

I nod. 'I can imagine, he didn't seem quite the gentleman.'

Donna Demetra smiles. 'Gentlemen are capable of worse than that, my lord, and that's why even your intervention today won't protect us against all professional hazards.'

'I understand. So as long as I'm here, Donna Demetra, I hope you will accept my services.'

Chapter 10

Pietro Perna harpoons a scrap of buttered bread, and between one mouthful and the next he launches into the description of the main course of the evening. 'Gentlemen, a little lesson in the ways in which the Venetian culinary arts have been able to flavour and revitalise a typical northern dish, salt cod. Our Nordic friends merely boil this fish after keeping it in the bath for two days.' He comes over and hugs me with an air of commiseration. 'I say: what an unforgivable lack of imagination. While we're on the subject, my friend, have you ever tried it?'

'Of course, many times.'

The Italian lets out a great laugh and raises his eyes to the roof beams. 'And I'm sure it slipped down your throat very quickly, too, without making much of an impression. The flavours you will taste today, on the other hand, will leave an indelible memory. So: after being boiled, our cod is dredged in flour, seasoned with salt and pepper and an oriental spice that we call cinnamon. Then you fry up some butter, garlic and onion, *capito*? And after a while you add some crumbled anchovies, some chopped parsley and some wine. Then, when the wine has dried you add some milk, *capito*? You pour it all over the fish and cook it until the milk has boiled away. Finally you serve it with the exquisite accompaniment of slices of polenta. It truly is a marvel!'

Bookseller Arrivabene's maid heaps abundant spoonfuls on to my plate, while Bindoni refills my glass with religious solemnity. He talks to me in a mixture of Latin, German and Italian, the latter a language that reminds me of the one spoken by Spanish merchants, of which I manage to make out a few words.

'No drink accompanies the fish as well as wines from the hills around Verona.'

Perna gives a start and turns to me, speaking in German. 'I hope you didn't understand what our printer here just said, because otherwise you're going to have to start keeping notes in your notebook, under the heading "Bollocks talked by Bindoni".' Then he switches to Latin. 'Our friends aren't aware that you've already had the opportunity to try the best Tuscan wines, *capito*? And they're trying to get you to believe that La Serenissima is unrivalled where wines are concerned.'

'Come on, Messer Pietro, you Tuscans have no idea what to drink with fish, everyone knows that!'

'Just as everyone knows that the Doge has demijohns brought to him from Mon-te-pul-cia-no!'

'I have heard', I begin in broken Latin, 'that the Venetian merchants, since the discovery of the New World, have been concerned that the western ports might increase in commercial importance. And it's true, if they sit down at the table and start talking about sauces and wines every time they're supposed to talk business, they won't be able to hold Columbus entirely responsible for their own decline.'

Perna studies me for a moment, takes aim and fires. 'On the other hand, if the merchants of the North don't stop talking about business and nothing else, they'll soon find themselves rolling in money, *capito*? But they won't have a notion what to spend it on, because smoked herring will be their only meal, beer their only drink and Luther's Bible their only book.'

'Fine.' Bindoni smiles. 'Then let's try to talk about books, where, at least in terms of printing, the Tuscans have some catching up to do. What do you propose, exactly?'

Perna speaks incredibly concisely, perhaps to allow me to catch every word: 'The *Benefit*. He finances and distributes within the territory of the Republic, you print, Arrivabene sells in Venice and I look after the area around Milan.'

Bindoni scratches his black beard. He's a man of about forty, a hint of a receding hairline and an olive complexion. 'Calm now, Perna, slow down a bit. You're making it sound far too easy.'

'What? How many copies have you sold so far?'

'About three thousand, the whole print run. But we have to be more cautious now. Since last year the Magistratura degli Esecutori has stopped merely supervising games of chance and blasphemy, and turned its attention to violation of the printing laws.'

Perna is careful to tell me in German, 'They're the Venetian censors.' Then, vexed, he looks at Bindoni and takes a sip of wine. 'But we've always printed everything here in Venice.'

Bindoni says, 'Yes, but now the Council of Ten are more cunning than they were. Before they're printed, all books have to receive the

authorisation of the Executors. I have serious doubts that they'd give
it to *The Benefit of Christ Crucified.*'

Perna looks at me to check that I've caught all that, then turns to
his two partners. 'Is there a problem with printing it clandestinely?'

Bindoni: 'No, but we'll need a cover title. If I request authorisation
for nine works, there's a good chance that the tenth won't be noticed,
you get me?'

Perna casts me a glance as I'm about to pick up my cod with my
fingers and holds a strange implement under my nose. 'Fork!' Then he
impales a piece of fish on it, brings it to his mouth and waits for me
to do the same. 'That way you don't get your fingers greasy.'

Arrivabene is a big fat man, he's about forty, same as me, with a
mop of sparse black hair and a rather simpering way of talking, lips
pursed. 'There shouldn't be any problems with printing, except
possibly financial ones. What sort of a run were you thinking of?'

A nod to the maid who arrives with a bowl of long black shellfish,
half open.

Perna performs the introductions. 'Mussels. These you do eat with
your fingers.' He takes one, opens it up, squeezes a few drops of lemon
juice on to it and sucks out the mollusc. 'Do you put parsley on them?
You should try them with breadcrumbs, chilli pepper and a little oil
. . . Tuscan, of course! I was thinking about ten thousand copies over
three years.'

The wine goes down the wrong way and Bindoni coughs while
Arrivabene slaps him on the back.

He gets his breath back. 'Are you joking? Who do you think I am?
Manutius? I can't invest all that money and energy in one single title.'

'That's because you haven't yet grasped the extent of the idea,'
Perna replies. 'Our German friend can finance the first ten thousand,
you see. And, along with me, he'll distribute them around Italy.'

Arrivabene isn't so sure. 'How can you be certain you'll sell so
many?'

Perna spreads his little arms. 'Because there's a good chance that it'll
be banned. You can sell a clandestine book at whatever price you like,
capito? And people have high expectations about its content. It'll sell
like hot cakes! Savonarolans, anti-Trinitarians, sacramentists, crypto-
Lutherans and everyone with any curiosity. Don't underestimate
people's curiosity, my friends, it can move mountains . . .'

'Hm. Here in Venice,' Arrivabene explains, 'the circle of buyers
consists of Strozzi's friends and the English ambassador: they're all
sympathisers of Luther and Calvin . . . and of course the wayfarers,
merchants and men of letters.'

'I'm convinced', Perna reassures him, 'that there's a good chance of the book being sold in Milan, and even more so in Ferrara, or in Bologna where there are plenty of students, or in Florence. First we'll start with the territory of the Republic, and then if things go well we'll start spreading further.'

Bindoni is thoughtful, smoothes his beard and rolls his reddened eyes around. He is weighing up the risks and the advantages, he's well aware of the former and far from convinced about the latter.

Perna's voice becomes urgent: 'Half the profits to us and half to you.'

Bindoni nods. 'If the print run has to be clandestine, let's not put my name on it.'

Perna holds out his hand. 'Done. If we were in Tuscany I'd close the deal in a more worthy manner, but seeing as we're on the lagoon, we'll have to settle for this more-or-less adequate wine from the slopes of the Veneto.'

Chapter 11

Venice, 10 July 1545

Donna Demetra's perfume is sweet and subtle, a more or less intense essence of lily of the valley that gives a clue to her presence, or to her passage through the rooms of the building.

She's sitting at the desk in her antechamber, dividing up the month's earnings with paper and pen. 'Come in, Don Ludovico, make yourself comfortable over here.'

Her grey-green eyes, inviting you to speak, and the few white hairs that have wilfully escaped her hair dye, are the only marks that forty years of life have left on the face of this woman from Corfu, the daughter of a Venetian captain and a Greek woman. Her body still emanates a youthful energy.

'You wanted to talk to me, Donna Demetra?'

'That's right,' she answers with an expert smile. 'But sit down, please.'

Distant memories of university help me to understand her mixture of German, Latin and Greek, a hotchpotch that seems to be the lingua franca to which the merchants of this city have adapted: the language of business, of spices, of fabrics and porcelain.

There is something magical, ancient and fascinating about the brilliance of her eyes. They shine with the intelligence of a woman well versed in the ways of the world, that many-faceted, multicoloured world that has made Venice an obligatory stopping-off point.

'Don Ludovico, I must confess a certain embarrassment.'

The phrase is studied, false in its content and not at all in its tone; it heralds the spontaneity that I am expecting.

Donna Demetra folds her hands in her lap. 'You are German and I know that in your parts it is not customary – in fact, it is rather rare – for a woman to talk business with a man.'

I reassure her: 'If that's the reason for your embarrassment, have no fear. My experiences have taught me that women's genuine practical sense is far preferable to men's narrow-minded materialism.'

Her smile broadens. 'I thought I was doing you a favour by acting naive: men usually take special pleasure in the idea that they can understand a woman's mind and look after the poor thing from the great heights of their own experience. To deal with you men as equals one has to fake disorientation and inferiority, or else risk giving offence by injuring your vulnerable pride.'

I nod, letting my eye slip to her olive-skinned neck and her ample décolletage. 'So let's leave pride to the inept and infringe the rule just this once.'

That's what she wanted to hear. 'I'd like to go into business with you, and turn this place into the most exclusive and most sought-after house of love in the whole of Venice. I have a few ideas, by the way, and you have the money to put them into action.'

I shift in my chair and rest my cheek on one hand. 'A singular suggestion, Donna Demetra, the guest becoming a brothel keeper.'

She raises a hand, bidding me to let her go on. 'I have no complaints about the way things are going at the moment. But experience tells me that a few modifications might increase the volume of business in the house by a considerable amount.'

Amused, I contain my surprise: there isn't a woman between the Rhine and the Oder who could talk so naturally about subjects of this kind.

'At present things work as follows: men accost the girls on the street, or else they come here, they walk down the passage that runs between the girls' divans, they sit down next to the one they like best, they ask her to join them and when they decide to go they pay for room and service. What do men like about this arrangement?'

She waits for a reply and I swiftly collect my thoughts in order to save face. 'A lot of things, I'd say, judging by their fondness for it. First of all the fact that the ritual seems so natural.'

'Exactly. As I'm always telling the girls, don't give a sense of being at work and when they invite you to join them, get up as though they'd asked you to dance . . . So what we need to do is make things even more natural. The customer should have the sense of having seduced the girl he fancies. There should be a very luxurious tavern on the ground floor, with a selection of excellent wines and food. A place where a wealthy merchant would want to go, even if only to eat.'

'Slow down, slow down, Donna Demetra, I can feel my head spinning already.'

She smiles and goes on, 'Think of it like this: at a given time, the girls come into the room. Some of them sit down, some serve at table, some go to the wine counter. The boldest customers invite them to sit at their table, the more timid ones ask a waitress to act as intermediary.'

Donna Demetra gets up slowly, and I'm sure she does so in a way deliberately designed to give me a new and fleeting view of her cleavage. She stands behind me and starts massaging my neck with the tips of her fingers. I shiver and heave a sigh.

'I think, Don Ludovico, that the act of conquering a woman over dinner, even if it's only a pretence, is much more pleasurable than doing the same thing on a couch in a corridor. Or am I mistaken?'

'You're quite right . . .'

'My second suggestion is that we extend the circle of girls. About fifteen regulars and another fifteen who turn up when they feel like it, when they need money. The greater the turnover the greater the illusion the regular clients will have that they aren't dealing with working girls, and that when they come here they'll have the chance of taking to bed a girl whom they wouldn't have the courage to approach elsewhere.'

The massage dissolves the tension along my neck and spine: these are the most skilled hands that have ever touched me. 'Why do you think I might be interested in a place like this?'

Her hair brushes my ear. 'If a foreigner comes to Venice it's because he's on business . . . either that or because he wants to hide. To the merchant I propose a business deal. To the fugitive I propose an activity that guarantees discretion and no interference from the authorities.'

I nod. 'I've been both. But I'll tell you that what I'm most interested in right now is information.'

She laughs brightly, like a little girl. 'Then, my lord, allow experience to speak for me: in bed, men reveal things they wouldn't even mention in the confessional. I know more about the Doge's affairs than his own counsellors do.'

This woman never ceases to astound me.

'You know, Donna Demetra, I think I'll make your fortune. Before you know it you'll be the Vittoria Colonna of the Republic of Venice.'

She slips her arms across my chest and brings her mouth close to my ear. 'With the difference, Don Ludovico, that Vittoria Colonna does the same job as I do and won't admit it. She comes on like a great seductress and pretends not to know what artists like Michelangelo expect from her.'

'Then let's just say that you're going to be rich.'

'And so are you. And perhaps you'll tell me a bit more about what you've come here to do. But I'd advise you to get a move on, if you want to have the pleasure of telling a woman something that her intuition hasn't yet suggested to her.'

Chapter 12

'Be gentle with that one, I've just brought it here from Padua!'

The workers are carefully rolling the barrel along the floor of the hall.

The big old tables have gone and have been replaced by new ones made by the best carpenter in Venice. Coloured veils cover the old damp walls, now repainted, and there's a big mirror behind the range of spirits. It reflects the image of a stout fellow, his face marked by time and grey hair. I stop and look at it for a moment, studying what I have become in my forty-five years. My body seems to contain a certain strength, still intact, but no longer quite as agile and alert in the eyes of the man who once used that strength on the barricades. What a ridiculous wonder is the mirror, and this city is full of them, there isn't a shop or a haberdasher's without one of the fine works of the local master glassmakers. A world reversed, symmetrical, where right becomes left: I didn't know my nose was so bent.

I immediately have to clear my head, there's still a lot to be done: we're opening tonight.

Donna Demetra comes towards me with a smile. 'The girls are ready.'

'And the roasted meats?'

'The cook's doing her best.'

She looks around, almost absently. 'This place looks completely different!'

'And it's mostly down to you; you've made some very tasteful choices.'

'Are you going to wear your new clothes tonight?'

'Don't worry, I didn't spend all that money on them to let them moulder in the wardrobe.'

Pietro Perna bursts into the tavern with his arms spread wide. He stops, open-mouthed, sees Donna Demetra, quickly tries to regain his composure and steps forward with a bow. 'My compliments to the loveliest jewel in the whole of Venice!'

'You are the most gallant admirer I have ever had, Messer Perna. But you're early, we don't start serving before sunset.'

'I know that and I assure you that I can't wait to taste the dishes that you have lined up for us.'

'So what brings you to these parts?'

'Before I crossed the threshold I was sure I knew the answer to that, but the light in your eyes has thrown my thoughts into confusion.'

Donna Demetra bursts out laughing, while I take Perna by an arm and lead him to the end of the hall. 'Enough of all this mawkishness, what's happening?'

He takes a step back and throws out his hands. 'Are you ready, my friend?'

'I'm all ears, just speak.'

'Martin Luther is dead.'

The wine flows from the barrels, while the glasses are passed from hand to hand in a long human chain winding through the crowd in the tavern. A lot of shouting, cheerful men and women, businessmen and even some minor aristocrats.

Bindoni is getting to grips with a pheasant drumstick, which he is gnawing at carefully, taking care not to stain his new clothes. Arrivabene is having his hair stroked by one of the girls and laughing at what she's whispering in his ear.

Perna is holding forth at one of the tables, telling anecdotes about a life lived between one city and another: 'Noooo, gentlemen, the Colosseum is an almighty con . . . a stupid great place, I assure you, full of huge mangy cats and rats as big as calves!'

At the next table four young members of the corporation of pharmacists are chewing what's left of a suckling pig, exchanging very explicit glances with the girls sitting at the end of the hall.

Behind a knot of heads, at the table next to the wall, a man and a young woman are whispering intimately to each other.

I get close to Donna Demetra, who is standing behind the counter. 'Who are those two sitting at the end? No one takes his lover to a brothel . . .'

She peers at them and nods. 'He does if she's someone else's wife. She's Caterina Trivisano, the wife of Pier Francesco Strozzi.'

'Strozzi? The refugee from Rome? The man who has dealings with the English ambassador?'

'The very same. And the man with her is her husband's friend, wait a minute . . . Donzellini, that's right, Girolamo Donzellini. He had to escape from Rome along with his brother and Strozzi because the cops were after him. He's a learned man, he translates from ancient Greek, I think.'

'And do you know why they were after him?'

Donna Demetra flashes her bright eyes. 'No, but in Rome it seems as though that's the only thing they know how to do these days.'

I laugh and make a mental note of the name. I've got a circle of dissident literati within spitting distance.

A little further away, three characters are sitting apart, enjoying the spectacle of the cheerful group that has gathered around Perna.

Donna Demetra anticipates the question: 'Never seen them before. From their dress I would say they were foreigners.'

I pick up a bottle and a glass, and walk over to their isolated table, but not before I've caught a fragment of Perna's tall stories. 'Florence, of course, Florence, my lord, I'll put it in writing if you want, is the most beautiful city in the world!'

Their clothes are elegant, the fabric and cut are very refined, their features indubitably Mediterranean: black hair, longer than normal, tied at the back of the neck with ribbons of dark leather. Very fine beards that descend from below their ears to end in a barely visible point.

I turn to them in Latin: '*Salve*, gentlemen, I'm Ludwig Schaliedecker, your host.'

A slight bow of the head. 'Unfortunately my Latin isn't a match for my Portuguese and Flemish.'

'Then we could converse in the language of Antwerp, if you wish. I hope you enjoyed the dinner that the Caratello has given you this evening.'

Somewhat startled: 'My name is João Miquez, Portuguese by birth, Flemish by adoption.' He points to the young man to his right. 'My brother Bernardo. And this is Duarte Gomez, my family's agent in Venice.'

If I had any doubts about this man's wealth, the massive gold ring that he wears in his left ear dispels them all. A little over thirty, intense black eyes, and a fine smell of leather, spices and the sea, all mixed together.

'Will you join me for a drink?'

'I'd be happy to drink the health of the one who has given us such a delicious meal. If you would honour us with your company . . .' He points to the chair with an elegant gesture.

I sit down. 'Really, you know, sir, today an old enemy has finally decided to accept his eternal reward. I'm tempted to drink to that happy event.'

The three cast each other inscrutable glances, as though they could communicate merely by thinking, but it's always the same one who speaks for them all. 'So will you tell us, who was the man that you hated so much?'

'Only an old Augustinian friar, a German like myself, who in his youth most vilely betrayed both me and thousands of other unfortunates.'

The Portuguese man smiles affably, showing perfect white teeth: 'Then allow me to drink to the painful death of all traitors, of which this world is so sadly full.'

The glasses are drained.

'Have you been in Venice for long, gentlemen?'

'We got here the day before yesterday. We're staying with my aunt, who has been living here for more than a year.'

'Merchants?'

The younger brother: 'Isn't everyone who comes to Venice? And you, sir, you said you were German?'

'Yes, but I've done enough business in Antwerp to speak the language of those parts.'

Miquez brightens. 'A splendid city, but not so much so as this one . . . and certainly not as free.'

His smile is impenetrable, but there's the hint of an allusion in that sentence.

I refill the glasses. I don't have to say anything, I'm in my own home. 'Do you know Antwerp?'

'I've spent the last ten years there; it's a wonder I never bumped into you.'

'So you've decided to transfer your affairs down here.'

'That's right.'

'When I first arrived, I was told that anyone who came to Venice was a merchant or a refugee. And often both at once.'

Miquez winks and the other two look embarrassed. 'So which heading did you fall under?'

It seems that nothing can take away his air of serenity, like a cat sunning itself on a windowsill.

'The wealthy refugees . . . Not as wealthy as you, though, I think.'

He laughs cheerfully. 'I would like to propose a toast to you, sir.' He raises his glass. 'To successful flights.'

'To new lands.'

*

The last customers slip through the door, unsteady on their feet, swaying back and forth like boats in the wind. I join Perna at the table where he's collapsed. 'Where did your audience get to?'

He makes a great effort, lifts his head, his eyes fogged, and regurgitates an inarticulate rattle. 'They're all arseholes . . . and they took the girls with them.'

'Oh, forget the girls, what you need is your bed. And it wasn't Tuscan nectar that finished you off tonight, either, it was Venetian wine.'

I help him to get to his feet and drag him towards the stairs.

Donna Demetra comes to meet us. 'What can we do for our gallant bookseller, who has been so kind as to entertain our guests?'

Perna, speaking in a shrill voice, springs into life with his eyes open wide: 'Queen of my sleepless nights! These deformed features do not prevent me from admiring you, extolling you, ad-or-ing you . . .' He dives like a dead weight into the skirts of Donna Demetra, who gives him an amused hug. 'If I didn't know you for the incorrigible seductress that you are, I would think you had a weakness for me, woman of great culture and infinite frailty.'

I pick him up, stopping him from falling backwards. 'Please!'

I manage to throw him on the bed, utterly harmless by now, almost lifeless. 'So, Tuscan, you've had enough for tonight, we'll meet up tomorrow morning . . .'

In a reedy voice: 'No, no . . . wait –' He grasps my arm. 'Pietro Perna is not going to take his secrets to the grave. Come over here . . .'

I have no choice, his terrible drunk's breath hits me.

He whispers, 'I am . . .' he hesitates, 'from Bergamo.' He's almost weeping, as though confessing to some unnameable sin. 'Stingy people . . . repulsive women . . . mountain folk . . . peasants . . . I've been lying, pal, I've been lying to everyone.'

I have to bite my lip not to laugh in his face. As I open the door, I can still hear him saying, 'My spirit . . . my spirit is Tuscan.'

Chapter 13

We leave the little bridge and enter the Calle de' Bottai. Marco struggles along with his cart, filled with crockery. I'm walking ahead of him, but I immediately notice that there's something strange going on: we can't get through, four heavily built men are blocking our way. One of them is the Mule.

Marco sees him too and slows down. We exchange glances, and I take the cart. 'You come along behind.'

I walk down the street very slowly, then charge, using the cart as a battering ram.

I block one of them against the wall, the others attack me, knives in their hands. A shuffling noise behind me and Marco's terrified cries. Three silhouettes come running, swords unsheathed, cursing in Portuguese.

The Mule and his men slow down, one of the Portuguese men comes up beside me, the other two run on ahead, swords raised. The Mule's cops run off.

Duarte Gomez holds the tip to the throat of the last remaining man. 'I could kill you like a dog, *señor*.'

The Miquez brothers come running back, João smiling and shouting in Flemish, 'It's not worth it, my friend!'

Gomez dabs a drop of blood on the man's cheek. 'Now clear off, you bastard.'

The man runs off towards the Grand Canal.

'It seems I should be grateful to you, Don João.'

The Portuguese sheathes his sword, a gold-inlaid weapon from Toledo, bows and laughs. 'Not much compared with the splendid hospitality the other evening.'

The younger Miquez brother, Bernardo, reassures Donna Demetra. 'You have nothing more to fear. These four hooligans won't bother you again.'

'I hope not, gentlemen, I really hope not. I'm infinitely grateful to you.'

'Can you really be that sure?'

It's the elder brother who answers. 'There's no doubt about it. In some circles rumours travel quickly. From this day onwards it will be common knowledge that a wrong done to you or your girls will be a wrong done to us.'

'So your family is that powerful?'

Don João speaks slowly, trying to gauge my reaction. 'The Sephardis are a big family, whose members are used to helping one another. It's a way of dealing with the problems that arise when you're always strangers in strange lands.'

A moment of silence.

'I'm surprised. I don't see how Donna Demetra and I could be part of your family.'

'If you'll accept my invitation to dinner, I'll be happy to explain.'

The long boat cuts across the Grand Canal and into the Rio San Luca.

The hunchback Sebastiano, the Miquezes' helmsman, is cursing endlessly at anyone who gets anywhere near the prow.

As a boy, that's how I always imagined the ferryman in Hades, in the classics lessons given by the learned Melanchthon. Dirty, with a mass of tangled grey hair that his headcap cannot contain, Sebastiano emanates a smell of putrescence that reaches all the way to us from the stern. He bends down and pushes the long oar almost vertically over the rowlock.

Miquez is a man of good sense. 'We've drunk to the death of traitors, remember? A fine appearance and good manners are as nothing compared with the loyalty of a faithful servant.'

We sail on to the Rio dei Barcaroli, crossing a wide stretch of water like a swimming pool, which narrows where it flows under a little bridge.

Miquez points out something on the left. 'The Church of San Mosè, or St Moses. Venice is the only Christan city where you will find churches dedicated to the Old Testament prophets. Don't imagine that this was granted out of generosity to the Jews who converted to Christianity, the ones they called the New Christians, or, more contemptuously, Marrani. We're pretty important here.'

'Don João, I'm very interested in what you're saying. Sympathy for refugees of all religions is almost an instinctive reaction for someone who has spent his whole life fleeing priests and prophets. I hope you won't be sparing with your anecdotes.'

'Sitting at such a well-appointed table, we will have no need to hide anything from you.'

We come out at the end of the Grand Canal, opposite the Doge's palace. I can't contain my astonishment at the huge volume of traffic going in and out of the canal. Boats of every shape and kind swarming into Venice's main thoroughfare. Brigantines and carracks docking on the great jetty of St Mark's: galleys on the open sea, a coming and going of rowing boats and sailing boats of all sizes. And Sebastiano yelling at them to get out of the way.

We make for the island of the Giudecca.

Chapter 14

Venice, 6 March 1546

Campo Barbaro. The tip of the Giudecca.

The Miquezes' splendid house faces St Mark's, which, on a clear sunny day like this, looks so close that you could reach out and touch it.

The house is seigneurial, with an internal garden abundant with unfamiliar plants and vegetation. The objects tell a story of endless wandering: carpets, porcelain, furniture, fabrics, from the shores of Africa that abut the territories of Spain and Portugal, to the gates of the Orient, to the Turk who now has his eye on the Adriatic, and the Moorish forms of Iberia, a bizarre and original mixture. Greek crosses and enormous silver crosses from Spain, but also seven-branched candelabra and reliquaries containing parchment rolls and coins, which look as though they might have come from the tombs of the biblical prophets.

I am shown to a chair on a wide patio, facing the garden. João Miquez carefully opens a wooden box and offers me a cigar. I feel a sudden rush of enthusiasm and pleasurable memories.

'I'm delighted to meet someone who's capable of appreciating the flavours of the Indies.'

A sudden shadow falls across my thoughts. 'Don João, throughout my life I have known little of splendour and luxury, and I have always had to trust my intuition.' A glance around. 'You must be one of the richest men in Venice. You come to dinner in my brothel, you save my life and invite me to your home. Why?'

A disarming smile and he nods. 'At long last, a reaction in the German style.' He pours me a finger of wine in a little crystal glass. 'And were it not for the fact that people say that's what you are, I'd have had trouble believing it. You know, when you turn up in a new city, determined not to sit twiddling your thumbs, you have to work out as quickly as you can what your opportunities are and who is worth knowing.' He gives me a telling glance. 'Your fellow countrymen call them business dealings. I would be inclined to call them affinities. They are what gives life its flavour and they open up interesting perspectives.'

I interrupt him. 'Are you sure that a man working as a brothel keeper is what you're looking for?'

'A German arrives in Venice from Switzerland. His past is mostly unknown, he has a considerable fortune probably accumulated in the northern ports; he associates on equal terms with the local printers and booksellers; he knows how to keep hotheads at bay and he opens the finest brothel in the city. And on top of that he bears the name of a heretic whom I saw being burned outside the walls of Antwerp: Lodewijck de Schaliedecker, better known as Eloi Pruystinck.'

My blood is racing like mad. I mustn't lose control. A deep breath: I exhale, to ease my tension.

I hold his gaze. 'Where do you think the conversation should go from here?'

His black eyes contrast with the brilliant white teeth glimpsed occasionally. 'We're all merchants and fugitives. We don't need to beat around the bush.'

'We agree on that. So tell me who you are.'

He makes himself comfortable in his chair, relaxed, cigar in one hand, glass in the other. 'My flight began twenty years before I was born, in 1492, when the most Catholic Ferdinand and Isabella, sovereigns of Aragon and Castille, decided to free themselves from the huge debts they had run up with the Jewish bankers and set the Inquisition on them. My ancestors had to flee in great haste for the first time, reappearing in Portugal, where, obviously for the sake of convenience, we embraced the Christian faith, safeguarding our inheritance. I was born in Lisbon in 1514 and my aunt, Beatrice de Luna, was born four years before me. We were rich and among the most respected families in Portugal. My aunt, Donna Beatrice, whom you will meet shortly, combined her fortune with that of the banker Francisco Mendez, just before 1530. Within a few years history repeated itself: the Portuguese monarchs, dramatically short of funds, called in the Inquisition and set it upon the Jews in order to get their hands on their properties. But this time we were ready, we'd been ready for forty years: my aunt was widowed and inherited the Mendez fortune, just as we were preparing to leave Portugal for good. It was 1536 when we reached the Low Countries.'

A pause. He shrugs. 'João Miquez, Juan Micas, Jean Miche, Giovanni Miches, or Zuan, as they call me here. There are as many versions of my name as there are countries that I've passed through. For Emperor Charles V I was Jehan Micas.'

The tension has subsided somewhat; my open face says that I trust him. 'Were you the Emperor's banker?'

He nods. 'Yes, but he wasn't as generous to us as he was to the Fuggers of Augsburg. We had to carve ourselves a little niche in the face of the greed of your fellow countrymen. They're not terribly keen on competition. After some time, the Emperor started to look to our fortune as well and suggested that my cousin marry one of his relations, a gentile, Francis of Aragon. My aunt, who had a healthy mistrust of the Emperor's matrimonial strategies, refused. And thus it was that the most Catholic one saw fit to accuse us of crypto-Judaism and we were denounced to the Inquisition as false Christians. Pretty shameless, don't you think? First they force us to change religion and then they throw it back in our faces. But money is money, and the Inquisition in the Low Countries takes particular care of the interests of Charles and his friends the Fuggers . . .'

He stops, waiting for me to grasp what, I'm almost sure, is more than a mere allusion. He can't know exactly whom he's speaking to, but he must be at least as troubled by his suspicions and presentiments as I am.

He goes on, 'We knew that Charles V wouldn't let us out of his territories without a fight, so we came up with a plan. I faked an elopement with my cousin Reyna and we headed for France. My aunt, on the pretext of following her wayward daughter, came after us. I stopped at the border and, once I'd brought the women to safety, I returned to Antwerp to prevent the sequestration of my family inheritance. I only succeeded after two years of exhausting negotiations with the Emperor and after buying off the inquisitors with quantities of gold. And finally, here I am in Venice.'

A servant glides up behind him and whispers something in his ear.

Miquez gets to his feet. 'Dinner is served. Are you still willing to dine with us?'

I hesitate, looking him right in the eyes. 'You saved my life today. You weren't there by chance, were you?'

He smiles. 'The advantage of having such an extended family is that you have lots of extra eyes and ears. But I hope you'll learn to appreciate us for all our other qualities as well.'

'How long have you been on the run?'

A luxurious library, long and narrow, inlaid wooden shelves, antique volumes; behind the desk, leaning against the wall, a Moorish scimitar.

'I told you, ever since priests and prophets claimed a hold on my life. I fought with Müntzer and the peasants against the princes. Anabaptist in the madness that was Münster. Purveyor of divine justice with Jan Batenburg. Companion of Eloi Pruystinck among the free spirits of Antwerp. A different faith each time, always the same enemies, one defeat.'

'A defeat that's left you with a considerable fortune. How did you manage that?'

'By defrauding the Fuggers, using their own weapons and paying a price that I'd rather not have paid. Eloi picked me up when I was dead and gave me back a life, possibilities, people to love. And the old instinct for battle, with different goals and different weapons. It worked until the Inquisition swooped on us. The irony is that we were waiting for the cops and the priests turned up instead.'

He interrupts me: 'And were you surprised? Our history should have told you something about that. I've always thought that business about tricking the Fuggers was a fairy tale. There were rumours about it going around Antwerp, but it didn't seem possible. How much did you get away with?'

'Three hundred thousand florins. With false letters of credit.'

A gratified expression. He whistles. 'And you really thought Anton the Jackal would stand and watch? I'd be inclined to say that he was the one who put the crows of the Holy Office on to you. In the Low Countries, even the Inquisition is a branch of the Fuggers and it must have suited Anton Fugger to expel you as heretics rather than admitting he'd been cheated. I think it's a miracle you're still alive.'

I go on thinking: Miquez's remarks are so simple and direct that they don't leave much room for doubt. 'What do you learn from it? They'll get you anyway. You've got to stand your ground, you mustn't stick your neck out.'

Miquez, with a serious face: 'Exactly the opposite: that you've got to move very fast. You've got to be faster than they are. You've got to blend into the crowd, have a goal to aim for, flatter your enemies and always travel light.' He spreads his arms to encompass everything around us. 'Otherwise what would we be doing here? In Venice, the brothel of the world?'

I become more insistent. 'Let's get to the point, then. What do you have in mind?

He relights the stump of his cigar and for a moment his regular features disappear behind the swirls. 'The printing press.' He searches for words. 'The printing press is the business of the moment. And it isn't just important from the point of view of profit; it conveys ideas, it fertilises minds and, very significantly, it reinforces relations between people. For a family that is important yet always under threat, like mine, and perhaps for the Jews in general, it may be crucially important to forge connections with men of letters, learned men, recognised and credible people who can influence other members of whichever community they happen to belong to. It's a kind of interested patronage, if you like, and that's why it isn't only the Jewish press that attracts me. I'm already in negotiations with the biggest Venetian publishers: Manutius, Giolito. With Donna Beatrice, my aunt, I've set up printing presses here and in Ferrara. We publish the Talmud, but also Italian writers like Lando, Ruscelli and Reinoso. We encourage a passion for literature. Donna Beatrice would happily abandon all her other activities apart from that one. I don't doubt for a moment that she's one of the most cultivated women in Europe.' He leans slightly forward over the desk. 'You'd have no trouble understanding why I'm interested in encouraging the tolerant, moderate party inside and outside the Church, and halting the spread of religious intransigence and spiritual war being waged by the Holy Office. I need people who can spot new currents of thought, works that are destined to move minds and change the course of history.'

I scan the titles of the books lined up on the shelves, Arabic, Hebrew, Christian texts, and I recognise Luther's Bible. Then I turn back to look at him. 'I can't claim the field is new to me. I'm working on just this kind of operation at the moment. Have you ever heard of *The Benefit of Christ Crucified*?'

He looks up, rolling his eyes. 'No. But that doesn't mean Beatrice hasn't.'

'Officially, the author is a Benedictine friar from Mantua, but there are important men of letters behind it, people who sympathise with Calvin and the representatives of the moderate Roman party, known as the *spirituali*. It's a cunning little book, designed to stir up endless hornets' nests, because it's ambiguous in its content and expressed in a language that everyone can understand. A masterpiece of dissimulation, and it's already causing all manner of dissent. It was first printed three years ago, here in Venice. From that point onwards its fortune has never stopped growing. We already have fresh copies to shift, not just here, but in the territories to the west and south of La Serenissima. We reckon we can get ten thousand out there in ten years.'

With a nod of approval, he drums the table with his slender fingers. 'Hm. Very interesting. An ambitious enterprise that needs proper funding. You've mentioned the territories to the west and south of the

Republic. So why don't we think of the ones to the east and north? If we called it twenty thousand copies, that would involve additional printing presses, we'd have to bring in more publishers to cope with the extra production. I have good connections in Croatia. Then there's England, a place of endless possibilities. I have the ships, the network of contacts and dozens of merchants who'd turn a blind eye to the distribution of anything at all. I hope you'll bear all this in mind. In any case I'd be delighted to have a copy of the book to give to my aunt. She's always after the latest source of scandal.'

'Your offers sound great. But I can't make decisions without first consulting my partners. If we went into business with you, we'd have to extend the range of the operation to a considerable degree.'

Miquez widens his arms and his smile. 'I quite understand. Take all the time you need. You know where to find me.'

'So do you. And I hope I'll have the chance to return your hospitality as well. Several of the girls had their eye on you.'

He shrugs and glances at me ironically. 'Alas, women are often attracted by what they can't have. Pleasure is a personal matter, it takes many different paths.' He registers my surprise and adds, 'But don't worry, Duarte and I won't deprive ourselves of the Caratello's good food and excellent bar.'

Letter sent to Trent from the pontifical city of Bologna, addressed to Gianpietro Carafa, member of the Ecumenical Council, dated 27 July 1546.

To my most reverend lord Giovanni Pietro Carafa.

My Most Honourable Lord,

The news that has reached Bologna from Trent over the past few months can only delight this zealous heart.

Indeed, not only has the Emperor seen his own hopes of the Lutherans taking part in the council go up in smoke, he has also been obliged to witness the definitive condemnation of the theology of the Protestants, the doctrine of original sin and justification by faith alone. Right now the Protestant princes of the Schmalkaldic League, his adversaries, are to be considered apostates and enemies of religion; and this has shattered Charles's hopes of reassuming control of the whole of Germany and bringing the German princes on to his side to fight the Turk.

Cardinal Pole's efforts to resist the council's decrees endorsing the definitive separation of the Lutherans from the Holy Roman Church have proved to be in vain, and that is perhaps the greatest triumph of Your Lordship and the party of the *zelanti*.

I am, in fact, able to confirm to Your Lordship that the reasons of health with which the English cardinal explained his premature abandonment of council work are merely an excuse: his withdrawal is due to the need to return to Viterbo to lick his wounds, rather than to Alpine fever.

But long years in Your Lordship's service teach me that we should not claim victory before the enemy is completely routed. Reginald Pole remains the Emperor's favourite, the man on whom the Habsburg places all his hopes of a change of attitude towards the Protestants, and there is no doubt that he will plot to promote the Englishman's career and fame.

For that reason the excommunication of *The Benefit of Christ Crucified* by the council fathers gives Your Lordship an additional weapon to employ against the underground strategies of the

spirituali and the Calvinist sympathisers within the papal
territories. The intention that Your Lordship announced to me, to
make the Congregation of the Holy Office set up an Index of
forbidden books, is now assuming enormous importance.
Benedetto of Mantua's dangerous little book has actually continued
to circulate, and to stir up minds predisposed to heresy, so much so
that possession of the work might now be enough to identify Pole's
sympathisers and indict them for heresy. I myself would already be
in a position to hand them over to the Inquisition.

But there we are. Today it may be enough to enjoy our
immediate victories, and wait to assess what is to be done when this
enthusiasm has died down, making way for wisdom.

Imploring Your Lordship's continuing favour and awaiting new
directives, I kiss your hands.

Your faithful servant

Q   Bologna, the 27th day of July 1546

27 July 1546

Luther is dead.

Reginald Pole has left Trent in defeat.

The Emperor is spewing bile.

The Viterban circle and all the crypto-Lutherans are terrified.

The *Benefit* has been excommunicated.

Perhaps old age is the only thing that keeps me writing words that no one will read. Madness.

I am keeping a record of names and places. Cardinal Morone of Modena, Gonzaga of Mantua, Giberti of Verona, Soranzo of Bergamo, Cortese. Some doubt concerning Cervini and Del Monte. Friends of Pole, but the last two are timid, little men.

His Holiness Paul III is choosing the members of the Holy College with a set of scales in his hand: one *zelante* for every *spirituale*; one intransigent for every moderate. This policy of balance will be short-lived; there are scores to be settled. Paul III, the Farnese Pope, is an old man, shrewd in his dealings and inclined to nepotism, with illegitimate sons to put in positions of power. The last Pope of a dying era, clinging for dear life to his throne and his ludicrous intrigues, unaware that his time is over, that new soldiers are advancing, down here as well as in the northern lands: the holy predestined people of Calvin, businessmen devoted to the cause of the reformed faith and their terrifying God; the men of the Inquisition, zealous and utterly devoted to their petty little policemen's jobs, tirelessly collecting information, rumours, denunciations.

Ignatius Loyola and his order of soldiers of God, the Jesuits; Ghislieri and the new Dominicans; and behind them all Gianpietro Carafa, the man of the future, an incorruptible man in his seventies and an efficient leader of the spiritual war, the battle for the control of the souls of men.

And myself in the middle. I too am one of those who have paid the price of the times, of the events they have lived through. Luther,

Müntzer, Matthys. I regret not those enemies left in the battlefield, but the man who stood up to them – the man I was back then. Now a man like Pole has been sent my way, a pious and lettered man who believes that God wants to be served with honesty. He and his friends do not know what true faith is; they have never had to sacrifice others on their own behalf, or sacrifice themselves by destroying others: murder, yes, extermination, the betrayal of faith. Müntzer, the Anabaptists and who knows how many others; so much damned good faith, so much innocence that was lost in that madness. So much waste. But it is much worse to assume that innocence is concealed behind honesty, the easiest form of penitence. And what we end up with is Thomas More, Erasmus, Reginald Pole. Crazed fools, ready to die because of their inability to understand the nature of power: either how to serve it, or how to fight it.

You are older than I am, lost behind a dream that is as far from the Papal Throne as it is from the mud of the stinking horde. You sicken me and I wish I had the stomach I once did, but I have lost it along the road that brought me here. The years do not strengthen the spirit, they weaken it, and you end up looking your enemies in the eyes, looking into them to see the void, the poverty of the intellect, and you discover that you yourself are willing to pardon stupidity.

In the middle. While these eyes are still fit for something, until they discover that your faith is abandoning you, and that it's only when you're drunk that you can wield the axe, like a befuddled old executioner.

Chapter 15

The little Italian gives me a firm, fraternal hug. 'My friend, I have struck an excellent deal. Milan is a big market, I assure you, full of krauts like yourself, but also plenty of Spaniards, Swiss and Frenchmen. The Milanese are good readers too, people who know their way around a book; I've sold almost three hundred copies of the *Benefit* and I've left another hundred to a bookseller friend of mine, who will let me have the statement of sales as soon as possible.'

The only way to stop him talking is to take him by the shoulders and force him to sit down. He shuts up, studies my eloquent expression and pulls a face. 'What's up?' It's the tone of someone expecting a disaster.

I sit down opposite him and ask one of the girls to bring us something to drink.

A cough. 'Listen, Pietro, a few things have happened. And they're not all terribly serious.'

He raises his eyes to the ceiling. 'I knew it, I knew I shouldn't have left . . .'

'Let me finish. Did you know about the council's excommunication?'

He nods. 'Of course I did, we're going to have to be more careful, but it was always on the cards, wasn't it? What's the problem? We'll sell it at twice the current price and we'll shift more copies . . .'

'Would you shut up for a minute?'

He folds his arms over his chest and narrows his eyes.

'Promise you're not going to interrupt me.'

'Fine, but go on.'

'Bindoni has said he's pulling out.'

No immediate reaction apart from the almost imperceptible twitch of an eyebrow. He doesn't move and I go on, 'He says that if the book faces an excommunication he's worried he might get into trouble and have his press shut down.' I raise a hand, anticipating his reaction.

'Just a minute! I think he's actually been waiting for an excuse to get out, because of . . . new associate.'

The other eyebrow rises as well and Pietro's face turns beetroot-coloured. He isn't going to restrain himself for long.

'I know. The agreement was that I would go to Padua to distribute the book to the friends of Donzellini and Strozzi. And I did. But I did a lot else besides.'

The red complexion fades, the light in his eyes goes out. Pietro's round head hangs over the table, anger making way for depression. With defeat in his voice he says, 'Tell me everything from the start and don't leave anything out.'

We pour ourselves some grappa. Perna drains the first glass and fills it again.

'There's a big banker, a very big one, who's interested in getting involved in the *Benefit* deal. He's offering us his commercial network to distribute the book.' Perna's expression brightens again. 'He could have it translated into Croatian and French' – his ears seem to prick up – 'he has contacts with big publishers and with clandestine presses inside and outside Venice' – his eyes gleam – 'and he'd be willing to increase the run by at least ten thousand copies.'

Perna jumps on to his chair. 'So what are you waiting for? I want to meet this man!'

'Calm down, now. Bindoni won't have anything to do with him; he says he's too big a fish, that we'll be crushed.'

'He's the one who's going to be crushed! By his own hopelessness! Who is this banker, what's his name?'

'He's a Marrano, a Sephardi, Portuguese by origin, João Miquez, he's done deals with the Emperor . . . He lives in a palazzo on the Giudecca.'

Perna gets to his feet. 'Bindoni can fuck right off. I told you the *Benefit* was a major deal and if a crappy little typesetter can't understand that, it's up to him.' He mutters to himself for a moment or two. 'In business with the Jews . . . in business with the greatest businessmen in the world . . .'

Francesco Strozzi. Roman. Man of letters, highly cultivated, has read Luther.

Girolamo Donzellini. Roman. Crypto-Lutheran man of letters. Knows ancient Greek. Student of the new science. Has been in the service of Cardinal Durante de' Duranti. Fled Rome because a Spanish monk working as a copyist denounced him to the Inquisition.

Pietro Cocco. Paduan man of letters. Owner of one of the most extensive libraries in the whole of La Serenissima. Enthusiastically acquired *The Benefit of Christ Crucified*.

Edmund Harvel. English ambassador to the Venetian Republic. Turned the volume round in his hands, puzzled and enthusiastic at the same time. He studied me with greater attention than the others did, trying to work out who I was.

Benedetto del Borgo, lawyer, Marcantonio del Bon, Giuseppe Sartori, Nicola d'Alessandria.

Affluent men of letters, in love with Calvin and with themselves.

Idiots.

Useful idiots.

They haven't a clue what's at stake, they just like the sound of their own voices, coming out with these fine ideas. They'll be the first victims of this spiritual war.

We want their breath to fog up the minds of respectable people, the literary salons. It doesn't matter a damn that they don't know what they're talking about, what's important is that they go on talking about it.

In the fog of diffuse dissent you can really cover some ground.

New vistas are opening up, broader ones. The information coming in from the Council of Trent confirms the feeble constitution of those good old *spirituali*. They're not warriors, even if that's the way Venetian men of letters describe them. We'll have to shake them up, but how? I never expected to find myself playing such a grand game, but neither did I expect to have such a powerful ally as the Jew Miquez, no less interested than myself in containing the advance of the Inquisition.

And what's my role in all this? To dissemble, so that others can go into battle? Encourage the *spirituali* without their knowledge?

Meanwhile keeping a closer eye on the enemy camp: splitting its forces, identifying its leaders, understanding its strategy.

Chapter 16

In this land that isn't land, colours are forever assaulting the eye and the bizarre apparel that the people wear seems to have been designed precisely to disorientate the passer-by, with bizarre geometrical shapes, extravagant make-up and uncovered breasts, oblong headdresses, fantastical coiffures and incredible footwear. It prompts weird feelings, nerves on edge, startling encounters in every *calle* and the sudden outbreaks of rage to which the inhabitants of this other-worldly city seem so curiously prone.

In this land that isn't land, the power of women changes the course of events, it suddenly puts a twist on poor tired old masculine reason, confirming a profound sense in my mind – and not for the first time – of the superior virtues of the fair sex, the fruit of resources inaccessible to the rest of us.

In this land that isn't land, laden with curiosity and a tension that keeps the senses alert, I am about to be welcomed by the woman whose fame, more than that of any other, seems to confirm how right my reflections are; Beatrice Mendez de Luna, or Donna Beatrice to the Venetians.

She is waiting for me in one of the sumptuous salons of the Miquez house: precious silks draped over delicately upholstered couches, arabesqued tapestries on the walls, along with scenes of Flemish life by Brueghel the Elder, a woodcut by Master Dürer, a very lovely portrait by Titian, the great local celebrity, and inlaid boxes by the tireless Venetian master carpenters, the first to rise and the last to go to bed, to the chimes of the Marangona, the great bell of St Mark's.

Bright black eyes study me. The explosive maturity of a Hispanic woman, face framed by raven hair lightly streaked with grey, a refined manner that reveals no fear. Brilliant white teeth forming the silent and ambiguous smile that welcomes me. With studied movements she rises from her sofa to come towards me, feline, stretching a neck sculpted with pearls from the east.

I take a bow.

'Lodewijck de Schaliedecker, the German, who has made such an impression upon João, my favourite nephew. Finally! German, but with a Flemish name, and what a name! Enemy number one of the civil and religious authority of Antwerp, I remember from those final anxious days before I left that hard-working, greedy land. What bizarre conjectures names provoke, don't you think? Men seem so fiercely attached to them, but you need only undergo an extra baptism, and pass through another country, to discover how useful, even pleasurable it can be to have several. Do you agree?'

I brush her bejewelled hand with my lips. I am sweating. 'Without a doubt, Donna Beatrice. I have learned to recognise men by the courage they can show and not by the names they bear. It is a very great pleasure to meet you.'

'Courage. Well said, Messer Ludovico. The name suits you, doesn't it? Well said. Please sit here next to me. I too have been anxious to meet you and here we are at last.'

In front of us, on a low little decorated table, a silver tray with wide handles in the shape of interlacing serpents. On it a steaming pot containing an infusion of aromatic herbs.

'The fame that precedes you is enigmatic at the very least, did you know that?' She pours the infusion into large porcelain cups. 'I don't want to dwell on it, but what my nephew has told me about you has certainly surprised me. Your contacts, past and present, your aura of mystery and the roads you have travelled, they all go to make an impossibly fascinating mixture. Believe me, I have insisted upon this meeting for many different reasons, first among them – please don't take offence – being to recommend that you take the greatest possible care about your every movement, your every word, even your every allusion. Please do not think my caution excessive.'

I watch her shifting position on the soft upholstery of the sofa we are both sitting on, bringing the cup to her mouth with both hands, sipping the hot, scented liquid. I hold my breath. 'Don't worry. I'll be as careful as I can. But forgive me for asking: to what do I owe such explicit instructions? Instructions that sound so pressing that they make me think of impending hidden dangers?'

She puts the cup back down on the tray. 'It's like this. Let me give you some information about the way things work. The immense power of Venice, a bridge between east and west, is not based on the water upon which mad and brilliant fugitives designed it, any more than it emerges from the crucible of the artists and men of letters who throng the city. For centuries now the rulers of this lagoon have been weaving an intricate web of power and spies, guards and magistrates that no one can escape. There is an extremely delicate balance to the relations that these people enjoy with kings and diplomats in all countries, with theologians, clerics and the highest authorities of every faith, and with wealthy people, crop growers and manufacturers in all parts of the world. Within the city an intricate network of control affects anyone who passes through it or who lives in it for any length of time. There is a police force for blasphemy and another one for prostitutes, one for panders and another for brawlers, there are police who control the ferrymen and others who keep the arms dealers under surveillance. No one can say who is in command here, but everyone fears the thousands of eyes that are always kept fixed on these streets suspended above the water. The strength of La Serenissima is guaranteed by a series of weights and counterweights. That is all that really counts, in a play of mirrors reflecting misleading images, where appearances deceive, where the real is often concealed behind heavy curtains. Take the Doge, for example, celebrated with those huge regattas, venerated by the people and appointed for life. Yet he himself counts for nothing, he can't even open the letters that are sent to him without the prior agreement of the advisers appointed to that specific function. Not to mention those sophisticated thinkers who channel the hatred of the lower classes by dividing them into factions and creating a thousand pretexts, a thousand games, for them to fight among themselves, with violence as bloody as it is unmotivated, never directed against anyone bearing a staff of office. Multitudes of prostitutes and lots of gaudy colours, hordes of artists and gastronomic delights, my dear Ludovico, are all used to conceal spies and policemen, judges and inquisitors who are constantly on the alert, surveying every inch of the city.'

My eye falls upon her décolletage, I still haven't quite become accustomed to the generous Venetian cut. Hot flushes. I study the bottom of the cup with apprehension: a pulp of black leaves. My bones feel soft, I melt into the couch. I laugh irrelevantly.

'Do you think that's funny?'

'Forgive me, but this agreeable situation doesn't accord with the sinister story you've been telling me. I have seen wars and massacres, and I'm not very used to the subtler weapons of power.'

'Never underestimate them. What I meant was that where authority does not lie in the hands of a single prince, but is distributed among various magistracies and corporations, it's possible to undertake the most daring manoeuvres. But only as long as you are able to acknowledge and gratify those powers when necessary. That is the freedom that prevails in Venice, not the city ordinance, which many praise but no one understands.'

She comes nearer and a sudden waft of perfume makes my head whirl. 'You see, we lend them the money. As ever, the same people who have flattered us will sooner or later begin to hunt us down. We've learned to do the same. We ally ourselves with important men, we support vital interests and activities, we decide when and how to untie our purse strings. The Rialto merchants are our debtors and so are the armourers in the Arsenal. The patrician families of the council, and the dynasties that supply bishops and magistrates to the Republic, owe us a fair proportion of the splendour with which they choose to surround themselves. For such people money is as important as the air they breathe: they have to think twice before opposing us. On the other hand we have to be aware that the bond won't last all that long.'

Her nephew's phrase: 'Travel light.'

She smiles. 'Corruption is a thin wire kept taut by weights and counterweights. That's the caution I was talking to you about.' An expression of anxiety flits across her face. 'You have to know whom to keep on your guard against, what forces might destroy your equilibrium. There's this new race of inquisitors, sly and fanatical, supported by Cardinal Carafa, who's the most dangerous of the lot. Always in the right place for decades now, he's the driving force behind the Congregation of the Holy Office, which the Pope set up for him, and since 1542 he's been in charge, breeding a pack of ferocious, devoted and incorruptible bloodhounds. And they're the ones to be on your guard against. They scent their prey, they spot it and pursue it till it falls.'

Beatriz manages to communicate to me all her anxiety, an ancient fear that seems to have been with her since the beginning of time. I shiver.

'I know these people. Fear is the weapon they use to subjugate mankind. The fear of God, of punishment, and of people like them. We can't train armies to combat them, but we can inspire other people to do so. There's this party of cardinals hostile to the Inquisition, the *spirituali*, but unfortunately they aren't much use in a fight: while the others are serrying their ranks, this is the only real landmark they've managed to produce.' I take the little volume out of my bag.

She nods. '*The Benefit of Christ Crucified*. I read it with great interest and I agree with you. It may not be enough to keep the dogs at bay, but it has a strength of which not even the *spirituali* are aware. There are plenty of priests, doctors, clerics, men of letters and other important people in the Church who are open to these ideas. Paul III is a coward, but if the next Pope were a *spirituale* – maybe that

Englishman everyones thinks so highly of, Reginald Pole – we might see changes in the air.' Another smile. 'Do business with us, Don Ludovico.' She takes my hand between hers.

'What an amazing couple!'

João Miquez bursts into the room, followed by Duarte Gomez. Gleaming teeth and the sound of boots.

'So, Beatriz, you've got our guest wrapped round your little finger. You'll notice that he, unlike your perverted nephew, prefers women.'

Donna Beatriz has a ready answer: 'But he surrounds himself with girls in the bloom of youth, from what you've told me.'

I look around uneasily. I'm overcome with embarrassment. 'Stop it, please.'

Miquez bows ostentatiously and Gomez bursts out laughing.

I extract myself from the crossfire. 'Friends, few people have welcomed me with such cordial familiarity as you have today. Your refined instincts are a constant source of amazement to me, opening up the possibility of fascinating vistas. The mark that has been branded on your people now appears to me in all its inconsistency. You would have to have travelled the length and breadth of the world to be able to depict it so clearly. I am grateful for the trust you place in me. I am still waiting for you to come back and honour my table, João. As to you, Donna Beatrice, every one of the girls who frequent the Caratello would have to be reborn three times before acquiring a fascination equal to your own.'

João and Duarte applaud with amusement.

'I shall keep my goodbyes brief: consider the contract signed on our first deal.'

Forty-five ducats. Plus thirty, eighty-one, sixteen. Subtract the girls' wages, food and wine.

'Demetra! We're out of ink!'

A jocular and irreverent voice comes from the kitchen: 'Use your memory, Ludovico, your memory!'

Forty-five plus thirty: seventy-five. Plus eighty-one: seventy-five plus eighty-one . . .

'. . . Those sons of bitches, darling, once they decide they're after you, you've had it, they're not going to let you go. And they'd like to sneak in everywhere, listen to everything . . .'

Yelling fit to wake the dead, and meanwhile that hand rummaging under her skirt. Seventy-five plus eighty-one makes a hundred and fifty-six, that's right, plus sixteen.

'Ah, but here in Venice Carafa's cops have a hard life, we don't let them walk all over us . . . we don't let them come and stick their noses into our affairs. We sort out our own problems with heretics and blasphemers . . .' Plus sixteen, and drop it you bastard, plus sixteen: one hundred and seventy-two.

'. . . so, my beauty, you know who Cardinal Carafa is? No? Then I'll tell you. He's a wrinkled, toothless old man and if you saw him at night you'd shit yourself with fear . . . I have met him, yes, but you don't see the old man about that much, no, he doesn't like it . . . he prefers the darkness, like demons and witches.'

With the corner of my eye I can make out a flurry of hands in skirts and cleavage. That's it, subtract the girls' wages and then . . .

'A nosy old spy, he wants to know everything about everyone, and then I, my darling, would be first on the list because I like wine and whores.'

Twelve, plus fifteen, plus . . .

'Nobody knows how old he is, he's been there for ever, he was spying when your mother and I were still at the breast. He spied on the Emperor, and the King of England, he spied on Luther, he spied on the princes and the cardinals. Then the Pope kept him happy by putting him in charge of the Inquisition, so he could really enjoy himself. And he's made his presence felt, indeed he has . . . He's recalled all his spies scattered around Europe, that's right, to infiltrate the Church with them.' The girls' wages. 'He was born to spy, that's what I tell you, he's dangerous, if it wasn't for the fact that we keep our ears open here in Venice, he'd want to get us all in line as well . . .'

He spied on Luther, twenty-seven scudi, *he spied on Luther, recalled all his spies scattered around*, twenty-seven plus forty-two, *the Inquisition, he's always been there, he was spying when you and I were still at the breast, he spied on Luther*, twenty-seven plus forty-two makes sixty-nine, there's still all the rest, *recalled all his spies to infiltrate the Church with them, the Inquisition, he prefers darkness*, sixty-nine *you know who Cardinal Carafa is*? Add fifteen for the wine, *no one knows how old he is, he's always been there, he spied on the Emperor, he spied on Luther.*

He spied on Luther.

I raise my eyes, the accounts melt away: only the girls, the groping hands have vanished. Empty chair. Pressure in my head, behind my eyes and at the base of my neck, heavy as a rock.

'Where did he go?'

A shrug, they show me the coins between their fingers.

Gone. It's night, slipping on the wet cobbles, a blethering noise in the distance tells me he's making for the Rialto. Running, quick or I'm going to lose him, running. A corner, another one, a little bridge, following the voice, a slurred version of a song in Venetian dialect, running at breakneck speed into the darkness, at the end of a street a fat shadow swaying drunkenly.

My heavy steps make him start, he draws a stiletto at least a foot long.

'Don't be afraid! I'm the manager of the Caratello.'

'I paid my bill, Messere . . .'

'I know. But you haven't tried the wine we keep in reserve for valued guests.'

'Are you taking the piss?' He narrows his red-rimmed eyes, his head must be fairly spinning.

'Not at all, it's on the house, I can't let you leave without trying this bottle.'

'Well, then, if that's the deal, and if you'll lead the way I'll be happy to follow you.'

I grasp him under the arm. 'You'll try not to fall into the canal?'

'Don't worry, Bartolomeo Busi's been drunker than this.'

*

'Bartolomeo Busi, formerly a Theatine friar. Before Carafa's black crows threw me out. Only two years ago, that's right, servant of God, and in my own way I still am, fuck it. I go with whores, certainly, maybe I overdo the wine a little, but that's all stuff you can explain, the good Lord isn't too worried about that, no. Now I find myself working my arse off in the Arsenal, sewing sails all day, look at my hands! Bastards! It wasn't like that in the monastery, it wasn't a bad life: I pottered about in the vegetable garden, spent some time in the kitchen, met a load of people, important guests, cardinals, princes. Do you think a monastery's a place remote from the world? Not a bit of it, people are forever coming and going, women especially. I was there at the start, the bastards, I didn't want to make a career of it, given that I've always been an ignoramus. Spies! Yes, fine, every now and again I would pinch a few spuds, a piece of beef, to sell it on outside, but nothing more than that. And instead they put this story about that I was a sodomite. A sodomite! They all knew I've only ever liked women, not little boys and all that filth the abbots get up to. Any excuse. The truth is that things had started to go bad some time before, my friend. It was understood that spies, informers and cops were taking charge. What's the point of taking the vow of poverty, renewing the Church, chasing the thieves out of Rome? All sorts of abuse went on behind the back of that pious man Gaetano da Thiena. And pious he was, the moron. And who was there? You know who was there, you know who was moving him as though he was a puppet? I'll tell you, the father of all spies: Giovanni Pietro Carafa. The big old man, that's right, he was always there, ptuh! That man, in a hundred years, when even the worms will turn up their noses at our corpses, he'll still be there spying. He'll be Pope, believe me. But just think about it, forty years ago he was already a bishop, forty years ago, my friend. A papal legate at the Spanish and English courts, listen to this, they used to say that he dandled the Emperor on his knees when the Emperor was seven years old! Before 1520 he was Archbishop of Brindisi, and then what does he do there? He smells the stench of shit: Luther, turmoil and Rome going to the dogs. And what does he do? He drops everything, so to speak, he gives up his jobs and puts his spies to work all through Europe. Meanwhile he's acting the saint along with poor Gaetano, the moron, and founding our order. So, after 1528, after the krauts have shat in St Peter's, everyone's slobbering all over him, begging him, pleading with him to sort things out. And what does he do? I don't have to tell you he accepts, but he says: things'll have to change, you're going to have to get serious or else

Luther's going to get rid of the lot of you. And then he goes on the attack. In 1537 they appoint him cardinal, he's in charge of issuing directives to rid the Church of corrupt clergy, sodomites and heretics, and it's full of them. So now you can't get the spies off your back. They're everywhere. And he's tireless, he's always plotting, as though he was never going to die. But what's the point, that's what I'd ask him. In 1542 the Pope, another fine character, gives him the Congregation of the Holy Office, a nice outfit made to measure for him. Bastards! He says: the time has come to sort things out. And what does he do? He recalls all the spies, all of them, even the ones making a note every time Luther went for a piss. I've seen them, you know, Spaniards, Germans, Dutchmen, Swiss, Englishmen, Frenchmen, all up at the monastery, they all passed through, taking the new orders. And he says: gentlemen, times have changed, there's a time to sow and a time to reap, this is the time to reap. Out they get, back out there spying, and they fuck me up because I've never liked that kind of crap, fair enough keeping your own house clean, but all this looking in people's underwear, waiting for you to say the wrong thing, to get you and put you on trial. God isn't a tribunal, God is love, fuck, that's what Jesus says, not me, Jesus Christ in person. They're not having any of that, though, you've got to be shit scared, and that's all. And then in they come with the accusations: Brother Bartolomeo the sodomite, with so and so many witnesses. The dirty fuckers! And guess what, it didn't turn out too bad. If I hadn't been small fry they'd have had my head off. And now I find myself working all day in the Arsenal for a crust. An old man, almost fifty. That's why I like whores and drink wine. Ah, but you're a fine gentleman, your brothel is like the garden of delights. What women! And I can't afford them, with the starvation wages I get. Just touch them and nothing more. Forgive me, you know, I've only to think of those pigs and I see red.'

Demetra's infusion has woken him up a bit and he's already casting interested glances at the bottle I've put on the table.

I uncork it. 'Germans. Did you meet any Germans at the monastery?'

'Germans, you say? They're his favourites, people you can trust, the krauts. Then there are the Spaniards, yes, but only because you tell them who to kill and they kill him. Bastards!'

'I'm interested in the Germans.' I fill his glass.

'Germans, of course I've seen them. Forever banging on about Luther . . .' He knocks back his wine. 'He said, Carafa did, that the Germans make notes of everything, they're very precise, not like us scruffs who can't stop chattering. They're the ones you can trust.'

'Do you remember any names?'

His belly bounces against the table. 'Hey, that's too much to ask. Names. In a monastery you're only ever Bartolomeo, Giovanni, Martino . . . Names don't mean a thing.'

'How many did you see?'

A red wine burp. 'Six, seven at least, maybe ten, although that's including the Swiss, who speak the same language. Germans . . . dangerous people.'

His head starts to wobble. I slip some money across the table. 'Tell my girls to look after you.'

He goes on, 'My lord, God bless you, I said you were a fine gentleman; if you want I'll tell you something else. When you want some tales from Bartolomeo, just whistle . . .'

The Rialto is overflowing with stalls, traders and passers-by who look as though they might topple into the canal at any moment. I elbow my way through, ignoring the shouted curses raining down on me. I make for the Mercerie, alleyways echoing with the yells of the goldsmiths and textile dealers, but at least you can breathe.

An old German sauntering about like so many others. My idea was to go to the Theatine monastery, but I don't feel like it, there would be no point.

The monastery. No one knows what happens inside a monastery, no one knows who you are: in the monastery your name is a name chosen at random, that's what Bartolomeo said. A spy headquarters in a place no one would ever think of.

Germans, at least half a dozen Germans. People who used to count Luther's visits to the toilet, installed in the right spots from the very beginning, since an unknown Augustinian friar nailed up his theses in Wittenberg.

I pass the Rio San Salvador, towards Campo San Luca. The shouts of the buyers and sellers fade very slightly.

Wittenberg. A life has been lived. Mine. Luther is dead. The Protestants have founded their reformed Church, the game's over. The spies are being recalled to Italy for new tasks. What's at stake is power in Rome, maybe the Papal Throne. New directives, it isn't hard to imagine which: infiltrate the enemy party within the Roman Church, the *spirituali*, the ones who want an agreement with the Protestants, spy on their every movement and report back to the boss. Even woo them, gratify their brilliant intellects, wait for them to make a false move and then strike them dead. Just like they did in Germany.

Like they did with Müntzer.

Like they did with the Anabaptists.

A time to plant and a time to pluck up that which is planted. Qoèlet 3, 2.

I sit down on a pillar, by the side of the Rio dei Fuseri.

The paper crumbles between my fingers, but the words are still legible where time's ravages haven't erased the traces of ink. Letters telling a story of twenty years ago, when Germany was aflame with the words of Magister Thomas; they've been guarded with care. Now I know why I carried them with me throughout all those years. To remind me of you.

Qoèlet.

I toss the coin in the air and catch it as it comes down. The writing is still clearly visible: ONE GOD, ONE FAITH, ONE BAPTISM. The relic of another defeat. A rare piece, almost unique, forged by the Münster mint.

A boatman calls his warning cry before turning the bend of the river and disappearing from view. The gulls float peacefully, studying the depths below.

You spied on Luther. You spied on Müntzer. You spied on the Anabaptists, in fact, you were one of them. One of us. Maybe I've met you.

Qoèlet.

The peasants in the plain.

The citizens of Münster imprisoned within the walls of the city.

Women and children.

Heaps of corpses.

You're here. Carafa can't do without an important pawn like yourself. You've served him well, but now they've got the Inquisition, they've no use for solitary pieces: collecting rumours, information, spying on the *spirituali* to choose the ideal moment.

You're here. Where the crucial game is being played, as always, as it was twenty years ago. My twenty years.

Heaps of corpses.

Magister Thomas, Heinrich Pfeiffer, Ottilie, Elias, Johannes Denck. Jacob and Mathias Ziegler, little more than children.

Melchior Hofmann, who died a few years ago in Strasbourg jail. Trusty Gresbeck and the Brundt brothers, imprisoned and executed outside the walls of Münster. And the Mayers and Bartholomeus Boekbinder who lent me his name, who fell in their courageous defence of the city.

And then there were Eloi Pruystinck and all the brethren in Antwerp.

A procession of ghosts on the bank of this canal.

You and I are the only ones left.

The only witnesses to an era that is drawing to a close. Two tired old shadows.

That hatred has left me now and not to my disadvantage: I can be more alert, even more cunning. More than you have ever been.

Now I can flush you out.

Beyond St Mark's Square the world stretches out towards the Arsenal, where the invincible ships of the Venetians wait to set sail.

Opposite, the island of San Giorgio Maggiore, with the Benedictine monastery. The basin of the Arsenal opens up on the left; the carpenters are at work on the skeletons of two imposing galleys.

I sit down to watch the mastery of these men, famed throughout the world, but I can't get my thoughts in order.

The elements in the picture are always the same. On one side you have an English cardinal, loved by everyone, looking towards reconciliation with Protestants, the favourite of the Emperor, who is hoping for religious peace in Christendom because the Empire is slipping away; greatly loathed by the cardinals who are fomenting the spiritual war of the Inquisition.

And on the other side there's the black prince of the Holy Office, Cardinal Carafa, who is building the machine one piece at a time and preparing to go into battle. He has recalled all his spies to Italy to set them on the *spirituali*. A throng of observers, an army of eyes and, clearly, of informers.

One of those is the most important, the most trusted. The bravest? Yes, if it's true that he was in Wittenberg and in Münster.

Münster.

The Anabaptists: old acquaintances.

An idea. Just an instinct.

No one down there has ever encountered Anabaptism. But he has, he was in Münster and he knew how to choose his moment for betrayal.

The elements at our disposal: a book, *The Benefit of Christ Crucified*, a Calvinist manual adapted for the Catholics; but I could still get something out of it. Just as the Anabaptists did with the writings of Luther. Setting the conflict alight. Radicalising the contents of the book: from Calvinism to Anabaptism.

I get to my feet; without stopping to think I chase off towards the square.

The inquisitors are hunting dogs, sniffing out their prey, pointing it and then not wasting a moment. That's what Beatriz said.

What we need is a hare.

A decoy to bring them into the open. And the hound would have to be the bravest, the most experienced of all. Qoèlet.

If the prey were an Anabaptist, or even better, a German Anabaptist, he's the one they'd send. The one who's already fucked them in Münster, the one who knows them well.

I cross St Mark's Square at a frantic pace, until I reach the Mercerie. An Anabaptist in Italy, someone who knows what needs to be done.

I stop in front of the Fondaco dei Tedeschi, panting for breath, my heart in my throat.

I take a deep breath.

A game for two players. Two men who've been fighting the same battle.

One old score to settle.

I can flush you out.

What would happen if *The Benefit of Christ Crucified* became a much more dangerous book than it is? What would happen if someone started going around rebaptising people, holding a copy of the *Benefit* in his hand?

Carafa and his sleuths would set off after him. But above all Cardinal Reginald Pole and all the *spirituali* would have to take to the fray and fight to defend themselves against an attack from the *zelanti*. It would be better if that happened before an intransigent, a zealot, a friend of Carafa's, or – even worse – Carafa himself was appointed Pope. Better to start settling scores right away, before the black prince's spies and informers got honest Pole and his naive followers penned in.

Speed up the conflict. Force Pole to fight back rather than being defeated in silence. Force that fine English mind to take up arms. He must be the next Pope. He's got to get rid of the old Theatine.

The mirror reflects the years all at once, but there's still a quickness in the eyes. Something that must have flashed on the barricades of Münster, or among the peasant armies of Thuringia. Something that wasn't lost along the journey, because the journey couldn't kill it. Madness? No, but as Perna put it: the desire to see how things will end.

The man in the mirror has longer hair. His beard's going to get longer too. The clothes won't be so elegant, not Venetian fabrics but old German rags.

The scarred face is pressed right up against the glass, a keen, piercing eye, glancing up every now and again to consult the Lord above. 'Yesterday I asked a five-year-old child who Jesus was. And he replied: a statue . . .'

The old madman grins in amusement.

I have found the Anabaptist.

Letter sent to Trent from the papal city of Viterbo, addressed to Gianpietro Carafa, dated 1 January 1547.

To my most illustrious lord and master Giovanni Pietro Carafa in Trent.

My Most Honourable Lord,

The strange fact that I am about to report to you demands proper consideration.

I know for certain that *The Benefit of Christ Crucified* has begun circulating again in various markets. Over the past few months copies have been bought in Ravenna, Ancona, Pescara and even further south, along the Adriatic coast. This means that they are travelling by sea, on boats capable of transporting considerable quantities of books. And we can't be talking about a few hundred copies, My Lord, but thousands, so many that it is difficult to believe that this is the work of a single press. Given the range of distribution, we must be talking about a printer in Venice or Ferrara, certainly a resident of the territories of those states most fiercely opposed to the entry of the Roman Inquisition.

I know that Your Lordship's authority does not extend to the territory of La Serenissima, but nonetheless it might be useful to raise the suspicions of the Venetian inquisitors and Duke Ercole II d'Este. I am not actually of the opinion that they will want to be seen as the kind of people who would allow publication of a book excommunicated by the council.

The strange thing is that here in Viterbo no one seems to know anything about the people who might be responsible for this new distribution. Indeed, it would appear that Cardinal Pole and his friends have nothing to do with it this time. One might have cause to suspect that this is a vast operation, directed by a brilliant mind, but someone outside the circle of the *spirituali*.

Well, as My Lord knows, many radical crypto-Lutherans have found refuge in Venice. So it might be useful to collect more information about their activities, without raising the suspicions of the Venetians, who, as we know, are rather sensitive about the Holy See interfering in their affairs.

Kissing Your Lordship's hands, I implore your continued favour. Your Lordship's faithful servant

Q   Viterbo, the 1st day of the year 1547

Q's diary

On the council

The Emperor wasted no time. The old lion still has his claws. He has brought his landsknechts down to the Trentino. And with them the plague, which has always come with them.

The message is clear: after the defeat of his champion in the council, the cardinals have to be careful. That fool the Pope has started sending signals of intent to the French. But Charles is always Charles, ruler of the Holy Roman Emperor, and no one's going to try to plot behind his back.

The council has been suspended, it's going to be transferred to Bologna, far from the pestilential breath of the landsknechts. They say.

On Carafa

Carafa's going to have to be careful: the Emperor isn't a man to be walked all over, as he has just demonstrated. Maybe that's why he's taking so long to set the Inquisition on the trail of *The Benefit of Christ Crucified*, on anyone who owns it and on the man who wrote it. Reginald Pole is still the favourite in many people's hearts, the Pope likes him and the Emperor likes him even more.

Or perhaps it's merely a studied delay. Perhaps the old man thinks that the time is not yet ripe, that many more fish still have to fall into the net and the book will have to go on circulating. But he's playing with fire, because it isn't just the book that's spreading: ideas are, too.

On the new distribution of the book

In whose interest can it be to risk so much just to print and sell *The Benefit of Christ Crucified*?

If Pole and the *spirituali* aren't involved, who's responsible?

A merchant, a man, or several men, with business sense. But why?

There are other ways of making money by printing books, there's no need to risk prison or your life for a vulgar compendium of Calvinism.

There's something I haven't yet understood. I've got to follow my instincts.

Titian

Chapter 19

'Yesterday I asked a five-year-old child who Jesus was. You know what he replied? A statue.'

Curious faces barely illuminated by the candle. About a dozen students huddled around the light, the only ones challenging sleep and the strict rules of the college. I met some of them this afternoon in the anatomy room, after the theology lecture. A little chat in the corridor was all it took for them to suggest that I follow them to the Benedictine college and spend the night there.

'What is Christ to a simple mind? A statue. Is that a blasphemy? No, because there is no intent to offend. So is it the lie of an ignorant person, then? It isn't that, either. I tell you: this child was not lying, in fact, he told the truth twice. First because before his eyes, as he was being trained to kneel, there was a stone crucifix. What instils life in that stone? What makes it different from the others? Knowledge of what it represents. Knowledge: that which gives a meaning to things, to the world, and also to statues. Hence, in order to bring that statue to life we must know Christ. Can we say in a few simple words who Christ is? Yes: He is love and grace. He is God, who, for the love of men, is sacrificed on the cross, redeeming them of their sins, saving them from darkness. And faith in that one act justifies men before God: that is the benefit that Christ brings us. The Benefit of Christ Crucified.

'So if it is knowledge and love that bring that statue to life, our task is to cultivate those two things as the most precious gifts and to shun, indeed to do battle with, anyone who attempts to remove them from us.

'Which brings us to the child's second truth. Now we are really witnessing Christ's agony. Not with love or with knowledge does the Church bring to life the Christ to which children turn. Christ becomes unconditional obedience to secular authority, to the corrupt hierarchy of Rome, to the simoniac Pope, He becomes the fear of divine punishment as dramatised by the Holy Office. None of this is the living God: it really is an arid, silent statue.

'So we ourselves must become children again, we must reacquire the simple mind of that child so full of wisdom and reaffirm the descent of grace within us. A new baptism, which makes us participants once more in the benefit of Christ crucified.

'With this renewed certainty we cannot be afraid to profess the true faith, even in the face of the hypocrisy of the courts and the corrupt men of the Church. Therefore I say to you, if anyone ever asks who has talked to you in this way, do not be afraid to tell them that it was I, Titian the Baptist.'

Chapter 20

'Just yesterday, leaving a church, I met a five-year-old child and asked him who Jesus was. Do you know what he replied? A statue.'

Brother Vittorio shrugs his shoulders and allows a smile to flicker briefly under his ample beard. 'If it's any consolation there's a man from our village, a carpenter who must be about forty years old, he goes to church three times every day, recites a *Paternoster* facing the crucifix and then goes back to work. I asked him how it was that he had become so assiduous in his visits to the Lord, and he told me it was I who had told him that if he prayed to Jesus three times every day He would cure his back pain. This is the nearest place I know where I can find Jesus, he added. I can't describe his face when I tried to explain to him that Jesus can be everywhere: in women and children, in the air and in the stream, in the grass and the trees.'

I clap my hands together and open them with resignation. The gesture attracts the attention of two other friars. They come over to find out what's going on.

'Your example gives me no consolation, brother. If a forty-year-old man believes that Jesus is a statue, just like a five-year-old child, it means that thirty-five years of norms and precepts, dogmas and punishments do not increase the Christian's faith by one iota. I ask you, how can a child be forced to receive the sacraments, to kneel down before what to his simple mind is nothing but a statue, to listen to the Gospel, when as far as he's concerned it's a fairy story no better than the ones told to him by the fireside? Does any of that seem reasonable to you? I say to you: it isn't only absurd, brothers, it's actually dangerous. What sort of believer are we really bringing up? What kind of sincere devotion to Christ can we hope to see maturing in that little creature if we make him accustomed, from the tenderest age, to passive acceptance of things that he does not understand? If we get him used to kneeling down before statues? I tell you, my brothers, that Christ can only be a deliberate and reasoned choice, not a fairy tale told to the naive. But today that is precisely what we are asked to do. We are asked to believe without understanding, to obey in silence, even to fear, living in the terror of being punished, of being tried, put in jail. Can true faith be born among such feelings? Certainly not, my brothers.'

The three Franciscans exchange an uncertain glance. They cannot break the silence that follows those last words. One of them nods to a group of others to come and join him.

I am Titian, a German pilgrim on his way to St Peter's. The Franciscans of this little country monastery have welcomed me with kindness and put me up with the greatest courtesy.

They talk quietly among themselves: a summary for the benefit of the latest arrivals.

Brother Vittorio freezes into the pose of a statue, but he can't help laughing. 'Don't put it like that, Brother Titian. Rather, think this way: near a village in our diocese there is an ancient poplar tree, perhaps the most impressive tree that you could ever set eyes on. Well, the peasants maintain that during the full moon in October, anyone who stands beneath the tree and catches one of the leaves carried on the wind, and then eats it, will acquire strength and longevity.'

A dark look. 'I don't see what you're getting at.'

'Twenty years ago,' he goes on, folding his hands behind his back, 'a pilgrim like yourself came for a rest in this monastery. We told him the story of the poplar and how to find it. He was convinced that miracles of nature could be proved to occur in places where the Madonna wished to show herself to her children. He went to the place and the Madonna appeared to him, saying, "The body and the blood of my Son give eternal life." Since then, every full moon in October, we celebrate the Madonna of the Poplar, and the peasants come to take the Eucharist, and the leaves of the tree that fall on the altar are blessed and distributed among the faithful.'

I take a seat on one of the stone benches along the wall. The monks have grown in number: at least ten of them now. The oldest ones sit down next to me, the rest squat on the ground.

'So,' I ask, turning to the whole group, 'what was your fellow brother getting at with the story about the poplar?'

A young monk replies, his face all nose and bony cheekbones, 'That to bring Christ to country people, you can't be too subtle. Some people think He's a statue, others will eat His body just as they ate the leaves of a tree in their youth.'

Now that I've got everyone sitting around, I suddenly leap to my feet. '"The body and the blood of my Son give eternal life." The

Madonna of the Poplar announced the heart of the Christian faith to that pilgrim. Country people don't understand Christ, because you make Him too complex. That's why they need a statue or an ancient legend to get close to him. God became man and died on the cross so that we too could attain eternal life. That is the faith that saves: nothing else will do. That is the faith that no newborn child can profess: for that reason I tell you that baptising a newborn child has no greater value than washing a dog. The only baptism is that of faith in the benefit of Christ crucified!'

He jumps up, almost tripping in his long habit, thick black eyebrows and a beard that reaches to just below his eyes. He leaps forward to hug me, kisses me and then gives me an incandescent stare. 'Adalberto Rizzi thanks you, Brother German. I have been living here for twenty years, since the Madonna appeared to me among the leaves of the poplar tree and gave many signs to bear witness to her presence.' The younger brothers look at him in alarm. 'Yes, yes, ask Brother Michele here if I'm not telling the truth. After the apparition I began to preach the same things as you, Brother Titian, have said today. Word for word, I assure you. But they told me I was confused, that I needed to rest and meditate, that the Madonna hadn't actually asked me to say the things I was saying. They persuaded me. But now I hear you restoring what was taken from me and with fiery tongue I shall proclaim it to the world: faith in renewed baptism, faith in the benefit of Christ Crucified!'

He throws himself on his knees, as though his legs will no longer support him.

'Baptise me, Brother Titian, because the splashing they gave me as a boy means nothing to me now. Baptise me, even with the dirty water from this well: my faith will be enough to purify it.'

I look around: everyone is standing motionless, open-mouthed, apart from Brother Vittorio, who shakes his head disconsolately. I have already done enough as far as this place is concerned. It would be better not to risk excessively blatant gestures.

'You can baptise yourself, Brother Adalberto. You're the witness to your own conversion.'

He looks at me for a moment with an expression of ecstasy, then plunges himself face first into the muddy water and starts rolling around in it, shouting at the top of his voice.

Rather blatant, all in all.

The secret storeroom of the Usque bookshop is underground. The only way in is through a trapdoor not more than a foot across, hidden between the floorboards. Then you go down a ladder until you find yourself in what looks like a cellar. But the place is dry, the Usque family have come up with an ingenious way to keep the damp away from the books they store down there, the ones that might turn out to be the most awkward and dangerous. Hatches at the entrance and exit allow the air to circulate, so much so that I can't help shivering: it's colder down here than it is at ground level.

Our printer leads the way with a lantern, until we reach a pile of volumes stacked up in expert fashion. 'Here we are, gentlemen. A thousand copies ready for dispatch. You'll have the rest within the month.'

Miquez points to one half of the pile of books. 'My men will come and pick up five hundred copies in a few days, and transport them to the coast. I'll take the rest right now and bring them to Milan with me. I'll bring you the statement of account by Easter.'

Usque cuts in, 'Leave me a hundred copies. I think I can sell them here.' His Mediterranean features stand out in the light of the lantern. 'Then take them out of my share. The cart's outside, you can load them straight away.'

We go back up to the elegant office of the most important Jewish printers in Ferrara. Six presses, a dozen busy workers. I'm spellbound, watching the synchronised rhythm of their movements: inserting the matrix, brushing it with ink, fixing the page to the platen, then lowering it and pressing down hard to print the letters on the paper. A little further on they are composing the pages, setting the letters one by one in the frame, fishing them out of large boxes, with one eye on the manuscript and the other on the little pieces of lead.

At the end of the chain the binders, armed with needle, thread and fish-glue, give the volumes their finished form.

Miquez comes casually over to me. In a low voice: 'Usque and his company only publish books to do with Judaism. They've made an exception for the *Benefit*.'

I grin. 'The reciprocal favours of a huge family . . .'

'That's right. And the persuasive force of a good business deal.'

Usque asks something in Spanish.

'Yes. You can go ahead. My brother Bernardo's out there, he'll make sure the load's tied on securely.'

The printer seems uncertain. 'There's one other thing, Don João . . .' A glance from Miquez convinces him that he can talk in my presence. 'I've had a strange request. From the court. A copy of *The Benefit of Christ Crucified*.'

We look at each other, puzzled, and then Miquez speaks: 'Was it the duke?'

'No. Princess Renée, the French one. She's interested in theology.'

Chiavenna. Switzerland.

Two years ago.

Camillo Renato and his circle of exiles.

I brought him books on behalf of Perna when I first came to Italy.

Camillo Renato, alias Lisia Fileno, alias Paolo Ricci. Sicilian, a man of letters, pro-Reformation, believer in predestination, sacramentist, scandalised everyone by celebrating the Last Supper with a banquet. When I met him he was playing host to Laelius Socinus and other lettered exiles. I stayed there for a short time, but long enough to know that he had travelled around Europe; he'd been with Capito in Strasbourg and faced the Inquisition in Bologna. Condemned to a life sentence for heresy in Ferrara, he had managed to escape with the help of a lady of the court. Princess Renée. Such was his gratitude that he had adopted the name of his saviour.

To Usque: 'It's important that we get a copy to her today.'

I take it out of the bag, and find a pen and ink on Usque's desk. I write on the first page.

No good work or deed can equal Christ's benefit to mankind. Only the grace received from the Saviour and the incommensurable gift of faith can mark the destiny of a soul. That rebirth is what unites true believers in Christ.

In the hope of meeting the lady who saved a mutual friend.

Tiziano Rinato. At the Baker's Inn.

The two Jews look at me, startled.

I hand the volume to Usque. 'This is the copy.'

To Miquez: 'Let him do it.'

He looks amused. 'You've been behaving very oddly since you grew that beard.'

'You were the one who taught me to cultivate friends in high places.'

He shakes his head and says goodbye to the printer in Spanish. Bernardo and Duarte are waiting for us outside; the boxes of books have been loaded up and secured with straps.

João puts his arm round my shoulders. '*Hasta luego, amigo*. See you in the spring.'

'Say hello to little Perna from me.'

A nod to his two accomplices and the cart moves off.

Chapter 22

The girl said the man was dark, fairly tall, with a mermaid tattooed on his shoulder.

The girl also said that he wouldn't stop fiddling with his dice, he always had one in his hand, because he liked gambling and he said the more he touched his dice the closer he was to luck.

The girl was crying. Because when it heals that kind of wound leaves a long white scar, which turns purple on cold days and looks like some kind of illness.

She cried as she told the story, despite the fact that it had happened some days ago, because her face was ruined for ever.

Demetra's eyes were icy. They were filled with disapproval, almost reproach: I wasn't there and she hadn't been able to do anything. Young Marco could have risked getting stabbed, but what would have been the point?

Between her sobs the girl said that the man spoke strangely, no, not with an accent like mine, different, maybe Greek, or Slavic. No, he hadn't hit her, he just had the knife, but she thought he was going to kill her, and he said that if she screamed he would slit her throat as though she were a lamb.

I didn't say a word. I really don't think I said a word. My eyes met Demetra's and that was enough.

What I had to do.

A Greek who likes gambling.

I don't remember crossing the city on foot. But I must have done, because by the time the bells rang I was outside the Moor's gambling den, staring at the giant on the door.

'Tell the Moor the German wants to see him.'

Goliath sneered, or perhaps it was just his natural expression, before he slipped in through the door.

I waited until the narrow doorway opened up again and the Moor's white teeth gleamed in the lantern light.

Dogfish smile.

No one noticed the lack of formalities. 'A Greek, maybe a Dalmatian, likes playing dice, elegant clothes and a tattoo on his shoulder, a mermaid. He's slashed one of my girls.'

The Moor didn't bat an eyelid, but his expression said he'd heard about this as well. 'On one condition, German. I pay the cops so that I'll be left in peace. Whatever you've got to sort out, do it outside. And leave your dagger with Kemal.'

I nodded, slipping the blade from its scabbard and handing it to the giant. The Moor stood aside to let me in.

The room inside was very quiet, nothing but the sound of dice rolling on tables and muttered curses.

Every race in the world had met up down there. Germans, Dutchmen, Spaniards dressed up to the nines, Turks and Croatians busy chalking up points on little boards hanging on the wall. No wine or spirits, no weapons: the Moor doesn't want any trouble.

I reviewed them one by one, concentrating on their hands. Hands that told stories, missing fingers, lucky gloves, rings that would be valued on the spot and put on the table.

Then I saw the dice rolling about in someone's right hand, a little object made of bone running between his fingers, back and forth, every time his left hand got ready to throw.

He can't have noticed anything till he felt the cobbles against his cheek.

Someone held his arm behind his back and at the same time bared his left shoulder.

He cursed in his own language, while the ivory dice rolled out of his pocket along with his luck.

Then all he could do was scream and watch the blade cleanly cutting off his fingers.

The fishmongers found them at dawn nailed up side by side on the market barriers.

In Venice, I'm Ludovico the German once again. And I've got to concentrate on the affairs of the brothel.

Chapter 23

Miquez and Perna are in Milan.

The German has made it clear to everyone that it's not a good idea to mess with him.

Titian has been spotted on three different occasions. In Ferrara he even met up with Princess Renée of France, friend to the exiles and very interested in *The Benefit of Christ Crucified*. The Anabaptist has made a big impression.

I could be satisfied, but it isn't enough. I'm thinking about a second trip. Treviso, Asolo, Bassano and Vicenza, then coming back to Venice. Now that I've got the measure of my Anabaptist preacher I can do things a lot faster. Ten days, two weeks at most.

Last night I dreamed about Kathleen and Eloi. Only confused images, I can't remember anything else, but I woke with the sense of something hanging over everyone's fate. Like a dark shadow pressing on the mind.

I dispelled my gloom with a walk to St Mark's and was greeted on the way by many people I don't know. On my way back I had a sense of being followed, maybe a face I'd already spotted that morning in Campo San Casciano. I came back the long way just to confirm my suspicions. Two strangers, long black hooded cloaks, thirty yards behind me. Police, perhaps. It can't have been hard to guess who'd cut off that Greek sailor's fingers. I'm going to have to get used to being tailed as I move about the city. Another reason for setting off again soon.

'Are you leaving again?'

She appears silently behind me, her emerald eyes fixed on the bag that I've just shut.

I try to avoid her eye. 'I'll be back in three weeks.'

A sigh and Demetra sits down on the bed beside my travelling bag. I waste some time knotting a handkerchief round my wrist: for a while now I haven't been able to shake off a rheumatic pain and I've had to restrict my movements.

'If you'd stayed here, Sabina would have kept her lovely face.'

Finally I look at her. 'That bastard paid for it. No one will ever touch a hair on that girl's head again.'

'You should have killed him.'

I try not to get too agitated. 'Then we'd have had the cops on us. They followed me to the market this morning.'

Another sigh, to keep herself from reproaching me with Sabina's scarred face again. 'Is that why you're going? You're scared?'

'There's something I've got to do.'

'Something more important than the Caratello?'

I stop. She's right, I have to tell her something. 'There are things that have to be done and that's all there is to it.'

'When men talk like that it either means they're about to go away for ever or they've got a score to settle.'

I smile at her wisdom, sitting down beside her. 'I'll be back. This time you can count on it.'

'Where are you going? Has it got anything to do with those Jews you've gone into business with?'

'It's better if you don't know. There's an old score to settle, you're right. It's as old as I am.'

Demetra shakes her head, a veil of sadness creeps over the green of her eyes. 'You have to be careful in choosing your enemies, Ludovico. Don't take on the wrong people.'

I give her a broad smile. She's more concerned about me than she is about the brothel. 'Don't worry. I've got myself out of worse situations. It's a speciality of mine.'

Q's diary

Imperceptible movements. Slowly creeping insects, which you can only spot if you stare very hard and allow yourself to be transfixed by tiny ripples in the stalks of grass.

It's hard to understand whether there's a secret order in that swarming motion, a harmony, a purpose.

I've got to follow my intuition. Discover where the anthill is. Identify its supply routes.

I'm setting off for Milan. I've written to tell Carafa that I'm following a trail to find out who is responsible for this renewed distribution of *The Benefit of Christ Crucified*. It's the truth. There isn't much left to do in Viterbo now. Someone is helping the *spirituali* without their knowledge, distributing the book all over the place. What do they hope to achieve? New supporters? Helping to unleash a pro-Reformation revolt?

It's essential that we understand who they are, that we discover what they want.

Milan. The inquisitors up there have arrested a converted Jew, accusing him of contributing to the distribution of a heretical work: *The Benefit of Christ Crucified*.

It seems he's Venetian, from Portugal originally: one Giovanni Miches.

What do the Jews have to do with all this?

João and Bernardo Miquez stand out against the door like two great giants, compared with the balding little man peeping out between them, a book smuggler and expert in fine wines.

He leaps out to meet me, grasping my outstretched hand. 'It really is a pleasure, my old friend, you can't imagine how things have been going . . . The books have been selling like hot cakes, practically up where the Most Catholic Emperor lives. Too bad we bumped into the Holy Office!'

I get Perna to shut up by greeting the two brothers: 'Welcome home.'

A clap on the shoulder. 'You're not going to leave us parched, I hope. We've had precious little in the way of sustenance on the journey.'

'I'll get a bottle. Sit down and tell me everything.'

Perna pulls up a chair and launches in. 'We managed to get away pretty well, thank fuck. They were about to get hold of your Jewish friend, that's right, you can laugh about it now, but things were looking pretty fucking hairy for a moment there, I can tell you, and if it hadn't been for the sack of money he gave that fat friar we wouldn't have been celebrating, if you know what I mean. Right now he'd be playing rummy with the rats in the dungeons of Milan.'

'Calm down now. Tell me the whole story from the start.'

Perna sits up straight like a good boy, his hands drumming nervously on the table. Bernard is the one who speaks, while João flashes one of his captivating smiles.

'The Inquisition kept him under arrest for three days. They accused him of selling heretical publications.'

I look at the older brother, who says nothing, encouraging his brother to continue. 'Loads of questions. Someone must have been spying. It turned out all right in the end, we just had to hand over some money to the right people and they let him go; they weren't that serious about it, but another time things mightn't go quite so smoothly.'

A moment of silence, Perna gets restless, waiting for João to say something.

He crosses his tapering fingers, leaning his elbows on the table. 'They're exaggerating. Those people didn't know a thing about the *Benefit*, they just had vague suspicions that something was up. Someone gave them my name and they came looking for me. That's all. If they really had been on the scent, they wouldn't have taken my money' – a dismissive gesture – 'or else they'd have asked more questions.'

Our bookseller butts in, 'Sure, sure, it's easy for him, but we've got to be careful. I'm well aware they didn't know a thing, those four black crows, but who's going to go back to Milan now? Who? It's scorched earth now as far as we're concerned, *capito*? The whole duchy's closed to us, there's bugger all for us there, we can't set foot in the place now without risking life and limb. How are we going to recover the outlay for the copies we've dispatched already?'

João reassures him, 'We'll make up for that money somewhere else.'

When we're on the second round of wine, Perna says, 'We might as well just forget about Milan. And yet we've all got to keep our eyes wide open: the Inquisition is getting better organised. Paul III is a coward, a plotter, but he won't last for ever. Everyone's fate is going to depend on the next Pope. Ours included.'

The three partners nod in unison. There's no need to say anything more: we all share the same thoughts.

Q's diary

Milan, 2 May 1547

Carafa's letter of introduction had the desired effect: I could tell from the sweat-drenched brow of Friar Anselmo Ghini, and the emotional gestures of his colleagues. Everyone suddenly busying themselves about the place. Ears pricked, eyes down.

Brother Anselmo Ghini, forty-two years old, the last two of those years spent minutely examining texts in search of heresy, on behalf of the Congregation of the Holy Office. He fiddled anxiously with his hands for the entire duration of the conversation, behind one of the desks in the reading room of the Dominican convent. The restless coming and going behind me didn't let up for an instant, as though I myself were the inquisitor. Everyone in the room clearly had frayed nerves. We talked in low voices.

Giovanni Miches: the name was given to us by a bookseller found in possession of ten copies of *The Benefit of Christ Crucified*. Once his presence in the city was confirmed, Miches was arrested on 13 March. He was accompanied by his brother Bernardo, their attendant Odoardo Gomez and the bookseller Pietro Perna, although the latter were not kept in custody. The first interrogation was conducted by Brother Anselmo Ghini.

Asked the reasons for his presence in Milan, Miches spoke of an imminent meeting with the Governor, Duke Ferrante Gonzaga, regarding an intercession with the Emperor to free some of the family's properties in Flanders.

He denied any kind of involvement in the distribution of *The Benefit of Christ Crucified*, but he admitted his interests in the printed word, explaining that he was a business associate of the biggest Venetian printers: Giunti, Manutius and Giolito. Miches added that he was aware of the existence of *The Benefit of Christ Crucified*, less so of its contents, which don't really interest him. He also said that he was amazed by our interest in him, given that it related to a piece of writing that has been circulating freely in Venice.

The next day, after a second discussion, of which there is no written record, Miches was released. In reply to my question about this omission, Brother Anselmo replied that the second occasion brought to light nothing that they had not heard the previous day.

First piece of evidence: Giovanni Miches is, without a doubt, a cunning character who brags about having the most surprising contacts. You don't show off about such elevated contacts if you're not in a position to prove them.

Who is Giovanni Miches?

Brother Anselmo isn't telling the whole truth: too much hesitancy, too many gaps.

Why weren't Miches's colleagues arrested?

Why is there no trace of any written record of the second interrogation?

I took notes today. Tomorrow I'm going to give some substance to Brother Anselmo's ill-concealed fears.

Milan, 3 May 1547

In Brother Anselmo's cell. No one eavesdropping.

It took less than I thought: Carafa's name provokes blind terror.

Miches paid up.

The monk began to blab the minute I told him to stop talking balls. He trembled, sitting on the couch, with me standing bent over him. It was no time before he started justifying himself.

They were informed in advance: Miches really is acquainted with the Governor of Milan. Many fine gentlemen do business with him, they depend on his purse. They don't do things hereabouts the way they do in Rome. Here it's the Emperor who calls the tune and Gonzaga doesn't like his friends getting into trouble. It isn't like Rome here, you've got to be careful.

They were informed in advance: a big shot, a powerful family. That's why the others weren't arrested. Bankers, the Emperor has borrowed from their coffers. How are you going to keep someone like that locked up in the dark? The Duke's own guards would have come to get him out. So they figured they might as well get something out of it. Something for the monastery. It isn't a matter of corruption, this is difficult work, you face a thousand hurdles. It's not like Rome here.

He begged me not to report him to Carafa. Blind terror.

I told him that from today he's going to be working for me, giving me all the useful information he can think of.

He thanked me; he kissed my hand.

*

Alejandro Rojas. Special Councillor to the Archbishop of Milan. Or Carafa's Spanish informer.

He has grown old, and much fatter: thanks to the bishop's table. He confirmed everything and added extra information.

Juan Micas, alias João Miquez, alias Jean Miche, alias Johan Miches, alias Giovanni Miches. Of the rich Sephardic Miquez family that married into the Mendez family, bankers to the Emperor.

A considerable inheritance and a convoluted past. Always on a knife edge between glory and ruin, but always able to find a way out. Their conversion to Christianity didn't stop their former friends from turning into their persecutors a day later. Peerlessly skilful and cunning, their fortune is tempting many, but they have learned to defend it. Some years ago they were transferred to Venice, where they undertook various commercial activities.

Converted Jews. Unscrupulous bankers. Known to the courts of half of Europe.

What interest could they have in distributing *The Benefit of Christ Crucified*? A simple business matter? I find that hard to believe.

Secret allies of the *spirituali*? Check that.

Certainly they have the means and the contacts to distribute the book very quickly indeed.

Other factors to take into consideration: the machine that Carafa has been constructing day after day is still far from perfect. Not everyone can be trusted. Milan and Venice aren't Rome. Each state has a patron, each patron establishes the acceptable levels of corruption.

Carafa is going to have to take that into account.

Milan, 4 May 1547

I can leave now. Brother Anselmo and the rest of the cowards leap to comply with my every request. The movements of the Miquez brothers or their associates in these parts will not go unobserved. Collect all useful details. I've got them all by the balls.

Letter sent to Bologna, to the Ecumenical Council, from the ducal city of Ferrara, addressed to Gianpietro Carafa, dated 13 June 1547.

To the most illustrious and reverend cardinal Giovanni Pietro Carafa in Bologna.

My Most Reverend Lord,

I have resolved not to tell Your Lordship the results of my inquiries until now, because that is how long it has taken me to obtain the elements required in order to compose the picture as a whole.

And I should add that in spite of this I can still not speak with absolute certainty on the subject on which I am about to expound, because the people we are dealing with here are unusually cunning and far-sighted.

But let us get to the facts. After travelling between Milan, Venice and Ferrara, and making contact with the inquisitors in those cities thanks to the letters of introduction given to me by Your Lordship, I managed to collect sufficient clues to assert that the inexplicable distribution throughout the whole of the Italian peninsula of *The Benefit of Christ Crucified* is to be imputed to one of the most important Jewish families in Europe, whose members, having converted to the true religion, are known at the imperial court as Mendesi, after the late Francisco Mendez, a Spanish banker close to the Emperor and consort of Donna Beatrice de Luna. The latter should be considered the matriarch of the family and is resident in Venice today. She has always taken an interest in publishing and in literature in general, as well as business and commerce. Along with her nephews, she finances not only the majority of publications on subjects related to Judaism, but also Christian authors, thus profiting from their own dual religion.

It is not a very extended family: Donna Beatrice has a daughter, Reyna, and a sister, one Brianda de Luna, who is widow of none other than the brother of Francisco Mendez, Diego, and who is in turn the mother of a girl of marriageable age, Gracia la Chica.

The men of the family are the sons of a brother now deceased:

Giovanni (whom the Venetians call Zuan) and Bernardo Miquez. No more than six relations in all, four of them women.

Nonetheless, the Mendesi family does an incredible volume of business with the most important Venetian merchants and ship-owners. Their wealth must be vast and their interests extend to some of the oldest patrician families in Venice.

But what will without a doubt be most interesting to Your Lordship is the intense trade in books. Here they enjoy the role of patrons and associates of the printers, and in which they are, not least, active as distributors. During my time in Venice over the past month I have carried out considerable research into this last activity and my discoveries have been quite fascinating, enough so to bring me here, to Ferrara, on the trail of the forbidden book.

But we must proceed one step at a time.

In Venice I came across certain clues concerning the involvement of João Miquez in the distribution of the *Benefit*.

The only person I thought capable of giving me some useful information was Bernardo Bindoni, the first printer of *The Benefit of Christ Crucified*. Bindoni is a small printer, rancorous in his dealings with the big players such as Giunti or Manutius, mean and all in all reticent, and disinclined to talk about the affair; an affair to which he always referred in the past tense, on the few occasions when he alluded to it at all.

But while I left his shop disappointed, he dared to suggest that if I was at all interested in acquiring a consignment of *The Benefit of Christ Crucified*, I would have to turn to the Jews.

This was amply confirmed.

In the end it was the Jewish printer Daniele Bomberg who pointed me towards his colleagues Usque of Ferrara.

And here I am in the territories of Duke Ercole II d'Este. If I had to print a book that had been declared heretical by the council, beyond a doubt this is the place that I would choose. Here, where the Inquisition's hands are tied by the Duke, a fiery character, intolerant of any attempt at interference on the part of Rome. Ferrara, halfway between Venice and Bologna, between La Serenissima and the Papal State, a small independent region with easy access to the sea.

It has been slow work, involving a great deal of waiting, but it has been worth the trouble. River boats come down the branch of the Po that leads from Ferrara to the coast, where they load the cargo on to merchant ships heading south. There are good reasons for assuming that the Usques are using the same means to bring their consignments of books to the Venetian ships that put in a few miles down the coast. That would explain the distribution of the books along the Adriatic, via the ships supplied by the Mendesi in Venice, which are sent along the Ferrara coast to add the books to their normal cargo, and then dispatched southwards, to circumnavigate the Italian peninsula.

And yet none of this tells us anything. Because, My Most Honourable Lord, what still eludes us is the reason why a wealthy Sephardic family would be interested in distributing a Christian book.

In order to favour Your Lordship's enemies, to bring aid to Cardinal Pole and the *spirituali*. That is the likely answer. To make it more and more difficult to isolate and strike the promoters of the heretical book, in accordance with Your Lordship's intentions.

In Venice I was able to observe the subtle survival strategies adopted by these wealthy Jews. The Mendesi finances rely on finely tuned balances of power, exchanges of favours, commercial involvements, bribery. That is how they have always managed to escape persecution in the past. People such as these would have everything to lose from an increase in the power of the Congregation of the Holy Office, from the advent of intransigence. In all likelihood they hope that it will be people like Reginald Pole who defeat the *zelanti*, that is, moderate and tolerant men of letters who are willing to engage in dialogue and negotiations with the Lutherans today, and might well do so with the Jews tomorrow.

These people are quite powerful in Venice, not so much so as to be untouchable, but certainly difficult to reach using normal channels. The Jews in general are an essential component of the life of this city, they are so much a part of it that without them Venice would risk sinking into the sea. As Your Lordship is very well aware, the state of order in La Serenissima depends on a delicate interlocking system of powers and authorities, politics and commerce, a system that is almost unbreakable. To attack a family like the Mendesis would be to touch a live nerve in Venice, with all the resultant consequences.

For the moment I shall stay in Ferrara, waiting for a reply from Your Lordship and seeking to collect additional elements about the development of the *Benefit* affair.

I kiss Your Lordship's hands, and beg Your Grace's continuing favour.

Your Lordship's faithful servant

Q   Ferrara, the 13th of June 1547

Letter sent to Bologna from the city of Viterbo, addressed to Gianpietro Carafa, dated 20 September 1547.

To the most illustrious and reverend Giovanni Pietro Carafa.

My Most Honourable Lord,

The news of the murder of the Pope's son, Pier Luigi, Duke of Parma and Piacenza, has reached us here, giving Your Lordship's servant some cause for concern.

Indeed, I think that the rumours attributing this misdeed to Gonzaga are not misplaced. Furthermore, it is not difficult to weave this murder into the intricate web of events taking shape before us; if we bear in mind the fact that Ferrante Gonzaga governs Milan on behalf of the Emperor, and that for some time he has had an expansionist eye on Piacenza, it is not difficult to imagine the shady exchange that has taken place: the elimination of Pier Luigi Farnese favours Gonzaga as much as it does Charles V, and it gives the Emperor the chance to pose a serious threat to His Holiness Paul III.

I believe that this is the imperial warning in response to the tentative signals given by His Holiness to the new French King.

But Charles has no intention of missing out on the valuable opportunity that fate has prepared for him: in a single year two of his oldest enemies have died, the schismatic Henry VIII of England and the bellicose Francis I of France. To this we might add the imperial army's victory over the Schmalkaldic League in Mühlberg: the Protestant princes suffered a severe defeat there and this has done much to reinvigorate the Emperor.

So we should not be surprised that the Habsburg is returning to the attack in Italy as well. What he could not achieve with diplomacy at the Council of Trent he might be able to obtain by placing his own papal candidate upon the Holy Throne, the man Reginald Pole whom Your Lordship would prefer to see banished from Italy once and for all.

Now more than ever we must proceed with due care, in order to ensure that the damage done is not irreparable.

Now I shall report on the most recent developments concerning the task assigned to me by Your Lordship.

Thanks to the references supplied to me by Your Lordship, I have been in epistolary contact with the police authorities and the inquisitors in some of the major cities in Italy. As a result I have been in a position to ascertain that the sphere of activity of the distributors of *The Benefit of Christ Crucified* is widening: ten days ago two hundred copies of the little book were found in Naples. This is the most notable of the six confiscations so far. In two of these we have found that as cover for the transport of the books there was business related to the wealthy Sephardic Mendesi family and we can now be more than certain of their involvement in the operation.

The local authorities have prepared for me an initial list of names of people I think it would be better to keep watch on from a distance.

Simone Infante, in the Kingdom of Naples; Alfredo Bonatti, for the Duchies of Mantua, Modena and Parma; Pietro Perna, in the Duchy of Milan; Nicolo Brandani, in Tuscany; Francesco Strozzi and Girolamo Donzellini in Venice.

These people are: a supplier to the court of Naples, a favourite courtier to the Duke of Mantua, an itinerant Bible seller who exchanges books with exiles from Basle, a member of the Florentine wool corporation and two men of letters who have fled the city of Rome.

These people tell us much about the uses to which *The Benefit of Christ Crucified* might be put in Italy. They are cultivated men, close to the courts of their rulers and in a position to carry ideas between the nobility and the members of the mercantile and artisanal classes. Little fish who could become dangerous with the passing of time.

My advice, should it prove impossible to interrogate the powerful Mendesi family, is that it might be useful to begin with the last links of the chain so that the Sephardis might feel the Holy Office breathing down their necks.

All that remains for me to say is that I await orders from Your Lordship, implore that I may remain within Your Grace's favour.

Your Lordship's faithful servant

Q   Viterbo, the 20th day of September 1547

Chapter 25

Dusk, in a drawing room in the Miquez house. Beatriz, now standing before me, in silence, outlined against a window that faces the setting sun. Lit from behind, her features now hazy and diffuse. Sitting on an ottoman, I am drinking Greek wine. They call it retsina. Aromatic wine, flavoured with resin of the maritime pine.

I was called to the house an hour ago, a message brought to me by a little boy. I thought something might have happened, but there's no sign of João, or his brother, or Duarte Gomez, there's no one. Even the servants were dismissed when I arrived. Once I had opened the door, two steps beyond the threshold: Beatriz, smiling.

Faint sounds, far-off voices come to me as I sip this wine – which Perna has never mentioned to me – among tapestries, paintings, objects and colours whose like I have never seen before, not even in Antwerp.

A peace one cannot have experience of in the midst of the alleyways and catacombs that I have been walking down every day and every night for ever. A peace that takes me somewhere far from this winter, from all winters. Not what I have to do, but the way things might be.

With this woman, unlike any woman I have ever met.

Her musical way with the Flemish tongue, something no Fleming could ever manage; free of all asperity, assembled from sibilants, elongated vowels and phonemes that are all quite new to me. Echoes of various Nordic and Romance languages, with hints now of Greece, now of Africa, along with fragments from the Levant and the Orient, resonate down my spine. Perhaps one day all men and women, in the four corners of the continent will modulate these same notes, a quiet pan-European sing-song, rich and polyphonic, with a thousand local variants.

Her smile. Alone. Alone here with me. The Queen Mother of the Miquez dynasty, a woman who deals with aristocrats and merchants, a protector of artists and learned men. A queen in a city of panders and courtiers. The poets whom she patronises dedicate their works to her. I flick through a book by a certain Ortensio Lando: 'To the illustrious and most honourable Beatriz de Luna'. She laughs, not with embarrassment, but with amused commiseration.

She asks me about the Caratello, about its management, about the girls. She sits down next to me. This woman who is not anxious to know what I have been, not desperate to know how many rivers of blood I have waded through. This woman who is not concerned about all my many names. This woman who is curious about me *now*. About me *in the present*. This woman who is now talking to me about my humanity, telling me she feels challenged by me, telling me she can sense my humanity beneath the carapace that I have worn for too long, beneath the resistant substance that I have made of my skin, to avoid being injured again.

Another sip of wine.

This woman. This woman who wants me.

Beatriz.

How things could be.

Now.

Chapter 26

Along the branch of the Po that links Ferrara to the coast, with five hundred copies of *The Benefit of Christ Crucified* loaded on to the two boats supplied for the purpose by the Usques. The sun is high over the muddy waters, which are studied by birds hunting for food above our heads and in the clefts of the river. Beneath our heavy woollen capes we are paralysed by the damp cold.

I notice it too late.

The boat carrying the first half of the load suddenly swerves ahead of us: the prow sweeps to the right, to avoid a barge that has all at once emerged out of the reeds, making for the middle of the river. Behind me, the helmsman curses. A moment later the boat disappears into a secondary canal, its opening invisible through the dense vegetation. The barge immediately behind it, with three silhouettes on board, crouching low.

I instinctively shoulder my hackbut and take aim, but they've already disappeared. To the navigator: 'After them!'

An abrupt change of course so as not to be left behind. We hear shouts and the sound of something splashing into the water. We slip into the narrow canal, only to bump into two floundering boatmen. Both barge and boat are moving away. We pull the two men aboard. One is bleeding from a temple, his face smashed in.

'Don't lose them!'

Sebastiano the Hunchback curses and plunges his long pole into the river bed, driving us forward.

As I wrap the injured man's head in a cloth, I turn to the other survivor. 'Who the fuck are they?'

He answers in a breath, 'Bandits, Don Ludovico, it was an ambush. Godless bandits. Look what they've done to him!'

I too grab a pole, over by the prow, to negotiate an unknown bend in the river. The cavernous voice of the Miquezes' boatman: 'Worse than a maze, lordship. Twists and turns and marshes, for miles and miles. No one ever comes back.'

I protest, 'They've got more than half the load on that boat. I have no intention of losing it.'

I glimpse the stern of the boat, they're not travelling too fast. Perhaps they didn't expect to be followed. Another bend to the left and then the mouth of another very narrow channel, which makes us lose our bearings. Midday, the sun at its zenith, the horizon out of sight: no landmarks. We're a couple of miles from the river now.

I push the pole with all my might, reflecting that I only came to Ferrara to pick up a cargo. If I allow myself to dwell on where I am and what I'm doing I almost start laughing, but I manage not to, with Sebastiano standing behind me spitting, cursing and dripping with sweat as he plunges his pole into the river bed.

I see the two boats disappearing before me, as though swallowed up by the water. I try to spot a detail, a landmark on the bank of the canal so that I can remember the exact spot where I lost sight of them. A dead tree, its branches submerged.

'Faster, faster!'

Sebastiano's curses supply a rhythm to our thrusts. There's the tree. I nod to the Hunchback to stop. I search the opposite bank with the pole, until I discover a spot where the reed-bed thins out slightly. It doesn't look like a navigable route, but it's the only place they can have gone.

'In there!'

Sebastiano insists, 'Lordship, listen, we're never going to get through there.'

A glance at the injured man. The blood's stopped flowing, but he's passed out. The other boatman looks at me with determination and picks up a small oar. 'Let's go.'

I clear a path for the boat by pushing the reeds aside. They close over our heads and behind us. Using the pole, I test the reed-bed inch by inch, a few yards beyond the prow. This forest of reeds could extend, compact and unchanging, for many miles around us. I've got to focus my concentration on the invisible waterway running through it, feeling for those spots where the vegetation offers least resistance. We advance cautiously, in complete silence. Suddenly the reeds come to an end. A marsh leading to a flat, sandy island.

The boat. Five men: one of them is mooring the barge, the other four are carrying the two boxes. They are advancing on to a spit of land. My two oarsmen resume their rhythmical rowing while I pick up the hackbut. They haven't seen us. We quickly slice through the stagnant water. He looks up too late, when I'm already taking aim. The shot sends clouds of birds flying in all directions. When the smoke clears I see him creeping towards his colleagues. One of the boxes is being left behind and they're loading him on to their shoulders. We push our boat on to the island with a jolt. I unsheathe my dagger and am the first to jump down; up to my belt in the slime, stuck there like a pole. I almost burst out laughing. Sebastiano goes ashore a little further along and pulls me free.

'Come on, come on, your lordship, they're getting away!'

To the other boatman: 'You load the hackbut and stay and guard the boat.'

Running the length of the spit. We see them limping along with the box and the wounded man. Sebastiano's curses are like projectiles fired at the fugitives. I'm out of breath, although I really want to laugh.

Another water-logged clearing, full of reed-covered islands. If I run any further I'm going to have a heart attack.

All of a sudden they stop.

I slow down.

Sebastiano catches up with me, spluttering. Breathing as deeply as I can, I load the pistol. We walk on, they appear to be armed only with sticks. The injured man is laid out on the ground, he might be dead. Pale, terrified faces, men dressed in filthy rags. Gaunt, their hair sticking to their heads like mud skullcaps. Strikingly gaunt, barefoot. Now that we're very close I aim the pistol, a glance at the poor man on the ground: he isn't unconscious, his eyelids are beating. I can't see any blood.

At that moment they appear.

A brief rustling in the reeds and about thirty ragged ghosts emerge, clutching raised sticks and sickles.

Shit.

All around there are marshes as far as the eye can see. I finally do burst out laughing, to shake off my tension and fatigue. That must come as something of a surprise to them, because they press their weapons to their chests and retreat suspiciously.

An almighty racket emerges from the depths of the vegetation. One silhouette looms over all the others. A mud-caked habit, two pieces of wood dangling from his neck, tied together to form a crucifix. He clutches a knotty stick, which he swings to left and right, babbling incomprehensibly.

He goes over to the box and opens it. I see him raising his eyes to the heavens, losing heart. He goes reproachfully haranguing the crowd.

He comes towards us. '*Perdono, perdono fratres, perdono.*' His grey beard is longer than mine, and encrusted with mud and insects. His eyes, two pale-blue embers peering out from wrinkles in which the mud of centuries appears to have accumulated. His hair falls to his shoulders, resembling a bird's nest. '*Perdonate fratres. Simplici ingegni, sicut pueri.* To eat, eat *solum. Numquam libres videro*, they don't know what they are.'

At that moment I become aware of movement on the islands. The reed-bed is artificially arranged, I glimpse holes, animated shadows. Wide nets held up by cords and sticks at water level.

A village. By God, the reed-bed's a village!

'They don't know about your mission. They can't read. They're not wicked, they're just ignorant. I' – he brings his hand to his chest – 'am Brother Lucifero, Franciscan.' He searches for words. 'Don't worry, most reverend *fratres*. I know. Missals from the abbey.' He points to the box. 'The holiest of books. They don't know that.'

He turns towards the gathering, uttering words that we can't understand, but which sound like reassurance. 'Come, come.'

As though in response to a signal, the clearing springs to life. Women and children creep out of the cabins and appear on the marsh. The men stream towards the dwellings, shouting indistinctly. The injured man is lifted up, he speaks, he too joins in with the general tumult.

Sebastiano stands there open-mouthed. I pull him along with me, frowning at him not to say a word.

Brother Lucifero, bringer of light to the rejected people, hidden in the marshes of the Po as though in an impregnable fortress. A bogland that stretches from the mouth of the river to the territory of Romagna. A no man's land, as wild and remote as the New World. Fratre Lucifero was sent to evangelise these forgotten people almost thirty years ago, and was in his turn forgotten and left behind. Far from contemporary speech and the vicissitudes of politics. Lost in an inkblot on the map, following the example of St Francis of Assisi, as though he had uprooted the cross of Christ to replant it in the shifting sands of these moorlands, as a challenge to pagan superstition.

Thirty years.

Almost unimaginable. Thirty years away from the fortunes of the Church. Away from Luther, Calvin, the Inquisition and the Council of Trent. Free to cultivate a faith based on pure charity towards humble people.

Ignoring our apparel, he has taken us for missionaries like himself, Friar Titian and Friar Sebastiano, sent from the abbey of Pomposa, to spread the doctrine and the book to teach it with. He has flattered us most sincerely and asked us to serve mass in his place. I couldn't get out of it.

And so it was that Don Ludovico, manager of the most luxurious brothel in Venice, in the garb of Friar Titian, found himself facing the entire population of the marshlands, celebrating the only religious rite he is capable of performing. He rebaptised all the adults. From the first to the last.

When the time came to turn back, we were supplied with a guide and a gift of a barrel of live eels, in exchange for a new faith and two copies of *The Benefit of Christ Crucified*.

Viterbo, 26 February 1548

If I know the old man he'll start with the little fishes as I suggested. The booksellers, the intermediaries, the printers . . . And if that isn't enough to frighten off the major players, the ones who are financing the operation, he'll come up with a way of getting them off the scene. The old man never acts on impulse, he knows how to wait. Death, in turn, seems to be waiting for him, it's as though it won't take him until he's accomplished his plan. You don't easily get rid of people like Reginald Pole, let alone influential families like the Mendesi clan. You've got to come up with something complex, you've got to unsettle the most stable arrangements. The wealthy Venetian Jews are cunning characters. They're used to being hunted out, they're used to paying out money to save themselves, forging strong contacts with merchants and men of letters, being treated as equals with them. You can't help admiring the Mendesi family, especially the women, who have had to learn the art of negotiation and subterfuge, business and politics.

But it's always a mistake to oppose Carafa. A fatal mistake. Who can say that better than I, who have served him for thirty years?

Meanwhile information from the Venetian inquisitors is bringing fresh concerns about the distribution of *The Benefit of Christ Crucified*. It seems it's causing a great deal of trouble in the countryside.

News from Venice

The Venetian Inquisition is on the trail of a Franciscan going by the name of Friar Pioppo, who is active in the Po Delta. Many peasants in those parts have revealed in confession that he has baptised them 'in the new faith of the benefit of Jesus Christ crucified'.

On the other side of the Po a family of fishermen refused to have their own son baptised, 'since he is not yet capable of understanding the mystery of Jesus Christ on the cross'. They made no mention of Friar Pioppo.

In Bassano a woman sought refuge in a convent because her husband beat her, in an attempt to persuade her to have herself rebaptised. A copy of *The Benefit of Christ Crucified* was found in the man's house.

This crude outpouring of popular religion is giving rise to the most ludicrous juxtapositions. Powerful ideas in simple minds. Where did the idea of rebaptising adults spring from? Certainly not from the material in that heretical little book.

We need more information.

Talk to Carafa about it?

27 February 1548

Why has the old man not yet used *The Benefit of Christ Crucified* as a weapon against Pole and the *spirituali*? Why has he not yet excommunicated his enemies? It wouldn't take much: the book faces excommunication from the council, and the old man would only have to put Friar Benedetto of Mantua in jail and make him give the names of his protectors, whoever it was who took delivery of the text and edited and printed it.

In all likelihood Carafa is worried about showing his hand too soon. He's still waiting. But what for? Paul III's days appear to be numbered and the Englishman could become Pope. That would delight the Emperor, who would expect him to set about establishing a reconciliation with the Protestants.

Perhaps that's the only reason why the old man is waiting patiently. He's waiting for the *coup de grâce*, delivered at the last minute. But how much longer does he think he'll be able to live?

Q's diary

Viterbo, 4 May 1548

Friar Michele da Este, prior of the monastery of San Bonaventura in Rovigo, heard by the inquisitors of La Serenissima on 12 March 1548, concerning the activities of a certain Friar Poplar, suspected of heresy.

A first name and a surname: Adalberto Rizzi, a Franciscan at the monastery of San Bonaventura, who disappeared at the end of January 1547 along with a German guest, a pilgrim who said his name was Titian and who allegedly rebaptised him with water from a puddle.

Additional information from the Venetian inquisitors

Vicenza, 17 March 1548: a carpenter and an innkeeper apprehended in the act of barking during a baptism. Interrogated about who it was who had persuaded them that 'baptising newborn babies is like washing dogs', they replied, 'Someone who professes the German faith, and is able to do so with authority, because he is German.'

Padua, 6 April 1548: the student Luca Benetti publicly maintains that 'baptism is useless for minds which cannot know the mysteries of faith, particularly the benefit of Christ crucified for the whole of humanity'.

Pressed on his statements, he maintains that they were suggested to him by a German man of letters, going by the name of Titian.

Elements of the picture

Rovigo. Bassano. Vicenza. Padua.

A trajectory, a path. A journey from one place to another? Or a semicircle, whose centre is quite definitely Venice.

A German. A German, whose presence may perhaps explain the origin of the idea of the second baptism.

(An Anabaptist?)

A German who says his name is Titian. Who hands out copies of *The Benefit of Christ Crucified* and rebaptises peasants.

Titian the German.

The Fondaco dei Tedeschi in Venice. The frescos painted by Giorgione and his pupil Titian on its external walls.

Our Anabaptist is a German living in Venice.

Like a needle in a haystack.

5 May 1548

There's a time and a place for everything that has a beginning and an end. And then, on the other hand, there are those things that return. They rise up to the surface from the dark places of the mind, like pieces of bark to the surface of a lake. Like dark threats, or reasons for living. Like vendettas, scraps, fragments.

There's a time for war and a time for peace. There's a time when you can do anything and a time when you have no choice, because all of a sudden twenty years of fire and courage have vanished beneath the wrinkles of your face.

And you begin to dread the arrival of a messenger. What will your next task be? I dread the disgust that runs the narrow path from belly to brain. Something you should be able to conceal behind the authority of missions accomplished, behind experience. And yet that feeling of nausea won't go away; in fact, it grows stronger by the day, however much you try to send it back down to the depths. You can't find a reason, you're held by a thousand faces, the faces of men and women dispatched to hell.

Then one fine day you find yourself telling yourself it wasn't you. That you didn't take up that sword. And when that happens you know you're finished.

Q's diary

Viterbo, 10 August 1548

The record of an interrogation, of one Brother Lucifero, reaches me from Ferrara. It concerns the spread of heresy in the community of the so-called 'Po pirates', already the plague of the Ferrara merchants, who were recently eradicated by Duke Ercole II d'Este.

The friar showed clear signs of madness, declaring that he didn't know in what year of grace we were living and declaring his conviction that Leo X was still the Pope.

Indicted for bringing heretical and pagan-influenced rituals among the outlaws of the marshes, and particularly for practising adult baptism, he defended himself by maintaining that he had taken delivery of the consignment from a missionary, one Friar Titian, who had in return received it from the abbot of Pomposa. The friar, he said, had sent him the '*librum de nova doctrina*', *The Benefit of Christ Crucified*, and had then conferred a second baptism upon him.

I took out the letter. The Venetian inquisitors are merely ignorant servants of the Doge. They haven't the faintest idea what Anabaptists are. They wouldn't find our Anabaptist missionary if they spent a hundred years looking for him. He never shows up in the same place twice. Every sighting comes from a different location and the epicentre of those locations is always Venice. It's almost a pattern. All you have to do is put all the pieces together. One single man moving between the territories of Venice and Ferrara, rebaptising people, allowing his chosen name to leak out. By the time the Inquisition gets there, he's already disappeared into the void, he's plunged back into the bowels of history, whence he came. It's clear enough: he's not on a pilgrimage, there's no way of following him. Just a series of single points, so that he knows he'll get away with it. He baptises people, he makes sure everyone knows his name and then he disappears. Otherwise why would he choose such a strange and celebrated name for himself?

17 August 1548

From the confession of Friar Adalberto Rizzi, also known as Friar Poplar, captured on the Ferrarese bank of the Po on 30 June 1548 and held in the prisons of the Duke d'Este:

'And he invited me to reflect on the fact that when he asked a little five-year-old boy who Jesus Christ was, he got the reply: a statue. And from that he deduced that it was not right to administer the doctrine to minds incapable of comprehension . . .

'He said that the worship of statues and simulacra opened up the way to an ignorant and incompetent faith . . .

'Yes, he affirmed that his name was Titian, and that he was on his way to Rome . . .'

The child and the statue.

Shivering. A shiver running through my head.

The child and the statue.

Something a long way away, hurtling towards me at very great speed, carried by a wind that sweeps memory away.

The child and the statue.

Chapter 27

Venice, 30 August 1548

A black shadow outlined in the doorway. Duarte Gomez takes one step forward, stops and stamps the heel of his boot. Olive-coloured face, delicate features, slightly feminine, but with a crease running across his brow.

A nod to Demetra, who takes the girls away.

'What's going on?'

'Please, you've got to come with me.'

The Miquezes' servant goes outside with me, first to the porch and then to the alleyway where there's only space for one person to pass at a time.

The two brothers are there. Like two hired killers waiting on the threshold for their victim.

João is taller, wearing a big black hat decorated with a leather strap. Bernardo, looking like a little boy, with the comical beginnings of a beard under his chin. Their Toledan swords point out from under their coats. The light fades from one moment to the next.

'What's happening, gentlemen? Why all this mystery?'

The smile he always wears looks somehow broken, as though it's at odds with his state of mind. 'They've got Perna.'

'Where?'

'In Milan.'

'What the fuck's he doing in Milan? Didn't we decide to forget that particular market?'

The three Sephardic faces darken and the light fades some more.

'He was supposed to stop in Bergamo, collect the money from the booksellers and come back. It seems he wanted to take the risk. He's been accused of selling heretical books.'

I listen to my breathing as it echoes from one end of the alley to the other and lean against the wall. 'The Holy Office?'

'You can bet on it.'

Gomez goes on nervously stamping his heels on the cobbles.

'What are we going to do?'

João takes out a rolled-up sheet of paper.

'We'll pay up and get him out before things get too serious. Duarte's setting off tonight. Gonzaga owes me some money: I've suggested wiping out his debt if he puts in a good word.'

'Do you think it'll work?'

'I hope so.'

'Shit. I don't like it, João, I don't like it at all.'

'It was just chance, I'm sure of it. Bad luck and carelessness.'

Bad premonitions, I can't think straight.

The elder Miquez gives me his sincerest smile. 'Don't worry. I'm still the most important financier in the city. They won't dare touch us.'

I press my hands against both walls, as though to push them apart. 'For how long, João? For how long?'

Venice, 3 September

Maybe someone has managed to put together the pieces of the puzzle. Bad news from Naples: Infante, our man down there, has been put in prison and is going to be interrogated by the Inquisition.

They're slowly unravelling the intrigue that we've woven over the past two years.

Cardinal Carafa still hasn't used his biggest guns: while Pole, Morone, Soranzo and all the other *spirituali* are still on top his hands are tied.

If Reginald Pole were to become Pope before Carafa managed to go on the attack, the Inquisition would be halted: the old games would start up again, even the excommunication of *The Benefit of Christ Crucified* would be suspended.

These networks are too extensive for one single man. It may even be fascinating for someone who's reached the fifth decade of his life, someone who's managing to appreciate its geometry, its design, but there's still something else to be done. Something personal.

Something that's been waiting for twenty years. When your muscles start stiffening and your bones ache, unsettled scores become more important than battles and strategies.

Titian the Anabaptist is going to have to strike again, but a long way from here: a strong wind is rising and I've got to keep our vendetta far away from Venice.

You've got to come and find me. So that I can get you.

Venice, 28 September 1548

Heresy is everywhere in Venice.

In the way the women dress, with their breasts outside their clothes, and heels a span high beneath their shoes. In the thousand narrow alleyways, where forbidden doctrines are whispered. In the impossible foundations that support the city.

In Venice the Germans are everywhere too. There isn't a *calle*, a *campo* or a canal that doesn't know the sound of Luther's language.

Venice: the ideal terrain for pursuing a trail.

The Fondaco brewery. Coming out with the occasional reference to Anabaptism: startled faces, references to the Münster massacre, no useful information. Titian: *Who, the painter*? Nothing at all.

A walk around the Rialto market, sniffing the air. Up and down the bridge, and then down to St Mark's, along the Strada delle Mercerie. People busy doing deals, Germans selling furs, impossible to imagine any of them baptising a friar in a convent in Rovigo, let alone among the students of Padua.

The students: Titian is a cultured man, someone who can speak the language of the universities at least as well as that of the innkeepers and carpenters of Bassano.

A sense I have: the man I am looking for doesn't frequent those places.

Venice, 30 September 1548

Archive of the Inquisition.

Three Germans implicated in heresy trials.

– Matthias Kleber, thirty-two, Bavarian, lutenist in Venice for twelve years, caught stealing consecrated hosts from the tabernacle in the Church of San Rocco, sentenced to exile, but rehabilitated with his repentance and conversion to the Catholic faith.

– Ernst Hreusch, forty-one, wood merchant, originally from Mainz, tried for writing words in praise of Luther on the walls of the churches of San Mosè and San Zaccaria. Sentenced to the punishment of rubbing them out, and of making payments of one hundred and fifty ducats to the two churches.

– Werner Kaltz, twenty-six, tramp, from the city of Zurich, found guilty of being a wizard for his work as a chiromancer, alchemist and astrologer. Escaped from the Piombi prison, still at large.

A semi-iconoclast, a Luther fanatic and a wizard. I try to imagine them in the various situations in which I have seen Titian as protagonist, but none of them really seems suited to the role of Anabaptist missionary.

Reverse the task: imagine Titian bringing his own ghost to life, moving through the streets and shops of the city like a puppet. No.

In Venice Titian isn't Titian. He's someone else. If he'd been rebaptising people here too, someone would remember. Titian is concealing his own identity; at the same time, though, it seems as though he wants to give his actions the greatest possible resonance.

Who is, who was, Titian in Venice?

Chapter 28

A letter preceded them. That's why we're here at the jetty, our eyes fixed on the Giudecca canal. They should be about to appear over there.

Bernardo Miquez walks up and down. João is as solid as a statue, very elegant as always, leather gloves slipped into his belt and wide sleeves on his jacket, flapping about in the wind.

Demetra has made me a woollen scarf for this frosty autumn. I'm grateful to her for that, because my throat's been playing up for some time.

I observe the boats gliding slowly towards the piers and discharging their weird and colourful human cargoes.

'For the Doge and St Mark!'

I give a start at the screeching voice of a massive black bird being carried in a cage.

João laughs out loud when he sees the expression on my face: 'Talking birds, my friend! This city never ceases to amaze.'

Bernardo leans forwards on to the edge of the bench, almost losing his balance. 'There they are!'

'Where?' I keep quiet about the fact that my eyesight isn't as keen as it once was.

'Over there, they've just disembarked!'

I pretend to recognise the boat, which is still a tiny dark blur. 'Is that really them?'

'Of course it is! There's Sebastiano!'

'By Moses and all the prophets! There's Perna. He's done it! Duarte's really gone and done it.' João allows himself a gesture of exultation.

'Bastards, scumbags, shitheads, fucking arseholes, I nearly died down there, Christ Almighty, covered all over with moss and mushrooms!' He draws breath, his eyes still terror-struck. 'Murderers, that's what they are. Crazy people, Ludovico, my friend, there were rats in there the size of puppies, you know? You'd never believe it, you should have seen them, that big, the bastards, a month in that shit-hole, prison, they call it, may the Turks impale the lot of them, fuckers, look, Ludovico, this size, the rats, and warders who looked like the monsters of the Apocalypse, hold a man in those dungeons for a year and he'll confess to anything, even . . . yeah, and they write everything down, everything, they don't miss out a single word, there's always some fucking little scribe writing down whatever you say, quickly, he writes very quickly, never taking his eye off the page, you sneeze and he writes it down, you know?'

His sparse hair is dishevelled, his eye sockets hollow and his jaws would pounce on the steak that Demetra's just served him, if they weren't in full flow.

He finally gulps down his first mouthful and seems to regain the requisite lucidity.

He barely lifts his eyes from his plate. 'Anyone else been put away?'

'Infante in Naples.'

He puffs.

'And that's not the worst.'

Perna's little eyes stare at me apprehensively. 'Who else?'

'Benedetto Fontanini.'

The bookseller runs his hand over the top of his head, smoothing down what's left of his hair. 'Sweet Jesus, we're fucked . . .'

'They've imprisoned him in the monastery of St Giustina, in Padua. He's accused of being the author of *The Benefit of Christ Crucified*. He could rot there for ever.'

Perna lowers his head again. 'We've got to be really careful from now on.' He looks at all three of us in turn. 'Everyone.' His eye falls on João: 'And don't you go thinking you're any safer than the rest of us, my friend. If they start getting serious we're all fucked. We're safe here in Venice for the time being, but they've given us a good warning.'

'What do you mean?' I refill his wineglass.

'They've worked it out. They know who we are, who's involved. First they arrested João, then me and poor old Infante. Then off they go after Benedetto of Mantua . . .' He chews and swallows.

Duarte looks at all of us. 'Who are we talking about?'

Perna's fork falls on to his plate. Silence. The Caratello is closed, we're alone, three Sephardic Jews and two inveterate unbelievers sitting around a table plotting: an inquisitor's delight.

Perna squats down like a cat. 'We're talking about the Hardest Man of all, gentlemen, yes, His Hardest and Toughest Eminence Cardinal

Giovanni Pietro Carafa. We're talking about the *zelanti*. The ones who want to make a nice little necklace for themselves from the balls of Reginald Pole and his pals. Bastards one and all they are, those men and their cops. They still haven't set them loose, but they will before long, you'll see.' A glance at João. 'And these men can't be bought, you know? Incorruptible bastards.'

I interrupt him: 'Milan, Naples, Venice – those cities are never going to let the Roman Inquisition poke its nose into their business.'

'And business it is. For the time being it wouldn't be worth their while setting their cops on us, you're right. But it all depends on who takes the Holy Throne, who makes the rules after Paul III croaks. And yet in order to avoid interference from Rome, the Venetians might think it best to settle their scores with us off their own bat, without waiting for Carafa and his friends.'

He swallows his mouthful. 'Oh, the filth. When I think about that latrine, I lose my appetite.'

Venice, 5 November 1548

The child who thinks Jesus is a statue.

I've travelled the length and breadth of the city. I'm looking for a German, trusting my intuition: the bookshops where he might have acquired *The Benefit of Christ Crucified*.

I visited the shop of Andrea Arrivabene, the bookseller at the sign of the Well, a place that Titian is sure to be familiar with. I pretended to take an interest in the doctrines of Anabaptism, hoping he might be able to suggest *someone* I could speak to.

Not a thing.

Venice, 7 November 1548

The child and the statue of Christ.

The child who thought that Jesus was a statue.

The *five-year-old* child.

The child that Bernhard Rothmann, the pastor of Münster, asked who Jesus was.

A statue.

The endlessly repeated anecdote, in the days of madness.

The days of King David.

It's hard to go back. Painful. Memories of conversations, long, interminable, stirring up the preacher's madness, suggesting the most deranged choices to a deluded mind.

Terror and slow dissolution.

The final days of Münster.

Outside those walls, the first shiver of uncertainty. I wanted to forget.

Titian, the German pilgrim who baptised Adalberto Rizzi, alias Friar Pioppo, Friar Lucifero and the pirates of the Po, knew Bernhard Rothmann.

Someone from Münster, someone I've met.

I went back into the street, this time in search of a face. I turned round with a start every time I heard a word uttered in my language. I scrutinised people's faces, beneath their beards, trying to see beyond their hair, whether it was long or short, peering among their scars and wrinkles. It was like a hallucination, a suspicion confirmed in every face I saw.

This won't do.

It isn't easy to explain to them that I've got to go. It isn't easy to tell them about an old enemy. Qoèlet, the constant ally, the traitor, the infiltrator.

It won't be easy, but it has to be done. Explaining the journeys of the past few months, this beard: Titian, the apostle with *The Benefit of Christ Crucified* in one hand and the water of Jordan in the other. Settling a score that was begun twenty years ago. Trying to set Carafa's cop – his best, his most cunning cop – on the trail of an Anabaptist heresiarch made to measure specially for him. There isn't much time left. The noose has begun to tighten earlier than expected, but I knew that would happen. I'm playing with fire and I can't put their lives in jeopardy. The same unforgivable mistake I've been making all my life: my past erupting into the present and turning into a massacre, ripping apart the flesh of friends, partners, lovers. Demetra, Beatriz, João, Pietro. The names of the imminent dead. Leave before it happens. Drag the Exterminating Angel and the eternal policeman along behind me, far from the loved ones of my final days. To the remotest corners, the very arsehole of Europe, this continent that I've travelled from coast to coast. Get him to follow me there and, in that foul-smelling sewer, wait and settle the scores for countless lives. Alone.

It doesn't matter how long it takes, Eloi can have his name back, I'll just be Titian the mad Baptist.

João will take care of the brothel and Demetra in my place. I'll move about, I'll leave clues, I'll keep going until I've dragged Qoèlet into the light.

Perna, you said it: you've got to see how things will end, you've got to put your life and your luck on the line if they're to mean anything at all. You have to supply a reason for each and every defeat, and for everything that's been spared. They're not going to give up the game and I want to bring it to its conclusion. Somehow.

*

Looks of astonishment, jaws set. The only sound that emerges is Beatriz's clear voice: 'Just because life has forced my family to dissemble, it has never stopped me from appreciating sincerity, Ludovico.'

She smiles. My words have done nothing to dim the light in her dark eyes. 'So allow me to reciprocate your candour. You aren't the cause of the danger that threatens us: we all knew from the start what risks we would face when we set out to distribute *The Benefit of Christ Crucified*. We've challenged the excommunication of the council, the Inquisition, the shady strategies of the powerful men of Venice. To what end? The spiritual war being waged by the black dogs of the Holy Office is a threat to all of us. Pretending not to know that won't save us. Look whom we've got here: an underground bookseller, the manager of a brothel and a wealthy Jewish family that's been on the run for half a century. Then there's you: a heretic, a reject, a thief and a pander. All of us the kind of people they want to sweep away. If they win they'll take everything, they'll fill every available space. We'll be locked up, the lucky ones will die.'

Beatriz walks over to the window, with its view of the Giudecca canal against the background of St Mark's. It remains a dark outline.

She goes on, 'You've spoken of personal fate, you've said you've got to settle a score. You mentioned the black wing that has been flying over your head throughout your life, destroying everything dear to you. Your concerns are noble and sensible, but everyone has a part to play. I, too, am convinced that it's a good idea for us to part, remaining united only in the interests of a common plan. The Titian trail, sowing heresy and confusion, may bring the dogs out, it may confuse their sense of smell, slow down their progress, as we await the new Pope. But if that's your task, everyone else is going to have to have something to do as well.'

João rises to his feet, unsmiling. 'Aunt Beatriz, you could keep the exit clear. Your charisma and your contacts at the court of Ferrara, where we are in good favour both because of your loans to the Duke and your great personal refinement, could guarantee a safe passage for everyone if things were to heat up. I'll stay here in Venice, to call in favours in return for the donations we've made. Now's the time for the patricians and merchants of the city to show their proper appreciation of the people who keep them in such splendid style and who keep their affairs afloat. Meanwhile I can take care of new business, the routes we've opened up with the Turks.'

He turns back towards Perna. 'You'd be better off staying out of sight for a while. I want you to be my agent on the eastern coast. Your job will be to spread the new translation of the *Benefit* in Croatia and Dalmatia, to Ragusa and beyond. You won't just be dealing with books, you'll be my link beyond the reach of the Inquisition.'

The little man jumps up. 'Selling books to the Turks? Am I dreaming here? Going up and down the coast on those stinking little tubs? Is that to be the fate of Pietro Perna, a man with a reputation, a man respected from Basle to Rome? Ludovico, say something!'

'Yes, you're right, you need a new name. Something less respectable, perhaps, but less well-known to the cops.'

Perna slumps into his chair, almost disappearing into it, his legs dangling.

João smiles at Demetra. 'The fascinating Donna Demetra will go on managing the Caratello as though nothing had happened, constantly on the alert for any indiscretions on the part of her affluent customers. Any information could be valuable. We'll keep an eye on her and the girls while Ludovico is away.'

Beatriz: 'There's no point denying that our fate depends to a large extent on the identity of the next Pope. Let's wait for that moment before we decide what to do in the light of that new situation.'

Bernardo refills the glasses. João raises his first, he's got his smile back. 'To the future Pope, then!'

We all erupt in hearty laughter.

Q's diary

Information picked up in places frequented or managed by Germans:

– 'Silver Lily' bookshop, specialising in Lutheran and sacramentist books, owned by one Hermann Reidel.

– Friedrich von Melleren, count, head of the small circle of German men of letters in Venice, has a *palazzo* just behind the Fondaco.

– 'Black Forest' inn, run by a German woman married to a Venetian merchant. It's the meeting place of the artisans: wood-carvers, goldsmiths, cobblers . . .

– 'Caratello' inn, owned by Ludwig Schaliedecker, known as the German, and a Greek woman. The brothel of choice for important Germans and for those with well-filled purses.

– 'Silk' inn, meeting place for merchants, run by Hans Gastwirt. Games of chance and favourable rates of exchange.

– Workshop Jacopo Maniero, glassmaker, every Thursday after vespers: meeting place of the Calvinist community (Italians, Swiss and Germans).

Venice, 15 November 1548
Spent a day in the Black Forest and in Hermann Reidel's bookshop.

Nothing.

A name that rings a bell: Ludwig Schaliedecker. Where have I heard it before? Among the German apostates? Something to do with Wittenberg.

Ludwig Schaliedecker, manager of the Caratello.

Check tomorrow.

Chapter 30

She leans against me to avoid losing her balance as she climbs aboard the boat that will carry us to the Miquez brothers' carrack, moored on the other side of the island. With the other hand she holds her heavy cloak, helped by a servant girl, taking care to ensure that her clothes don't get wet. She manages to preserve a boundless dignity where other noblewomen would simply have appeared clumsy, encumbered by all their flummery. I can't help reflecting that Beatriz is a special, luminous creature.

I help her to settle on the seat, with her cloak rolled up under her arms.

Hunchbacked Sebastiano is ready with the oar at the stern.

João and Bernardo embrace us.

'Don't be afraid, Aunt Beatriz, I'm leaving you in good hands. Write to me when you reach Ferrara, and do pass on my greetings to Duke Ercole and Princess Renée.'

'And you be careful, João, these streets can be more treacherous than the castle dungeons. And keep an eye on your brother Bernardo; if anything were to happen to him I'd hold you responsible.'

'Don't worry. We'll all meet up again very soon.'

João flashes his smile. 'Good luck, my friend. Keep your powder dry and don't be too impulsive. These people are dangerous . . .'

'I can be too, if the occasion calls for it . . .'

Sebastiano has already unmoored the boat from the jetty. The two brothers say goodbye to us, their hands raised to the sky.

The news arrived at dawn. A Franciscan who came to the Caratello for a quiet fuck: the Venetian Inquisition is planning to arrest Beatriz. Today they would have interrogated her concerning some informer statements identifying her as a crypto-Jewess, a false Christian.

An act of intimidation, a feeble attempt to pressurise a family whose presence is awkward for everyone, perhaps to blackmail them to obtain discounts on credit. The patricians of La Serenissima are shitting themselves. Who hasn't had loans from the Mendesi, as they call them here? Who doesn't covet their vast family wealth?

João immediately prepared the carrack, there was no time to lose.

So we're leaving without even having time to think.

Ferrara. That will have to be the starting point of Titian's journey. A long journey, this time, using the city of the Este family as a safe house to which I'll return to pick up news about the situation in Venice. My plan is to head south, towards Bologna, and cross the Apennines, get to Florence. Before I bade him farewell, Perna told me I couldn't die without having seen Florence. Poor little Perna, dispatched along the Croatian coast. I have no doubt that he'll be a great success down there; Pietro the bookseller weeps and wails, but in the end his big balding head always pops up again, unharmed and ready to resume its endless logorrhoea.

So here we are. We're on the home stretch, the last bit of our journey and a new adventure. I'm a madman, an old bird perched here on this seat with my grey beard and aching bones that won't leave me in peace. I'm mad and I still want to laugh. I still can't believe I'm off on my travels again, preaching up a storm. I find myself thinking about how it all began. I find myself thinking that my life has coincided with war, with flight, with sparks that set the plain alight and waves that covered it over. I should leave my tired old bones in a hole somewhere and slip serenely away, a little bit at a time, reviewing the faces of my friends and lovers in my memory. And instead I'm still here, dogs snapping at my heels, settling the score on behalf of all those faces. The obsession of an old heretic who can't find peace.

The last challenge, the last battle. I could have died in Frankenhausen, in the squares of Münster, in Holland, in Antwerp, in the prisons of the Inquisition. But here I am. And finishing the game, solving the mystery, is the last thing that remains to be done.

Venice, 16 November 1548

Visit to the Caratello. Ludwig Schaliedecker, or 'Don Ludovico', the manager, isn't there. He's left, no one knows where he's gone. I throw out the occasional question, I don't want to arouse anyone's suspicion.

Clearer memories: Eloisius de Schaliedecker. Wittenberg, more than twenty years ago, a man who came to challenge Luther and Melanchthon. He was the talk of the whole university, because of his strange notions about sin and perfection.

He might have come from the Netherlands or Flanders, I can't remember.

Try to get some information. Write to the Inquisition in Amsterdam and Antwerp. A letter of introduction from Carafa might be useful. And that would mean telling him of my suspicions.

It would still take a matter of months.

Keep on searching here in Venice. Keep an eye on the Caratello, in case he comes back.

Write to the inquisitors in Milan, Ferrara and Bologna to get fresh information about Titian the Anabaptist.

Letter sent to Rome from Venice, addressed to Gianpietro Carafa, dated 17 November 1548.

To the most illustrious and honourable Giovanni Pietro Carafa.

My Lord,

I have just today received your most urgent communication. You will receive this reply at most two days before I arrive in Rome. I will immediately be available for whatever tasks Your Lordship may wish to assign to me.

It is my duty and my wish to inform you that the sudden deterioration in the health of the Farnese Pope is taking me away – with a displeasure that I am unable to conceal – from a promising trail concerning the distribution of *The Benefit of Christ Crucified*. My immediate assumption is to imagine that this little treatise features largely in Your Lordship's plans to obstruct Reginald Pole. I therefore hope that the precipitation of events involves only the suspension of the investigation that I have been conducting for months, since it is still far from its conclusion and has certainly not exhausted its fascination.

Trusting in the speed of Italian horses to put me at your disposal as soon as possible, I kiss Your Lordship's hands.

Your Lordship's faithful servant

Q   Venice, 17 November 1548

Chapter 31

*Finale Emilia, on the border between the Duchies of Modena and
Ferrara, 2 April 1549*

The way station is an isolated farmhouse in the middle of flat, even land. A few scattered little bushes break up the monotonous line of the horizon. The horse is tired, and so are my back and legs.

The internal courtyard is a hubbub of chickens and sparrows fighting over invisible crumbs among the pebbles. An old dog barks at me without a great deal of conviction, probably out of duty, after all the years he has wasted guarding this place.

'Hey, groom, do you have room for this nag of mine?'

A stout character, moustache down to his chin. He points to a low door, the upper panel of which is closed.

I dismount with some difficulty and take a few steps, legs still splayed into the shape of the saddle.

He takes the reins. 'Bad day to be travelling.'

'Why's that?'

A vague gesture towards the west. 'A storm brewing. The road's going to be a river of mud.'

I shrug. 'That means I'll have to stop here for a bit.'

He shakes his head. 'No beds. Full up.'

I look around in search of any traces of overcrowding, but the courtyard is empty and there isn't so much as a sound from the house.

The stableman clicks his tongue and the tips of his moustache spring up. 'We're waiting for a bishop.'

'You could stick me in the barn.'

Another shrug of the shoulders, as he disappears into the stable with my horse.

The dog has returned to lie down in the sun. The tufts of grey hair around its muzzle make it look like an animal replica of the groom. When I see him coming back out of the stable, I smile at the resemblance. 'How old is it?'

'The dog? Oh, eight, nine, more or less. It's old, it's losing its teeth. I'll have to kill it before long.'

Eyes narrowed to slits and paws outstretched, just a slight movement of the tail and one raised eyebrow. Even its facial expressions look like its master's.

I stretch myself and my bones make a curious cracking noise.

'There's some hot soup indoors if you want some. Ask my wife.'

'That's great. But won't you want to serve it to the bishop?'

He stops, puzzled, and scratches the sweaty back of his neck. 'You see, we don't get fine gentlemen in these parts all that often. We've never had a bishop here before.'

I bend down to check that my knees are still working, roll my head around and I'm as good as new.

He thinks about it. 'It's actually a bloody nuisance. His whole entourage, all those lackeys . . .'

'His secretaries, his servants, his personal guards . . .'

He gives a worried sigh and shrugs his shoulders. 'They'll have to be content with what they get.'

He climbs the stairs back into the house.

'Soup'll do fine for the guards and the lackeys. But the bishop's going to want some game . . . By the way, who is he?'

He stops in the doorway. 'Cardinal Bishop His Lordship Giovanni Maria Del Monte Ciocchi. He's coming from Mantua, on his way to Rome.'

'Ah yes. That'll be for the Conclave . . . they say the Pope's ill, but as we know, popes take a long time to die . . .'

He looks perplexedly at the tips of his shoes, uncertain whether to encourage me or tell me to go to hell. 'I don't know a bloody thing. I just have to put the bishop and his entourage up for the night.'

'Of course, of course. But you haven't got any game for his dinner.'

He turns purple and if the stairs weren't between us I'd fear for my throat. 'We haven't got any today! It's a way station, not an inn!'

He goes into the house.

I chuckle to myself and walk over to the dog. It seems to have calmed down and allows itself to be stroked. It doesn't seem particularly keen on snarling at me, or even, particularly, on living. Soon its hour will come.

'You're no better than the Pope. And at least you haven't got an army of vultures flying over your head at all hours.'

Cardinal Del Monte.

Zelante or *spirituale*?
On Carafa's side, or Pole's?
Mantuan.
The old dog yawns toothlessly into my face.
Mantuan, like Friar Benedetto Fontanini.
Zelante or *spirituale*?

The bishop's insignias on the doors of his carriage are splattered with mud. A dozen armed men are bivouacked on the gravel of the courtyard. A lot of people coming and going up and down the stairs. The groom is busy polishing the episcopal crest with a rag.

The soldiers barely give me a tired glance. The fine clothes I'm wearing must make me look like a courtier.

A slimly built man trips daintily down the stairs, enveloped in an elegant cape and with a ludicrous hat on his head. He looks about thirty. He turns to the groom. 'His Lordship would be grateful for some hot water *before* his lunch.' An arrogant and scornful tone.

The man with the whiskers nods with the stupidest expression in the world, stops working on the carriage and hurries up the stairs.

I walk over. 'The service always leaves a lot to be desired in places like this.'

I take him by surprise, he can only manage a nod. 'It's really scandalous . . .'

'A man of such calibre . . .'

He can't look at me, my cordial manners have knocked him off balance. 'After travelling for so long, at his age . . .'

'And with such terrible worries . . .'

He decides to react, grey little eyes looking down from above. 'Are you by any chance from the same parts as His Lordship?'

'No, sir, I'm German by origin.'

'Ah.' He adopts the expression of someone who has suddenly discovered a profound truth. 'I am Felice Figliucci, secretary to His Lordship.'

'Titian, like the painter.' A slight mutual bow. 'I imagine you're headed for Rome.'

'Indeed we are. We set off again tomorrow morning.'

'Hard times . . .'

'Quite so. The Pope . . .'

We stand there in silence for a moment, eyes lowered, as though reflecting on deep theological questions; I know he wants to say goodbye, but I don't give him time. 'If there's anything I can do for His Lordship, don't hesitate to ask.'

'Most kind of you . . . Of course . . . For the moment, you will forgive me if I dash upstairs and check that all is well.'

Embarrassed, he takes his leave.

It's pouring with rain, but I have a terrible urge to smoke a cigar. Taking shelter beneath an awning, I inhale the smoke as I stare at the storm. No sign of the old dog. A cat's eyes flash before it disappears through a grille.

I will baptise people methodically, the people needed to form the nucleus of a genuine sect. Inquisitors are partial to sects, you can go on about them till the cows come home, you can blame them for all kinds of things: popular discontent, plagues, prostitution, your wife's infertility . . . I need apostles to go around the place rebaptising people, just as old Matthys did. I already have a few people in mind, from Ferrara, but I've got to go further afield than that: Modena, Bologna, Florence. Then there's Romagna. The inhabitants are said to be the most turbulent of all the Pope's subjects. It might be interesting to meet up with someone down there. Heresy and rebellion: what else?

I clench the cigar between my teeth and fold my hands behind my back. A shiver tells me it would be better to go back inside. I can't risk falling ill.

The fire is still lit in the hearth. Someone's stirring the coals with a poker, a black outline from behind, sitting on one of the inn's wooden chairs. A flannel shirt to his feet, covering his bulk, and a purple skullcap perched on top of his tonsure.

He turns round slightly when he notices my presence.

I hasten to put him at ease. 'Don't worry, Your Lordship, just an insomniac's footsteps.'

A strange sound, halfway between a mumble and a sigh. Round eyes deep-set above his wrinkled cheeks. 'Then that makes two of us, my son.'

'Can I help you in any way?'

'I was trying to get this fire back to life so that I could read a few lines.'

I pick up the bellows and start blowing on the embers. 'Insomnia's a dreadful thing.'

'You can say that again. But when you've reached the age of sixty-six there's no point complaining, you humbly accept what the good Lord sends. We should be grateful that our eyes are still good enough to read and take us through the hours of night.'

The fire has started crackling again, Cardinal Del Monte picks up the book that lies open on the floor. I glimpse the title in the firelight and can't contain my surprise. 'You're reading Vesalius?'

An embarrassed murmur. 'May the good Lord forgive the curiosity of an old man whose sole pleasure lies in keeping up with the bizarre excrescences of the human mind.'

'I've read that book, too. It certainly is strange, manhandling corpses like that, but what you're left with, it seems to me, is a wonderful homage to the glory of God and the perfection He has created, don't you think? If more people cultivated their curiosity as you do, we might avoid a lot of misunderstandings, like seeking evil where there is no trace of it.'

He gives me a crafty look. He's like an affable old bear, crouched in his chair. 'So you've read it? But what do you mean when you speak of misunderstandings?'

Let's give it a try. 'So many fervent Christians today risk being imprisoned for their wish to revive and bring fresh blood to the Roman Church. They are fingered as members of dangerous sects, as alchemists, magicians and plague spreaders. They are tried as enemies of the Church, Lutherans, when they have never even dared to question the infallible authority of the Pope and the theologians. If only someone would pay one hundredth the attention to their ideas that you are showing now, I don't think it would be too hard to tell them from the heretics and schismatics beyond the Alps.'

Del Monte gives me a paternal look. 'My son, sitting by this fire, right now, you and I are merely two insomniacs. Tomorrow morning I will once again be the Cardinal Bishop of Palestrina, and in that persona I could never allow myself to be as liberal as I am about to be. It is difficult to reconcile one's responsibility of defending a beloved flock with the measures needed to bring back the sheep that have been lost along the way, led astray by their intellects, by bad books and bad logic.'

I decide to take the bull by the horns. 'What I fear is both the rashness and the excessive caution of the judges, I'm worried that they will destroy the spirit of renewal, that they will lump everything all together . . .'

The cardinal narrows his eyes. 'You have something specific in mind, don't you?'

'I have. I don't know if I can risk talking to Your Lordship about it, but the late hour, and the opportunity to talk privately to you, are encouraging me to say a few words about an affair that has been troubling me for some time, and which concerns one of your fellow countrymen.'

'A member of my diocese?'

'A pious man, Your Eminence. Friar Benedetto of Mantua.'

No reaction. I've taken my step, I'll have to keep going. 'For months he has been isolated in the monastery of Santa Giustina of Padua, accused of being the author of *The Benefit of Christ Crucified*. He's suspected of apostasy.'

A brief coughing fit. 'That little book is threatened with excommunication, my son.'

'I know, Your Eminence. But follow my reasoning, if you will. The excommunication of the book by the Council of Trent dates back to 1546 and for a very particular reason: it was only then, in fact, that the doctors of the Church definitively fixed the Catholic doctrine of salvation, declaring the Lutheran teaching on the subject to be heretical. Well, Friar Benedetto wrote the *Benefit* in 1541, five years before the council's definitive pronouncement reached us.'

He nods in silence.

I go on, 'When Friar Benedetto wrote that book, he was driven to do so by the sincere intention of offering a chance of reconciliation with the Lutherans. There is not a single page in *The Benefit of Christ Crucified* that calls into question the authority of the Pope and the bishops, there's nothing even slightly scandalous about it. It merely sets out in the clearest terms the doctrine of salvation *by faith alone*. But you know better than I, Your Eminence, that there are passages in the Bible that lend themselves to that kind of interpretation . . .'

'Matthew 25, 34 and Romans 8, 28–30 . . .'

'And Ephesians 1, 4–6.'

Del Monte sighs. 'I know what you mean. I've read the *Benefit*, and the fate of Brother Benedetto is of great concern to me, too. But there are very delicate balances that must be taken into account, difficult conflicts to resolve . . .'

I lean towards him slightly. 'So I hope Brother Benedetto's incarceration doesn't have more to do with the internecine war currently rocking the Church than it does with the Lutherans. If that were the case, there would be more need than ever for the intervention of important figures independent on both sides, lest any innocent people fell victim to a conflict that didn't really have anything to do with them.'

He gives a very faint nod. 'You're making your point very clearly. But I assure you that it isn't easy, particularly now that the Pope is ill and the gruesome wind of negotiations is blowing in from Rome. It isn't easy for someone seeking to be a man of peace to stay aloof from the conflict. At the moment, any gesture, even one of the simplest charity, would be interpreted as siding with one party or the other. For those who wish to prevent the punishment of the innocent, the only way forward lies in an appeal to charity and to the good sense of the men of the Church.'

I interrupt him. 'Humble gestures can sometimes be significant.'

He stares into the dying flames as though searching for something. He looks tired and resigned. 'I know the General of the Benedictines very well.' For a moment it looks as though he has nothing more to say. 'A letter to Monte Cassino is the kind of thing that I might still be able to get away with . . .'

'That would be something.'

'I think I'll be able to sleep now.'

A fairly explicit message. Time to say goodnight.

'Your Eminence, such magnanimity as you have shown is a rare thing these days. There aren't many holy men of the Church who would agree to talk to a stranger in the depths of night, let alone grant him his wishes. My name is . . .'

He raises a hand. 'No. Come tomorrow, the Bishop of Palestrina won't be able to afford to make the confidences he has made tonight. As far as I'm concerned, you will simply be the erudite insomniac who happened to keep me company.'

Viterbo, 25 June 1549

Farnese is dying. It might be tomorrow, equally it might be in three months' time. The negotiations are getting more frantic by the day, as the life slips from Paul III's exhausted body.

Things are not balanced in the *zelanti*'s favour. The Emperor is backing Reginald Pole and his fame is sky-high. The champion of the faith seems to be able to bring many different people together. If the Conclave were held tomorrow, the die would be cast. In that case, the plot that Carafa has woven over the past few years would unravel at a stroke. His great adversary on the Papal Throne, elected by his most vehement enemy: the Emperor. There isn't a day to lose. Carafa is inciting his French ally to make a move. He wants to tear up the picture as it stands, slow things down and start the game all over again.

The King of France, Henri II, following in his father's footsteps, has renewed his alliance with the Protestant princes. Carafa is spurring him on to fight again, but there is a lot of resistance: finances are always shaky, internal balances uneasy, people are becoming increasingly detached from Italian affairs. The head of the Holy Office will have to employ all his skill to overturn an outcome that would be fatal to him.

The atmosphere is one of score-settling. The winner will have no scruples about sweeping his adversary away. The calculation never stops: every vote cast could be crucial. Everything is being promised to everyone. The conflict is entirely driven by the privileges that are to be distributed and the time that remains.

Carafa will face his most crucial moment when the fortunes of the hated Emperor are at their zenith; you can almost touch his black moods and his icy determination. Here in Viterbo, on the other hand, people's faces are much more relaxed, people are confident that they will soon see the 'harvesting of an ancient seed', as they call the outcome that seems to be on the cards. The Englishman dispenses smiles and a few calm words, while euphoria grows within him.

Viterbo, 7 September 1549

Farnese is a long time dying. The *spirituali* are starting to stamp their heels, their smiles are looking forced: all this waiting is getting to them. They are afraid of events that might alter a balance that is currently in their favour. No longer hiding it, they fear Carafa's every move.

And they are right to do so. The old Theatine always has a secret weapon in waiting, the *extrema ratio* of a war that he cannot lose: *The Benefit of Christ Crucified*.

If the outlook remains unchanged, he will not hesitate to use it. He told me to stay alert, but he is still keeping his plans secret.

He could use the *Benefit* to attack Pole and the *spirituali* head on, accusing the Englishman of being the real author of a book excommunicated by the council. He could put the pressure on some of the smaller fry in the Viterbo circle, to make him confess. But he would have to do it now, which would mean exposing himself personally. It would be risky. Carafa doesn't like putting himself in the middle of enemy fire. If I know him, he'll choose another way: he'll circulate rumours, increasingly insistent, increasingly detailed, about the potential consequences of Reginald Pole's ascent to the Papal Throne. The Pope supporting doctrines excommunicated by the Council of Trent. Images of disintegration, dark omens of a paradoxical and irresolvable conflict, the dramatic weakening of the Church of Rome, its total dependence on the secular authority of the Emperor.

A gloomy picture designed to instil fear in many people and one which could cause decisive votes to be cast.

Only then will Carafa become involved, once the Conclave is under way, as the bringer of order and superior reason. Carafa the Conciliator.

It makes me laugh.

Rome, 10 November 1549

Paul III Farnese is dead. One of the most influential dynasties in Europe has come to an end.

A slow death, and now they are all holding their breath, as though frozen by a sense of something imminent. The question is no longer which family will be next to hold the reins of pontifical power. That no longer comes into it. What is at stake is the role of the Church and the conception of the power that it will have to exercise. We have reached the end of an era, and find ourselves in the midst of a very fierce confrontation between two factions, two opposing conceptions of Christianity.

One thing alone is certain. There's no turning back.

No longer will we see powerful families taking their turns on the throne, forming and breaking alliances. Instead, a whole constellation of forces, apparatuses and new entities that are emerging with great vigour, will have to be kept in balance. The Lutheran Church, Calvin and his followers, the Inquisition, the charitable orders, the Jesuits, with that man Ignatius who won't leave anyone in peace. And all that in order to face the changing fates of empires, kingdoms and principalities.

However different the aims of these most bitter adversaries may be, both Carafa and Pole know that the Church will have to be something different now from what it has been in the past. They are looking ahead, far away from the old models.

Rome, 29 November 1549

The cardinals have gone into the Conclave. In the alleyways of Rome the betting is on Pole. The favourite.

I have bet against him.

Following Carafa's instructions, I am going around the groups of priests, clerics, onlookers, gamblers and working men who crowd the city squares. I disorientate them with indiscretions concerning the true authors of *The Benefit of Christ Crucified*. I'm not alone.

The *spirituali* will try to resolve matters very soon, taking advantage of the fact that the French cardinals have been delayed. They have had a difficult journey, both by land and sea, passing through the territories of the Emperor, who is trying to obstruct their arrival.

They don't have the numbers to withstand the *spirituali*. Carafa is going to have to instil his proverbial terror into the hearts of those who are wavering.

Rome, 3 December 1549

Black smoke. Twenty-one votes for Pole. He would need twenty-eight to win the two-thirds majority that he needs.

It's always a mystery how information manages to get out of the Conclave, but a few times a day out it comes, always punctual and highly detailed.

Rome, 4 December 1549

Black smoke. Pole got twenty-four votes. The consensus is growing, but rumours are circulating that the French cardinals are about to arrive. If Carafa can defer Pole's election by one more day, the Englishman could be out of the game.

Rome, 5 December 1549

Rumours indicate that Carafa has delivered his accusation.

Not a head-on attack, that isn't his style. More of a warning, an invitation to reflect upon the risks that need to be avoided. He will certainly have suggested to those venerable ears what a paradox it would be, and what a huge problem, to have a Pope who had co-authored *The Benefit of Christ Crucified*, a book excommunicated by the council. He is sure to have summoned up, for the benefit of those old men, images of the terrible battles between bishops and popes that the Church knew in times past.

He has instilled doubt into those who have already returned that seraphic English smile.

The vote will be held this afternoon.

He has got a message through to me. A short one, just enough to suggest the tension that the old Theatine must be feeling. The *spirituali* have reached an agreement with three neutral cardinals: if Pole wins twenty-six votes, they will transfer their votes to him. If that happens, my instructions are to contact Dominican headquarters straight away.

If that happens it's all over.

The vote is in an hour.

I pass the time nervously.

Twenty-five votes. There was one missing, only one.

They stared at each other for a long time.

No other hand was raised.

Black smoke.

Rome, 6 December 1549

French cardinals in the Conclave. Pole can't win now.

We have been dangling from a thread, and it hasn't broken.

Rome, 14 January 1550

Exhausting. They've been shut in there for forty-eight days now. There is no agreement: a new name comes up every day and no one can believe it.

They're even betting on who won't get out of the Conclave alive. Very powerful old men wearing themselves out in sealed chambers amidst the stench of piss and excrement. I can imagine the tired voices, the enfeebled bodies, the fuddled brains. Ideal for Carafa.

Rome, 8 February 1550

White smoke.

Nuntio vobis magnum gaudium. Habemus papam. Sibi nomen imposuit Iulius III.

Seventy-three days to get halfway through this century and reach a compromise: Giovanni Maria Del Monte, Cardinal Bishop of Palestrina.

Julius III.

Chapter 32

We slip silently down the alleyway, without a backward glance. Stop and pretend to chat: no one is following us.

We carry on till we get to the house: three knocks, then another one.

'Who is it?'

'Pietro and Titian.'

The door opens, a round face with a curly black beard and pointed moustache. 'Come in, come in. We've been waiting for you.'

He leads us through a workshop cluttered with tools and workbenches. The floor is covered with shavings that crunch beneath our feet.

We climb a staircase to his apartment. There are four men waiting for us, recruited over the past year and rebaptised by Titian in person.

The carpenter shows us to some chairs that smell of freshly cut wood.

'Have you explained everything?'

'It's better if you do . . .'

I nod before he finishes his sentence.

I study them carefully: deferential faces.

'It's quite simple. Pietro and I are planning to call a council and bring all the brothers together. We've got to know one another and know how many we are.' A couple of them give a start. 'So far all I have done is baptise. Preach and baptise, never stopping for a moment. Over the past few months Pietro has travelled the length and breadth of the Great Duchy and the Marches. Now it's time to meet. And for you to do your part.'

One man has no scruples about interrupting me: 'When?'

Disapproving glances from the others, but I'm not bothered. 'In the autumn. I haven't decided where yet. Right now we're going to have to get moving to contact all communities between here and Abruzzo. Each community will have to send two representatives. The location that we choose for the council will be announced once they have reached Ferrara. It's better not to run pointless risks.

Ferrara, 21 March 1550, an hour earlier

'What do we need a council for?'

'We have to know how many there are of us. We've got to get organised.'

'It's dangerous, Titian, the Inquisition . . .'

'The Inquisition barely knows who I am. It knows nothing about you and it certainly doesn't suspect there are large numbers of us. Don't worry. Just go on using my name, it's the only one the brethren need to know.'

'But if one of them was captured, you'd be the first to go down.'

'I would. Just me, no one else. You know them: they're not interested in the proselytes, it's the heresiarch they're after.'

We laugh.

'May God preserve us, but a council would expose everyone to the risk of discovery.'

'It'll be clandestine. Listen to me carefully, Pietro, that's why I don't want more than two representatives per community. There won't be fewer than fifty of us, but there won't be more than a hundred.'

'Why don't we wait to see what the new Pope does? We don't know if he's going to side with the *zelanti* or the *spirituali* . . .'

'He isn't going to side with anyone.'

'What?'

'He isn't going to side with anyone, I've met him. He isn't going to go along with one group or the other, it's the most difficult path to take, because it means he has to keep everyone happy and the interests of some are the ruin of the others.'

'What . . . When did you meet the Pope?'

'Before he was elected. I spent a long time talking to him. He has the same opinion of the Inquisition as we do. He's against the methods of Carafa and his friends. He knows that if he gives them carte blanche we'll end up with a massacre of the innocents. He promised me he would personally intercede with the General of the Benedictines to get Fontanini out of prison.'

'What Fontanini? Benedetto of Mantua? The author of the *Benefit*?'

'He's out now. Isn't that a sign that we can breathe a bit easier? We'll have to hold our council as soon as possible, before the balance shifts again, perhaps even forcing the Pope's hand. I'm almost certain that Julius III is basically open to dialogue with the reformed faith, except that he can't say as much or state it explicitly, because he knows that his election was the result of a compromise. He has to behave accordingly. What is it you lot say? Run with the hare and hunt with the hounds.'

'If you think it's the right thing to do, I'm with you.'

Pietro Manelfi walks beside me down the Via delle Volte. I met him in Florence: he was a cleric from the Marche, an unruly subject of the Pope. His spiritual torments had begun years ago, leading him to abandon his seminary and slide ever faster down that thin line that separates mystical inspiration from heresy. I gave him the answers he was looking for and he attached himself to me like a dog to its master: Titian's first disciple. To put him to the test, I sent him to his own part of the world to recruit proselytes. Then he joined me here, full of hope. He prays too many times a day, but he has an exceptional memory, he remembers the home towns, names and professions of everyone who's been baptised, and he helps me to stay in contact with all the brothers. He tells everyone about me: outside Ferrara no one knows anyone else apart from the mysterious Titian. If they were to be arrested, they couldn't betray each other; just Titian, the hare, the target.

We pass underneath the arches that stretch over the street, a street that never sleeps: a great hubbub of tanners, blacksmiths and cobblers by day; breasts and thighs by night. We slip silently into the alleyway, without a backward glance. We stop and pretend to chat: no one is following us.

We carry on till we get to the house: three knocks, then another one.

'Who is it?'

'Pietro and Titian.'

Ferrara's fine. It's a city where everything moves at a particular pace, where everything fits together nicely. But it isn't like Venice. Venice is complicated, in Venice if you so much as move a pin you always run the risk of sticking it in a giant's arse.

Ferrara is small and clings to the edge of the river, but even so you can still get lost in the older alleyways. Ferrara is freer, lighter, less crowded, without so many cops and spies. In Venice there's always someone keeping an eye on you; not here, you walk without ever having to stop, pretend you've taken a wrong turning, see if there's someone in yet another absurd disguise walking behind you. A salutary habit, but pointless in Ferrara, you can rest easy here. Ercole II is wreathed in smiles about the new Pope, but at the same time he allows the most active and dangerous minds in Italy to find refuge here. He likes to have his palace filled with men of letters and he never allows the flame to go out on the tomb of the poet Ludovico Ariosto, whom the people here venerate like a saint. It really must be irksome for him to know that there's no one of that calibre in his court. Then there's Renée, the widow of Alfonso d'Este, who has no scruples about displaying her Calvinist sympathies. A considerable number of people have taken refuge behind the princess's skirts, to escape the police and the inquisitors.

As in Venice, no harm is done to the Jews, but here they chiefly practise usury, lending money at a lower rate of interest than their cousins in the lagoon, and they do excellent business. The money keeps on circulating, it never stops, and that's a sign of the city's good health. Justice is administered equably, without too many magistrates and policemen and courts taking months to decide the respective competences if someone dies during a brawl. They act swiftly here: if you attract too much attention they walk you to the border. If you kill someone they walk you to the executioner, an old drunk who lives on the northern walls and sings obscene ditties to himself as he works. If two people have a score to settle they make an appointment to meet in the duelling alley, a narrow little street closed on both sides by densely barred gates: two go in, only one comes out. It's all done without too much noise, without disturbing the city's peaceful activity.

My Anabaptist is right in his element here.

I've assembled half a dozen adepts, not all of them Ferrarese, who are willing to leave for other towns to spread the new faith and go around rebaptising. At the same time I'm taking care of the other part of myself, meeting Beatriz in her house, which I enter via a narrow passageway at the back.

The Miquez brothers have brought me messages sent by Chiú, landlord of the Gorgadello, the best cellar in the city, right beside the cathedral. It's said that Ariosto used to go and get drunk there and some of the regulars can even remember hearing him declaim the verses of his *Orlando Furioso* on more than one occasion. Chiucchiolino, or Chiú as he's known to everyone who's run up a tab with him, is an impressive creature: he has eyes on either side of his head, like a toad, pointing in different directions. His forehead is covered with a leonine mane of black curls, thick and coarse like a boar's bristles. He's an important man, an essential part of the city. If you have a problem you can talk to Chiú about it and he'll be able to recommend someone who will almost certainly be able to sort out your difficulties. Chiú is the bank of secrets. You can tell him everything and be sure that he won't open his mouth to anyone; he'll accumulate information in his safe and return it to you with interest in the form of advice, names and addresses for you to make use of as you will. My secrets are in that bank as well. The key: a few conventional signs. Wine: no news. Spirits: important information.

Spirits today. To the Miquez house at dusk.

Across town to my house. A little room where I can shed Titian's clothes for a bit and get a few hours' rest.

I light the fire in the little hearth and put the water on to heat up. Venice has got me accustomed to washing frequently, so much so that it's become a habit. An inconvenient and expensive habit for someone who's always on the move.

I stay naked and investigate what the accumulation of fifty years has done to my limbs. Ancient scars and the odd white hair on my chest. Fortunately, I've never given my muscles time to relax too much: the strength is still there, it's just more solid and leathery. But I have permanent rheumatism. It only ever lets up in the summer, when I stretch out in the sun like a lizard, drying out all the humidity of these low lands. I've also discovered that I can no longer bend my spine completely, or I get the most terrible pains, and where possible I avoid riding on horseback.

Strange how in old age you learn to appreciate simple actions, how you're more willing to waste time rocking yourself in a comfortable chair, in the shade of a tree, or rolling over in bed trying to think of a good reason to get up.

I meticulously dry every corner of my body, lie down on the bed and close my eyes. The minute I find myself shivering I take my clean clothes out of the trunk that is the only other piece of furniture in the room. My elegant Venetian clothes. A broad-brimmed hat to hide my face, my sharp stiletto to wear in my belt. The bells: it's almost time to go.

The black hair on her shoulders smells of rich perfumes. I become aware of that warm body, still pressed against mine, that I can wrap in an embrace of hands and legs and feet.

They could barely believe what I told them. My meeting with the future Pope, his intercession to free Fontanini.

I can't see her face, but I know it's awake and possibly smiling.

A paradox. Either the council was wrong to excommunicate *The Benefit of Christ Crucified* . . . or else the Pope's a heretic, João said.

I'd like to tell her something, something to describe the emotion that's clenching my stomach and almost making me cry.

Neither a *zelante* nor a *spirituale*, Julius III is performing a balancing act. In the end he'll come down on whichever side wins. The game is still open.

I'm too old to talk about love, something I've relegated to the dusty corners of life and which I've always managed to sacrifice, denying myself the intimacy of moments like this one. I've denied myself the chance of extending those moments over the years, allowing them to change my life.

How were we to get out of this stalemate, Duarte asked. What were we going to do with the *Benefit*, now that it was top of the list of forbidden books that has just been promulgated by the Venetian Inquisition?

It must be much the same for her. Our stories are basically similar. Stories we haven't told each other. Questions we haven't asked.

Keep at it, she said. Confident, surprising us once again. The Inquisition can't do a thing without the support of the local authorities. Venice can defend itself against interference from Rome. Keep at it. Keep on fomenting discontent against the Church.

Beatriz lies motionless and lets me listen to her breathing, as though we both had a natural sense of what mattered, as though we were both thinking the same things.

'Have you found him?'

'Who?' My voice sounds as though it's echoing from a cave.

'Your enemy.'

'Not yet. But I can feel that he's nearby.'

'How can you be sure?'

I smile ironically. 'It's the only thing that could give me the strength not to stay here with you until I die.'

Rome, *17 April 1550*

The new Pope has reformed the Congregation of the Holy Office: Carafa and De Cupis, *zelanti*, Pole and Morone, *spirituali*, Cervini and Sfondrato, *non-aligned*. He wants to keep everyone and no one happy. Julius III is a temporary armistice, a cover that the *zelanti* and *spirituali* will fight over to the death.

Carafa spends his days in close negotiations, as though the Conclave were still going on. He wrote to tell me that he caught lice 'among those old men, more dead than alive'. Seventy-four, older than the Pope, and he hardly ever sleeps.

I wish I had his energy. Instead, here I am, waiting for orders, not moving for weeks, strolling aimlessly among the hills of Rome, enjoying the mild climate of the season, like an old fool at the end of his days.

I have written once again to the inquisitors of half of Italy for information about Titian. Still nothing.

Rome, *30 April 1550*

Titian in Florence.

Pier Francesco Riccio, butler and secretary to Cosimo de' Medici.

Pietro Carnesecchi, an old acquaintance from Viterbo, already tried in 1547 and absolved by papal intercession.

Benedetto Varchi, lecturer at the Florentine Academy, a member of the circle of the *Infiammati* in Padua.

Cosimo Bartoli, magistrate at the Florentine Academy and a reader of *The Benefit of Christ Crucified*.

Anton Francesco Doni, man of letters, mounted courier operating between Florence and Venice.

Piero Vettori, friend of Marco Antonio Flaminio and correspondent of Cardinal Pole.

Jacopo da Pontormo, an excellent painter, and his pupil Bronzino.

Anton Francesco Grazzini, known as 'the Fish', a poet who fulminates against the Church.

Pietro Manelfi, cleric from the Marche.

Lorenzo Torrentino, printer.

Filippo Del Migliore and Bartolomeo Panciatichi, patricians.

The tight circle of Florentine crypto-Lutherans. Different career paths, all ending up in the same place under the protective wing of Duke Cosimo I de' Medici, a great patron and a bitter enemy of Farnese, always ready to revive the flames of anti-papal polemic for his own ends.

Titian has spent the whole of the past winter splashing around in that particular pond. It was there that he spent the days of the Conclave, among the most dogged supporters of Reginald Pole.

The inquisitors point out that his preferred company was the painter Pontormo and his pupil Bronzino.

Now in his sixties, Jacopo da Pontormo is spending day and night on what seems to be his greatest work, the fresco in the basilica of San Lorenzo, commissioned by Pier Francesco Riccio for Cosimo I. The work is shrouded in the greatest secrecy, even the boxes containing the preparatory sketches are sealed shut. Only Bronzino and a very few others are allowed a glimpse of what the master is doing.

Rumours, anonymous messages that have reached the Florentine Inquisition, the indiscreet eyes of certain friars: Pontormo is representing *The Benefit of Christ Crucified* in detail in the apse of the church where Cosimo de' Medici is to be buried.

After the end of the Conclave there is no more news of Titian in Florence.

Rome, 8 May 1550

Carafa was counting on the French. But according to the information that reaches us from France, Henri II cannot afford to resume the war against the Habsburgs where his father left off, because he would need finances that no one is prepared to give him.

Carafa says the Emperor is preparing to reach an agreement with the Lutheran theologians, and if he succeeds in this the *spirituali* might win.

Carafa wants to remove Pole from Rome. He wants him out of Italy.

Carafa says a war of succession is about to break out in England. Henry VIII is dead, leaving behind him a host of children fighting for the crown.

Carafa says we must prepare the ground for the reconquest of

England by the Catholic Church, and that we must ensure that the undertaking is entrusted to Pole.

Carafa says I must go to England to make contact with the supporters of Mary Tudor, a devotee of the Pope, who seeks to contest the crown against the claims of her younger brother.

Carafa speaks of a delicate and most important task that he can assign only to his most trusted servant. Carafa has never spoken to me like this.

Carafa serves hemlock in a silver chalice.

It was bound to happen sooner or later.

Carafa has taken me out of the larger game, the one I've been following from the start.

The star of Qoèlet is in decline.

In England. Dealing with four ignorant and badly dressed noblemen.

In England. Operation *Benefit* is no longer mine.

I'm not sure that I will go back. I may not even make it to London. I'll find myself on the wrong end of an assassin's knife somewhere along the road, unseen by anyone. My days are over. Thirty years of secrets are frightening to anyone preparing to begin a new chapter in the struggle for absolute power in Rome. There are ignorant young fanatics: there's Ghislieri, the Dominican. There are the Jesuits. There's no room left. Time to call it a day.

I'm tired. Tired and frightened. My luggage is ready and I look at it as if it weren't mine. A few rags inherited from a life that is drawing to a close, far from the eyes of the world. The thought has been with me for some time now, but I didn't think it would happen so quickly, or with this feeling of banality in my heart. This isn't the way to prepare for it.

I'd like to leave these pages to someone, the testimony of all that has happened. But to what end? For whom?

We plough our way through the twists and turns of history. We are shadows unmentioned in the chronicles. We don't exist.

I have been writing for myself. Only for myself. And it is to myself that I dedicate and leave this diary.

London, 23 June 1550

Days of rain and discussion. Stolid aristocratic Englishmen plotting in broad daylight, incapable of any kind of diplomacy. They are skilful practitioners of the sword, which they all carry in full view. That's it. Everything will be resolved by blood and the winner will be the one with the bigger army.

Three contenders, three sides. Unlikely balance.

Edward, a little boy with the crown on his head, who has chosen as his private tutor no less a man than Martin Bucer, the great Lutheran theologian. Mary, the daughter of Henry VIII's first marriage to Catherine of Aragon, and thus half Spanish, great devotee of the Pope. Then young Elizabeth, born of the blood of her mother Anne Boleyn, who seems to admire the schismatic path chosen by her father.

The families supporting Catholic Mary would love to see Reginald Pole returning to his homeland as a champion of Catholicism, and some of them are keeping the throne of Canterbury warm for him. For centuries these aristocrats have been busy eliminating one another, wiping each other out in clan wars more closely akin to the barbarian customs of the Celts than to the art of politics.

It's worse than exile here. I have no news from Italy.

That knife never came. Carafa has granted me more time. Perhaps he's deciding what to do with me. Or perhaps it's all part of the plan.

The resolution adopted by the Stoics has nothing to do with me. I have no disappointment to expiate. Nothing to lament.

It's raining here. It's always raining. An island without seasons, cramming all four into a single day.

I'll die somewhere else.

London, 18 August 1550

My task is completed. There is no stability in sight: I am coming back burdened with promises and the certain knowledge that the English nobles are entirely untrustworthy. Mary isn't just knocking on our door, I've seen Spanish advisers here as well. Charles V has a son to remarry, although he is ten years younger than Mary. If Carafa predicts that Pole is to return to his homeland, he will have to take into account the fact that this might mean a rapprochement between Spain and England, very much to the Emperor's advantage.

Lack of interest in these events has made it difficult to write the reports that I have been sending to Rome and now that I am preparing to leave, I am not in any great haste to return. What remains is my curiosity about a certain mystery and my sense that there is one last thing to be done.

I want to give myself time to retrace my footsteps. To understand what it is that is trying to force its way to the surface.

Chapter 33

'Men of letters, painters, poets, printers. And also palace secretaries, university lecturers, clerics. There is an underground world of dissent against the Church. A transverse world that touches key points, major figures in the courts, people who distribute ideas and advice to the princes. They are all unhappy about the growth in the power of the Inquisition and the intransigent cardinals. Every city now has circles in which a profound discontent has formed, along with an awareness that a choking noose is being tightened. The Waldensians of Naples, the Florentine crypto-Calvinists, Pole's friends in Padua, the pro-Reformation groups in Venice. And then there's Milan and Ferrara . . . Princes like Cosimo de' Medici and Ercole II d'Este see these figures and ferments as a bulwark to keep the Inquisition away from their borders, and have thus been obliged to inaugurate a phase of liberalism and tolerance. The old power of the noble dynasties could be useful in impeding the advance of the new inquisitorial power. For these rich families, Roman interference is like an intrusive eye focused on their dominions, a menacing and invasive presence. If they saw popular dissent mounting against ecclesiastical privileges and hierarchies, they might decide to stand up to the courts of the Holy Office.

'The task for us Baptists will be to vanquish the chronic indecisiveness of those literate circles, to goad them, force them to come out into the open before it's too late.

'But there is also a popular discontent that has spread through the countryside and everywhere else. An instinctive and almost innate aversion to the excessive power of the clergy, the result of the pitiful conditions in which the people are kept. Our task – and it is a difficult one – will be to bridge the gap between the spirit of plebeian evangelism and cultivated dissent and cultured dissent.

'This will not necessarily have to happen in broad daylight, but it will have to be accomplished with due care: we will have to dissemble our true intentions and our faith. Our council must provide a unity of intent for the immediate future to all the brethren scattered around the Italian peninsula. It will be held in Venice in October and it will be clandestine. I will not be there.'

'What? You're the only thread that links the whole community together! You're the central point of reference for everyone . . .'

'The document that I am giving you will speak for me. If it is true that I am your only spiritual authority, it's better that I stay in the shadows. It's better if they don't know Titian's face, just the power of his words.'

Manelfi lowers his eye deferentially and spreads the sheet of paper out on his desk. Jottings in a tiny hand. That will be Titian's spokesman at the Italian Baptists' council.

Antwerp, 3 September 1550

Lodewijck de Schaliedecker, alias Eloisius Pruystinck, alias Eloi.
  Roofer by trade.
  Suspected of the distribution of heretical books, of denying the substance of God, of denying sin, of insisting on the perfection of man and woman, of practising incest and concubinage.
  Burned at the stake as a heretic on 22 October 1544, along with many members of his sect, the so-called Loists.
  His name appears several times in the annals of the authorities in Antwerp, in association with those of David Joris, Johannes Denck and some notable and wealthy local merchants.
  As early as the 1530s, some of his followers and associates were arrested.
  Despite his humble origins, Pruystinck was an integral part of the machinery of anti-ecclesiastical activity in Antwerp, but was also hostile to the Lutherans.
  He was tried and given a lenient sentence in February 1526 after being denounced by Luther, who, after meeting him in Wittenberg, wrote to the authorities in Antwerp to tell them how dangerous he was. He escaped that mild punishment thanks to a complete retraction and the feeble sanctions then in force.
  In 1544 he was tortured to make him confess his practices and his blasphemous ideas.
  He never acknowledged any of his accomplices or followers, signing the death warrant with his own hand.
  The warrant was countersigned by Nicolas Buysscher, Dominican, who received his final depositions.

The German I am looking for is a dead man who fills an entire file in the archive of the Antwerp Inquisition.
  The dead man is now the titular owner of a luxury brothel in Venice.

The German I am looking for travelled through these parts during the years of the Anabaptist revolt.

Antwerp, 4 September 1550

Today Nicolas Buysscher is the right-hand man of the inquisitor of Antwerp.

Forty or so, tall, gaunt, the expression of someone who has held the fates of men in his hands.

He welcomed me very cordially. He remembered everything, holding nothing back. The details of an incredible experience.

The heresiarch of Antwerp was an astute and cultivated character, capable of weaving a complex web of connections both with the common people and with the important figures of the city. Even today, many people consider him a martyr and a hero. If you mention the name of Eloi down at the port, people still smile.

Eloi the roofer was a very special kind of heretic. He denied the notion of sin with a series of arguments that were difficult to refute. He seemed to want to build paradise on earth. He managed to persuade wealthy craftsmen and merchants to share their goods and property with the plebeians. A master in the art of trickery and persuasion. His followers in Antwerp lived together, in properties placed at their disposal by wealthier men. Over the course of the years dozens and dozens of men and women passed through the Loist community. Eloi welcomed them all, regardless of what misfortunes they might have fallen into. A very special kind of heretic, in contrast with the more extreme and bloody fringes of Anabaptism. Nonetheless, several of those survivors of Münster or Batenburg's gangs found refuge in his house. Expert dissembler as he was, he could have gone a lot further had he not trodden on the toes of the wrong people.

What the records had to keep silent. A complex fraud perpetrated upon the Fugger bankers, false letters of credit, hundreds of thousands of florins. An incredible thing: even the bankers had trouble explaining how it could have happened. And that isn't clear even today.

The spoils have never been recovered.

Eloi had partners in this enterprise. One of them was a German merchant by the name of Hans Grüeb, of whom there is no trace.

The Fuggers could not afford for this affair to become known, so they knocked on the door of the Inquisition. The order to take action against the Loists came directly from Rome.

They weren't all arrested. It is believed that many of them fled to England.

As regards former Münsterites, it is hard to say how many of them there were among the ranks of the Loists. One of them is known to have died some time ago, in prison. He was Balthasar Merck.

No other names are known. Not among those who were arrested.

The unknown German merchant who was Eloi's partner.
A colossal swindle of the Emperor's bankers.
Money never recovered.
A luxury brothel in Venice.
Strategy of dissimulation.
Former Münsterites.
The child and the statue.
Titian the Anabaptist.

This mystery is taking me back in time. Outside the walls of Münster.

Perhaps it's a hallucination, information retrieved at random. In pursuit of a corpse.

Who? It could be myself. The final chase, to defer the coming end. What does a man do when he knows he's dead? Old scores have to be settled. Starting with memories the mind had erased. Outside those walls.

In a muddy ditch, my whole life hanging on my filthy hands as they claw the earth. The arrogant whiskers of the mercenary holding his knife to my throat.

The smell of wet grass; lying like an insect in no man's land, between the city and the rest of the world. No turning back. Ahead of me, the unknown: an army of paid soldiers ready to shoot anyone who crosses those walls.

Mud slipping through my fingers: the great towers, the easiest points to enter. Your life isn't worth shit, he tells me, just imagine you're dead already.

I agitatedly describe every fortification, every passageway, the roster of the guards, how many sentries there are at each gate.

You can extend your life in the captain's tent, he says, laughing. He thumps me and drags me away.

Captain von Dhaun saved my life and gave me a chance.

His exact words: if you manage to climb up on to the walls tonight, and come back without being killed, you'll have shown that you merited my trust.

That was how the betrayal was accomplished, planned and jealously guarded since I reached the city of the mad, living side by side with them for over a year.

The last months of hunger and delirium are a black stain that the mind has erased. I never turned back throughout all that time. Fifteen years, to look for those people's words and faces. Perhaps because I wanted to hide from myself the fact that I too had vacillated, for a moment, down in that ditch, as though I too had become infected with madness, my mind distracted from the task at hand. Perhaps because, that day, I risked failing miserably, risked being run through by the bishop's mercenaries, who by some quirk of fate chose instead to bring me before their captain.

Over the days that followed, after the massacre, the Bishop of Waldeck, who had returned as absolute lord of Münster, his throne a pile of corpses, said that people such as myself, the heroic warriors of Christianity, would never be forgotten, commemorated in works and effigies.

He was lying, the bastard. Every trace of people like myself has vanished. The people who carried out the project, who were ready to be consigned to the dustbin, from which they would be picked up by noble lords to do their dirty work for them.

Then I asked My Lord, Christ's black standard-bearer, to take me away from those lands, from the horror that had lacerated my flesh and crushed my faith.

And now that is the place to which I must return, faithless now, to open up my scars again.

Scenes of poverty are always the same. Thin, ragged children. Bellies swollen with nothing, bare feet. Filthy little hands begging for alms. Women filling sacks of grain, up to their knees in the great vat that holds a season's harvest, babies tied behind their backs with scarves so as not to interrupt the work.

A few old people, bony, crippled, sightless eyes.

The road of dry mud outside the southern gate. The shacks leaning against the walls like a shapeless excrescence of the city, spreading slowly into the countryside. Not a man in sight. They're probably all in the fields, bundling the straw for beds for the coming winter and hay for their lordships' animals.

Only three men loading sacks on to a cart, bent-backed and sweating.

The district of shacks. Wood and stinking rushes, along with the mud and the mosquitoes.

I break up the bread and cheese that I have in my bag and distribute it among the children swarming around me. There are tiny ones that can barely walk, and bigger ones, busy firing their catapults at the sparrows raiding the grain. One of the quicker ones gives me his weapon.

I greet them all with a smile and a blessing. Slight nods of the head in reply.

The three men glance at me uncertainly. Massive great men, big heads.

Poverty is misshapen.

A whistle echoes from the walls.

All eyes on the gate. The three men hurry to cover the cart with a big piece of sackcloth.

Their agitation suddenly erupts, the men curse furiously.

Something's about to happen.

A troop of knights passes through the archway. I count about a dozen of them. Armour and lances at the ready. A standard with the bishop's ensigns.

They ride in amidst the protests of the women, they stop, they can't go any further, excited shouts.

One of the women who were filling the sacks, the most furious of the lot, stands up to the head of the troop.

They scream at each other in ungrammatical Latin mixed with the almost incomprehensible local dialect.

'. . . to receive a tenth of the grain . . .'

'. . . in the middle of the month . . .'

'. . . getting earlier and earlier . . .'

'. . . we're not going to do it any more . . .'

'. . . non-negotiable . . .'

'. . . His Lordship has decreed . . .'

The three men have stayed by the cart. Furtive looks. One of them climbs on board, the other two secure the canopy very tightly with ropes.

The tax collector notices them.

He points in their direction, muttering something.

The woman grips the horse's reins and tugs on them.

The bastard strikes her in the face with a riding crop.

I leap to my feet on a rickety bench. 'You son of a pox-ridden whore!'

The bastard turns round, I've already taken aim.

The stone gets him right in the face.

He collapses on his horse with his hands over his face while everyone around unleashes an infernal hubbub. The boys throw rocks in unison like a line of archers. The women creep under the horses, severing their hamstrings with little knives. The cart sets off at breakneck speed. The blood-covered fucker shouts, 'After it! After it!'

The horses rear up, fall to the ground, a hail of stones rains down on the cops. Sticks and work tools are raised in the air. Alerted by the shouting, the men run in from the fields.

The two men who were loading the cart gesture to me to follow them. They slip into a gap in the middle of the shacks. We make our way down ever narrower alleyways, with me bringing up the rear, hurl ourselves into a hut built of worm-eaten boards, come out the other side, on the banks of a stream, little more than a ditch.

A flat, narrow little boat: in we go, pushing like crazy, among curses that I can't understand.

Ahead of us waits the dense pine forest.

The Jüdefeldertor is the gate through which goods go in and out. The peasants go in with their harvest, the merchants go out with their manufactured goods. Carts loaded with fabrics announce that Münster's most lucrative activity has been revived with fresh vigour. There is no memory of Knipperdolling, the former head of the weavers' guild.

The streets are filled with men and women, playing out their daily life.

The convent of Überwasser is now a hospital. Perhaps some nuns are still here. There's certainly no sign of Tilbeck and Jüdefeldt, the two Lutheran burgomasters who barricaded themselves in there during the days of the Anabaptist revolt.

In the main square in the centre of the city, the cathedral and the Rathaus still stand facing one another. The cathedral has been completely restored, adorned with statues and spires that exalt the Roman Church. Outside the council building there are troops of guards, whose presence is apparent everywhere.

Then there's the market square. The stalls are arranged in a line along its edge, displaying their products. Voices are shouting prices, striking deals. St Lamberti.

Three cages hang from the bell tower. Empty.

No one looks at them.

Bockelson, Knipperdolling, Krechting.

I alone stood there with my nose in the air for I don't know how long, while everyone walked past me: some on their way to the market stalls, some going into the church.

No one looks at them.

The past hangs right over their heads. And if they try to lift their heads too far, the cages are there as a reminder.

Münster is a warning to the whole of Christendom: everything returns to the way it was, nothing remains of evil but the eternal symbol of the most terrible punishment.

Before they were displayed in the cages, the bodies of Bockelson, King David, Knipperdolling, Minister of Justice of the Kingdom of Zion, and Krechting, Counsellor to the King, the men were dismembered with red-hot pincers and then run through by the executioner.

The church walls no longer echo with the incendiary sermons of Bernhard Rothmann, the preacher of revolt. Those sermons that always began with the anecdote of the statue of Christ and the child.

No point asking what became of him, since his body was never found among the piles of corpses.

Old as he must be by now, I sometimes wish that he were this Titian who's making his way around Italy.

He should at least have recovered from the madness that I helped plunge him into. Long discussions in that nave, about the practices of the patriarchs in the Bible, about polygamy, about the finality of Mosaic law, feeding the fire of delirium. Bernhard Rothmann, the spiritual guide of the Münsterites, pastor to the insurgents, prime enemy of the Bishop of Waldeck. Then hurtling down, into the abyss of despair and Apocalypse from which there is no return. No. Not Rothmann. Whether he is alive or dead, he could never start all over again from the beginning.

If there had been one just man in the whole of that city, Sodom would have been saved.

But that one just man had left Münster. For that reason alone I was able to do what I did, living shoulder to shoulder with the court theologian, day after day, on that road to ruin. And even today I think I only hastened the pace of the inevitable.

The one just man had gone away.

He had escaped the nightmare and the killing.

From the steps of St Lamberti I looked down at the square. The stalls piled up as barricades, the torches, the weapons, the orders shouted from one end of the market to the other.

The hopes and illusions of the Anabaptists, who had risen up in this square; it was Rothmann, Matthys and Bockelson who betrayed them.

Not me. I only betrayed the one just man.

It was to this square that I had to return, to settle my scores with the man I was. Not the lecture theatres of Wittenberg, or the palaces of Viterbo. Thomas Müntzer, Reginald Pole: naivety, like the madness of the prophets, betrays itself. Not the sense of possibility of those days, those actions, not the determination of the one who instilled their beliefs.

He should be the one settling the score, not Carafa's knife. But he should still be alive, having escaped fifteen years of defeat, having survived the Dutch rebellions. He should have been received into the Loist community in Antwerp, he should have escaped the revenge of the Fuggers, taking with him the fruits of his fraud, he should have arrived in Venice, the land of fugitives, becoming the manager of a luxury brothel and, at the same time, bearing the name of Titian, he should have travelled around Italy spreading Anabaptism.

Yes. And the Turk should convert.

I can now return to Rome, to meet the fate that awaits aged and exhausted servants. The banal epilogue to a life played out amidst events too great to take into account the uneasy emotions of a spy in his sunset years. In the face of all this, and in the face of those cages up there, I can say that I have never lived, I have never taken risks, except in the days of the wicked and perfect betrayal of the greatest enterprise that the courage and madness of men could come up with. The lucid reason of a spy and a lieutenant's passionate fidelity to the captain he had admired from the very first day: these days overflow with memories, the only real memories, as charged with discordant sensations as life itself, memories that I have kept at arm's length as I fearfully put those grandiose plans into action. I should have killed you then. Only that way could I have expressed my supreme respect for your deeds. Only that way would I have been able to help myself, fifteen years on, almost at the end, from wanting to see once again the fire in your eyes, feel the cold blade of your sword, Captain Gert from the Well.

Chapter 35

No moon. I can barely make out the darker outlines of the trees and the murmur of the waves on the beach.

Malcantòn, on the other hand, studies the darkness as though he can tell exactly what things are and how far away they are. Hard to tell his age, a grim sailor's face, with a permanently worried expression. Hands like spades and a scar stretching from his ear to his shoulder. Someone must have tried unsuccessfully to chop his head off. Someone must have regretted that. Malcantòn, the bad zone, the North-West, where the sudden storms come from, hail that ruins the harvest, hurricanes that capsize the ships. Anyone interested in finding out his real name can go and read it in the square in Ravenna, where it is nailed up in full view, along with the price on his head.

The others have prices on theirs, too. Mèlga and Guacín, the Rasi brothers, wanted for more than a year for the murder of a customs officer.

Tambocc, not more than twenty, with an angelic face, black curls and limitless strength. An accomplished fraudster, a trade that he inherited from his father along with a hatred of priests and the authorities. He is squatting by a tree trunk, staring into the night behind us. Noises emerge from the pine forest, rustling sounds and the beating of wings, which he recognises one by one.

This strip of land and sea is a geographical intersection, contended over by Venice, Ferrara and the Pope, and at the same time a no man's land, a labyrinth of customs, duties, taxes that all the lords attempt to impose upon all kinds of goods in transit, all kinds of agricultural products. With the result that the poor are even more oppressed here than they are elsewhere, and traffic and trade are brought almost to a standstill.

That's where the smugglers come in.

They know every inch of the flat coastline from the Po Delta to beyond Rimini. Makeshift landing places, disused jetties, abandoned canals from Roman times, providing access to the hinterland, a vast, marshy bog that extends for many miles beneath an unchanging roof of maritime pines. A maze of water and mosquitoes where only those outlaws can find their bearings, scattered with unlikely landmarks, traps, cleverly disguised stores.

It's in the interest of the Dalmatian merchants, and the Venetians as well, to negotiate with the smugglers of Romagna – there's none of that endless waiting around in the ports, no tolls or taxes, no rake-offs for the local highwaymen. Much of the traffic comes along this coast, along a line of invisible points in the open sea, where the merchant ships meet up with the smugglers, disguised as fishermen. It isn't easy work, nothing on the sea is certain: they can end up waiting for hours, days, depending on the weather. When they finally meet up, goods are transferred, bills are paid. Or else the merchants are guided towards secret landing places by agile little launches, and the cargo is unloaded on to the beach, the price is agreed and the deal is completed.

Ambushes happen frequently. The smugglers risk their lives and face very serious punishment if caught.

But it's only thanks to this invisible commercial network that the people here don't die of starvation. To choose the life of a smuggler you have to have come from the most terrible poverty, you have to have the instinctive and well-motivated hatred that everyone here feels for all figures of authority; they are almost always men wanted for some crime or other, forced to hide in the dense pine forest to escape the police.

There are no women, no old people or peasants in any of the villages around here who wouldn't protect them, if only by remaining stubbornly silent. Because a proportion of the goods in circulation is regularly distributed among the people. That's the only duty paid.

Before the bishop unleashes his tax collectors to call in their tithes, a share of the harvest is hidden by the smugglers in various places in the forest, to reduce the burden and to guarantee the survival of the communities during the winter.

That was what was happening a month ago when the troop of the tax collectors turned up, as they do earlier each year.

Malcantòn, Guacín and Mèlga were the men who carried the grain to the hidden stores in the marshes.

All it takes to win the lasting esteem of these people is a catapult and a good aim. All it takes is a bit of fire in your blood.

Moonless night. We're waiting to see the sign of the torches. I wrap myself up in my coat, damp and chilled to the bone, while Malcantòn keeps his eyes fixed on the sea.

Mèlga, the swindler, is ready with the boat, oars in the rowlocks. His brother holds the lantern, ready to light it in reply.

Tambocc keeps listening out for noises in the pine forest.

For them, this night means the start of a new trade, one that they're both surprised and curious about.

They'd never have believed it. They laughed. They asked lots of questions. Forbidden? Why on earth? Nobody understands them anyway.

No. They'd never have dreamt that there was money in smuggling books.

Rome, 1 November 1550

There's one last job to be done. Carafa reserved it for me. As delicate and as important as the others. Perhaps even more. So important that it can't be accomplished by anyone but the most trusted, the most meritorious of his soldiers. He knows he has put me to the test several times, that he's always demanded the very best of me. After this final mission I will be able to enjoy a well-earned rest, as long, of course, as I want one.

I accepted enthusiastically. This time the old man wasn't able to read my mind.

Fucking over the Jews, those hateful parasites, unrepentant Christ killers, who have often converted to the true faith for the sake of convenience, with the sole aim of going on getting money out of their sordid deals, he said. A disease that infects the whole body of Christianity from within. A disease that must now be eradicated. And we must begin where its roots are deepest.

Venice.

He said my reports had once again suggested to him to understand that I was the man best suited to this particular task. Indeed, the very importance of the matter became clear to him when he read how much wealth those wicked families of usurers had been able to accumulate. For some time he had been studying the ideal solution to the problem, and now the time is ripe, everything is in place, the agreements have been drawn up.

The enforcement of the Index of prohibited books in the territory of La Serenissima is seen as a clear signal that the Venetian authorities have finally understood the need for a compromise, choking back the vanity and arrogance that have always been their distinguishing features. And the reason is clear: the patrician families of Venice are up to their necks in debt, their fortunes depend entirely on the purses of the Jewish bankers, the Marrani. A debt so great that it could be extinguished only with the extinction of the creditors. The exchange is one of mutual satisfaction: for Carafa it is a demonstration of the strength of the Holy Office in the city most hostile to Roman interference, a prelude to the iron fist that the power of the Inquisition is about to wield in every Catholic territory; while the Venetians will have their finances restored as a result of the confiscation of the property of the wealthy Jews.

The mechanism is already under way. The Inquisition and the Venetian courts have begun putting marginal members of the Sephardic community on trial, on charges of crypto-Judaism. But it's the big fish they're really after.

And to get them they need someone like me. Someone with thirty years of spiritual warfare behind him, and capable of creating a diffuse hostility against the Jews in the city, identifying them as the source of all ills, preparing the ground for an offensive that will put the entire community under attack.

I accepted enthusiastically.

I concealed my surprise at seeing my time extended.

I showed the mask of the zealot, which does not belong to me any more.

The last job before my well-earned rest.

One last vile deed.

Reserved for the one who has always been privy to Carafa's secrets.

I thought I'd reached the end. I've been given a reprieve. For how long? And why?

The robust and ravenous Dominicans who crowd these corridors would not be able to conduct intrigues of this kind. They're too fanatical. They're too full of the role entrusted to them, they're incapable of subtle strategies, however effective they might be in their blind persecution of the prey that has been pointed out to them. All in broad daylight. Carafa is preparing them for the most important offensive of the spiritual war. The day of reckoning, after ten years of accurate planning. The construction to which I have contributed, brick by brick, will be completed by others, and very soon. The coming council, strongly desired by the Emperor, seems to be the moment when Carafa will reveal his cards, unleashing his frontal attack against the *spirituali*. The tension on the faces and in the voices of the young followers led by Michele Ghislieri, a hawk flying high in the old man's consideration, tells me that all hesitation is about to come to an end.

I will not be involved in that part of the game because I know all the moves leading up to it: Carafa is very well aware that two people can keep a secret only if one of them is dead.

In the meantime he is entrusting me with the last dirty crusade, one for which I no longer have the stomach: inventing the new enemy and guiding it towards the Christian army. Anyone who goes into this battle is guaranteed an ample recompense: the wealth of his victims and a place in heaven. The Venetians are the first, others will inevitably follow.

My task, as ever, is to prepare the ground for the first slaughter. Then all I will have to do is keep my secret. Under six feet of earth.

I accepted enthusiastically. Venice. There's still time to solve the mystery. This time I won't be the tireless and efficient servant that Carafa has known in the past. The mystery, and its imminent solution, will occupy all the time remaining to me.

Chapter 36

'Dalmatia was a great success, pals!' Perna skims a stone across the surface of the water. 'The people eat pretty badly, you know? But they're choosy about what they read. If we keep on like this we're going to be famous as the distributors of the best-selling book after the Bible.'

A chilly wind that smells of night, sea and resin. On the beach, with Pietro Perna and João Miquez, a meeting to exchange information and plan our immediate future. A meeting of pirates, like the one many seasons ago on the shores of Holland. My hand sinks slowly into the cold sand, the sun does the same beyond the pine forest.

We go into the fishermen's shack. Inside, the fire is already going. The nets hang drying from the ceiling.

I try to catch João's eye. 'Any word of Demetra?'

He turns with a nod. 'That woman's making you a rich man. The last time I passed by the Caratello there wasn't a free table. As far as I can see she's fine, I don't know of anyone giving her any trouble.'

'And what about here in Romagna?' Perna shakes me by an arm. 'I hope you haven't missed out on the chance of a drop of that extraordinary Sangiovese Sangue di Bue. They say it's an absolute dream, *capito*?'

I take the bottle out of my pocket and uncork it under his nose. 'Be my guest.'

Perna takes a series of thirsty gulps. 'I had to come and unearth you down here so that you'd offer me some more of your splendid wine. What else is there to delight the palate in the middle of these marshlands?'

'The people of these parts hate the clergy from the depths of their guts. I've met a great variety of people, baptised peasants and fishermen, merchants and drunkards: all of them stubborn in the same way, all of them with fire where their blood should be. I don't think it should be difficult to stir up people's minds around here.'

João: 'What about the *Benefit*?'

'The cargoes have been turning up regularly. I've been selling them well. I work through the smugglers around here. A pretty rough crowd, grim-looking, speaking a dialect that I can still barely understand, but they're shrewd and close to the people. Not one of them can read or write, but they immediately understood how useful this business could be.'

João whistles through a seashell and then shakes his head. 'It's better that way. I think it's best if you stay on your travels for a bit longer.'

I look at him, hoping for an explanation.

'The authorities have caught wind of the Anabaptist council. There haven't been any arrests as yet, but they're all on the qui vive. Venice is crawling with cops, spies, informers, you can't trust anyone . . . Since the promulgation of the Index, they're keeping a particularly close eye on the printers and books aren't circulating as easily as they were before. And there's something else that's new: some converted Jews, friends of ours, people we know well, have been arrested on charges of crypto-Judaism. The first trials are being announced, they're all pretty marginal for the time being, they're not high profile, but these are things I've seen before. The first cloud that heralds the storm, the indelible mark of the Inquisition, as in Spain, as in Portugal.'

Perna: 'You know that mate of yours? You know, the Pope? Big bloke, dodgy line in reading matter? Well, it doesn't seem to me that he wants to keep the slavering hounds of the Holy Office under control. All hell's about to break loose around here and we could have our cocks on the block if we're not careful.'

Miquez: 'I'm using all the diplomacy at my command to sound out the mood of the merchants who do business with us. I'm trying to hint that there are concrete concerns for what might happen to them if we were incriminated. I don't think it's enough. Diplomacy and corruption are indispensable weapons at the moment, but they still aren't enough. It's better to be prepared for all eventualities. However, the way the wind's blowing it's better if you stay a long way away from Venice for the time being.'

'Fine, but not for much longer. I'm slowly getting fed up to the back teeth acting the prophet at my age. Titian's sown enough seeds for now. The Anabaptist council has affirmed the union of the community in its dissent from the Church. Circles frequented by prominent figures in every state in Italy are putting pressure on the authorities. One great painter whom I've been lucky enough to get to know, Jacopo da Pontormo, is painting a fresco of *The Benefit of Christ Crucified* in the chapel where Cosimo de' Medici is going to be buried. A wonderful work, I've seen the sketches and part of the finished painting, which he's carrying out in secret. All the communities are active: the first stone has been cast and we're about to see the consequences. Meanwhile you must keep me informed about what's happening in Venice. The details are important, too.'

We sit there in silence. The wash of the tide lulls our sleepy thoughts, our heads are heavy. Our elongated shadows slide along the walls to the ceiling.

Perna jerks up his head, as though woken by a sudden sound, his eyes small and red with fatigue: 'Could I have another drop of that nectar of yours?'

Q's diary

In Venice I'm one among many. A spy in the land of spies. There are many of them observing, taking notes and then referring back to whichever boss they happen to be working for, and they're often in the service of several bosses at once. Turks, Austrians, Englishmen: there is no power, party or commercial enterprise that doesn't have an interest in keeping its eyes and ears in every corner of this city. Everyone's spying on everyone else, in a baffling system of double, triple, quadruple games. Within this maze of conflicting strategies and conspiracies I should be able to bring out the common interests required to capture the Jews.

How?

Meanwhile I am keeping my mind alert with the intrigues designed to lubricate the pact between Carafa and the Venetians.

On the 21st of this month the Council of Ten banished the Barnabite Fathers and the Angelic Sisters from Venice, on charges of passing on restricted information, gathered in the confessional, to the governor of Milan, Ferrante Gonzaga, a vassal of the Emperor. In this way Carafa managed to shake off a competitor, and at the same time close the eyes and ears of Charles V in Venice. The old Theatine's cunning is breathtaking. Not only does he manage to clear the field of his enemies in preparation for major manoeuvres, but he allows the Venetians to confirm their reputation as upright custodians of their own affairs, unique in their unwillingness to tolerate interference from anyone, not even from Rome. The old man pretends to be sorry as he tightens the vice.

I've been in Venice for a few months. I don't frequent many places myself, but I have many eyes in my pay, observing the things that interest me. The brothel of the dead heresiarch of Antwerp above all.

Not so much as a shadow of him: he's more of a ghost than anyone. I must be patient. Collect additional information about Titian. And meanwhile pursue the task assigned to me.

Venice, 9 March 1551

My eyes in the offices of the Magistracy devoted to foreigners mention a strange influx of people to the city in October last year. Shady characters, minor artisans, businessmen, clerics, men of letters, including some from a long way away. About a hundred whose presence is hard to explain in relation to the affairs of Venice. None of them stayed more than a week. A black mark in the archives of the local authorities.

The names tell us nothing. Apart from one. Pietro Manelfi, the son of Ippolito Manelfi, a cleric from Ancona.

The same name that appeared among the acolytes of the crypto-Protestant circle in Florence.

The same circle frequented by Titian between 1549 and 1550.

A clue.

Report this name to the inquisitors of the neighbouring territories: Milan, Ferrara, Bologna.

Venice, 16 March 1551

A missive has arrived from the Father Inquisitor of Romagna.

Some artisans in Ravenna have been interrogated about the practice of adult baptism. They state that they have heard of a certain Titian who was devoted to this no more than a month ago, in the low lands around the city. They also say that this Titian spoke out against the authority of the clergy and ecclesiastical property. They say he won the sympathy of the ordinary people thereabouts, who always welcome any opportunity for imposture and turmoil.

Venice, 18 March 1551

Report from the inquisitor of Ferrara.

He confirms that the name of Titian the Baptist is known in certain circles in this city.

Venice, 21 March 1551

The whole night was spent reflecting on the strategy to be adopted towards the Jews. There may be a way.

Write to Carafa.

To the most illustrious and honourable lord Giovanni Pietro Carafa.

My Most Respected Lord,

The three months of my stay in this vast, bizarre city have been enough to suggest to me what I believe is the only practicable strategy against the Jews. I am therefore hurrying to give Your Lordship an account of it, so that you can express your most wise opinion upon it and grant me the privilege of once again serving our common goals.

The balances of power in Venice are as intricate and complex as its streets and waterways. There is no information or event, secret or not, that will not somehow reach the eyes or ears of a spy, an outside observer or a mercenary in the pay of some powerful man in the course of his movements about the city. I myself, in order to get hold of underground information, have had to adopt much the same method. The business constantly being carried out in broad daylight is matched by an equal, or perhaps even greater, volume of schemes, illicit trafficking and shady agreements affecting every area of life in La Serenissima. The Sultan has his spies in the Rialto, as do the English King and the Emperor Charles. Gonzaga had his own informers among the very ranks of the Venetian clergy, as Your Lordship is well aware. The big merchants do their manoeuvring in the shadows, to prevent information about commercial agreements from trickling out and avoid seeing their best financial opportunities going up in smoke. No one, be they princes or merchants, could survive in Venice if they did not have at their disposal a network of skilful spies, capable of reporting quickly on the power games both within and without St Mark's Republic.

The Jews do not play a secondary role in these relations, indeed, the fact that they only half belong to Venice, their role as bankers and financiers and their double religion, all make them one of the cornerstones of the commercial and political life of the city. This position makes them appear impregnable, while at the same time showing us their weak point.

Many Jewish families have converted to the Christian faith in order to remove all possible obstacles to their affairs and to defend themselves against attacks of any kind. This dissimulation could be thrown back in their faces and could itself become a source of widespread loathing towards them. To this we might add the fact that in many cases the Turk himself is able to call upon the skills and advice of the Jewish financiers in order to represent his own interests in Venice. One very fine example of this is the Mendesi family, already responsible for the diffusion of *The Benefit of Christ Crucified*, who are in commercial and diplomatic relations with the Sultan. If one could trace the network of Turkish spies active in the territories of La Serenissima back to the great Jewish families, it would not be difficult to expose them to the authorities as being responsible for a conspiracy that threatens the interests of Venice.

Because the Jews are great experts at persuading people that their ruin would mean the ruin of all, it is vitally important that everyone should understand the advantages of such a vast operation against them. If we were to attribute all intrigues to the Jews, everyone else could conduct intrigues of their own to their heart's content. No one could fail to see the usefulness of such a ruse.

The charge of false conversion would allow the Venetians to confiscate the wealth of the Jews, fattening the coffers of the state; the charge of conspiring with the Sultan would rule out possible intervention in their favour on the part of the Christian powers.

I confidently await Your Lordship's advice, imploring your continued benevolence.

Your Lordship's faithful servant

Q   Venice, the 22nd day of March 1551

Q's diary.

Venice, 2 April 1551

The operation's under way.

Michele Ghislieri is in Bergamo. The local bishop, Soranzo, is charged with agreeing to the diffusion of *The Benefit of Christ Crucified* in his own diocese. A copy of the excommunicated book has been found in his private library.

Ghislieri will torture him until he falls.

Venice, 21 April 1551

The Bishop of Como has also come under investigation. The *Benefit* has met with no obstacles in that diocese, either.

The *spirituali* are aghast. They weren't expecting a direct attack.

Ghislieri, the Dominican, is roused.

As one might expect, Carafa has waited for the resumption of the council in Trent before launching his final offensive.

Venice, 16 May 1551

The Bishops of Aquileia and Otranto are falling as well.

The charge is the same.

One by one: Carafa's strategy is proceeding unhindered. There is a double advantage: cleansing the Church of its internal enemies and at the same time blocking the plans of the Emperor, who was calling all the tunes around the time of the resumption of the council.

Venice, 25 June 1551

The biggest rock of all, Morone, the Bishop of Modena, a member of the Congregation of the Holy Office and trusted adviser to Reginald Pole, an impregnable figure until a few months ago, has crumbled beneath the blows of Ghislieri the Dominican, the new hammer of Christendom.

All those people currently under investigation will have to defend themselves from now on. And the rest will be quaking in their shoes.

When heads such as these start falling it is a warning that no one is safe. No one touched by the poison of *The Benefit of Christ Crucified* escapes unscathed.

The ripe fruits of my work are dropping one by one. I should be dead already, taking to the grave the secrets of an operation conceived ten years ago.

An act of rashness, or perhaps an excess of confidence or even the burning desire to annihilate the enemy. I still have a little time, enough to impale the crucifix in the heart of the Jews.

Venice, 10 July 1551

New letter from the inquisitor of Romagna. The presence of a German by the name of Titian was reported in the town of Bagnacavallo, between Imola and Ravenna.

Venice, 29 July 1551

In the city everyone is talking about the investigation of the *spirituale* cardinals. The report is unambiguous: with the Bishop of Bergamo, Soranzo, facing charges, Rome has planted its flag within the borders of La Serenissima and it has been brought there by Ghislieri, one of Carafa's men, via the Venetian inquisitor.

Meanwhile my anonymous letters to the local Inquisition have borne their first fruits: the Jews are already being treated with some diffidence; there is talk of the persistence of certain old religious practices on the part of the Marrani, and of the shady interests of the biggest Jewish families. The merchant community of Venice lends no credibility to these rumours: its affairs are too closely tied up with the Jewish bankers. The trials under way are feeding a hostility that looks as though it might spread. But we need a spark to make the flames flare up.

I have my eye on certain louche Levantines who might be useful in the current circumstances. If properly instructed, a Turk confessing to the Venetian authorities that he was a spy of the Sultan, in the pay of a powerful Jewish family, would provoke the reaction we are waiting for.

Venice, 8 August 1551

The inquisitor of Ferrara writes to report the presence of Pietro Manelfi in the cities of the Este.

Venice, 21 August 1551

Carafa has appeared in person. Speaking to the council, he has accused the *spirituali* of negligence, of never having done anything to prevent the diffusion of *The Benefit of Christ Crucified*. He maintains that Pole and his friends had no wish to admit the heretical scope of Fontanini's book because of their shady desire for reconciliation with the Lutherans. He is accusing them of allowing themselves to be taken in by Protestant ideas. The charge is a very serious one.

Never before had the old Theatine gone into battle in person. If the *spirituali* cannot react in time, they are destined for defeat.

Via della Gattamarcia: Rotten Cat Street. People's names don't tell you anything, place names always do.

Stench of carrion and corruption. Dried-out corpses of cats, crushed tufts of feathers that must once have been chickens, before the rats gnawed their bones. Shit all over the place, it's almost impossible not to step in it. No one comes along here except for furtive and shady encounters, the real paths are within the buildings, whole covered districts, tunnels, passageways, in a complex system of dwellings, offices, shops. This narrow street is an open-air drain for excrement and rubbish.

Pietro Manelfi is agitated, pedantic, frightened. '. . . and I've often had a sense of being followed, spied upon. But above all, as I told you, there are all these questions going around, my name's being mentioned in pubs, people I've never seen before are asking questions. And then there are all the things you hear people saying; even outside the city they're starting to breathe down the necks of the brethren, in Romagna, in the Marches. You hear so many things, there's the Index of books and all that palaver about *The Benefit of Christ Crucified*. Things weren't supposed to turn out like this. You said this Pope would be more moderate and instead, it seems no one's safe any more, not even the cardinals, let alone us. There are too many people going around asking questions, they're on to us, they're up to something. Even here. Did you hear about what happened to Giorgio Siculo? The Duke didn't think twice about burning him. In Venice, at the council, they were talking about "Nicodemism", about concealing our true faith, but when they get their hands on you what do you do? They start torturing you, they use red-hot pincers, if you're lucky they throw you in jail for the rest of your life.'

'Pietro, that's enough! I understand your anxiety about being hunted down, but the foul stench of this shit-hole where you've arranged to meet me is fogging your mind up. Did you think the clergy in Rome would become our ally? Or that the princes might be persuaded to put in a word for us? If they did, why would we have anything to hide? Don't you understand that they're trying to put the frighteners on us? This is their strategy: put everyone under suspicion so that the ones with reason to be frightened will make a false move and reveal themselves.'

He stinks too, of sweat and fear. 'But what if they get me? I don't want to end up like Siculo!'

'Talk about me, just about me, and deny everything. Say I was the one who stuffed you full of false beliefs; say that you were weak and I was skilled at presenting a pack of lies as the true doctrine.'

He agitatedly wrings his hands. 'And what if they get you?'

I press him up against the wall, feet off the ground, my face against his. 'Listen to me, Pietro, leave Ferrara. Go back to the Marche. Shut yourself up in a monastery, head off to the top of a mountain, anywhere you feel that you're safe and you can let your fear pass away. I don't like cowards who freeze with terror every time someone asks a question.' I let him slip back down the wall, stiff as a rake. 'Fear can be an ally if it helps you become more cautious and more astute. If you're shitting yourself, the enemy will be able to find you just by following the smell.'

I leave, to get away from that appalling stench.

Chapter 38

Chiú poured spirits. A joke and a quick goodbye, off to the Miquez residence.

Beatriz is standing by a big birdcage. A minah bird is pecking at an apple in her hand.

Every time I see her I understand why I don't much feel like running after people like Manelfi. I stand and watch her, waiting for her to notice I'm there.

'Ludovico! Are you trying to scare me, looking such a fright?'

'Forgive me, I didn't have time to make myself more presentable.'

'I have a message from João for you here.'

'João-João.'

I turn round with a start and look at the cage, and Beatriz bursts out laughing. 'It's amazing how well they can imitate people's voices.'

She hands me the sealed letter.

It seems puzzling at first glance: a sequence of words singing the praises of the rural life.

'Try it with this.' Beatriz hands me a thin sheet of iron riddled with little holes, the same size as the page. 'It's our family code. We've been using it for years to protect ourselves against prying eyes. Put the grid over the page.'

The spaces cut into the sheet isolate individual words, fragments of sentences, syllables, which suddenly start making sense.

A new . . dog . from the Roman countryside . German . hunter . of weeds . Studying . reading . advising . Always inside . the menagerie . never showing . his face . helping the shepherds to count their sheep . to . separate . the grain from the chaff . He helps his boss . without . donning his garb . Do not attempt . to return . to the lagoon . They are seeking . the painter . News . will come.

One of Carafa's men is helping the Venetian inquisitor. A German. A layman.

Looking for Titian.

Qoèlet.

We're there.

What I have to do.

Qoèlet

Dead of night. The Giudecca is a long strip of houses and trees outlined against the sky. The boat glides gently up to the jetty behind Ca' Barbaro. I beckon to the oarsman to stop and tie the hawser to the post.

I pay in a hurry, as long as it takes to count the money, and push the boat towards the open water, nearly toppling in.

My footsteps drum on the planks. The door.

I knock.

Nothing.

Louder.

The sound of a window opening above my head. 'Who goes there?'

'It's Ludovico. I've come back.'

All of a sudden the door flies open, a suffused light falls on the barrel of a gun.

'Duarte, it's me!'

He rubs his sleepy eyes. 'Bloody hell! Are you mad? What are you doing here?'

'I've got to speak to João.'

I walk into the garden of the house. Noise from the stairs. 'Who is it?'

'It's Ludovico!'

A curse in Portuguese.

He's wearing an embroidered lace shirt, his hair loose on his shoulders. 'Why did you come back? I wrote to you . . .'

'I know what you wrote. But there's no time. We've got to talk.'

João presses an eye with his thumb and his middle finger. 'Damn it but you're a madman. Come in.'

He walks me over to the desk. 'The Inquisition is investigating the council being held by your Anabaptist friends. The name Titian has been mentioned more than once. Coming here was a stupid move on your part.'

He stirs the embers in the hearth. Then he sits down, still rubbing away at his eyes to wake himself up.

He looks at me with the air of someone who's waiting for an explanation.

'How long have you known about the German?'

He stifles a yawn. 'A few weeks. You never catch sight of him, he's unapproachable.'

'When did he get to Venice?'

'I don't know. Six months ago, maybe more.'

I hiss a curse between my teeth. 'I'd say it was round about the time that the Jews started being arrested.'

João's expression turns serious. 'They say he's a special consultant to the inquisitor and that he spends his whole time reading the books published in Venice in search of the tiniest sign of heresy.'

'Forget the rumours. There's something worse than that.'

'What do you mean?'

'Doesn't it strike you as strange that Rome should send one of its men to Venice and all of a sudden start arresting Jews?'

He leaps to his feet, suddenly wide awake, takes a few nervous steps, staring at the floor. 'Do you think they've made up their minds to get us all?'

'Obviously. And if it's the German I think it is, he's one of Carafa's men. The best man he's got.'

He runs a hand over his beard and exhales noisily. 'If that's how things are, we've got to know for certain. But for some time now it's been becoming increasingly difficult to get hold of information. They're turning the place into a desert all around us. And as though that weren't enough, they're keeping their eyes on us all the time. Even the Caratello is under surveillance. I've had to put spies on to their spies.' He stops, avoiding my eye.

I press him: 'Tell me everything.'

'We found out it was a Turk, a threepenny conman who hangs round the Arsenal. He started throwing all kinds of shit at us. He says he's been receiving money from a rich Jew to pass on information about the Venetian fleet to the Turks.'

A twinge in my wrist makes me grit my teeth. 'We've got to try something, João. Before it's too late.'

He starts shivering. He picks up a heavy dressing gown and puts it on. The golden arabesques gleam in the firelight as he sinks back into his leather armchair. His fatigue has fled and his voice has resumed its normal tone. 'Tell me what you have in mind.'

Venice, 20 October 1551

Three days ago Pietro Manelfi spontaneously gave himself up to the inquisitor in Bologna.

Chapter 40

Venice, 2 November 1551

The little boy knows what he's got to do. The little boy is ten years old. When the bells ring he's to deliver the message to the *palazzo*, with the agreed counter-signature pressed on to the back of the folded sheet, the mould of a snake wrapped round the blade of a sword. The message reads:

The German is in Venice. Place and time established.

The little boy knows he must insist that His Excellency receive him immediately, or else he'll be whipped, he sobs; the master who sent him there told him it was urgent, that there would otherwise be trouble 'for me and for you'.

The little boy, blond curls to his shoulders, teeth white as the driven snow, is no one's fool; he insists, he sobs, he delivers what he had to deliver and he's off.

The place is the Church of San Giovanni, behind the Turkish Fondaco.

The faceless man is on time. As agreed, he is sitting in the confessional, waiting.

The bald little man on the other side of the grille begins his story.

He tells of his life as a sinner, how infrequently he attended mass, how many years it has been since his last confession. But he likes churches, he says, they convey a sense of peace, and particularly this one, so small, so far from the hubbub of the city, filled him with the desire to unburden his conscience.

The faceless man curses to himself. This pedantic midget with the Tuscan accent wasn't at all what he was expecting. He remains silent, waiting for the man to finish.

The voice croaks on about how he can't resist the temptation to gamble. About how it weighs upon him that he has won this money and the need to turn it into good works.

Something is pushed into the gap under the grille, it gleams in the light filtering through the cloth, balances on the rim and with the final shove topples into his lap.

The faceless man is confused.

The voice descends into a series of words of thanks, he really needed to shake off that burden, luckily there are always holy men who are willing to listen, and then gradually fades away. The final words are a reminder that sooner or later we all end up before the Supreme One.

The confessional is empty.

The faceless man gives a start. He goes out into the nave: not a soul.

He opens the palm that holds the coin. The inscriptions are printed on both sides, he has to bring it up to his eye to decipher them. They speak his language.

ONE GOD, ONE FAITH, ONE BAPTISM.
ONE RIGHTEOUS KING RULING OVER ALL.
THE WORD MADE FLESH.
MÜNSTER 1534.

The faceless man dashes out of the church.

The light dazzles him. He stops. There isn't a trace of the little man.

The Kingdom of Zion. Münster. Venice.

In between, an ocean of time filled with a mystery.

The German. With a dead man's name.

The ghost who brought that coin here.

It's all happening too quickly, too suddenly, where the sky is reflected on the cobblestones.

The little square is becoming animated, there's a strange agitation in the air. Some stout young men, their faces contorted like those of men possessed, come running from both sides: the jackets of the Nicolotti versus those of the Castellani. First insults and curses, a few stones, sticks raised, then a tangle of crazed bodies fills the scene.

The faceless man, astonished, back to the wall, tries to get to the very narrow alley that runs alongside San Giovanni.

A huge creature appears beside him, driving him in that direction. The faceless man steps back, impressed by the incredible vision of a woman about six feet six inches tall, wearing a hat as wide as the alley, from which there spills a tall arrangement of hair like the snakes of the Medusa, white face, blue-ringed, carmine-tinted nipples on display pointing straight into his face, on impossibly high heels, she totters towards him as though on stilts and smiles.

The faceless man is no longer quite sure he can believe his eyes. He turns round and tries to quicken his steps as he runs down the alley, which gets narrower by the second.

At the end of it the little boy is waiting for him. He waves broadly: come, sir, come this way.

The little boy is ten years old and he knows what he has to do.

The faceless man has no option but to turn towards that cascade of golden curls. By the time he sees the gaping door in the darkness on his right, it is too late to try and turn back. Right beneath his bollocks he spots the gleam of a knife, which the little boy is clutching firmly in his hand.

The faceless man isn't sure what to do.

The Sephardi's brother takes delivery of him, the cold blade now at his throat. This man has pleasant features and something like a smile on his face. The door is closed behind him. The faceless man goes down the narrow stairs towards the faint light of a torch. He notices the acrid smell of mildew, the damp that is penetrating his bones.

The Sephardi's loyal friend slips a hood over his head and ties his wrists behind his back. No one speaks.

He sits him down on an unsteady bench.

The faceless man can neither see anything nor feel the passage of time. The Sephardi's brother says he'll have to wait, the explanations will come at the proper time and not before. Then silence falls again.

The hooded man's limbs are filled with torpor, it's very cold, he arches his back, stretches his legs, starts succumbing to fatigue.

After an endless period of time, three dull knocks come from the far end of the cellar. The Sephardi's brother and his friend take him beneath the arms and lift him, carrying him to a narrow passageway. The hooded man puts up no resistance, his legs are unsteady, he feels the rocking of a boat on water. They bring him on board.

The hunchback plunges the pole into the water and guides the boat towards the maze of canals, shielded by the darkness.

The hooded man doesn't know what to expect.

The Sephardi is waiting in a safe house overlooking the Sacca della Misericordia. They lead the hooded man off the boat and walk him into the house. A lot of coming and going up and down stairs, then he is made comfortable in an armchair.

The Sephardi is seated opposite him. The hooded man smells the aroma of a cigar and becomes aware of a faint light.

The Sephardi has pleasant manners and expresses his thoughts clearly. He says that the unpleasant condition of being a prisoner makes anyone, even the strongest of men, incapable of predicting his immediate fate. If that state is imposed on someone accustomed to deciding the fates of others, it is not hard to imagine his utter confusion. Anyway, a little information, some clarification of what was happening, would certainly alleviate that burden.

The Sephardi says that you have to be particularly careful in Venice when choosing your informers. That here in Venice informing is probably the most widespread profession after prostitution, and one might even say that it differed in no respects from the latter. In Venice, informers are quick to switch allegiances. And furthermore a spy asks only a decent wage and his own personal safety; anyone capable of offering him those will enjoy his services. So it could be that inconveniences of this kind are due either to the sparse remuneration offered by the inquisitors, or to the excessive generosity of their enemies. And the funny thing is that in this case the generous payment has come from someone who is constantly being accused of greed and usury.

The hooded man hears the other man's footsteps moving in a circle.

After a few seconds the voice begins again. It says that trusting faithless informers was certainly an act of carelessness, but it was not the only one. Indeed, not leaving your enemies with an escape route is equally imprudent. Tightening the noose around an entire community, leading them to predict a future of suffering and death will inevitably unleash surprising reactions. The man with his back to the wall is the man who will defend himself best. War, not only spiritual war, is an art as refined as diplomacy, which derives from it. And in this art, against their will, the Jews have been obliged to excel. When you are encircled, you come up with plans; faced with death, you fight.

The Sephardi announces that there will be much more to talk about, such as, for example, that Turk who brags about having been in their service on behalf of the Sultan. But all in due course. Because first, after a few hours' rest, another journey awaits him.

The hooded man is laid out on a hard bed and falls into a troubled sleep.

Chill light of dawn.

I study the short, rippling waves of the lagoon, which will bring defeat to me. Will bring me face to face with it.

The island of San Michele. A church, a cloister, a cemetery.

A whole life's actions concentrated into a few short days. Endgame is approaching and no one could predict its outcome.

Now there can be no delays. The old Baptist, the heretical hare, Titian, finally hunted down. His hunter in Venice. The Jews caught in a trap leading straight to the scaffold.

Decades of intrigues and attacks, betrayals and retreats, rashness and remorse, are rushing together all of a sudden. The prophets and the king of a single, tragic day; cardinals and popes, and new popes; bankers, princes, merchants and preachers; men of letters, painters and spies, and counsellors and pimps. Everywhere, involving everyone, the same war. Those people, myself among them, were the most fortunate ones. They enjoyed the privilege of fighting the war. Wretches or noblemen, bastards or heroes, wretched spies or knights of the humble, sordid mercenaries or prophets of a coming age, they chose the battlefield, they embraced a faith, they stirred up the flames of hope and vanity. And in that battlefield they found the one who ripped their flesh to pieces; that faith is the one that betrayed them on the final day; the flames are the pyre on which they are burning now. They were responsible for their shifting fortunes and their own unstinting ruin. Day after day they filled the poisoned chalice that would finally kill them.

We ourselves must ask forgiveness for having had too propitious a fate. Enjoy our privilege to the dregs. Work out a final plan. Test out that crazed conclusion.

Not much longer to wait. The faint light of dawn is starting to give shape to the tombstones and the white crosses, a scattered army leading down to the water.

The campanile of San Michele looms over the whole flat island, standing out against the stars that are going out one by one. A sea breeze swells up beneath my woollen cloak. I can feel exhaustion spreading through my limbs and in the throbbing pain behind my right eye. My attention is captured by each little thing, each detail, it needs a break after all the long sleepless nights, with João at my side, planning the operation down to its tiniest particulars. In the distance, returning fishing boats, keeping to the open sea to avoid the treacherous shallows at low tide. The first gulls are either starting to fly or settling on the calm water.

I should be tense, agitated. Instead, I am aware only of the exhaustion in my bones, my rheumatic pains and also a certain hesitancy. Perhaps deep down I don't want to know. I'd rather preserve intact the suspicions that have travelled with me throughout all those years. Turn the page and start a calmer story, a tale of soft beds and welcoming loved ones. Tear myself away from the battlefield and rest, for ever.

But the dead would return to interrogate me. All those faces insist on memories. They say that it's down to the last man left alive to settle the scores. To discover the truth. Perhaps I owe more to them than I do to myself, perhaps I owe more to the ones who were left in the field, the prophets betrayed by their own prophecies, the peasants who used their hoes as swords, the weavers who turned themselves into soldiers to topple the bishops and the princes, all the people who have travelled with me throughout my life. I also owe it to the Jews, that strange breed of pilgrims with no destination who have gone with me the last part of the way.

Or maybe not. Sometimes I think this is the illusion that has kept me going, trying out new paths, never stopping to admit that more than anything else it was the years that betrayed me.

Or perhaps it's both at once. I can no longer give things the same importance as I once did. And yet I should do. Now that I'm about to have the confirmation that I've been seeking for such a long time; now that the story is about to reach its conclusion. Now I'm almost sorry. Because I know that I'm just going to be disappointed. Disappointed at having reached the end, disappointed at recognising the man who has been selling us to the enemy for thirty years. It's stupid, it's absurd, that more than anything else I feel the desire to ask him to remember the past, to bring out all those faces once again. The only one who really knows my story, who can still talk to me about that passion, that hope. It's the desire, stupid and banal, of an old man. That's all it is. Or maybe it's only fatigue that's taking me back, the heedless sleep that blots out the mind.

A boat appears on the horizon, making straight for the island.

Fine, it's time to finish things off.

The Hunchback moors the boat to the little jetty. The hooded man is helped out. The Sephardi unties his hands and removes his hood. Then he turns back and gets on board.

The old man rubs his wrists, blinks his reddened eyes; his face marked by exhaustion, grey dishevelled hair. He brings a hand to his eyebrow and rubs a deep scar, then fixes his eye on me.

I try to scrub away years from that face.

Qoèlet.

He speaks first: 'An action worthy of Captain Gert from the Well.'

'When did you work it out?'

His palm presses on his old wound. 'I went back to Münster.' He coughs, wrapping his dark cloak around him. 'I've been looking for you for years and in the end you were the one who found me.'

'But you'd worked it out already.'

'It wasn't that difficult: Titian the Baptist, a pimp with the name of a heretic. Antwerp, and the survivors of Münster. Three days ago I had my final confirmation. A well-constructed trap. Only you could have prepared it.'

'I'd been told you died in Münster, trying to force the bishops' blockade.'

He leans on one of the tombstones, hands on his knees, eyes on the ground. Like myself, he is no longer of an age for chilly dawns like this one. And, more important, he no longer has a reason not to remember.

'You left in the spring of 1534, in search of money and ammunition in Holland. You did me a favour. I'd have been sorry to see you engulfed by the hastening destruction along with the rest. I had arrived in Münster with a task: to join the Anabaptists in their struggle against the bishop, to become one of them, with all that entailed, help them to turn the city into the New Jerusalem, and when the time came to send that hope up in flames. I introduced myself to Bernhard Rothmann with a large donation for the cause, telling him I was a former mercenary who had been away from Münster for many years. Money achieved what my story could not.'

I look at this bent old man, having difficulty recognising him as the man I entrusted with the defence of the market square in the days when we took Münster. Now he's only the relic of my lieutenant, Heinrich Gresbeck.

He goes on, 'I attached myself to you because they said you had fought with Thomas Müntzer; you were the only one I could depend on. The arrival of Matthys, his swift end and the sudden acclamation of Bockelson as his successor made the work much easier. All I needed was for you to go. I became the confidant of Bernhard Rothmann, now a mere shadow of the fiery preacher who had led the Anabaptists against the bishop. I dusted down the Wittenberg lectures, spent days and nights with him discussing the regulations of the New Zion, the practices of the patriarchs in the Bible, to help his vacillating mind bring forth the most lethal absurdities.

'That wasn't so difficult either: it wasn't long before Bockelson proclaimed himself the New David, the King of Zion, and at the suggestion of the court theologian Rothmann he instituted polygamy, in order to restore the customs of the Fathers. That was the end. I don't remember how many women were executed for refusing to submit to the new ordinances. I have a vague memory of those months, like the memory of a dream. Hunger, houses ransacked for the last loaf of bread, the child judges, death in their eyes, pointing out undesirables in the streets. Pale, haggard bodies dragging themselves through the city, almost unconscious. I could have gone away and let the end come of its own accord. Instead, through some strange alchemy, I felt that I had to be the one to make the last compassionate gesture. I had to put an end to that agony.'

He straightens his back with some difficulty, as though his shoulders were very heavy. His eyes stare at an indefinite point in the lagoon.

'I jumped the walls, travelled the half-mile separating them from the bishops' front, risked the bullets, squatted in a ditch and stayed there for hours, sure that if I had lifted my head up I would have presented an excellent target to von Waldeck's mercenaries. I was captured and escaped death by rebuilding a model of the walls with mud, and indicating where the walls could be penetrated. It wasn't enough: I had to demonstrate the truth of what I said by climbing back up the walls at night and returning to the camp unharmed. You remember? You were the one who entrusted me with the control of the defences. I knew every inch of them. I alone could do it. It was up to me to deliver the *coup de grâce*.'

He bends over again, overwhelmed by the weight.

I hand him the yellow pages, dust between my fingers. He reads, holding the pages at a distance and narrowing his eyelids.

'You've kept them all this time . . .' He hands me back the letters he wrote to Magister Thomas twenty-five years ago.

'Were you already in Carafa's pay?'

'I was one tile in a mosaic assembled over a period of years. When they recruited me I was only the library assistant at Wittenberg University. My task was to keep an eye on Luther. At that time only a few people realised what an obtuse little Augustinian friar was capable of unleashing. Carafa was the first to understand that the German princes would use him as a battering ram to bring down the gates of Rome and to punish the arrogant scion for whom the Fuggers had bought the imperial crown. Within that intricate design my duty was to ignite the fiery mind of Luther's greatest antagonist, Thomas Müntzer, to feed the fire of the peasant revolt against the princes and their apostate at the court. While the rebellion raged across Germany, Rome took its time and Carafa tried to convince the cardinals of the danger that Luther represented. But then things got going. The boy Emperor showed himself to be more ambitious than expected: his emergence as a champion of the Catholic faith over a territory stretching from Spain to Bohemia made him much more dangerous, in the eyes of Rome, than the little German principalities. From that moment onwards, Luther's protectors became potential allies against the Emperor. In the meantime the insurgent peasants had become a source of alarm. The revolt had to be stopped. Those letters were used to oil the whole machine. They won me my promotion on the battle-field.'

Old Gresbeck takes a breath, coughs again and looks at me. A grimace. 'After the sack of Rome, in 1527, Carafa took advantage of his own predictions, no one dared to contradict him, he had been right about everything from the start: the Lutherans were wicked people who cared nothing for excommunications and blithely pillaged the papal city. He started to accumulate power, he climbed his way up through the ecclesiastical hierarchy and had many more sound premonitions.'

The words come out unbidden: 'A network of spies in every state.'

He nods. 'He always managed to have information before anyone else, thanks to all the many pairs of eyes that he kept in all the key places. Wherever something significant was taking place, it was a safe bet that the old man had one of his people there.'

I interrupt him: 'Why did he order you to destroy the Anabaptists in Münster? What did that have to do with Rome?'

'Rome is everywhere, Gert. The spirit of revolt against the powerful survived in you people. Luther had preached unconditional obedience. That was fine: you can always negotiate with sovereigns. Not with you, though, you wanted to shake off their yoke; you preached freedom and disobedience, and Carafa couldn't afford to let

ideas of that kind spread. Thanks to my detailed reports he understood the strength of a tightly organised unit and he had seen what a
single preacher like Thomas Müntzer could do. The Anabaptists had
to be crushed before they became a serious threat.'

'Carafa called a meeting of all his spies at the end of the thirties. The
monastery of the Theatines was where you were to assemble.'

He looks astonished. 'You've done your homework.' A shiver passes
along his shoulders, but he goes on talking. 'We were needed in Italy.
The Pope was about to give Carafa approval for his plan: the
constitution of the Holy Office. His motives were very noble: to resist
the spread of heresy with new means. In fact, the old man would use
those means against his internal enemies in Rome. The highest job of
all was at stake.'

'The Pontifical Throne.' My turn to shiver.

'And the annihilation of all his adversaries. The Englishman, Pole,
was causing him problems, in his own way he was a tough nut to
crack, but Carafa played his cards very well. And he got him. He did
it by a hair, but he did it.'

'*The Benefit of Christ Crucified.*'

'Exactly. I took care of the whole operation. At least until Carafa
needed me again. From the start we knew that the circles of Pole and
his friends were behind Fontanini and his book. We knew that the
spirituale cardinals would read the book and would take it as their
starting point in their approaches to the Lutherans. If they'd
succeeded, Charles V would have brought together the whole of
Christendom under his banner for a crusade against the Turks and
today he would have no enemies. But Pole didn't become Pope, and
now the *spirituali* are falling, one after another, beneath the blows of
the Inquisition. Once again the old Theatine has outwitted everyone:
he has taken his enemies' weapon and turned it against them.'

The sun has appeared above the lagoon, a blood-red disc casting its
glow across the water. The thoughts pile up in my mind, but I have to
force myself to hold them back. I have to know; time is precious.
'What do the Jews have to do with all this? Carafa struck an agreement
with the Venetians, didn't he?'

Another nod of assent, his eyes getting smaller and deeper with
exhaustion. 'The Jews are goods to be exchanged. Everyone will
benefit from their ruin: if the Marrani are found guilty of perpetrating
Judaism in secret, the Venetians will be able to confiscate all their
goods. Carafa is handing them over on a silver platter and in return he
is planting the banner of the Inquisition in Venice, launching an
operation in the grand style, in the state that is famous for its

independence from Rome. A good few sovereigns in Europe will break out into a cold sweat when they hear the news. You're on the wrong side once again, Captain.'

Silence, nothing but the slow surge of the tide and the cry of a gull.

'Is that your task? To round up the Jews?'

A shadow falls across his face, as though he had to force himself to speak; his voice is a murmur. 'That's why I was sent to Venice.'

Exhaustion runs through every inch of my body, my headache has worsened. I press a finger to my temple and I too lean on a tombstone to support my legs.

Heinrich Gresbeck scans the horizon, then he turns to look at me. The years haven't spared him, the night has been long and sleepless for both of us.

'What will your reward be, this time?'

He smiles. 'A quick end, probably.'

'Is that the reward for the most faithful servant?'

He shrugs. 'I'm the only one who knows the whole story from the beginning: Carafa can't risk keeping me in circulation. Not now that he's preparing to seize all the power for himself.'

I let my eye wander to the gravestones. On every one of them I could read the name of a companion, I could run all the way back through the various stages that have brought me to this place. But I can feel no hatred. I no longer have the strength to despise anyone. I look at Gresbeck and all I see is an old man.

Chapter 42

Venice, 3 November 1551

The boat sets off again. Bernardo and Duarte row in unison, with Sebastiano at the stern, ready to avoid the shallows with the pole, or to take over. João is at the prow, next to me. The hooded man is on the seat opposite.

One of the Miquezes' cargo ships is waiting for us, another mile beyond the city, in the silence broken only by the strokes of the oars in the water and the cries of the gulls.

A duel that has lasted a lifetime. Is this how it ends?

A rope and a rope ladder are thrown down to us from the Miquezes' carrack. From his very depths, I hear Gresbeck bursting into indecorous laughter. It sounds lugubrious to my ears, like a foretaste of death. And perhaps to João's ears, too, because, just for a moment, he loses his proverbial smile and snarls, '¿Porque coño te ries?'

'Gentlemen, I know you have many things to tell each other. But unfortunately the situation does not permit us to wallow in our memories.' He looks Gresbeck straight in the eyes. 'As you will have understood, Excellency, I am João Miquez. The very man you're trying to destroy.'

Gresbeck doesn't turn a hair, doesn't say a word.

This isn't one of João's smiling days. 'Your accord with those ten scoundrels on the council must be important enough – and explicit enough for both parties – for you to support even the most ludicrous exaggerations. Like the one that you have based around the confessions of . . . what's his name? Tanusin Bey, I think, the one who's accusing my family of being in charge of the Sultan's spies in La Serenissima. I wonder what gutter you dragged him out of. I don't imagine it can have taken much to persuade a common cut-throat to offer you his services.'

Gresbeck remains silent, impassive.

Miquez goes on, 'And what about the trials for crypto-Judaism? You used to force us to kiss the cross when the fires of the stake were already lit, and now you come and tell us we did it out of convenience, and we're all exactly the same as we ever were.' He nods to himself. 'Fine. They've sent you here from Rome to finish us off. And the Venetians will let you do it, they'll help you in your undertaking. They're madmen, heading for their own perdition. You and I know that. There isn't a single one of those merchants who hasn't had dealings with my family over the past five years. There isn't one of those jackals sitting in the council who hasn't taken loans from us. Without the Jews Venice will lose its trade routes, the Sultan will take them all, one after the other, business will dry up, the city will go back to being a spit stain on the map, squashed in between the empires. These smug aristocrats are condemning themselves to become irrelevant little country squires.'

He sighs. 'But there we are. If that's what they've decided, you know very well, Excellency, that we won't allow ourselves to be captured without a fight. The merchants who depend on my purse strings have already announced that they're going to suspend all traffic with the Orient unless the authorities put a stop to this indiscriminate Jew baiting. And as far as you're concerned, if what this old acquaintance of yours tells us is true, I think that this time Cardinal Carafa is going to have to get by without his foremost agent.'

Gresbeck continues looking at him without batting an eyelid, a tired, inoffensive expression on his face, breathing with difficulty.

João gets to his feet and walks pensively up and down. 'You're pretty shrewd, my dear sir, and I'm sure you can understand where my interests lie.'

He sits back down again. Silence. Only the surge of the waves and faint footsteps on the deck. The daylight shines in from two big side windows to illuminate the captain's cabin: a table, two armchairs and a bed.

I get up with enormous difficulty. Gresbeck glances at me serenely. I sit down on the edge of the desk, moving aside the chart of the Adriatic. It's my turn.

'The advantage of having come this far is that we need no longer deceive one another. At the age of fifty, I don't have the holy fire of rebellion in my veins and I haven't slept for two nights. My fatigue will help me speak clearly and keep my words to a minimum.' I press my fingers to my temple to ease my headache. 'Your prick of a boss is seventy-five. Most men are under the ground by that age. What I wonder is what that wicked old man is demanding of himself, of his men and of us. I wonder what plan he has truly been urging on for all those years. Defeating heresy? Punishing beggars for trying to stand up for their own redemption? Setting up tribunals of conscience to control people's thoughts? I wonder what use it was to him, accumulating all that power. And even now that the heads of the *spirituali* are falling one by one, and attention is being focused upon the Jews in Venice, I wonder why. It isn't the money of the Sephardic Jews, or the affairs of Venice, or a settling of scores with Carafa's enemies among the *spirituali*. And it isn't the Papal Throne either, Heinrich. Not at seventy-five. Carafa has never suggested himself as being eligible for the papacy. What is at stake is something higher than all those things put together. Something that is hanging over all our heads. To understand what's going on here, what awaits us, we must have a complete understanding of his project.'

A suspicious smile under Gresbeck's moustache. Hoarse breath, a deep voice: 'The Plan. What Carafa has been working on all his life. That phrase that fills the mouths of the humblest country priest, that is written on the standards of the armies, on the swords of the conquerors of the New World, on the façades of parish churches and cathedrals alike.' He lets the words fall like stones. 'The greater glory of God.'

He barely shakes his head. 'Imposing an order on the world. Enabling Peter's Church to remain the unquestioned arbiter of the men and nations of the world. Carafa has understood the foundations of a millennial power better than anyone else. A simple message: fear of God. A gigantic and complex apparatus that inculcates that message in people's thoughts and deeds. Spreading the message, managing the knowledge, observing and assessing the minds of men, investigating every impulse that dares to go beyond that fear. Carafa has assumed the enormous task of opening up the foundations of that power to the light of the new age. The ambition that he embodies has drawn out all the weakness of the body of the Church and turned it into a concentration of strength. Luther has been both his most vehement enemy and his best ally. Without diminishing the fear of God, the Augustinian friar made everyone aware of the need for change. The first ones to understand this were the most intelligent men, like Carafa, like Pole, like the founders of the new monastic orders. More than thirty years on, they're the only ones still in the game. He had to respond with the right weapons to the gauntlet thrown down by Luther. And it was there that the conflict came into being: Pole and the *spirituali* were willing to mediate just to preserve the unity of Christendom. Carafa wasn't. He preferred to abandon the Protestants to their fate rather than allow so much as a tiny crack in the absolute authority of the Church: he had to strike back at the Lutherans blow for blow, make a clean sweep within his own church body and establish new apparatuses that would rise to the challenge. If the *spirituali* had won, Rome would have lost its primacy. If some friar, or even a layman like Calvin, had been allowed to discuss matters as an equal with a descendant of St Peter, what would have become of the millennial order? What would have become of the Church of Rome? What would have become of the Plan?'

Gresbeck stops, exhausted.

Miquez can't contain himself: 'From our present vantage point, my dear sir, the question is a rather different one. What will become of us?'

The same calm tone: 'You will be sacrificed.'

I look into his eyes. 'To the greater glory of God.'

'Exactly. And this time, Messer Miquez, it won't be as it was in Portugal, or in Spain, or in the Netherlands. This time it will be for good. Inquisition proceedings concerning Donna Beatrice are already in preparation; they will be put into effect within a matter of days. The Venetians are only interested in your money. Carafa wants a demonstration of strength by the Inquisition. He wants to reduce you to powerlessness, to leave a desert around you and crush you. And may the lesson be a warning to everyone. You can't buy your safety as you have done in the past: Carafa's men are incorruptible, they have a mission to accomplish and they're very good at their work. The merchants can't frighten them with boycotts, they simply don't matter. You're right, Venice will do itself irreparable damage, but he who does not adapt to changing times is destined to perish.'

João is black-faced, stiff in his seat like a mahogany statue, he isn't speaking.

Gresbeck turns back to me. 'And your Anabaptists are about to be swept away, too. Every single one.'

'That's impossible.'

'The idea of Titian was a clever one. But no plan is perfect; trusting the wrong person is the kind of mistake you end up paying for.'

A twinge in my stomach.

'Two weeks ago Pietro Manelfi gave himself up to the Inquisition in Bologna. He really has an astonishing memory. He gave us all the names, professions and places of origin of the members of the sect. Of course, he talked about Titian as well. If he carries on being as helpful as that, he'll win himself a pardon.'

I breathe deeply, thoughts rushing into my head. Then I have a sudden realisation: 'You've met him.'

He coughs. 'I was on his trail for a while. I hoped he'd lead me to you. When I got the news I dashed to Bologna. Just in time to meet him, because Leandro Alberti, the inquisitor, had already decided to send him to Rome so as not to have the responsibility of dealing with such an important affair. At this moment Manelfi is repeating his confessions before the Congregation of the Holy Office. All the people he's baptised over the past few years are going to be for the chop.' His grey eyes pass from me to João. 'You've done well. Printing *The Benefit of Christ Crucified*, contacting all those men of letters. Pontormo's coup was admirable. Anabaptism was a ridiculous enough idea to be able to work. But you couldn't make it. Not when you were up against Carafa.'

João draws his sword with a swift and elegant gesture. 'So, Excellency, at least allow me the satisfaction of sending you personally to hell, depriving you of the pleasure of witnessing the fruits of your vile labours.'

Gresbeck doesn't move. He doesn't look at the blade.

I raise a hand. 'No. You haven't told us everything. You knew what your fate would be, you knew it the moment you looked me in the face. You could be silent. You could say nothing and meet your death while leaving us all in a state of uncertainty.'

He smiles. 'My time is over, Gert. When the Jews are on their knees, Carafa will want me dead. I know too much.'

'There's something else, isn't there?'

'No plan is perfect. No plot is safe from contingencies. And there's always a flaw, a little detail that risks ruining everything at the last moment, something that has been thought irrelevant and forgotten, but which suddenly becomes the spanner in the works that could demolish the whole machine.'

João has lowered his sword. 'What are you talking about?'

Gresbeck: 'I no longer have that fire in my veins either, Gert. I'm dead already. Whether it's you or one of Carafa's hired killers doesn't make much difference. I've been carrying out orders all my life. I can allow myself an ending other than the one that lies in wait for me round the next corner. I can give that privilege to you, Captain Gert, my lifelong adversary.'

'Why?'

'Because we're two sides of the same coin, because we've been fighting the same war and neither of us is going to emerge the winner. The field belongs to Carafa, the hope of the ragged ones has been sunk in the mud, but Qoèlet, too, must make his exit.'

This time I'm the one to smile, the words come out slowly, as though I were weighing them on my tongue: 'You're wrong, Heinrich. While it might seem easy to believe, you and I aren't actually the same. You've been fighting someone else's war, you've been obeying orders, you've been carrying out a part in his Plan. You've served other people all your life, for a goal that you won't even see accomplished: that's your defeat. You weren't beaten in the battle-field, like those thousands of ragged men and heretics who fought against their masters and against the power of Rome. You have nothing, not even the sense of what you've done. That's why you must give me the last chance, because it's yours as well, the last chance to take back the life that you've sold to someone else.'

He says nothing. He slips his hand under his jacket and hands me a sheet of paper. 'Manelfi didn't just give me the names of his brethren. He told a story when he faced the inquisitor. The story of a heretic who went around rebaptising people and a cardinal who then became Pope. A story which, if it reached the right ears, would blow Carafa's whole Plan away.'

Et in primis interrogatus de quis eum initiavit doctrinae anabaptistae, respondit:

> In Florence Titian began to preach the Anabaptist doctrine to me and rebaptised me, telling me that I was not baptised because I had not faith when baptised as a child, and telling me of other ancient beliefs of the Anabaptists, that Christians may not hold magistratures and seignories, dominion or kingship, and this is one of the first principles of the Anabaptists; but we did not find that these Anabaptists denied the divinity of Christ or fall foul of other articles determined and concluded in the council that was held in Venice, as I have said above.
>
> And this Titian said that the Anabaptists had the blessing of Our Lord Julius III, and that he was able to bear witness to this because he had met him before he was made Pope.

Interrogatus an credat dectum Ticianum convenisse ad cardinalem Ioannem Mariam Del Monte, respondit:

> The said Titian told me he had spoken to the above most reverend Cardinal for an entire night discussing various matters. And in particular that most notorious book, Beneficium Christi, and its author, Friar Benedetto Fontanini of Mantua. Titian told me he had asked His Lordship concerning the heresy of this book and His Lordship

agreed that there was none. Item: he asked His Lordship to intercede on behalf of the said Fontanini, imprisoned in Padua, insisting on his innocence. He ordered that Fontanini be freed. I believed Titian's story.

Item: Titian frequented many men of letters, courtiers and even fine lords, seeking to persuade them all of the goodness of the Anabaptist doctrine and the aforementioned Benefit of Christ Crucified. *This he did in Florence with the courtiers of Cosimo de' Medici, and also in Ferrara, and with Princess Renée d'Este.*

Item: the same office of persuading Our Lord of the Anabaptist doctrine was performed by Titian, named in my confession, for whom I have no surname and for that reason I know he brought this Anabaptist doctrine to Italy, and is always going around preaching and teaching this doctrine.

He waits for João to finish reading as well. 'This is the most surprising part of the Manelfi confession, the deposition that Pietro Manelfi made to Leandro Alberti, the inquisitor of Bologna. One copy has already reached Rome along with the penitent man himself, and you can be certain that it will be duly purged from the files the moment one of Carafa's men has the opportunity to set eyes upon it. The second copy, complete with signatures and counter-signatures, I received from the same Alberti, with the task of delivering it to Carafa in person. I copied out this passage before depositing the whole dossier with the branch of the Fuggers at the German Fondaco. It is certainly the most precious deposit that they have ever had in their coffers, and fortunately they are unaware of the fact. Here it is clearly written that the man most wanted by the Inquisition, Titian the Baptist, was able to approach Cardinal Del Monte before he was elected Pope and persuade him of the innocence of *The Benefit of Christ Crucified*, to the point of driving him to intercede in the matter of the author's incarceration. Fontanini really did leave prison thanks to the intercession of a powerful man. The General of the Benedictine order knows Pope Del Monte personally. There is tangible proof of the veracity of the story.'

My laughter rings out in confirmation. 'It sounds crazy, but it's the truth.'

Miquez is still puzzled. 'I still don't understand what's so precious about this confession.'

Gresbeck says in a serious voice, 'Ghislieri and his mates are nailing the *spirituali* one by one as responsible for the distribution of *The Benefit of Christ Crucified* in their dioceses. Carafa, at the Council of Trent, is openly accusing them of failing to obstruct its circulation and in many cases of having encouraged it. What do you think would happen if the inquisitors themselves became aware of the Pope's interest in the author and the contents of *The Benefit of Christ Crucified*? What would happen if the cardinals under investigation availed themselves of this deposition and used it to free themselves from the accusations that have been brought against them?'

João leans on the table. 'Carafa would be fucked. But who's to guarantee that this document really exists?'

'Neither of us has anything left to lose.'

Two days' vigil and only eight hours of sleep is enough to prevent an aching fifty-year-old from doing up his jacket properly. Only at the third attempt do I finally regain the confidence to perform my everyday activities. I drag up from my stomach the agitation that is required to banish fatigue.

Gresbeck is already in the hall, wrapped in his coat, his back leaning against the chest of drawers and his head thrown back, as though trying to concentrate by taking long, deep breaths. He won't be carrying firearms. A short blade, the absolute minimum. He's as old as I am. More exhausted. I can trust him.

A twinge in my wrist, always tightly wrapped in a light and brightly coloured oriental fabric, folded over itself several times, five inches long, covering a little less than half of my forearm.

He will go into the agency without arousing suspicions. He has carte blanche there. The Fuggers know whom they have to side with.

Tight gloves of black leather, gleaming, soft, tanned by Spaniards, given to me by the young Bernardo Miquez.

Fate's strange; scores aren't settled as you would expect. I catch my reflection in the sumptuous mirror – same height as myself, twice as broad – of the Miquez residence at the far end of the Giudecca. Not as you would expect. A sparse grey beard frames my face.

He'll have to stick around there for as long as it takes to withdraw the dossier; no time for niceties.

That old bump squashes the tip of my nose slightly to the left. My hair is pulled back behind the nape of my neck and smoothed with oil, a gift from Beatriz. My guns are crossed in my belt, I brush my hand over the handle of the knife fastened behind my back.

He's going to come towards me, passing me the little cloth bag that holds the document.

I cover my arms by pulling the hem of my cloak over my shoulder. A glance at Heinrich, reflected in the mirror, in the same position.

Sebastiano is waiting for us by the boat.

After the swap, we will exit on the opposite side of the Fondaco, straight on to the Grand Canal. From there to the Caratello. Then to the mainland.

All of a sudden João appears and everything is in place. A nod to Gresbeck and off we go.

We turn into the Rio del Vin, between the domes of St Mark's and the campanile of San Zaccaria. Sebastiano is in charge of the boat, Gresbeck and I are seated opposite one another. He rubs his neck for a long time to ease the tension in his muscles. No one feels the need to speak. After a wide bend we turn into the broad, winding Rio di San Severo. We pass beneath a few bridges before we get to the Rio di San Giovanni, and then on the left the canal opens up and continues straight ahead.

Once we're on the mainland, head at breakneck speed for Trent, going up the Brenta Valley. Two days' gallop, stopping only to change horses, escorted by the best men the Miquez brothers can supply. We have to get to Pole at all costs.

At the crossing with the Rio dei Miracoli we turn left, into the Rio del Fondaco. We disembark.

To deliver Manelfi's confession into the hands of the English cardinal. Only Heinrich can do it.

Twenty-five yards or so and we're in. The great commotion of groups of people talking by the entrance; my glance meets Duarte's. Just a nod of the head. Gresbeck is beside me. We enter the square courtyard of the German Fondaco.

At its centre stands the well, raised up on its two stone steps. My place. Businessmen coming and going, the inevitable pouring of beer.

Gresbeck walks beneath the portico to the left, making for the Fugger agency. When he reaches the third arch he goes in.

I touch the gun handles under my cloak.

Three porticoed storeys rise up along the four sides of the courtyard. Five arcades, ten on each of the upper floors, diminishing in size the higher they get.

To the right four people are engaged in an intense discussion, counting on the tips of their fingers.

A man leaning against a pillar, by the exit leading on to the canal.

In the corner, behind me, some Germans pass pieces of paper to each other.

My gaze continues on its way. Other busy men are constantly crossing the portico. From the first floor comes the sound of the customers of the brewery facing on to the courtyard, lost in chatter.

At the main entrance, away from all the coming and going, two men dressed in black, keeping to the sides.

Swellings under their capes.

They're staring at the door of the bank.

Shit.

Gresbeck is still inside. The four men to my right haven't stopped counting. The furthest one away gestures towards the agency. He glances towards the upper arches, behind me.

I turn round. Another cop is keeping his eye on the bank.

The one leaning against the pillar is still there. His eyes facing in the same direction.

It's a trap.

They've got us.

Back to the main entrance. The two black crows have been made agitated by the racket coming from outside.

Duarte walks into the Fondaco at the head of the Rialto merchants. The noise mounts.

The agency.

Gresbeck comes towards me. He raises his arm, aiming his gun.

He's fucked me over again.

He fires.

A man behind me collapses, falling back into the well. The clank of iron hitting the ground.

The merchants invade the courtyard.

Gresbeck holds the bag out to me. 'Move it, damn you!'

An indistinct uproar, I'm swallowed up by the crowd, I push my way through the sea of people shielding me, shouting in every imaginable language.

Pietro Perna grabs the bag off me, swapping it for an identical one. He winks. 'Habemus papam!' He slips out of the throng, towards the main entrance. Manelfi's confession is safe.

I yield to the tide of Rialto merchants swarming in the opposite direction, towards the canal-side exit. I can't see Gresbeck. I get back to the front entrance, driven along by a knot of shouting men who appear to have lost their minds. Blows, shouts. The policeman at the door is quickly overwhelmed. Gresbeck reappears at my side, a doorway opens and we are flung on to the boat.

Away, away, to the Caratello.

We pass beneath the Rialto, Sebastiano driving the boat with all his strength, and slip into Rio San Salvador.

My hands are trembling with agitation. I'm on fire, from head to toe.

I'm not sure what's happened. Opposite me Gresbeck's face seems calm, surprisingly impassive.

As we turn right into the Rio degli Scoacamini, he takes out some gunpowder and reloads his gun. He turns round and nods with a reassuring expression: they're not following us.

I put my ideas in order, run my hands over my face. 'Where did you get that?'

'Gert, you can deposit anything you like with the Fuggers. I know what you were thinking. But as you see, your trust was not misplaced. Neither was it in Münster: Heinrich Gresbeck has been a good lieutenant.'

'I thought that bullet was meant for me.'

'Those were Carafa's hired killers. I was the one they were after. I wonder how they could have been there waiting for me.'

Rio dei Fuseri, we go up it as far as the Rio di San Luca to emerge back on to the Grand Canal. We head straight up the Rio dei Meloni.

'The Fuggers know who they're dealing with, Heinrich. Their proverbial reserve evaporates in the face of people who can guarantee that God is on their side. They were the ones who alerted Carafa.'

We spot the mouth of the Rio Sant'Apollinare and turn into it. We're nearly there.

Gresbeck shakes his head. 'The chase has barely begun. How are we going to get to Trent? Even if we were to succeed, Carafa would be waiting for us with open arms.'

The boat pulls up.

A grimace trying to look like a smile. 'We're old, Heinrich. We'll try.'

He takes a little notebook from his pocket. Yellow pages, wrapped in a strip of leather tied together with a lace. 'This was in the Fuggers' coffer as well. It's the only trace of my passage. Keep it, Captain, it's yours.'

I slip it into my sleeve. We go up.

We make our way up the narrow alley in single file, until we get to the back of the Caratello.

Scores aren't settled the way you expect.

Chapter 44

'Filthy fuckers, queer lovers, Jew lovers!' A slap. 'The party's over!'

Pietro and Demetra are tied to the chairs, bruised and swollen.

'You horrible fucking dwarf, I want to have a bit of fun with you before I see you roasting in here!'

Smell of pitch.

I go stomping in, weapons at the ready, the Mule hasn't time to turn round before a bullet fired at point-blank range blows his shoulder apart. He falls heavily to the floor.

I aim the other gun.

Gresbeck aims his.

There are three of them.

They haven't had time to get their guns out.

Wide eyes fixed on the barrels.

Motionless.

In the corner of my eye: the bag. On the counter. Manelfi's confession.

Slip forward and get it.

But Heinrich is moving, slowly, along the wall, he leans his hand on the smooth marble.

He's got it.

A shadow on the staircase behind him.

'Look out!'

He turns round in a flash, the blade flies past his face, his gun fires, catches him right in the chest, the Mule's henchman falls back against the stairs.

The man next to the fireplace kicks the barrel, the pitch tips on to the glowing embers, a flame reaches all the way up to the ceiling.

He hurls himself at me, knife in hand.

Pain like the bite of a dog above my left arm.

I give a shout.

I grab him by the hair at the back of his neck as he loses his balance and smash his face against the edge of the counter.

The flames climb up the curtains and run along the floor to the feet of Perna and Demetra.

Quick, ignoring the searing pain.

I untie them.

I free Demetra.

Then Pietro. He hisses between his sobs, 'Sons of bitches!'

On the other side of the wall of flame I see Gresbeck drawing his dagger.

One against one.

He hesitates.

Heinrich smiles. All of a sudden he flings his blade.

A groan and the bastard gives up the ghost.

I cough, the smoke has filled the room. Demetra faints and I carry her with one arm. To the door. We're out. A trail of blood. Mine. My head spins, my legs won't move.

Perna coughs. 'The bag . . . the confession . . .'

I turn round, Gresbeck isn't there.

I've got to go back. I'm very weak, nausea crushing my stomach, my vision blurred. I take deep breaths, I mustn't faint. I stumble the few steps back to the door, an endless distance.

From the doorway I glimpse his silhouette in the middle of the room: the bag in his hand.

There's a wall of flame between us.

A narrow passage between two overturned tables.

'Over here!'

One of my knees gives way.

The Mule's shredded mask rises through the smoke, behind him. He's clutching a poker.

I cry out as he brings it crashing down.

They both fall.

I can't see them now. No, Gresbeck's staggering to his feet. He hasn't got the bag, he looks around.

Just one moment.

The moment it takes to see the architrave of the ceiling fall down and crush him.

Chapter 45

The sailors haul the long narrow boat on to dry land.

With my good arm I help Demetra to pull up the hem of her water-logged cloak. Perna, on the other side, up to his waist, whispers a curse.

We stop on the sand, beneath an opaque sun that gives no warmth.

Demetra touches my bandage. 'Careful not to bathe the wound. And eat a lot of meat, you've lost a load of blood.'

I smile at her – her make-up barely covers the bruises on her face. 'Don't worry, you did a fantastic job with that wretched arm of mine. It'll be as good as new.' João and Bernardo shake hands with little Pietro.

'Are you sure?'

Perna spreads his arms, the stitches on his cheekbone mean that he has to keep one eye half closed. 'Let's go, João, can you imagine me among the Mohammedans? Turbans don't suit me and those people don't even drink wine. They drink nothing but water! No, thanks, that won't do for Pietro Perna of Lucca. I'd rather stay here.' He casts a contented glance at Demetra. 'I'll be in good company.'

Bernardo hugs him and lifts him in the air.

Duarte kisses him on his uninjured cheek, making him blush.

Demetra's emerald eyes are bright.

I stroke her cheek. 'What are you going to do now?'

'I'll start over again somewhere, I think. Or maybe I'll accept Pietro's proposition. I'll be fine, don't worry.'

Perna's embarrassed. 'Ferrara's always a good market, you know? A good place to start. I still have a few contacts scattered here and there around Italy, there'll be a lot to do. If they go on printing books, my friend, don't worry, men's ingenuity will find a way of getting around Indexes and maybe, who knows, they might one day abolish them altogether. They'll always need someone going around selling books, you can bank on it.'

'When you say that, Pietro, it sounds like a guarantee.'

He laughs, moved. We hug.

João points to the path along the edge of the pine forest. 'Your carriage awaits you.'

Pietro picks up his bag. 'Bye, kraut.' He lowers his voice. 'Watch your arse among the Mohammedans and careful where you stick your cock, do you hear me?' Then he smiles. 'Bye, everyone!'

Demetra says, 'Good luck, Ludovico. And bon voyage.'

'The best of luck to both of you.'

They are walking on the damp sand. He small and fat, she tall and elegant. On the edge of the trees, Perna turns towards us, to wave a last farewell. He shouts something that disappears on the wind.

We watch him vanishing among the pines.

João comes up beside me. 'We've got to go. Beatriz's boat will have reached the ship already.'

She welcomes us on to the deck of the flagship of the Miquez fleet. The wind has loosened some locks of hair, without taking away any of her feminine fascination; in fact, giving her a sensual air that sends the stomach and the heart plummeting.

I kiss her hand, holding it between both of mine for a moment. 'The prospect of travelling by your side makes defeat less bitter, Beatriz.'

She gently brushes the hair out of her face. 'Defeat, Ludovico? Do you really think so? Aren't we still alive and free to plough the waves?'

Bernardo calls some orders to the captain of the ship, and whistles and warnings run from one end of the deck to the other.

I smile at her. 'You're right.'

I don't add anything else. Her daughter and her young servant go with her to her cabin.

From the quarterdeck João beckons me to join him. 'The captain says the wind is with us. Better not to waste it. You'll reach Lissa in a few days at the most. Then Ragusa. Two more days to Corfu. Once you've made it to Xanthe you'll be out of reach of the Venetians.'

'What do you mean by that?'

He lowers his eyes. 'Bernardo and I are going back to Venice.'

'Are you out of your mind? They want to kill you.'

The Sephardi stares at the coastline, blurred by the mist.

He sighs. 'Ludovico, you can't understand. We're a family: we have an inheritance to defend. My task is to get back as much as I can from the claws of the Venetians. And believe me, it's not a task that I've chosen for myself.'

I instinctively turn towards Beatriz's cabin.

The Miquez smile. 'In a sense I'm on the payroll as well.' He stares at the coast again. 'We can't leave everything in Venice.'

'Do you think they'll let you take all the loot right out from under their noses, after all they've done to fuck you over?'

'Not at all. I'll have to use diplomacy, deceit and maybe even a bit of force. All the weapons in the Miquez arsenal.'

He gets a laugh out of me.

'And then there's another reason for going back. The family I'm telling you about is as big as a nation. In Venice there are five thousand Marrani and they all risk imprisonment or death. I have to find a way to get as many of them out as I can.'

I nod. 'What are we going to do in the Sultan's lands?'

'You'll like Constantinople, you'll see. The biggest city in the world, more than half a million people. Many people there owe us favours as well, Suleyman most of all.'

'What kind of favours? The ones a certain Tanusin Bey was accusing you of?'

He smiles. 'Ludovico, the house of Miquez is as big as the world. For each door that closes, another must open.' A stout clap on the shoulder. '*Hasta luego*, my friend. We'll meet up again in Constantinople.'

João goes down on to the deck, where Duarte is already waiting for him along with his brother.

They reach the little boat moored under the ship. The sail fills with a snap.

I watch the boat slip away, while the captain of the flagship gives the order to hoist the anchor.

Off the coast of Romagna, paralysed with cold, I stopped studying the horizon.

Below deck I stretch my aching bones on a folding bed. Beatriz is waiting for me, but first a muddle of thoughts and sensations cries out to be untangled.

Decrepit pages, now nothing but dust on the past thirty years.

The coin of a kingdom that lasted only a single day.

The copy of a book that will leave no trace.

A notebook full of jottings.

The strangest legacy that fate could have entrusted to me.

Heinrich Gresbeck, or whatever his name was, is the final face to take its place in the gallery of ghosts. Maybe his best days were the ones he spent by my side. Maybe that's how I should remember him.

He wanted to be killed by my hand, rather than by one of Carafa's assassins. Instead, he fell victim to the most ludicrous of my enemies and his own machinations. The Mule: a miserable pimp who wanted to avenge an insult, taking advantage of the fury that had been stirred up against the Jews. I should have killed him then. I find myself laughing again, as I have done a lot lately: the destinies of the powerful, the destinies of men all hanging on the actions of one stupid arsehole.

Manelfi's confession was consumed in the flames. No one will ever know that those few pages could have changed the course of events for ever. Details are escaping, the minor shades who populated the story are slipping away, forgotten. Rogues, mean little clerics, godless outlaws, policemen, spies. Unmarked graves. Names which mean nothing, but which have encountered strategies and wars, have made them explode, sometimes stubbornly, as part of a deliberate struggle, at other times purely by chance, with a gesture, a word.

I was one of those. On the side of the ones who challenged the world order.

With each defeat we tested the strength of the Plan. We lost everything each time, so that we could stand in its way. Barehanded, with no alternative.

I review the faces one by one, that universal parade ground of men and women that I am taking with me to another world.

A sob shakes my chest and I spit out that muddle, unresolved.

My brothers, they haven't beaten us. We're still free to plough the waves.

On the deck the wind lashes my face as I gaze towards the sunset. I turn the notebook round in my hands. I untie the lace that holds the pages together. I glance through it. Dates, places, names. Thoughts written in a smaller hand.

A folded page falls into my lap. Different paper.

To Giovanni Pietro Carafa

My Lord,
    This is the final missive from the one who has served you for more than thirty years.
    The new age that you are preparing to inaugurate will have to forget its anonymous architects, the ones who have seen to it that events fitted together in accordance with the plan. The illustrious names of the defeated and the victors remain in the chronicles, available to anyone who wants to reconstruct the intricate events of

an era and that which it produced. When those deeds are long gone and those lives have made way for the future, not a trace will remain of that silent army of soldiers of fortune and obscure labyrinth builders. So it is only a matter of hastening the moment of that disappearance, just enough to allow us to escape the final execution.

Innocence has been lost over the half-century that lies behind us, along with the hopes that I have helped to destroy: I nurture no illusions of escaping the fate that I know awaits me. It is not life that concerns me, because apart from the Plan I am nothing but an old unarmed mercenary, surrounded by corpses. The ones who were left in the battlefield, and the ones who are taking over the world. I will not flee in the face of any of them, but my task ends here. Others will take the Plan to its conclusion. I am preparing to meet one last old adversary, I hope that he will be the one to take the light from the eyes that have served you so loyally throughout my life. A life that has slipped away along with the thousands of others who have, decade after decade, drowned in blood. A life that I am choosing to finish in my own way.

There is nothing you can do; you cannot even reproach yourself for your failure to predict the defection of your finest agent on the last mile: the minds of men move in strange ways, and no plan can take account of them all.

This will keep any victory from coming to its final conclusion. Even yours.

This means that no one will have died in vain, not even he who, with his final gesture, is teaching you this lesson.

Your Eye

Q

Epilogue

Cuius regio, eius religio. To each land its prince's faith.

You can always negotiate with princes. You can always do good business with them.

This one was decided in Augsburg two months ago, sealing an agreement sanctioning the division of goods, territories and religions throughout the Empire. The new Pope, Paul IV, is allowing the Protestants to retain all the possessions they have confiscated from the Church until the present day and blessing the peace that has been restored.

This slams shut, once and for all, the lid that Luther, the puppet of the German nobles, lifted almost forty years ago, opening decades of hope, rebellions, revenge killings and restorations. Forty years, that's how long it has taken to strip the people of the power to choose their own fates, and men of the right to choose their own faith.

This is the end of an era. Charles V, the now enfeebled ruler of an empire on the brink of collapse, is preparing to abdicate, leaving young Philip with a legacy of debts and wars yet to come.

Even the star of the formidable Fuggers is in decline, darkened as it is by credit that they will never be able to collect. For almost half a century they have financed the pretensions and aspirations of the Habsburg: now they're paying the price.

Cuius regio, eius religio. He who has refused to accept the rule of a prince, or to ally himself to a single land, has no choice. The fate of the Jews in Venice was exemplary of that.

By the time copies of the Talmud were burned on the Rialto, on 21 August 1553, João had already succeeded in finding an escape route to the East for almost a thousand Sephardic Jews. After the edict of Julius III, after the burnings, the arrests, the ghetto, there was no other option. Now the same thing is happening elsewhere, at the hands of Paul IV.

Heinrich Gresbeck knew this. Venice is going to bear the brunt of all this, for opening the way to the most hypocritical and ferocious persecutions. The people of the Bible are carrying with them the treasure of their experience, their knowledge, their skill, on yet another flight. The portals of another empire are opening up to them, one that will welcome them and acknowledge their courage. But along with the Jews will go many Christians, other landless men and women, who will start a new life beyond the banks of the Mediterranean, among those Infidels whom we have been taught to hate and who are now alone in accepting us without requiring acts of faith.

Their undisputed sovereign, Suleyman the Magnificent, the mere mention of whose name sends a shiver down any Venetian spine, is the wealthiest and most powerful man in the world, the ruler of an empire stretching from the Crimea to the Pillars of Hercules, from Hungary to Baghdad. A keen judge of character, both of men and of nations, he sits on Constantine's throne with the air both of an invincible warrior and of a sage tyrant. No one may appear in his presence without remembering that he is the conqueror of Mesopotamia and that it was he who brought his troops beneath the walls of Vienna, that he defeated Charles V at Mohacs, that he is the man who with so much as a nod of his head could close the trade routes with the East, reducing Venice to an inconsequential little port.

If he asks me about the continent adjacent to his possessions, I shall tell him my story, in the certainty that he will appreciate something more than an ambassador's report.

There is nothing to be learned from it. There is no plan to follow. I'm still alive, that's all. Since I left the other half of the world behind, that distant land that I saw slipping away into the mist one winter day, I no longer have anything to share. I leave it all to the princes, to strengthen their thrones and choose the faith their subjects must follow; to the new bankers who are preparing to take the place of the Fuggers, reciting Calvin's words from memory. To Calvin himself, putting Michael Servetus, scientist and theologian, to the stake. I leave it to the book-burning inquisitors; to Reginald Pole, who yesterday was the champion of conciliation, and who is today Archbishop of Canterbury and persecutor of the Protestants in England.

But to more than anyone I leave it to the architect of the Plan that is finally being put into effect. To Giovanni Pietro Carafa, who ascended the Papal Throne with the name of Paul IV, at the age of seventy-nine, on 23 May 1555.

'Still in bed?'

I didn't hear her come into the room. I roll over, mumbling.

Beatrice lowers her head to look me in the eyes. 'The Sultan won't be too pleased if he has to wait for two infidels of your standing.'

Sitting on the bed, I put one arm round her waist, imprisoning her with the other in a firm embrace.

'That's right, and he'll take your head clean off.'

We laugh. I pull myself up and go to the bathroom, the relief of my old age. Every time I put a foot in there, at least twice a day, I feel a mixture of emotion and contentment about my condition. Blue and sea-green tiles gleam on the floor and the walls. The big basin occupies one whole side, two yards in length. It can be filled continuously from two pipes that pour in hot or cold water. The water, heated in a cistern on the floor above, is allowed to flow in as one wishes, and mixed with the cold water that comes down through the other pipe.

In this dream city baths are a sign of a superior civilisation and of a consideration for bodily hygiene unknown in Europe. They are everywhere, in every size and design, all of them adapted to restore the limbs and the mind from fatigue and the sultry climate.

I immerse myself in the warmth, motionless. Let the Sultan wait.

Jossef gives me a start by bursting in as noisily as possible. 'Don't tell me you've drowned, old man?'

He is wearing his best clothes: his favourite knee-high boots, wide pale trousers; a long buttoned blouse, embroidered across the chest; his curved knife in his belt, its inlaid hilt; the headgear typical of these parts wrapped round his head, blue, with a white feather fixed to it with a gold pin.

'There are other people we have to meet before we see the Sultan. Hurry up, Samuel's been waiting for you for ages. The comforts of this city are making you lazy.' He throws a piece of soap into the water, splashing my face. He hands me a big towel. 'Get a move on!'

You can find anything you like in the great covered bazaar. After walking among a myriad of benches and narrow corridors that run between the shops, following Samuel and Jossef who are guiding my inexpert steps, we walk into a shop displaying grains and spices.

The air is filled with all kinds of aromas. All around stand low little tables, carpets and cushions, occupied by men intent on their business, chattering and smoking narghiles.

Two fat and smiling Ottomans come towards us, making ample bows.

One of them embraces Jossef warmly and then turns to the other. 'This is the most honourable Jossef Nassi, a legend. And this is his brother Samuel, no less courageous.' He brightens up. 'In Venice these men, known as João and Bernardo Miquez, are considered to be the chief enemies of La Serenissima, by virtue of the fact that they have always been our friends. If they returned to Venice, you can be sure that they would be impaled upon the pillars of St Mark's.'

They laugh heartily: my mate is clearly admired.

It's Jossef the Sephardi's turn to speak. 'But that's not to say that we won't return one day. In spite of its rulers, Venice is a splendid city. Gentlemen, I present my colleague, Ismael-the-Traveller-of-the-World, the one who has been through every kind of adventure between the cold North and here, the enemy of all the powerful men of Europe.'

The two opulent merchants bow deferentially again.

They ask us to sit down. One of them begins to fill the bowl of the narghile, while the other asks Jossef to tell his colleague all about his incredible flight from Venice.

'Some other time. We are awaited at court and I wouldn't like to waste the little time at our disposal in idle boasting. Let's talk business.'

'Of course.' A swift clap of the hands and a boy in a white tunic brings a tray with a steaming pot and some cups.

The servant pours a dark liquid, with an intense and unfamiliar scent.

I look at Jossef.

He talks to me in Flemish, the language of those far-off days in Antwerp. 'This is the business we're going to talk about. Try it.'

A diffident smile. The hot liquid goes down my throat, a strong, slightly bitter taste, then a sudden sensation of vigour and a sharpening of the senses. A longer sip and the grains that had settled on the bottom of the cup are left on my tongue. 'Fine, but I don't understand . . .'

'It's called *qahvé*. It comes from a plant that grows in the regions of Arabia.'

The merchant hands us a little bag of green beans and Jossef takes out a handful.

'You roast them and grind them to powder, and they're ready to infuse in boiling water. They'll go crazy for it in Europe.' He senses my puzzlement. 'The Sultan is demonstrating his appreciation of the services and information that we're supplying to him, but it's always wise to have a few other projects, a few good deals to develop. Believe me, the coarse people of Europe are going to appreciate, one by one, these little pleasures that make life worth living.'

I smile and think of my tub full of warm water.

Jossef goes on, 'They're already setting up shops here where you can drink restoring beverages. Places like this one, where you can talk, do business and smoke tobacco from these fantastic water pipes. You'll see, it won't be long before we introduce similar habits to Europe. We'll just have to start sending bags of these precious beans along our commercial routes and showing people how to use them.'

'Europe isn't keen on pleasures, Jossef, you know that.'

'Europe's finished. Now that they've signed their agreement, they'll start fighting each other again, chasing a dream of barbarous supremacy. The world is ours.'

The boy refills the cup.

I draw a good mouthful of smoke from the mouthpiece of the narghile. My limbs relax and I sink into the cushion.

I smile. No plan can take everything into account. Other people will raise their heads, others will desert. Time will go on spreading victory and defeat among those who pursue the struggle.

I sip with satisfaction.

We deserve the warmth of baths. May the days be aimless.

Do not advance the action according to a plan.

Characters, cities, documents

Acknowledgements

For their indispensable contribution the authors would like to thank:
Silvia Urbini, Andrea Alberti, Susanna Fort, Guido Novello Guidelli
Guidi, Gianmassimo P. Vigazzola and Antimo Santoro.

In a flyer of 1616, the chief stages of the life of Martin Luther. 'Therefore let everyone who can, smite, slay, and stab [. . .] remembering that nothing can be more poisonous, hurtful, or devilish than a rebel. It is just as when one must kill a mad dog; if you do not strike him, he will strike you, and a whole land with you.' (*Against the Robbing and Murdering Hordes of Peasants*, 1525)

Thomas Müntzer in a sixteenth-century engraving by Christoffel van Sichem. 'So tell me, wretched and disgusting vermin, who it was that appointed you prince of the people?' (Letter to Count Mansfeld, 12 May 1525)

IOAN MATHYS VAN HAERLEMO

TOHAN MATHYS VAN HAERLEEM EEN PROPHEET DER GEE STDRYVERS.

Jan Matthys in an engraving by van Sichem. In the background, his death during the siege of Münster. 'God is going to sweep his threshing floor!'

IOHAN·VĀ·LEIDEN·EY·KONĬNCK·DER·WEDERDOPER·
THO·MONSTER·WA   ERHAFTĬCH·CŌTER·

HÆC·FACÍES·HÍC·CVLTVS·ERAT·CV̄·SEPTRA·TENE·
REX·ἀναβαπτιστῶν·SED·BREVE·TĒPVS·EGO·
HENRÍCVS·ALDEGREVER·SVSATÍĒ·FACÍEBAT·
·ANNO·M·D·XXXVĬ·
GOTTES·MACHT·ÍST·MYN·CRACHT·

John of Leyden in a 1536 engraving by Heinrich Aldegrever. 'The epic of the Anabaptists and the legends of the enemies have turned us into monsters of shrewdness and perversion. Well, in truth, they were the Horsemen of the Apocalypse. A baker prophet, a pimp poet and a nameless outcast, an eternal fugitive.'

WAERHAFTICH·GEKONTERFET·BERNT·KNIPPERDOLLICK
DER·XII·HERTOGEN· EYN·THO·MONSTER·

IGNOTVS·NVLLIS·KNIPPERDOLLINGIVS·ORIS·
TALIS·ERA·SOSPES·CVM·MIHI·VITA·FORET·
HINRICVS·ALDEGREVER·SVSATIE·FACI
1536

Berndt Knipperdolling in a 1536 engraving by Heinrich Aldegrever. 'We have begun the struggle, and we will see it to its conclusion.'

MELCHIOR HOF-MAN VAN STRASBVRG.

Melchior Hofmann in a print by van Sichem. 'One of the most eccentric prophets I have ever met, quite unique of his kind, and, in madness and oratory, second only to the great Matthys.'

Out of Europe: Beatriz de Luna and João Miquez in a 1932 illustration by Arthur Szyk.

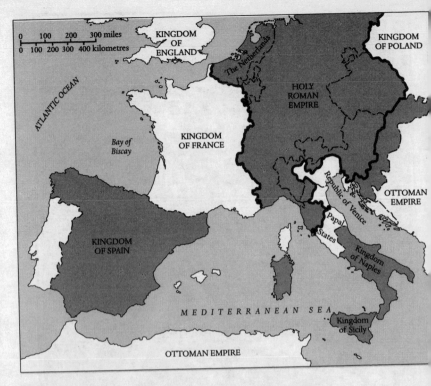

Possessions of Charles V

Holy Roman Empire

'A Europe in which political changes are determined by German bankers; in which religious faith is raised on the banners of mercenary armies; in which entire populations are subjected to martial law. A Europe criss-crossed by columns of refugees, in which the rebellion of the desperate faces a compact front made up of the old families and the emerging mercantile powers. The same shitty response as always: cannons and genocide, and then fire and the sword . . .'

'We have never been interested in generic calls to peace: there is an extremely strong rationale for the existence of war today, just as there was four centuries ago. It is deeply rooted in the criminal economic and political choices made by states and multi-national powers, whether they are the United States or the empire of Charles V. And similarly there is a rationale behind the ethnic cleansings and reprisals, one to which we do not adhere, and which we have always fervently opposed. [. . .] It would be immoral and incoherent not to use every space and every public occasion to denounce the madness of those in government and the apathy of those governed by them.' (From the press communiqué by the authors of *Q* against the NATO bombings of Yugoslavia, 1st April 1999.)

View of Nuremberg from the south. Woodcut by Wilhelm Pleydenwurff and Michael Wolgemut, 1493. 'The imposing towers of the imperial fortress remind us of what we know already: this city is one of the biggest, finest and wealthiest cities in the whole of Europe.'

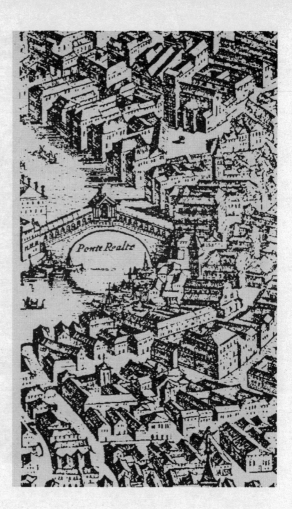

View of Antwerp. At the bottom, the port of the same city in a drawing by Albrecht Dürer. To the right, the Rialto bridge from Jacopo de' Barbari's view of Venice. 'The need of a constantly expanding market for its products chases the bourgeoisie over the entire surface of the globe. It must nestle everywhere, settle everywhere, establish connections everywhere.' (K. Marx and F. Engels, *Manifesto of the Communist Party*)

Beheading of peasants after the battle of Frankenhausen. 'So the sum total is: 80 beheaded, 69 of whom had their eyes put out and their fingers cut off, which comes to 114 florins and two cents. From this should be deducted: 10 florins, received from the citizens of Rothenburg; 2 florins received by Ludwig von Hutten; leaving: 102 florins. To this should be added two months' pay; for each month 8 florins = 16 florins, which makes: 118 florins and two cents.' (The receipt of the executioner Augustin, known as Awe, addressed to the Margrave)

Dye Grundelichen Vnd rech=
ten haupt Artickl / aller Baur=
schafft vnd Hyndersessen der
Gaistlichen vnd Welcli=
chen oberkaytē / von
wölchen sy sich
beschwert ver=
mainen.

Frontispiece of the *Twelve Articles* of the peasants of Swabia.

Ein erbermkliche aufrür der Pa
Thoman Münzer in Thüringen/r
poret sich das volck wider die fürste
wider die geistlichen. Sölicher aufr
100000.erschlagen vnd gericht. Dr
büchstaben des nachgesetzten verfli

Peasants being tortured in a chronicle from 1548. 'I was tortured in the barracks of the Second Paduan Brigade. Tied to the table, my head dangling, I was made to swallow litres of salt water. They beat me, breaking some of my ribs and causing me a internal lesion to one eye. They gave me electric shocks to my testicles and burned my groin. They cut my thighs and my calves, then sprinkling them with salt.' (Cesare di Lenardo, May 1982, quoted in: Luther Blissett Project, *Nemici dello Stato*, Derive Approdi, Rome 1999, p. 63)

emeinden erhůb sich durch
gantz Teütschland/do em
oberkeiten/ vnnd merteils
r wurdend allenthalben ob
aurenkriegs stadt in den zal

The 'Company of Anabaptists', defamatory illustration by Heinrich Aldegrever. 'Horrendous processions of twenty or thirty paedophiles staged in the avenues of the cemeteries of the Modenese lowlands, dissolving into boundless orgies, destroying the innocence of their own children and the children of their acquaintances.' (The chronicler Luigi Spezia, *ibid*, p. 149)

Top: Dislocation with red-hot pincers, from: R. Vaneigem, *The Movement of the Free Spirit*, Nautilus, Torino, 1995.

Bottom: 'One God, one faith, one baptism', slogan engraved on a coin from the kingdom of Münster.

The cages in which the corpses of the heads of Münster were displayed. 'No one looks at them. The past hangs right over their heads. And if they try to lift their heads too far, the cages are there as a reminder.'

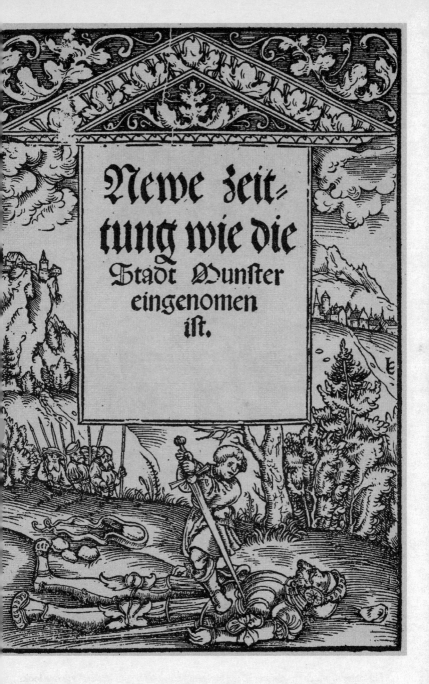

From an anti-Anabaptist 'Newe Zeitung': John of Leyden dressed as Goliath, brought low by David.

Anti-clerical flyer of the late 16th century. 'A sodomite! They all knew I've only ever liked women, not little boys and all that filth the abbots get up to.'

Lieber Du Solt Lang Fragen Nicht   Ehr Heist Mit Nam Der Antechrist
Wen Dis Bilt Gantz Annlich Sicht   Schaue Ann Die Sprich Inn Heilligenschrifft
Doch Wiltu Wissen Wer Ehr Ist   So Wirstu Kennen Das Odern Gifft.

Bust of the pope in the manner of Arcimboldo, from a drawing by Thomas Stimmer.

DE ORTV ET ORIGINE
MONACHORVM.

Gestabat fœtum magna prurigine Pluto,
   Plena venenati stercoris aluus erat.
Hoc tandem enitens ut laxo uentre profundit,
   Non est materiæ simplicis illud onus.
Nanqȝ cucullati dirupto podice fratres
   Exiliunt, uaria ueste, colore, animo.
Miratur Pluto portenta tot edita ab aluo,
   Miratur tantum se genuisse malum:
Et simul obtorto inspiciens sua pignora uultu,
   Vulgus & insuetum, progeniemȝ nouam:

Non equidem frustra, uideo, mea uiscera tanto
   Dudum tormento mota fuisse, refert.
Ecce, malum peperi, lemures quod crimine, & oës
   Exuperat, Stygij quos tenet aula ducis.
Hei mihi si cunctos uno ordine, tempore eodem
   Dij linteam, Regnis pellar ego ipse meis.
Dixit, & arridens totum dispersit in orbem
   Tet Monachos, Mundi crimen, & exitium.
           Iohannes Villicus.

'The origin of the monks', flyer of 1545 from the workshop of Lucas Cranach.